Rudy Wiebe

COLLECTED STORIES | 1955–2010

Rudy Wiebe

COLLECTED STORIES | 1955–2010

The University of Alberta Press

Published by

The University of Alberta Press
Ring House 2
Edmonton, Alberta, Canada   T6G 2E1

LIBRARY AND ARCHIVES CANADA CATALOGUING IN PUBLICATION

Wiebe, Rudy, 1934–
     Rudy Wiebe: collected stories, 1955–2010 / introduction by Thomas Wharton.

(Currents, a Canadian literature series)
Includes bibliographical references.
ISBN 978-0-88864-540-1

     I. Title. II. Series: Currents (Edmonton, Alta.)

PS8545.I38A15 2010   C813'.54   C2010-905511-X

All rights reserved.
First edition, first printing, 2010.
Printed and bound in Canada by Houghton Boston Printers, Saskatoon, Saskatchewan.
Copyediting and Proofreading by Meaghan Craven.

A volume in (cuRRents), a Canadian literature series. Jonathan Hart, series editor.

The University of Alberta Press is committed to protecting our natural environment. As part of our
efforts, this book is printed on Enviro Paper: it contains 100% post-consumer recycled fibres and is
acid- and chlorine-free.

The University of Alberta Press gratefully acknowledges the support received for its publishing
program from The Canada Council for the Arts. The University of Alberta Press also gratefully
acknowledges the financial support of the Government of Canada through the Book Publishing
Industry Development Program (BPIDP) and from the Alberta Foundation for the Arts for its
publishing activities.

The image on the part pages is the Iron Creek meteorite.

In memory of

Peter Frank Bargen (1922–2004) and
Frederick Millington Salter (1895–1962)

who challenged me to continue

CONTENTS

XI *Preface*

XV *Introduction* THOMAS WHARTON

ONE | FACE TO FACE, LOOKING NORTHWEST

3 Broken Arm

22 Where is the Voice Coming From?

32 Watch for Two Coyotes, Crossing

52 Along the Red Deer and the South Saskatchewan

63 The Year We Gave Away the Land

72 From Montreal, 1848

75 Games for Queen Victoria

94 A Night in Fort Pitt, or (if you prefer) The Only Perfect
Communists in the World

107 The Fish Caught in the Battle River

116 Oolulik

133 Dialogue at an Exhibition

142 The Naming of Albert Johnson

TWO | SO MUCH TO REMEMBER

156   After Thirty Years of Marriage

167   Sailing to Danzig

178   All On Their Knees

191   The Power

197   Tudor King

204   Scrapbook

210   The House Smashers

213   Lake Isle of Innisfree

216   They Just Won't Believe

221   Growing Up in Rosebud

224   The Darkness Inside the Mountain

231   Speaking Saskatchewan

235   Chinook Christmas

THREE | PARALLEL REALITIES

248   The Angel of the Tar Sands

252   Seeing is Believing

267   Millstone for the Sun's Day

276   Did Jesus Ever Laugh?

292   Believing is Not Seeing

310   Life Story

312   Crash

314   Urn Burial

316   A History of the New World

321   Bluecoats on the Sacred Hill of the Wild Peas

330   In the Ear of the Beholder

346   The Blindman River Contradictions

FOUR | NOW AND WHEREVER

358   Shadow of a Rock

367   The Shells of the Ocean

379   An Indication of Burning

398   The Good Maker

408   There's a Muddy Road

420   Sleeping (Uneasily) with Franz Kafka

435   Home for Night

442   Except God, Who Already Knows

458   Bears, All the Time Bears

462   Someday Soon, Before Tomorrow

472   The Funny Money of 1980

476   The Oil Capitals of Canada

485   Finally, the Frozen Ocean

513   *Appendix* Predestined

519   *Selected Bibliography*

527   *About the Author*

PREFACE

IN A LIFETIME OF WRITING, hundreds of stories meander, drift, leap up, collapse or vanish, and occasionally reincarnate themselves in your imagination. Some of their vestiges—to me the German word *Bruchteile* (literally "fractured parts") seems even more apt—remain in files as beginning sentences, images, characters, places, actions or events. Of many more no written words have ever existed, and the fifty stories included in this collection are those I have completed. Whole books, both fiction and nonfiction, and story scripts have demanded most of my writing concentration.

Human beings are the story-making species. You ask me, "How are you?" and if I care to explain, I'll tell you a story. A fiction writer glimpses stories happening anywhere; as out of the corner of his eye; as in passing.

The tiny high school I attended had no athletic program to lure me into relentless physical sport. I had enough daily chores at home and other labour jobs to build muscles; besides, in my early teens our family had no car and riding a bicycle in southern Alberta wind was excellent exercise. In such an environment, an obsessive young reader with eyes wide open has time to feel and see and hear stories everywhere, can at times perhaps imagine himself a writer even if he has never met one. Especially stimulating for my imagination was the fact that, though I experienced endless stories as a boy, and heard them told in three languages, I never read a single one about the life I was personally living in boreal Saskatchewan or prairie Alberta. Only the occasional glimpse of frontier landscapes in Zane Grey's Ohio or Ralph Connor's Ontario, the shimmer of indomitable characters in the Bible or Greek myths or Victor Hugo or Charles Dickens.

So when I finally met W.O. Mitchell's *Jake and the Kid* on CBC Radio (Is that when voice subliminally rooted itself in my fiction?), it was a delight; Sinclair Ross's "One's a Heifer" an evocative revelation. It was possible to write stories about my worlds, involving my peculiar Canadian peoples. And Sheila Watson, Frederick Phillip Grove, Margaret Laurence, Robert Kroetsch made what was now obvious inevitable.

The first of the stories collected here was begun in September 1955, the last completed in January 2010. Isolated immigrant traders and settlers, the worlds of the original Turtle Island peoples: an unplanned but suitable symmetry for this collection. Gathered together, it is obvious that numerous stories here are integral to many of my longer fictions: a minor character from a novel becomes the protagonist of a short story; the focused event of a story becomes an adapted scene within a novel; the lives of some novel characters continue decades after the original book has been published.

Except for very minor changes—typos, an occasional punctuation mark or paragraph—these stories stand as they were first published, their style, attitudes, opinions left intact. To attempt to "contemporize" them would only falsify whatever merit they have. I was, however, strongly tempted to add a sentence to my best-known story, "Where is the Voice Coming From?" For almost forty years the text has stated, concerning the character Ernest Grundy: "The gravestone, if he has one, of the fourth man Almighty Voice killed is more difficult to locate," but, as a matter of fact, Grundy's gravestone obelisk is very easily found. After 113 years it still stands beside what remains of the tiny Anglican Church in Duck Lake, Saskatchewan. While visiting the village last summer I again felt I should rectify this false statement. Was it originally deliberate? I could not remember. Finally, after months of pondering, I concluded that this reputed "difficulty," too, was one more particle of historical facticity crucial in creating the fragile web of the story's structure. So stet: add nothing; let the original error/omission/lie stand.

On the other hand, I did feel it essential to add a concluding paragraph to the original version of "Broken Arm." The brutal historic facts of the last, and largest, inter-tribal battle on the Canadian prairie must not be avoided; rather, the facts draw the tragic irony of a magnificent life into its full, completed, circle.

❋ The story is told that when the Gitskan People of the Pacific Northwest heard from officials that their lands belonged to a distant government, they were astounded into silence. Finally, an Elder asked: "If this is your land, where are your stories?"

Indeed. It seems to me that the stories of our lives are a kind of convergence of streams, which, gathering together over a vast landscape, eventually flow into rivers, lakes, perhaps as far as the possible oceans of history. As if all stories, wherever told, about whomever, had endless sources and continuations within and out of each other, with innumerable others still waiting to be recognized and mapped. As if, like a boreal aspen tree of roots, parent stem, countless saplings sprouting out of the roots, branches, leaves, flowers, seeds, there could be no ultimate beginning or end, ever, to any one story within any one lifetime.

RUDY WIEBE
Edmonton, February 2010

NOTE: *The first date at the beginning of each story is the year it was written, the second date that of its first publication. A single date indicates the story was written and published the same year. More complete details are given in the selected bibliography.*

INTRODUCTION

Thomas Wharton

He will listen to those voices speaking now for as long
as he lives

IN RUDY WIEBE'S SHORT FICTION, story becomes an almost tangible element of the world, like stone, or river, or a piece of white bone glimpsed through the glass of a museum showcase. Story has weight, presence, a shape one can almost hold in the hands. Story is a gift or a burden, or simply a necessity, a "living closeness" that people carry with them in their migrations and wanderings, something they could never imagine leaving behind, even when almost everything else must be abandoned in order to go on. The story journeys, and often in these pages the story turns about and tells of the journey itself; the story is the journey.

Wiebe's parents fled hunger and oppression in Stalinist Russia, and one of the writer's own lifelong journeys, both in fiction and memoir, will be to double back through the history of his family and his farflung Mennonite ancestry, tracing in words the migrations of his people in search of tolerance, peace, or mere survival: across Europe, across the steppes toward the blue mountains of China, across the seas to the United States and Canada, to South America.

So that it is no wonder one of his characters asserts that the quintessential human story is wandering—of the peoples on the earth eternally without rest—and searching "...the restless, inexplicable wandering back to where you have been, or have not..." ("Except God, Who Already Knows," p. 455).

Where you have been, or have not. For the stories do not deny that they are imaginings, of course. The hands and voices that carry them shape them and reshape them, like wood or stone or clay, sometimes through a lifetime, sometimes across many lifetimes, many countries, many languages. In "Except God, Who Already Knows," Wiebe's recurring character Adam carries an almost-erased family story with him on a canoe journey into the Arctic with his son Joel, a terrible, inexplicable story passed to him by others and one that he can only tell haltingly, aware of the gaps in his knowledge, his inability or perhaps unwillingness to fully understand. The Arctic tundra, the otherworldly landscape through which he and his son are travelling, intrudes upon his telling, and yet opens up new vistas on the history that Adam has gathered. The wind and the water and the mosquitoes add their own insistent voices to the narrative. And when the story is finally passed from father to son, it has the power to open fresh wounds. The story does not end in the telling. It merely adds another layer, takes another path. As Robert Bringhurst has suggested, we rarely have a choice about which stories will move through us: "Stories find the tellers they need. They nest in us as saw-whet owls and wood ducks nest in trees. More than that, they use us to reproduce themselves."[1]

Like tangible things, the stories here are found, or made from what is found. Seldom is it remarked by the many self-conscious narrators of these fictions that the stories are, ultimately, written. And often it is that unease between the impulse or imperative that moves the teller to make the story, and the fact that the end result is a tidy sequence of silent letters on a page, that the story itself turns upon. The anonymous Plains Cree narrator of "Broken Arm" marvels that "to fix words on a white piece of wood or leather, not merely signs but words which always say exactly the same thing... that goes beyond strange" (p. 13). Here, as in many of the stories, the effort to make the story is the attempt to hear a voice and recreate it on the page. The power of words to make voices from the past or from imagination speak upon the page is what indeed moves the text "beyond the power of sign or declaration into mystery" (p. 13).

Wiebe is a writer of voice, of voices. Throughout these pages one can hear the author trying on different voices, venturing into the world or worlds around him through voices. There is an almost theatrical preoccupation with voice in many of these stories, as Wiebe reconstructs the history of the Canadian west through a multitude of speakers: aboriginal people, prairie farmers, traders, British colonels, politicians, artists, children. And of course one of his most well-known and anthologized stories, "Where is the Voice Coming From?" turns upon itself to ponder the making of story as an act of hearing a voice, interrogating the mysterious process by which the past, our own or that of others, can speak to us, can insist on being heard, through the mute evidence of historical records and artifacts. "This story ended long ago," says the narrator in this imagining of the life and death of the Cree fugitive Almighty Voice, but of course it hasn't, and the writer knows it. The story of Almighty Voice's brief, futile stand against White authority becomes a prelude to the larger narrative of Big Bear and his people in rebellion and flight from an alien world of "threatened incomprehensible law" (p. 30). And the narrator of "Where is the Voice Coming From?" discovers in a more personal way that the story has not ended, that it has in fact "run me aground," as if the writer is a fugitive like the title character. The maker of story, the hearer (and vessel?) of this inescapable, almighty voice, can "no longer pretend to objective, omnipotent disinterestedness. I am no longer *spectator* of what *has* happened or what *may* happen: I am become *element* in what is happening in this very moment" (p. 29).

Sometimes the voice is not that of an individual but of a community, a voice that transcends time, distance, the limitations of the individual perspective. For almost all of Wiebe's protagonists, the community that surrounds and shapes them is a defining force of their lives, to be embraced in some cases, to be struggled against in others, but always an inescapable presence. There are few figures without community in these stories. Two that come most powerfully to mind are, perhaps significantly, both killers: the anonymous murderer in "Did Jesus Ever Laugh?" and Albert Johnson, the "mad trapper" of Rat River, fugitive, legend, enigma.

The historical Johnson's seemingly supernatural ability to conceal his tracks and travel impossible distances through the harshest conditions baffled and ultimately awed his pursuers. Even a recent exhumation and DNA testing have not unearthed the truth of Johnson's "real" identity. And so the refusal of name and community becomes the story. In "The Naming of Albert Johnson" the narrative runs backward from Johnson's death on the Eagle River in February 1932, to the moment of his rage at being found and named, when he believed he had left names behind. The story doubles back on the historical record, as Johnson himself doubles back on his own tracks, until he is ultimately confounded by the landscape's own capacity for deceit, when he discovers that "the sluggish loops of this river doubling back on itself have betrayed him" (p. 144). But even in death the fugitive goes on eluding his pursuers, and becomes, strangely enough, a figure for the writer, doubling back through his own past, refusing to be pinned down, caught at times when the landscape of story plays its own tricks. No wonder Wiebe seems to be having so much fun in "The Blindman River Contradictions," where he invents a fictional British past for himself to evade the inevitable, tiresome questions about his Mennonite upbringing (a joke that has tripped up more than one serious biographical researcher).

Compared to a selection, which maps the writer's journey as a simplified set of landmarks, a "collected stories" is unkempt, meandering, a palimpsest of possible journeys, glimpses of roads not taken. And of course all of these voices. In a comprehensive gathering of fifty years of fiction, one might expect to get a fuller sense of the author behind the work but in fact, reading these stories in the sequence given here, something surprising begins to happen: the author recedes even further into the multiplicity of his voices.

And perhaps behind or within all of these voices is the voice of the land. Maskepetoon's people in "Broken Arm" listen to the voice of the wind and it carries to them news of those "who are white as a peeled log with iron axes and knives stuck in their belts and who will make dreadful sounds which no one has heard before. So we knew of Whites long before we ever saw them..." (p. 12). The land speaks, and when the Whiteman comes, it will be his monolithic Word, more than his guns or other technological marvels, that will destroy the traditional world of the Plains Cree. The land speaks to the Mennonite boy in "Speaking Saskatchewan." Out in the bush beyond homestead and town, "everything spoke: warm rocks, the flit of quick, small animals, a dart of birds, tree trunks, the great lights in the sky at night, burning air, ground, the squeaky snow....Everything spoke, and it spoke Low German" (p. 231). In this story, the unnamed boy who hears in the world only the language that his family speaks at home, finally goes to the local school and learns that the world also speaks a startling new language called English. A discovery of strangeness that will lead the boy to a greater discovery of "human voices speaking from everywhere and every age, saying everything, things both dreadful and beautiful, and all that can be imagined between them...and he will listen. He will listen to those voices speaking now for as long as he lives" (p. 234).

Wiebe himself has talked elsewhere of his puzzlement at not being able to remember when he first learned the language in which he would one day write his stories. Surely a foundational moment for a writer, but for Wiebe the moment is lost in time. And perhaps it is that absent discovery that Wiebe imagines again and again in his fiction, as his characters grapple not just with the conflicts and challenges of their lives but with the fact of the world itself, and the words one must use to attempt to speak it. Again and again in these stories the narrators find themselves stunned or baffled by the world, and by words. Again and again their sentences are broken, or unfinished, or their thoughts turn back upon the words themselves. The world is impossible, dazzling, unrelenting, often moving too quickly for the eye to comprehend what it has seen. In "Sleeping (Uneasily) with Franz Kafka," Adam Wiebe remembers a visit to Prague with his lover, where they scour the city for its memories of Franz Kafka. In the old Jewish ghetto they meet a woman who eerily displaces the author's remains, and at the same time Adam finds the memories of his lover receding from him, uncertain. In the magnificent story "The Shells of the Ocean," a father searching for his lost daughter can only endlessly *look*: "And he has looked, he would certainly always look now into every crowd: so many people, especially in cities, thousands, millions....sometimes he did see her, even among the black heads of Jakarta and Singapore, the incredible complexions of Lima, Kuala Lumpur, Sao Paulo: bits of her, a profile, a momentary back, a jacket fold or flip of hair and shoulder shift, and his heart would lurch for he already knew he must certainly be disappointed; and he was" (p. 372).

The world (and the story) almost always comes in fragments, scattered images and words that must be stitched together by the storymaker. The world tricks the eye and the ear, as the Arctic river looping back and forth across the tundra ultimately "out-doubles" Albert Johnson's own doubling trail and confronts him with his own pursuers. For a moment, Johnson and the land almost seem to share an identity, although it is one at odds with itself. Johnson is a marvellously skilled reader of the landscape, but his impulse, *away* from voices and community, ultimately turns the land against him as well. Sometimes the landscape trips up a character's cherished preconceptions and allows a new vision. The convoluted, impossible world, whether it be tundra, prairie, boreal forest, history, or one's own past, continuously demands that it be read, interpreted, gathered somehow into words, into story.

Wiebe introduces his own anthology of short fiction, *The Story-Makers* (1970, revised 1987), by looking at our need to make story and suggests that its early forms developed from five immemorial human impulses: "dreaming how we wish things were; recounting what happened; explaining why things are as they are; instructing ourselves and our children; making an imitation."[2] One can see all of these impulses at work in Wiebe's own fiction, often all five in the same story. Even in the brief, often comical pieces written for the Alberta Centennial ("Lake Isle of Innisfree," "The Funny Money of 1980," "The Oil Capitals of Canada") there is instruction (the lessons we never seem to learn from history), there is explanation and recounting of the past we are always in a hurry to shed, and perhaps there is a little dreaming about the way things should be. But in his preface to the revised edition of *The Story-Makers,* Wiebe suggests that the modern short story has developed not only from these ancient impulses: "it has also developed from *the very desire to make story.* That is, making a short story now is justification enough for its existence; it needs neither to dream, recount, explain, instruct or imitate anything, though in the process of becoming itself it may do all five. The process, the making itself often seems the writer's primal objective, and the question of *where* that making takes place—in the act of writing or in the act of reading—then becomes the further point at issue."[3]

The stories in this collection, then, always turn toward the reader, asking us to double back on our reading tracks, and then to look outward from the story into the unwritten world. Our task, Wiebe suggests, is to look and listen for the stories around us with all that we are. The most recently finished piece in this collection, "Shadow of a Rock," tells of an anonymous narrator searching the Battle River region of central Alberta for the original (so to speak) site of a meteorite now lodged safely in a "mechanically controlled museum" (p. 364). The meteor has been labelled the "Iron Creek Meteorite," but its oldest known name, given to it by the Blackfoot and Plains Cree, is Old Man Buffalo. The narrator finds the stone gone from the hilltop, another moment of absence, but the hill is still there, and it is a place where vision is still possible. Where one may see this world, or perhaps glimpse a world beyond. You will need to look, and listen, and with patience you may see and hear "Old Man Buffalo's black face shimmering in the unbearable light of the sun, his long bent nose, his great mouth open, will you listen!...If you can see in silence, you can also hear. Feel this enduring stony earth, under your knees" (p. 366).

NOTES

1. Robert Bringhurst, introduction to *The Dreamer Awakes*, by Alice Kane (Peterborough, ON: Broadview Press, 1995), 12.

2. Rudy Wiebe, introduction to *The Story-Makers*, 2nd edition, edited by Rudy Wiebe (Agincourt, ON: Gage Educational Publishing, 1987), xiii.

3. Wiebe, preface to *The Story-Makers*, 2nd edition, ix.

ONE | FACE TO FACE, LOOKING NORTHWEST

Broken Arm

1. IN THE BEAVER HILLS

In those days long ago when the Mountain and River Cree were never
sick because there were always enough buffalo to keep us strong, we
had a great chief called *Mas-ke-pe-toon*, Broken Arm.

No one knows now where he got that name. Perhaps as some say
it was from fighting a grizzly, or in a raid or battle, or perhaps from a
vision he had on the Medicine Lodge Hills above the Blindman River
when he was young. At that time all the Blackfoot Peoples already
knew him as The Young Chief, but even before that we called him
The One-With-Eyes-In-The-Back-Of-His-Head and one spring he left
our band with the Young Men and rode as far as they pleased from
our country on the North Saskatchewan, south through the lands
of our fierce Blackfoot enemies, the Siksika and the Bloods and the
Peigans, and then the Assiniboines and the Crows, all the way to the
Missouri River where they traded at the mouth of the Yellowstone.
There they also met White soldiers whose guns ended in long bright
knives. These soldiers took him with some other People down that
river for many days and up another and another and over mountains
until finally they showed him a man with a black beard they said was
their Big White Father in a place called Washington who hung a large
silver medal around his neck. But when after three years he came

back to the North Saskatchewan with all his Young Men still alive and more horses and rifles than the Mountain and River People had ever seen, he would not say one word about it.

"If I told you everything I saw by that Stinking Water," he said, "you would only call me a liar."

He stayed with his People then for eight years. His wives gave him sons and daughters, he hunted buffalo and killed Blackfoot as any man of our People must, and everyone might have forgotten his journey if he had not kept rubbing the silver medal which he had never removed from around his neck. It was worn so smooth now that the profile of the man on it, the bearded man who gave it to him, could barely be seen even when it was held flat to the light. Once he told his wife Matono-wacap that while he was on the boat going down the river one Whiteman had made an exact likeness of his face with paint on a piece of leather, but she clapped her hand over her mouth in astonishment and quick terror that he had not killed such a devil immediately. After that, every morning when he awoke she was bent over him, staring into his face, for she knew that just as he was wiping away that White Chief with his fingers, so that painter would one day destroy him; and paint on leather cannot last as long as silver. So he smiled at her every morning, his smooth face more powerful and sharper than ever, and said nothing at all about the boat which had brought them back against the current of the river without either sail or paddle.

In those days when our Mountain and River People traded at Fort Edmonton or Rocky Mountain House they could only trade one at a time because the Hudson's Bay Company mounted cannon in the forts and locked the gates and opened nothing but one small door with an armed man standing guard behind it. Maskepetoon traded hides and pemmican there sometimes for tobacco or tea, or a rifle if they let him, but during those eight years when he rode against the Blackfoot every spring, what he had seen fasting as a youth on the Medicine Lodge Hills kept coming back to him. One day when his second wife, Susewik, enraged him, he drew his knife and with one swift, brutal motion, scalped her. She did not, however, die of that. Gradually the top of her skull healed white and dry like a buffalo-skull at the Thirst Dance and she protected it with a small cap she

Rudy Wiebe: Collected Stories, 1955–2010

sewed of fur, but sometimes when she lay in his arms, laughing or crying with him, he again saw the Blindman River valley open below him, the shining mountains at his back and Gull Lake a silver coin among the trees where the earth flattened away. And then the thunderstorm would come up from the south again, from the Red Deer River canyons there, and he would see his Mountain and River People riding south and the Blackfoot and Blood and Peigan warriors galloping north to meet them with war cries shrilling high above the thunder and his People screaming in turn and his left arm would reach out between them, would grow huge until it split the prairies, a giant swelling log laid between his People and their endless enemies. "What does it mean?" he would whisper in Susewik's ear. And his left arm, which could bend a bow or pull the largest horse to its knees in one easy, unstoppable motion, would cramp around her in agony and she would laugh at first, happily, and then recognize the pain in his face. "What is it?" she said then. "What is it?"

His father had told him something, though he really did not want to hear what the old man said. Every time he rode out against the Blackfoot his father, who could no longer walk and lay between robes all day long and thought, would say, "Is a man's true greatness to be sung in the scalp dance? What do your powerful eyes, what do your travels to unnamable places help if you see only what everyone sees, that war is glory, that killing is revenge? You have always seen different, why can't you see different about being a brave man?"

But there were always so many mothers in camp wailing for sons and daughters lost forever to the Blackfoot, or fathers for sons and grandsons and brothers for brothers and nephews for uncles and young men for their blood friends and sweethearts and little boys growing slowly older on hate for their fathers' killers, that Maskepetoon could not listen. The Blackfoot had named him The Young Chief after his first raid when he killed three of them with two arrows and an axe and often now they avoided his camp as if the very sight of his long shadow on the lodge hides were enough to terrify them; there were always so many Blackfoot that needed killing.

"There is truth and there is lie," his father continued to say. "Hate and love, war and peace, goodness and shame. What do you want? What do you see?"

Then, seven years after he had come back from his first long journey, in the spring when the first grass is green and beautiful for horses, Maskepetoon and eight warriors rode south as usual out of the parkland to the prairies. They swam their horses across the Red Deer River and two days later as they came up between The Three Hills he heard birds chirping. At his signal the riders stopped, listened; it seemed the wide prairie about them was dancing with meadowlarks. "That is the enemy," he said and thrust his rifle, the only one they had, back into its scabbard. "We will ride slowly towards that low hill." They did that, and suddenly from the west a man appeared, coming towards them. The man rode very tall, blurred huge in the heat that shimmered over the plain. "Form a line behind me facing him," said Maskepetoon. "And no one touches a weapon unless I give the signal."

So the warriors circled into line and Maskepetoon rode forward a little from them on the hill. He was peering into the mirage, the immense rider slowly, slowly floating closer and after a moment he said, "That's not a Blackfoot, that's a Blood." One of the eight Mountain People kicked his horse to run from the most magnificent and terrifying warriors of the plains, but Maskepetoon wheeled and seized the horse's bridle and hurled them both back into line. "Sit still," he said. "They are all around us."

The Blood on a beautiful bay stallion rode a wide half-circle about the base of their hill. Our People sat motionless facing westward as he slowly rode up the hill behind them, then between them in the line. That horse carried that big Blood through them, it seemed, without so much as a thud of a hoof on stone, up behind Maskepetoon sitting rock-like on his horse and then past and a hand reached out, drew the rifle from the scabbard against Maskepetoon's left knee as smoothly as if it were plucking a berry. Maskepetoon did not move. The Blood rode on, his back towards them all, then suddenly whirled his stallion and faced them. He held the rifle he had taken flat across his horse's withers.

You are a brave man, he signalled with his left hand.

"All those birds sing so beautifully," Maskepetoon said in the Blood language.

"And you are very wise too," the Blood said after a moment. "Come."

He turned and raised his hand, and it seemed the earth all around them grew warriors like grass, none of them had ever seen so many Bloods, not even Maskepetoon on the Missouri. So they rode into that huge camp in a bend of Kneehill Creek and the buffalo started coming south then so they helped the Bloods hunt and feast for sixteen days and then rode north again driving a herd of gift horses loaded down with presents, including meat and four better rifles than the company had ever traded them, and they easily avoided a large circle of Siksika and galloped out of the trees into our home camp beside Battle River Lake whooping their triumph. But there was no one to greet them. The bright green trees by the lake were black with funeral platforms. The Siksika had come and killed over half the camp, men, women, dogs, everything including Matono-wacap with all their children. And Maskepetoon's father under his robes.

"I cannot wail any more," Susewik told him. "Your two oldest sons are alive. I think they will heal by fall."

She had been up early that morning, the two boys getting water with her from the lake. She had dragged the boys into the rushes but she had been unable to hold them back as long as it took the Siksika to destroy our camp and when they got loose from her the warriors were already so full of killing they casually cut down the two little boys charging them with hands full of gravel from the beach and left them for dead. Who needed to bother with children's scalps on such a morning?

Four of the men could find no one of their families alive to mourn with them, so they came to Maskepetoon that same evening. "There are only fourteen warriors left now," they told him. "We are going to ride south again." But he would not go with them. Two days later seven of the thirteen came back and showed him the scalps they had taken. "We know who killed your father," they said, and before he could stop them, they told him that name. "We left him for you."

Not even that stirred his terrible rage; he refused to fight but took our People north and east to the Beaver Hills, beside the shallow lake where geese nested white as snow all year and there they healed that summer and fall and winter. The buffalo came easily to their autumn pounds and in the spring, when so many birds came north they could barely see the water, the eighth spring since he had come back, he heard of a new Whiteman in Fort Edmonton who spoke for The Great Spirit. The Cree who told him this said some Blackfoot were so impressed they were giving that God-man the hand nearest their heart to shake because they thought he had floated down from the sky in a small piece of paper which Factor Old Man Rowand at Fort Edmonton opened and he became big enough to step out of it.

Maskepetoon laughed aloud at that. When the man came to our camp shortly after he saw exactly what he had expected: one of those Whites with a fringe of beard and white collar he had seen often on his first journey and to whom he had never spoken. But this man, whose White name, Rundle, as usual meant nothing, was very gentle; he carried a small cat on his arm so the camp dogs would not tear it apart and he prayed every morning and evening bent down on his knees with his black book in his hands and so Maskepetoon let him touch Susewik's new son with water and give him a White name, Jo-seph. A very strong name, Rundle said through the interpreter, a name to save his people.

For Maskepetoon now knew two things certainly: though the Young Men looked at him every day, he could not ride against the Blackfoot that spring; and he had not seen the Medicine Lodge Hills vision since his father was killed. And a third thing was fixed also: his left arm, which looked as thick and powerful as ever, sometimes hurt so much at night he had to talk to it. When he went outside then to look for the dawn it seemed the light was rising in the west, that the world had been turned inside out. And when he faced the sun there growing large above the Beaver Hills, praying as he always had with his eyes wide open, he saw the crimson light gradually darken into another colour through his tears.

That summer, eight since he had returned, Maskepetoon heard that Governor Simpson of the Hudson's Bay Company needed a guide through the mountains to the western ocean. Though he had never journeyed in that direction, he said he would take the Governor there, and he did. He left Susewik and her baby with us and took his two oldest sons with him. The mountain passes with their terrible roaring rivers frightened them, and the smell of the bitter, undrinkable sea clenched between hills covered by trees as monstrous as the rivers and vines crawling everywhere alarmed Maskepetoon in a way he could

Rudy Wiebe: Collected Stories, 1955–2010

not remember of himself eight years before; though he knew now he was more and more aware of the powers beyond things. The Governor went onto the boat waiting there for him. They called it Amisk, *Beaver*, and invited Maskepetoon aboard to sail around the harbour, so he and his sons went and the boat moved slowly on the water without sails or paddles, shuddering deep within itself as it did so. This time he insisted they take him into it. There below deck he saw a stinking fire and machinery turning which they said made the ship go, but he could not see what made the machinery turn. Fire they said. So he had the Governor write on a piece of paper that he had been on such a ship and when he stood on land again beside his two sons he took the now featureless silver medal off from around his neck and threw it into that western ocean. When they got back to the Beaver Hills again, the paper with its incomprehensible marking was all he would show our People. And his two sons would tell us nothing either.

He would not kill our traditional enemies now. He said it was useless to fight, peace was the way people should try to live, and after a year he heard Rundle talk again. This time the God-man spoke of a "Prince of Peace" and so Maskepetoon invited him to sleep two nights in his lodge. The story of Jesus who finally died hammered up high on a tree was worse than anything he had ever heard, but the story of creation and fall stung him with happiness. He told Rundle the Mountain and River People were like young birds reaching up with their mouths open, waiting for food. And that summer for the first time Maskepetoon rode with his two sons into a Siksika camp carrying only a peace pipe, and the Siksika smoked peace together with our People, a truce that lasted all summer. The Company Factor at Rocky Mountain House was very happy for that. He offered to teach Maskepetoon how to read his own language and in a few days the chief had learned the syllabics and could pronounce anything written in Cree, though it took a little longer for him to learn to write it. His sons learned the writing even more easily than he and a summer later Rundle touched them both with water and named them: Benjamin and Joshua. Benjamin went to Fort Edmonton and started to learn English from Rundle.

The next Easter Maskepetoon went with twenty men to trade hides at Fort Edmonton above the river bluffs. That evening they

drank whisky at Whitemud Creek and suddenly his terrible rage
overcame him again and he took a man in his hands and very nearly
killed him. He left then, south, without talking to Benjamin, and so
met another God-man called Father Thibault who said Rundle did
not really know the right way about Jesus, the Prince of Peace. For
three years Maskepetoon thought about what these Whites said again
and again and again. He made another, longer, truce between us and
the Siksika and one entire summer made another journey, guiding a
fat English lord down the Saskatchewan River east past Fort Carlton
to The Pas. There he met another God-man named Reverend Hunter
who said both Rundle and Thibault were wrong; he alone knew the
way to heaven because he had a building with a bell which he rang
when it was time to pray. Maskepetoon looked in Hunter's black
book, which looked just like Rundle's, but he could read nothing
there; it was all English. So he returned the two-month journey back
to Fort Edmonton. Rundle told him immediately that Hunter was
of the Church of England and it did not matter what he claimed, no
more than the Roman Catholic Thibault, but Maskepetoon told him
Benjamin was now coming back with him to the Beaver Hills.

"Each of you three," he said, "say you know the only way to
heaven. Who can tell what you know? You should call a council
among yourselves to agree on what you do not know. Then I would
go with all of you."

Rundle gave him parts of the black book transcribed in Cree
syllabics and Maskepetoon promised to read it, perhaps every day if
he could, but said it was time for Benjamin to return. That summer
Joshua and a young man with six fingers stole Sarcee horses; the
young man was killed in the raid so Joshua gave all the horses to
his family. Later that summer Rundle and his cat went east with
the brigade down the river to return to his home over the Stinking
Water. And that fall, eight years after Maskepetoon had first laughed
to hear that Rundle had come from the sky in a folded piece of paper,
the Siksika passed our camp in the Beaver Hills on their way to Fort
Edmonton. Maskepetoon with Benjamin and four other men rode
out and smoked a truce with them so they could trade for winter in
peace. The Siksika gladly accepted these words from the man they
still called The Young Chief and that evening their leading men came

to eat meat with us. As they rode into camp without any paint or feathers, our women and children welcoming them with dancing and laughter, one of the warriors who had ridden with Maskepetoon when they faced the Bloods nine summers before came close to the chief and, pointing to a grey-haired man among the visitors, shouted the name of Maskepetoon's father's killer. The welcoming shouts died. The chief stood motionless, a dreadful blackness hardening in his hard face. The Siksika looked about at the Cree warriors suddenly surrounding them, bristling with weapons; they could not deny either the name or the deed which had been sung long ago in so many of their dances.

"Bring him to my lodge," Maskepetoon said at last. The Siksika stood alone in front of the lodge with the small group of his friends behind him and our People surrounding them, all waiting to see what weapon Maskepetoon would bring out. But our chief emerged with nothing but his embroidered ceremonial suit in his hands, the old suit of beads and quills and scalps he had not worn for years. "Put it on," he said in Blackfoot, and very slowly the old warrior did that. "Bring my horse," Maskepetoon said then, and when it was brought he gestured. "Get on." The Siksika looked at his friends without hope, then mounted in one swift movement and waited, his face clenched to accept whatever hit him first. Maskepetoon looked up at him.

"Both my hands are empty," he said then. "You took my father from me, so now I ask you to be my father. Wear my clothes, ride my horse, and when your people ask you how it is you are still alive, tell them it is because The Young Chief has taken his revenge."

Slowly the old Siksika slid from the horse and faced Maskepetoon empty-handed. Then he took him in his arms and held him hard against his heart.

"My son," he said, "you have killed me."

That night Maskepetoon had a vision again. It was not a dream because he was not sleeping. He saw one of the Mountain and River People who had walked in the way of Jesus and been good, doing more than it was possible for a person to do. This man died and was taken up into the White heaven. There the man found everything beautiful, and numberless White people all happy and singing among their friends for there was everything that could be desired, and more. But for the man it was all strange. He knew no one, there was no welcome for him, he met none of the spirits of his ancestors, there was no riding or hunting and no feasts around the fire; and finally he grew very sad. At last God heard of it and called to him, "Come here," and he went. God asked, "Why are you sad in this place I made for your joy and happiness?" So the man told him. And God looked at him sadly. "I can't send you to the People's heaven," he said. "You chose this one. But you were a very good man, so I will send you back to earth again. I will give you one more chance."

Maskepetoon lay under his buffalo robes staring into the pointed darkness of the lodge above him. He could hear his wives and sons and daughters and grandchildren breathing in sleep all around him. His left arm throbbed faintly, a drum beating perhaps or a bell ringing, he could not tell which. His long journeys spread like bright rivers, searching across the mountains and plains of his life. *I will give you one more chance.*

"What does it mean?" he said aloud. "What does it mean?" he whispered.

2. PEACE DANCE

Our ancestors knew that nothing ever happens which someone was not listening for; everything has already been heard. They taught us we must rise before dawn and listen very carefully for the voice of the wind; it sounds like two people singing the same song together. As they sing they come nearer and nearer and they have picked up a leaf, a stone, a bone and they are passing these three back and forth so that each always holds one and the third is moving between them, as is their song, which is the fourth thing that they pass. We listen and we hear in their endless dreamlike song of those who have been and will be carried ashore by the tides, who are white as a peeled log with iron axes and knives stuck in their belts and who will make dreadful sounds which no one has ever heard before.

So we knew of Whites long before we ever saw them with their inevitable rifles in their hands, in the same way that long before we first saw a horse we had already heard of them from the dawn, how they were larger than four dogs and so strong they could carry a grown man on their backs and still gain ground on a running buffalo. That is why our name for horse is "skydog."

No one doubts what he hears in the dawn songs of the wind; the world is too amazing for anyone to doubt any possibility. It is astonishing to us that Whites can carry the gruesome smallpox about with him in a small bottle that looks empty, and which he threatens to open any time he pleases, but we do not doubt that he can do this any more than we doubt that he has another bottle which contains the killer of the smallpox. After all, the sickness is his own and he should be able to do with it what he pleases (though sometimes, when he only has one bottle and not the other, it turns on him and kills him too); all this is merely astonishing, at most strange. But to fix words on a piece of wood or leather, not merely signs but words which always say exactly the same thing and which can make you say the same thing when you have touched the pen, that goes beyond strange. When we first saw words on things we could lift and put down with our hands, we thought such words would destroy both listening and memory altogether. However, after many long thoughts around a centre fire, we understood that this was not so. Rather, the knowledge of how to fix words in wood or leather or paper gave them their ultimate power: now one could handle them, make them and send them in silence, see them as well as hear and remember. That moved words beyond the power of sign or declaration into mystery, and if we had thought about it further, as some of the wisest among us surely did, and if we had listened even more intently at dawn, we would soon have understood that it was not Whiteman's gun or his diseases which would end our living as we did, no, no, it would be his words that would destroy us. As it was.

"But mystery is that which is hidden to some and revealed to others," our great chief Maskepetoon told us around his centre fire. "Once we were deaf but now we hear; once we were blind but now we see. The mystery of words and the world is revealed in the Book for those who truly want to know."

He was the first of our People to make words, and also the first to read them, and he understood mystery in the same way that it was given to him to read. When he first tried to make the three- and four-edged curves and lines and tails of words, whatever he made was smudged, he said, though the shapes were very sharp to us who could not understand them. He said they were all smeared, dragging like the tracks of an old person in river mud. Then Rundle gave him two pieces of Christian glass with a wire to hold them in front of his eyes and suddenly he laughed aloud, roared in his huge voice so that women and men and children from all around the camp came running.

"I can see," he cried, "I see!"

And he saw not only the sharp limits and edges of words but also the gnarled old scar of his broken left arm, which had always been so close to his eyes yet he had not been able to see it distinctly since his vision of heaven. That glass on his nose, which clouded the world for us when we put it on, made everything he could touch as exact as his memory and fingertips told him it was; wearing that he could say words slowly, saying them in parts in the same way that they were made on the paper:

"In the be-gin-ing God made the heavens and earth...."

After that his favourite words in the Book were about creation, the way things were made and held together by the Great Wind, the Spirit that made all things and gave them to all people, and the young missionary John McDougall later told the story again and again of when he first met Maskepetoon: he was seated with the log wall of the mission house at Fort Victoria against his back, the Book in his hands and the glasses on his nose. The North Saskatchewan River endlessly repeating itself between the striped banks of clay and shale and coal in grey-green reflections as he read aloud, slowly:

"...our sufferings of this time are not worthy to be compared with the glory which will be revealed to us then. For all creatures, the whole created universe waits with eager longing for God's sons to be revealed....Because then the universe itself will be freed from the chains of mortality and enter the glorious liberty of the Sons of God. For we know that until now the whole creation groans in all is parts as if in the pains of childbirth, and we also groan while we wait for God to make us his children and set our bodies free."

Maskepetoon looked up at young John, who had spoken our language since he was a child, and who therefore also understood the laughter of our old chief as it bounced off the cliffs across the wide river and came back to them, its image repeating itself like the river in their ears.

"I will be set free," Maskepetoon said then, "free from the groaning of my heart in the day, the cry of my heart at night. And I will walk across the waters of the river and up the cliff and over the buffalo prairie to all the Blackfoot and give them my two empty hands and we will sit down together and make words of peace forever."

Perhaps somewhere beyond flowing water and rock and time there was waiting that completed paradise; Maskepetoon brought us as close to it as we ever were that fall when he and his grandson faced the united Blackfoot warriors at the Blindman River below the Medicine Lodge Hills. We had moved that far south because the buffalo had not come north and in those short days before the snow starvation was already visiting our camps. But of course our enemies needed the great herds as much as we and they followed them north toward us until there did not seem to be so much as a grass blade to separate our two Peoples. And the camps of their fierce relations, the Bloods and the Peigans, were at the Red Deer River crossings less than a day behind them. In the Falling Leaves Moon some of us had already eaten our dogs and were going to start on our horses.

Then Maskepetoon said he would ride to the Blackfoot and six of us, only six, said we would go with him. Our horses had barely broken through the slivered ice of the river when their scouts noticed us and disappeared south up the spruce of the valley draws. Maskepetoon rode after them and we followed, saying nothing while we stared at the skyline ahead. We were half across the wide valley when heads bristled up there, at least thirty of them and with a whoop they charged us on their summer-fed horses. We swung around and rode back hard for the river, there was nothing to fight for against such numbers on such a day when the snow whispers it is coming, but when we dashed through the water and turned to look at the pursuit, we saw that the Blackfoot had not followed us. And we also saw that we had two riderless horses running with us; Maskepetoon and his grandson were standing where we had turned, facing the wide line of charging warriors alone and on foot.

And then, as we looked at each other and were about to gallop back to die with them, they sat down on the ground, both of them, and in an instant they were surrounded, Blackfoot horses running around them in three and four circles so that we could see nothing but our furious enemies and hear their screams; and our own hearts pounding with fear.

So it was Chief Child, Joshua's son who was only sixteen years old then and stayed with him, he told us the story.

"My grandfather stood looking at those horses, there was nothing to see but heads and knees coming, their riders so low on their necks, and I stood beside him. Then he said to me, 'It is time to read,' and put his hand inside his blanket and took out the Book and the glasses, and he sat down. So I sat down too. He set the glasses in place and began to read from the opened Book, his voice strong as if he were seated in his own lodge in the circle of our People:

"'…in the same way the Spirit comes to help us when we are weak; we do not even know how we should pray, but through our inarticulate groans the Spirit himself pleads for us.'

"And that is how the Blackfoot rode their circle around us, my grandfather not looking at them but reading on while the hooves of their horses threw grass and dust over us until the riders finally stopped their screams and just sat there on their shivering horses, staring. They had not shot a single arrow or bullet; I suppose not even Blackfoot kill a man sitting on frozen ground and speaking words into the air breathing winter over him, and suddenly the oldest of them shouted,

'It is The Young Chief!'

giving him that old name they had first given him when he was young and killed them better than any man of our People, and my grandfather looked up and said in their tongue,

'Yes Red Sky Bird, I am that one,' and he stood up and the Siksika slid from his nervous horse and they took each other in their arms. Red Sky Bird said,

'What is that you hold in your hand?' and my grandfather said,

'My friend, I do not need to ask what it is you hold in your hand.'

"The warrior looked down and seemed surprised that he still held his Hudson Bay rifle in his hand, its long barrel rubbed so blue you could see it lay with him under his blanket every night. And then he understood that my grandfather had embraced him even while he

Rudy Wiebe: Collected Stories, 1955–2010

was holding it, and he dropped it to the ground and said very gently,

'Forgive me. What have you?'

"And my grandfather smiled. 'These are the words of the Great Spirit,' and he showed him the marks in the Book and translated them into Blackfoot. Then Red Sky Bird and some of his men put the glasses on their noses and looked but the words were more smudged than ever and they still could understand nothing without Maskepetoon as interpreter so finally Red Sky Bird said,

'It must be the will of the Great Spirit that we meet as brothers today. You are the only one who can tell us his words.'

"And his warriors agreed, so they sat down with us and our men came back from the river and all the horses grazed the fall grass of the Blindman valley together while we smoked the Blackfoot pipe. Even I who was not yet a warrior, but had stood by the side of my grandfather."

That is how Chief Child told his story. And that very evening eight Blackfoot men came on foot into the large camp of our People, and Chief Child rode out with sixteen young men to escort them in. Hundreds of us would have been happy to kill them all for who did not have blood vengeance crying in his heart, but we honoured Maskepetoon's word and Chief Child's young courage and the Blackfoot walked through our camp as if they were being led through a great bluff of silent trees. Straight to the centre of the camp where our chief waited to greet them at the door of the great lodge. And that night the drums called us to Peace Dance.

Our war leader at that time, Starving Young Bull, stood up first to the beat of the drums. He was following the guidance of The One He Dreamed Of, he said, and he began to move in the rhythm of the drummers. Long and marvellously he danced, finding a song that reached up from the ground and through his voice and under the raised edges of the lodge past the People watching all around to the sharp cold stars of the winter sky. He danced around Maskepetoon's centre fire and The One He Dreamed Of gave him words, gave him courage and he lifted his blanket from his shoulder and gave it to Red Sky Bird singing, "Starving Young Bull has been given the courage to live in peace," and he stripped off his beaded shot pouch and powder horn and gave them to a second Blackfoot singing,

"Starving Young Bull hunts only buffalo." How we cheered him as he sat down in the circle, exhausted and naked.

Then one by one our greatest warriors danced agreement with Starving Young Bull, and when they had given their most precious possessions as gifts to all the Blackfoot, they all smoked the Pipe of Peace, round by round. Then Red Sky Bird, sitting beside Maskepetoon on the side of his heart, rose to his feet. He stood in gifts to his knees and he held the blue rifle in his hand as softly he began to sing. Our drummers passed the drums to the Blackfoot and they beat out the rhythms of our enemies, but different too for the words we knew were strong like the man standing motionless in his great song, singing of courage and peace and trust, words that a mother or a father could have sung to a snuggling child though his hands reaching out were like a black tree with the rifle grown blue into its branches. Then he bent at last to our chief Maskepetoon and laid the long rifle at his feet.

Maskepetoon sat motionless gazing into the fire; it seemed now as if he had seen and heard nothing. The Blackfoot drums grew quieter, quieter, and then Maskepetoon's broken arm reached out, picked up the rifle and laid it in front of Chief Child sitting on his right side.

But Chief Child said nothing either, nor did he move. He sat beside his grandfather as if he were one with him like the roots hold a tree and slowly the drums died away and silence came upon us all, silence as when one person is alone on the prairie and all things under the sky make their sounds but they mean nothing; it is their endless silence you must be able to hear. So we waited for that other silence. And it too came, walking like mountains opening their mouths or soft bones when they move into the order of birth. And in this silence at last we heard a song, whether from the fire or the ground or the poles and skins of the lodge or the rifle or Chief Child's hand we could not say; perhaps it was Maskepetoon's Book itself talking to each of us in our language, words none of us had ever until then been ready to hear:

The wind at dawn
Gives me the words
To teach stones to speak.

The knives of the wind
Open my eyes to see
the hills cry yes, yes.

That was the best peace we made with the Blackfoot, and it lasted
longer than any we had in all those years of our ancestors when we
rode anywhere on the prairie that our horses would carry us and we
had friends to meet. In a few years we would be forced to agree with
Whites that we had to live on little reserves, the "bits of land left
over" as we call them, and the Blackfoot would have to agree to that
too because the buffalo were suddenly all gone and there was nothing
to eat except what Whites agreed to give us and they would agree to
nothing unless we touched the pen to the words they made on their
paper. We did not have the power then, neither the strength in our
arms nor the words to hold what the Spirit had given us we thought
forever; our heads then seemed to have been shaken loose somehow,
it could have been by disease or whisky or fear or starvation, or all
four; or perhaps we had never truly understood what our most coura-
geous leaders tried in many ways to tell us, but the Blindman River
Peace sung in the shadow of the Medicine Lodge Hills lasted three
years, and it was the last peace we ever made with the Blackfoot. This
is how it was.

It was summer three years later, in the time of the Hatching Moon
and we were south much farther than ever, on the Bow River trying
to find buffalo. Two hundred Blackfoot lodges were on the Little Bow.
We stayed away from each other, hunting in different directions, but
one night three of our women went to the Blackfoot camp to play
and in the morning four of our men went after them. They all came
back alive, but now the peace was broken.

So our ancient chief Maskepetoon asked us to help him onto his
horse and with Chief Child and two others he rode to the Blackfoot.
When they came over the hill above the bend in the Little Bow where
the huge camp was, Blackfoot warriors came riding from four directions but Maskepetoon rode on, holding the Book and his Peace
Pipe high. And Red Sky Bird was coming to meet him, smiling and
holding his hands up, empty, when suddenly from the back of the
pushing horses a shot was fired. Maskepetoon pitched forward, and

fell from his horse. Red Sky Bird screamed so loud his voice was heard high above the warriors.

"What have you done?" he cried. "What have you done, stop, stop!"

And he stretched his empty hands to the sun, praying for them to stop. But the warriors had smelled blood, they beat their horses and rode circles around our men and cut them down screaming, there was no power could stop them and when their frenzy was at its highest they threw ropes around Maskepetoon and dragged his body down the hill and round and round through the camp for the women to see, screaming their triumph as the dragging dust churned up behind them.

A young man was living in that camp. His name was Rattlesnake Boy, his father was Blood but his mother Cree, and he ran to see what was happening. When he saw the torn, insulted body of Maskepetoon being hacked to pieces for the dogs, he went back into his lodge to cry. That night he slipped away, stole a horse and rode to our camp. So we learned what had happened to our great chief, and ah-h-h-h, how we wailed.

But, before we could finish wailing, there was something we had to do and next morning at dawn every warrior in our camp was at the bend in the Little Bow. There was nothing there however; the Blackfoot knew we would send a war party and had broken camp and fled. We pursued them south all the way to the Medicine Line and they crossed that and later met American traders there who gave them whisky and smallpox and that winter they came north again to escape that and then in spring we finally found the few that were left, weak with disease and hunger. And we killed them, we killed every one of them we could find screaming, "The Young Chief! The Young Chief!" Our peace chief Maskepetoon, Broken Arm. Whom they killed when he held only the Book in his right hand and the Peace Pipe in his left, the one nearest his heart.

Our greatest peace chief, and how we tried to honour him with a war of revenge. Sometimes, some of us can almost forget. For in that last, dreadful, battle, the small camp we attacked had, unknown to us, several huge camps of allies nearby, and they were armed with American repeater rifles. Four times as many Cree as Blackfoot died that day, October 25, 1870, in the Oldman River coulees now surrounded by the city of Lethbridge, Alberta. In their winter count for the year 1870, the Blackfoot named that place *assini-etomotchi*: "Where we slaughtered the Cree."

Where is the Voice Coming From? [1970/1971]

THE PROBLEM is to make the story.

One difficulty of this making may have been excellently stated by Teilhard de Chardin: "We are continually inclined to isolate ourselves from the things and events which surround us...as though we were spectators, not elements, in what goes on." Arnold Toynbee does venture, "For all that we know, Reality is the undifferentiated unity of the mystical experience," but that need not here be considered. This story ended long ago; it is one of finite acts, of orders, or elemental feelings and reactions, of obvious legal restrictions and requirements.

Presumably all the parts of the story are themselves available. A difficulty is that they are, as always, available only in bits and pieces. Though the acts themselves seem quite clear, some written reports of the acts contradict each other. As if these acts were, at one time, too well-known; as if the original nodule of each particular fact had from somewhere received non-factual accretions; or even more, as if, since the basic facts were so clear, perhaps there were a larger number of facts than any one reporter, or several, or even any reporter had ever attempted to record. About facts that are simply told by this mouth to that ear, of course, even less can be expected.

An affair seventy-five years old should acquire some of the shiny transparency of an old man's skin. It should.

Sometimes it would seem that it would be enough—perhaps more than enough—to hear the names only. The grandfather One Arrow; the mother Spotted Calf; the father Sounding Sky; the wife (wives rather, but only one of them seems to have a name, though their fathers are known as Napaise, Kapahoo, Old Dust, The Rump)—the one wife named, of all things, Pale Face; the cousin Going-Up-To-Sky; the brother-in-law (again, of all things) Dublin. The names of the police sound very much alike; they all begin with Constable or Corporal or Sergeant, but here and there an Inspector, then a Superintendent and eventually all the resonance of an Assistant Commissioner echoes down. More. Herself: Victoria, by the Grace of God, etc., etc., QUEEN, defender of the Faith, etc., etc.; and witness "Our Right Trusty and Right Well-beloved Cousin and Councillor the Right Honourable Sir John Campbell Hamilton-Gordon, Earl of Aberdeen; Viscount Formartine, Baron Haddo, Methlic, Tarves and Kellie in the Peerage of Scotland; Viscount Gordon of Aberdeen, County of Aberdeen in the Peerage of the United Kingdom; Baronet of Nova Scotia, Knight Grand Cross of Our Most Distinguished Order of Saint Michael and Saint George, etc., Governor General of Canada." And of course himself: in the award proclamation named "Jean-Baptiste" but otherwise known only as Almighty Voice.

But hearing cannot be enough; not even hearing all the thunder of A Proclamation: "Now Hear Ye that a reward of FIVE HUNDRED DOLLARS will be paid to any person or persons who will give such information as will lead...(etc., etc.) this Twentieth day of April, in the year of Our Lord one thousand eight hundred and ninety-six, and the Fifty-ninth year of Our Reign..." etc. and etc.

Such hearing cannot be enough. The first item to be seen is the piece of white bone. It is almost triangular, slightly convex— concave actually as it is positioned at this moment with its corners slightly raised—graduating from perhaps a strong eighth to a weak quarter of an inch in thickness, its scattered pore structure varying between larger and smaller on its polished, certainly shiny surface. Precision is difficult since the glass showcase is at least thirteen inches deep and therefore an eye cannot be brought as close as the minute inspection of such a small, though certainly quite adequate, sample of skull would normally require. Also, because of the position it cannot be determined whether the several hairs, well over a foot long, are still in some manner attached to it or not.

The seven-pounder cannon can be seen standing almost shyly between the showcase and the interior wall. Officially it is known as a gun, not a cannon, and clearly its bore is not large enough to admit a large man's fist. Even if it can be believed that this gun was used in the 1885 Rebellion and that on the evening of Saturday, May 29, 1897 (while the nine-pounder, now unidentified, was in the process of arriving with the police on the special train from Regina), seven shells (all that were available in Prince Albert at that time) from it were sent shrieking into the poplar bluffs as night fell, clearly such shelling could not and would not disembowel the whole earth. Its carriage is now nicely lacquered, the perhaps oak spokes of its petite wheels (little higher than a knee) have been recently scraped, puttied and varnished; the brilliant burnish of its brass breeching testifies with what meticulous care charmen and women have used nationally advertised cleaners and restorers.

Though it can also be seen, even a careless glance reveals that the same concern has not been expended on the one (of two) .44 calibre 1866 model Winchesters apparently found at the last in the pit with Almighty Voice. It is also preserved in a glass case; the number 1536735 is still, though barely, distinguishable on the brass cartridge section just below the brass saddle ring. However, perhaps because the case was imperfectly sealed at one time (though sealed enough not to warrant disturbance now), or because of simple neglect, the rifle is obviously spotted here and there with blotches of rust and the brass itself reveals discolorations almost like mildew. The rifle bore, the three long strands of hair themselves, actually bristle with clots of dust. It may be that this museum cannot afford to be as concerned as the other; conversely, the disfiguration may be something inherent in the items themselves.

The small building which was the police guardroom at Duck Lake, Saskatchewan Territory, in 1895 may also be seen. It has subsequently been moved from its original place and used to house small animals, chickens perhaps, or pigs—such as a woman might be expected to have under her responsibility. It is, of course, now perfectly empty, and clean so that the public may enter with no more discomfort than a bend under the doorway and a heavy encounter with disinfectant. The door jamb has obviously been replaced; the bar network at one window is, however, said to be original; smooth still, very smooth. The logs inside have been smeared again and again with whitewash, perhaps paint, to an insistent point of identity-defying characterlessness. Within the small rectangular box of these logs not a sound can be heard from the streets of the, probably dead, town.

> *Hey Injun you'll get hung for stealing that steer*
> *Hey Injun for killing that government cow you'll*
> *get three weeks on the woodpile Hey Injun*

The place named Kinistino seems to have disappeared from the map but the Minnechinass Hills have not. Whether they have ever been on a map is doubtful but they will, of course, not disappear from the landscape as long as the grass grows and the rivers run. Contrary to general report and belief, the Canadian prairies are rarely, if ever, flat and the Minnechinass (spelled five different ways and translated sometimes as "The Outside Hill," sometimes as "Beautiful Bare Hills") are dissimilar from any other of the numberless hills that everywhere block out the prairie horizon. They are bare; poplars lie tattered along their tops, almost black against the straw-pale grass and sharp green against the grey soil of the ploughing laid in half-mile rectangular blocks upon their western slopes. Poles holding various wires stick out of the fields, back down the bend of the valley; what was once a farmhouse is weathering into the cultivated earth. The poplar bluff where Almighty Voice made his stand has, of course, disappeared.

The policemen he shot and killed (not the ones he wounded, of course) are easily located. Six miles east, thirty-nine miles north in Prince Albert, the English Cemetery. Sergeant Colin Campbell Colebrook, North West Mounted Police Registration Number 605, lies presumably under a gravestone there. His name is seventeenth in a very long "list of non-commissioned officers and men who have died in the service since the inception of the force." The date is October 29, 1895, and the cause of death is anonymous: "Shot by escaping

Indian prisoner near Prince Albert." At the foot of this grave are two others: Constable John R. Kerr, No. 3040, and Corporal C.H.S. Hockin, No. 3106. Their cause of death on May 28, 1897, is even more anonymous, but the place is relatively precise: "Shot by Indians at Min-etch-inass Hills, Prince Albert District."

The gravestone, if he has one, of the fourth man Almighty Voice killed is more difficult to locate. Mr. Ernest Grundy, former North West Mounted Police constable, was postmaster at Duck Lake in 1897; apparently he shut his window the afternoon of Friday, May 28, armed himself, galloped east twenty miles, participated in the second charge into the bluff at about 6:30 p.m., and on the third sweep of that charge was shot dead at the edge of the pit. It would seem that he thereby contributed substantially not only to the Indians' bullet supply, but his clothing warmed them as well.

The burial place of Dublin and Going-Up-To-Sky is unknown, as is the grave of Almighty Voice. It is said that on May 30, 1897, their bodies were blown up. It is said that a Métis named Henry Smith lifted Almighty Voice's body from the pit in the bluff and gave it to Spotted Calf. The place of burial is not, of course, of ultimate significance. A gravestone or obelisk is always less evidence than a triangular piece of skull, provided it is large enough.

Whatever further evidence there is to be gathered may rest on pictures. There are, presumably, almost numberless pictures of the policemen in the case, but the only one with direct bearing is one of Sergeant Colebrook who apparently insisted on advancing to complete an arrest after being warned three times that if he took another step he would be shot. The picture must have been taken before he joined the force; it reveals him a large-eared young man, hair brush-cut and ascot tie, his eyelids slightly drooping, almost hooded under thick brows. Unfortunately a picture of Constable R.C. Dickson, into whose charge Almighty Voice was apparently committed in that guardroom and who after Colebrook's death was convicted of negligence, sentenced to two months hard labour and discharged, does not seem to be available.

There are no pictures to be found of either Dublin (killed early by rifle fire) or Going-Up-To-Sky (killed in the pit), the two teenage boys who gave their ultimate fealty to Almighty Voice. There is, however,

one said to be of Almighty Voice, Junior. He may have been born to
Pale Face during the year, two hundred and twenty-one days that his
father was a fugitive. In the picture he is kneeling before what could
be a tent, he wears striped denim overalls and displays twin babies
whose sex cannot be determined from the double-laced dark bonnets
they wear. In the supposed picture of Spotted Calf and Sounding Sky,
Sounding Sky stands slightly before his wife; he wears a white shirt
and a striped blanket folded over his left shoulder in such a manner
that the arm in which he cradles a long rifle cannot be seen. His head
is thrown back; the rim of his hat appears as a black half-moon above
eyes that are pressed shut as if in profound concentration; above
a mouth clenched thin in a downward curve. Spotted Calf wears a
long dress, a sweater which could also be a man's dress coat, and a
large fringed and embroidered shawl which would appear distinctly
Doukhobor in origin if the scroll patterns on it were more irregular. Her head is small and turned slightly towards her husband so
as to reveal her right ear. There is what can only be called a quizzical
expression on her crumpled face; it may be she does not understand what is happening and that she would have asked a question,
perhaps of her husband, perhaps of the photographers, perhaps even
of anyone, anywhere in the world if such questioning were possible
for a Cree woman.

There is one final picture. That is one of Almighty Voice himself.
At least it is purported to be of Almighty Voice himself. In the Royal
Canadian Mounted Police Museum on the Barracks Grounds just off
Dewdney Avenue in Regina, Saskatchewan, it lies in the same showcase, as a matter of fact immediately beside that triangular piece
of skull. Both are unequivocally labelled, and it must be assumed
that a police force with a worldwide reputation would not label
such evidence incorrectly. But here emerges an ultimate problem in
making the story.

There are two official descriptions of Almighty Voice. The first
reads: "Height about five feet, ten inches, slight build, rather good
looking, a sharp hooked nose with a remarkably flat point. Has a
bullet scar on the left side of his face about 1½ inches long running
from near corner of mouth towards ear. The scar cannot be noticed
when his face is painted but otherwise is plain. Skin fair for an

Indian." The second description is on the Award Proclamation: "About twenty-two years old, five feet, ten inches in height, weight about eleven stone, slightly erect, neat small feet and hands; complexion inclined to be fair, wavey dark hair to shoulders, large dark eyes, broad forehead, sharp features and parrot nose with flat tip, scar on left cheek running from mouth towards ear, feminine appearance."

So run the descriptions that were, presumably, to identify a well-known fugitive in so precise a manner that an informant could collect five hundred dollars—a very considerable sum when a police constable earned between one and two dollars a day. The nexus of the problems appears when these supposed official descriptions are compared to the supposed official picture. The man in the picture is standing on a small rug. The fingers of his left hand touch a curved Victorian settee, behind him a photographer's backdrop of scrolled patterns merges to vaguely paradisiacal trees and perhaps a sky. The patterned moccasins he wears make it impossible to deduce whether his feet are "neat small." He may be five feet, ten inches tall, may weigh eleven stone, he certainly is "rather good looking" and, though it is a frontal view, it may be that the point of his long and flaring nose could be "remarkably flat." The photograph is slightly over-illuminated and so the unpainted complexion could be "inclined to be fair"; however, nothing can be seen of a scar, the hair is not wavy and shoulder-length but hangs almost to the waist in two thick straight braids worked through with beads, fur, ribbons and cords. The right hand that holds the corner of the blanket-like coat in position is large and, even in the high illumination, heavily veined. The neck is concealed under coiled beads and the forehead seems more low than "broad."

Perhaps, somehow, these picture details could be reconciled with the official description if the face as a whole were not so devastating.

On a cloth-backed sheet two feet by two and one-half feet in size, under the Great Seal of the Lion and the Unicorn, dignified by the names of the Deputy of the Minister of Justice, the Secretary of State, the Queen herself and all the heaped detail of her "Right Trusty and Right Well-beloved Cousin," this description concludes: "feminine appearance." But the picture: any face of history, any believed face that the world acknowledges as *man*—Socrates, Jesus, Attila, Genghis

Khan, Mahatma Gandhi, Joseph Stalin—no believed face is more *man* than this face. The mouth, the nose, the clenched brows, the eyes—the eyes are large, yes, and dark, but even in this watered-down reproduction of unending reproductions of that original, a steady look into those eyes cannot be endured. It is a face like an axe.

It is now evident that the de Chardin statement quoted at the beginning has relevance only as it proves itself inadequate to explain what has happened. At the same time, the inadequacy of Aristotle's much more famous statement becomes evident: "The true difference [between the historian and the poet] is that one relates what *has* happened, the other what *may* happen." These statements cannot explain the storymaker's activity since, despite the most rigid application of impersonal investigation, the elements of the story have now run me aground. If ever I could, I can no longer pretend to objective, omnipotent disinterestedness. I am no longer *spectator* of what *has* happened or what *may* happen: I am become *element* in what is happening at this very moment.

For it is, of course, I myself who cannot endure the shadows on that paper which are those eyes. It is I who stand beside this broken veranda post where two corner shingles have been torn away, where barbed wire tangles the dead weeds on the edge of this field. The bluff that sheltered Almighty Voice and his two friends has not disappeared from the slope of the Minnechinass, no more than the sound of Constable Dickson's voice in that guardhouse is silent. The sound of his speaking is there even if it has never been recorded in an official report:

hey injun you'll get
hung
for stealing that steer
hey injun for killing that government
cow you'll get three
weeks on the woodpile hey injun

The unknown contradictory words about an unprovable act that move a boy to defiance, an implacable Cree warrior long after the three-hundred-and-fifty-year war is ended, a war already lost the day the Cree watch Cartier hoist his guns ashore at Hochelaga and they begin the long retreat west; these words of incomprehension, of threatened incomprehensible law are there to be heard just as the unmoving tableau of the three-day siege is there to be seen on the slopes of the Minnechinass. Sounding Sky is somewhere not there, under arrest, but Spotted Calf stands on a shoulder of the Hills a little to the left, her arms upraised to the setting sun. Her mouth is open. A horse rears, riderless, above the scrub willow at the edge of the bluff, smoke puffs, screams tangle in rifle barrage, there are wounds, somewhere. The bluff is so green this spring, it will not burn and the ragged line of seven police and two civilians is staggering through, faces twisted in rage, terror, and rifles sputter. Nothing moves. There is no sound of frogs in the night; twenty-seven policemen and five civilians stand in cordon at thirty-yard intervals and a body also lies in the shelter of a gully. Only a voice rises from the bluff:

We have fought well
You have died like braves
I have worked hard and am hungry
Give me food

but nothing moves. The bluff lies, a bright green island on the grassy slope surrounded by men hunched forward rigid over their long rifles, men clumped out of rifle-range, thirty-five men dressed as for fall hunting on a sharp spring day, a small gun positioned on a ridge above. A crow is falling out of the sky into the bluff, its feathers sprayed as by an explosion. The first gun and the second gun are in position, the beginning and end of the bristling surround of thirty-five Prince Albert Volunteers, thirteen civilians and fifty-six policemen in position relative to the bluff and relative to the unnumbered whites astride their horses, standing up in their carts, staring and pointing across the valley, in position relative to the bluff and the unnumbered Cree squatting silent along the higher ridges of the Hills, motionless mounds, faceless against the Sunday morning sunlight edging between and over them down along the tree tips,

Rudy Wiebe: Collected Stories, 1955–2010

down into the shadows of the bluff. Nothing moves. Beside the second gun the red-coated officer has flung a handful of grass into the motionless air, almost to the rim of the red sun.

And there is a voice. It is an incredible voice that rises from among the young poplars ripped of their spring bark, from among the dead somewhere lying there, out of the arm-deep pit shorter than a man; a voice rises over the exploding smoke and thunder of guns that reel back in their positions, worked over, serviced by the grimed motionless men in bright coats and glinting buttons, a voice so high and clear, so unbelievably high and strong in its unending wordless cry.

The voice of "Gitchie-Manitou Wayo"—interpreted as "voice of the Great Spirit"—that is, The Almighty Voice. His death chant no less incredible in its beauty than in its incomprehensible happiness.

I say "wordless cry" because that is the way it sounds to me. I could be more accurate if I had a reliable interpreter who would make a reliable interpretation. For I do not, of course, understand the Cree myself.

Watch for Two Coyotes, Crossing [1996–1997/1998]

*And Cain went out from Jahweh's presence
and lived in the land of Wandering.*
—GENESIS 4:16

1. MY NAME WAS KANE. Paul Kane, painter. The work of a painter is to lend his eyes out.

I was born in Mallow, County Cork, Ireland, on September 3, 1810, and died suddenly (as they say in newspapers) in Toronto, Ontario, on February 20, 1871. If anyone remembers me now one and a quarter centuries after my death it is because of a singular journey I made across North America. When I started it, I had already been wandering for nine years, living as I could by my painting in the United States, England and Europe, and even a bit of Palestine and Africa. But who can count the thousands of painters, many gifted beyond the imaginable grace of God, who have endlessly repeated for us the images of those lands, seen with much the same eye because the painters have already made us see them so often? No painter had ever looked at what I saw on my ultimate journey, I started all the seeing. Perhaps I should say, I could have.

Love enters at the eye and, like it, is a circle; but moving I think.

When I was almost nine my parents immigrated to Upper Canada, to York, the village at the head of the Toronto Portage which a few years before the Americans had attacked and largely burned. From our ship entering Toronto Bay that muddy little place was difficult to see among the prodigious oaks and maples. Even the steeple of the first St. James's Church, which had not been destroyed and was grand enough at the time (though nothing like what it was later), looked lost on the quarter of a million acres of forest the Empire bought from the Mississauga Indians in August 1805, for ten English shillings—it still has to be cleared, you know—paid for in their own Indian tobacco, I heard them say, and largely smoked on the spot.

Money. Who knows about that so-called "Toronto Purchase" for ten shillings? Few if any of the millions now living there. Can a travesty be dignified by an honest word like "purchase"? My father Michael Kane, who had somehow survived Napoleon and retired a corporal of the Royal Horse Artillery, tried for years to be a wine merchant on the corner of Yonge and Adelaide, and he always preached the practical English dictum, "A deal's a deal, it's only good or bad in the eye of the dealers." And his sole other legacy was like unto it: "Just remember, money makes the world go round."

And I do remember, still. He said it so often I have no choice. Even though my mother Frances never agreed with him; she was Irish and insisted the world went round on something else.

2. I left Toronto on May 9, 1846, and returned to it October 13, 1848. Two and a half years, over six thousand miles on foot or by boat, canoe, horse, snowshoe, dogsled—not a single step of road, nothing of railroad—through the lands of eighty different Indian nations, I could not have imagined such visual richness existed in the north of America; in Europe wilderness is mostly thought of as always one, and "wildly" picturesque. I returned massively long-bearded and gaunt, but with a pencil journal of 119 pages and 500 paintings and sketches: stories and images to overflow the twenty-three years that remained to me.

On November 18, 1847, I was forced to leave behind my smudged, water-stained sketches in a tin trunk among the frozen brush of the frozen Athabasca River because—ugh, dates, statistics! the muck of accounting, money, money, how can I—the following spring voyageurs brought them to me again in Edmonton. I re-made them into some one hundred large oil paintings, I lost count of exactly how many but I lived on the money they brought, yes I painted to sell them, and the journal eventually became a book illustrated by my paintings and published in London in 1859: *Wanderings of an Artist Among the Indians of North America from Canada to Vancouver's Island and Oregon through the Hudson's Bay Company Territory and Back Again*. It also appeared in French, German, and Danish.

Why I mention in the title that company name, now the oldest continuous business enterprise in the world, should be obvious to anyone living in the advertising nightmare of the 1990s: to go on my journey I had to convince the most relentless money-maker in Canada that my wanderings would be profitable to him. Sir George Simpson himself who, when not being carried about his fathomless domain on the shoulders of French Canadian voyageurs, sat occasionally in his mansion overlooking the Lachine Rapids, Montreal, Lower Canada; with his much younger, beautiful but white invalid wife Frances Ramsay, Lady Simpson. Through his governorship of the Hudson's Bay Company he had long ago decided that he controlled, by money, a land three times the size of Europe, from York Factory on Hudson Bay to the arctic Beaufort Sea and the mouth of the Columbia River on the Pacific Ocean, to say nothing of the northern latitudes of what is now Quebec fronting the Atlantic. For him money decided everything, a true twentieth-century man a century ahead of his time—but with an added dollop of nineteenth-century aspiration: nobility. Sir George, Governor-in-Chief of the Hudson's Bay Company, but better known as "The Little (for his short legs) Emperor."

Immense colonial wealth, untouchable colonial power: surely achievements of true nobility for the illegitimate son of the eldest son of a Scots Presbyterian minister.

3. I stared too much into the deadly light of the sun on snow during the two long winters of my journey. And yet it was a journey too brief, I often thought later, an entire lifetime of preparation and then so little time, a little more than a dozen years of eyesight really, to exploit it.

Exploit. A fine Simpson word that, so effectively ugly. Whatever I saw was overlaid with his voice always as it were at my shoulder: "What a magnificent landscape—all it needs is *development*." For without his permission and his expenditures, I would not have been there to see it.

During the journey itself I had no time to notice that the light had begun to destroy my vision: I was too busy moving, staying alive, absorbing what I could in the strange changing worlds that confronted me, that tried to transfix me into motionless parts of themselves. In those later years, the 1860s in Toronto, when my wife Harriet would let herself into my studio on King Street where I kept trying to re-see what my often hasty sketches—fur brigades move seventeen to twenty hours a day in the long northern light of summer—provoked like an illusion of spirits dancing beyond control in my memory, she often found me crucified on the floor, my burning eyes hidden under an arm, no brush or pencil in my hand. She had such heavy work of it caring for me and our four small children, but her hand then was delicate as prairie mist in the morning.

"Harriet...Harriet," the tips of my fingers see every tiny particularity of her face, though I know I will never again be able to draw it. "You could be Margaret Harriott, my Harriet."

She laughs; it is a game she has created for the sake of her participation in what she in loving kindness accepts as my to her inexpressible memories. "But that, Mr. Kane," she says, "is merely an accident of sounds—*my* name is Harriet Clench."

Frances Lady Simpson was no "accident of sounds," and so easily avoidable as a play of verbal memory. A secret that lived in my most solitary visual recesses, her hand and extraordinary skin almost exactly mine, a quarter of a century younger than her stumpy husband's. And my finest paint then dared a glance, to dream it.

But to continue the play with my loving wife, I always answer. "Your name *was* Harriet Clench," gathering myself again with a small laugh. "Marriage changes names."

"Only for women."

"Miss Harriott's name was then not changed, not yet."

"Nor was mine, then," laughing too. "Though it might have been."

"But not to Celtic 'Kane.'"

"Who can say—you told me yourself, in the North-West only certain kinds of marriage changed names, for certain kinds of women."

"Yes, I told you...yes...." my contemplative fingers.

"And did you see Miss *Margaret* Harriott with your fingertips as well, Mr. Kane?"

Sometimes she shifts her repartee that way, meaning whatever she means, and I am forced to scramble if I wish to retain our comfortable, to us acceptable, blind exchange. As I do, I do; though on occasion I wonder why she will never dig deeper. Almost I think I wish it.

4. The first time I saw Margaret Harriott there was no possibility for fingertips. On the frozen North Saskatchewan River, the winter afternoon light so silver where the cliffs broke away raw across the river to bend east and steam wisped up through the ridged ice like intermittent spirits, breathing. My eyes were still superb in December 1847, careful and swift as a painter's must be to catch the instant, and keep it, and I saw her coming towards us in the second sled quicker than Young John Rowand—though no quicker than his wife Mary, to judge from her face.

Young John Rowand's Mary. Whatever her real name was, a Cree "daughter of the country" as such "reputed wives" were then called by white men or the legitimized sons of white men who took these women to live with in the fur territories. Cree Mary—what other mothering name could she have had?—was laying spruce chunks on the fire while I sketched her, leaning forward at the waist like any lady into what leaned away from her as pale flames strangely silver against snow. Her classical nose nudged a bit, beautifully, askew, her skin warm as fondled brown stone. Under her hooded fur I could discern the body of a slender Greek but sadly, as always, her face must suffice me.

"You better get in the teepee," Young John grunted behind me. "Out here you'll freeze your fast fingers."

5. "Young" John was the son of Chief Factor John Rowand, the "King of Edmonton," and nearly as enormous as his father: three hundred

pounds nurtured on thirty-six years of buffalo meat and dripping. But even walking on snowshoes as long as my body, he had come up through the creek bush soundlessly behind me. I lost my pencil line for an instant, though he had startled me before with his silence, his massive shape beaked suddenly over my shoulder.

I had only one skill, as mysterious to him as to the Indians who crowded about me when I drew—See, powerful medicine, it makes your face appear out of paper!—but Young John considered my skill supremely useless; he spoke to me only in order to help keep alive, as he thought, a helpless man in inexplicable high favour with the supreme Sir George.

"She's so—" but I dared not utter "beautiful," not to his bearish, glowering face. "My oils are hard as rock, right beside your fire or I'd—"

A shout from below on the river, the voice of their son. And the distant ring of sled bells as all the camp dogs about us burst into their apocalyptic howl of enraged greeting. I don't know why I was looking at Mary then, but I saw sharp as if I'd painted it how her smooth face froze. She had recognized the second sled coming around the bend of the river: a cariole, and in it a white woman.

Young John was rumbling at Mary, Cree too rapid for me to decipher any words except "Fort Pitt," but then he broke off; he too had recognized the cariole woman.

6. Margaret Harriott. Not bothering to lift her arms in her furs to greet us, the sled long as a sarcophagus thumping her over the broken, shelved river ice. At least seven days out of Fort Pitt with four men who could speak nothing but Cree or doggerel French carrying her around like the untouchable, cocooned insect she was for them, Chief Factor John Edward Harriott's daughter to be deposited with her father in Fort Edmonton. Going there for Christmas, going there to become a bride, going there to have her wedding portrait painted by me. Fortunate girl.

Young John's Métis companion, the hunter François Lucie, had emerged from his teepee and, with the boy by the river below, was hallooing mightily, arms waving wide. But Young John barely acknowledged the whistling, dancing whips of the drivers as the three sleds slid by. He merely flicked his hand at Mary, who

immediately vanished into their teepee, and then as he himself
stooped to enter, said over his shoulder to me,

"Tell François to take you back, to the Fort."

7. The HBC flag that snapped on the flagstaff over Fort Edmonton's
inner square was precisely the same throughout the fur territories.
By December 1847, I was twenty months into my wanderings and I
had learned, exactly, how everyone inside a Hudson's Bay fort lived
within the Company's particular customs, its own peculiar laws.
The reasons for that were simple enough: in 1670 King Charles II
of England gave a charter to an enterprise designed to make money
for its shareholders, in a land he had scarcely heard of and certainly
cared nothing about. That solitary purpose remained for each fort
factor: make money for the Company and you will make money for
yourself. I was, therefore, surprised when I came through the river
gate of Edmonton into its Inner Square.

More than surprised—utterly amazed. Not by the exploding dog
fights, which are usual enough when new teams arrive among the
hundreds of local beasts and which only indiscriminant beatings by
all the drivers will subdue—no, amazed at the livid white face of Miss
Margaret Harriott screaming, above the dog bedlam, at her father:

"Wedding? I come for Christmas—*my wedding*?.."

And John Harriott standing like a bent sheep in the fort where he
was, supposedly, absolute despot. While his wife Nancy shouted back
at the furious girl, their voices bouncing from log walls and palisades,

"...plenty of time...after New Year's...what is all this.."

Questions and answers shouted or not given, what were they
about? Did Miss Harriott not know? Had she not been informed
of her own marriage? The Company clerks and maids and workers
stood motionless about the square and on the Big House balconies,
clouds of excitement snored in the frozen air; a regal spectacle acted
out before every servant, a celebration of arrival indeed!

8. Two nights before the ravenous dogs of Edmonton very nearly
devoured the Reverend Robert Rundle. Methodist Rundle was the
first missionary Simpson ever permitted to enter his territories and
he, as was usual for him, was carrying one of his small fluffy cats in

his arms across the inner square to his quarters when he stumbled and fell among the dogs.

Not a hair of the cat was recovered, and often I had seen in the eye of a Company worker the same gleam with which several went out of their way to tell me that story: I with my papers and many little pencils was a similar, fluffy indulgence of Company royalty. Fort Edmonton was not, of course, the court of the Little Emperor; that followed Sir George wherever he went in his immense flotilla of canoes with his irrefutable decrees, met him at every Company establishment as bowing factors and always available harems (and occasional children, some sometimes acknowledged; born as he was, Simpson understood well the inevitable vagaries of illegitimacy), harems of Indian or Métis (his preference varied) beauties of endlessly accommodating, delicate shades of brown.

And for continuing services rendered in a remote posting, the Edmonton Rowands and Harriotts were known to be his favourites; definitely the families of the Princes Royal. Therefore, when I set up my easel the next morning to paint Margaret dressed in her wedding splendour of lace, I existed merely as a servant hired for his eyes and fingertips, nothing else.

"Father, you tricked me!"

Harriott had the surface evasions of a decent man who, when sober, knows his shortcomings only too well. This early in the day he could only plead like maudlin melodrama:

"My beautiful daughter! I so wanted to explain all this to you before, but letters are so very difficult—"

She was not beautiful. Handsome perhaps, as seventeen can be under high emotion. Obviously the best the English governesses at the Red River Academy could do, but she would never be shaped into a "lovely, tender exotic" for the highest possible connections: there was too much the tough sturdiness of her "bit of brown" visible in her. And in her voice.

"Daughter!" she burst through his words. "I've seen you five times in my life, and now you arrange this overnight marriage to a man more than twice my age who's been—"

"Your mother died," he interrupted quickly, "in that horrible mountain snow! You know that story, how could I keep you? The

Company sent me, year in, year out, from one wilderness post to the next, how—?"

"You needn't have married a child bride."

"What?" His tone hardened then. "My Nancy—no Company trader could ask for a better wife."

"You married Old John Rowand's daughter at sixteen because he told you to, and this—arrangement—for me with his son, who everyone knows has wives and children behind every bush on the Saskatchewan, this is his plan as well!"

"Margaret!"

"Because I'm white enough to dignify him? Because I am, God knows! a virgin?"

I couldn't believe it. Was this how the imported governesses trained old traders' daughters in that "little Britain in the Wilderness" of a Red River Academy? She had gone too far, even for Harriott, her face blazing with incontrovertible facts.

"You will *not* speak that—I am your father!" Harriott's tone became that of the chief factor explaining the day's orders to his voyageurs. "Among us, a father makes the best possible arrangements for his daughter's marriage because he best understands our situation. Young John has the best possible connections in the entire Northern District, with all the governors, with Sir George himself. With you for his wife, you will both rise to the top of the Company."

"Like his father," she spat at him.

"Yes! Like his father!"

"Because I'm 'white' enough?"

"Yes, that helps!"

And then she truly astounded me because she had a more powerful word than "virgin" to use:

"How 'white' was my mother?"

For a moment Harriott could not speak. He tugged at his greying sideburns, so carefully trimmed for Christmas celebrations—or the anticipated wedding. Like many traders he drank too much, but he had not been sufficiently obsessive about money: he had a library of several books, he was no Simpson or Rowand; this, his only child from his first marriage, whom he had always disposed of as seemed necessary to nurture her, was his best hope for a comfortable Company old age.

"Old John Rowand," Margaret said in a tone so abruptly sweet as her lips curled—if only my brush could catch that twist, a superb transformation! "has had a Cree wife for forty years. Though he's never actually married her. And he's considered to be just below the Emperor himself. Vacationing alone now, as always, doing what he pleases in the 'imperial palace' in Montreal."

"Such marriages," Harriott said, relieved at her apparent change, not at all sensing her sarcasm, "'in the way of the country' were fine, long ago, but their time—my dear, please, consider our situation, yours and mine. The Company's land is so large, large! Sir George insists his leading men must now have wives as white as possible, and properly married—there's a Methodist minister here in Edmonton right now!—it is the determined policy of the future, my dearest Margaret, don't you see? You have travelled it, summer and winter, this endless land!"

He was waving his arms wide. To fill the sitting room with all the prairies and mountains I had struggled to cross, all the ranges and plains and hills and forests and rivers and grass and glaciers I had seen vanishing into continuous distance wherever I looked. And I knew that no lifetime of copying Old Masters in Rome or Amsterdam could ever help me actually *see* such a land. No painter can choose vision by another's eye, much less love.

"Your children will have all of it," Harriott pleaded. "This is your inheritance, this land, think of it! Larger than Europe!"

"Yes, think of it," Margaret said, strangely abstracted. "What if... when I marry...like my mother I go—" and there she stopped. She did not say "mad." "...like my mother...I...walk away."

Harriott groped for liquour. Perhaps at that moment Margaret's voice, words, were like her mother's. A month before, when our brigade was struggling towards Edmonton on snowshoes through the high snow of the Athabasca Pass, the men showed me a desolate valley and told me the story of how seventeen years before Elizabeth Harriott had left this tiny girl carefully wrapped in blankets on the snow there, on the trail, and vanished into her own particular wild. Her body was never found.

9. Another person besides me heard this astonishing conversation in the Rowand sitting room of Fort Edmonton. Mrs. John Rowand, Senior, though to my knowledge she was never openly called that. It was of course her room, and she must have been there all along, for she certainly did not enter after me, but I only saw her, suddenly, when Harriott took up his bottle and ran.

How could I not have seen her? Seated on the floor, her ancient head beside the fireplace bent into the firelight over a needle and leather. The woman Old John would later describe on her death certificate as "my reputed wife, the mother of all my reputed children." In English she was called Louise Umfrieville, a woman of the Saskatchewan, as much brown as white, though until she saved John Rowand's life and he "married" her she had lived Cree.

Harriott did not seem to notice her as he left; nor did Margaret.

10. Margaret Harriott was considering me. Or perhaps she was glaring; certainly her eyes burned in that loggish room of dull, frosted windows. I had not actually achieved much on my paper, barely a quick outline of features, the planes of posture on the chair. Too much to see, to hear.

"Do you often paint brides, Mr. Kane?"

"If I am commissioned, I...." I responded too quickly, stupidly, and stopped; she had no interest in a revealing honesty from me.

"Brides who refuse to be brides?"

I could only work, furiously now. "Well...in Europe, painting, I found most young ladies agreed with their fathers."

"Most."

"Most...a few...may convince their father *he* is telling them to do what *he* wants...."

"When actually it is what *they* want."

"Yes."

"Perhaps I would agree to be a bride, if you agreed to be the bridegroom?"

Luckily I was holding a pencil, not a full paintbrush. "I...I don't...."

"Our educations are, I think, compatible, and at this moment I know you better than I know John Rowand."

"We...we've just met, this minute...."

"Exactly. You heard my father: marriage in the 'Empire of the Company' is an arrangement between the prospective son-in-law and the father of the bride."

"Well...I'm flattered, I...."

"So, would you care to speak to my father?"

And finally I could laugh; the fundamental subject of every sitting room with any social pretensions, anywhere in the English-speaking world, here discussed not by gossiping aunts but by the possible principals themselves, direct confrontation—it suited our smoked log surroundings! And so I blundered on,

"But I have no...almost no connections, it took me two years to persuade Sir George Simpson for permission to travel in his brigade! And the great inheritance your father so eloquently—I can offer... really, nothing."

Margaret Harriott let me bumble on in my gaucherie, my uncomprehending reason against her precise irony. But finally she did relieve me, her voice abstracted, gentle:

"Presumably I already have all the inheritance possible, Mr. Kane. From my mother and my grandmother."

Obviously she did. Sitting thus, she was the Queen of Edmonton without attachment to grotesque Young John Rowand. Was if she wanted to be. Certainly more so than Frances Ramsay Simpson, no matter where Sir George might have her carried, his cousin and wife enduring the ongoing illness of rich monotony in Lachine, the lovely China rapids just beyond which in 1532 a deluded Jacques Cartier thought he could already see the coming spices of the Far East. My painting of Kakabeka Falls facing her on the dining room wall, reminding her of her endless canoe-brigade honeymoon in 1830, a slender child dragged along three thousand miles of roaring fur-trade rivers with their people staring without words but with knowledge at her, a growing awareness of the driven five-foot-two mechanism of a man she had in complete ignorance, except for his wealth, agreed to marry. But there was another painting, one I made just for her, that Sir George never permitted her to see. Not even after he was dead.

If you paint by commission, you never own what you paint. But then, if you're lucky, you never have to see it again either.

"You want to see Young John, he's outside there."

I was in Fort Edmonton, in the sitting room of the Big House. The soft, almost expressionless English words of the old woman by the fire.

And so he was: even from the second floor window of the Big House her huge son towered above a herd of shaggy Blackfoot ponies twisting about half-terrified in the yard below; around the flag-pole. He was choosing one, rejecting another as the Blackfoot argued their qualities. I had not noticed the din of trading outside until that moment.

Margaret had stood up too, but she did not look through the parchment window at her possible husband. She stood before my sketch with her slim body of white wedding lace poised—as if alerted to a bug. I hastened to explain:

"I'm a bit slow, tomorrow you'll...."

"What are these...pillars? Throne?"

"Your father wanted a...you know, regal. And, personally, if I may... it is appropriate."

"You find me 'regal'?" For a moment she looked at me wide-eyed as if she might possibly become interested in who I actually was.

"I'm a painter, I paint what is asked for, I...." I laughed, "My English father always said, you'll excuse his language, 'You dance with the bloke who brung you!'"

Her black eyes were deep enough to vanish me.

"I was born here, in the western mountains, here," she said with a peculiar emphasis. "I grew up on the Saskatchewan, at Fort Carlton where my mother's father John Peter Pruden was the chief trader. A Scot of course, working forever for a Company pension. My grand-mother died when I was nine, my grandfather just called her 'Anne,' he lived with her for thirty-seven years, why would he mention her true name? I spoke better Cree than English when I was dispatched by cart to Red River after she died. Perhaps I still do.

"Mr. Kane, do you actually think Cree royalty is best presented on a Victorian throne with a vague background of Corinthian columns?

"You accomodating ass."

11. The facade of the post office they built in 1852 on Toronto Street still exists. When I was alive it was just around the corner, north, from my office on King, and I had to pass its four elegant Greek

columns at least twice a day; fortunately they are Ionic. There are parts of my journey I never wrote down in any way, nor coded into my impossible notebook spelling, nor told. Not even to my good wife Harriet, nee Clench. Nor of a painting I made that was destroyed by the stubby despot who commissioned it.

It may be I could have told someone, anyone, these stories; if I had been a better painter.

12. But my eyes were what I had, and they were for hire. With my hands. Whatever I had, it could always be bought and paid for. I saw Margaret Harriott once more before her wedding on January 6, 1848—at the Fort Edmonton Christmas banquet where I was given the honour of carving the dried moose nose. I danced with several "dusky beauties" as they called them then, dried wild flowers woven in their wild black hair, but Margaret never so much as glanced at me or said a word, neither then nor when I stood as witness to the wedding ceremony conducted by the still catless Reverand Rundle. Why me? Perhaps someone anticipated I might someday be famous, but more likely because I could write my name. Margaret did not acknowledge my existence even when I had to stand within inches of her, her husband bulging black and bearded over her. Her shoulders bare, my hands clenched together behind my back.

In any case, to paint her I did not actually need to see her again. All my life I had an excellent visual memory of a certain formula kind.

I often wish I had had the perception to paint—or at very least sketch, I did hundreds of every possible animal, scene, person—but I never sketched Louise Umfrieville, Mrs. John Rowand, Senior. Her sitting room was full of chairs and thick, furred sofas, but she sat on the worn stones beside the fire, sometimes feeding it with split logs, her right hand forever poised as a swift, silent needle. She never spoke a word that I heard to run the household; with Old John gone once again, she too had decided to let her daughter Nancy order the house, as Nancy's husband old Harriott ordered the business of the Fort.

What did she say to me, beyond telling me her son was among the horses? What was her true name?

I comprehended too little of names and my own aging then. Despite what I thought of as my insatiable, omnivorous eye, I now know I was always looking for what Sir George had ordered so explicitly in his letter—I was to draw "...buffalo hunts, conjuring dances, warlike exhibitions or any other scenes of savage life with a view to their being coloured and framed, and of equal size so as to match each other." The European obvious: the picturesque. That which could be hung on a proper wall in a room in a rich house, no matter what possible world of image, make it small to fit such a wall, all one size for any landscape, all one size—but larger for portraits of savage manliness, especially as seen in wildly decorated chiefs and warriors. And for those beautiful, strong young women with their incomprehensible skin. Cun-ne-wa-bum in her embroidered elkskin dress, her beads snaking in spiralled layers around her neck and over her breasts moving as I danced around her, as she danced so gravely, moccasined feet together in one spot while she turned, dancing, always to face me, her fluid skirt shaped by her long legs, fringes dancing. Cun-ne-wa-bum, "One that Looks at the Stars," she told me. Holding her white swan's-wing fan by its exquisite porcupine-quill handle above her eyes while I painted her, sat motionless, patient, looking past me with a slight smile; so near in unfathomable distance.

A father's or a husband's name attached to her would mean nothing. And hanging in a room on a wall....

How was I so ignorant as not to ask "Louise" her name? Perhaps she would not have told me—why should she? I could not see her, then. Though I do now; every decade more clearly. She endured in the enormous four-storey "Rowand's Folly" of John's house, a soft mound on the floor of the largest sitting room in the North-West. Her despotic "reputed husband" never took her anywhere, even if she had wanted to go, no more to Montreal where their second son Alexander was a medical doctor than to Hawaii in 1842 when Simpson took him along on his travels around the world. An inexplicable incarnation of much Cree and a little English, always useful, always used, always there.

To me, remembering, "Louise" is the incarnate spirit of that place: the people of the Saskatchewan whose names no White knew. Over whom Sir George imagined himself the emperor. As I laboured to finish John Harriott's commission, she told me two things.

One was: "Margaret's mother, you know she had bad luck. She went a little bit crazy, that's okay—but in a bad place, that's bad luck. Lucky thing, she left that baby wrapped tight in a blanket, the men brought her here, ten days sucking a leather tit soaked in buffalo blood. I'm too old then, but there's lots of women here, lots of good milk."

The second: "Hunnn, maybe two coyotes crossed her path and she didn't notice. They say her mother was her father's cousin, but they got married anyway, had a baby anyway. Cree people don't marry that way, a man marry his aunt's daughter, because your aunt is really your mother and so you're marrying your sister. Real bad luck."

Luck. I think now the story she was telling me concerns Cree "medicine," power that can be experienced as either good or evil, depending, but actually English has no word that can deal with such "medicine." Just as Cree has no word for English "sin." I should have understood her then.

And would have; if I had dared to be a better painter.

13. Two days after the wedding, on January 8, 1848, a party of thirteen people started from Edmonton for Fort Pitt two hundred miles downriver. Young John Rowand had been appointed head of that Company establishment, and so he led the three carioles and six dogsleds out onto the river-ice trail.

A cariole is intended for one person only, a thin, wide board curled up at the front with a straight back to lean against; the sides and top covered by green buffalo hide with the hair scraped off, dry and white like parchment. When I slid myself down into the cariole I was to ride, it seemed I had slipped into a beautifully bound book. Or white coffin.

Later I painted a picture, without sketch, of our long caravan around two bends in the river, the standing spruce piled over, weighed low by snow and the dogs running furiously as they always do at first. Each cariole is painted with sprays of flowers, every team decorated in celebration, their collars and cloths fringed and embroidered with fantastic colours, feathers waving, tiny bells ringing clear above the sleds' swish and thump. "A Wedding Party Leaving Fort Edmonton" now hangs occasionally in the Royal Ontario Museum in

Toronto. Standard landscape size, nineteen by twenty-nine inches. I am stretched out in the last cariole, my wilderness hair streaming. Margaret is in a sled so far ahead it is indistinguishable from her husband's.

I also painted a picture of François Lucie, Young John's former hunting companion, complete with plumed buffalo hat, embroidered sashes and rawhide parfleche. On the afternoon before the wedding he took me hunting and showed me how to "make a buffalo calf." Our Fort Pitt caravan passed François's camp a few minutes out of Edmonton. It still stood on the same spot where I had tried to draw Mary bending at her fire. There she stood, between François and her young son (by Rowand) in front of François's teepee; she did not raise her hand in greeting as the wedding party passed, though the other two did.

The buffalo were extraordinarily numerous that winter; sometimes they nearly surrounded the fort, grunting, farting, and sometimes they broke into an inexplicable run of dusting snow and thunder. Several came so near pawing for grass that they were shot dead from the corner palisades. At night the wolves howled outside the walls and sang us to sleep; they were after the horses herded inside for protection, a horse being much easier to hamstring than a buffalo, and perhaps tastier too.

As for hunting, rather than blaze away at a skittish buffalo from a distance, dull sportless work at best, François, who hunted for the Company, showed me how a herd can be approached close enough for excitement. Two men "make a calf" when one covers himself with a wolf skin, the other with the light brown skin of a buffalo calf. They crawl through the snow on all fours until they are within clear sight of the herd, and then the "wolf" pretends to pounce on the "calf," which begins to bellow as in fear.

I played the wolf and François the calf, and his terrified bellowing was so perfect that a buffalo cow immediately turned from the herd and ran towards us. However, an enormous bull near her seemed to understand the trick, he tried to stop her by running between her and us, but she was too agile, she dodged him and charged so that François had to throw up his hide and shoot her. The bull charged up, smelling her all around where she had fallen. We had no interest in him, in hard winter only the sweet meat of cows is eaten, but he would not leave. He tried to raise her up, he shoved his immense head under hers, grunting as they do, almost like a groan. He was so unmovable that in the end François had to kill him too.

"Pretty strange, eh," he said, his knife in the warm body of the cow faster than my pencil on paper. "Sometimes...a bull is like that, he won't leave her. And she for sure never leaves her calf."

The bull was magnificent in full winter fur, a massive "bell" hanging under his great hump at his throat. But only his tongue was worth eating.

14. Why did Margaret Harriott marry a huge, obese man more than twice her age? To be eight years the mistress of the cluster of log huts that was Fort Pitt? By 1856 her husband had left the Company, no king he, and moved to Red River to live away his wealth doing nothing.

By then Old John Rowand was dead, of an apoplectic fit suffered while, typically, swearing at a voyageur. It happened at the York boat landing under Margaret's Fort Pitt window. When the old man collapsed, screaming, the voyageur fled and two days later was shot in what Young John recorded in the fort journal as "a hunting accident." They buried the old curmudgeon at Fort Pitt, but George Simpson, when he heard about it, had his own ideas of proper royal fur burial. He had the body dug up, the half-rotten flesh boiled away (voyageur rumour had it by an Indian who was kept drunk the whole time, and that the fort women made soap with the gallons of fat thus rendered), had the bones sealed in a barrel and shipped, via Norway House and York Factory, and from there across Hudson Bay and the Atlantic Ocean to London (because Simpson feared the superstitious voyageurs—who had suffered Rowand's abuse for forty years—would dump his bones in some deep rapid as soon as their canoes left the Saskatchewan waterways) and from there back across the Atlantic and up the St. Lawrence River to Montreal where over four years later the barrel was opened and the bones buried at last, November 10, 1858, in Mount Royal Cemetery. In the plot beside Simpson's Lady Frances, dead then for a year.

My wife Harriet says, as I try again to forget that travesty, Frances lying forever between rotting little George and the clutter of John's immense boiled bones, "What else could Margaret do?"

"His thick lips...his bulging, ugly face...grotesque." Behind the underground darkness of my eyes, my memory grows uglier than when I could see the light. "Eight men could barely lift his coffin, he weighed four hundred pounds when he was finally dead!"

"So, Margaret could deal with Young John I'm sure, why wish him on your beautiful Cree Mary?" my Harriet asks.

"At least with Mary he was a hunter, that's what he really was, and maybe he'd have been lucky and died young...crashed off his horse, broken his neck...gored by a buffalo."

Harriet says gently, "He 'turned her off,' the way the white men did then, to François. Took care of Mary as well as...as necessary."

After a time she continues, "Did Margaret tell you about her new grandmother at Red River?"

She told me nothing; she just called me an ass. But the loutish royalty of the fur trade had no recreation beyond drink and gossip: I heard a great deal resting as the mosquitoes permitted around evening fires. Gossip of the white pretension of governesses brought from England; of how old John Peter Pruden, John Harriott's ancient uncle and so both Margaret's grand-uncle and grand-father, hauled Miss Anne Armstrong with her face like the bottom of a slop-bucket to a Fort Garry altar four months after the death of his "reputed wife and mother of my children"—that is, Margaret's grandmother—before he heard the rumours that she had spent every night of the three months' voyage from London to York Factory in the captain's cabin (though that would hardly have stopped him since, though well soured, she was white); gossip of Margaret's youngest aunt, Caroline Pruden, known everywhere as the most beautiful woman in Red River, being married off to the retired money of another groping old Indian trader.

"Did Margaret have children?"

I lie quickly: "No."

And my wife grows thoughtful. "How did...could she do that?"

"Maybe two coyotes crossed her path, and she noticed."

"What?"

But I cannot explain what I do not comprehend.

"Seventeen years," Harriet muses, "to survive her 'grotesque'

Rudy Wiebe: Collected Stories, 1955–2010

husband as you call him, and now she's the wealthiest woman in the North-West. She lives in Silver Heights above the Assiniboine River, a house certainly grander than Rowand's Folly with no old Simpson to tramp over her every year. Why do you keep wondering, 'O, why did she marry him?'"

But I do. I lie on the floor, my arm over my blind eyes forever. It may well be, if you will not see, the time comes when you cannot.

Along the Red Deer and the South Saskatchewan

[1972/1973]

To the memory of Little Bear and F.W. Spicer

THIS IS LONG AGO. Before Whites dared to come into our country, when they built the Big House they call Edmonton now and then Little Big House at the edge of our country and barred the doors and put cannons on the corners and let our people through one small door one at a time when we came to trade. We were camped along the Red Deer that winter for the buffalo would go there under the trees and we followed them. One day that winter Appino-kommit was gone. We didn't think about that, since he never said where he was going, or when. He was a very young man who thought longer than he spoke, and the Old Men sometimes called him *crazy head* because he had already led boys his own age in a good raid and the older warriors hated him because they were jealous of the coups he brought back. But we, we loved him.

After many days my younger brother told me Appino-kommit had come back and wanted to see me at the Antelope Butte. So I went there. His face was burned by the wind and his moccasins worn out; I saw war in his face and I loved him. He told me he had gone three days down the Great River from the forks where the Red Deer joins it and he had found a camp of twenty-five lodges. When he said this he swung his hand flat across his throat, the sign for our enemies the Plains Cree, and I was very happy. He had watched that camp till the sun went down, but then it began to snow and he had to leave because they would see his trail in the snow. He had wanted to watch them one more day, it was foolish for such a small camp to be there alone but the snow made him come away.

"We start this tonight," he said. "I want three hundred young men to meet me at the Lone Tree Crossing when the moon rises. Tell them just that, no more, and they are not to talk to me today because then the chiefs will guess something and tell us not to do it."

I did as he said, and when the moon came up over the Great Lone Tree the young men started coming out of the darkness, all quiet; no one knew that anyone but himself had been called. But when they saw all the faces around them, their faces shone with happiness for they saw there was much to do. Silently we followed Appino-kommit and he led us across the white flats and into the thick trees and willows. There, where we could not be seen, we built small fires and made our quiet prayers to The Great One, asking help, and when that was done every one told the others of each wrong he had done, both great and small, so that if he didn't come back no one could say, when his deeds were told in the Great Medicine Lodge, that any shame had been hidden in his heart to blacken the glory of his death; that he had faced the enemy with his warcry and his name the last brave sound he would make.

All day we lay under the trees and at night we ran until the line of light grew so wide in our faces that we had to return to the river valley for the day shelter of trees. On the sixth night our run was short. Appino-kommit told us we should sleep till he called us, but I don't know if anyone slept. Just at dawn he came among us and said we should put out the fires.

"Eat all you can," he said. "Who can say who will eat again."

The snow was almost to our knees and the sun shone on it like fire leaping in the cold. Appino-kommit led us through the brush of the coulee and soon we heard dogs, then horses, and children laughing, and I think I have never heard so many women sing so happily or their axes ring as loud as they did that morning, but I may have forgotten it. But that day I will never forget, and we were not listening for such happy sounds that day, we were very busy. The fire of war burned in us, our enemies were there and we looked at each other and saw war paint. We stripped off our clothes very fast, everything but breechcloths and moccasins lay on the snow, a great pile of clothes and my young brother had to stay there with them. This made him very sad, but Appino-kommit said it was glory enough for someone so young to be one of a war party as famous as this one would be, so we left him there smiling. I don't know what happened to him; I never saw him again.

We were divided into two equal parties, Appino-kommit leading one and Kristo-koom-epoka the other. One party would follow the coulee to where it spread out into the river valley and the edge of the camp, the other would go higher, along the edge of the brush above and then, on a given signal, both would rush into the camp from opposite directions and meet in the centre, as nearly as possible. Women and children wouldn't be touched if they didn't fight. My friend, that was the time to see Appino-kommit; you would have known as we did that he was born to be a warrior. He told every man what to do, nothing was forgotten.

"The Cree make it so easy for us," he said. "Such a small camp should have scouts out all the time."

We looked at each other and then our swift feet carried us apart, but I like to remember that little bit of time, to remember us all together and how I felt the fire of the coming battle jerk my heart for happiness, remember my sad young brother sitting on the pile our clothing made and Appino-kommit, our leader, his war feathers quivering about his proud head in the sunlight so bright and cold, his eyes finding each one of us down to our very hearts as we stood around him. Proud and happy.

The last legging had fallen on the pile and my brother was hardly seated when the word came and we broke into our two parties, running silently, crouched, to the proper place. I was with Kristo-koom-epoka on the left, running with my good friends down the coulee and already I could hear the roar of victory, the brave deeds being sung again in the Medicine Lodge and I thought of two eyes shining and soft skin flushed soft red as I sang the song of what I had done, I, a warrior with coups at my belt who needed to fear nothing, certainly not to ask for a girl since everyone knows a warrior needs a wife to keep his lodge. My heart was pounding so hard with these happy thoughts my chest ran sweat under those frozen bushes, and we had hardly reached our place and squatted, peering under branches past the bottoms of the hills set there like giant grey hoofs when through the morning air rang the signal. The warcry of Siksika, The People!

As in that instant before a man's hands meet to clap again, there is silence. It all seems so peaceful, the sound of singing women and children, horses just hanging there as if not yet quite gone and everything motionless and so quiet with the sunlight dancing on the snow, smoke going straight up from lodges against the river hills and into the blue sky. Then! A roar as three hundred men leap up, teeth glistening into sunlight, screaming we run, stretched out towards our enemies with our knives and plumes and spears pointing the way A-a ha he ha, a-a ha he ha, I yo ho i yo ho, Ha koc e mat, Spum o kit, Spum o kit, I yo ho, i yo ho, our voices thunder in the joy of it as lodges split themselves before our sharp knives and the enemy staggers out, snatching at weapons and falling, snatching and falling, and trying to stand zipp! Arrows hiss some of us down but who sees that, we are forcing them back, they are summer flies, their clubs and knives just flies brushed aside and crushed I yo ho the joy of knife thudding in bone and blood spray I yo ho I am here now! and we hear our brothers' voices bellowing towards us above the screams and smoke and know we will meet soon to grasp their bloody hands a-a ha he ha.

But listen! There is a far sound above the roar, the screams, there, between the lodges, the white dust of snow rising with the thunder of hooves down the valley, back back! Back! Each desperate voice cries to each, back! for the open jaws of horses swirl up towards us through the snow of their running with spears and knives and warcries of our enemies bristling above them, shout to your brother that death is running us, back. "All stay together!" Kristo-koom-epoka cries, and we gain the coulee's shelter fast, and we still feel there may be hope but we must turn to face those charging horses.

You see, my friend, this is how it was. In the bend of the Great River below that small camp we attacked, where we could not see it, was the main Cree camp. So big a thousand warriors could jump up in a moment. Appino-kommit knew that early in the morning Cree horses are always in camp, and he knew that if we attacked at that time it would save us the trouble of rounding them up to take them. So the thousand warriors in that big camp he didn't know about had to take no more than one running step before they could gallop.

Rudy Wiebe: Collected Stories, 1955–2010

We could tell by the sound of guns, the Cree had six or seven and we altogether had two, that the others led by Appino-kommit were also retreating to the coulees of the river hills and we would have to get together to stand, if possible. I have told you, my friend, that we wore only breechcloths and moccasins, but that is not true; I also had a shirt which I'd traded the fall before from the traders when we got those two guns in the north at Big House. It was cotton and only reached my belt but it was a great comfort to me as you will see. Ai he ha, I see it all now, the rush for our lives to the coulee, we reach it and turn just in time to stop them with arrows and a desperate charge against those horses' swinging heads with axes. Ahhh, they are so tight now stabbing around us that horses can be killed with knives, they jam the coulee so tight in their rage to trample us into the frozen ground. They charge again, and again, wheel away and charge again, and four times we meet them on foot, leaping among the foaming horses, smashing their heads, tearing off riders and gutting horses and smashing knees, smashing them down, our knives driving between ribs and gulping blood straight from pounding hearts I yo ho I yo ho I am here now! the dead piled up in that coulee so high we can't see over them, the bright sunshine and the red circles on the snow as the Cree whirl around once more, and charge again. I can taste my own blood in my mouth here they come again, the fourth charge and I hear their roar as they hurdle the dead and we meet Ha koc e mat! and I am among the horses, my enemy's arm lunging a spear past me and I have that arm, he starts to fall down towards my face and I step slightly aside, knife straight up and it is gone in him to the hilt. The horse rears, screaming, and I twist my knife out, up, and with both hands drive one long red line down through his white and bay belly while he is still on his hind legs pawing above me and his warm curled intestines pour out in one great steaming puddle about his hoofs in the red snow. That hot smell now! Down, he is down like a spilled mountain and the club of a friend splatters his rider's brain in my face and we roar with laughter. They are gone. Gasping I pull another friend from under a floundered horse.

A voice is behind me. Kristo-koom-epoka has to tell me his name for my breath roars in my ears and he is unrecognizable, as if poured over red. "Take cover," he shouts, "they'll come on foot now, with bows! Cover." And they do that, but we are sheltered by the coulee, they have to shoot high into the air and the arrows falling down straight hurt only a few.

"Friends," the voice of Kristo-koom-epoka again, "I don't think anyone wants to stay here. This place is mostly cold and falling arrows. We should go back in threes, two strong take one wounded between them, I'll go first. That way we can get back to the others. Keep close together, come now."

Like a wounded grizzly we started. In an instant our enemy answered our warcry and rushed to meet us. That wasn't the kind of fight a warrior likes to remember, carrying his wounded friend and trying to cut his way out; no joy, no joy. I only remember that as soon as we started an arrow killed the wounded friend I was helping carry and I took his axe in my right hand and my knife in my left and pushed towards the front to Kristo-koom-epoka. We stood side by side and I helped him chop our path through Cree. How long that was I don't know, but at last they drew back with only a few arrows spitting at us. We could see then not far away our other party slowly retreating and carrying the wounded as we were. The Cree tried to keep us apart, but up there on the flats they seemed to have worn off their fierceness against our knives and the terrible cold; soon we were together with what was left of our friends. About then some late Cree arrived and put more heart in the enemy, but now we were prepared for them. Appino-kommit sent all the wounded ahead and formed a rearguard of the strongest that were left. And on the flat plain there and the one shallow line of a beginning coulee we fought for a long time, driving them back again and again until the sun was low. It was the middle of winter, but it took the sun a long time to get there.

Then Appino-kommit said to me, "You are a great runner and your legs are still good. Run ahead of us to the place where we were camped this morning. Tell anyone you find there we must meet in the tall timber we passed through last night, down in that bend. Then you go ahead there and build big fires, the Cree have all our clothing. Run, or many more will die in this cold."

So I left them and I ran. I passed the wounded ones, giving them my message. I ran till there was only one track in the snow and a narrow line of blood for me to follow.

Soon I saw someone running in front of me, not steadily but as if drunk and as I overtook him I looked into his face. He was a boy of fifteen. A shot close in had blown his lower jaw away and his tongue was frozen on his breast with long icicles of saliva and blood. I only looked once and said nothing but ran on. I saw what rode his shoulder. Soon he would go slower, and then he would stop and lie down in the snow, and then sleep. Even now sometimes in a dream I see how he looked at me as I passed him, I running without bad wounds, and I could not stop to help. I saw him and the lives of all depended on me but he did not know that or what I saw and his look told me that he would feel it even when he couldn't feel his wounds any more. The heat of battle was gone and we were retreating; we had to get to fires; we had to tie up the wounded.

As I ran my heart wanted to die because I had to think of all that faced us. Without clothing, home and safety were five long nights and days away, and we had no food. Would our wounded need us after one night of this cold? Of course the Cree would track us, and get the scalps of those who fell, and they would make sure that no one survived the cold; they would be all the happier if we froze like dogs rather than on their knives with our warcry sounding. Do you wonder my heart was stretched out?

The sun was cut in half when I reached the grove where the fires were to be built, and there I found some comfort because four sweat lodges made of raw buffalo hides stood under the trees. These could give shelter to some wounded, they would gradually warm if we built large fires outside them, and the hair could be used to stuff the mouths of wounds. If any still bled in the terrible cold. After I had started the first big fire I scraped hair from one of the robes, tied my shirt sleeves tight and pulled my belt very tight around the bottom of my shirt. Then I stuffed hair inside, and I can still feel the

warmth that came over me as I worked hard, doing this. And soon
people began to arrive, the hurt ones first, and among them Otat-
to-ye, the brother of the girl whose shadow I often tried to follow
in my dreams. Any child could see he would not reach home. Blood
oozed from a hole in his chest and froze on his skin; an arrow had
cut through his entrails and its head was buried in his backbone.
Only his great heart had brought him this far ai-ha-he-ha, our hearts
so heavy.

No one said a word as we worked to staunch running blood, to tie
sticks around crushed limbs. At last Appino-kommit, with the rearguard. I looked around in the firelight to see who was there, and
nearly half of all those who had run east under these trees so happily
were now lying, somewhere, in the trampled snow. And of the ones
here, over half were badly wounded. But as I looked around I had
more courage; in every face burned fierce resolution and revenge;
oh the early summer sun, may these Cree live long enough to see
that! And before dawn our trek had to begin, the strong helping the
weak, and those who had died at night we placed in a line against
trees facing where the enemy would come so that they could, even in
death, glare at the enemy they hated now more than ever.

I and a friend went to Otat-to-ye and lifted him to his feet and,
each of us with an arm about him, held his arm over our shoulder
with the other hand. We had moved this way only a few steps when
he asked us to take him back and place him on the ground beside the
dead fire. We did that. Then he said, "Take half of my breechcloth and
cover my face." I did that; then he said, "Go fast, the Cree will soon be
here, go fast and don't look back."

As we went I heard his voice again, I could barely hear it calling
my name. He said as I stood by him again, "Take the cloth off." I did.
"Kiss me," he said then, and I did. His eyes were wide open and so
black I could look through them and through his skull and see the
very inside of blackness. "Now put the cloth back, I don't want to see
them." And I walked from him again, and I heard nothing behind me.

Friend, can you know how I felt? Do you know pain? That was
what made us men, then, such happiness and such pain, that could
turn quickly as a hand turning. Our hearts had to know and hold
both, and though we were very young we were the children of this

land and sky and we did not cry out and make women of ourselves by groaning and cutting ourselves. We were already cut enough; our hearts could bleed in silence. I see by your face you understand some of this: the story I would have to tell his sister, that I had left him alone to wait for their knives because I could not kill him.

All day they ran our flanks like wolf shadows on the snow and happy the man whom the wolves got before they, our enemy. And as the sun sank Appino-kommit came and said I would have to run again. I would have to be the one to go ahead and tell all this to our camp, and ask that food and clothing be sent.

Now you will understand about a man bringing such a story into the great camp of our people. When sorrow strikes so swift and hard sometimes a hand flies up and kills the messenger who has dared to speak such words; friend or stranger, it doesn't matter, our love for our own is so strong. As soon as it was dark I started. It was colder and the snow had begun to drift before a northwest wind and I had to run against that all night. I rested a little when I could not twist my strength tighter, then all next day, taking only a short sleep by a fire in the middle of the day, then on, day and night. In the evening of the third day I came near our great camp. I had eaten only rose-bush berries as I ran and slept no more than half a night altogether, watching for what might be following me, and I could barely walk as I came in, my face frozen and legs cut by the crusted snow. I moved towards the chief's lodge, for only there was there safety for me, but the children recognized me and ran through the camp crying that one had come back alone who could scarcely walk and had gone to the chief's lodge. The whole camp ran together.

I entered the lodge and seated myself under the Medicine, and I will tell you what that means, my friend, for you will not know it. The door of a lodge is always towards the rising sun and the chief's bed is always exactly opposite the door, that is, against the back side of the lodge equal distance from the door if you go either to the right or to the left when you enter, and the head of the bed is always to the west so that when the chief sits during the day his face is always east towards his own fire in the centre of his lodge and the rising sun. There are reasons for this. At the head of the bed on his left is a tripod, his robe rests on one side of this and under the tripod he keeps his war bonnet, his tobacco, and the other sacred things, and over this, but outside the lodge, hangs his Medicine. Now whoever comes in and sits down on his left before the tripod also sits under the Medicine, and even if he is an enemy, if he gets to the middle of the camp where the chief's lodge is and gets inside and gains that place, he is safe as long as he remains there. Once out of that place anyone may kill him, provided he hasn't convinced them otherwise. So I got in, and got under the Medicine, sitting there in the warm, safest place of my people with my head hanging to my knees, and I couldn't say anything as the people ran together outside.

For a long time the chief sat with his head bowed. He had not said a word when I jerked open his lodge door so naked and bloody, and he said nothing while the sounds of people outside grew and one by one the councillors came in silently and looked at me and seated themselves on my left. At last the chief reached behind him for his tobacco board and prepared a pipe of tobacco and slowly filled his great pipe. He passed the pipe to one councillor, who placed the stem in his mouth, turning the bowl towards another, and that one took a live coal from the fire and placed it on the tobacco. When it was lit, the councillor passed the pipe back to the chief. He pointed the smoking stem toward the rising sun and prayed to The Great One, to the sun, stars and moon, to earth and sky and water, that they have pity on his people. Then he passed the pipe to me; he bid me smoke, and called his women to prepare food. When I had smoked and eaten in silence the chief took my hand and said,

"Do any live?"

"Yes."

He repeated my answer to the people.

"Are they in danger?"

"Yes, from starvation and wounds."

"How far are they?"

"In two days they should be here, those still alive."

Again he cried this out to the people, and orders were given that warriors take food and robes to them.

And then began the hardest of all. The people began to ask about their loved ones. One would enter the lodge and call a name and I would make the sign for living; then rejoicing would echo in the

warm lodge and all around it from those outside, but perhaps at
the next name called I, I would have to make the sign of death, or
wounded, and the sounds of mourning began and soon there was
nothing but that sound surrounding me. I could not lift my head
under it and I heard my mother's voice asking about her youngest
son, three times she asked and I couldn't answer. I had no power left
to lift my hand, there was nothing left in me hearing her voice for my
father was dead and she was already bent under great sorrows. But I
made that sign too. And the wails grew and still I made the dreaded
sign and still I had not heard that one voice, the one I loved and so
dreadful now and on and on until my heart gave way. I sprang to my
feet, shouting,

"Don't ask me for Otat-to-ye, don't ask! How can I say his last
word beside the dead fire!"

And when I had said that I heard a low cry in front of me and the
world turned black. When I knew something again two days later
they told me fifty young men had been brought back. The relief party
reached them just in time, or not ten would have returned. Fifty out
of three hundred.

It is late, my friend, and time to sleep. That was our life then,
that was what made us men, such happiness and glory and pain that
could turn quick as a hand turning. When the Old Men still taught us
and we lived with the great buffalo and the rivers on this land which
had been given to our people before us and we had the strength to
breathe and run wherever our eye moved across the land under this
sky. Yes, we wailed that winter in the cold valleys of the Red Deer,
and the Cree, ai he ha, the Cree that summer! You see, white traders
finally dared come closer to us because we were friendly and we piled
our robes up against their guns and the longest of them could kill
farther than any gun I ever saw. No, he was too young, it was Ok-ki-
kit-sippe-meotas the war chief who led us. And how the Cree wailed
that summer along the Great River, ahhh, how they wailed.

The Year We Gave Away the Land

I REMEMBER each year of my long life as easily as I finger a string of beads; each bead is one particular thing that happened. But no Blackfoot can forget the year the Whites count 1877. That was the year we gave away the land. I will tell you how it was.

SUNDAY, SEPTEMBER 16

The Queen's white commissioner came with eighty Mounted Police and forty wagons over the round hills of the Bow River at the Crossing. Up on the prairie we had seen their dust curl all day, but still their white helmets and red coats shone in the sun, a long stiff worm of red and white and gleaming horses coming down into the valley with a white-fisted drummer rattling them ahead as they rode. Two of the wagons had those guns so big you can stick your fist into the barrels.

But at Blackfoot Crossing there were only Old Sun's and Crowfoot's bands of the Siksikas to watch them, and the Stoneys camped across the river running together to stare. Not a single Peigan or Sarcee had come, and I and my forty young men were the only Bloods. Without women or children, we could have been on a raid. We sat on our horses, watching. They came across the river flat, straight like Whites do everything, straight, one wagon with a square canvas to keep the sun off the commissioner's blotchy face. They came bumping under the flags, straight to where the trees open on the Crossing. There Colonel Macleod lifted his hand and everything stopped. The police swung down and after a minute the blotchy man unbent himself, long and bony, out of his wagon.

"Tall Man," someone behind me named him.

And we laughed a little. I had a better name for him later, though I never said it; he was too strong for me. But he did not seem so then, just long and thin, and we stopped watching him because there were more police on the south hills. They were trying to chase grey cattle into the valley.

"There come the presents," someone said, and a few of us laughed again.

MONDAY, SEPTEMBER 17

A little after noon they fired the guns. The sound rumbled down the valley and sent children and dogs running for shelter. Then all the chiefs went to see Macleod and Tall Man under the canvas inside the squares of police tents, Bear's Paw and his Stoney councillors riding their best horses through the river. But no more people had come in. Old Sun would not open his mouth and Crowfoot said they would have to wait two days, maybe four. Macleod said to me,

"Medicine Calf, do you think Red Crow and Rainy Chief will be here with your people in two days?"

For a minute I looked at Jerry Potts, the guide and interpreter. His mother was a Blood killed in a whisky brawl before the police came and stopped that; he got paid well by Macleod, and when they had it he got quite a lot of confiscated whisky too, though he always wanted more.

"Why doesn't he ask Crowfoot again?" I said.

Potts swore, carefully under his hand. "He never understands, he still thinks the Blackfoot nation has one big head chief."

"That one," I nodded at Crowfoot, "doesn't mind pretending we do." Though if we had, it would have been my chief, Red Crow of the

South Bloods. But Red Crow never wanted to talk to Whites, so how could they know how powerful he was?

"What is he saying?" Macleod asked Potts.

"He doesn't know," Potts said.

Tall Man was talking. The Mounted Police would give us food, the things piled inside the square and the bony cattle if we needed them, and Bear's Paw stood up and said he wanted everything, yes. But Crowfoot was studying Tall Man, whom none of us had ever seen before.

"We still have buffalo," was all Crowfoot said. And his tone meant what Big Bear had said three years before about treaties: "When we set a fox trap, we scatter meat all around, but when the fox is in the trap we knock him on the head. We want no bait, let your chiefs come like men and talk to us." I fought Big Bear four times. He was a Cree, our enemy, but that time he spoke true.

Macleod and Tall Man looked at each other when Potts translated Crowfoot's four words; they understood meanings. Then Old Sun stood up, and every Blackfoot stood up with him.

TUESDAY, SEPTEMBER 18

We rode east before dawn along the prairie above the river, and there we ran buffalo as the sun came up blood red. O Great Spirit, the land and the sky. When we returned dragging our travois heavy with meat, Sitting on an Eagle Tail with all his Peigans was at the Crossing, about nine hundred of them. And so were the traders from Fort Macleod and Edmonton, chopping down trees for walls to protect their goods. Many were Montana men. They carried their Winchesters naked on the saddle across their knees. We surrounded them, all bloody from hunting, and told them no treaty had been made and they would not chop down one more tree at this sacred place. So they went to the Mounted Police and Macleod said we were right. While we sat on our horses watching them they stacked their goods back inside their tents.

We danced and ate meat all night with the Peigans. Eiyan-nah, the stories and the singing!

When we came to the tent inside the police square the Whites were already there, including six white women, more than any of us had ever seen. After the long, hot summer their faces were still like snow under their wide hats, their bright dresses pulled in so tight around the tops of their bodies. My young men stared and stared, such dry women looking shamelessly back at us, but laughing and whispering to each other like Blackfoot women.

We chiefs sat down in a half-circle in front of Tall Man and Macleod, and behind us our prairie people gathered, several thousand now though Red Crow and the Bloods had not come. Tall Man began in a high singsong, and after a moment he stopped, waited. But Jerry Potts could say nothing. Such speech was impossible for him, he never translated more than five words, no matter how long the original statement. Finally an old white man who had lived with the Peigans for years, he was called Bird, stepped forward. He could talk like a medicine man and Tall Man started again.

"The Great Spirit has made all things, it is by that Spirit that the Queen rules over this great country. She loves all her children, both white and red alike, but she hates wickedness. And that is why she sent the police to punish the bad men who robbed you with whisky."

"Did your father ever tell you a woman had our country?" Eagle Ribs asked me. He was war leader of the Siksikas as I was of the Bloods; we would have to explain all this to our warriors.

On his left Eagle Calf, leader of the Many Children band, said, "The Whites are coming anyway, like in Montana. We should at least get some of those presents for our land."

"Twenty years ago," I told them, "I signed the Blood treaty with the Americans in Montana. And now you can't ride anywhere there without a White watching you. Treaties mean nothing."

"But look, this is Macleod," Eagle Calf said. "He talks for the Great Mother, he's different."

"He's just white too," Eagle Ribs said staring at the pale smiling women, their hands folded in their flowered laps.

"Last year," Tall Man was saying, "we made treaty with the Crees, and now we come to make treaty with the Blackfoot. In a few years the buffalo will all be destroyed and for this reason the Queen wishes you to live in some other way. She wishes you to allow her white children to come and live on your land, raise cattle, grow grain, and she will assist you to do the same."

"There are so many Whites along the Oldman's River already," Eagle Ribs said, "they have ruined the hunting."

"She will also pay you," Tall Man shouted, "money every year, money as a gift so you cannot be cheated. Twenty-five dollars for each chief, twelve dollars each for signing, and five dollars every year after that, forever."

Forever is a long time.

"How can we give away land?" Eagle Ribs muttered.

"Maybe we can't give it," Eagle Calf said, "but those Whites can sure take it. We better take their presents."

Eagle Ribs was looking at me. "What's 'money'?"

"Sometimes it's metal, sometimes a piece of paper with a picture. If you have enough of it, the traders give you a gun."

"Or a dipperful of whisky," Eagle Calf laughed.

"If you sign the treaty," Tall Man shouted, "a reserve of land will be set aside for you and your children forever, for every five persons you will have one square mile of land set aside. Cattle will be given to you, and potatoes like those grown at Fort Macleod. And we will send teachers so your children will learn to read books like this one...."

Tall Man was holding up a black missionary book, and Macleod just sat, nodding his heavy head. But I was hearing the mutter of young men behind me. That blotchy man had said that soon the buffalo would be destroyed. There were so few left now, and the Crees from the north and Sioux from the south were hunting those few also, I knew he was right. Eagle Ribs beside me was thinking my thoughts: the land and the buffalo, how else can prairie people live?

That evening I rode up to the prairie. Bull Head and the Sarcees had come in, they were raising their lodges in the circles of the valley. But Red Crow and Rainy Chief, my wives and children with them, had not come. The sun was gone behind the white teeth of the mountains, and a wind—as if the earth were breathing...hissss uhhh... hissss uhhh—cold and hard, I could smell winter, I could smell dying. Like the terrible year of the Rotting Sickness when we scraped ourselves bloody against the traders' gateposts, trying to rub off the disease that killed us piece by piece, to give it back to the Whites who gave it to us but themselves never suffered from it. The moon bulged up, white and blotchy, out of the land. Who had ever asked for them to come, if we could just kill them all, who would not pray a lifetime if only they could be wiped away like dirt in a sweat lodge?

My horse grazed a little in the dry circle of my reins. The earth under me was hard, warm; it moved so certainly with my breathing. But the police had stopped the whisky trading, the terrible drunkenness that killed us as surely as disease. And now Macleod said, "Sign." But how will we live? How can we live with them? Forever is a long time.

When the moon was down, I stood up. And prayed. After a time it came to me that war, raid and defence, which were my life with my people, these were not enough. Words had to be made here. And then Pemmican came to me in my prayer, the old medicine man of my people.

"The buffalo make you strong," were his words. "But what you eat from this money will bury our people all over the hills. You will be tied down, Whites will take your land and fill it."

When I opened my eyes, I saw that the long light that comes before dawn had spread my shadow wide, grey across the prairie. A thin grey stick pointing west.

THURSDAY, SEPTEMBER 20

After the guns fired, Crowfoot and Old Sun and Sitting on an Eagle Tail and Bull Head all said they would speak tomorrow. Then I stood up.

"My chief, Red Crow, is not here, but it is time now for defence so I will speak. The Spirit, not the Queen, gave us this land. The Queen sent Macleod with the police to stop the whisky. At that time I could not sleep, any sound might be my drunken brother coming to kill me or my children in his drunkenness. Now I can sleep, without being afraid. But there is still the land."

While Bird translated, Crowfoot watched me with his hard, beaked face. He understood Whites better than anyone, he had thought about them for years.

"The Great Spirit," I said loudly, but really to Crowfoot, "it is hard to understand, but He must have sent the Whites here to do what He wants. We Bloods signed a treaty with the Americans twenty years ago, and the first year they gave us large bags of flour and many blankets, the second year only half as much, and now it is nothing but a handful of flour and a rag. The Queen must give us fifty dollars for each chief, thirty dollars for every man, woman and child. Every year. We must be paid for all the trees the police and the Whites have already cut, for there will soon be no firewood left for us. The land... the land is too much to give away for so little."

And Tall Man was laughing. "If our police have driven away the whisky traders," he said, "surely you cannot expect us to pay for the timber they used. For helping you so much, by rights you should pay us!"

And I burst out laughing, and all our people with me. Tall Man and Macleod and the police laughed too; but for a different reason, I think.

Crowfoot, however, did not laugh. And that night Red Crow and Rainy Chief with almost two thousand Bloods rode in. The whole valley was now filled with lodges, with the laughter of people and the running of horses. That was the last free gathering of the Blackfoot nation for though we talked all night in Crowfoot's lodge, though I said again and again that the treaty was too little, and though the North Peigans and Eagle Ribs wanted to wipe out every policeman and the commissioner at dawn and then ride east to the buffalo, nevertheless Red Crow stated he would agree with Crowfoot. And Crowfoot said, "The Whites are coming. The Americans make treaties and then their army kills people like rabbits. Macleod treats every White and every Indian exactly the same. What can we do? We have to trust Macleod."

I walked to my lodge and saw the faces of my wives and children. But I did not sleep. At dawn Pemmican came to me again. "The Whites will lead you by a halter," he said. "That is why I say, don't sign. But my life is old, over. Sign if you want to. Sign." I could hardly hear his voice, it was so old and broken.

FRIDAY, SEPTEMBER 21

All the tribes of the Blackfoot nation, Siksika, Blood and Peigan, and our allies the Sarcees, gathered with the Stoneys at the Crossing. And Crowfoot made the long speech the Queen's commissioners had sat up stiff all week to hear.

"Take pity on us with regard to our country, the prairies, the forests and the waters, the animals that live in them. Do not take them from us forever. We are the children of the plains, and the buffalo have been our food always. I hope you look upon the Blackfoot as your children now. If the police had not come, where would we all be? Bad men and whisky were killing us so fast, but the police have protected us as the feathers of the bird protect it from the frosts of winter. I am satisfied. I will sign the treaty."

And Red Crow spoke also.

"Three years ago, I first shook hands with Macleod at Oldman's River. Since that time he has made me many promises. He kept them all—not one has ever been broken. I trust him entirely, I will sign with Crowfoot."

They all said that, and finally I had to stand.

"I cannot be alone. I must say what my people say. I will sign."

And then Macleod opened his square, bearded mouth. "I am gratified to hear your kind words. I told you when I came that nothing would be taken from you without your consent, and every promise we make to you here will be kept as certainly as the sun now shines upon us."

So on Saturday, September 22, 1877, we touched the pen and "did thereby cede, release, surrender and yield up forever" fifty thousand square miles—as much land as the Queen's entire country—for five dollars per year and a medal and a new suit of clothing for each chief every three years. Oh, there was a great deal of eating and hand-shaking, and four hundred of our warriors dressed their horses as for war and charged down the hills to circle the square tents of the police, shooting and screaming their war cries. But it meant nothing. The life we had lived since before the memories of our oldest fathers was gone. Four thousand three hundred and ninety-two of us had been paid off.

That winter three of our chiefs died. Crowfoot had to go to a white doctor to be cured of an illness. No snow fell on the prairies, and no buffalo came toward the foothills. Instead, prairie fires burned the earth black. And in two years there was not a single buffalo left on the land we had given away; in three, we had only flour "not quite

unfit for food" to eat; and in four, one thousand five hundred of us
were dead.

I touched the pen. My x is on the treaty. It is there following
Crowfoot and Old Sun and Bull Head and Red Crow, the fifth of fifty-
one chiefs and councillors.

I knew about money then, but I did not know what the treaty
meant by "reserves to allow one square mile for each family of five
persons." I know now, since I have lived on this "small place, land set
aside." I and my children will live here, remembering; forever.

But there is still the land.

From Montreal, 1848

MY FAMILY EMIGRATED from Berwick-on-Tweed, Scotland, in 1832, and I was born in Montreal on December 20 of the same year. On March 3, 1848, I bound myself to the service of the Hudson's Bay Company for five years at ten pounds a year and in early April we left Lachine in three Rice canoes, eighteen paddles to each canoe, for the wild, unknown West. I was fifteen, and my contract had mentioned nothing about bedding so the first night I spent blanketless before the fire and cried out my homesickness.

Next morning I felt much better and bought two blankets from a trader. We paddled via Bytown (now Ottawa), French River, Lake Huron, Fort William, Rat Portage and Norway House to York Factory on Hudson Bay where we met the Saskatchewan Brigade on July 10. From there we paddled and tracked with the brigade (thirteen canoes of eight men each led by Chief Factor Rowand, an incarnate fiend who would curse you blind if you looked sideways) back to Norway House, across Lake Winnipeg and up the Saskatchewan River past Forts Carlton and Pitt to Edmonton. When we arrived there on September 26, I discovered I had been assigned to Rocky Mountain House, 250 miles farther upriver. I was given a horse (I had never been on one before) that looked like a box of cutlery and told, "Ride." We finally reached our winter quarters on November 2. Seven months to the day.

That endless season was the worst part of my life, so far. I had two
quarrels with fellow greenhorns; both times the brigade boss ordered
us to fight it out and both times I was pounded flat and kicked
purple. Life was all work, eat and sleep. The sleep was merciful
oblivion, the work of paddling, tracking and portaging was labour
(not much), drudgery (more), and exhaustion (mostly). I do not
remember seeing anything, what I remember is food.

We began at Lachine with the old staples of pork and peas and
black quarter-pound biscuits. When we wanted coffee, we burnt
the biscuits and added water. But our real drink was three drams
of rum per day, strong and warm in your gut. When we reached
Sault Ste. Marie we recruits were locked in a warehouse for fear
we would "skip" to the American side. We discovered a sack of
raisins in a corner and ate so much that during the night our grand-
mothers came and made faces at us. After that we got nothing but
corn, greased with tallow to make it slide down, till we reached
Rainy River and saw our first pemmican. We crowded around a
hundred-pound hide sack (hair outside) and nibbled a sample. My
first mouthful made me sick, but I got over that. We made rab-a-bo,
pemmican mixed with a little flour and boiled in water. When cooked
it looked something like soup and could be eaten either with spoon
or knife, and since our rum ration had been stopped long ago, we
had nothing to help it down. We ate that for forty-one days to York
Factory where we each received a loaf of bread, two pounds of pork
and a whole quart of rum! You can understand why all the brigade
men were big powerful men: weak chaps got killed quick.

For two days out of York (beginning July 24) we ate "regal," then
we were back to rab-a-bo. We called it a-bo-rab and bo-rab-a but
it tasted more or less the same, so we dreamt of buffalo. We were
tracking now (that is, hauling loaded York boats upriver with ropes
over our shoulders) and at The Pas we laid in a welcome stock of
potatoes. Finally, on August 31 at Wives Hill near Carlton, the Cree
appeared with fresh buffalo meat. Every manjack of us ate until he
could hold no more, and a good number were seasick among the dry
bushes for it. Then all the way to Edmonton, tracking four hours on,
four hours off, from morning till night, we had twenty-seven days
of uninterrupted buffalo. Edmonton itself was flour, pemmican and

buffalo, so our first camp out of Edmonton, at White Mud Creek on October 9, we killed seventy-five rabbits and stuffed ourselves. Then we had nothing but rabbits until we reached winter quarters November 2.

Work, sleep, and eat: that was my first Rocky Mountain winter. Evenings were endless and I had nothing to read. I did not get my first mail (three letters from my mother and two copies of the Montreal *Witness*) until a year later, September 1849. By that time, however, I had won my first fight and begun visiting the women. Being young and quick to learn, I soon spoke as much Cree as was necessary.

Games for Queen Victoria

IT SEEMED that at age thirty-one I was being passed in the race
of life. Everywhere in the world there was nothing but peace. The
Great Powers were bent upon disarming; no Bashote or Beloochee
or Burmese or any other "ee" or "ese" anywhere in the Empire could
muster so much as a skirmish. At my birthday celebrations—such as
they were, considering—in October 1869, it seemed as if the noble
spirit of military adventure—of the square, the red coat, the bugle
at dawn, my twelve-year dream—had vanished. That very day I had
been given to understand that a Company in Her Majesty's service
would be at my disposal if I could produce £1,100, plus £450 for over-
regulation items, but as a sixth son I had obtained this position of
first-for-purchase by the slow process of existence, nothing else.

"Oh for a Napoleon across the Channel...Napoleon...."

Donkin, who had arrived at this juncture two years before me,
slowly raised his head, then his glass.

"Sixty years too late, my dear Lieutenant Butler, s-sixty years....We
can but drink today and, for tomorrow, pray that the...indomitable
s-s-spirit of independence has not yet complete...ly *died* among the
s-s-s-savages of the world."

I drained my glass to that. However Francis Dickens, last son of
that international scrivener, refused all comfort.

"There's nothing left but barrack duty in Madras," he mumbled. "There you get promoted for yellow fever and then *finis*...governor of a gaol for infant diddlers in the Midlands...God save us everyone."

"Like the Queen," said Donkin morosely.

We could but raise our empty glasses.

"There is a speck, of something perhaps, in North America," I said. "The *Times* last night...."

"Those North-West rumours?" At my nod Dickens's face dropped gloomier than ever. "Wolfe and Brock were the last soldiers they allowed into Canada."

"Not a hope," Donkin muttered. "Canadians are all s-s-Scots, they can afford...nothing but talk."

If such was the case, and my subsequent experience with the converted lumber town of Ottawa revealed little to oppose Donkin's opinion, then I thanked God that in the wilderness of North America Louis Riel was quite French and Indian. Time revealed that he and his fellow Métis were not disposed to accept the arbitrary arrangement for government of the North-West reached between Ottawa and the Hudson's Bay Company, and since the Métis hunters were the only effective military force on Red River, they suddenly seized armed possession of Company headquarters at Fort Garry and sent the proposed Canadian governor scurrying back behind the protection of the United States border.

Reading of these developments in the English papers, I was impressed with the early leadership of M. Riel. Even primitive resistance...resistance that perhaps borders on rebellion, if accomplished with some—a modicum of style, with...one hates so much to see a thing bungled.

And in truth, what knew the wild Métis, unreclaimed as the prairie and the bison they hunted with savage joy, of State, of duty, or of loyalty? Doubtless they had heard of England, in a shadowy way, but Canada? The Company had hitherto provided what little law and government they needed; for protection they had their guns and untiring horses; the produce of their summer hunt filled their few wants in trade: blue capotes with shiny buttons, ball and powder. So when Canadian surveyors came attempting to cut squares out of the great lone land which was theirs through the aboriginal rights of their mothers, when the leading Canadian politician stated, "They are only eaters of pemmican," why, who can condemn them that their proud Indian blood leaped within them, that they reached for their guns? The least Englishman would have done no less.

Unfortunately M. Riel's *coups*—taking the fort, routing the governor, imprisoning his local opposition, and, greatest of all, sending personally chosen delegates to Ottawa to negotiate the entry of Red River into the Canadian union not as a governed territory but as a full-fledged, independent province—inevitably such achievements went to his head. With all the vanity of the Indian peeping out, Riel began to imagine himself a very great personage indeed and in a few months his Provisional Government went from violence to pillage to robbery, all accompanied by that debauchery which ever follows the mendicant suddenly placed in equestrian position. Finally, on March 4, 1870, disregarding appeals for mercy and with many accessories of the coldest cruelty, they shot to death a helpless Canadian named Thomas Scott. Such an act bears only one name— the red name of murder—and in April 1870, the Colonial Office advised the Canadian Government to send an armed force against the malcontents of Red River.

When news of this projected expedition appeared in the *Times* I was making one final effort to procure an unattached promotion; however, a younger colleague purchased the captaincy over my head. My fortunes thus reduced to the limits of a single throw, I sent a telegraph message under the Atlantic:

To Colonel Wolseley, Winnipeg Expedition.
Please remember me.
—WILLIAM F. BUTLER

Then I caught a hansom to the Cunard Steamship Company in Old Broad Street, City.

"What steamer sails on Wednesday for America?"

"The *Samaria* for Boston, the *Marathon* for New York."

"The *Samaria* broke her shaft last voyage, didn't she?"

The clerk hesitated, but had to concede the matter.

"Good," I said. "Book me a passage in her; she's not likely to play that prank twice in two voyages."

For four weeks I ran the social gauntlet of cards and unending analyses of American politics on the *Samaria*, of Bunker Hill memories in Boston, and the glistening wonder of Niagara still half-frozen and so without the hawkerism and nigger melodies of the tourist season, only to discover in Toronto that the Red River Expeditionary Force had already been mustered. At headquarters I was everywhere greeted with, "You should have been here last week"; "Too bad, you haven't a chance"; "That's right, we leave tomorrow," until such overly informative condolences stopped perforce at the commander's door.

"I'm so sorry, old chap," he said, rising to greet me. "I did get your telegram, but every British regular in Canada wanted in. There really is nothing for you."

Colonel Wolseley's five-year seniority gave him advantage of the entire Crimean War where a shell had smashed his face and blinded one eye, but that encounter had served merely to sharpen the most brilliant mind I ever met in the British Army. He was of that order of officer who regards an impossibility merely in the light of an obstacle to be overcome; he would lead his five hundred regulars and seven hundred Canadian volunteers anywhere, to do anything that men in any shape of savagery or of civilization can do or dare. And I was prepared to convince him I had not spent the last month simply polishing my gear.

"I think, sir, there is one berth still vacant."

"And what is that?"

"If you will allow me?" I gestured to the map behind his desk and he nodded. "From Toronto here to Fort William here is one hundred miles by railroad, about five hundred by water. The Americans control the canal at Sault Ste. Marie and you may encounter some delay there? American politicians...." I glanced at him.

The colonel nodded, but his expression gave nothing away. I continued,

"Whatever that delay, your travel to Fort William will be rapid compared to the six hundred miles of wilderness between there and

Fort Garry. You will be cut off from all communication for weeks, perhaps months, along these wild rivers and—"

"There are plans to complete the cart road from Lake of the Woods to Fort Garry."

"In time for your use?"

"Perhaps."

I had not expected this offer of information, and I continued with greater confidence. "That could of course expedite your movement, but if you had any question about the road when you arrived at Lake of the Woods you would doubtless continue on the much slower but militarily more judicious canoe route, via the turbulent Winnipeg River. In either case, however, you have at present no one to inform you about conditions along the American flank of your march, what regarding annexation is being hatched in Minnesota, whether rabid Fenians are gossiping support for Riel in Dakota, what these settlers—"

"Very good!" the colonel interrupted, his handsome face almost smiling. "And in the meantime, what are you?"

"Why, I am an English gentleman with private means and sporting intent travelling west along the easiest available US routes. I am particularly interested in the sharp-tailed grouse of the British North-West, but am also a convivial sort who seems to enjoy hearing locals talk."

Sir Garnet laughed, eyes flashing as he turned on his heel. "Start for Montreal on tomorrow's train, and two days after you arrive go to see General Lindsay."

That general, then commanding in Canada, quite agreed with my solitary appointment. And even while I was waiting for Ottawa's sanction, a tiny flame of action suddenly presented itself fifty miles south of Montreal: armed Fenians were reported crossing into Canada from the United States. I immediately offered myself as reconnaissance officer, was accepted, and so was the only soldier actually to see these pretend revolutionaries march in "fours" across the border into Canada. No one else saw them because when I brought up our officers and troops they had hidden themselves along the Trout River in some June-green hopfields—excellent cover for belligerent Irishmen!—and when we fired one volley into it they all vanished as the morning mist. Rumour had it we killed one, but I never saw a drop of evidence. Years later a Haymarket barber told me his brother had been in my regiment in Canada but he had suffered so much there in war that he was henceforth good for nothing but rest behind the family stove.

"What war was that?" I asked, mightily intrigued.

"The War of Trout River, sir, 1870. It was their stomachs got them, they had no food and lay for days in a forest all overhanging with terrible creeping vines till they had to eat their own blankets."

I convulsed so suddenly with laughter that he almost cut my throat.

This terrible Trout River—or Hopyard—War dealt me, however, back into the race: confirmation of my orders for Red River was waiting when I returned to Montreal. General Lindsay told me, "We leave matters entirely to yourself, just draw on us for any funds you require. If you find it feasible, perhaps you should drop down the Red River and join Wolseley before he reaches Fort Garry. Take care of those northern fellows for us," and I embarked on the Grand Trunk Railway for the golden gleam of the setting sun. In Toronto I paused to find a wardrobe suited to the country where I would travel. A Canadian tailor assured me the only possible thing was "colonials," designed perhaps on the pattern of the American flag since the tops presented mainly star combinations and the bottoms had a tendency toward stripes. All in all, "colonials" at ten dollars were impossible to resist, especially when the tailor included, gratis, a broad green and yellow necktie. With the gear I had already packed and the addition of a large dog, I felt myself quite prepared for M. President Riel strutting on the graves of his victims at the heart of the vast continent.

By July 20, five arduous weeks later, I was on the muddy Red River and steaming north aboard the *International*. I was quite convinced by then that, for certain purposes, I was playing in the wrong league: I had met dozens of American soldiers, not one of whom could be addressed below "Colonel." Perhaps it was the enormous, and bloody, efficiency of their Civil War, lately concluded. Whatever the reason, at thirty-one in the United States I must have been no less than a field marshal patrolling half a territory, rather than the lone subaltern I was watching the flat prairie creep by so totally empty and unused as to humiliate any Englishman conscious of empire, watching two riders keep pace and then gradually outdistance our ponderous paddles as the widening loops of the Red River drew us ever farther north, and ever closer to Fort Garry.

"Those horsemen move like centaurs," I commented to the man beside me, a Canadian returning to Winnipeg where he had lived for two years.

"I wouldn't know about that," he replied wisely, "but them coyote French sure can ride."

I hid my laughter behind my hand but he, only too eager to continue my acquaintance, noticed nothing.

"They pretty well live on them horses, and every summer they haul all their women and kids, even their priest out on them big buffalo hunts. They don't even get off except to eat and sleep. Maybe not to sleep—they're just animals."

Though the *International*'s roof presented the entire immensity of billiard-table-flat Red River prairie, not a single buffalo had yet been visible; until I spied the riders it had seemed that the renowned half-breed picket line, rumoured to stretch almost two hundred miles along the border from Lake of the Woods to the Pembina Mountains, was as non-existence as the great beasts. When we crossed the border not so much as a dingy customs officer had presented himself. However, the effortless horsemen confirmed my faith in frontier rumour, and when shortly thereafter the fireman from below decks informed me confidentially that the arrival of a mysterious stranger with a huge black dog was already known to the triumvirate of Riel and his "General" Lepine and his Fenian O'Donoghue—the woodcutters at the last stop had said so much—clearly it was time to plan my next play.

I returned to my cabin and once more spread out my inadequate map. The steamer must dock at Fort Garry, and what if Riel's guards awaited me there? Obviously I must get to the English settlements twenty miles downriver, at the centre of which stood Lower Fort, still controlled by the Hudson's Bay Company. Once there, Lepine and his hunters could not touch me. I could not allow myself to be arrested. I must make up a small package of essentials, step ashore as soon as the steamer touched quay, and if anyone offered to delay me, win out of the situation either by wit or by my Colt revolver and fourteen-shot repeating carbine, weapons of very equalizing tendencies but quite useless until a certain stage in confrontation is reached. There was nothing else for it.

My sporting gear and baggage I left in care of the captain. Then I stowed papers and extra ammunition in a pocket and, with a small package of personal stuff, my Colt and carbine concealed under my capote and my dog on leash, I proceeded on deck. It was nearly midnight but some light still remained, a faint orange line along the bank of prairie.

After a moment, my awareness...it is difficult to explain...my senses seemed to...as if some hitherto impossible perception sang like spirits along them: the slightly rain-freshened air cool on my skin and crisp in my nostrils, the clucking of the river as the steamer murmured forward, the grouped stars above like sprays of ice meeting again in the gleaming river, the yellow dots of Métis village lights. Somewhere a dog barked, the black shape of houses moved by, of barns, church steeples slender between roofs and trees, dear god, for an instant I thought a bell was tolling the Angelus—the peace of simple homes, of people...and I with the hard bulge of my guns there under my arm—who had so colossally bungled the transfer of government in this place as to make me necessary? The Hudson's Bay Company, which surrendered for £300,000 their territorial rights? The Imperial Government, which accepted the surrender? Or the Canadian Government, to which the country was in turn transferred by the Imperial authorities? A sensible man would have come here, talked to these simple people, and ordered everything in a few hours. But the great and puissant bodies of governments and companies must hedge, negotiate, speechify, pass papers, pass money, money until all is such a hopeless muddle that store clerks can begin to imagine themselves messiahs and suddenly there is nothing left but that twelve hundred good men must win through primeval wilderness, rifles on their backs, to perform that particular and ultimate duty only men with rifles can perform. There was no glory here, only stupid necessity.

My dog growled softly at my feet. Somewhere, hundreds of miles to the right, British soldiers were sleeping beside some awesome cataract; they would wake at dawn to another torturous day. It was not their role to question, to reason why. And neither, as the steamer carried me slowly between the half-breed villages towards Riel's stronghold, was it mine. Though alone, I remained a British soldier. The slowing beat of the paddles and the dim figure at the bow railing reminded me of pressing necessities.

I had to verify my plans with some local confidant, and the Canadian of copious "coyote French" information was there before me. It was unnecessary to explain to him exact particulars about my position: he had that invariable colonial intuition that anyone with an English accent and a modicum of dignity could be nothing less than an Imperial Importance. He effusively agreed that I must avoid initial contact with Riel, "that bastard" was not to be trusted "near his own mother." But rather than brazening it through at the quay, he had another suggestion: the Fort Garry dock was on the Assiniboine River, just around the point of its juncture with the Red. When the steamer turned that point it must momentarily touch the north bank, and in that instant it was possible to leap ashore. I could then flank Fort Garry in the darkness and make my way north to Lower Fort via the good north road through the village of Winnipeg. He would personally supply me with a horse. How could we meet in the darkness? Why, he intended to leave the boat with me; he was as interested as I in avoiding that "tin-can Napoleon."

The title he used raised my hackles—but there was no time for a history lesson. I agreed with what grace I could and, leading my dog; followed down to the lower bows of the boat. As we went, steam was being shut off. The boat rounded ponderously from the Red River into the narrow Assiniboine. The western sky was now quite black, and a short distance ahead and above us, lights, figures shifted against the blacker mass of what must be the walls of Fort Garry. They loomed massively higher than I had supposed possible. And the torchlights sparked as they do when moving between men holding rifles at guard.

For an instant the bow nudged the soft mud of the north bank and the Canadian's eyes glinted up at me. With a conspiratorial hiss, "Here it is, here now!" he jumped. And I hesitated—that sweaty expression, the dark sneaking manner of it all in the face of men at

arms in the shadow of the haughty fort, why not—but with a whine
my pointer leaped and I, his chain short about my hand, perforce
leaped also. Under my feet was shingle, then mud. The boat was
swinging away; ahead of me the fellow, still with his silly hiss, was
already scrambling up a very steep bank. There was nothing now but
to follow.

The dog pulled me mightily, almost as if he were returning

home, but I was much impeded with my arms and small baggage.
The weeds and willows of the bank snagged at my legs, the cliff
was almost perpendicular, and when I finally gained the plain, the
Canadian having paused unnecessarily to give me a hand over the
lip of the bank, I immediately unhooked the dog from his leash. The
stern of the *International* was gliding by behind the huge corner
bastion; there were shouts in French from the quay now hidden to
us. I could feel the limestone slabs, the rounded curve of the fortress
like an immense cliff against my back. If its men and gates were of
this calibre, the taking of Fort Garry would not be without honour.

The Canadian was hissing we must hurry, and already he was
moving away along the path that skirted the wall. I followed, past
the northern bastion and soon we were in the vicinity of straggling
houses. This, I was told, was Winnipeg, and the north road leading
between the houses was under my feet. Just on the other side of the
village a bridge lay across a deep ravine; he would meet me there with
his horse. Before I could protest this assistance, he had hurried away.

I certainly had no intention of hissing after him. The white walls
of the village houses, an occasional tiny light gleamed in the darkness; the bastioned fort lay silently behind me. My unease, which
had grown all evening, suddenly focused; back in Canada I had
bungled my play. Badly. I should have informed myself of the highest
personage at Red River compatible with Imperial interests, brought
a letter of introduction to him, and then stayed with him while
awaiting Riel's move in the knowledge that I was present. I should
have grasped this when the general so blandly said my major move
here would be to "drop down the river to join Wolseley." For me to
tiptoe past Riel like a pimp in the dark—but obviously I had not been
on board the steamer when it docked, so how could I appear there
now? How could I pretend I was an ordinary British officer passing

through simply to facilitate the coming of a peace force? The half-breeds had never had more than seven hundred men under arms, and here was England's most brilliant colonel with twelve hundred men—no—I had cast my uncomfortable die with that jump ashore. I must now avoid Riel and recoup what I could after I was safely in the English settlement. I must think that through.

Whistling for my dog, I strode forward between the silent houses. When the villager appeared with his horse, I would refuse to use it: despite its travel comfort, I could not afford to be further entangled in whatever petty difference its owner had with Riel. My dog, however, did not appear, and as I whistled loudly for him again I became aware that I was approaching a narrow wooden bridge; at its centre stood a solitary figure. Villager? Sentinel? Guard? I advanced without breaking stride, poised for the worst, and passed him at arm's length without a word. He never moved. The prairie night had swallowed my dog as silently as the ghostly figure immobile on the bridge.

So, leaving Winnipeg behind me, I strode forward into the dark plain spread mistily about me. A sense of mystery, the unknown, shaped itself in the shadows, in the distant sounds of animals; I felt extraordinarily exhilarated. I decided that if I heard pursuit I would fling my capote to the road and conceal myself. When the pursuers halted to examine the strange object in their path, some rapid firing from my fourteen-shot would send them flying. In the meantime, road and stars led me ever north.

Daylight breaks early in July; the first dawn began to glimmer when I had been three hours on the march and was, I estimated, at least sixteen miles beyond Fort Garry. No pursuit had come near me. I had slaked my thirst at successive creeks and now the square tower of what could only be a Presbyterian church arose on the riverbank. I reached the gate, was run at by a mongrel who very quickly thought better of it, and pulled a bell at the manse. The moon's crescent still hung in the reddening sky. I pulled again, then again. Finally the door creaked and an apprehensive face presented itself.

"What do you want?"

"How far to Lower Fort?"

"Four miles."

"Could I hire a horse, or wagon, to—"

"No."

The door was closing. I realized from his expression that I looked like nothing so much as a bandit and I added hastily, "I am an English officer, arrived last night by steamer, and I must get to Lower Fort."

No "open sesame" could have worked more magically in that misty red morning: an upholstered chair, breakfast, and horse and buggy materialized so promptly that they might have been apparitions had they not transported me to Lower Fort and dissolved in dreamless sleep under a featherblanket; only to solidify again as a hand on my shoulder, a whisper in my ear.

"The French are after you?"

"The French...." Was I in France?

It was my friend the Presbyterian clergyman, and behind him my Company host. Apparently the docking of the *International* at Fort Garry last night had provided the finest of half-caste spectacles: all citizens available arrested on the spot, including the captain, and my supposed Winnipeg accomplice dragged from his house; the enraged President literally foaming about the quay at the strange Englishman of colossal proportions who had vanished with his gigantic dog. The dog—ahh, that was a masterstroke—huge stranger and brute stalking the gloomy, nightshrouded prairie! "After him!" screams the President. "Bring them in dead or alive!" And armed men gallop off fearlessly in all directions. One large and particularly fearless party is evidently only minutes behind me on the Lower Fort Road when it itself is suddenly arrested eight miles north of Winnipeg—by a house known as "Whisky-Tom's."

Over an excellent mutton chop my host assured me that daylight and leadership would alter the complexion of my pursuit; Lepine, for one, was no rum-swiller. He advised me to proceed immediately to the Indian settlement on Lake Winnipeg; there I would find both protection (the Ojibways were all faithful Anglicans) and canoemen to help me try to find the Expedition. Wolseley? Well, all they had heard of him was he had lost thirty-one men on his first portage and was already down to starvation rations.

The two men were observing me closely and for a moment I kept my face down, concentrating on my tea. The ration detail must be false, but the thirty-one men...that was almost too precise for fabrication. It was impossible that a mere loss of men would halt Sir Garnet, but whatever the case it was now more important than ever that I get inside Fort Garry, perhaps even talk to Riel...above all, I must avoid arrest. Yes, get inside Fort Garry.

"The Indians are completely reliable?"

"Henry Prince, the chief, will tell you he is the most faithful child of the Great Mother."

And so he did, at incredible length, striking his hand upon his very broad and hairless chest. Throughout the oration I felt that the interpreter, with perhaps two hundred monosyllabic English words at his command, was not quite intercepting the entire message; he was certainly out of measure with the chief's large voice, the savage pomp and ceremony, the deep half-circle of brawny warriors with their outmoded flintlocks firing in salute, their rolling "ho ho's" of agreement as Prince spoke of watching the lake for the great chief coming with many warriors to give presents to the red children of the Great Mother. Ho ho.

Poor noble red man of the great North-West. I have found you at last, here on the far shores of stormy Lake Winnipeg. I have long heard of you, and the smoke of your teepee does blur the evening air to blue. You now clothe yourself in the white man's garments, and in his religion, but your dark eyes are still wistful for feathers and war paint, for the dream omen. For what mean price have you sold your past—and future—glory?

When Prince concluded at last I played my simple, but I hoped effective, gambit; any listening Riel informant had to get the matter straight. I affirmed that the Great Mother's chief was coming from the east—I, standing before them was evidence of that—and and he would punish those who set themselves against her, but he would also give rewards to those who had been faithful to her. I was going forward tomorrow to meet him, and I wanted the very best canoemen they had to assist me. In the meantime, I wanted them to accept my present of tea, flour, and pemmican, for I knew they had been faithful subjects. A universal "Ho!" testified that my speech was good.

As they ate and drank I went about grasping Red Deer and Big Apron and Long Claws and others by their bony hands; momentarily, at least, their simple paradise was at hand: ceremony complete and full stomach in process. And I had set my line.

And Riel took it. Early next morning as I was examining various canoes and canoemen, a messenger arrived for me from the south. Would I visit Fort Garry? On the night of my arrival there had been an error in the proceedings—no doubt! The Provisional Government was actually most loyal to Her Majesty. But was it not true that my baggage had been confiscated, and several persons arrested on my account? Was not a flag other than the Union Jack flying over Fort Garry? Yes, this was true. I declared: "While these things remain, I will not visit Fort Garry."

It seemed however, that these things need not remain as they were; in fact, they were already being altered. Further, a message from Colonel Wolseley had come through which urged construction of the road between Fort Garry and Lake of the Woods; such work could not be done, however, unless I visited the fort.

I had not expected so much from Riel: the Wolseley message was a counter-gambit, since Sir Garnet would not have sent it any later than his leaving Toronto. Of course, it suited my purposes exactly to accept, if my minister friend could accompany me. The prisoners had already been released, the flag—well, that might be arranged—but certainly my friend could come.

It was then the Indians who raised a great wail at the prospects of my going to Fort Garry. Their chief medicine man, Bear, tried to impress me that Riel was "on a track of blood," indeed, the three pegs of wood from which he had gleaned this particular information implied a fatal ending for me if I travelled south. He held the pegs up for my inspection: one of them represented Riel, one his Satanic Majesty, and one myself. Old Bear shifted them swiftly in the manner of a thimble-rigger and it seemed my peg did have a damnably hard time of it, but I could make nothing of either his mutterings or his peg gymnastics so, with thanks for the warning, I turned to the laconic messenger. He had seemed indisposed to dismount when he first arrived and had now swung onto his horse again; at my agreement he gestured silently and a horse was led forward. Telling the

Rudy Wiebe: Collected Stories, 1955–2010

factor that I would be back before nightfall, that I expected to begin my river journey that very evening, I mounted.

The sun was so brilliant that July day I felt as if I held in my very hands the heat shimmering between the copses of oak and beyond over the prairie. My horse followed the others down a grassy creek bank and up again, his steady gallop holding me close to the messenger's side. This man, with the warlike, angelic name of Michel, though his appearance was quite non-heavenly, said nothing further to me; he simply rode as if every day of his life he had done nothing else. The minister assured me we were following the road I had walked in darkness, and, as is my habit, I had then continually oriented myself toward particular shapes and landscapes. But now I could not seem to recognize anything I had noted then. Galloping, the half-breed riders silent around me, the tiny groups of farms along Red River, the green prairie burning out of sight into the distant west—all was simply...strange. If I could have set my foot on the ground, strode through a blackened landscape, perhaps a recogniz-able world would have returned to me.

Suddenly I was struck with the thought: if French and English were united in these settlements, isolated as they were and with these superb horsemen to protect them, they would be extremely difficult to dominate by an imported force. Perhaps impossible. Perhaps Macdonald had been very judicious to grant them provincial status. With such calvary, these plains one immense manoeuvring ground...and yet, there across the river in the haze of noon heat was St. Boniface, its cathedral low and mean-looking; straight ahead lay tiny Winnipeg, and beyond that the flagstaffs of Fort Garry. Where was the bridge on which I passed the sentry? The scattered lights of Winnipeg had been transformed into two rows of saloons facing each other across a pig's wallow; the fort bastions themselves squatted old and dirty. Really, there seemed to be nothing here of what I had seen. Had I dreamt it? Then, or now?

A sentry leaning lazily against a wall, a part of which leaned on nothing, jolted me back to my purpose: I was practically inside Riel's so-called fortress. Two gun-muzzles protruded through the embra-sures flanking the wooden gate; the sentry there did not so much as straighten up as we rode through. Inside, eight neglected field-pieces were ranged in a semi-circle with their muzzles pointing toward the entrance. A few dusky men, ragged, with rusty flintlocks, lounged about; the buildings behind them were bare to crumbling whitewash. The entire place looked ruinous, except for a trim bit of bunting flapping on one of two flagpoles: the half-breed flag of fleur-de-lis and shamrock on a white field. On the second pole, in deference to me,

twitched the Union Jack. It was insultingly dirty, and tattered.

Our laconic guide left us in a large room with Louis Schmidt, secretary of the Provisional Government. This short person with a nose grown ponderous from drinking immediately revealed himself so ignorant of the strength of their position that I almost laughed in his face.

"Will you," he asked, "see Monsieur the President?"

I replied, "To call on him, certainly not."

For a moment Schmidt could not intercept what I had returned him so very promptly, but he recovered to play my game.

"But if he calls on you?"

"Then I will see him."

The bumpkin smiled, extremely pleased with himself; I returned the smile fully. And so he hurried away.

After the brilliant sun the room we were in was gracelessly bare, dingy, but suddenly I saw at its centre a billiard table. Its balls were racked in position, a cue laid out as if for play. That precise triangle, the faultless level sward gleaming in a shaft of sunlight which imperceptibly spiralled with dust...from somewhere my Presbyterian friend responded to a question I may have—I suppose I must have asked but his voice seemed strange, and distant.

"I know nothing of such games."

"That is unfortunate," I said. The cue-tip was rosined, I was already planning my breaking shot. "Pocket billiards consists entirely...of angles and positions. It is superb for partner or solitary play...if you plan ahead at each individual shot, it is always...possible you could keep your run going until every single ball dropped... without mis-cue...."

I broke. Incredibly, the one-ball dropped in the centre right pocket, and near the opened cluster of balls the "two" lay open for

me. It ran dead true, and by changing my position slightly I saw
the "three" was free. I made shot after shot until I felt caught in a
precise, infallible rhythm of unbelievable accuracy. It seemed my
hands played a delicate machine, a lock perhaps whose tumblers
clicked into place wherever my hand moved; I saw each shot immediately, my legs moved, my hands made each exact stroke as if
propelled by a power beyond their own. Finally, I had made a particularly intricate two-bank play that left my cue ball in direct line to
drop the "fourteen" in the top right pocket and I was moving easily,
perhaps humming a little, to make that unbelievably simple shot
when I sensed I must pass two moccasined feet at the corner of the
billiard table.

They belonged to a stocky man in formal black trousers and coat,
sallow, puffy face and large head whose square-cut, massive forehead
was overhung by thickly clustered hair—altogether a remarkable face
driven almost to hypnosis by glaring black eyes. The face, the formal
clothes and the buffalo-hide moccasins on the carpeted floor—I could
not for a moment comprehend who this mixed apparition might
be, how it had exploded out of nothing into mystery when I had so
nearly completed the most perfect billiard game ever to form itself
under my hand—I still could not quite credit the ball movement, the
accuracy of my shots which seemed so little of my doing—if I had had
this billiard set at the officers' club in Ceylon I could have purchased
a captaincy in three different regiments—almost as if, instead of
playing, I was being played—

"This is Monsieur the President, Louis Riel," Louis Schmidt's thick
voice blundered somewhere in the background. "Lieutenant William
F. Butler, 69th Foot Regiment."

I almost laughed, perhaps at the fortuitously bungled order of
introduction, but I felt a powerful hand. I still held the cue in my left,
and Riel said nothing. He simply stared as if he would know everything of me at one glance.

"How do you do?" I said, and dropped his hand for I found myself
in the perfect position for the penultimate shot. I bent to it; it was
so unbelievably simple after what I had now completed that I could
keep on talking. "Do you ever indulge in billiards, M. Riel?"

"Never."

"That is a loss," I said, and shot. The balls clicked, the "fourteen" vanished dead-centre in the pocket. "A capital game, a truly...." The cue ball rolled precisely into position for the last shot—but it kept on rolling as if driven quite beyond its proper place and suddenly, before I could put out my hand to stop it—absurd notion—it dropped in the bottom left pocket. Scratch.

I could not believe it. The simplest possible shot! I put my hand in the pocket and took out the single ball—yes, the white—I looked up and saw the minister looking at me incredulously. And Louis Schmidt also. There was no Riel—hadn't I shaken Riel's hand, why, where... hadn't he been here, a moment ago?

Schmidt hurried out. My companion came and took the ball and cue from me. And then Riel was there again; I motioned him to a seat and took a chair myself. Our two companions left the room. I sat face to face with the still silent "tin-can Napoleon."

When our regiment returned home from Ceylon in 1864, our clipper anchored for two days, April 15 and 16, off the desolate volcanic rock of St. Helena. Nothing so lonely, so age-riven, so thunderous with the sound of the sea exists anywhere on earth. Those seas roar with the legend that, when the powers of Good and Evil destroyed the ancient world between them, the vanquished spirits of Evil prayed that St. Helena might remain. When the Almighty asked why, the Evil Spirit answered: "So that one day, in the new world, there may be brought to that rock a mortal all but godlike in his genius, and on its black altar he shall undergo a lingering death at the hands of evil men."

If I live a thousand years, those two days steeped in thoughts of glory and grief will live with me, for I saw Longwood where he was penned behind sentries standing shoulder to shoulder day and night, and touched the rotten stumps of the gum trees smashed by the storm the night before he died.

And the man before me, self-chosen leader of this new nation of the North-West...why, he had the youth, the appearance, perhaps the brilliance to create a glorious empire. He certainly had the people, and their power. With a thousand of his horsemen riding the plains and rallying thousands of their savage kin out of their torpor—what hadn't the few Minnesota Sioux in their unorganized hit-and-run tactics been able to accomplish in 1862? Terror, destruction, absolute conquest was possible for this man; by securing a source of ammunition and supply from any American or British entrepreneur, perhaps with some maverick British officers to teach his superb hunters basic cavalry strategy, this half-caste could wash the western half of North America clean of all whites with their own blood and rule an empire larger than Europe. He could be a veritable New World Genghis Khan—he could be....

But Riel sat and talked: like a priest. Of peace; of preventing bloodshed; of resigning immediately when the proper Government authority arrived. He had a glorious face, voice, his very tones were electric and I could feel like ice drawn down my back how that voice would send soldiers screaming defiance into the flaming mouths of cannons—but he had no emperor's spirit, he had no emperor's eye to gain an indescribably glorious prize. Half the New World, and he could only mewl over the bits of blood it would cost....

He must have read the disappointment on my face. Undoubtedly even my disgust at the meanness of his ambition. A leather-clad Indian on the prairie grass has presence, has dignity, but to suppose that this half-caste could ever play the part of the greatest man on earth since Alexander, dressed in the garb of a priest and the footwear of a savage, was simply absurd. Absurd.

He had risen abruptly. Since I would not move, he had to lean down to give me the final benefit of his piercing eyes.

"Had I been your enemy, you would have known before now. You would not visit me and, though I felt humiliated, I came here. I want peace."

And with those sentiments, truly worthy of the linen-draper's assistant he had been before he seized this pretence of spokesman for an unknown, nameless people, M. Riel darted from the room as silently as he had entered; twice.

And I? I too must rise. To face the ride north, the pathless solitudes of great inland seas where the red man's canoes ride the waves like gulls. Perhaps they will not disappoint me. Perhaps they, at last, can help me run my elusive quarry to his haunt.

But...for a time, I sit, motionless. The sunlight slants across the billiard table. Ah yes. Yes.

A Night in Fort Pitt, or (if you prefer) The Only Perfect Communists in the World

LATE ONE NOVEMBER EVENING in the thirty-third year of the reign of Queen Victoria, a solitary horseman might have been seen riding along the hills that parallel the North Saskatchewan River. He had been riding west since before daybreak, but now long after sunset the giant sweep of the frozen river suddenly confronted him, forcing him south, or as nearly south as he could surmise from the stars that glittered occasionally, momentarily, between storm clouds. And the wind which had been threatening snow all day now roared, it seemed, with a malignant fury up the cliff down whose steep slope he could not risk his exhausted horse, though he knew that he must somewhere, somehow get across the valley if he was to find shelter at Fort Pitt, the only white settlement along three hundred miles of river between Fort Carlton and Victoria House.

The night before the rider and his small party had endured among bare poplars in the fold of a creek; when they emerged that morning onto the prairie before dawn to continue their journey, they discovered the entire sky brilliant with aurora, torn sheets of light gently glowing and leaping into blaze above them and smouldering away again. The man had stopped his horse, watched, stunned; felt himself

shrink as it were into and then grow incandescent in that immense
dome of brilliance until sunrise burned it into sheer light, and he
became aware that his Indian guide and Métis companion had
vanished into the apparently flat earth; leaving nothing but the line
of their passing in the hoary grass. The quick winter afternoon was
already darkening before he caught up with them in their relentless
track. The radiance of aurora still informed him and he told them
they had veered too far south; sunset perhaps verified his perception, for after the long day's ride they still had not encountered the
river. He refused to accept another night in the open and swung onto
his weary mount. His men had already unburdened theirs, preparing
to weather the storm they insisted was driving up from the west in
a brushy hollow. So they watched him ride west alone, the prairie so
open he could inevitably be found if lost, as impatient and as supe-
rior with all necessary knowledge as every white man they had ever
met, riding into darkness following stars.

And now in stinging snow the stars were lost, though it did not
matter since he had found the North Saskatchewan River. Well, it did
matter, because he knew that every Hudson's Bay settlement was on
the north bank; he must cross over the river or he would miss Pitt,
he could ride as far as he had already ridden in a month, another
five hundred miles across prairie into the glacial mountains themselves and not encounter a white man. As if at the thought, his horse
stopped. No urging could move it so he slid off, straightening his
long legs against the ground with a groan. The horse turned its long,
squarish head to him, nudged him, breaking the icicles off its nostrils
against his buffalo coat and then finding the warmth of his armpit.
Perhaps this hammer-headed bay from Fort Carlton could become as
superb a companion to him as Blackie had been—the storm shifted
an instant and he realized they were on a point of cliff. Perhaps a
tributary cut its way into the river here as steeply as the main river.
Where was he? Even if he got down into the valley, if Fort Pitt was
built half a mile back from the river in a bend like Fort Carlton, he
would never find it. He sheltered his crusted eyes against the whistling snow that enclosed him: the air seemed as solid as any frozen
prairie. He would walk on it easily as dreaming out into the sky....

The cheek-strap of the bridle hit his frozen face when the horse moved. He felt that, his arm slid onto its neck.

He knew he could not lose this one certain warm body also, his mittens clamped on to its stiff mane and so suddenly he was led forward and down, sideways and down, the incline almost vertical and shifting like relentless sand, but that one body was solidly with him, there, whenever they slipped they slid closer together, their six feet all one and always somehow set certainly into the side of that incline of what might be rock or frozen clay, deadly as ice, but so reliable, so trustworthy he would never let go of this horse, never leap aside even if river ice parted into water as it had when he leaped from Blackie sinking, scrambled to safety while seeing his horse sink into blackness and there was its beautiful head bursting up, its front legs, neck arched, and knees clawing ice with its deadly shod feet, trying to climb up into the bright air by sheer terror, nostrils flaring bloody and the ice smashing now again and again in ringing iron, and he turned away, sprinted for his rifle—he was an English soldier, soldiers can always offer the ultimate mercy of running for their bloody rifles—and he knelt there expert sharpshooter on the white, deceptive ice until the shots hammered back at him tripled from the cliffs and the long water ran flat again and implacably empty; on his knees, crying.

But this hammerhead bay led him so easily down...down five hundred feet or a thousand—instinctively he was counting steps, an officer must always carry some facts, even if they are estimated—and they scrambled out between broken boulders (or were they frozen buffalo?) and there was river ice again, certainly, hard as the cliff here and he was still clutching the horse. But with his arms and legs now, completely, and it moved with his frozen face in its mane, he could smell prairie slough hay, hear scrub oaks at Fort Garry scarlet as cardinals in October light, the chant of Te Deum prayed by monks in a roofless Irish ruin, and he became aware that the sting of snow had quietened: there was an upthrust, darkness moving beside him, a dense blackness, and he loosened one hand, reached out: it was most

Rudy Wiebe: Collected Stories, 1955–2010

certainly the usual twenty-foot spruce palisade. Never anything in stone like the permanent ruins of Ireland. And a gate in the wooden wall; hanging open. Perhaps the Indians here were all dead, the gates hanging so open.

The bay followed him through that hanging gate like any dog and the storm was so abruptly quiet he felt himself breathing. High-peaked roofs, gabled, around a square, he could not distinguish a light or a sound. Perhaps smallpox had discovered them all, Indian and Métis and white alike, as in Fort Carlton. Winter would keep the bodies perfectly, death already blossomed over them like spring flowers. He limped across the open square to avoid what lay at the edge of every shadow, what might move, dreadfully: a door, darkness in the centre building. He seemed to have reached the heart of something, corpses were keening all around him, at the very hoared edges of his fur cap and he wheeled around, listening. But there was only his own small breathing, nothing but the horse snoring, bent low like grass behind him. So he turned back to the door and began to pound on it. Nothing. The plank door would not budge to his fists, its cracks blacker than its wood, and he tilted forward, hands, face clutching the frame, they were all dead, O open up, *o miserere mei*...he heard a sound. Inside. Against his face an opening, of light, the skin of a face, a young woman's face. Impossibly beautiful.

Such materializations are possible out of the driving blackness of a prairie blizzard, lantern-light and such sudden woman's beauty as perfect as it is unbelievable? He found himself bending forward slowly, past the worn planks of the door frame, tilting slowly into her light, his frozen cheek, his still tactile tongue...and felt...nothing. Those eyes, the black brows and exquisite nose, was it white, that skin in the golden light? Was it believable though impossible?

It is possible that when Lieutenant General, the Right Honourable Sir William Francis Butler, Knight Grand Cross of the Order of the Bath and member of the Privy Council of Ireland died in his bed in Bansha Castle, County Tipperary, on June 7, 1910, died as his daughter then wrote, "of a recent affection [!] of the heart...that was brought to a crisis by a chill," it is possible that on his deathbed thirty-nine and a half years later Sir William could still not decide: was that face he instantly loved at Fort Pitt on the North

Saskatchewan River in the North-Western Territories of Canada on November 18, 1870, loved as only the truest Victorian male who believed all his life that Jesus Christ and Napoleon Bonaparte were the greatest men in all of human history could love, a latter-day romantic when romanticism was still acceptable in a male if he was also practical and above all heroic, dear god, was a man who championed the innocent and detested the brutalities of war all his life while becoming one of Victoria's most honoured and decorated soldiers, a member of Field Marshal Wolseley's brilliant Officers' Ring that fought for the Empire on four continents, and who dreamed for forty years of "the Great Lone Land" as he called the Canadian prairie and never saw again and idealized every Indian person he lived near for those few months in 1870 and 1871 when they were either dying of smallpox or more or less starving despite their unselfish greedless tradition of sharing everything, which makes Indians, as he wrote then, "the only perfect communists in the world, who, if they would only be as the Africans or the Asiatics it would be all right for them; if they would be our slaves they might live, but as they won't be that, won't toil and delve and hew for us, and will persist in hunting, fishing, roaming over the beautiful prairie land which the Great Spirit gave them: in a word, since they will be free—we will kill them"; this Butler who on the same journey contemplated the parklands of the Saskatchewan, observed their remarkable similarity to the English downs and found it "mortifying to an Englishman" that they were, as he so concisely put it, "totally undeveloped": this Butler was forced over an unseeable landscape by a November blizzard to be confronted by a woman's face, her thick black braids hanging to her hips; wearing a loose nightgown.

The nightgown was probably not thin. More likely it was heavy flannel since any Hudson's Bay fort at the time (they were really nothing of forts but rather clusters of log buildings surrounded by log palisades, all of which could and did, as easily by accident as by design, burn to the ground) was badly heated by cavernous open-hearth fireplaces, doubtless she wore that heavy flannel of solid red or delicate floral design which cloths the Company traded with the Cree and which those people suspended as gift offerings to the Thunderbird on the Centre Tree of their thirst dance lodges in June.

And here it would hang as gracefully, draping between braids, shoulders and arms and nipples and hips a slender revelation. And the very handsome, six-foot-two and always brave and presently very hoarfrosted Lieutenant Butler, late of her Majesty's 69th Regiment in India and the Fenian Raids in Quebec across the Canadian border from New York, and most recently renowned as intelligence officer of the Colonel Wolseley Red River Expedition against the Métis founder of Manitoba, Louis Riel: frozen or not, Butler must fall instantly in love.

As he stood there, erect and frozen, clamped to the hand-sawn plank of the door frame, his faithful pony having discharged its final faithful duty of carrying him to safety and about to collapse in faithful exhaustion behind him, did Lieutenant Butler say, "Madam, I very nearly gave up hope of ever reaching succour"?

And did she reply as stiffly, "O sir, our rude abode is but little better than the storm, nevertheless..."?

And he, accepting her hesitation: "Madam, if I may be so importunate...."?

And she, accepting his: "O sir, of course, do come in, sir, come in out of the storm"?

And did she turn to send the dark servant woman standing behind her scurrying to the kitchen to revive the fire that was no more than embers in the hearth?

Perhaps that was how Fort Pitt, named after the great prime minister but doomed never to be as famous as Pittsburgh, named after his father the Great Commoner, perhaps that was how Fort Pitt offered itself to him. Or did she exclaim out of the lamplight, "O la sir, what a storm brings you here!" And he, bursting into laughter, reply, "What you see is mere weather, my fine wench. There will yet be greater storms than this!" Staring so closely down into the luminous whiteness of breasts her nightgown made but small attempt to contain.

Her father, Hudson's Bay Factor John Sinclair, had only a brutal litany of disease and starvation and death to offer him at Fort Pitt. He always kept the palisade gate locked—some damn Indian had tore it loose—every building locked, they were under siege and if thirty-two of sixty people at Fort Carlton was dead, including the factor, and half the McDougall missionary family at Victoria dead too, then Pitt had been saved because he wouldn't let one goddamn Indian into the place, trade or no trade, locked them all out, and he had been damn quick in summer when he first heard the smallpox spreading and he got some blood out of a Saulteaux Indian vaccinated at the mission in Prince Albert and used that to vaccinate everybody—well, damn near everybody—in Pitt and he had kept every Cree locked out, every bloody one of them: Butler could barely restrain himself. Use them, use them any way you can, use their very blood...but he sat at the kitchen table devouring (with perfect army manners, of course) the mound of buffalo steak and potatoes Mary (now properly dressed, of course) served him before the pine fire blazing on the hearth—where was the mother, the inevitable Indian, at best Métis, mother? The free traders, muttered Sinclair into his rum, had destroyed the hide and fur trade anyway, what did they care about Indians, just soak the buggers in whisky, steal all they could from them today and to hell with tomorrow, so now even at Pitt, the very heart of buffalo country, the beasts were gone, not enough robes this summer to make three decent bundles and he'd have nothing at all to eat except potatoes if Big Bear, that ugly little bastard that never got sick, hadn't dragged in ten to trade and he'd risked taking them even though half of Big Bear's band was spitting blood, they caught it fighting the Peigans near the border who got it from the American Bloods, hell, they said it was the US Army deliberately infecting the Indians down there to wipe them off the face of the earth because it was costing them damn near a million dollars each to shoot them! The smallpox was sure cheaper, about as cheap as wolfers throwing strychnine all over the prairie, and about as effective. There'd soon be nothing but corpses stinking up the whole goddamn stinking North-West.

Butler looked at him carefully: Sinclair was typical enough, a poor Scot forced to spend his whole life remembering home from the other side of the world, living who knows how in what over-whelming monotony of daily life and endless, endless miserable seasons repeating themselves, too old now for even the occasional Indian woman to rouse him, and suddenly a government official appears out of the night at whom he could momentarily blurt what-ever he wanted, an official not on the summer boats but riding an assignment in the dead of a deadly boring winter on orders from the Lieutenant Governor of the Territories—there was one at long last—someone who had been within breathing distance of all those invisible Hudson's Bay lords in London barely seven months before, who had often smelled the "goddamn heather" and actually glimpsed the Queen herself who had finally survived her grief for Albert and was now the emerging mother of a world empire: what poor lonely sot of a homesick Scot wouldn't seize such an opportunity to snore every pessimistic worry he had aloud into his grog?

To be starving in Pitt, Sinclair suddenly roared, is like freezing to death in Newcastle! This is buffalo country, one herd moved over these hills for seventeen days and nights in '62, over two million, there was no end of them summer or winter and he'd fed every fort from Rocky Mountain House to Vermilion and The Pas, every goddamn fur dragged out of this country and every bloody ounce of stuff dragged back into it in every bloody York boat—every fuckin' trader had Pitt pemmican in his gut and now Big Bear brings in ten jesus carcasses and he has to burn the hides and boil the fuckin' jesus christ out of the meat! But at least that old bugger knew what he was doing, telling his people to leave the fort and scatter in the bush and maybe the winter would be cold enough to kill the white man's disease, though what they would live on, even their dogs and miserable horses so far gone....

Butler saw Mary Sinclair turn like a flame in front of the fire. After a month of half-fried bannock and pemmican—which had all the taste of boiled shoe-leather—her baked potatoes were beyond any remembered cream and butter, dear god their very aroma— and she facing solitary winter darkness, a lifetime of that incredible skin drying up in cold and mosquito-and-blackfly heat, such a shape hammered slack by year-after-year pregnancies. At her bend by the hearth for another rack of buffalo rib he felt his body thaw and stretch completely, his powerful legs, toes flaring so fluidly, a kind of tensile vividness she awoke in his hands hard from cold and clenched reins all day, a touch of, somehow, flesh and resistance needed; despite heavy cotton the length of her leg, her curved thigh, her quick smile past her shoulder, her extraordinary face even when seen sideways or upside-down. Her father snored, fat arms flat on the table: every night such a lullaby and every night lying somewhere innocent, somewhere in this clumsy building, every night she was here naked against cotton and he rolled in his deerskin sack on the frozen prairie, sweetest jesus why is there no comfort in the world ever together?

The Métis servant came sluffing down the stairs. The bed for the gentleman was warming with hot stones between buffalo robes, would he go up? It was Mary who spoke, Mary who led him up the narrow stairs through her own shadow to the door, opening it without so much as a glance: she gave him the lantern and was gone, not a gesture of her lithe body even at his stumbled good night, and thank you again...the hall was empty before he grasped her going. Wind moaned in crevices. Well, doubtless to help the Métis woman hoist her father back into his bed again. He stripped quickly, blew out the light. The stones were too hot, the robes total ice; he felt his body slowly shrinking into a huddle. Be I as chaste as ice, as pure as snow, I shall not...he sensed a footstep and sat up: she was there, he knew. But it was several seconds before the rustle she made told him she was lifting the heavy cotton nightgown over her head.

Could he say anything when she came in beside him, he the Irishman of endless easy words, when she laughed aloud so gently at all his sweaty underwear? And she peeled it off him, chuckling again at the memory of his good night, did he think Pitt was a hotel and she a chambermaid? Hot stones in bed were no better than camp-fires: you were always roasted on one side and freezing on the other. He may have had a small hesitation.

The bed...is too narrow.
Wide enough for one is wide enough for two.

And her skin fit completely around him, her head warm as opening lips in the hollow of his neck. If despite twelve years of Her Majesty's army his body still did not know what to do, she doubtless helped him to that too; and perhaps his own skin and various tongues in that black room taught him something of her invisible shape.

Perhaps this happened to William Francis Butler in Fort Pitt in the North-Western Territories of Canada on the night of November 18, 1870. Perhaps, if he was really lucky and Mary Sinclair was, thanks to her mother (certainly not her father), one of the world's perfect communists.

There is of course another story; the one Mary Sinclair told forty years later. Before things went wrong in 1885, she said, when I was only a young girl, an English officer came to Fort Pitt. He was tall and very good looking and he talked and talked and he could talk so well I thought perhaps I could love him. He told me about his home in Ireland, he came out of the snow and storm one night like someone from a different world and then when his men arrived after him he rode on to Fort Edmonton and I could only think about him. But he came back again, and he asked me to marry him. He asked me to go live with him in the Old Country. There I was, a child of the Saskatchewan, what would I do in another country? Perhaps I cried a little, but I sent him away. And after a while I did not remember him so often.

I sent him away. That is how Mary Sinclair later told it. But not Butler. He wrote his story in a book, and he mentions her only in the same sentence as "buffalo steaks and potatoes." For these in Fort Pitt, he writes, "I had the brightest-eyed little lassie, half Cree, half Scotch, in the whole North West to wait upon me," and he mentions this "lassie" not at all on his return journey from Fort Edmonton at the end of December 1870 when bitter cold and a lack of sled dogs forced him, so he writes, to wait at Fort Pitt for seven days. Did she then also with steak and potatoes wait upon him? Serve him? Such a handsome Victorian soldier wrapped in tall furs on govern- ment assignment would perhaps not have remembered that she sent him away, especially not after he discovered in Ottawa a mere four months later that all the "excellent colonial ministers," as he calls them, had large families and that "an army officer who married a minister's daughter might perchance be a fit and proper person to introduce the benefits of civilization to the Cree and Blackfoot Indians on the western prairies, but if he elected to remain in single cussedness in Canada he was pretty certain to find himself a black sheep among the ministerial flock of aspirants for place." Premier John A. Macdonald's only daughter Mary was handicapped beyond any possible marriage, and the most beautiful girl on the prairies could certainly not have helped Butler be an "aspirant for place"

in lumber Ottawa so, despite letters as excellent as excellent colonial ministers could make them for his excellent service, the tall
officer returned to the heart of empire still a lieutenant, still without
a permanent government appointment, still without a steady war
in which to achieve the fortune that could purchase his promotion.
He could not then know that soon the kingdoms of hot Africa would
provide him with a quarter of a century of men he could, with his
enormous organizational efficiency, help to kill. In Fort Pitt on the
North Saskatchewan in November and December, 1870, during cold
so severe no Englishman could imagine it, a beautiful young woman
"waited upon me," as he said; "sent him away," as she said.

Or is a fourth story possible? Did they dream together, narrow
bed or not? Did they see those enormous herds of buffalo that once
flowed along the rivers there, such a streaming of life never again
seen anywhere on the surface of the earth or even in the depths of
the sea? And in the darkness did they see the long, hesitant parade of
the Cree chiefs in 1876 approaching Treaty Number Six that ordered
them thereby to cede, release, surrender and yield up all that land
forever, and behind them the one chief who would not, the chief
Big Bear as the whites called him, but perhaps better translated
"Too Much" or "More Than Enough Bear," who would ask them all
how could one person give away forever what they had all forever
had, who had more than enough of everything except the power to
persuade his people of his defiant vision until years later Fort Pitt
was burning, was becoming a great pillar of smoke bent over the
river and the empty hills and all that flour and rancid treaty pork
they had never wanted, had abhorred as soon as ever they saw it,
surrounded them, rained on them, dripped black and stinking out of
the very air they were forced to breathe?

She knows that darkness alone can offer what he longs to accept.
Smell and touch and the tongue in the ear, yes, taste itself, yes,
yes—but not sight. Eyes for him are impossible.

The fire locked inside each palisade log, the factor's house, the
spruce walls close about their narrow bed springs into light, fire
lifts Fort Pitt, transforms it into air and its place, here, on this earth,

is lost to any memory, the valley and the hills changed as they are
already eternally changed beyond the going of the animals and some
day the Hutterite farmers will break through the bristly poplars,
domesticate them into wheat fields and a plough furrow along the
bank of the still relentless river one day reveals a shard of blue
willow china; its delicate pastoral a century's confirmation of her
waiting upon him, of her serving him?

Behind the double darkness of his clenched eyes he sees again
the length of his rifle barrel and the black hair whorled behind
Blackie's straining ear: the blood explodes exactly there! They
had to cross today, an officer's daily plan must be followed,
iron shoes or not on thin ice or no ice they must cross, and his
groans, his unplanned and most irregular tears.

They may have dreamed something together. Possibly they
dreamed the scarlet riders of the police he would recommend the
Canadian government establish to force English law upon the
western plains, the police whose thin implacable lines would weave
the red shroud of the old Queen's authority over every child of the
Saskatchewan until Inspector Francis Jeffrey Dickens, the great
novelist's third son who aspired to his appointment by patronage,
not by excellent merit of excellent colonial service, would at Fort Pitt
become the most infamous officer in the history of the world-famous
force. Force indeed.

Or they dreamed again the gaunt Cree dying, scraping their pustu-
lated legs and arms and breasts and infants' faces along the gates,
the door frames, the windows of the locked fort to force the white
man's disease back upon him, to somehow smear him with his own
putrefaction. And perhaps they also dreamed Big Bear walking so
emaciated among his people, his magnificent voice persuading them
they must scatter to the woods and the animals, that only on the
solitary land would they be given the strength to destroy this invisible, this incomprehensible evil that rotted them, his words and his
scarred face proof of his lifelong power over the white diseases, his
name certain and forever More Than Enough Bear for everything
except the white words on the white paper, words he could never

read that would one day endlessly whisper to him behind the thick, sweating walls of Stony Mountain Penitentiary.

Was it Big Bear who helped her say to him then: Go away.

Only she could dream that. It is impossible for Lieutenant William Francis Butler to dream such a hopeless dream; even in a narrow bed in Fort Pitt, even in Mary Sinclair's warm and beautiful arms.

The Fish Caught in the Battle River

ON WEDNESDAY, MAY 27, 1885, southwest of the barracks in Battleford I met these two men with a fish they had caught in the Battle River that day. They had a young poplar stuck through its gills and on their shoulders, and then the tail trailed on the ground. It must of been at least six feet. I don't know what kind of fish and I forget the names of these men, but maybe they're still alive and still remember.

※ That's what I remember, a long dripping fish or the dust on this girl's ankle where her moccasin was cut through to her brown skin— dust, or grease on the top of long hair—but hardly ever names that didn't get written up from that time. Or numbers. There were exactly twenty-one yoke of oxen in our freight train divided into two companies with a leader for each and a driver for every three yoke. That way we were supposed to form two circles together fast when we got attacked or for night, and we practised that too with all us men and teams inside. They never give us soldiers for protection on the first trip, nothing, not even a guard till fifteen miles out of Battleford and the trail goes right by these big Indian reserves and we camped like that and our leaders sent in two men to bring a guard so we could come past and get in. Then this Colonel Otter sends out a squad of twenty North West Mounted Police to bring us in, but on the second

trip from Swift Current we never got that close to Battleford and we
sure never had time to form circles among the young poplar of the
Eagle Hills when these painted feathered-up Indians were sprouting
all around us, Bang! without so much as a horse-fart to warn us
before they were all over like the grass itch. That was Thursday,
May 14, 1885. Ten o'clock in the morning. Late enough if you've been
switching ox-ass since half past five on that Battleford trail. In a half
hour we'd of been stopping for a feed but there were these maybe six,
seven hundred Indians and half-breeds all looking only too happy
to blaze away and then nothing was ever luckier than us not having
more than a few hunting rifles or they'd of rubbed us right out. I
guess at least three hundred of them had rifles and the rest axes
and war clubs and stone-headed clubs they were swinging over their
heads like loosening up for some nice game after a short night on
hard ground. I was on the last wagon and in charge of food for that
part of the train. So I had one of the rifles. One of our leaders he still
had his head on straight and he got up with a white handkerchief—
white as it was two hundred ox miles from Swift Current—on a stick
while I covered him. I guess I could of gotten one or maybe even two
if Frank—yeah, that's his name, Frank—and lots of good it would of
done him too, but he says, "Cover me, Dan," and I guess that's the
way it's supposed to be done, but eight hundred Indians, what the
hell. As it turned out, there were heads worn straight with them too.
They said we had to leave the oxen and everything and they'd take us
men as close to Battleford as they dared. It looked to me they'd been
eating a bit pinched for a while and our heavy wagons looked real
good to them. We weren't more than eighteen miles out of Battleford
as it was and twenty men started us in, all on horseback and us
holding on to one stirrup-strap, running beside them.

※ On Tuesday, April 28, 1885, we were starting from Battleford to get
this second load of supplies, over four hundred miles round trip, and
it wasn't actually us that was so stupid. We wanted escort through
the Eagle Hills and we asked for it. Both for then and when we'd get
there coming back. That Colonel Otter sent a policeman with orders
to either move in fifteen minutes or get arrested and our teams given
others to drive. That Otter should of stayed at home, in Ontario,

yelling orders on parade and knitting spare time, thinking his two
hundred men lying around the Battle River flats was shaking any
Indian feather in the Eagle Hills. So our guys weakened and obeyed
orders, and his little skirmish at Cutknife Hill on May 2 of attacking
a sleeping Indian camp of over half women and children just got him
eight men killed including a teamster name of Charles Winder shot
through the head. He was no Custer at Washita Creek, that's for sure.
And on the 14th he damn near got our hair creased and lifted too.
These were Cutknife Indians, low on powder and tight in the belly.
Poundmaker Crees with Stoneys thrown in, and they're madder than
the Crees, any day.

✺ We hadn't run more than a mile or so when these other Indians
galloped out of the bushes on the left and stopped us. One of the
half-breeds was translating a word here and there and said they were
Poundmaker Indians too, but it came out we had to either go back
to camp or these new ones that hadn't been in on the original agreement would maybe shoot us right there. And there were too many
of them for our Indians to shoot it out, though one or two were
waving their guns around, like what the hell, let's do it! I couldn't
figure this out till after a few days. Our Indians, the ones we were
running beside and who had first captured us, had given their WORD
they'd take us close to Battleford alive but these other Indians, the
same tribe and I guess the same chief and everything, hadn't given
their WORD on anything. They hadn't been there to argue and so
if they felt like it they might shoot it out with their friends so they
could shoot *us*. You ever hear of such a thing? It wasn't as if we were
enemies or anything, hauling supplies to a army that had already
tried as hard as it could to surprise them and rub them out; our
Indians had given their WORD.

✺ One of the big troubles Indians have is they've got no general who
gives out orders. Even if they are stupid. Stupid orders are anyways
orders, but with Indians even a really big chief like Poundmaker or
One Arrow can only say, "This is how I think," but if a lot of others
don't think like him then it doesn't happen. If a war chief like
Poundmaker's war chief Fine Day wants to lead, he makes a long

speech and then he rides off and if anybody agrees with him, they follow; if not, everybody sits around looking at the ground and after a while the war chief comes back and he may still be war chief or he may not. Any Christian could tell them that's no way to run a war.

✷ We got run back to the main camp and they had a council. All of them this time, about thirty of the main ones sitting down in a circle and all the other men standing around listening to the talk. Indians have any amount of time for talk. Talk, they're never rushing anywhere. We stood there too, looking out of the corners of our eyes and over our shoulders; the smell was pretty strong too, considering the leaves were out all over the hills. I wasn't looking that much at leaves then, and no nice dusty ankles either. This was business and the women stayed where they belong, over the hill. You didn't need a word of Cree to understand mostly what was happening. If the speaker wanted to kill us he'd dance around the circle with his rifle crooked in his arm, talking loud and fast. If he felt otherwise he'd leave his rifle or club on the ground and walk around, talking like he wanted to quiet a ox or horse. It was a long time touch and go but finally they agreed to keep us alive if nobody tried to run away. If anyone did, then any Indian that wanted to could kill as many as he wanted of the rest of us. So how do you like that? I mean us freighters weren't any tribe of Indians; we'd just been working together two trips up and down the Swift Current–Battleford trail and most of us hadn't known each other before that and sometimes you don't care to continue the acquaintance longer than absolutely neces- sary, if you see what I mean. We accepted the terms, of course, but I could see some of them bloodthirsty ones were counting on maybe one or the other of us trying a White act. Poundmaker talked to us then, wearing his fox-skin hat like always and said our lives were safe and said we should thank God. He also gave us a nice quiet man to interpret so we would know what was wanted. When an Indian visited us and expressed a wish to kill one of us, this man always let us know his wish. They took our bedding and also my coat and vest. I had thirty-four dollars and I did not like parting with that (Scotch) but the interpreter said maybe I should let it go when one Indian was swinging a loaded rifle near my head. I did then, and the whole camp started to move southeast. A minor chief had me drive his oxen, his wife and I sitting on the front seat and he sitting behind on the supplies with a four-foot cutter bar of a grass mower in his hand, all the knives broken out except the top five. An ox-cart isn't actually that big and it bumps a lot. My Indian was sitting right behind me, that thing bouncing pretty loose in his hand going over the bumps.

❋ On Monday, November 16, 1885, I was driving four yoke of oxen with four loads of fifty-two bushels of wheat each on my way to Regina. When I was just west of the North West Mounted Police barracks I was stopped by a policeman who told me to turn to the right and keep outside the stakes with a red flag on them. Nobody would come inside the red stakes. Going around the stakes was all turtleback, no road at all, just ruts and buffalo trails and prairie bumps. If these oxen hadn't been really trained to go by the voice alone I would have had a big job. We got back to the main road, then two miles and we were in Regina. The first words I got were, "Riel is dead." He was being hanged while I was going turtleback around them stakes.

❋ We were travelling in these five columns and about half a mile wide winding between the poplar bluffs and just out on flatter country going southeast when the guard up front rode back waving everybody back into a ravine we'd just crossed. The rest of the riders went forward, and when they came back they said they'd shot a redcoat. It was a Mounted Police, or a scout at least, and who knows what he was doing there alone and I did not see the shooting, but heard it. He was shot in the back of the head by a Stoney and they buried him a little by carrying ground from a badger mound close by. We camped for supper about 5:30 and my Indian's wife and her sisters, all pretty young, and mother made supper of peeled potatoes, bannock, hardtack, tea, milk and sugar, all from our supply wagon. We sat on our heels in the teepee around the food. I at the wife's right and she saw that I had plenty to eat. They didn't know about cans so I put a two-pound can of Armour's beef in front of her on a board and took the axe and cut it in half with one cut. They all looked serious but didn't move when I picked up the axe and all burst out laughing when the can fell apart and they saw what it was. I did it twice more but signed that they should leave the rest for another day. My Indian never opened one of the cans, he always gave me the axe and stood a little away like he could never be sure what might be inside those tight little white man's boxes. Once one lay too close to the fire and exploded; that one I had to take away and bury. I always had to take a bite too before they would, but the women were always good to me, both young and old. On passing a creek I let my Indian know I was going to have a drink and I let the oxen go themselves. When I got a drink I ran to catch the team and there was a old squaw. She just had her few things tied in a bundle on the back of a skinny dog and nothing in her hand. She took me by the wrist as I went past and I stopped and she rubbed my open hand slowly all over her head, smiling all the time at me.

◉ The third night, Saturday, May 16, 1885, was very cold with maybe an inch of ice on the slough where we camped. The water was good, not a bit alkali. We were sleeping on the ground between two wagons with a canvas thrown over them. The first night we were in a tent and they gave us some blankets too but when these were divided I got none and not being much good at pushing for a place I got left to the door of the tent. Every little while a Indian would come to look at us and one of them saw me shivering and come back with a beautiful braided rabbit-skin blanket under which I went sound asleep and warm and forgot my troubles. I had that only one night and between the wagons we only had two double blankets for six men so two thought they would be warmer in the wagons and climbed up. We had a guard all around and every hour or so a Indian who didn't trust us come and counted to see if we were all there. All of a sudden there was a terrible racket. A Indian was standing with one foot on either side of my head, a burning piece of wood dropping sparks in one hand and using a butcher knife in the other as a pointer while he counted. Only four men on the ground—good, good—then they could start killing. I didn't move my head off my boots (my pillow), just covered my face with my hands because of the sparks and the interpreter was yelling for everybody to lie still, he was telling them again and again that everybody was still there, and after a while the guys in the wagons dared show themselves and so we were all there and everybody went back to sleep. Of course no Indian camp is ever all asleep. There's always something moving, a dog snarls sniffing around, a child stands up to take a leak, horses snuffle. There are night birds too, little night hawks that seem to split over your head with a whirrr—enough to really scare you with ghosts if you don't know what they are. There's just a shadow over your face and at the same time whirrrr. On cold nights there aren't mosquitoes and the sky lights up deep blue like a lake with diamonds. Sometimes the northern lights come too, washing back and forth over the sky all quiet. Then the Indians are really quiet. They say they can get you, the spirit dancers up there. I'd rather have slept with the Indians and was glad I was with them in the day. Then I'd get away from the only thing anyone ever talked about in English:

"How long do you think we'll live."

All I ever said to that was,

"Maybe five minutes, maybe till our teeth rot."

We moved every day a little, talking and talking and waiting to hear from Riel. They were fighting at Batoche.

⁕ On Sunday, April 26, 1885, we were coming into Battleford with our first load of supplies and Colonel Otter sent out the police to bring us in when we sent in our two riders. We camped about eight miles from town, putting the wagons in a ring for protection, the men and the teams inside. I was put on guard on the west side and the police gave me a heavy revolver. About eleven o'clock a scout of Poundmaker's come close and had a look at us but not doing any more and so we didn't either. Everything was quiet about one o'clock, horses quit stamping and the oxen lay down with their long breathing groan, men went to sleep, police walking around with almost no sound. I was lying under a wagon with head and shoulders outside the ring under the sky, the revolver under my hand. Then I heard, "Are you asleep?"

"No, sir," I said, and that was the truth or I would not have said anything.

◉ Poundmaker was head chief of the big camp of quite a few reserves together and he was at least six feet, with very long hair in two braids hanging in front, a long straight nose and always wearing his whole fox-skin hat with the brush hanging down his back. He's the finest looking Indian I ever saw, dressed in blanket chaps, moccasins, buffalo-hide coat tanned and covered with rows of round-headed brass tacks and sometimes carrying his heavy pukamakin. It had four knives sticking out in four directions. The runners were expected to bring good news from Riel but they come and said Middleton had overrun Batoche and Dumont was wounded and going to the States. Then the Indians and half-breeds in camp put down their arms and after a couple of long councils decided to take us prisoners to Battleford and ask for terms. The squaws came often to look at us. They did not say much, just sat on the ground nursing their papooses that were mostly naked. The children would come and look too. Sometimes the children laughed at us but one old squaw who was poor and alone with all she had tied on the back of a spotted dog let me know she was sorry for me. We were taken to Battleford in four or five wagons and just as we were ready to start a Indian struck each of us on the shoulder with a quirt. That was on the 22nd. Middleton sent a message that they were to come in or he would come down and also defeat them utterly. On Tuesday, May 26, 1885, Poundmaker and his warriors came to Battleford and surrendered without terms. The flat between the Battle River and the fort called Fort Otter was covered with the white tents of the soldiers when the Indians come out of the sand hills to the south, a long, wide column of them with the two wagons piled up with guns and rifles, every kind ever sold by the Hudson's Bay Company in two hundred years, flintlocks to sixteen-bore single-barrelled to fourteen-shot Winchesters.

◉ On Tuesday, May 26, 1885, a soldier pulled the tent-flap back. General Sir Frederick Middleton sat on a chair north of the Battle River facing west. At about fifteen feet sat Peter Hourie, the interpreter, on a chair facing east. The Indians sat a little lower in a semicircle on the ground to the south. I stood about fifteen feet north of the general, inside the soldier lines. Poundmaker got up from the centre of the Indians and stepped closer and held out his right hand. Middleton sat still leaning back in his chair, so after a while Poundmaker pulled his blanket tight and turned around and sat down on the ground again. Middleton asked why he had taken up arms and murdered innocent settlers. Poundmaker said he had murdered nobody and had defended himself when attacked at dawn which he thought he was entitled to do. Middleton asked why he had promised to help Riel fight the Queen with two hundred men, and Poundmaker said if he had promised that he would have done it. Middleton said he hadn't helped because he was scared, like a squaw. Poundmaker sucked on his long pipe and after a while he said, "I am sorry. I feel in my heart that I am such a person as I am."

Middleton sat there and said very loud, "Poundmaker, you are accused of high treason. What have you to say?" Then Hourie and Poundmaker talked back and forth for some time and soon Hourie made a statement.

"There is no such word as 'high treason' in the Cree language."

The general stared at him and the interpreter leaned forward talking back and forth with Poundmaker again. Then he announced: "You are accused of throwing sticks at the Queen and trying to knock her hat off."

All at once a fat old wrinkled woman standing with the hundreds of Indians behind the seated chiefs started to talk and scream and wave her hands. The interpreter did not interpret. You could've heard her in the hills over the Battle River. Poundmaker said one loud sound without moving and she was quiet.

⚙ Sir Fred just nodded to Peter Hourie, and asked more questions.

Oolulik

IN THE STOREROOM is where I am that afternoon, getting ready
two sled loads of supplies when the dogs began to howl outside.
From their tone a team must be approaching so I climb out, up on
the drifts that cover all but the roofs of Tyrel Bay post. The short
February afternoon is grey over the snow and the wind rising in a
falling temperature. Paliayak and several of his people are already
beside the mounds of their houses, looking west.

In that direction we still hope. The fall caribou must have gone
south there, for only stragglers came down the usual eastern branch
of migration and Paliayak's camp, which hunts east and south, just
made Tyrel Bay the week before. With three of nineteen people lost
to the long January hunger. Squinting against the gloom, I finally
make out the dot moving where the curve of the bay would have been
except for the level drifts. The figure seems barely to move; there can
be only two, at most three, dogs on the sled. I shout to John on the
blue roof of the store, swept bare by the wind, "Take the light sled
and four dogs!" In a few moments he is gone, dogs running madly. I
go down into the store to brew tea and stir the beans. Beans. Eight
hundred pounds of uncooked beans neatly labelled "Emergency
Rations" for a land without a natural fuel supply. And the one
government plane that came in just before the darkness hasn't

116

returned to correct what may be mix-up, may be stupidity. Even after soaking six hours, it takes a rolling three-hour boil to cook a potful.

Beside the stove two of the four children staying in my room because of their frostbite play intently with a ball of string. I watch them rolling the ball back and forth, the string running out like a track over the floor and then rolling up again. They are warm and full of food; the aroma of beans drifts through the store. The children play without a sound.

When the barking approaches, I go out. It is bitterly cold now with the wind still rising, but all the people are standing by the two houses watching the approach. In a few moments John draws up; he has picked up the driver, two dogs and little sled without bothering to unhitch anything. The dogs are barely skeletons. They lie motionless on the sled, and when the man lifts his face to us for a long moment I can see only starvation; then I recognize Keluah, Ikpuck's younger brother. We lift him from the sled and into the store. The little children look up as we come in, then run quickly to their mothers who are in the group that follows.

After he has drunk three mugs of tea I ask Keluah in the language of the people, "You come from Ikpuck?" He nods. "Does his family have meat and fuel?"

His mouth moves, reluctantly, "No."

The circle of brown faces stirs but no one says a word. I ask, "Where is the camp?"

"On Dubawnt Lake, with the others."

"Turatuk. Vukarsee. Nakown. Lootevek." He speaks as if behind his closed eyelids he sees the grouped humps of snow houses on the long shore of the lake. It is at least ninety miles from Tyrel Bay, and there is no need to ask whether the others had food.

"Why did you all camp at the lake?"

Keluah lies on the blankets against the counter; it takes a long time for him to speak. "Some deer came last fall, but not much. We hunted, shooting stragglers and here and there a small herd. But there were not enough for caches, we always ate everything we killed. A little after the twilight came Ikpuck found a good herd at Dubawnt Lake. We killed them all, and we could again lick the blood from our hands and our bellies were full. But the others had found nothing for many days, and they camped at Dubawnt one by one when they had no food. We fished. But we have no meat since the middle of the darkness."

Incredibly, not one clear hint of this has reached the post. But there has been no movement this winter: the weather unbelievably bad and the foxes at low ebb. If only the reconnaissance plane had come after I sent John to Baker Lake in early January—but it did not and that thought is useless. Three weeks without food during the darkness. Forty-five people in six camps traded west last fall— and then I remember. "Keluah," I say quickly, "where is the camp of Itooi?" The largest of the western camps, it contains ten people, the families of Itooi and his brother-in-law Ukwa.

The man lifts his gaunt face from the cup of broth John is giving him. "Itooi would not stay at the lake when the deer were gone. He said the few fish would give out too and we would all die in one place. He and Ukwa went south to the Front River, they said."

"Have the fish given out at Dubawnt?"

"Yes."

"Have some of the people died?"

Keluah is slowly drinking the soup, the muscles of his cheek working to control himself before his hunger. Finally he pulls back and lifts seven fingers. "I left so long ago, with the last dogs. But some had died." There is no need to say he was the strongest man left in the camp. Ninety miles in seven days, with a blizzard only two days before.

Paliayak is looking at Keluah, reading every hour of that fight in the frost-black face. I say to him carefully, "Can you make up two teams from your dogs? Are there three men who can travel?"

He nods his huge head. "We can."

"I wanted us to rest at least another day, but now we cannot. One could take four of my best dogs and the small sled to Baker Lake. If the weather holds, perhaps in three days. I could send a message to take to the Mounted Police, to fly out with food. Two could come with me, with loads for Dubawnt."

Paliayak says heavily, "It will blizzard soon—two, three hours."

"Will it be too bad to travel?"

"Perhaps." He shrugs.

I look at them all standing in a circle around Keluah who is almost slumped down, his mouth hanging slack as in sleep. They are the people of this land and they know better than I what is ahead on this trail, but I do not have to ask them if they will. "The blizzard will have to take care of itself; we have no time to wait for it." A fleeting smile touches the faces of the people. Then we move quickly to complete our preparations.

119

Oolulik

Though the wind continues to rise from the north and the ground-drift whirls about our legs and over the dogs, especially in the hollows of the land, it does not snow and the sky remains clear. We have the moon and the trail at first needs no breaking. As I jog along this seems an ordinary dead-of-winter trip, where the only matters to watch for are frostbite and over-fatigue. Ordinary, if I did not have to keep sharp eye on my two companions to make sure they keep up even though my sled is too heavy for six dogs. And if, above all, I did not know that waiting for us were the people and that even an hour longer could make all the difference for some of them. That Paliayak's son Atchuk will get through to Baker Lake is as sure as anything can be; next to his father he is the best man in the band and with the light sled and fresh dogs he cannot fail. Except for the unexpected. But Itooi early taught me that the margin of safety on the barrens is so narrow that if the dangerous unexpected comes it is almost inevitably fatal; therefore it can be disregarded. Do your best and if it fails you will not likely have another chance. Atchuk: a hundred and fifty miles in about the time we make ninety. If the weather is even barely flyable the plane will be in Dubawnt within two hours from Baker Lake; arriving perhaps as quickly as we. They will fly immediately, beyond doubt; emergency sloughs bureaucracy aside, thank God. But verified emergencies are often already too late. That too is a fact of the Arctic barrens. For the whole matter depends on the plane. With no more dogs left in the camp, we cannot hope to get all the people out with our three sleds. Besides, the bigger the loads we haul in, the more dogs we need and the more food for them we need and if we are held by a blizzard even for a few days—and in this season we cannot expect to get away without one—then it is a question whether the food and fuel oil we are pulling down the trail now against the side-blast of the wind will be of any help at all to the thirty-five persons at Dubawnt, except to slightly prolong their pain. And as for Itooi's camp—

I stop thinking about it. If the people are to be saved at all it will have to be the plane; if it comes the loads we are now hauling will make a difference. What we need now is a mug-up. I whistle to the dogs.

My oil-stove is already warm under the tea-pail when Paliayak and Nukak pull up out of the darkness. We slump in the lee of my sled, faces near the meagre warmth. Presently Paliayak says, "Maybe the blizzard won't come. See, the lights." They have emerged as we ran, out of the east and northern sky: a great white-frozen band tinged pink that flimmers and shifts over the endless level of the land. There are still no clouds, and now perhaps there will be none for a little. Under the lights the winter darkness softens and the land spreads blank around us to a horizonless silver. Once when we rested on the trail Itooi told me that the lights were the souls of unborn children playing with their umbilical cords. Even after years between this land and sky, the lights can touch terror. I look at the other two and they smile grimly. "It is good," I say. "We will move until the weather turns."

We cannot do quite that. Eighteen hours later we are two-thirds of the way to Dubawnt and we must make a sleep-stop. The weather has held, fiercely cold but steady; for five hours I have been pulling with the dogs. Quickly we build a snow house, feed the dogs, gnaw some frozen meat washed down by tea and crawl into the robes. In ten hours we are on our way again, not rested but moving. And the weather holds, the temperature about fifty below. I pull with the dogs immediately as do the others but we are moving across the coarser grain of the land now and we make less than twenty miles in eight hours. In the last two the snow begins to sting head-on. We are almost to the lake-ice then and still perhaps ten miles from the camp, but we have to stop and risk the storm getting worse. We waste no thirty minutes on a house but simply pull the sleds into a triangle and huddle in the robes in that shelter. Exhausted, we sleep. When I next look at my wristwatch in the darkness of the robe it is four hours later. Nearly noon. I cannot feel my left foot and I pull off mukluks and socks, massaging, until the pain comes back. Then I push half-erect. The wind shrieks but it is not yet full blizzard.

The wind shifts to the northeast after we take to the trail, which is lucky because the dogs could not have faced it for ten miles. Nor we. The lake, at least, has no eskers. There is still a trace of daylight left when we corner the last headland and see the mounds of the people's snow houses. The dogs rouse their last efforts and break into a trot at my urging. My leader even raises his head and howls, to be echoed feebly by some of the other dogs, but no answering sound comes from the camp. No figure emerges from the scattered houses even when I halloo as loudly as I can, running.

I stop at the first circle of houses and halloo again. Entrances blocked, I cannot see any tracks from one house to the next. I dig out my flashlight as Paliayak and Nukak pull up. Their faces are gaunt with exhaustion and without a sound the dogs drop in their traces. We trudge together to the nearest tunnel entrance. Paliayak pulls the block of snow aside; I bend to crawl, calling as cheerily as I can, "Someone from far has come for a visit," following the beam of my light down the long entrance.

The tunnel opens up into the house and when I get to the end I raise my head with the light. The beam flashes around the domed roof and against the worn caribou of the figure crouching almost at my face beside the entrance. My heart thuds as I struggle erect, the two behind me in the passage, "Hello! We've come from Tyrel Bay!" But the figure does not move, it is hunched forward over the stove, its hands palm-out to the heat and even as I lean forward I comprehend the house is dead cold. Paliayak's face emerges out of the entrance hole as I touch the shoulder. It topples like a stone; Turatuk, frozen rigid.

We stare at the face fallen over in the dirt against the empty oil can, the body visible here and there through tatters of fur. No sound at all in the house, not even our breathing, and then I remember the sleeping bench along the back. Only a bumpy robe; I jerk it back and there lie Turatuk's wife and his seven-year-old son and baby daughter, in a row, as they slept.

Paliayak and Nukak have not moved out of the entrance. I fling the beam of light around the small house, but there is only the useless tin stove, dog skulls, bones, the empty oil drum, a few scattered pots, and the bodies. They have eaten everything—extra clothes, hides, the very dog bones are split for marrow. Someone has chewed the leather braided handle of Turatuk's dog whip. I say, "The other houses—there must be some still," and Nukak plunges out of sight with Paliayak behind him.

We go the round of the death encampment. In some houses weak voices answer when I call at the entrance and we crawl in. We empty one of the larger houses and Paliayak and Nukak help or carry the living to it, setting up stoves and melting snow and heating meat while I run on, from house to house. I find several where the people, though alive, cannot answer my call so each must be searched. The darkness has long come when I have finished all the houses I can find. Of thirty-five people who should be here, we have found seventeen alive. Of the men only Ikpuck and Nakown remain; the hunters inevitably go first. I squat beside Ikpuck and in his face I cannot see the brightness of the isymatah, the leader of his people. He says, in my silence, "We sent Nayak to you in the middle of the great darkness. Then at last we sent also Keluah."

"Yes. Keluah told us. But Nayak never came."

"Ahhh," it is a sound deep in his throat.

"Ikpuck, we have searched all the houses here, three in this group and four to the west, where you were. Are there others here? And have you heard of Itooi and Ukwa?"

Beyond Ikpuck, where Paliayak is doing woman's work, the fragrance of thawing meat fills the snow house with warmth and strength. Ikpuck does not move as he speaks, "One has not heard from Itooi. They were going back to camp on Front River, but one has not heard of them since the darkness."

"Yes," I say in his silence. "When the plane comes we will find them. Perhaps they have found the deer. Are there others here?"

After a moment he says, "Long ago Lootevek and his oldest son went on the hunt, but they did not come back. His wife—and his other children—are in their house beyond the others, over the little creek."

"So far away? If she is alone, why—" I stop.

Ikpuck says heavily, "She was asked to come here, several times. But she would not." As I move quickly to go Ikpuck looks up, fleetingly. "It would perhaps be well if two men went to that house."

I look at him an instant, at a loss to decipher his tone. "How many children?"

"Three."

Impossible. Outside I find Nukak unloading the last from my sled, and in a moment we are beating west along the shore. Under the overcast the wind drives like needles across the lake; it must be clear tomorrow if we are to expect the plane from Baker. One or two of the seventeen may not recover, but the rest surely will. And if Itooi's band has escaped with only one or two deaths and if Lootevek's wife and two children, or perhaps even three, remain, why out of the forty-five that had traded west at Tyrel Bay last fall twenty-seven or even twenty-eight are alive to—but I cannot face the thought at the moment: nor the fact that in ninety miles of travel we saw only two rabbits, no owls or fox tracks; nor that as far as I know only two men and three teenage boys are left to this group of the people. I think rather of the people as they were last summer, friendly, laughing together with their friends in the sunshine on the bay when the land briefly burst open with flowers. I rub the frostbite on my cheek. It seems very long ago since I heard their laughter.

"There," says Nukak as the lead dog barks, then all howl in chorus. A small mound barely pokes out of a drift. We drive up, the dogs hushing. Lootevek always was a loner and his wife, a large strong woman, hardly even smiled, but in the camps he seemed to lose some of the moroseness which fell on him when he lived near the store. I brace myself and push aside the entrance block. "Hallo! We have come from Tyrel Bay," I call, bending down into the tunnel.

And suddenly out of that black tunnel rises laughter.

The sound echoing in the narrowness is beyond measure more horrible than the silence we fear. I stop and Nukak's scramble behind me ceases. I cannot unravel thought; I can only shout, "We are coming," and lunge forward, Nukak at my heels. The house is dark but I fling the light-beam up before me and we are inside. It is as cold as the other houses, but on the sleeping bench Lootevek's wife

Ooluti̇k

sits erect, wearing her outside parka, her eyes glaring through matted hair, her mouth still hanging slack from the sound which greeted us. We stare at her. I move the light, but she is obviously the only person in the house.

"Where are the chil—" I begin but Nukak jogs my arm, gesturing to the floor. There are so many split bones lying about that I stumbled coming in. As I blink down at them now suddenly the woman laughs again. And in that shriek I understand.

There is no way to get her from the house but tie her in the sleeping robe and kick through the wall to the sled. We bring her to main camp and put her in a house by herself where her laughter will not terrify the rest of the people. Then, after several hours of feeding broth to those who cannot sit erect, I crawl into my sleeping bag.

Paliayak rouses me after eight hours; we go out, and clearly the blizzard that has been holding off is moving in over the lake from the north and east—the direction of Baker Lake. No plane on earth can get aloft in that. There is nothing to say, so we go back in and heat food. As we eat I explain a plan. He shakes his head, but helps load the sled. He stands looking after me as I urge the rested dogs out on the lake. Perhaps, with a light sled and rested dogs, I can cover the twenty-odd miles somewhere along which Itooi's Front River camp may be before the weight of the storm hits. And if forced to stop I can wait out the blizzard as well on the trail as in this dreadful camp. So we run.

When the blue shadow that precedes dawn comes up over the long white land breaking trail for the dogs is no easier for the wind rises inevitably, nagging loose snow, and the bank of cloud more clearly rolls higher behind me. About dawn I make out the ridges on the lakeshore between which the Front River breaks to the lake and I turn south. Once on the twisting river I cannot lose my way: I simply follow until I reach the camp. If Itooi has left the river—well, it is useless to think of that.

The diffuse sun-blob is as high as it will rise when between the van lashes of the storm I think I hear the echo of a plane. I am chewing meat as I run, not daring to stop for tea, but at that I stop and tear back my hood. There it is again! I stare around, the blood pounding in my head, searching for direction from the wind-torn sound. The dogs prick up their ears, and then I see the flash of it, between tags of drift, coming up over the esker from the southeast. I jerk the covering from the sled, clamber up a rock ridge and wave frantically. The snow swirls around me and the plane noses on obliviously west and north. Then, suddenly, it banks towards me. A red and silver Norseman; they must have radioed from Baker to Churchill and they risked a try into the storm. The plane roars over and I wave northeast towards the lake. It circles right, red lights flashing. Don't be so stupid! And you know there's no place to land on the riverbed or on the ridges! He passes over again, very low, so slowly the stall warning must be roaring in his ears. He dips and I see his face: Jimmy Hughes of Churchill. Swinging the tarp towards the lake, I scream at him though he cannot hear me, and he lifts up again into the wind. The wings waggle. He understands; and knows as well as I he's daring the face of the storm to try and unload, take on some of the people and get out before he's grounded. In a few moments he will be over the camp from which I've been struggling four hours. If the storm had held off we could have searched—but there is no need for such thought, and I clamber down to the team.

Two hours later it is impossible. The blizzard has been upon us in full fury for over an hour and only because it is behind us could we still trek. In its blindness now I realize I could go within twenty feet of the camp never knowing. And I have to stop while I have enough strength to build a snow house. Suddenly the dogs whine behind me. I stop, look back at them and then ahead. There is nothing except the streaking snow. I get my mitt on my leader's collar. "Okay, c'mon."

We move ahead slowly, and then abruptly the snow darkens and a shape is floundering towards me. "Hallo!" I reach for the shoulder and head bent into the white wind. The figure jerks and straightens. I am staring into the sunken frostbitten face of Oolulik, wife of Itooi.

I hold her by the shoulders then, for when she recognizes me she seems almost to crumple. After a moment I can ask, "Are you breaking trail for the others? Are they behind you?" I brush the ice from her face and she shakes her head with a shudder. "Where are they? Can we get to them before the storm is highest?"

She says through frost-broken lips, "They are in the camp by the Lake of Little Men." Somewhere beyond—perhaps five, perhaps eight miles, where the Front River runs out of the lake, where the deer cross and where for generations the people have hunted them by setting up inukshuk, rows of rock mounds that at a distance look like short men, to channel the deer into the river for easier spearing. Three years before Itooi took me there for the fall kill; there were full meat caches that winter. I stare at his wife now, trying for a moment not to think what her being out in this storm alone means, trying not to understand the small bump on her back under the parka. She murmurs, "They are without breath in the snow houses, Itooi also. Only the baby."

For a moment we hunch there, our backs to the storm. "Come," I say finally, "we must find a drift for a snow house."

There is little time to look, and the house we manage to build is tiny. But it is shelter, and when I get the oil-stove and the food inside from the sled there is warmth. I melt snow for water and give Oolulik the soup to drink from around thawing meat. She soaks a bit of hide in it and gives it to the baby to suck, but he seems almost beyond that. I should have remembered milk but she looks at me and murmurs, "Tomorrow one will have milk for him." I crawl out to feed the dogs; the storm is so intense now that I cannot see my feet. I check the dogs' chains, pull the caribou sleeping robe off the sled and struggle back into the house. Oolulik is holding her child to her under the parka, bending back and forth over the little stove as if rocking in sleep. I rouse her. "The storm will be long, and we must save the oil. Here." I spread my heavy robe on the sleeping bench; she looks at it. She herself sewed it for me three winters before. "I know," I say at her look, "you could carry nothing but the child. But we must stay warm." I squat by the stove.

She lays the naked boy in the robe, then pulls off her own worn, frost-hardened leather clothes, spreads them out on the floor and gets into the robe. I blow out the stove and in the darkness I quickly undress and I lay out my clothes to freeze. Then I crawl into the robe also. It is just large enough. I can feel the ice of her emaciated body against mine but I know that together we will soon be warm, and as she hunches closer the wind's whine over the house is already dying in my ear.

For the first three days of the storm we do little but sleep. Oolulik eats what she can and cares for the child. He is her only concern and as she grows stronger she has milk for him but he does not improve. She rocks him gently, holding him to her under the parka, and in the long hours she tells, in snatches, the story of what had happened at the camp by the Lake of Little Men. If we were not alone in the cramped snow house and her strong handsome face haggard as I have never seen it, I could almost think we were in the hunting camp as we have been so often and that any moment my friend Itooi will crawl through the door and lift his laughing face to us and shout, "Telling old stories again? No one bothers with them now, only a few women! Ha! But just now a deer happened to run under the guns. Perhaps it will be enough for supper!" But no deer will ever again just happen to run under Itooi's unerring rifle. He lies where he has fallen over the fish hole in the ice, Ukwa's knife-wounds in his back. For Ukwa, big simple childlike man who could never hunt very well, and did not have to as long as his brother-in-law cared for him and his family, broke mentally under the long hunger. In his madness he may have believed Itooi was deceiving him in dividing the few fish on which the two families subsisted, so he—who knows—the fact was he went to Itooi jigging for fish, stabbed him, then went to his brother-in-law's house and before Oolulik knew what was happening had already stabbed the oldest girl as she lay beside her brother. Oolulik, strong in terror, succeeded in wrestling him down and tying him because he kept crawling back to the sleeping bench, insanely intent on the ten-year-old boy, Mala. Then, the baby on her back, she went out to get Itooi to do what had to be done with the madman. She found her husband face down in the ice hole. There was only one law left her: survival. She returned to her house, pulled a thong taut around Ukwa's neck, dressed Mala in what hides were left and, with the baby still on her back, leaving her dead and Ukwa's wife—her sister—and children she could not know in what condition, with time only for one desperate effort for her two sons, she began the trek for Dubawnt Lake under the threat of the storm. But Mala was too weak; in an hour he collapsed. She waited beside the boy until his panting stopped, then covered him with snow and turned again to the storm. Some hours later I found her.

We are safe now; we have food and shelter. But it is too late for the baby and on the third day he dies.

On the fourth day she gives me the body and I take it out. Finding my marker, I dig out the sled and lay the body under it where the dogs cannot reach. The blizzard howls without cease. There is no way to help Ukwa's family even if they are alive. The storm roars over me for a time, then I return into the house. Oolulik is sitting as I left her and I begin to melt snow to make tea. We have said nothing since the child died, and I cannot endure the silence. But how to break it? We

128

have known each other since I came to Tyrel Bay and though we are about the same age, she is my mother as Itooi has been my father in the north. Now I can only make her tea.

She drinks a little. Eyes closed, she squats on the sleeping bench, swaying silently. I drink tea, listening to the storm, and presently I sense her singing beside me. It is not a Christian hymn such as the people love to sing together when the missionary comes to Tyrel twice a year and which they sing together when they hold their daily morning prayers. It is the old song of the people that I heard only once or twice during my earliest days in the north, a song as I have long since not been able to beg from Oolulik. Like the singers of the people long ago, she is composing as she sings, and it is her own song:

Where have gone the deer,
The animals on which we live?
Who gave us meat and blood soup to drink,
Our dogs strength to run over the snow?
Once their strong sinews sewed our clothes,
And their bones gave the sweet-brown marrow;
Then our houses were warm with the fire of their fat
And our cheeks smeared with their juices.
Eyaya – eya.

And when they would not come, Long ago,
The angakok would send his soul beneath the lake
Where lives the mighty spirit Pinga
And there sing a charm for her that would soothe her
And the deer would come
In great herds that covered the land
And the birds that follow them hide the autumn sun.

We would hunt them at the sacred crossings
Where the little men stand guard,
And the angakoks would sing their songs,
And the people would keep strictly to the taboos
And not offend Pinga,
And in the winter the storm would wail about the house,
The dogs roll up, their snouts under their tails,
On the ledge the sleeping boy would lie
On his back, breathing through his open mouth,
His little stomach bulging round.
Eyaya – eya.

Were it not Oolulik, the wisest woman among the western people
who is singing, and were her song not so terrible in beauty, I would
think her mind has given way. For though she is the daughter of a
great angakok and it was whispered among the people that even as a
child she had already shown some of his power, she gave her name to
the missionary as a young girl and all her life she has been a fervent
Christian. She told me the legends of the people only after much
persuading. Itooi was the church catechist for the band, leading the
services during the long months the missionary could not visit them.
Like all the people, they were profoundly devotional. The two times
I was with them at Baker Lake they attended church services every
day six days of the week. The angakok to them had long ago been
declared the power of Satanasi, the devil. And now Oolulik sings on:

When all the people came safely from the hunt
Then we knew our amulets were strong,
And the angakok who had gained his strength
In the lonely way of the barrens
Would sing of Sila, the great spirit
That holds up the world and the people
And speaks in no words
But in the storm and snow and rain
And sometimes through unknowing children at play,
Who hear a soft gentle voice,
And the angakok knows

That peril threatens.
When all is well Sila sends no messages.
He remains solitary, silent.
And there is meat in the camp, and the drum dance
Calls the people for dance and laughter and song.
The women lie in the arms of the song-cousins of their husbands;
And the angakok speaks through the fire of the seance.

Rudy Wiebe: Collected Stories, 1955–2010

She has stopped, her face tilts back towards the low roof of the house, her eyes closed. Her song in its short endlessly repeating melody has grown loud, but now it drops away:

Eyaya – eya
Where have gone the deer,
And the people of the deer?
Eyaya – eya.

When I can bear to look at her again she is motionless on the sleeping bench, looking at me with bright dry eyes. Suddenly she says, "When the white man came to the people with guns and oil for heating, it was almost as if we no longer needed shamans or taboo for we could hunt the deer wherever we wished, from far. Then the missionary came and told us of Jesus and we listened and soon our old beliefs seemed of little use for us to live. We have lived this way most of my life, and every year the deer have been less. And our prayers to God do not bring them back. In the old days the shaman did."

Finally I can say something. "Oolulik, you do not believe that. The shaman could not bring the deer if there were none."

"There always were deer."

"Yes, but they have been over-hunted, here, in the north, in the south."

"Because men have guns."

"Partly, but also—"

"And they no longer keep the taboo of not killing more than can be eaten. The missionaries tell us that we must believe other things, and the white men do not even believe what the white missionary says. We have seen them in Baker Lake. Many never go to church, and yet they are fat and warm and never hungry. We believed and prayed, and see—" she gestures about the tiny house. "There is nothing left to believe. The deer and the people are gone."

"The people are not all gone. There are many left in the eastern bands, and to the north, and the deer will come back in a few years. The government is beginning to make surveys and soon we will know why the deer—"

She is looking at me with a gentle smile and I cannot continue. "Abramesi," she says. "You are a good man. But you did not go with us to church. You do not believe either."

Finally I can murmur, "But you have believed for many years, long before you met me. And you still believe."

She does not look at me but stares against the wall of the house as if studying the storm that howls beyond. She says at last, "The deer are gone and the people of the deer are gone. I also wish to go away."

There is nothing to be said. Later I crawl out and feed the dogs; there is only one skimpy feeding left, but from the sound of the storm it may break tomorrow. I go in and prepare food for us. Oolulik eats little, squatting silently on the floor. She will remain that way all night, swaying back and forth, singing softly to herself. I undress, crawl into the robe, and pull it tight over my ears.

I awake to the smell of food. Oolulik is at the stove and there is no sound of wind outside. I dress quickly and crawl out. Stars sparkle in the fierce calm cold; when the sun comes up the world will blaze white. In a few moments we have eaten, loaded, and are on our way. Oolulik rides the sled with the body of her child. She leads us unerringly to the spot; we find the body of her other son and take him with us also. Travelling is fast on the wind-hard drifts. In an hour we are at the camp, and even as I clear the entrance of Ukwa's house I hear the plane coming from the north. It will spot the dog team so I concern myself no further with it for the moment but scramble into the house. Amazingly, Ukwa's wife and two of the three children are still, if barely, alive. They know nothing; only that Ukwa has not returned. I start the stove, put on frozen meat and crawl out. The plane is landing on the ice of the lake and with a jolt I see it is the RCMP craft from Baker. A little luck now would have been too much to expect.

Corporal Blake must, of course, examine all the bodies. Oolulik has brought all hers to the sled, and after he crawls into what was her house and examines Ukwa. There is no way of concealing the way he died and I translate while the policeman questions her. Nothing can be done: she has killed the man and she must be arrested. It seems we will have to take the bodies of the two men with us for medical examination, but then it leaps in me and I curse him, long, completely. When I can control myself he says only, "Yes, it would be too much for the plane." And he permits Oolulik and me to take what is left of her family out on the wind-swept hill overlooking the lake. There is, of course, no way to dig a grave. We do what the people did long ago: lay them on the ground, cover them with the few wind-cleared rocks we can pry loose, and leave them to the elements and the wild animals. In the house I had found Itooi's prayer book and now I hand it to Oolulik to read a prayer over the four graves. But she takes it from my hand and, without opening it, thrusts it under the rocks. Then, squinting against the blazing sun on the snow, we drive down the hill. Blake has helped Ukwa's family to the plane, and when we arrive the two sisters look silently at each other, one knowing, one unknowing though without hope. We climb in; four adults, two children and five muzzled dogs make an awkward load but soon we are airborne. We circle over the hill with its patch black against the snow, and head for Tyrel Bay.

Two days later when the plane comes in from Baker again to evacuate the last of the people from Dubawnt Lake, the pilot tells me that the first night Oolulik spent in jail she hanged herself. She too had gone away.

Dialogue at an Exhibition

THE OBJECT, the plaque tells me, is a shaman's dance garment. It comes from the land of the Copper Inuit, which is Victoria Island and around Coronation Gulf on the Arctic coast. I thought that all traditional wearing apparel there had hoods, but this item is hoodless and so it cannot be called "parka." There are here no animal ears sticking up pertly on a hollow suggestion for a head, though it is certainly made of fur, in fact of several fine textures of fur in tan and reddish brown with the long shape of a predator's tail outlined in stunning white fur on the back. The front is overlaid with white male patterns, but this maleness elongates downward into a female's rounded maternity, her white curves outlined by three elegant lines of ochred red hide. This coat seems to embody both animal and human, both female and male. But with no suggestion of head.

I realize that this garment is become an art item; displayed here at an exhibition, draped over what could be a dressmaker's dummy adjustable to any size, the long gallery walls intense under tiered, directed lights. Nevertheless, when it was made it must have been intended for someone to wear. Here now it is an object, merely visible, stripped of every dimension except one; stripped like a requiem mass overheard from a distant concert hall. Yet every passing viewer knows that a garment is made to be worn; is equipment; vestment; armour. To be garmented is to be fitted out, dressed for whatever one imagines one's task to be. To be garnished (the same word), armed properly for an occasion.

The garment declares, "The occasion is to stay alive."

"What?"

"That is the essential 'occasion' of every Arctic person: to stay alive. And that is never so simple. There is no more difficult place in the world to live than in the Canadian Arctic."

"That is why," I say, "you do not make sense: how can anyone in the Arctic be properly garmented if nothing covers the head?"

The garment responds slowly, as if conceding something to human logic, "You understand perhaps one thing about garments, but perhaps not another. A garment is a small house, yes, in which you live all the time, a small, moveable, fitted house that makes living in winter or in wind or in ground drift and blizzard possible, even in the long darkness when you have only the memory of the endless summer sun to tell you that somewhere it's light may still exist and you may live to see it return with your prayers. 'House' is the basic understanding of garment, yes. But if that were the only one, it would be like saying that the only reason a shaman had to travel to the moon would be to bring back stones for people to feel. Any child looking up knows there is more to the moon than a few stones."

"I've never really been interested in moon stones, why..."

But the garment is talking on, implacable as weather.

"You need to know what Payalliq told the big white explorer Stefansson when he was going through our country in 1915 looking for Copper Inuit he thought looked like Whites and he heard our shaman Payalliq had a song for good hunting. Payalliq could fly to the moon, I saw it myself, but Stefansson didn't care about the moon either, he wanted to buy Payalliq's power for good hunting so his dogs would never have to go hungry again and he offered her his Primus stove and six gallons of kerosene for the hunting song. She said, 'Sure, you're the boss, I can show you how to say it,' and she told him what to sing. 'If you're going to use the power,' she explained, 'you have to tie this wood around your mittens and then you sing and ask the Big Boss, sing right and the wood will get really heavy. But if it doesn't get heavy, it won't work.' Then Stefansson wanted to try it right away but Payalliq said of course it wouldn't work now because he didn't need it yet, he had lots of frozen seals in his caches. So Stefansson gave her the Primus stove and the kerosene.

"He was going back and forth all winter, going east to find more 'blond Eskimos' as he called them and he had Pannigabluk as his wife then, she was travelling with him and sewing his clothing and Natkusiaq was with him too, hunting and driving the other dog team. They had over thirty dogs in two teams and when they came to the Smoking Mountains they were running out of dog food. 'Don't worry,' Stefansson said, 'I've got the power, I'll do it tonight and we'll shoot plenty of animals tomorrow, don't worry.' So that night he tied the power to his mittens and he was singing and singing but the wood wouldn't get heavy. Pannigabluk didn't laugh but Natkusiaq had to crawl out of the snowhouse really fast and he didn't even get out of the house tunnel before he was laughing out loud. But nothing whatsoever was happening with Stefansson's song, and finally he had to give it up. He was really mad. 'That Payalliq,' he yelled, 'she got one of my Primus stoves and my dogs are going to starve anyway!'"

"He expected dog food forever for six gallons of kerosene?"

The garment says severely, "Don't think White. Any good thing can be given away as a gift. And the song was a way of hunting. People have guns now for that but those old-days people sang to hunt their animals. Their songs were so strong that was all they needed."

I cannot resist the question: "So, were you sung into being a hoodless dance coat?"

"Only a woman can make me."

"Didn't a man hunt the skins?"

"Understand me, a skin is merely a skin, and only a woman can make a new water bird which is a man in a kayak, or a new animal which is a person in a fur garment. I came from thirteen thin summer skins in the hands of a singing old-days woman. From her bone needle and her song."

"Then why are we telling stories about dog food?"

It seems the hollow garment is echoing with laughter, the fringes at its shoulders and hem swaying gently.

"You should ask that! You don't know how often human beings long to be only and simply animals? You don't remember how close animals and people are? You need to know another story, about the woman who, it is said, refused to take a husband. It seemed no man on earth was good enough for her, so finally her exasperated family took her to a barren island and left her there with dogs. And there, it is said, she became the dogs' wife; she was really a good woman and all the dogs had her and soon she gave birth to a litter. Half the litter was white people, the other half Indians. Neither of them had existed before that."

"Your story tells us that all Whites and Indians are the children of an Inuit woman mating with dogs?"

"So they say."

"Who are 'they'?"

"The ancient ones, the people who knew everything. They knew how close to animals people are; they knew that when people wear animal skins they are as properly hunted by a polar bear as they hunt him. And that is why they knew that garments alone are not enough to survive in the Arctic. A human being needs songs, and dancing. To have no song in the dance house is like standing naked in a blizzard; it is to be dead. In the great dance house built of snow during the long darkness that is where I was worn, a garment without hood, animal tail behind and woman and man markings all one in front so that wearing me the person becomes animal or woman or man and the singing can be happy, the dancing violent with transformed happiness. Then everyone sings the song, and everyone feels it:

> *Yai – ya – yuya*

> *How glorious to see*
> *The great muskoxen gathering in herds,*
> *Their rumps all in a row*
> *Across the autumn hills.*

> *Yai – ya – yuya*

> *How glorious to see*
> *The round-cheeked girls gathering in summer*
> *And together telling the manly men*
> *Some small lies.*

Yai – ya – yuya

But there is a fear in
Turning the mind away,
Longing for loneliness
Among so many laughing people.

Iyaiya – ya – ya

And how glorious to feel
The bright warmth of the sun
Walking in its old footsteps
Across red summer hills.

Yai – ya – yuya

But there is fear in
Feeling the cold moon step over the world,
The moon, full moon, new moon,
Following its old footsteps
Through the deep blue winter night.

Iyaiya – ya – ya

"Those are the happy songs, but often songs have to be louder than that, and wilder. Especially the shaman songs to the spirits of the air, or to the one down there who is Nuliajuk, The Mother of All, of all sea animals and all land animals as well, mother of every-thing on which people live. Nuliajuk is always down there in the sea, and when you hear of her she will certainly be angry. To soothe her, to keep her quiet the shaman has to sing wild, wild songs. When the woman shaman sings to her, all the men in the dance house repeat the chorus and they dance naked, every man has to take off his skin coat and be only his own bare animal, bouncing himself in front when they sing many verses of such a song as this led by the woman shaman:

There are such big men, here!
Is it an animal track, this one
With a polar bear's face?
I have such a...hanging face.
Is this the polar bear's intestine?
I have such an...intestine.

There are such big men, here!
Is it an animal track, this one
With the little puppy's face?
I have such a...hanging face.
Is this the little puppy's intestine?
I have such an...intestine.

There are such big men, here!
Is it an animal track, this one?
Is this an animal intestine, this one?

"Does a man shaman sometimes sing such ribald songs with naked women?"

"No. Naked women are too dangerous. The Mother of All, Nuliajuk is female also and human females, through their uncleanness, often break her taboos and so bring illness and hunger on every person. Therefore very old songs are sung with women, songs so old their meanings are no longer known but that does not matter, since Nuliajuk and the spirits of the air know the meaning of everything:

Ayai – ye – rershe

How is it that I feel
I wish to explore down there?
That woman down there, perhaps.
And the taboo broken under the man.
Her boot straps,
Let her loosen them on her feet.

I feel I wish to explore down there,
But how shall I look
Under the man.
Look at cheeks, smooth out wrinkles.
   Her boot straps,
   Let her loosen them on her feet.

Let me look under the woman;
Look at cheeks.
Explore secrets.
Smooth out wrinkles.

"Such words must simply be uttered, but their wisdom is concealed."

"I don't understand, why is The Mother of All always angry?"

"No one understands Nuliajuk. To live one needs to know she exists and behave with the deepest respect towards her. She is queen of everything: of both food and clothing and therefore of all animals and all humans, and her anger never dies. The ancient ones said that it may be she is the woman who lived with dogs on the island, and when she sent her young out from there to live she gave her inner boots to her Indian children for boats, telling them that wherever they travelled they would be opposed to people. And they have been; the Indians and the Inuit or the Whites have often fought each other. To her White children she gave her outer boots for boats, telling them to be smiling and friendly. But when she tried to leave the island and enter the boats she had given them, her children threw her into the sea. She clutched at the boat, and they chopped off the first joints of her fingers, and then the second joint, and the third as she clung desperately and so she sank, the stumps of her hands bleeding, to the bottom of the sea. But the joints of her fingers became all the sea animals, the seals and the whales and the walruses, and all the land animals too. Nevertheless her anger remains, and who can blame her? Nuliajuk sees every taboo that is broken and she forgives nothing; when she is angry enough she hides all her animals under her oil lamp at the bottom of the sea so that there is nothing for anyone to eat. Then only a shaman, singing the sacred songs to her and moving in a sacred way, can discover the taboo that has been broken and go down into the sea and charm her with songs so that she releases the animals again. Then the people are able to live again."

The garment is silent, but what more do I need to hear? The anger of Nuliajuk is now certainly traversed by steel ships, penetrated by the iron pipes of oil drillers, threaded through by nuclear submarines hunting as silently as only a machine driven by a human being can hunt another machine-driven human being. It would be far better, this hollow garment is telling me silently, if people were merely and nothing more than animals. Can Nuliajuk hide her finger-joint children under her lamp at the bottom of the sea so that they escape being cored by a diamond drilling bit? What will the bleeding stumps of her hands accomplish with a torpedo armed with thirteen different nuclear warheads, any one of which is capable of incinerating twice the total of all the Inuit that have ever lived on this land in eight thousand years?

If somehow I could soften the blinding light that reflects from these long walls, the hoodless dance garment before me might tell a further story.

It might say: "When at last, out of the long winter darkness the sky at noon begins to brighten in the southeast, the ancient people would say to each other, 'Today we will go up on the hills and greet Sirenek, the Sun.' Oh, to see that first ray of light level over the snow! Every tip and curl of wind pattern is lined with gold and our shadows lean away behind us longer than we can see! Then we raise our bare hands to the sun, laughing, and wave a little, but we say nothing; nor do we sing. For once again we have lived to see the sun return, and now is the time to return silently to our snow houses and throw out the old oil in the lamp and fill it with new for the sun has once again transformed our dark world of ice into unfathomable, soft beauty."

These gentle words of ceremony and joy pluck at my spirit: I am in the presence of a hollow garment; headless, though retaining the crafted imprint of body—female?—male?—animal?—no, it contains nothing. Mere surface enclosing a shaped, possibly animalhuman, space. In a world of ice Inuit life grew and, despite much frozen misery, flourished joyously for eight thousand years. Now half of

Nuliajuk's litter, her "friendly" white children are everywhere; no barren Arctic island, no sea lair is safe from their irresistible developer smile. And The Mother of All is reduced to the memory of a solitary, hoodless item in an enormous urban exhibition.

The Naming of Albert Johnson

1. **THE EAGLE RIVER, YUKON:** *Wednesday, February 17, 1932,*
   Tuesday, February 16, 1932

There is arctic silence at last, after the long snarl of rifles. As if all the
stubby trees within earshot had finished splitting in the cold. Then
the sound of the airplane almost around the river's bend begins to
return, turning as tight a spiral as it may up over bank and trees and
back down, over the man crumpled on the bedroll, over the frantic
staked dog teams, spluttering, down, glancing down off the wind-
ridged river. Tail leaping, almost cartwheeling over its desperate roar
for skis, immense sound rocketing from that bouncing black dot
on the level glare but stopped finally, its prop whirl staggering out
motionless just behind the man moving inevitably forward on snowshoes, not looking back, step by step up the river with his rifle ready.
Hesitates, lifts one foot, then the other, stops, and moves forward
again to the splotch in the vast whiteness before him.

The pack is too huge, and apparently worried by rats with very
long, fine teeth. Behind it a twisted body. Unbelievably small. One
outflung hand still clutching a rifle, but no motion, nothing, the
airplane dead and only the distant sounds of dogs somewhere,
of men moving at the banks of the river. The police rifle points
down, steadily extending the police arm until it can lever the body,

142

already stiffening, up. A red crater for hip. As if one small part of
that incredible toughness had rebelled at last, exploded red out of
itself, splattering itself with itself when everything but itself was
at last unreachable. But the face is turning up. Rime, and clots of
snow ground into whiskers, the fur hat hurled somewhere by bullets
perhaps and the whipped cowlick already a mat frozen above half-
open eyes showing only white, nostrils flared, the concrete face wiped
clean of everything but snarl. Freezing snarl and teeth. As if the long
clenched jaws had tightened down beyond some ultimate cog and
openly locked their teeth into their own torn lips in one final wordlessly silent scream.

143

The pilot blunders up, gasping. "By god, we got the son, of a
bitch!" stumbles across the back of the snowshoes and recovers
beside the policeman. Gagging a little, "My g—" All that sudden
colour propped up by the rifle barrel on the otherwise white snow.
And the terrible face.

The one necessary bullet, in the spine where its small entry
cannot be seen at this moment, and was never felt as six others were,
knocked the man face down in the snow. Though that would never
loosen his grip on his rifle. The man had been working himself over
on his side, not concerned as it seemed for the bullets singing to
him from the level drifts in front of him or the trees on either bank.
With his left hand he was reaching into his coat pocket to reload his
Savage .30-30, almost warm on the inside of his other bare hand, and
he knew as every good hunter must that he had exactly thirty-nine
bullets left besides the one hidden under the rifle's butt plate. If they
moved in any closer he also had the Winchester .22 with sixty-four
bullets, and closer still there will be the sawed-off shotgun, though
he had only a few shells left, he could not now be certain exactly how
many. He had stuffed snow tight into the hole where one or perhaps
even two shells had exploded in his opposite hip pocket. A man could
lose his blood in a minute from a hole that size but the snow was
still white and icy the instant he had to glance at it, packing it in. If
they had got him there before forcing him down behind his pack in
the middle of the river, he could not have moved enough to pull out
of the pack straps, leave alone get behind it for protection. Bullets
twitch it, whine about his tea tin like his axe handle snapping once

at his legs as he ran from the eastern riverbank too steep to clamber up, a very bad mistake to have to discover after spending several minutes and a hundred yards of strength running his snowshoes towards it. Not a single rock, steep and bare like polished planks. But he had gained a little on them, he saw that as he curved without stopping towards the centre of the river and the line of trees beyond it. That bank is easily climbed, he knows because he climbed it that morning, but all the dogs and men so suddenly around the hairpin turn surprised him towards the nearest bank, and he sees the teams spreading to outflank him, three towards the low west bank. And two of them bending over the one army radioman he got.

Instantly the man knew it was the river that had betrayed him. He had outlegged their dogs and lost the plane time and again on glare-ice and in fog and brush and between the endless trails of caribou herds, but the sluggish loops of this river doubling back on itself have betrayed him. It is his own best move, forward and then back, circle forward and farther back, backwards, so the ones following his separate tracks will suddenly confront each other in cursing bewilderment. But this river, it cannot be named the Porcupine, has out-doubled him. For the dogs leaping towards him around the bend, the roaring radioman heaving at his sled, scrabbling for his rifle, this is clearly what he saw when he climbed the tree on the far bank; one of the teams he saw then across a wide tongue of land already ahead of him, as it seemed, and he started back to get farther behind them before he followed and picked them off singly in whatever tracks of his they thought they were following. These dogs and this driver rounding to face him as he walks so carefully backwards in his snowshoes on the curve of his own tracks.

Whatever this river has done spiralling back into the Yukon hills, his rifle will not betray him. Words are bellowing out of the racket of teams hurtling around the bend. His rifle speaks easily, wordlessly to the army radioman kneeling, sharpshooter position, left elbow propped on left knee. The sights glided together certain and deadly, and long before the sound had returned that one kneeling was already flung back clean as frozen wood bursting at his axe.

He has not eaten, he believes it must be two days, and the rabbit tracks are so old they give no hope for his snares. The squirrel burrow may be better. He is scraping curls from tiny spruce twigs, watching them tighten against the lard pail, watching the flames as it seems there licking the tin blacker with their gold tongues. The fire lives with him, and he will soon examine the tinfoil of matches in his pocket, and the tinfoil bundle in his pack and also the other two paper-wrapped packages. That must be done daily, if possible. The pack, unopened, with the .22 laced to its side is between his left shoulder and the snow hollow; the moose hides spread under and behind him; the snowshoes stuck erect into the snow on the right, the long axe lying there and the rifle also, in its cloth cover but on the moose-hide pouch. He has already worked carefully on his feet, kneading as much of the frost out of one and then the other as he can before the fire, though two toes on the left are black and the heel of the right is rubbed raw. Bad lacing when he walked backwards, and too numb for him to notice. The one toe can only be kept another day, perhaps, but he has only a gun-oily rag for his heel. Gun oil? Spruce gum? Wait. His feet wrapped and ready to move instantly and he sits watching warmth curl around the pail. Leans his face down into it. Then he puts the knife away in his clothes and pulls out a tiny paper. His hard fingers unfold it carefully, he studies the crystals a moment, and then as the flames tighten the blackened spirals of spruce he pours that into the steaming pail. He studies the paper, the brownness of it; the suggestion of a word beginning, or perhaps ending, that shines through its substance. He lowers it steadily then until it darkens, smiling as a spot of deep brown breaks through the possible name and curls back a black empty circle towards his fingers. He lets it go, feeling warmth like a massage in its final flare and dying. There is nothing left but a smaller fold of pepper and a bag of salt so when he drinks it is very slowly, letting each mouthful move for every part of his tongue to hold a moment this last faint sweetness.

He sits in the small yellow globe created by fire. Drinking. The wind breathes through the small spruce, his body rests motionlessly; knowing that dug into the snow with drifts and spruce tips above him they could see his smokeless fire only if they flew directly over him. And the plane cannot fly at night. They are somewhere very close now, and their plane less than a few minutes behind. It has flown straight in an hour, again and again, all he had overlaid with tangled tracks in five weeks, but the silent land is what it is. He is now resting motionlessly. And waiting.

And the whisky-jacks are suddenly there. He had not known them before to come after dark, but grey and white tipped with black they fluffed themselves at the grey edge of his light, watching, and then one hopped two hops. Sideways. The first living thing he had seen since the caribou. But he reaches for the bits of babiche he had cut and rubbed in salt, laid ready on the cloth of the rifle-butt. He throws, the draggle-tail is gone but the other watches, head cocked, then jumps so easily the long space his stiff throw had managed, and the bit is gone. He does not move his body, tosses another bit, and another, closer, closer, and then draggle-tail is there scrabbling for the bit, and he twitches the white string lying beside the bits of babiche left by the rifle, sees the bigger piece tug from the snow and draggle-tail leap to it. Gulp. He tugs, feels the slight weight as the thread lifts from the snow in the firelight, and now the other is gone while draggle-tail comes towards him inevitably, string pulling the beak soundlessly agape, wings desperate in snow, dragged between rifle and fire into the waiting claw of his hand. He felt the bird's blood beat against his palm, the legs and tail and wings thud an instant, shuddering and then limp between his relentless fingers.

Wings. Noiselessly he felt the beautiful muscles shift, slip over bones delicate as twigs. He could lope circles around any dogs they set on his trail but that beast labelled in letters combing the clouds, staring everywhere until its roar suddenly blundered up out of a canyon or over a ridge, laying its relentless shadow like words on the world: he would have dragged every tree in the Yukon together to build a fire and boil that. Steel pipes and canvas and wires and name, that stinking noise. In the silence under the spruce he skims the tiny fat bubbles from the darkening soup; watches them coagulate yellow on the shavings. Better than gun oil, or gum. He began to unwrap his feet again but listening, always listening. The delicate furrow of the bird pointed towards him in the snow.

2. THE RICHARDSON MOUNTAINS, N.W.T.: *Tuesday, February 9, 1932, Saturday, January 30, 1932*

Though it means moving two and three miles to their one, the best trail to confuse them in the foothill ravines was a spiral zigzag. West of the mountains he has not seen them; he has outrun them so far in crossing the Richardson Mountains during the blizzard that when he reaches a river he thought it must be the Porcupine because he seems at last to be inside something that is completely alone. But the creeks draining east lay in seemingly parallel but eventually converging canyons with tundra plateaus glazed under wind between them, and when he paused on one leg of his zag he sometimes saw them, across one plateau or in a canyon, labouring with their dogs and sleds as it seems ahead of him. In the white scream of the mountain pass where no human being has ever ventured in winter he does not dare pause to sleep for two days and the long night between them, one toe and perhaps another frozen beyond saving and parts of his face dead, but in the east he had seen the trackers up close, once been above them and watched them coming along his trails towards each other unawares out of two converging canyons with their sleds and drivers trailing, and suddenly round the cliff to face each other in cursing amazement. He was far enough not to hear their words as they heated water for tea, wasting daylight minutes, beating their hands to keep warm.

The police drive the dog teams now, and the Indians sometimes; the ones who can track him on the glazed snow, through zags and bends, always wary of ambush, are the two army radiomen. One of the sleds is loaded with batteries when it should be food, but they sniff silently along his tracks, loping giant circles ahead of the heaving dogs and swinging arms like semaphores when they find a trail leading as it seems directly back towards the sleds they have just left. He would not have thought them so relentless at unravelling his trails, these two who every morning tried to raise the police at Aklavik headquarters on their frozen radio, and when he was convinced they would follow him as certainly as Millen and the plane roared up, dropping supplies, it was time to accept the rising blizzard over the mountains and find at last, for certain, the Porcupine River.

It is certainly Millen who brought the plane north just before the blizzard, and it was Millen who saw his smoke and heard him coughing, whistling in that canyon camp hidden in trees under a cliff so steep he has to chop hand-holds in the frozen rock to get out of there. Without dynamite again, or bombs, they could not dig him out; even in his unending alert his heart jerks at the sound of what was a foot slipping against a frozen tree up the ridge facing him. His rifle is out of its sheath, the shell racking home in the cold like precise steel biting. There is nothing more; an animal? A tree bursting? He crouches motionless, for if they are there they should be all around him, perhaps above on the cliff, and he will not move until he knows. Only the wind worrying spruce and snow, whining wordlessly. There, twenty yards away a shadow moves, Millen certainly, and his shot snaps as his rifle swings up, as he drops. Bullets snick from every-where, their sound booming back and forth along the canyon. He has only fired once and is down, completely aware, on the wrong side of his fire and he shoots carefully again to draw their shots and they come, four harmlessly high and nicely spaced out: there are two—Millen and another—below him in the canyon and two a bit higher on the right ridge, one of them who slipped. Nothing up the canyon or above on the cliff. With that knowledge he gathered himself and leaped over the fire against the cliff and one on the ridge made a good shot that cut his jacket and he could fall as if gut-shot in the hollow or deadfall. Until the fire died, he was almost comfortable.

In the growing dusk he watches the big Swede, who drove dogs very well, crawl towards Millen stretched out, face down. He watches him tie Millen's legs together with the laces of his mukluks and drag him backwards, ploughing a long furrow and leaving the rifle sunk in the snow. He wastes no shot at their steady firing, and when they stop there are Millen's words still

You're surrounded. King isn't dead. Will you give

waiting, frozen in the canyon. He lay absolutely motionless behind the deadfall against the cliff, as if he were dead, knowing they would have to move finally. He flexed his feet continuously, and his fingers as he shifted the rifle no more quickly than a clock hand, moving into the position it would have to be when they charged him. They almost outwait him; it is really a question between the coming darkness and his freezing despite his invisible motions, but before darkness Millen had to move. Two of them were coming and he shifted his rifle slightly on the log to cover the left one—it must have been the long cold that made him mistake that for Millen—who dived out of sight, his shot thundering along the canyon, but Millen did not drop behind anything. Simply down on one knee, firing. Once, twice, bullets tore the log and then he had his head up with those eyes staring straight down his sights and he fired two shots so fast the roar in the canyon sounded as one and Millen stood up, the whole length over him, whirled in that silent unmistakable way and crashed face down in the snow. He hears them dragging and chopping trees for a stage cache to keep the body, and in the darkness he chops handholds up the face of the cliff, step by step as he hoists himself and his pack out of another good shelter. As he has had to leave others.

3. THE RAT RIVER, N.W.T.: *Saturday, January 10, 1932, Thursday, December 31, 1931, Tuesday, July 28, 1931*

In his regular round of each loophole he peers down the promontory towards their fires glaring up from behind the riverbank. They surround him on three sides, nine of them with no more than forty dogs, which in this cold means they already need more supplies than they can have brought with them. They will be making plans for something, suddenly, beyond bullets against his logs and guns and it will have to come soon. In the long darkness, and he can wait far easier than they. Dynamite. If they have any more to thaw out very carefully after blowing open the roof and stovepipe as darkness settled, a hole hardly big enough for one of them—a Norwegian, they were everywhere with their long noses—to fill it an instant, staring down at him gathering himself from the corner out of roof-sod and stove pipes and snow: the cabin barely stuck above the drifts but that one was gigantic to lean in like that, staring until he lifted his rifle and the long face vanished an instant before his bullet passed through that space. But the hole was large enough for the cold to slide down along the wall and work itself into his trench, which

would be all that saved him when they used the last of their dynamite. He began to feel what they had stalked him with all day: cold
tightening steadily as steel around toes, face, around fingers.

In the clearing still nothing stirs. There is only the penumbra
of light along the circle of the bank as if they had laid a trench-fire
to thaw the entire promontory and were soundlessly burrowing in
under him. Their flares were long dead, the sky across the river flickering with orange lights to vanish down into spruce and willows
again, like the shadow blotting a notch in the eastern bank, and he
thrust his rifle through the chink and had almost got a shot away
when a projectile arced against the sky and he jerked the gun out,
diving, into the trench deep under the wall among the moose hides
that could not protect him from the roof and walls tearing apart so
loud it seemed most of himself had been blasted to the farthest granules of sweet, silent earth. The sods and foot-thick logs he had built
together where the river curled were gone and he would climb out
and walk away as he always had, but first he pulled himself up and
out between the splinters, still holding the rifle, just in time to see
yellow light humpling through the snow towards him and he fired
three times so fast it sounded in his ears as though his cabin was
continuing to explode. The shadows around the light dance in one
spot an instant but come on in a straight black line, lengthening
down, faster, and the light cuts straight across his eyes and he gets
away the fourth shot and the light tears itself into bits. He might
have been lying on his back staring up into night and had the stars
explode into existence above him. And whatever darkness is left
before him then blunders away, desperately ploughing away from
him through the snow like the first one who came twice with a voice
repeating at his door

I am Constable Alfred King, are you in there?

fist thudding the door the second time with a paper creaking louder
than his voice so thin in the cold silence

I have a search warrant now, we have had complaints and if
you don't open

and then ploughing away in a long desperate scrabble through the
sun-shot snow while the three others at the riverbank thumped their
bullets hopelessly high into the logs but shattering the window again
and again until they dragged King and each other head first over
the bank while he placed lead carefully over them, snapping willow
bits on top of them and still seeing, strangely, the tiny hole that had
materialized up into his door when he flexed the trigger, still hearing
the grunt that had wormed in through the slivers of the board he
had whipsawn himself. Legs and feet wrapped in moose hide lay a
moment across his window, level in the snow, jerking as if barely
attached to a body knocked over helpless, a face somewhere twisted
in gradually developing pain that had first leaned against his door,
fist banging while that other one held the dogs at the edge of the
clearing, waiting

Hallo? Hallo? This is Constable Alfred King of the Royal
Canadian Mounted Police. I want to talk to you.
Constable Millen

and they looked into each other's eyes, once, through his tiny
window. The eyes peering down into his—could he be seen from
out of the blinding sun?—squinted blue from a boy's round face
with a bulging nose bridged over pale with cold. King, of the Royal
Mounted. Like a silly book title, or the funny papers. He didn't look
it as much as Spike Millen, main snooper and tracker at Arctic Red
River who baked pies and danced, everybody said, better than any
man in the north. Let them dance hipped in snow, get themselves
dragged away under spruce and dangling traps, asking, laying words
on him, naming things

Yukon, you come across from the Yukon? You got a trapper's
licence? The Loucheaux trap the Rat, up towards the Richardson
Mountains. You'll need a licence, why not

Words. Dropping out of nothing into advice. Maybe he wanted a
kicker to move that new canoe against the Rat River? Loaded down
as it is. The Rat drops fast, you have to hand-line the portage anyway

to get past Destruction City where those would-be Klondikers wintered in '98. He looked up at the trader above him on the wedge of gravel. He had expected at least silence. From a trader standing with the bulge of seven hundred dollars in his pocket; in the south a man could feed himself with that for two years. Mouths always full of words, pushing, every mouth falling open and dropping words from nothing into meaning. The trader's eyes shifted finally, perhaps to the junction of the rivers behind them, south and west, the united river clicking under the canoe. As he raised his paddle. The new rifle oiled and ready with its butt almost touching his knees as he kneels, ready to pull the canoe around.

4. THE PEEL RIVER ABOVE FORT MCPHERSON, N.W.T.:
Tuesday, July 7, 1931

The Porcupine River, as he thought it was then, chuckled between the three logs of his raft. He could hear that below him, under the mosquitoes probing the mesh about his head, and see the gold lengthen up the river like the canoe that would come towards him from the north where the sun just refused to open the spiky horizon. Gilded, hammered out slowly, soundlessly towards him the thick gold. He sat almost without breathing, watching it come like silence. And then imperceptibly the black spired riverbend grew pointed, stretched itself in a thin straight line double-bumped, gradually spreading a straight wedge below the sun through the golden river. When he had gathered that slowly into anger it was already too late to choke his fire; the vee had abruptly bent towards him, the bowman already raised his paddle; hailed. Almost it seemed as if a name had been blundered into the silence, but he did not move in his fury. The river chuckled again.

"...O-o-o-o..." the point of the wedge almost under him now. And the sound of a name, that was so clear he could almost distinguish it. Perhaps he already knew what it was, had long since lived this in that endlessly enraged chamber of himself, even to the strange Indian accent mounded below him in the canoe bow where the black hump of the stern partner moved them straight towards him out of the fanned ripples, crumpling gold. To the humps of his raft below on the gravel waiting to anchor them.

"What d'ya want."

"You Albert Johnson?"

It could have been the sternman who named him. The sun like hatchet-strokes across slanted eyes, the gaunt noses below him there holding the canoe against the current, their paddles hooked in the logs of his raft. Two Loucheaux half-faces, black and red kneeling in the roiled gold of the river, the words thudding softly in his ears.

You Albert Johnson?

One midnight above the Arctic Circle to hear again the inevitability of name. He has not heard it in four years, it could be to the very day since that Vancouver garden, staring into the evening sun and hearing this quiet sound from these motionless—perhaps they are men kneeling there, perhaps waiting for him to accept again what has now been laid inevitably upon him, the name come to meet him in his journey north, come out of the north around the bend and against the current of the Peel River, as they name that too, to confront him on a river he thought another and aloud where he would have found after all his years, at long last, only nameless silence.

You Albert Johnson?

"Yes," he said finally.

And out of his rage he begins to gather words together. Slowly, every word he can locate, as heavily as he would gather stones on a Saskatchewan field, to hold them for one violent moment against himself between his two hands before he heaves them up and hurls them—but they are gone. The ripples of their passing may have been smoothing out as he stares at where they should have been had they been there. Only the briefly golden river lies before him, whatever its name may be since it must have one, bending back somewhere beyond that land, curling back upon itself in its giant, relentless spirals down to the implacable, and ice-choked, arctic sea.

TWO | SO MUCH TO REMEMBER

After Thirty Years of Marriage [1978]

AFTER THIRTY YEARS of marriage and six children, Papa and my
total worldly wealth was a mortgaged house in Rockford, Illinois, and
a plot in the Rockford cemetery where little John Wesley had been
lying for sixteen years. Land in Illinois cost a hundred dollars an
acre; we cleared a thousand dollars from the sale of our house and on
March 20, 1906, Papa and our second youngest son, Jolson, boarded
the train for Red Deer, Alberta. With three men over eighteen left in
the family, we could file on 480 acres of free land; a few years of hard
work on that much land and we believed we would return to the
States with enough money so our three youngest sons, Ethan, Jolson
and Billings (still too young to file, unfortunately), could go to school
and Papa and me retire in some comfort.

There was, of course, no land available near Red Deer. Actually, of
the thirty-six sections in any Alberta township, sixteen are already
owned by the CPR, one by the Hudson's Bay Company, and two
reserved for schools, so that only seventeen widely scattered sections,
the even-numbered ones, can ever be homesteaded on. When Ethan
and Billings and I arrived in Alberta near the end of June, we travelled to the railhead which was then at Stettler. There we found Papa
and Jolson shingling, their lips purple with nails, and after many
colourful kisses they told us they had filed sight-unseen on land
seventy miles east and our first problem would be to get there. I had

a migraine headache from sitting up four days and nights on trains but I managed to cook my first Canadian meal to hugged and kissed acclaim.

I had been able to borrow an extra two hundred dollars in Illinois. That was not nearly enough for a team of horses, but together with what Papa and Jolson had earned building in Stettler, we purchased two oxen. One was a blotchy red, the other coal black, and both had great extended ears that waved in time with their majestic pace. They were immediately christened Tom and Bruce, good short names for yelling, Papa said, and when we harnessed them, put bits in their mouths, and hitched them to the wagon, we found them as fundamentally opposed to motion as any mountain, but ever faithful and above all patient. That compensated for almost everything. How often I leaned against Tom's powerful shoulder and cried until I had no tears left, and he would turn his flat, triangular head towards me, his eyes so steady and unchanging. We had them both as long as we were in Alberta.

Papa and Jolson had taken a hunting knife and shotgun with them, and Ethan (not to be outdone) bought a .30-30 for eighteen dollars. It seemed a very large amount of money to me, but it proved its value the second day out from Stettler. There were ducks on the sloughs (as they call the ponds here) everywhere, but far too wary for a shotgun so when we saw a lovely goose stretching its neck at us out of the bullrushes, Ethan got out his big gun. Papa laughed, "You'll blow it to pieces!" And sure enough, when Ethan leaned on the wagon and fired, the goose vanished as the ducks rose in a frightful clatter. Billings waded out and discovered the bullet had slit its jugular vein! Ethan never fired that gun again—we never saw an animal around the homestead that needed it—so his marksmanship became a family legend, and though the goose was excellent, I always thought it too dear at eighteen dollars plus a bullet. Later that summer Jolson stacked hay; by saving every single penny, he brought home twenty dollars for a month's work.

When we found the iron peg with four square holes dug around it that marked the corner of one of our quarter sections, we all went a little daffy. We had been travelling for five days at ox-pace over open land the colour of burnt bread, land which none of us could have ever imagined. We would see a settler's sod house or board shanty four hours before we passed it, and at most we saw three a day. Papa jumped from the wagon, "I want to enter first," and Ethan said, "I'm with you," and then all three boys had jumped off, even young Billings, and with their hands on Papa's shoulders they walked onto the promised land together while I watched them over the backs of the oxen. Then we oriented ourselves to the sun and by the end of the day had found our other two quarters. There was one homesteader near us, three miles southwest, and Ethan got a pail of water from his barrel and with the wood we had carried with us we made camp. That Mr. Williams, who had been a Union soldier during the Civil War, brought us luck: when Papa and the boys began digging a well beside our tent the next morning, they struck cold fresh water nine feet down; the land looked so featureless, slightly rolling and covered with buffalo grass, that the only reason we camped there was because I felt I had to be in sight of Williams's cabin.

Though it was barely July, all the things that had to be done before winter almost made us dizzy, just to list them. When our eyes grew accustomed to distance, we discovered other homesteaders about us: almost all of them from the States, but no one had time for a July 4 celebration that year. We had a well, a very great blessing, but we had to buy a cow and chickens, fence, put up hay, and above all build a house and barns for ourselves and our animals. Besides that, we had to find wood to burn and also break land so that next spring we could seed and grow our first cash crop. In the meantime, we had to live on our resources, such as they were, and so instead of all the boys being able to help Papa steadily, both Ethan and Jolson hired out to neighbouring ranchers and settlers for fencing, haying, any kind of heavy work that could be got. We needed the cash to buy food and clothing for the hard winter that everyone who had lived in the country for a year took great joy in assuring us was certainly ahead. If I had known then that the winter of 1906–07 would be the worst in the living memory of anyone on the Canadian prairies, I know I would have despaired. But I did not know, and I suppose that was for the better.

Actually, the summer was very pleasant, and at first I was not really afraid of the endless space all around. The mosquitoes were

Rudy Wiebe: Collected Stories, 1955–2010

more or less over after about two weeks, though not completely gone till September, and Papa discovered that there were wooded hills southwest of us, enormous numbers of gnarled and dead aspen so we could haul as much firewood as we pleased. I refused to live in a sod shanty; I knew it was cheap and warm but I also knew it was like a tent—quite impossible to keep clean—and though the trees were too short to build a conventional house of horizontal logs, they gave me an idea. I sketched it on the back of a milk-can label and within a week Jolson had dug a trench for the foundation of the house twenty-eight by eighteen feet. Its walls were to be made of two rows of vertical poles with the space between them filled with mud from the lake. There was not another house like it in the entire country, and after we had spent the winter in it we knew why. But it seemed fine at the time, though it required nine loads of logs and forty tons (as the boys estimated) of mud just for the walls. We moved out of the tent into it on Saturday, October 20, 1906. The roof had not been completed and that night I was as cold as I had ever been in my life. The wind howled so dreadfully I did not know how I would have endured it in the tent hammering, jerking on its ropes. That is perhaps the worst of living on the Alberta prairie: the wind. There is not a bush anywhere, and it gets a two-hundred-mile clean run at you from the mountains.

But that was the coming of winter. Summer was beautiful, and I had never seen such skies or light. From the wooded hills the prairie spread east like water falling away, wind brushing the grass and the small sloughs everywhere dark green and blue and indigo and the horizon merging with the sky in a bluish dust. On the CPR section beside us lay the perfect circle of a pond surrounded by willows, the water so sweet it must have been fed by springs, and the paths of the buffalo radiated from it like the spokes of a wheel cut two and three feet into the ground; in the long evenings when the light settled down like a slow blanket, you could so easily imagine those huge black shapes coming single file from all directions towards the last bright centre of water, silent, moving lower and lower into the earth cut by their paths. Then suddenly the ducks would begin talking: gossipy old women among the rushes so loud I could hear them a mile away in the tent complaining, comparing children, and bang!

Billings's shotgun would explode, bang again as the ducks splattered up and away, and soon I would be plucking—hopefully mallards because they were the largest and always the fattest for some reason—and at sunset Papa and Ethan and Jolson would have meat to fill their stomachs, empty from all day cutting and stacking hay: they each wanted half a duck at least or a whole prairie chicken.

The Alberta sunsets were beyond description. Such burning reds I never saw anywhere again, either in nature or art. It seemed to me then that if this world is finally to be judged by fire, surely that fire has been kindled already.

Cooking? How did I cook. Like a squaw at an open fire mostly, bending there until I was more smoked than my meal cooked. I had few enough cooking worries; there came a time when eating potatoes and oatmeal was nearly as monotonous as cooking them. Until our stove arrived from Illinois—in September—I had to walk to Williams's every other day with my dough and an armful of wood to bake four loaves in their stove. Often, on that endless walk with my arms numb with those seemingly light things I was carrying, I found a rock or badger mound to sit on and cry. An especially good place for this was "Buffalo Rock," a huge stone in a hollow worn out by hooves of buffalo itching themselves. I sat there, my head against the rock rubbed smooth as marble, but when Billings came with me, we two swinging the dough pan between us and both of us with half an armful of wood, then we stopped there to rest only, to drink some water and laugh at the gophers chasing each other so easily across the prairie. How handy to live in the ground, he said once, to have a smooth pointed body that could whistle in and out of narrow tunnels. No tent to clutch desperately in wind or thunderstorm, and covered with fur against both flies and mosquitoes.

That was best about outdoor cooking: the soaring pests disliked smoke. Of course we had smudges in the evening, but the tent could not be tied up tight in the hot nights and no one can sleep in a cloud of smoke, so we really had no protection. Sometimes towards evening the oxen were neither red nor black, simply grey with mosquitoes. As Papa said one late supper, "It's a great comfort to eat in the dark. You don't know what all you're eating."

Every time I was down with my two- or three-day headaches, I felt these terrible insects would finish me, whining, crawling, burrowing everywhere. Actually there were homesteaders who gave up their claims because of them. Perhaps the women did it. The men had hard daily drudgery to weary them so they slept through insects and storms too; above all, they had visible results of a house wall or an acre of ploughing to prove themselves, but women have to keep at the same few things over and over and wait for their men to come from wherever they are. I could never see my men haying because, though it appears flat, the prairie is filled with slopes and hollows; wherever I looked there was simply the endless horizon. For days then I saw no living, moving things from the tent, and I never dared venture from it for fear I would be lost—I never did lose myself, but I always had the numb ache that I would. When I finally saw a distant moving wagon, or a herd of cattle filing at noon towards the sweet pond to drink, I felt a relief, a companionship I rarely knew in Rockford when my neighbours came for afternoon tea.

I have never been one to complain, and I won't begin now, but pioneering is work for very strong people, or a group of people like ourselves who have various strengths between them. Many people came to Alberta not knowing that. For someone alone, or if Papa had had only me, we could not have lasted a month. But our boys were unbelievable; I never knew my oldest three children, grown up and happily married in Illinois, the way I now knew these last three, the way they tackled problems that would have turned an old person grey, worked for months on ranches or on railway crews where gambling and loose living destroyed many married men while our boys brought home every penny they earned, laughing and telling us endless stories. I remember one terrible day when the heat and flies had literally hammered me flat and my migraine had built to such a pressure that I knew the plates of my skull were bouncing, grinding together in agony, and then towards evening I heard Billings come home singing at the top of his voice, "Back, back, back to Baltimore!" his high boyish sound floating as if it came from everywhere around me and I struggled to my feet and came out of the tent and the sun was low and mellow beyond the horizon like a burning town; I just hugged him all sweaty and he gave me a fast squeeze, not seeing my tears.

"There are so many flowers," he said, pushing back, "it's too bad we have to tear them up with the plough."

And the people. The best thing about homesteading is that everyone begins at the same place, really with nothing but themselves on the empty land. That's true no matter how many "things" you bring with you: you struggle with the mosquitoes, the water, the wood, the loneliness, the space and distance all around; that is, the land. After a year this begins to change, and by the end of the second summer when the hail had smashed some of our crops into our new ploughing and others got fifty bushels to the acre, the pioneering oneness clearly began to go, go forever. But the first year: I used the Williams's stove, they came to our good well for drinking water; Papa used Erik Olsen's haymower while he ploughed with our plough. If you had something a neighbour needed, or ate a meal when a neighbour came by, you shared. Community. That was the strange, human effect the first year with a new land had on all of us, and for some it was so strong that it did not vanish, Billings told me later, to the end of their lives.

The prairie fire of May 12, 1907, had the entire country fighting it, together. Though we had seen a few distant fires in the late fall, the worst season is early spring just before the green grass comes. The fire travels on the wind, and with its own terrible heat creates such a draft that often no running horse can stay ahead of it; the only protection is a slough or ploughed land or a backfire—anything which deprives it of fuel—and if these barriers are too narrow the headfire will simply leap over them. That day a father six miles south of us had gone to the timber—why he would leave when the smoke had been visible all day before and the smell of burning on the evening air, I don't know—and left a girl alone with an invalid mother and three little children. The house was poorly fireguarded, and the girl led the children to the ploughed field and told them to sit there together and not to move or look anywhere while she went back for the mother. But the children must have been terrified: they started back towards home and so when the father returned home, driving furiously from the hills when he noticed the fire, he found his house and stacks and barns in ashes and himself the only survivor of his entire family.

We saw the high smoke when we got up that morning, and the
wind was from the southeast. Ethan rode south (we had a pony by
then) to the ridges while Papa and Jolson ploughed a wider fire-
guard and Billings and I laid out sacks and set pails of water. Soon
Ethan returned as fast as his horse could gallop, but by that time
we could already see the flames and smoke driving across the hills
only three miles away. The men quickly began setting a line of small
fires farther and farther south, very carefully: if you set too wide a
backfire, you can create a prairie fire of your own. A family north
of us started a backfire two miles from their house, just to be sure,
and burned down their homestead before the wildfire even reached
them. But despite the black wedge of prairie on two sides of us, the
approach of that fire was awesome. The men went forward with the
neighbours to see if they could turn the headfire; but Billings and I
had to stay at the house with sacks and pails: if the fire got past the
men and jumped the guard, we would have to scream for help and
try to control it until help came.

The fire burns in a wedge. The headfire at its point creates such
a flaming whirlwind that it rushes ahead as if it were following a
trail of gunpowder. Nothing can stop a headfire in May prairie grass
on a windy day. The boys fought towards it with sacks soaked with
water, the smoke suffocating, and then suddenly the smoke lifted
in the wind and they saw a wall of flames driving towards them
and they ran, desperately, and if the freshwater pond had not been
within twenty yards of them, they and the horse would have burned
alive. Ethan rode, Jolson jumped right into the water, and the flames
passed them like a giant locomotive roaring through a station.

"Maybe it caught Papa!" Ethan gasped. "On the other side."

Jolson was already pulling himself out of the muck. "Come on!"
he shouted and ran across the smoking grass leaping with scattered
patches of fire. Ethan had a longer struggle to get the frightened
horse across.

But Papa was all right; he and the neighbours had stopped the
western sidefires so when Jolson sprinted up their only concern was
us and the homestead. I saw that headfire approaching, and with
Billings beside me felt so totally helpless, a puny human nailed to
the ground with a wet sack in her hands and that inhuman scourge

roaring...the backfire and guards made it hesitate, just for an instant, and Billings screamed, "It'll stop, Mama, see, see!", but it would not have, I know, that momentary hesitation was nothing to that horrible furnace driving at us but then like a breath from heaven a westerly crosswind wafted over us, unbelievably, and perhaps all the people in the country were praying with me and Billings and Papa and Ethan and Jolson. For like a startled animal that headfire leaned, suddenly leaped sideways and roared around us along the east side of our guard, northward. When the men ran up, scorched and gasping, Billings and I were slapping out the last bits of flame on the haystack and the house roof. Papa kissed me, right in front of everyone, and then they ran off north and east after the slowly spreading sidefires. The headfire didn't die until it ran into the big lake seven miles north of us.

Such a black smoking world you cannot imagine. We were a grey island in the deepest corner of hell. Wherever you stepped your feet burned, smoke sprang at you. But a day later it rained, a warm, soft, penetrating rain and the glory of grass and flowers that grew out of those ashes within a week I cannot describe. The wonders of the world are endless, how out of the greatest terror God surprises us again and again with more beauty and goodness than we ever had before.

That was our first spring, after we had come through the winter of 1906–07. We had lived it in our unique house, of course, and that was a mixed blessing too. The house was clean enough after the tent: once, during the summer I had gotten out my broom and leaned it against the front of the tent, not with the intention of sweeping anything (after all not even I, as Ethan pointed out, could clean up the whole prairie) but just to remind me of a future hope; however, the house was cold. Indescribably. The wall of lake-mud dried, cracked, and we could not fill the cracks carefully enough. I put on my heaviest clothes for bed, and in the morning granules of snow were sifted over me, my breath frozen into ice on my pillow. I have never been so cold, and during my headaches the house became worse than Hades. The men could not, of course, stay all day with me during my sickness, not even Billings, because there was so much work to do and I did not want them to stay: I preferred my agony alone, to their restless impatience, but how often I prayed for the understanding hand of a woman.

Very few homesteaders wintered on their claims; they returned East or moved into town, but since so much of our summer energy had gone into building the disastrous house at my insistence, we could not afford that. However, one of our absent neighbours had a little organ which they permitted us to use for the winter, and I do believe it saved my sanity. I would play, pumping furiously, singing every song I knew and pieces I made up so loudly that Ethan swore he heard it all the way to Mr. Mason's store and post office, three miles above the howling wind. I told him he'd freeze his ears if he didn't keep them covered.

But one day in February not even the organ helped. Both Ethan and Jolson were working away at the time and Papa and Billings had been fixing the barn against the hard storms; I was the second day into a migraine and about three o'clock Papa said he should go to Mason's as there had been no blizzard and probably the mail had come in. Billings looked at me so longingly that I said he should go along, but please, come home quickly. So they trudged off into the snow, and I waited.

Five hours! I made supper for six o'clock, as usual, but nothing. I wanted to rush out, search, but of course there were two of them and besides I was terrified of the winter prairie. My head hammered; my feet were blue with cold no matter how much wood I banged into the stove. And outside lay that vast motionless stillness which comes only before the worst storms, a night where the moonlight turns the endless waves of snow into rigid, frozen steel. And when those two men finally came in, with no mail, they said they'd been choring in the barn for half an hour, just so they could save putting on their mackinaws again and oh they were sorry they hadn't bothered to tell me they were back!

I got out of bed, thrust my feet into my old slippers, and started for the door in my nightgown.

"Sara," Papa said, "where are you going?"

"Outside. To stand on my head in a snowdrift."

Papa and Billings sank back into their chairs, their arms hanging down limp, the most marvellous expression of helplessness on their faces.

"Why Sar," Papa said finally, "I believe you're crazy."

"I *know* it," and I got the door wrenched open and marched
around to the west side of the house where the drifts were the
deepest. I broke the crust, knelt down and stuck my head into the
snow as deeply as I could without smothering and I held it there
until it felt quite frozen and all the rest of me too. Then I picked up
a big piece of snow and went back into the house. The men sat there,
looking at me, not having moved a muscle. I wrapped the snow in a
towel and lay down on it like a pillow and I slept without waking or
dreaming and in the morning my headache had vanished and so had
my temper.

We stayed five years in Alberta, and we stayed that long because of
Billings. Our first crop was smashed by hail so we couldn't sell out or
leave that year, but then the crops were steadily better as we ploughed
more land and also bought cattle so that in three years Ethan could
enrol in the winter session at the University of Chicago and Jolson
was taking correspondence courses from there too. They both studied
until they finished their PH.D.'s and became professors in the States,
thanks to our Alberta homestead, but Billings returned to Alberta
after a year of high school in Illinois and he refused to go back.

We could not talk him out of it. So we stayed for five years: he
was nineteen then and he bought Ethan's and Jolson's quarters with
money he borrowed against our quarter, which we gave him outright,
and he stayed on to become one of the old-timers of the district.
He even became a Canadian citizen and celebrated the first of July
instead of the fourth. Papa and I returned to Illinois, more bent and
no richer, but we had been able to give our last three sons a good
start in life, though one life was very different from the way we had
foreseen it.

Rudy Wiebe: Collected Stories, 1955–2010

Sailing to Danzig

MY NAME is Adam Peter Wiebe. As far as I know, there hasn't been an Adam in the family since the name Wiebe was first recorded in 1616 in Danzig, which is now of course Gdansk, Poland. The first Adam Wiebe was Frisian, and in Danzig he had two sons, Abraham and Jacob. Oddly enough, my own father, who was born in Chortitza Mennonite Colony, the Ukraine, was called Abraham Jacob, which in the Russian Mennonite tradition of naming meant that his father's name before him was Jacob. My oldest brother, who was born in a Mennonite village in the foothills of the Ural Mountains, was named Abram Abraham, my second brother Daniel Abraham, the Daniel coming from my mother's father. How is it then, I asked my parents years ago, that I, the last son, was named Adam Peter?

"Actually you weren't," my mother tells me without hesitation. "In the government papers in Saskatchewan, wherever they have them, your name was Heinrich."

"Heinrich?"

"In the papers, yes, and Abraham your second, like always. You were Heinrich Abraham."

"I'm not Adam?" At age seventeen I am about to discover my name?

"Of course you're Adam," she says calmly. "That was just those government papers. But we were living so far in the Saskatchewan bush when you were born it was seven weeks before your father got to town and he registered your name 'Heinrich Abraham.'"

My father, across the kitchen table from me, has continued to study his *Mennonitische Rundschau*; his reading glasses, bought at a counter in Eaton's, tilt at the end of his long, almost patrician nose. He sits this way every Sunday afternoon, the only day of the week he does not have to feed cattle on the farm where he will work as a hired man until he is sixty-nine, another seven years, never able to find the one Canadian dream he still has: a job where he can work inside and be warm all winter. He says nothing now, not even at my mother's teasing irony which, we all three know, will prick him eventually into some response.

"He had the day wrong, too," my mother continues suddenly. "He remembered it was a Saturday but he got the date wrong a whole week and when we got the registration when he was going to become a citizen Mrs. Graham says to me, 'My Lloyd was born the same day as your Adam, the midwife came from you to me, how come your day is wrong?' and then I noticed that too."

"It was eight weeks after, not seven," my father mutters finally; as if correcting her fact will balance his.

"But my name, Pah, you didn't remember my *name*!"

He seems particularly intent on the *Nachrichten*; he will never understand more than the barest English and it is in the weekly *Rundschau* that he learns what he knows of the news of the world.

"Mr. Graham wrote the names in then," my mother says, "'Adam Peter,' and so we corrected both the date and your names."

"When was this?" I ask.

"Well, Father, when was it, you became a Canadian citizen?"

"Nineteen forty-one. You want my registration number too?"

My mother is knitting and ignores that, easily. She knows he memorized the number immediately in case he was ever forced to cross the border again; when they got to Canada at last on March 5, 1930, he vowed he would never leave of his own free will and he never has.

"But you always called me...."

"Yes, we always have."

"So how come you called me that, Adam?"

"Oh," my mother looks up from her knitting, dreamy like the look I now see again on my daughter's young face, "there was a little boy, a Penner, he was a little Adam and he died just before you were born, he was so beautiful, always singing and only four and so good, laughing in the children's room in church and playing with all the babies to make them laugh too, it was so sad when he drowned in the slough behind their barn. That was a nice name, he was an Adam, so good."

"Well," I say bitterly, "you tried your best, with the name."

"Adam," my mother says softly, and touches me. For an instant her voice and fingers seem about to find tears behind my eyes, but my father says gruffly,

"Where did you find out about this Adam Wiebe, in Poland?"

"In a book."

"Books, books, all your books they'll ruin you."

If I only had the chance. What's ruined him? Being born in 1889 in Russia he always says, a Mennonite hauled into the Czar's forests in lieu of compulsory military service and he had finally finished his four years and come back to his village to marry my mother when World War I erupted and he was dragged back again, another four, or three rather, because the glorious October Revolution ended all that, they got so busy killing themselves, all those Communists, and playing games with him forever, what could anyone do but do what he was told? But finally, at forty, he did one thing: he left what little he had, they were poorer than Russian meadow mice, and took his wife and six kids to Moscow to try and get out of there; forever. Astonishing, he did that one thing, after a Mennonite father and four older brothers and over seven years of the Czar's army and then ten years of Communists, the Communists, oh he had learned to do what he was told.

"What was this Adam?" my mother asks.

Adam/Peter—ground/rock, surely a name significant enough for anyone. Adam/Peter/Abraham—ground/rock/exalted father of a multitude, dear God more than enough, all earth and exaltation too, with Wiebe a solid Frisian name to anchor it; a people stubborn and implacable as water. In a class I taught years later at the University of Leeuwarden there was a long blonde girl named Wiebke den Hoet, her father the dike master on a new polder slowly forming itself out of the North Sea. But I could not know this when I was seventeen, did not yet know Wiebe was a Frisian given name transformed by deliberate centuries into a patronymic, my mother knitting mittens for poor children on a hot August Sunday in Alberta. That first Adam Wiebe sailed from his fishing village of Harlingen on the North Sea for Danzig in 1616 because that Hanseatic free city needed a water engineer and he was the best in the world. Harlingen is still a village in the Netherlands; its labyrinth of dikes and canals, many of them probably built by Adam, still thrust it out in alternating loops of earth and water against the grey sea. The aerial (KLM) photo I have shows it almost as neat as the 1624 copper engraving of Danzig which in the top-left corner features the city's coat of arms and the top right a portrait of Adam Wiebe himself.

"Look," I say to my mother, and read for my father's benefit, since he won't look up, "Wybe Adam von Harlingen."

"That's your father's nose," my mother says, and so it is. But a higher forehead, heavier eyebrows in a narrower face; an unstoppable genius who served Danzig thirty-two years and before he died had streets and gates and even squares named after him.

"Where's my long nose?" I ask.

My father laughs then. "It got lost for a turned-up Loewen. Her mother's family."

"Does your book have pictures of a Loewen?" my mother asks.

If I could answer her now, I would tell her the Loewens were Flemish believers from the other great Hanseatic city, Antwerp, probably jewellers who escaped religious persecution and arrived in Danzig even earlier than Adam Wiebe. But perhaps now, rather than parade all my dubious facts of history, I would ask her to sing, that beautiful soprano now lost forever except in the folds of my memory. Any of the songs she sang when the leaves came out green as frogs in the Saskatchewan poplar May and she began to cook on the stove outside to keep the house cool for sleeping. It would be a song from the *Dreiband*, their pocket-size Mennonite hymnal without notes but of course a person who sang in a church choir then knew at least five hundred songs from memory, and my father across the yard somewhere within earshot would answer her in tenor harmony, their voices floating like lovers hand in hand high in the bright air. By some genetic shift more drastic than my nose the two musical rocks of Flemish Loewen and Frisian Wiebe have faulted into my tunelessness: though I can recognize any melody, I cannot reproduce or mirror one either close or at a distance. Not even the overwhelming choir of thirty-six Peter Wiebe descendants in Gladbach, West Germany, last year helped me to one tuneful sound—the over two dozen children from two families finding hours of melodies in that tiny apartment, their heads filled endlessly with identical words and notes.

"Peter Wiebe," my father would have slowly raised himself erect. "That was my brother, the rich one with us in Moscow in 1929, he always—"

"Leave that old story," my mother would have said quickly. "We have to forget such things."

"Forget!" my father's thick worker hands are crumpling the paper. "You forget when your own brother who's as rich as the dead Czar keeps saying to you, 'How do you think you'll get out to Germany, you and your Marie and six kids, when you don't have three kopecks to rub together?' How do you forget that?"

"Abraham," my mother murmurs, "God needs money for nothing."

"And the Communists don't either, thank God," my father laughs sardonically at his own wit. "Having money in '29 was the end of any going, no beginning."

"So forget that old story, it—"

But I would have to interrupt her. "This isn't your brother Peter, Pah, it's his son, he was in Moscow with you too, young, he—"

"Peter Wiebe is in Germany now? Did he finally buy his way out, now?"

"It's your nephew, not your—"

"That young Peter was nineteen in '29," my mother says dreamily. "Short, very thin and very bright eyes. Such an open Wiebe face."

And he still has it the first time I see Peter Wiebe. In 1982. He was coming towards me through several thousand Mennonites at their annual reunion in Germany to celebrate their '70s escape at last from the Soviet Union, exclaiming, "That's a Wiebe face, a Wiebe face!" And for that moment he appeared to be my father reincarnated in a slight, short body, his thin blond hair which would never turn grey and that patrician nose and square jaw, limping towards me through the crowd that turns to stare and then laugh aloud at our happiness, at our embrace and enfolding double kiss. I had to bend down to him, over him, my arms surrounding his narrow bones, and suddenly between my fingers there spread an enormous, overwhelming silence. I might have been holding my father, alive again after seven years; though he had never in a lifetime held me like that.

"I never wanted a Peter in my family," my father says. "An Adam I didn't care, but a Peter, another Peter...."

My mother is singing. She will be singing not to avoid my father: they did not live sixty-one years with each other that way; rather, that wordless sound suspended by her voice, a broadening colour which does not hesitate at sadness or laughter, or break because of anger, unforgiveness, even hatred; it is a sound which slowly, slowly threads brightness over the glowering, stifling Sunday afternoon. It is like the story young Peter Wiebe, now seventy-two, will tell me of his second arrest and his second transport to the Gulag in the last fierce days of the dying Stalin. He will say:

"We had religious freedom, of course, it was official, guaranteed by the Soviet Constitution. But no more than three people could talk politics together and the police must suspect everything so when our village met every Wednesday evening for Bible reading, faith became politics. I had the only Bible and the room was full, always tight full and I read in German, no one ever said a single word not used by Luther—where would you get a Russian Bible? This German Bible from my father was the only one in the village, and even if we had spoken Russian, who knew what person had been pressured by what police, and why? Your own sister or cousin or even husband would never dare tell you if they *had* to inform to prevent something worse. That was the way they controlled us, fear, and if *you* had to inform, at least you knew how to protect yourself because you knew at least something they knew because you'd told them—well, why would Soviet police or party members believe us when we told them again and again we never spoke anything at all but the words of Jesus? And sometimes his words, well, the way you say them can sound like something a little slanted and people will smile as if they know

Rudy Wiebe: Collected Stories, 1955–2010

something, just for a second they know and can think, something.
So that time they came in as I was reading John 15: 'I am the vine,
you are the branches. They that abide in me...' they were pounding
loud on the house door, and of course it takes a while to get the door
open and there's always so many big men and women around the
door that they can't actually get in for a while and when the knock
came I had to leave the room, like I'd done two times before but this
time they are smarter: two of them greet me by the kitchen door as
I come out. 'We just want to ask you a few questions, nothing more,
don't worry, Katerina Petrovna, he'll be back for night.' Of course, but
which night? Four years later, when Stalin is dead three years and
Khruschev reviews all the ten or eleven, maybe it's thirteen, million
political prisoners' records, I am released just as quick, I can go not
even into free exile as they call living anywhere in the Soviet Union
except within five hundred kilometres of your home village, I can
go, go home. I am alive only because I am small, and because I can
keep books. Even sitting on a stool in a heated room all day you get
barely enough food to keep a body as small as mine breathing year
after year, but if you have to labour in the mines or the forests in the
terrible cold, especially if your body is big like yours, you don't last
a month; the smaller people last longer, sometimes almost half a
year, but me they would have stuffed with black bread gladly forever,
sometimes even a fish-head in the soup because every camp admin-
istrator has to have a bookkeeper who will keep him ahead of his
boss—you cannot imagine the unbelievable records that have to be
kept, every turnip peel weighed and written down to whom it went
and to have a prisoner in camp who can add and is honest, well,
honesty is so unbelievable that every camp boss I ever had kissed
me and cried when he had to let me go. By God's grace there I am,
four years of a twenty-five year sentence, the food ration is the same
whether you have to meet an impossible quota set in the Kremlin
of trees cut in waist-deep snow or add numbers all day, columns
like forests down page after page growing themselves green in your
head until you are an adding machine, your eye sliding down their
wrinkled bark and clicking so exactly even the unexpected Kremlin
inspector with machines can't do anything faster, leave alone find a
mistake in books stacked to the ceiling, thank the dearest God who

gives you this year after year mind of numbers and denial, nothing more, 'No, I did not....No, I never said....No, I know of no one....' the unending questions that come to you at any time of any night, always only at night, and only the numbers are constant, solid as rock and the frozen spruce piling up like corpses around the camp you have no idea where it is buried in the taiga but you know exactly how many bodies there are, trees or people. You become numbers; soon an axe blow no matter how feeble in the farthest swamp is already written on the paper of your mind, eleven to seventeen chops per tree up to thirty centimetres in width for a fresh prisoner, seventy-six to ninety-three for the same tree for someone who will be dead in her bunk rags tomorrow, the skin stretched stiff across her torn teeth and you have another statistic: longevity calculated in relation to declining rations, in relation to quotas not filled, how long can rations be cut for the prisoner coming in weighing thirty to forty kilos, forty to fifty kilos, do women last longer than men even though their initial production is never as high and they have the same quotas, same food ration? The largest men always die first. But I am small, I work inside where it's warm, I last four years; until Stalin is dead. It is Wednesday evening again when I get off the train and walk to my village along the empty farm roads and I open the door of our house, the same door where they took my father in 1936, and the woman inside who is reading stops and she gives me back my father's German Bible and I open it and read as if I had never left, read aloud in that room crowded with the same white, silent faces the words of Jesus, 'They that abide in me and I in them, the same bring forth much fruit, for without me you can do nothing.' That was my second return, the first time was in the war when I was falsely accused and our collective farm worked two years to get me out. But my father never came back the first time. They came for him in 1937, and Stalin still lived then for almost twenty years."

. This story, and all the other stories I will hear from Peter Wiebe are already there in my mother's song as she sings until my father joins her, their voices singing this story which has already taken place but which they will never hear nor speak about sitting at the worn kitchen table in Alberta, Canada, my memory of them like their memories of Moscow, like Peter's memories of his father, my uncle

Peter Jacob, the rock and the deceiver, my father's older brother
having to live on in the Mennonite village in the Ural foothills to
which he and his family are returned from Moscow in 1929 while
my father and his family travel to Germany and finally Canada. My
uncle has to wait seven more years until that knocking on the door
he has always known will come finally comes, and he disappears into
the winter darkness leaving only memory and his German Bible, a
tall, strong man like my father who has no mind for numbers either
but can chop down a thirty-centimetre tree in nine strokes of an axe,
easily, and so fill his quota. At least for the first three or four days.
With the square Wiebe face we all have, but a nose unlike mine; a
patrician nose like Adam Wiebe in 1616, the year Shakespeare died
and Adam sails to Danzig to lay the city's first wooden watermains
and set artesian wells in its squares and drain the marshlands along
the Radaune River by building dikes and canals and wind- and horse-
driven mills that lift the turgid water up into the slate-grey sea.

"What is this," my mother says, pointing with her knitting needles,
"these strings here?"

She is studying the grey picture of the copper engraving of Danzig,
the coat of arms in its top-left corner, the narrow, energetic face of
Adam in its top right. Below the coat of arms is a line drawing of a
high hill labelled Bischoffs Berg, the centre is low sagging land along
the river and marshes with the church spires and gates of the city
beyond; but below Adam's picture on the right there is an elevation
almost as high as the hill: it is labelled Wieben Bastion.

Adam built that fortification to protect the city from the army
of King Gustavus Adolphus of Sweden, and he constructed the city
walls and the bastion above the swamps of the river by using earth
from the Bischoffs Berg. The strings between the two my mother is
puzzling over is the double cable Adam Wiebe strung on poles so
that, by means of an endless stream of moving buckets attached to
this cable, the earth could be carried over the river and the swamps
from hill to bastion. So exactly were these buckets designed, so
precisely were distance and weight calculated that no power was
needed to make them move: the weight of the filled buckets at the
top of the hill carried them down across the valley to the bastion
while returning the empty buckets back up to the top. And though

the gigantic Gustavus Adolphus and his mercenaries destroyed much of Europe for hire and the unending glory of the Protestant Church, they never got inside the walls of Danzig, leave alone near its central bastion, because in 1622 my ancestor invented the cable car to defend a defenceless city.

"When did this Wybe Adam von Harlingen die?" my father asks abruptly.

"Sixteen fifty-two. Pah, he built all that for them, and Danzig never even made him a citizen."

It is then my father looks up. "Yeah, yeah," he says, heavily, "that's the way. It always is. When those Communists hammered on our door in Moscow and told me to get on that train to Germany, they gave me a yellow card. 'Stateless refugee,' that's all it said. A hundred and fifty years in Russia and they send us out, a piece of yellow paper and fill in your own name. 'Stateless refugee.'"

I had not known that either. I suppose it doesn't really matter. After all, over how many lakes and rivers and parts of oceans, across how many fairgrounds, up how many mountains on how many continents have I sailed through air suspended somehow from a cable and not known about my ancestor Adam Wiebe? My ignorance has, of course, never made any of those cables less real, any sailing less beautiful. Or potentially dangerous.

And in my memory my parents sit at our kitchen table in Alberta suspending the thin thread of their songs across the marshes and bitter rivers of their memories building what bastions? Against what fearfully anticipated or remembered war, against what knock at what door, "We just want to ask you a few questions, come, you'll be home for night"? Slight, bent Peter, the rich Wiebe's son having to live a sort of a life in the Soviet Union, I the poor Wiebe's son living a different sort in Canada: which would one actually prefer? Peter Jacob who vanished in 1937, Peter Peter bringing that Bible to Germany when he is too old even to keep other books and still so immovably honest and absolutely immovably stubborn and he is told to go at last, go, who wants you, you old bastard, you troublemaker— these are facts, were already becoming facts one August Sunday afternoon long ago when I was a teenager and discovering that my mother and father could tell me so little about the names I had, could tell me only small facts that explained nothing; facts like intermittent needles in compassionate wool, or poles sticking up out of sinking ground, holding up cables no one could explain what genius, what vision had once made them possible so that all that solid earth could be moved so beautifully over swamp from the Bischoffs Berg to build the Wieben Bastion.

Wybe Adam von Harlingen, where are you now? Your cables are gone. Only the memories of songs remain.

177

All On Their Knees

[1964/1968]

ONE

Down on one knee he thrust his arms under, groping for a grip.
It was curled, head and arms balled round to belly and knees.
He fought the blizzard's weight and that unyielding curl, sweat
bursting from his pores. For a long moment he curled over, around
it, fumbling and hugging at its iron cold as if in love, then he got
his arms locked and heaved erect. He staggered: the world wheeled
over under the gritted snow and, incredible wonder, balanced on the
sleigh track, a hard sure line for his feet.

Gradually a shadow bunched in the streaking white and he was
floundering beside the sleigh. He tipped it in, felt for the reins; the
horses moved as he clambered up. He tugged his robe over it and
hunched behind the dash, heart violent in his chest.

Turn-off, make the turn-off, there's nothing beyond. Head down
and mitt over his mouth, he breathed deeply once and again, then he
stood up. No bush alongside; he could not even see the horses' heads
now; only their rumps, occasionally bellies, remained, dark and
heaving. My god if the tracks are drifted too much and they miss—
in the wind—something—he thrust back his hood and the blizzard
awakened his numb face. Nothing. He forced his lips to a whistle, the
thin sound swallowed as it left his mouth, but suddenly a wild bark,

and Roarer was plunging beside the sleigh. He yelled, "Hey, hey! Get up there!" reaching down. The dog sprang at his mitt and then vanished ahead.

The wind shifted to eddy and bush formed on the right. Once they turned, the blizzard's sweep was broken by poplar and spruce but the drifts were higher. The black was nearly finished, the reins told him this, and its momentary lag behind the bay in leaping at each new snow-ridge. The timing staggered so badly that once the black's haunch jammed the sleigh an instant before it leaped, the sleigh struck the drift at an angle and he had to hurl himself flat against the tilt. Something struck him behind the knees then and he crumpled across the dash. Rein pressure gone, the horses almost floundered but he jerked erect, screaming, slapping, and they plunged on. On the hard level between drifts, he shoved the balled shape away from his feet, back under the robes.

Mutt's barking welcomed them to the homestead clearing and the wilder storm. He snapped the icicles off the horses' nostrils and left them spent in their stall. At the sleigh again, he got one leg in, heaved it against himself and staggered to the door. Its very rigidity calmed him; like a heap of firewood he propped it up on his knee to lift the latch.

Where in the—well—he hooked a table leg and dragged the table from the wall. As his lamp caught the match flame, the dogs growled in the doorway. "Good fella! Good girl! But out now, come on, out." He eased them into the lean-to and pulled the door tight.

His glance slid around the little room—god what if—but his hesitation broke before it stopped his movement and he shrugged off his hooded sheepskin and was at the table, tugging, prying for a hold. Finally his hand found a doubled limb; he braced himself. Gelidly a knee rose, straightened; the other leg moved as hardly, but moved, and he could thrust up under the parka to feel a bare warmth seemingly hugged together there. He edged farther, searching, his fingers felt a frazzle, prodded roughness that suddenly slipped like grease. He jerked back, knowing before the light etched his bloody fingers.

Herman saw the red smudge, blackening, the familiar room opening into darkness. He shook his head; come on, blood is blood, everybody has it—but who expects a frozen lump—the tracks, maybe there were sleighs on the road just before—it was warm! Swiftly he unbent the arms and pulled back the head. An Indian, about his own age and, perhaps, alive—breathing, yes. He stretched for a dishcloth behind the stove, plunged it into the water pail and began wiping the dark face. No cut in the shaggy parka; maybe wounded inside a house. Maybe dropped for dead.

The man twitched. Suddenly his head jerked his cheek down against the table and his muscles knotted in spasms here and there; stomach, thigh, shoulder, ankle. Herman held him to the final long shudder, and the limbs relaxed. He got the bottle of whisky from the cupboard then and took one long swallow. Only the features remained contorted, the mouth hanging open a little.

Night had long since thickened the storm when Herman finished bedding his stock and returned to the house. On the hides beside the stove, the Indian had not moved. Unconscious; or dead? Sleeping. Thick hair in a jagged cut at the neck; skin almost transparent over sharp bones; he knew all the Cree on the reserve across the Wapiti River but this man—he looked starved. Perhaps he was no Cree.

Tossing off coat and mitts, Herman washed, then lifted the blanket to study the sprawl of dried blood gluing the shirt against the chest. There it couldn't be fatal and it wasn't bleeding now, no frostbite. The long fingers seemed all right, curled like that. He pried at the moccasins; stockings worn thin, and the skin blotchy to the ankle.

He was testing a basin of lukewarm water with his finger when his glance met the Indian's, eyes wide, staring. The pupils shone as strangely, intensely black and unblinking as two polished knobs on some wooden—Herman shuddered. Then the broad nostrils flared in breathing and he said, "Hey! You're lucky I was crazy enough to try going to town. You okay?"

The eyes did not waver.

"I was crazy, yeah, and to stop too," Herman laughed, too loud in the little room and he turned to pull up a bench. "You'll have to be higher so I can try to fix those feet." He lined two chairs against the bench; the other shifted an arm feebly and Herman stooped, "Just easy with it, easy." He lifted him, holding his torso rigid, and eased him to the bench so that below the knee his legs hung to the floor. He got the basin and began bathing the icy feet.

When he had changed the water twice the blotchiness seemed to be fading. An enormous hunger suddenly moved in him. He propped the Indian's legs so that his feet hung free in the water, then got out meat and bread. In the pan the meat spit, its aroma drifting through the smoked moose-hide smell, strange in this room. He offered him a piece of meat on a fork; he gnawed as if it would stick in his throat. Herman dipped some bread in milk.

When the Indian had eaten bread and, with his head supported, drunk some milk laced with whisky, Herman soaked away the shirts and the filthy scarf. A wide gash lay across the left lower ribs, glancing off one and then another. Blood welled in red beads here and there but, oddly, it seemed clean, inflamed only at the apex. He got his medicine box and fished out the needle and catgut boiling in a pot on the stove. Even for his stubby fingers the heavy gut fit the needle easily. "This is just for cattle, you know, but it works. Fixed my leg good, once, when a crazy boar ripped her from here to here."

He reached for the iodine, and the Indian's look flicked up at him, abruptly alive and blazing as the blizzard roared outside. But as swiftly his eyes closed, and he said no word. "Hey," Herman said, "you better have some whisky, straight."

After he cleaned up and sat down at the kitchen table, elbows spread wide. The bay shying and his own stupidity, as he thought it then, at getting out to see what it might be and the instant of terror, as totally violent, as totally strange to him after all the Saskatchewan blizzards he had outfaced, when the track vanished under his feet just before he saw the drift forming over the mound—he was not even sleepy, now. The storm whined about the cabin. In eight years no one but himself had ever slept in the bedroom until a half-dead—aw, he had done with those thoughts. No one visited him; that fact required no thinking. No more than the Mennonite deacon's remembered voice when, at Herman's persistence in marrying his daughter, he had named him the bastard of a woman long since dead and left him to stumble out, past the rigid face of the church minister, into that long ago summer night. His washbasin mirror had stared back at him and his face bloody with mosquitoes crushed in the trudge home.

He stirred. The things he had brought from town: he had ordered them long ago, carefully, and risked a dash to town before the storm

181 All On Their Knees

for them, but now they could wait. He piled packages and mail on the table, and a magazine cover made him pause. "Christmas is coming!" it stated. A doll lay among blankets: through the frosted window behind it a child's face stared in. Round eyes staring at the doll white as frosting. After a time he roused: the title was high enough, trim it and hang it up. He flipped the page; just a poem centred in a grey-outlined barn and he had already begun the tear when he saw the title and first line.

"The Oxen." "Christmas Eve and twelve of the clock." His glance slipped down the stanzas: he had never heard of Thomas Hardy. It was short so he read it deliberately. At the third stanza he was shaping the words under his breath,

> ...Yet I feel
> If someone said on Christmas Eve,
> 'Come; see the oxen kneel
>
> 'In the lonely barton by yonder coomb
> Our children used to know,'
> I should go with him in the gloom,
> Hoping it might be so.

"Barton" and "coomb" were explained at the bottom of the page. He could not remember when he had last read a poem. And impossible too. Maybe when he was very small, the arms of whom he then believed his mother around his chest, her warm chin on his shoulder while what he then believed to be the flat German voice of his father murmured on about Jesus, yes, born in a barn on such a night, yes— maybe then. But his barn now, the two heifers, his yearling—old Brindy buckling to either heaven or hell!—he roared aloud before he remembered the Indian.

Almost eleven. The poem was as good as an evening verse. He got up, stretched, listening to the dark bedroom. Strange smell they always had, different from any white. Not just dirt; on the reserve Mrs. Labret was as clean as they come but you knew it walking in the door. A whiff of alcohol, a snore audible above the storm; strange too, here. He stripped to his underwear, flicked the hides straight and, rolling his sheepskin into a pillow, snubbed the lamp and lay down.

Firelight wavered against the ceiling. Shapes of Indians stumbling, sticking out legs and arms like sticks towards barns swaybacked under snow where cattle leaned, legs tucked under them, before cribs piled with hay. Strain as he would, there was a weight on his shoulder; he could not see what his tangled exhaustion seemed to insist. And, as the blizzard continued worrying at the house, his grimace faded to vacant sleep.

TWO

Next morning the man's gaunt body shook in fever. After redressing the wound, Herman wallowed into the storm to feed his stock. The yearling nuzzled his sleeve and while it ate mash he scratched its ears. The white markings lay on its broad curly face in perfect symmetry. To hunt deer was impossible, and he no longer raised pigs.

Abruptly he untied the rope, tugged the pail away, and led the big calf out. It plunged about in the wind's bite, butting him playfully as he dug at the toolshed door. In a surge of emotion he wrestled it a moment, its body big and flinging, then he got his arms clenched around it and tossed it bodily into a drift. When it gambolled up he had the door free. Inside he put down the pail and, snorting, it reburied its nose in the mash. He reached for the mallet on the shelf; just as the yearling began raising its face to him, he struck down hard.

THREE

Two days later noon sunlight blazed through the iced window onto the table between them eating. The man could sit and so there was no longer need for fresh beef borscht. Herman watched him work at the heap of steak and bannock. Like a hammer mill, but silent, without a pause as if there would never be an end until there was nothing. His wide mouth no longer pulled so gauntly against his teeth and he limped without apparent pain. But then he had never shown pain. And since that momentary flicker of—what it had been

Herman was no longer sure; sometimes he wondered whether he had not been hoodwinked in what he thought he saw that night, threading the needle. Since the fever the man had muttered perhaps ten words to necessary questions, face expressionless, black eyes blank beyond reach. Sometimes it seemed to Herman the man was not even there; he would come in and the house as silent, as empty as ever, and he would look into the bedroom: the man lay on the bed, face empty, staring nowhere. Well, the beef disappearing was proof! He grinned and said,

"You from the Cree, over the river? I don't think I ever saw you."

The other held a last piece of meat speared on his fork. "No."

"What's your band then?"

The pause stretched. "Chipewyan."

"That's a long way north." Herman wiped bannock around in his plate. "Real cold too this winter, so early too. Hunting?"

"Yeh. No deer there."

Finality in his tone, almost like resentment. Herman pushed the dishes together. When he looked up the other's glance slid away.

"No deer," the man's voice repeated behind him.

"Yeah. And a family to feed too, eh?" But the other said nothing.

He was placing the last dish in the cupboard when the dogs barked outside and he went to the door. Two figures plodded over the blinding drifts. Herman squinted; the dogs were silent now, leaping about them. In the immense cold the world shone with a hard, implacable brilliance, lifeless in a sheer light with which the sun seemed to have nothing to do; it hung above the bush as if frozen on the sky.

No one was at the table when he turned, and it was a moment before he could make out the Chipewyan standing in the bedroom door. His parka, which had padded the chair, he clutched to his chest. Herman said, "It's two men. I can't see who but—" and then he realized that the expression on the man's face was terror. Its very density seemed to hunch him together so that the shirt of Herman's he wore hung even more baggily, his body coiled to leap into flight. Herman said quietly, "From the dogs, one of them—" but stopped. In two and a half days the man had slept or accepted bandaging, spoonfeeding, washing of frozen feet, lying aloof and motionless as if waiting for his body to get over its weakness and catch up to wherever his will had long since been. No emotion; not even a twitch when iodine touched the sewn wound. Now, this, as they stood, hearing the approaching sounds. The unbalanced door scraped; the man was gone.

Feet stomped outside and he thrust open the outer door.

"Hello, Herman."

"Hey!" His breath caught in his throat. "Hello, Bill. Hello," to the other shape against the unbearable snow. "Come—come in, outa that."

"Thanks." They kicked off their snowshoes and the room was packed with them. Herman pushed forward two chairs.

"Sit down, warm up."

Bill was fumbling with buttons. "Christ that sun's awful. Even with the glasses I'm blind." His mackinaw opened to a vee of scarlet police tunic. "Herman, this's Constable Brazier, from Saskatoon."

The constable was tall, younger than the corporal and his blistered face drooped at a long, heavy jaw. "How do you do," he said in a strangely toneless voice.

Herman nodded. "You never hiked all the way from Hany?"

Bill groaned, "I bet. We had to leave the snow rig at the road, your drifts are damn well over the trees!"

"And it's quiet on foot." Herman laughed, "Except for the dogs!"

Bill's laugh bounced about the room. "Yeah, dammit, I guess I forgot them dogs!"

"They haven't forgot you—"

"Why are you so concerned about our coming quiet, Mr. Paetkau?" The dry voice was the constable's.

Herman glanced at him momentarily, shrugged. "Dunno. Guess we, Bill and me, try to joke sometimes." He turned to the stove. "Anyways, it's cold. I'll heat some borscht."

"By god that's what this god-forsaken cold needs—more people with a good pot of Mennonite borscht on the stove!" Bill got out of his coat entirely. "You might as well have some too."

There was a brief silence before the constable answered, "I'll check the barn in the meantime."

Bill said heavily, "Look, there's hardly—look, Herman, we're—"

"Sure," Herman swung around, poker in hand, "go ahead." Brazier, already at the door, stopped as Herman followed him.

"I won't need help."

"I wasn't coming—it's just the dogs." The growl that greeted the policeman faded at his: "Let him alone, you hear. Mutt!" The dogs sat down again, ears cocked at the black figure pushing into the glare.

Bill stood before the picture tacked by the bedroom door. "Nice," he cleared his throat gruffly. "Coming all right, hmm. December 24 and a cop hasn't even time for a Christmas picture."

Herman went to the cupboard. "I'd join you but I only got two bowls."

The corporal swung around. "Look, this Brazier and his—he's okay all right. It's just his first big job, just out of Regina and head crapfull of theory. You know." They had known each other since Bill Gent's first Treaty Day in Hany more than two years before when Herman, one of the few whites who spoke any Cree, helped quiet a brawl behind the livery barn.

"Sure. Who you looking for?"

"A Chip from west of Reindeer Lake, name of Carbeau. His sister's Joe Sturgeon's wife—you know, Tough Joe, on Stony Point. He came there the day the blizzard started, had a fight and Joe got killed and Carbeau got away on a stolen horse. They say he's cut pretty bad."

Herman stirred the soup. "What'd they fight about?"

"That's the funny part. It started when Carbeau got there, right away, but nobody'll say why. Yet. Maybe Joe was beating up his sister. She wouldn't say but she looked pretty bad. You ever hear of Indian men fighting about that?"

"Yeah."

"Yeah? Well, maybe them Chips up there learned real fast from the whites," Bill guffawed. "They steal about like them anyway. More likely Joe owed this Carbeau meat from last year. Reports are there's nothing of anything around Reindeer this winter, not even rabbits."

Out of the corner of his eye Herman saw Bill's bright scarlet move from the bedroom door; perhaps he was now looking at the bracket above the table, at the alarm clock there, or the faded gothic letters on the German Bible. But it was in the room like a presence, that abrupt unfathomable terror, seeping through, choking the room. Bill talked on, "...relatives cut him off back north and they just about had him this side of Poplar Lake when the blizzard hit. We found the horse dead on the road this morning three miles west with a leg bust. He probably tried walking this way. You see any sign of the poor dev—"

A growl flared outside and Herman sprang to the door. "Mutt! Drop it!" Brazier was stooped at the door of the kennel, his gloved hand clamped rigid in the dog's jaws.

The constable straightened, face livid. "That's a vicious dog. Ought to be chained." He was rubbing his hand. "And that one followed me every step."

"They're not pets."

"Look, I'm no prowling Indian—"

Their looks met, held, and fury roiled in Herman. "You figure they should know your uniform?" Then he saw the constable's track around the house. "If you looked at tracks, you'da seen there was just dogs around the doghouse. It'd be pretty cold in there, through that storm."

Bill in the doorway was looking at him oddly; he had said too much. Too much? It was impossible. Even if he wanted to.

"The borscht's hot," he said, turning.

The two policemen ate quickly, silently, and in a few moments Bill pushed back. "Thanks Herman. That old touch is still right there!"

"Yes," Brazier said. "I've never tasted it before, but it is very good. Thank you."

Herman nodded. Take him and get.

Bill said into the awkward hush, buttoning his coat, "Yeah. As I was saying when the dogs caught Brazier—ah—" he snorted, "red-handed, you get home before the blizzard?"

"Huh-uh. It got me a couple miles south of the church."

"I figured. See any sign of Carbeau?"

So say it so they get. He opened his mouth and met the tall constable's look; cold, as if performing some drill of inhuman precision. He said to Bill, "I can't say nothing that would be enough for him."

The policemen glanced at each other. For a moment only the fire snapped in the stove. Bill jerked, "All right, take the bedroom, I'll get the cellar."

Staring down at the cabbage stuck to the rim of the borscht-pot, something turned over in Herman and he felt spent, filthy. When they came in the door he should have just said, "The bedroom. Sic 'em" to that long-jawed—Brazier had not come out. He twisted, peered into the bedroom. The constable was dropping the end of the cot, turning irresolute, eyes probing the tiny room. If he's got a nose, he can smell him! After a moment he came out leaving the door ajar. His glance circled, moved to the ceiling and Herman heard him catch his breath.

"Where's your ladder?"

"Huh?"

"Your ladder, for the attic." Herman stared at him and the policeman seemed almost to smile for the first time. He said, "I want the ladder to get into your attic. Understand?"

In his confusion Herman nearly laughed. "It's just a loft, a little—I don't—" The other's look was hardening. "Stand on a chair."

The constable jerked one around, stepped up and nudged the trap-door with his hand. A shower of dust fell in his face; he started as if a current had struck him.

"That's enough." Bill stood on the cellar steps, pushing away his flashlight. "Nobody's been there." As the other two stood motionless he emerged entirely and pulled on his mitts. "You see no sign at all, eh, coming home?"

Herman lied, without comprehension, "No."

"I'm sorry, Herman," the corporal hesitated, his face mottled red. "It's my fault. The first thing you're supposed to know in this job is who to ask and who to search. One of the drivers ahead of you on the road remembered his horses shying somewhere after the church, but he hadn't thought much of it. We never found nothing; I knew you'd of stopped if your nags shied. All right! Thanks again for the borscht. So merry Christmas!"

Herman watched them slip on their snowshoes. His eyes followed them across the clearing until they were lost in the unrelenting light. There was no sense anywhere, neither his lies nor the nothing in the bedroom. Or the world with its sun and inhuman, mocking white-ness. He turned back at last into the black house and he did not know how long he stood, arms propped on the table, head hanging, before he knew Carbeau was watching him from the bedroom door.

"My god," he said, and sat down.

Carbeau limped to the other chair. "Never saw me behind the door."

They looked at each other; laughter burst from Herman, a roar that fluttered the cupboard curtains and hushed. The other smiled. Herman exclaimed suddenly, "They won't quit, what's the use of running? It'd be a year or two for manslaughter, at most. Why didn't you come out?"

Carbeau's lean finger poked along the edge of sunshine on the oilcloth. "Why didn't you say?"

Herman said, finally, "I dunno."

After a time Carbeau said, "I was getting to Labrets now." He nodded slowly.

"They won't come back—" but stopped. "You know Labrets?" he asked irrelevently.

"My uncle."

"Hey, I thought they're Cree. Didn't he say—"

Carbeau was looking away. "Yeh. My uncle."

"You know the way from here?"

"Yeh."

Herman stood up heavily. "You'd better sleep, and start when it's dark."

He put on his barn coat and went out. He cleaned the barn thoroughly for the first time since the storm and, as the sun set, did the chores. He returned to the house and heated the last of the borscht. When he went into the bedroom, Carbeau awoke and they ate supper.

Herman said, as they finished, "Even five miles with them stitches—well—if it don't open, take them out in two, three days. Mrs. Labret can do it." He pointed to the worn knapsack he had gotten from the bedroom. "There's some meat and bannock. Labrets don't have much either, this winter. Here, you'll need another shirt."

The other was staring at him and Herman continued, almost loud, "Hey, where's your gun? You run your deer down?"

Carbeau said slowly, "In the fight—I—"

"Sure sure," Herman got up and reached above the door to the gunrack. "I don't need these both. Some shells," he rummaged in a drawer, "here, you can bring it back when—when you don't need it."

Carbeau stood looking down at the little mound of things. "You better start," Herman said. "You ain't going fast."

When Carbeau was dressed at last, the knapsack on his back and the gun in his hand, Herman hooked his snowshoes off the nail in the lean-to. The other man could not seem to move; then he said almost inaudibly, "No."

"Look, it's over five miles, belly-deep! I'm not going no—" but Carbeau jerked up to him, frost-blackened face contorted,

"Joe, I—I come jus'—jus' to ki—"

"Hey, hey!" Herman was shouting the words away, "you'll have time, to make yourself a pair! Leave these at Labrets! You hear me!"

Carbeau's face slowly hardened. He seemed to stoop forward, as if accepting a weight, then turned and limped heavily out on the porch. He stepped into the snowshoes. The two dogs sat at attention as in the gentle moonlight he moved into his stride. At the clearing's edge Herman thought his figure hesitated, but then it was gone.

When he became aware of the cold, he went in. He sat at the table a long time before he got up and took down the picture. He glanced at it, turned it over and, with lips moving, read the poem. Gradually his broad face softened, as if a fathomless serenity blossomed like child's laughter in him. He folded the paper carefully and put it in his shirt pocket. He again pulled the hides before the stove, stretched out face downward, and fell instantly asleep.

FOUR

He awoke, lifting his head from his arms. In the absolute stillness the lamp burned, sputtering on its wick. He pushed himself up and looked at the clock. Then he pulled on his barn coat, blew out the lamp after lighting the lantern, and stepped out into the silver, frozen world. The northern lights flamed a path down the endless sky. He could not have explained what he expected to see as his hands pulled the barn door open.

The Power

THE GAUNT TREES crowding the road were shivering spectres, staring through him in the passing wagon. The spring, the summer, even the autumn had gone now, and the winter had not yet come. The stillness of no season at all filtered through the thin November wind as it slid, moaning, between the creaking branches of the poplars. It was no season at all, only a kind of suspension that was waiting for him to get on and do something. Yet he could do nothing, for he seemed to be, like the season, suspended by an everlasting thread in a void, and he was twisting slowly, futilely, like a strangled rabbit in a snare. He opened his eyes wide once more and stared about him, pupils fixedly dilated. The trees seemed to look, the road and wagon and horses, the huddled log church they were passing, the two men in front of him, even the woman leaning against his shoulder seemed to look and be there, yet somehow they were not there because they were flat like shadows, and, like shadows, though he could reach out and touch them, he could not *feel* them.

His big hand closed upon the hard muscles of his thigh. For a moment it was absurd that he should think of himself as one of the silly rabbits he snared in winter, but it passed in an instant. He could not feel the presence of anyone, stare as he would, and he could hardly feel his empty self.

The wagon halted by the cemetery and he got off quickly. The thin wind seemed to rattle through his bones, and he looked at his bare hand, mildly surprised that the horny skin was still there. He noticed that the woman had taken his arm and was leaning heavily on it, so he walked forward with her through the creaking gate, their feet crunching the twist of dead leaves swirled up behind the gatepost. They walked towards the little heap of fresh-broken clods, and it struck him that the few mounds were huddled and lonesome in the barbed wire enclosure. Even the inscriptions of the rotting pine boards were spidery—with aloneness, as if an old feeble hand had traced each stroke far apart and by itself. Everything, including the fresh hole he had gnawed from the iron ground—yes, only that morning—and by which they now stood, appeared to have lain there for ages. It was all so old, and each thing by itself.

Then the two men got there too, from the wagon, and put the coffin down beside the hole at his feet. The men removed their hats and the knifing wind cut the hair on their heads into streaky pennants, wavering and falling. His wife was shaking convulsively on his arm as he looked down into the waiting hole and at the waiting coffin. His right hand clenched tighter in the worn coat pocket.

❀ "Hey Dad, you'll bring me a present eh, Dad, huh? Willya Dad, please?"

"Daddy, if Johnny does, I please get one too?" begged Jeanie, jumping up and down on his knee, her round little body aquiver with anxiety.

"Now, Toots," his deep voice growled at her in the tone she loved, "it's Johnny's birthday tomorrow, and he should get a present, shouldn't he? Remember last summer? You got Betty and he got nothing."

"But Daddy, now too?"

"Daddy hasn't the money for two presents. You play with Betty now and wait a bit—Santa Claus will bring you something for Christmas, okay?"

"Oh—Kay—, but I'll get a really present at Christmas?"

"And you'll get a 'really present' at Christmas." He rumpled her curly head as his wife came from the other room, pulling on her coat.

He wondered, as he had a thousand times, how she could put both arms through the sleeves at the same time. He had tried it the first time he met her. "John," she was saying, "it's getting late, and it's such a long trip."

"Yes, I know, but as you see, I'm waiting for you, eh Toots?" And he tossed the little girl in the air. She squealed happily as her short skirt parachuted about her, and he caught her strongly, his two hands not quite meeting around her little chest, feeling along his arms and through his body the grip of his love for her. He had consciously to force himself not to hold her too tightly, and then put her down. Johnny moved closer and whispered in his ear.

"Dad, remember the little silver trumpet in Maxwell's window...."

"Well, that was summer, might not be there now—but we'll see."

His wife was checking the wood-box and the stove. "Johnny, you play paper dolls with her, and don't go out. Here"—she opened the cupboard curtain—"your lunch is here and after you've had it you both have a good nap, and when you wake up, we'll be home."

"Aw, Mom, we'll be okay—we've been home alone lots of times."

"I know, dear." She kissed them goodbye.

"So long, kids," he said and opened the door. Outside, the grey overcast was like a leaden bowl inverted over the world. As his wife went out to the waiting wagon, he turned and looked at the two in the doorway. Jeanie was smiling a little too bravely, but Johnny glowed all the confidence of his eleven years. He stooped, kissed them, and closed the door quickly. As they drove from the yard, two faces were pressed against the window, and three arms waved good-bye.

The clearing with its log house and the barns under the trees were soon left behind. His wife said, "I'll never get used to driving away and leaving them alone like that—"

"Well, we both have to go. Better to let him stay at home with her than take her on this miserable trip. It'll be okay. Besides, he has to feel responsible."

They had fifteen miles to town, so he kept the horses trotting steadily. Just before noon they arrived at the hamlet. They drove down the one street, which was merely a wagon-rutted strip of land bounded rather vaguely by the single-track railroad with two peeling red elevators on one side and a scattered motley of false-fronted "business establishments" on the other. The wrinkled little veteran in the land office was, as usual, very busy at a cluttered old desk without any apparent reason for being so. "Well, there she is." His hand shook badly as he handed the title over to be signed. "Didn't think ya'd stick 'er that long, but ya picked the best land anywhere north of here. Just th'other day a chap comes in here and files in your district—heard about your wheat, he sez. Gonna start clearin' in spring." The watery eyes slanted up, half hoping, "I don't suppose ya knew ya were gettin' a neighbour...."

"Huh?—Oh, ya, he came around after harvest. Ahh, I want to buy another quarter, so I'll mortgage th—my land."

"Well, in that case—" Immediately the old man became the official again, disappointment forgotten in the importance of it, fingers fluttering around forms and stamps. "She'll have to sign too. Good thing you brought her along."

Half an hour later they came out of the building. He felt tremendous, as if he were pushing the world around with each expansion of his chest. After five years of drudgery, they finally owned land, and soon would own more—land to pass on to the two children. To his wife's embarrassment, he seized her by the shoulders, lifted her level with his face, and kissed her ringingly. "It's ours!"

"John, right in the street—!"

"What do I care! I've got land, a wife, two terrific kids—I'm King of Canada! Look," he reached in his pocket, "I—ah—found two dollars in my pocket this morning. Get yourself some cotton at Maxwell's and dress Jeanie and you up real fine, okay?"

"John, you old—'"

"No back talk. Come on!"

In an hour they were on the road home, wagon loaded with supplies for the month, the horses chipper after their oat bundles— and at being headed home. On her lap under the robe lay the brightest cotton in Maxwell's, and in his pocket, just below the breast pocket that crackled with the land title and mortgage application, was Johnny's present.

It was a cold, bumpy trip, but neither of them noticed as they sat close, feeling themselves move against each other as the wagon bounced on the unimproved road allowance. They were full of the future—it had been hard, but worth it to leave the worn land in the south and come up here where it lay fertile and waiting for any who would dare take it. And others were coming now, the hardy ones, those who would not lean back on their fathers' labour—those who could take and hold this land. The razor-spined slough grass and the cattle were fabulous, but the wheat—there lay the future. They both felt close as they leaned together and sang loud folk songs to the listening forest and the unsettled land. Then they turned the corner into their isolated clearing, and their song dropped dead.

The clearing was empty, save for a little heap of black rubble. The smoke wavered up to mingle indistinguishably with the leaden sky.

He lashed the snorting horses into the yard. They must have escaped! The barn! "Johnny, Jeanie!" They shouted madly through the barns, but there was only the empty echo. They rushed out again and stopped, staring wildly at the rubble and at the mild-faced cattle bunched behind the barn fence, patient to be fed. "Johnny! Jeanie!" From afar, out of the silent forest it came back weakly, in heartless mockery, "Johnny—Jeanie—"

"No!"

He leaped over the blackened fence into the ashes and kicked and clawed insanely. The black mounds disintegrated into flakes and dust at his blows. But there was nothing. Only loafing spirals of smoke, some puddles of hard glass, and a char-black stove with a hole in the firebox. Tiny granules of snow began to fall, streakily, hissing softly on the ashes. In the corner where the bed had stood.

❋ The snow was starting again now as he stared at the black-draped box. His wife, her young figure stooped and thin, had sobbed more than she could, and now moaned softly, intermittently, through the sodden handkerchief clutched over her mouth. The minister from town, who in his kindness visited the little church once a month, seemed to be finishing his remarks.

"—the Lord hath given and the Lord hath taken away,"—the iron-grey, gentle eyes looked at the box hesitantly—"blessed be the Name of the Lord. Amen."

He watched as his brother-in-law, the only homesteader near them, jumped into the hole and the minister handed down the little box which contained a few unidentifiable ashes from the bed corner. There was no coffin—a shoe-box was enough. Even if they were gone, you had to have a place you—or your wife at least—could call theirs, where you could visit them. The man crawled out, his face streaked. As he stared down, his fist clenched in his pocket. It didn't mean anything—that box. There were some ashes in it—he had gathered them himself—that was all. They might be ashes from the wall or the ceiling—anything. But they had been alive and breathing and he had held them—they were not in that box. It was empty. And as the man threw down some straw, the little box did not even make a hump in it. The box was buried before they threw dirt down. He turned away before his brother-in-law could pick up the shovel.

His wife would not leave. She stared down at the scattered straw; the minister, seeing his move, came and gently took her arm from him.

He walked towards the wagon. Near the gate he turned and looked at the three figures, and they were silhouetted, timelessly and alone, against the skeleton poplars and the vacant grey heaven.

His hand came out of his pocket and looked at the silvered little trumpet. Then he threw it, glinting dully as it fell, into the dead grass among the graves.

The thud of falling earth and the whisper of snow in his face was his only sensation as winter came.

Tudor King

"WILL HE BE ALL RIGHT?" the boy asked again. Against the cold his breathing came in short gasps and his normally round face was pinched together expectantly to the huge parka-ed figure beside him.

"I told you—we'll see when we get there," his brother Frank flipped the reins gently against the flanks of the horses. Encouraged, they butted their way into another drift driven behind the brush skirting the road. "Don't talk. Just stop wriggling, keep the robe up—tight."

Immediately the boy settled back and resolved again not to make another move until they got there. The question, however, ran on through his head in circular repetition, like Little Black Sambo's tigers around and around the tree. Remembering that naked little fellow, the boy involuntarily hunched lower into the blankets for warmth, eyes squinting at the storm-wasted world. His father had said it had been the worst snowstorm to ever hit the district. For five days the blizzard had whipped the pellet-snow across the land; one evening only the ropes they had strung between house and barn had brought Frank safely in from feeding the stock. But last night when the boy awoke there had been no storm whine. What he heard as he lay, limp from sleep and staring at the red bulge of the heater, was the sad howl of the wolves, hunger-desperate after the storm. He had heard, and felt something finger down his spine even as he curled more tightly, pulling the wool quilt up and over, and then

he had heard his father just beyond the bedroom partition make a
sound in his sleep and the long moans had lost their hold and he
had lain snug, his eyes wide again to the cheery heater. Abruptly he
had remembered the old man, thought of all the after-blizzard nights
he must have lain in his sagging cabin, hearing the wolves. With no
father to clear his throat in the darkness.

Now, the team plowing steadily ahead, the boy shuddered again.
He sensed Frank looking at him, and to cover up he rubbed his nose
fast with the back of his mitten. Somehow that did not seem enough;
he crouched lower in the seat of the cutter and lifted the heavy robe
over his head. The musty smell of the cowhide brought him back to
the old man again because that was his cabin smell too. Mixed with
some others.

His father had said the old man was already there when they
came to their homestead. Probably he had always lived there, bent,
scum-grey hair projecting from his face and under his cap, pants held
up by twine, stitched together with string, old. On warmer days in
spring and summer he shuffled past their farm every week towards
the store which was also the post office, his hand folded behind his
back, a greyish sack held in place by cord over his shoulder. And
at his heels followed the dog, small, brownish, and always bald at
varying spots from his truceless battle with fleas. Like the other children of the settlement, the boy stared at the stooped figure almost
apprehensively from behind a tree or barn-corner. The name, hissed
at bedtime, was enough to quiet any restless youngster.

But once, last summer, the boy had faced him. On a long Sunday
afternoon the boy and two friends, daring each other into a corner
beyond their courage, had inched up to the cabin where the old
man lived. Someone, with gritted teeth, knocked. And then the door
squeaked open and they were inside where the litter, gathered home
over years in the greyish sack, left them barely room to shuffle their
feet. The dog, squatting on the sack-heaped bedstead too, looked
more miserable than ever, but something had happened to the old
man. In the darkness under the robe the boy, now as then, saw him
in awe. And heard his voice.

"Think I'm in bad shape, huh? You," jabbing a finger at the tallest
of the three, "you've taken history?" He said it as if there were only

Rudy Wiebe: Collected Stories, 1955–2010

one bit of history to be known and it could be taken like a pill.

Henry nodded hastily.

"It says the Tudors was once kings of England. Eh!" The last was not a question; his whole body jerked as he shot it out.

Henry, whose head was still bobbing from the previous question, said quickly, "Uh-huh!" because that was one bit he did seem to know.

"Well, what's my name?" The boys could say nothing, quite floundered that the old man should ask such a thing. Even the dog had stopped scratching. "Eh!"

Henry ventured, very gently, "Mr.—Tudor."

"Eh!" The ejaculation snapped at them like a whip; in the gathering wonder of that moment the three suddenly comprehended. Under the robe, the boy could again see the flash of the grey eyes and again he was mesmerized. "That means I come from them same Tudors that was kings of England. You know what that means?" The voice not creaking now, but full and deep. "I'm a Tudor. I should be King of England."

As if suddenly aware of their numb comprehension, the old man relented a little, but the flame in his eye did not die. "Now I ain't saying I'm against the King. I ain't really, no, only I don't think he's running the war right. Look at what Hitler's doing to people. Even bombing them! I ain't against him but if George was to come out from England and say, 'Tudor, will you take over?' why, I wouldn't refuse him. Eh!"

As on that summer day, the boy heard no more of the voice but in the musty, seeping coldness under the robe he again saw the old man before him. And the dingy flesh obvious through the rags, the bedraggled whiskers, the rotting shoes, even the dog with his ceaseless scratch, were transformed. If before him was the nadir of humanity, the flashing eyes and the compulsive spirit moving there revealed the stuff of majesty. The lined face was no longer directed toward the palpable ambitions of youth; no longer toward an actuality or even a probability. Whatever had crushed any achievable ambition had not been able to erase a fragment of history, or prevent it from blossoming in the failing mind of the old man.

The boy had not actually known this on the last summer afternoon as he and his friend stood dumb in the cabin. He did not even know it now under the robe on his way to see how the old man had weathered the storm; if asked directly, he could have shaped no words to explain himself. He simply knew what he had seen in the wreck before him, and the two miles home had vanished under his feet as he sped to tell all he could put in words: I saw a king! And the disappointment struck him again as he remembered how Frank had laughed.

"Ah, Andy. That's his dream. Told me years ago. Dream—what else can he do, now?"

He stood sullen in the warm dust of the barnyard. The Tudors *had* been kings of England; it was in a book at school. And the old man's name *was* Tudor. So he must be from the same family, and so the throne belonged as much to him as King George VI. And the way he had looked and the way he had spoken—

Frank put down the book he was reading and leaned back against the haystack. "Sorry Andy, I didn't think you really believed him." He looked over the trees into the sky and added slowly, "But you're almost ten. You've got to learn sometime that you can't believe everything. It's okay to dream about chasing wolves and flying planes—every boy does—but you can't go around believing every old tramp that says he's a king. Even if his name happens to fit something four hundred years ago."

Seeing the boy stare wordlessly at the ground, Frank insisted, "Kid, you can tell. He's not really right any more, in his head. He's lived alone and with that dog too long. A man can become low and mixed-up if he just lives with himself too long. He can become no man at all. How can a man live like he does—in a shack full of junk and that filthy runt. That's what you saw. Listen. Just last week Ted Martin was missing some eggs again. He had a good idea where they were going, so when he met old Tudor on the road he said, 'You know, I've been losing eggs out of my barn again.'

"'Oh,' says old Tudor. 'Say, there must be a snitcher around. Just yesterday I was missing some—' ·

"'Yah,' Ted interrupted, 'but I'm fixing him. I'll plant some poisoned eggs in that barn and we'll see what's what.'

"Ted said Tudor's eyes got all big and scared, 'Hey Ted, you wouldn't do a thing like that to an old friend, would you?'"

After a moment Frank said heavily, "All these years he's lived alone, in dirt. Too long. All the truth and pride in him—everything's rotten away. What can you believe him?"

But no logic or facts could budge the idea caught in the gleam of the old man's eye as he sat enthroned among the sacks of his bed. The boy could no more deny it than he could understand it. But it was there.

He heard Frank shout, "Haw!" and he felt the cutter lurch to the left. He thrust his head above the robe; they were turning off the main road up the drifted track to the cabin now, the greys steaming, heaving themselves forward together. The jack pine and scrawny outline poplars crowded closer here. It was too cold for wind or even clouds; there was just one massive concentration of cold. The sunlight blazing on the drift-driven snow only added ironical emphasis.

But the cold, sting as it might, could not hold his thoughts. *Around the copse and then we'll see*, he thought, keeping even the cold at arm's length. *Just around the corner. A few more steps—that one more big drift and there it will be—*

Only it was not. When they rounded the last pine they saw no cabin in the clearing. The boy jerked to his feet. Where the cabin should have been hunched in the lee of a small hill there was only the straight waste of a giant drift that had levelled the clearing to lose itself at the edge of the spruce. Then, his eyes skipping back over the drift, he saw the bit of stovepipe sticking up and he knew that the wind had only buried the shack and that beneath the hard surface it was snug and—then he looked at the stovepipe again.

"Frank," he said.

His brother was standing too, huge, his weathered face rimmed by the frost on his parka. "Yah," he muttered.

The horses fought their way a bit closer, then halted at a word. Frank muttered, "Hang on here," giving the boy the reins, and stepped out to pull the blankets over the hot horses. "I agreed to watch him, but the Mounties can't blame me. Not for a five-day blizzard."

"Frank—"

"Stay in the cutter! Get under there and stay warm. Y'hear!" The boy, knowing his brother was rough because he had just said what he need not have said, and yet having to say it though useless, sat down slowly and watched him bull himself into the deepening snow. From this angle the boy could see that the wind had eddied the snow clear within a few feet of one side of the cabin, leaving a curving rift in the drift. He saw the iceless glass of one small window; he looked at the stovepipe. No smoke. He remembered the look of the old man. He dropped the reins and was out, his legs churning along the straggled trail. Frank wheeled at him, mouth open to thunder, then after an instant stooped without a word to continue clearing the door.

The inner door ground a cracking protest on its leather hinges. Beyond the flash of snow the interior was black as Frank pushed back his hood and stepped inside. He completely blocked the opening, but the boy, hunching over, slipped past his legs. As he stood there facing the gloom he could feel the old trunk against his leg and he knew from the shadows that the clutter of pottery and worn-out harness of the summer before still lay upon it. Through a corner of the east window the sunlight now managed a faint reflection, outlining in ragged silhouette the heaps of stuff crowding the room. The stovepipe stood above the hump of the heater against the middle of the low ceiling. The boy's mittened hand reached up to the edge of Frank's parka in the silence of their breathing.

"Uh—Tudor," Frank cleared his throat gruffly. Then more loudly, "Tudor, you here?" His voice bounced about.

After a moment Frank started into the room. "He saw a hundred storms—had enough wood for four days if he skimped." He leaned into the gloom about the heater. "Maybe he tried to go out for more—there's none h—Oh."

He straightened instantly, brushing away the boy's hand. "Andy, you better get back to the cutter and..." but there was no need to finish. More accustomed to the half-light, the boy had already seen the figure curled tight against the heater, the back cramped against it as though to plead some touch of warmth from its rigid flank. They both leaned closer as sunlight from the door fell on the granite face. An icicle of saliva had frozen the mouth and beard to the floor.

Frank said, "Wonder, where's the dog."

The boy, still gripping the parka, pointed.

Rudy Wiebe: Collected Stories, 1955–2010

"Huh?" Frank's glance moved slowly around the room, ending on the bed bare to its rope springs. His hands fumbled slightly as he thrust his mitts more firmly onto them, then, with an abrupt movement he bent down. Rigidly, as a welded iron framework, the whole shape moved. He half-straightened and said strangely, "No weight to it." Then quickly he reached down and pulled the dog out from where it was cradled, hugged, in the nest of rags. It seemed only at this moment to be turning stiff. Even as Frank pushed something aside and eased it to the floor, the hairless limbs stretched rigid also.

Frank said slowly, "He tried his best for the dog. Knowing we'd come when the storm dropped. Old Man Tudor."

Then he suddenly turned. The boy felt himself lifted up in his brother's strong arms, held close as he had not been since he was a small child. But he did not find that strange. Something was breaking through his numbness, painful and wet, and he pushed his face against his brother's cold, hard shoulder; as if he were already remembering his own fierce happiness at once having recognized the fleeting stuff of human majesty.

Scrapbook

IN THE DARKNESS under the rafters he awoke to the screaming.

It was like his dream of being crushed by a huge tree and waking up to find his brother's arm lying on him, inert and solid in sleep. But now he had had no dream. Rather, he had felt something a long, long time, as if it stretched back without end into his slumber, even as if he had felt it forever: the leaping rise, the rasping plateau of sound, and then the moaning fall of it down to a whimper, before he awoke and heard it.

All was quiet for a moment after he awoke and these things groped through his thought, when suddenly he knew that David was not in bed beside him. Why wasn't he there? The strangeness of his absence and the sleep-remembered sound—had he heard something after he awoke?—welled fear in him. The straw-tick squeaking, he snuggled over into the big hollow and it was not warm at all. Where was David—*had* he heard—and then he jerked erect, careless of the dark, because the stovepipe which reached up through the middle of the attic seemed surrounded by light. It was! a light from below shone up through the opening around the pipe. Then he heard movement there. Were they all up, with the light burning? Perhaps he had heard—

The screaming came again. It occupied his bent body completely, that inhuman scream, as if he and it were alone in a universe; it drowned his brain until he could not hear it for the sound, and then it fell horribly, as if stretched beyond elasticity, down to a burbling moan.

He snatched the quilt up and over, but the half-warm darkness was not enough. He had to find them. His small bare feet were cold on the rough boards as, hunched against the darkness, he felt for the top of the ladder-like stairs near the oblong of grey that showed light below. Then he felt it and slipped down, feet quick on the familiar steps. The moaning had almost died now, and he could hear movement beyond the curtain of the living room. He crept over and pulled it aside.

He did not know what he saw as he stood for a long moment, fear forgotten. It was not that the lamplight was strong on his sleep-rimmed eyes. Rather he did not know why his big sister Marg, who had lain on the bed in the corner of the living room for months because she had an enlarged heart, his mother said, was now in the middle of the night so stiffly erect in a chair, as if nailed there. And why David and his father should be holding her down. He had never seen her face like that. Like a crumpled paper doll. Her black hair was stuck in strings over her forehead as his mother wiped her face, and then he saw the clothespin gripped in her teeth and the blood oozing from her lips. In the wonder of it he stared, rooted, and suddenly the pain within her tore the shell that held it and he heard the scream again, saw it ripped from her throat and saw the muscles of the men's arms bulge as they tried to hold her in the chair.

The fear numbed him now. He looked here and there as the sound seared him. If it was near David and his father, where—then he felt arms around him. His sister, five years older than himself, sitting crying by the door, clutched him to her.

It was not so long as last time, and he could look up as his father, face beaded with sweat and tears, said desperately, "Mother, we have to do something—we can't stand this," and David, almost maddened, hissing fiercely,

"Do something! *We* can't stand this! Look at her—thinking about yourself!"

And his mother, wiping the tortured face again, saying, "David, don't. That doesn't help. She bites her lips so much when she can't stand it—if we could only stop her burning. Maybe the Samsons—"

"Mrs. Samson would know *something*—get her—or do something. Get Bud to ride and get her."

They noticed him then as he huddled with his sobbing sister, not knowing himself what to do, cry or not. He didn't want to cry in front of David, who said crying was sissy, but Marg seemed to hurt so terribly. And everyone was so different. David said, "Bud, get Prince and ride for the Samsons. Quick!"

His mother bent over him. "I have to go out—I can't stay to see her—Toots, get some colder water and wipe her face. I'll take the lantern, Buddy."

In a rush he was dressed and out in the coolness where the spring frogs croaked hoarsely through the morning dark. He liked to ride, but now—when they were near the barn they heard the scream again but it seemed far away and unattached to him. Like a coyote howl in the night when he lay in bed. He jerked at the door, and the warmth from the horses moved around him. Straining, he reached up and lopped the bridle off its peg. The only sound was the horses' breathing in the dark and his mother's half-held sobs as she raised the lantern in the doorway.

"Whoa," he said softly. "Easy, Prince, old boy," as he stroked the black object in the stall. The horse moved over, waking up, and he went into the narrow space murmuring quietly as David had taught him to do with animals at night. The teeth would not open for a bit so he scrambled up on the manger and strained over to lever them apart, slipped the bridle over the flattened ears, snapped the strap, undid the halter shank and, grabbing the long mane, half swung, half jumped to the smooth back.

"Okay Mom."

The light swung away and he backed the sleepy horse out of the stall, wheeled it, and, hanging over the left side, right arm and leg clinging, rode out the low door. He was glad he didn't have to walk out of the black barn.

"What shall I say, Mom? Mom?"

Her voice sounded choked. "Tell them Marg's terribly sick—to come quick and help."

Rudy Wiebe: Collected Stories, 1955–2010

Somehow her expression of those few words made him feel her dread for the first time. Someone, a neutral person, had to share this horrible night with them and he knew then he had to do something so he kicked the reluctant Prince sharply. As the horse moved he could hear her say, "Be careful, my little Buddy," and then her voice fell into prayer. He was so busy getting Prince into a gallop he did not hear the high distant sound reaching after him as he swung through the gate and onto the narrow road.

The clouds raced across the moon and its light flicked over the landscape as if whipped by a fierce wind. Down among the trees, however, all was still as he heard and felt the rhythmical clop of hooves carry up through him and into the night. With a shudder he knew he didn't like the spruce now. They were too solidly black. And grasping. He kicked Prince hard to get him past the muskeg. Where the moonlight slid out spasmodically, the violet blots of the spruce shadows leaped up and poured around him, and when there was no moon the darkness held all. The last stretch was an opaque tunnel, with the horse's withers rocking up at him, solid and living, in the (he knew abruptly) senseless fear that gripped him; just at the end the scream seemed to stab out of the blackness and he was terri- fied. But then he twisted the corner out of the forest to where poplars bordered the road on one side and the dull greyness of the Samson field stretched out against the pale, moving sky on the other.

The open was better; his thoughts raced on with the hard-running horse. This was like the dreams of riding through the night for help— all by himself, just as he had read in *Black Beauty*. Not many boys, perhaps not even most men, had ever done this. He'd tell them at school!

There was a clump of trees now, then the wooden bridge over a spring creek that burbled between sloughs filled with croaking frogs. The hoofs clunked hollow twice, and he was over, then in an instant saw the outline of the Samson gate. Prince turned up the lane. The farmyard lay black and violet under the half-bare moon.

The dogs barked raucously out of their sleep as he slid off. Holding the reins taut, he banged on the door. "Mr. Samson! Mr. Samson!" Except for the dogs, he knew he could not have opened his mouth against the night. He hammered again and again, suddenly desperate for movement from the still house. Then, as he finally stopped for his numb fist and tilted over, panting, suddenly footsteps came. The door creaked.

"Mr. Samson—" he was staring at the long night-dress, "Mrs.— Marg's awful sick. Mom says, come quick, and help...."

"What's wrong?"

"She—she (he did not know what to say) she bites herself and she sits in the chair and David and Dad are holding onto her and—and—"

"Ride home quick, we'll come right away. George—" she was turning to the figure joining her in the lean-to.

He yanked Prince over to the wagon in the yard, scrambled up, jumped to his back and was headed home. He was cold now, and he saw the eastern treetops were just tipped, as with gold foil. Prince galloped with a will so he closed his eyes and hung on. The road was endless. The horse seemed to run so hard. He felt shaken apart and once he barely caught himself slipping off in sleep. He did not even see the spruce.

His mother was waiting, alone, in the yard. "She said they're coming, right away," he mumbled. He rode in, unsnapped the bridle, tumbled off, snapped the shank on and, dropping the bridle in the corner, went out. His mother took his arm at the door.

"I went in once, but it's too terrible. Oh my Buddy, she's burning up and I can't do anything. It came just like that—so quickly—and she's burning up!" They were near the woodpile and she dropped to her knees by the chopping block. He could feel her frantic clasp on his small body as she prayed, the same words over and over.

"Aw, Mom," he said when she choked, crying, "it's—"

He didn't know anything to say. Where was the word to say when his mother was like this. She who could do everything. Then his crying rose and fell with hers at the great unknowing fear, the helplessness he felt through her. The scream in the distance was very weak, and did not come again for a long time.

Suddenly a jingle of harness and, in a moment, the Samson wagon whirled up. As Mr. Samson tied the horses, Mrs. Samson came to them by the woodpile and put her arm around his mother. She clutched his hand, sobbing, "She was getting so much better and all of a sudden, in the night—"

"We brought some laudanum—that should help some."

He knew it would be all right. They walked to the house; sleep kept pulling his head over as the house came closer. There was a dark door opening, closing them inside.

In the late morning when he awoke and came downstairs, his mother told him Margaret was dead.

The house did not smell right. Everyone seemed to be struck dumb, and cried unexpectedly. He could not find David anywhere. He did not want to go into the living room; he could not think of anyone as dead.

"Mom," he said, "I want to go to school."

His mother didn't seem to hear him. After she had told him she had turned away and was washing dishes, alone in her grief for the child she had nursed so long.

He went out, and the early spring sunshine was fresh and good. No one noticed him as he slipped into the barn, bridled Prince, and rode off.

Yet, somehow, school wasn't right either. When he got there he didn't feel like saying anything about his ride, or even why he arrived late during recess. He sat in his small desk in the one-room school and the teacher said, "Grade three, take out your Healthy Foods Scrapbooks." He opened his desk and there, slightly dog-eared and crumpled from much looking, lay the scrapbook. He and Marg had made it for health class. Actually Marg had done all the work, he had just watched. That was why his book had been first in class. On the cover was the bulging red tomato she had cut from the tomato-juice label, and there was the kink she had made when he bumped her because he was leaning so close as she sat propped up in bed, cutting it out. He said, almost aloud, "She's dead," and he knew that "dead" was like the sticks of rabbits he found in his snares.

And suddenly he began to cry. Everyone stared, but he could not stop.

The House Smashers

EDMONTON'S FIRST MAYOR was a Conservative named Matt
McCauley, and its first federal cabinet minister Frank Oliver—a Liberal,
believe it or not. Now they've named a skyscraper-shopping centre after
the one and a town with a big mental hospital after the other, but in my
time they were best known for being convicted house smashers.

It was about the time the CPR didn't come to Edmonton, a few
winters before the Louis Riel scare on the Saskatchewan downriver
at Batoche. One warm Saturday in February an American named L.
George drove stakes at the corners of a river lot east of where the
Macdonald Hotel now stands and before anyone noticed much had,
with several men he hired, put up a rail fence and started building a
house. The lot was the usual two hundred yards wide and ran north
from the river up over the high bank and all of two miles back to
Rat Creek: a very nice bit of land if you could get it by knocking up a
hundred-dollar shack.

"Well, have *you* got title to it?" L. George hollered from behind
some two-by-fours he was holding for his carpenter.

"You know nobody's got title, only the Bay Reserve's been surveyed
yet!" McCauley yelled back.

"So go...." and L. George gestured, turned to hammering again.

That night he set up a tent on the wooden floor and slept in it.
Sunday in Edmonton, then, was always a day for church and restful

thought; a pondering of life and its possible meanings. Sunday night was very cold, but early Monday morning L. George emerged from his tent and soon was sawing with all his hired help. Sleighs and pedestrians kept passing in the snow ruts of Jasper Avenue— as they'd just renamed Main Street. Many passersby were men who had bought small expensive lots west on Jasper from the Hudson's Bay Company, and others men who had lived there for ten, twelve years and always believed that the land on which they built their businesses and homes would surely be theirs when the government finally got surveyors out of central Ontario as far west as the North Saskatchewan River valley. But if this American had discovered a new way, and the North West Mounted Police continued to have nothing to say about land, why, someone who looked like Frank Oliver was heard to mutter, "Let the facts be known at once so that shotgun law can prevail."

The sun was low in the winter sky. More men gathered to inspect the new building, and they did not leave. When one loud voice requested that somebody better get his goddam shack outa there, L. George put down his hammer and drew a large revolver from his carpenter's apron. By this time the brittle rail fence had disap- peared, and one of the several hundred men milling about slipped behind L. George and grabbed him while someone else deprived him of his revolver. The carpenters now picked up their tools and left; hands were reaching everywhere for L. George, and the only reason he remained in the building was because he was being assisted to leave it between so many different wall studs at the same time. But then ropes arrived, and the building began to move south toward the riverbank.

There were some problems. The bank is two hundred feet high at this point, more or less straight down, and the tent and bed were removed but still the building hesitated; it merely teetered. Then L. George stepped out and the building lost its balance, fell, bounced down in more and more pieces until it spread itself over a small patch of frozen river. The rest of the lumber went flying after it, and then L. George accepted his revolver back.

I think only Matt McCauley and Frank Oliver were ever tried for smashing that house. One was pure Conservative, the other pure

Liberal, and for some reason they walked into Inspector Gagnon's NWMP office together just when L. George was filing damages there for ten thousand dollars and they were both immediately arrested, with complete political impartiality. There were two dozen witnesses ready to swear they had seen both of them with their hands on ropes, on corner studs just before the house fell; Oliver had even been heard verbally encouraging others in similar acts. So Gagnon committed them for trial in June. They were convicted with overwhelming evidence, fined a dollar each, and in October the surveyors arrived from Ottawa.

A dollar was worth a lot in those days, for sure, but I still think McCauley and Oliver were lucky. Sir John A. might have sent an English general after them. I mean, Louis Riel tried to get surveys and land titles for thousands of people who had been living on the prairies for generations, and you know what happened to him? They hanged him. And they haven't named a mental hospital after him yet.

Lake Isle of Innisfree

THE CANADIAN NORTHERN RAILWAY built through Del Norte,
Alberta, the summer of 1905 and it came right through my homestead on the east-west road under the hill where travellers had been
stopping for the six, seven years we'd been trying to make a living
there. Actually, my wife ran the Del Norte post office out of our house
and that plus wagons stopping overnight helped us make it. But then
they wanted to move the post office close to the tracks of course, and
we thought maybe we could get a town started. Elevators, stores,
everything, and the Canadian Northern said sure so all us farmers
were happy. But Mannville and Vermilion were down the line east
and Vegreville west so Del Norte couldn't seem to get going. The
trains roared through and we hardly even had any wagons stopping
by for three, four years. Then one spring day a train with a private
car stopped and Sir Byron Edmund Walker and ten, twelve reporters
got off.

He wasn't actually "Sir" at the time. King Edward VII knighted
him a year later but he was already so important I've always thought
of him as—well, at sixty he was president of the Canadian Bank
of Commerce plus president of the Canadian Bankers Association
and vice-president of the American Bankers Association, and also
chairman of the Board of Governors of the University of Toronto and
of the Trustees of the National Art Gallery and one of the founders

of the Royal Ontario Museum—a list of everything he was doing, and did after, would fill a book but they say he's the main reason Canada has just seven, eight big banks with branches everywhere and not the thousands of small local banks they have in the States where hundreds regularly go broke and you lose everything.

Anyway, when Sir Edmund stopped his private car at Del Norte he was looking for towns where he could build branches of the Bank of Commerce. He said to me he wanted to see the town so I said come on up the hill. Most of those reporters started with us but by the time we got to the top on that rough path there was only him and me left.

The hill's all covered with poplars now. When we first moved there it was bare as any prairie but by 1908 they were already shoulder-high, and as far as you could see from the top there were more and more trees growing, everywhere. The farmers' fields were black-and-tan patches and the trees shimmering yellowish green because there weren't any fires any more, and long, long no buffalo, to keep those tough poplars from spreading. The lakes lay blue in hollows, the land all around us rolling beautiful like the green knuckled back of God's hand my wife used to say. I told Sir Edmund that.

He was looking as if he wanted to remember forever. Then he pointed to Birch Lake a mile or two away. Its little islands had always had a bristle of trees on them even when all the rest was bare prairie.

"That looks just like my summer place," he said. "In Ireland. Innisfree, beauty...beauty...."

He was so quiet, I looked at him. In size he wasn't even as big as me: soft grey suit and that climb had hardly put a speck of dirt on his shining shoes. He seemed to be looking past the horizon; the way some people can when the land doesn't scare them.

"I will arise and go now, and go to Innisfree,
And a small cabin build there, of clay and wattles made:
Nine bean-rows will I have there, a hive for the honeybee,
And live alone in the bee-loud glade.

And I shall have peace there, for...."

I hadn't heard of William Yeats then but I know poetry when I hear it, and he just stopped saying it for some reason. Below us were the ten, twelve buildings of our town and the red elevator with "DEL NORTE" on it and the tracks straight out of sight in either direction. Just an ordinary day in Alberta, clear as rubbed glass.

"Mr. Puckette," he said suddenly. "I was my father's oldest son, born on a farm in Seneca County, Ontario, and I left school at twelve to work for my uncle and...."

I was going to tell him I never got past grade five either but I could see what he had started was far too personal for a big man like him to blurt out to a stranger on a prairie hill, no matter how beautiful. So I shut up and let him say what he suddenly wanted to tell me.

"Mr. Puckette," and he was looking me straight in the eye then, "you tell your community that if you rename this town 'Innisfree,' I'll build you the most beautiful bank on the prairie."

Well. I got him to write that name for I sure didn't know how to spell it and then we shook hands and walked down. You should have heard those farmers holler when I told them. You'd have thought "Del Norte" fell on us from heaven instead of something somebody already dead had remembered from Colorado. Nobody even knew what it meant till I wrote to the new university in Edmonton and a month later found out it was really the tail end of the Spanish "Rio Grande del Norte": Great River of the North. What could that mean to us? The North Saskatchewan was big enough but thirty miles away and there wasn't a Spaniard around, anywhere. There's no Irish either somebody yelled, which was true. Were we going to let some eastern bigshot tell us what to call our place when it'd had a perfectly good name for at least ten years?

"You better call it Innisfree," my wife said knitting our kids the usual winter socks. "You'll never see that Mr. Walker again anyway, and you just might get a bank out of it."

She was right, on both counts. Sir Edmund's word was as solid as his bank. Come and see it. Standing over seventy years, the hill high and green behind it. And still the most beautiful town bank on the prairies.

They Just Won't Believe [1978–1979/1979]

I DON'T KNOW WHY, but Albertans are known as being big liars. Maybe lately there is some reason for it, writers like Bill Mitchell and Bob Kroetsch telling stories here now, but there was a lot of liar talk going around already over a hundred years ago, like for example the two sons of the Reverend George McDougall. He was the Methodist missionary that froze to death in a buffalo hunt by Nose Creek in 1876. His sons were called the three biggest liars on the Canadian prairie, son David being one and son John the other two. Well, David was a businessman, so okay you can believe that, but John was an ordained minister, for two years chairman of the Canadian Methodist Assembly. I mean, really.

Actually, I think a lot of this liar business comes from Alberta nature. People who've never lived here can't believe the most natural stuff that happens, like big mosquitoes. There was a carpenter from Ontario name of August Bessai come to work on the heavy oil pilot plant at Cold Lake. One day he finally got tired of knocking mosquitoes aside with two-by-fours and crawled into an oil barrel to get some rest. When the brutes drilled their stingers through the barrel at him, he just bent them over with his hammer and for a while he was okay. But he only did that to seven mosquitoes, and then they flew away with the barrel. Any Albertan would have taken his hacksaw in there, but easterners, they just don't believe.

Or a perfectly natural thing like the power of the Alberta sun. Dick Harrison, a Peace River farmer, made a rawhide harness for his team and he was halfway up the Dunvegan Hill with a load of wheat when a cloud came up and it started to rain. Of course, that wet rawhide started to stretch. He finally got the horses to the top, but it was a real soaker and those rawhide traces had stretched so much his heavy wagon had slid back all the way down to the bottom of the hill, a mile and a half down. The rain stopped just then, so he knew he had to work fast. He got the harness off the horses and buckled it onto a big spruce just as the sun came out and he barely had time to roll and smoke a cigarette before the heat of the sun had shrunk that rawhide right up and brought that load up Dunvegan Hill so fast he had to cut the traces or the wagon would have smashed into the spruce.

People outside Alberta won't believe that. They've heard stories about our chinooks for over a hundred years and you'd think— David McDougall in 1877 told them how that winter he drove a sleigh and team from Morley to Fort Calgary and the chinook blew down through the Kicking Horse Pass and started licking up the snow so fast he whipped those horses to a dead run and they could barely stay ahead of it. His horses were ploughing snow, the front runners of his sleigh were floating easy on a river of water, and the black runners were dragging up such a dust that his dog running behind choked to death in the dust storm. Eighteen seventy-seven, and other Canadians are calling that a lie to this day! They could come out here any winter, but oh no...it's like our premier said just the other day, the just won't believe *nothing* about Alberta till they see it on the TV.

Well, if nobody believes stories about our nature, they believe even less about our people. Like Eric Harvie, for instance. This silly story has been around for about forty years that Eric Harvie became our biggest oil millionaire by a legal accident: that instead of being paid lawyer's fees of something like forty-eight thousand dollars, he took over the mineral rights to some Alberta land from an English company—absentee capitalists, of course—and then they found both the Leduc *and* Redwater oil fields under it. Harvie had those mineral rights, okay, but do you actually believe a lawyer born and raised an Ontario Methodist would skip that kind of fee by accident, in 1943 dollars? You have to be crazy.

I'll tell you what really happened, and if you've had a hard time
with what I've told you so far, I don't know what you'll do with this.
Eric Harvie was born in 1892, in Ontario. That wasn't his fault, of
course, and he left Orillia for the West as soon as he was old enough
and graduated from law at the University of Alberta in 1914. He was
wounded in the elbow, knee, and hip in the Battle of the Somme
(1916) and had a fever all his life, about once a year, from that.

He was so careful as a lawyer he wouldn't even smile during business hours, it might give a client the wrong idea, but with his own
money he was a gambler. Not the idiotic, lottery, slot-machine kind:
he gambled on the resources of this province, especially oil, right
from the start. So in 1921 he was in with R.B. Bennett—later prime
minister of Canada—and the Turner Valley oil field, in 1925 with
Home Oil at Wainwright, 1928 at Lloydminster, and Vermilion in
1941. All these fields were small, but Harvie put his legal head and
money into every one of them and in 1943 he took the gamble that
could have wrecked him as easy as it made him the richest man in
Alberta, some say Canada.

The Social Credit government about 1941 set a tax on mineral
rights of half a cent per acre owned. That doesn't sound like much,
but this English outfit called the Western Land Company owned
rights to 487,342.8 acres. By 1943 they were going to let those rights
revert to the government for taxes when Harvie heard about it and
offered them ten thousand dollars; they sold immediately, but then
Harvie was stuck with all the back and ongoing taxes. He paid over
a hundred thousand on his "Moose Pasture," as he called it, to keep
the titles clear before he finally persuaded Imperial to drill, and
on February 13, 1947, Discovery No. 1 exploded at Leduc. That's no
accident, that's high-roller gambling. They drilled 1,278 wells at Leduc-
Woodbend, most of them on Harvie's rights, and when Redwater blew
in, four times the size of Leduc and dead centre on Harvie rights that
Shell Oil had once tested and told him were completely useless—
reporters suddenly started figuring Harvie was worth about fifty
million dollars, take or give ten. By 1954, from rights sales, organ-
izing so many companies nobody except he could keep track of them,
and a steady flow of oil royalties, they figured he was over a hundred
million. And that's when the strangest thing of all happened.

He started giving the money away. He always kept his hand in—
organized Western Minerals to drill the first holes north of the
Arctic Circle, for example—but he started big giving through foundations he organized: the Glenbow to collect paintings, artifacts,
manuscripts, photographs—anything of western history value—and
the Devonian doing things like underwriting cold-ocean research
in Newfoundland, building a Fathers of Confederation Centre in
Charlottetown and a glassed-in park in downtown Calgary; he set
up statues to Robert the Bruce and General James Wolfe; through
the Woods Foundation he donated both River and Heritage Park
to Calgary—in fact, he gave so many millions away that in August
1974, *Time* magazine (you should believe it, it's American) called him
"The-Man-Who-Gave-Everything-Back-And-Then-Some."

I'm not saying Harvie's family was—is—poor. No way, but after
Leduc he and his wife never changed houses; he drove one car until
it wore out and then he got another one. He hated publicity, honestly,
and besides the hundred odd millions everybody knows he gave
away there's probably as much again nobody knows about because
he wouldn't talk. I watched him over thirty years, though we never
said a word to each other, and I figure Eric Harvie was setting a new
world style in millionaires. I mean, can you imagine J. Paul Getty or
H.L. Hunt or Howard Hughes stopping piling it up so they could give
it away? Well, nobody much in Alberta's followed him either, at least
not yet. And when the press kept asking him, all he'd say was the
province had been very good to him, why shouldn't he give it back?

I know this is harder to believe than any chinook story. Just don't
bother Mrs. Harvie trying to check it out, she still lives in that house
in Elbow Park, Calgary, or their children Donald, Neil, Joy. They're
like Harvie, they don't talk to snoops, but you'll never see them in *the*
places in London and New York either. And don't bother the Herron
brothers who were in with him on the Turner Valley excitement in
the twenties, or Jim Gray who tried twenty-five years for one good
interview, or Jack Brooks who kept Harvie's bird dogs in his kennels
for forty years, or—heck, three thousand people worked for Harvie at
any given time, I can't name them all. If you're really interested, why
don't you just go to the Glenbow Archives, 9th Avenue SE, Calgary. It
was built for twelve million dollars to store some (it's not big enough

for all) of the things Harvie had collected, and he gave five million to keep it open for the public. The archivist there, Hugh Dempsey, tells me they're trying to persuade Mrs. Harvie to let them make a video-tape of Harvie's life, so you can watch it all in black and white.

That's the best proof I can give you, now. But I know that the good that people do lives after them, and I'm sure it'll be at least another three, four generations before the Harvie heirs change so much they become "personalities" and start fighting in public and stuff like that. So it'll be a while before the Toronto CBC will hear about him and make a TV documentary drama of his life so you can know for sure.

Growing Up in Rosebud

IN 1896 when I first went to school in a log building near Rosebud,
Alberta Territory, we often saw men fighting over politics. You know,
grown men knocking each other down if they could, or at least
breaking a few teeth. Whenever the Conservatives were getting the
worst of it, one of us little Conservatives would run for the North
West Mounted Police constable. The Liberals that year had made up
a song for school kids to sing, and when any of them sang it we were
supposed to start fighting too. I never did. I thought Frank Oliver, who
became Minister of the Interior in Laurier's Dominion Cabinet, looked
far more impressive than the Conservative candidate, but my dad
said Oliver just had that huge, droopy moustache so you couldn't tell
which side of his mouth he was talking out of and when they sang,

Oliver rides on a big white horse,
Cochrane on a mule.
Oliver is a gentleman,
And Cochrane is a fool,

I better start swinging or I'd explain myself to him behind our barn.
So whenever I heard the song begin I was always swinging as I high-
tailed it for the bush of Rosebud Coulee.

The nearest polling station was at Elliot's, west of Carbon about twenty miles from our place, but my dad said he had to go and vote even though it would take him almost two days to get there and back. I bumped along on the wagon with him and I remember the Conservative scrutineer at the booth, though I won't mention his name. He'd say to anyone who looked him straight in the eye, "See Angus in the barn." Angus was taking care of good Conservatives there, and he took care of my dad so well that I drove the team home all the way while he lay in the bottom of the wagon box and watched the stars and sang songs I had never heard before and didn't again for quite a while after. Politics were more important then, I think.

My mother was the local medicine woman. She had learned a lot from the Blackfoot about herbs and roots, and always had a big bag of them hanging behind the stove. If you had a sore that wouldn't heal, you came to her and she'd take out a root, chew it, and tie the mash tight over the sore. I never knew whether it was the root or my mother's spit, but the sores always healed. She even healed my dad when he spent three days in a snowdrift in January 1907.

The Blackfoot weatherman told him not to go, the low heavy haze in the north looked bad, but the sun was bright and he started north, thirty-five miles to my uncle's. When the blizzard hit we thought he had probably stopped at a ranch, but he was in a snowdrift ten miles away and for three days lived on flour and snow. After a while he thought he heard voices, that all around him in the drift were the people he knew and they were calling to him. So he was still alive when the storm was over and he found his horses frozen solid to the sleigh and started to walk home. But his feet were too frozen, they wouldn't carry him. He rested and crawled, rested and crawled until he saw the banks of Rosebud Creek near our house in the setting sun, but he was too weak by then to lift his head. He lay down to die, and suddenly a strong voice told him to get up. The sun had gone down, but he felt stronger then and he crawled a little farther to the top of a hill, and my mother who had been looking out the window all day, praying, saw the dark object in the snow and told me to go see what it was. So I found my dad and carried him home.

After a while there was nothing wrong with him but his feet. When his toes started to rot, my mother held the butcher knife and

I hit it clean and sharp with the hammer, once for each toe and that fixed him. She healed him up otherwise, but he could just wear moccasins after that. He died in the General Hospital in Calgary twenty-two years later.

The Darkness Inside the Mountain [1978/1979]

NUMBER THREE HIGHWAY west of Lethbridge, paved, leads through Fort Macleod where at seven-thirty in the morning the Hutterite men in their black overalls are already swinging off their staked cattle truck beside the New American Café—"To buy ice cream cones till the back door of the beer parlour opens," Daddy tells me, laughing—and then there's the high prairie of the Peigan lands—"Watch for Horse-drawn Vehicles"—and in the emptiness against the foothills a tree has been set up. It couldn't have grown there so thick and all alone, its huge sawn-off branches holding up what at that distance looks like a platform of branches and blankets.

"That's the way Indians bury them," Daddy says. "Chiefs. High for the crows."

"Crows?" I can see one flapping across the summer shimmer of heat already buckling the hills.

"It's okay, better to fly off than be dragged deeper by worms."

That was one reason Mama didn't want me to go with him all day on his truck run to the Crowsnest Pass. "A girl of ten, Wendell, doesn't need *soaking* in cynicism." "Don't 'Wendell' me." "I didn't give you your name." "You don't have to use it, 'you' is enough." So I am in the red Coca-Cola truck he has driven since spring, bottles leaping in their crates when he can't miss a pothole, the mountains south of Pincher Creek like broken teeth with very bad fillings. The three

224

Cowley elevators drone past, then Lundbreck with half-boarded-up square storefronts—"There's no mine here now, not even a sawmill"—and the pavement ends with a crash and slither of gravel, the bottles going crazy. The railroad bounces doubly under us and against a hill, curves, and suddenly the road silence of a bridge, and thunder. Spray in clouds between cut rock—

"Daddy! Daddy!"

"Yeah, Lundbreck Falls. We'll have a look coming back."

The falls are gone behind an inevitable shoulder of rock and I'll have to wait with a memory of water hanging like brushed grey corduroy, vivid grey, not like irrigation falls, and the quick flash of rapids between trees and rocks, a shimmer spreading behind my eyelids as I squeeze them shut. When I open them there is the smoking cone of the Burmis sawmill but a tiny church also, you'd have to bend to go in, and over a hump the peaked and mortared stone walls of a—no, surely a castle! With all the wooden core of it burned out by a year-long siege, don't tell me!—and I look at Daddy and he doesn't, just grins and gestures ahead to the sudden upthrust of Crowsnest Mountain. Straight down the highway, over the narrow railroad track that cuts the gravel at right angles in front of Bellevue slouched on little hills ahead. We have to stop there while a string of mine cars tugs across the road in front of us.

"You must be good luck," Daddy says. "I never seen them going into the mine before."

Past our broad red nose the little cars are now all seated tight with blackish men facing each other knee to knee, hip-roofed lunch buckets in their laps. Each single giant monster eye on the top of each head turns, stares, and one by one they slide into the hole in the hillside, click *click*, click *click*, box after box of them slipping past where the sunlight of the trees and the blue sky stops like a wall. And for one instant that single eye glares from the darkness, and is gone, click *click*, click *click*.

The sun sits on the eastern mountains and I would like to curl up, arrange all this behind my eyelids, there is too much already, how can I possibly remember it all, but Bellevue is there, old stores cut into hillsides and a Chinese café and a Ukrainian café with bottle cases stacked in cellars, behind gaping fences, crashing as my father

225

The Darkness Inside the Mountain

heaves them about single-handedly and the blackish faces of the off-work miners leaning across the porch rail of the Bellevue Hotel swivel with us as our long red truck flashes past in the window behind them. We bend around a large grey school and the road splits, straight ahead or down into the valley to a scatter of houses across the river and around a green hill. We drive straight on.

"What about those?"

"There's nobody there," Daddy says, "in Hillcrest, there's nothing there now."

Behind my eyelids I imagine I can see into one of those little houses, look inside its one large room, and there is no ear to hear it as slowly, without a sound, the floor crashes soundlessly into the dark hole of the cellar below and the corners of black begin to move—I jerk my eyes open and a girl, tiny like me, tilts against the iron-mesh fence of the schoolyard with her hands up as if wired there and I wave, she is the first girl I have seen and I wave with both hands, desperately, but she does not move. Her face is early-summer brown like mine but she does not even blink, only her head turns like a mechanism and then we are plunging into the pale limestone wilder- ness of the Frank Slide under the ruptured face of Turtle Mountain. The highway and the railroad so smooth over and through it, a monumental cemetery for eighty people buried in two minutes; 1903, Daddy says, and on the edge of it they found a baby still sleeping in its cradle untouched. Through piled fields of boulders and past a store beside Gold Creek and then Turtle Mountain Playgrounds, and we stop in the noon shadow of that threatening overhang to eat sandwiches. Last night my mother packed them, and we wash their dryness down with Coca-Cola ice cold because my father exchanges two of our extras for cold bottles from the cooler he services inside.

"See that man," he says, chewing. "He's starting on his third million. Finished the first two, too."

A slim man—he has arms, legs just like everyone, how could you see he is rich?—opens the door of a silvery green convertible for a thinner woman with hair like a cloud of gold piled upon her head. Oh, she is. Rich. The convertible murmurs, spins away, their heads leaning back together, they almost touch.

"He was just born," my father says, "that's how he got all that."

Blairmore is one long street facing lower green mountains, the CPR station, and the water tower. And a longer alley black with heat and the fried stink of food, the blackness moving, settling, settling down out of the sky like granular snow in the blistering day, every-where. I sort bottles, my hands like the miners' faces but sticky with pop too, and my father stacks cases five-high and hauls them in and out, up and down on the two-wheeled dolly until finally we drive the length of the street again, bumping through the sunken sewer ditches that cross in front of every business and past green mine timbers squared up like tunnels on the cinder space beside the railroad— a banner, "Welcome to the 52nd Annual Mine Rescue Games"—and finally, finally, there is air at the open window and only the grainy blue of Crowsnest Mountain. By itself like a blessing, and the road folded left and upward in green arcs towards Coleman. My father is sweating; his thick hands shake as he rides back and forth through his ten gears into the hills.

227

"I can't work a whole day on that horse-p—" He gestures behind him but looks straight ahead. "Not such a killer day."

I had never thought he could. After three grocery and one drug store, four cafés, the miners' clubs and the Canadian Legion, he pulls up tight against the bright shade of the alley behind the hotel—"Take a rest, I won't be long"—and is gone. I lock the doors, stretch out and fall into sleep that breaks in sweat, I am gasping on the sweat-hot seat. I pull myself loose, clamber out and up, hand and toe up to the top of the cases on the truck. The bottles burn my fingers. And I cannot open them anyway like my father does by levering two caps together because my hands are far too small, and weak.

"I'll open one for you." A whiskered man, grey, his layers of clothing so black with dirt they shine below me in the terrific sun. He reaches up, his horned, gleaming hand takes one bottle from me and his lips draw back on his teeth and he places the top of the bottle there and at one slight grind of his head the hot liquid boils out between his whiskers and over his chin and down his layered front, but he does not notice. Just spits out the cap and looks up at me easily, offering me the hissing bottle.

"It'll make you sick," he says. His voice is as gentle as if he were touching me. "Hot like that."

The Darkness Inside the Mountain

But I cannot put the bottle to my mouth. Not where his enormous teeth have been. He is something that has risen out of this day, out of the black and overwhelming power of these towns strung between and under mountains and over mines, a heat-blister out of the day, his green eyes glittering through his hair with the snore of the fan blowing beer fumes over me.

"Did you deliver in Hillcrest?" his soft voice asks.

"Hillcr...wha...no, no...no."

"You wouldn't. Not today, that's when it happened, June 19, 1914. Forty years, today."

His hands clutch the top cases and I cannot move. He is so close the dirt stands grained and polished in his skin bit by bit.

"A tiny fire jumped up, poof! In the miles of tunnels crossing each other two thousand feet inside Hillcrest Mountain, and then the fire licked along the methane gas bleeding along the tops of the tunnels and found the coal dust, here, there, the pockets where the miners were working and it exploded...waugggghhh!...and the ventilator shafts blew out and then all the oxygen left in the tunnels burned, bright blue like thunder and lightning breaking, and all the miners...." his face, hands, body are changing like a rubber horror mask, bursting from one contortion into another, his body curling up, jerking open spastically..."they breathe fire...the last oxygen burning, explosion after explosion...in the darkness inside the mountain they begin to come apart."

Gradually his face hardens again, his arms, head, shoulders are all there, together.

"Only their brass identification tags gleam in the stinking smoke when the rescue lamps...Hillcrest Collieries Limited, June 19, 1914. One hundred eighty-nine men. From Peter Ackers to Michael Zaska."

The coated bottle still sticks in my hand. The truck is twenty cases long: each narrow body is a row of cases, to lay them tight side by side will take nine...nine and a half....

"That was my shift," his soft voice goes on. "I was called, yes, I was called but my leg ached. So my friend took my shift. There was never a body found with his brass tag on it. His unchangeable number. We found, we assembled one hundred eighty-eight bodies, and then we had one leg left over."

The sun winks between the four chimneys, the immense crossed tipple of Coleman Collieries. A tiny smoke forms there, disappears grey into the brilliant sky.

"Forty years ago, today," the old man says. "Listen, I will tell you their names. Listen, there was Ackers, Peter. Adlam, Herbert. Albanese, Dominic. Albanese, Nicholas. Anderson...."

I have to run, run! But he is below me, between me and the hotel bar door I must reach so I scramble, clanking over the empties and scrape my leg along a case wire but I am down, somehow half-falling and look under the truck—will he move, will he?—and I see one leg there, motionless, beside the tire and then his hair, his head lowers, upside down, it looks like nothing human and at the top of it the terrible mouth is opening on another name and it reaches out for me like a long black tunnel, Oh, sweetest, sweetest Jesus....

"I have only one leg," it whispers, "I have only one...."

The truck spins past me, his head coming up—"Androski, Geor"— and the door under the beer-scummed fan, and darkness. Like a moist hand clapping shut over me...but it is open too, and high everywhere, I reach out my arms and there is nothing. Only this moist, slipping, darkness.

"Daddy...."

But there is a light, behind a high narrow table and a shadow moves there, light and glass, misshapen bottles everywhere. And there are other shadows too: quick little double movements of light that come and go, and then I know suddenly that those are the eyes. Turned to me from the vastness of the cavern which I cannot see the end of, that is breathing around me like an animal opening itself endlessly for me into close, moist terror—

"DADDY!"

"Del," a huge voice from the light and as my heart jerks I feel my father's hands on my shoulders, his big hands hold me as only they can. They lift me, completely, and his chest, his neck is there too. His gentle breath.

"...Prosper. Davidson, John. Demchuk, George," murmurs the mound between wall and telephone post. My father places two warm bottles of Coca-Cola beside it. "Demchuk, Nicholas. Dickenson, Matth...."

The Crowsnest River burbles between boulders around a small island and then bends, vanishes over Lundbreck Falls in quick, slipping silence. In the water I can see that the western sky between the Crowsnest mountains is covered with giant flames. They do not vanish but grow motionlessly larger, upward from the limits of the world and if it were not for the deep sound of water below, I know I could hear the sky burning there.

"The mines are finished," my father says. "Everything's oil and gas now, coal is nothing."

We move slowly east towards the flat darkness of the prairie. I curl up on the seat, my head in the bend of his thigh. I can hear his muscles shift against my ear as he controls the pedals, the levers, and when we are level at last and up to speed his right hand comes to rest heavy and cupped on my hip. But behind my eyelids I am not asleep; in fact, I may never be able to sleep again.

Speaking Saskatchewan

IN SUMMER the thick green poplar leaves clicked and flickered at him, in winter the stiff spruce rustled with voices. The boy, barefoot in the heat or trussed up like a lumpy package against the fierce, silver cold, went alone to the bush where everything spoke: warm rocks, the flit of quick, small animals, a dart of birds, tree trunks, the great lights in the sky at night, burning air, ground, the squeaky snow: everything spoke as he breathed and became aware of it, its language clear as the water of his memory when he lay in the angle of the house rafters at night listening to the mosquitoes slowly find him under his blanket, though he had his eyes shut and only one ear uncovered. Everything spoke, and it spoke Low German.

Like his mother. She would call him long, long into the summer evening when it seemed the sun burned all night down into the north, call high and slow as if she were already weeping and when he appeared beside her she would bend her wide powerful hands about his head and kiss him so hard his eyes rang.

"Why don't you answer, you?" she would speak against his hair. "Why don't you ever answer when I call, it's so dark, why don't you ever say a word?"

While he nuzzled his face into the damp apron at the fold of her thigh, and soon her words would be over and he heard her skin and warm apron smelling of saskatoon jam and dishes and supper buns love him back.

His sister laughed at his solitary silence. "In school are twenty-seven kids," she would say, "you'll have to talk, and English at that. You can't say anything Low German there, and if you don't answer English when she asks, the teacher will make you stand in the corner."

"R-r-r-right in front—of...people?" he would ask, fearfully.

"Yeah, in front of every one of them, your face against the wall. So you better start to talk, English too."

And she would try to teach him the English names for things. But he did not listen to that. Rather, when he was alone he practised standing in the corners of walls. Their logs shifted and cracked, talking. Walls were very good, especially where they came together so warm in winter.

But outside was even better, and he followed a quiet trail of the muskrat that had dented the snow with its tail between bullrushes sticking out of the slough ice, or waited for the coyote to turn and see him, its paw lifted and about to touch a drift, its jaw opening to its red tongue laughing with him. In summer he heard a mother bear talk to her cubs among the willows of the horse pasture, though he did not see them, but he discovered their sluffing paw prints in the spring snow and his father said something would have to be done if they came that close to the pig fence again. The boy knew his father refused to own a gun, but their nearest neighbour gladly hunted everywhere to shoot whatever he heard about, and so he folded his hands over the huge, wet paw prints and whispered in Low German, "Don't visit here any more. It's dangerous."

The school sat on the corner, just below the hill where the road turned south along the creek to the church and the store. In the church every Sunday there were hands waiting for him. At the top of the balcony stairs that began in the corner behind where the men sat, up there among wooden benches, with the visiting sound of people talking like heavy rain below them, were hands that could find things inside him. Huge hands with heavy broad thumbs working against each other on his neck, pressing down, together, bending his small bones until through his gaping mouth they cawed:

"C-C-C-CAT!"

"Yes, yes, like that, try to say it again, 'cat.'"

And he would, try; desperately, those marvellous hands holding him as if everything on earth were in its proper place and all the brilliant sounds that he could never make when anyone listened coming out of him as easily as if he had pulled a door, open.

"Cat."

He never looked at the school, the tiny panes of its four huge windows staring at him, staring when they passed. The day before he had to go there every day like his sister, the planes came over for the first time.

Their horses were pulling the wagon up the hill as slowly, steadily as they always did and it happened very fast, almost before he could look around. There had been a rumble from somewhere like thunder, far away, though the sky was clear sunlight and his father had just said in a week they could start bindering the oats, it was ripening so well, and his mother sat beside him broad and straight as always, her braided, waist-long hair coiled up for church under her hat, when suddenly the thundering planes were there as he turned, four of them, yellow-and-black, louder than anything he had ever heard. West over the school and the small grain fields and pastures and all the trees and hills to the edge of the world. His father would not look around, holding the horses in carefully, muttering,

"Now it comes here too, that war training."

But the boy was looking at his mother. Perhaps his own face looked like that next morning when the yellow planes roared over the school at recess, so low he saw huge glass eyes in a horrible leather head glare down at him before he screamed and ran, inside to the desk where his sister had said he must sit. When he opened his eyes the face of the teacher was there, her gentle face very close, smiling almost upside down at him between the iron legs of the desk beneath which he crouched. Her gentle voice, speaking.

"Come," she said, "come," and after a moment he scrambled to his feet. He thought she was speaking Low German because he did not yet know that what that word meant was spoken the same way in English. "Come."

Not touching him, she led him between desks to a thin cupboard against the wall opposite the windows and opened its narrow door.

Books. He has never imagined so many books. There may be a million.

She is, of course, speaking to him in English and later, when he remembers that moment again and again, he will never be able to explain how he can understand what she is saying. The open book in her hand shows him countless words: words, she tells him, he can now only see the shape of, but he will be able to hear them when he learns to read, and that the word "READ" in English is the same as the word "SPEAK," *raed*, in Low German and by reading all the people of the world will speak to him from books, he will hear them, when he reads he will be able to hear them, and then he will understand. He is staring at what he later knows are a few worn books on a few shelves, and then staring back at the few visible but as yet unintelligible words revealed by the book open in her hands, and slowly, slowly he understands that there are shelves and shelves of books in great stacks on many, many floors inside all the walls of the enormous libraries of the world where he will go and read: where the knowing she will now help him discover within himself will allow him to listen to human voices speaking from everywhere and every age, saying everything, things both dreadful and beautiful, and all that can be imagined between them; and that he will listen. He will listen to those voices speaking now for as long as he lives.

Chinook Christmas

THE WINTER I TURNED NINE was our first in southern Alberta, and the white scars of irrigation ditches circling lower and lower into the long, shallow hollow of our town uneven across the Canadian Pacific Railway seemed to me then like the trenches of some besieging army: the grey wrinkled snow driven there off the tilted fields, long, long welts carved in parallels below the square top of Chief Mountain sixty miles west where the implacable General of the Winds stood forever roaring at his troops: Advance! Relentless wind whining, roaring in one's head all fall, the trees bent so low east that one day I straightened up on the pedals of my bicycle and discovered I could stand motionless, balanced, the wind's weight a wall, a power that held me shivering uneasily facing into it.

But then I was nudged, pushed, clubbed and I let the wind wheel me round like always and I spread my arms akimbo, my jacket held wide at the waist and went no hands sailing along the gravel street, through three ridged stop corners on the fly to Jakie's house and leaned into his yard like a racing sloop, all canvas spread, and met him wobbling forward on his bike beside the little irrigation ditch that was filling their cistern for winter so I knocked him into that grey water and then he knocked me into it too.

"Let's ride to the main ditch," he said, trying to blink through the mud in his eyes.

"Sure," I said. "We'll get it anyways, we might as well get it good."

He was three years older than I and that summer we had become uneasy friends with the town's whole length of one-way wind between us because we were second cousins (twice removed at that, my father said, but for Canadian Mennonites that means a lot sometimes) and because of Anni and mostly because neither of us had any other friends. My sister Anni always knew what she wanted.

"We have to have a Christmas tree," she said. "How'll we ever find one here, nothing but sugarbeet fields and ditches?"

She was fourteen and the spring before when we left our bush homestead up north so my father could work on an irrigation dairy and Mama and Anni and I could thin beets, she had already been kissed there once or twice under a full moon, and she still thought that a good deal better than getting sunburned between endless beet rows, wrinkling up, hunched over like every other poor woman and child she saw stoop-shouldered in every field. Up north she and I had always ploughed our Christmas tree out of the muskeg, our dog bounding high through soft cushions of snow, the air so motionless between the muskeg spruce—flounced, layered and blazing white with brown and green edges.

"There's a tree on old Heidebrecht's front lawn," I said. "It's real pretty."

"Oh sure," and Anni sang, "Chop chop, hoora-a-a-il, Christmas in ja-a-a-il, how can we fa-a-a-il, they will throw out our heads in a pa-a-a-il."

"Anyways," I told her, "a Christmas tree isn't even Christian, it's heathen."

Old Emma Rajcht—"Always Right," (but in Low German it rhymes, Emma Rajcht Heidebrajcht)—had the biggest Mennonite house in town. He had finally sold his farm to one of his sons for an unbelievable price—that was what he was mostly right at, buying low and selling very high—and now he drove a black Buick to church twice every Sunday with his ancient daughter as stiff and erect as himself beside him; he always roared the motor until a cloud of bluish smoke was visible through the rear window before he slowly let out the clutch and began to move, shoving in the clutch a little as soon as the car threatened to go too quickly but never easing his foot off the gas.

All summer his lawn, shaded by giant cottonwoods and blue-coned spruce, was bright green like a frog's belly.

"A Christmas tree's heathen? Who said, smarty head?" Anni twirled around me.

"In Sunday school, Mr. Rempel," I said. He was tall with broad shoulders and had "adorable," Anni had once confessed, curly blond hair.

That stopped her; for two seconds. But I saw immediately it was astonishment at my still holding that outdated opinion that was spreading like a cat's tongue licking over her face. She laughed aloud. "He's no fun," she said irrelevantly. "In fact, he's kinda dumb."

"How do you know?" I hit her with all I had: "You've never even talked to him."

"He's a curly blond," over her shoulder, going into the kitchen. I never had enough for Anni, of anything.

The Christmas kitchen was a whole pasture of smells gone crazy in spring, not only from two kinds of cookies, oatmeal with one choc-olate chip topping each and pale almost brownly bluish shapes of ammonia creatures Mama had let me stamp out of thick dough, but also cinnamon rolls with their bottoms up exuding sweet brown syrup and dimpled raisins like twirled targets to aim an uncontrol-lable finger at—"Mama, Eric's poking the rolls!"—and tiny square pereschtje with their tops folded up into peaked and quartered little tents of ridged golden crust that oozed juices, red strawberry and royal purple saskatoon and pale creamy apple, how for the love of Christmas and stomach could anyone keep their hands—

"Eric!"

And outside was chinook. The night before a small bow of light had grown along the western horizon under the ceiling of clouds hammered down overhead like solid rafters; at the end of the day, the monolith of Chief Mountain sat for a moment against blue and an orange streak like a knife-tip about to slit open the rest of the horizon, a faint smell of crushed irrigated clover in summer slip-ping through to wander over the glazed drifts. And also a touch of warmth, very nearly a flare of mad possibility in the cold; today it blazed into actuality, my head huge as if its plates were unhinged for I could breathe that clover without sniffing after it, all the air burned

with it, the drifts already wrinkling down into sodden sponges
and the air swimming limpid like creek water on a May morning.
Chinook! It fondled my bare head. Our chickens sang behind their
windows, I opened the door and their acrid avian mist was swallowed whole, disappeared into the morning brilliance of chinook; our
white-faced cow lifted her head above the dry alfalfa of her manger,
her ears gesturing gently as they did whenever she was moved to
ponderous, liquid-eyed bovine contentment. Go on Boss, you bulgy
hay-chewer, your warm flanks to butt my head against, your long
soft teats swishing hot milk between my rhythmic fingers, go on you
globed warm femaleness, and breathe all that spring, that momentary maddening spring the day before Christmas.

"There are still some trees left, Mrs. Orleski on her lot," I said to
Anni, shifting the basket of tweeback to my other arm. She carried
two pails of layered pastry for Taunte Tien and though they were
heavier, they were actually easier to carry because she could walk
balanced. The basket in the basket of my bike would have been best,
but the chinook had only licked the gravel street dry in blotches
and left the rest wet, running everywhere under the snow-levelled
ditches. It was everywhere slurp and slide and temptation to not
catch your balance before you tucked your head and rolled soft and
squitchy and were all over coated with three-times gumbo like your
laden boots.

"She told us, a tree costs at least a dollar," Anni said.

"Yeah, the miserblist one, we'd never—"

"That's no word, 'miserblist.'"

"Miser-erbilist?"

"Miser-erbalist, rhymes with 'herb-alist.'" Anni sang, skipping a
puddle too nonchalantly perhaps and slipping beautifully but sliding
herself into balance so that nothing but her left pailbottom came
up small gravel and heavy, heavy gumbo. We wiped it off with snow,
left the food in Taunte Tien's barren kitchen with her small horde of
children rolling their small barbarian eyes at the steamy warmth of
things and ran out before the small barbarian fingers could—"Eric
and I have to get back because Mama needs us and Father is coming
home right after supper and the...." Anni hauled me out with her long
arm and swinging muddy pail and there was Jakie leaning against

the cottonwood in the front yard. Looking absolutely Chicago gang-
ster to the very bend of his leg and cap pulled tight over his eyes.

"If you want a tree so bad," he said, "why don't you take it?"

Anni actually stopped and looked at him. Chinooks touch
everyone differently: all he needed was a short machine gun.

"There's never nobody there at night," he said.

It was very hard to read Anni's expression, and Jakie must have
made the same mistake I made because he continued, still looking at
his fingernails which were very long and smooth with nice moons at
their base, "Anyways, who'd miss one shitty little tree?"

"I presume," Anni said, and her tone warned me instantly, "I
presume that if there is never nobody there, there must always be
somebody, and I presume further that not even an habitual criminal would be so idiotic as to steal under such conditions, leave alone
someone honest at Christmas when a chinook is blowing."

Her statement would have been stronger without either Christmas
or chinook, and I think Anni felt so too because we hadn't left Jakie
more than half a block behind, still leaning against the tree and studying the perfect moons of his fingernails, when she inexplicably
commented, "He won't even get as far as his stupid dad, he'll just
end up in jail."

"What's the matter with Onkel Willm?" I asked. To tell the truth, I
liked Onkel Willm. He was certainly the strongest man in town, not
much taller than me but so broad he had to shift sideways through
any door and he could place his thick arms under half a beef and
hoist it around and up onto a hook in one immense motion without
breathing hard or slipping on the sawdust under his butcher's chopping block. Unlike any other Mennonite grown-up, he cracked jokes
with me and so did Mrs. Cartwright who sold the meat for him. Mrs.
Cartwright was always dressed so perfectly, her face as careful as a
picture, and when she leaned over the counter, laughing, I always
wanted to laugh with her like every man who bought meat there
though I never saw a woman who did, her lips and teeth so red and
white and marvellously, smoothly exact. She laughed like no woman
I had ever seen, deeply, powerfully, her entire vivid body pushing
itself out at me and moving with it until I felt tight and awkward,
somehow—inexplicably then—ashamed.

"He's not our uncle, thank Jehoshaphat," Anni snapped, and then seeing me goggle-eyed said quickly, "There's Mr. Ireland, let's catch a ride!"

Mr. Ireland's dray with its unmatched greys was moving toward the train station, but it seemed that in any case Anni had intended not to go directly home but rather "downtown" as we called it— our town had three parallel streets south of the tracks and three north with avenues at right angles numbered 100 at the centre, and higher and lower on either side in anticipation of more or less measureless and endless expansion—so we hopped aboard and bounced along dangling our legs off the tailgate. The horses trotted while Mr. Ireland sang, the biggest grey plopping out hot, steamy buns, and Mr. Ireland interrupted himself to mutter, "Enough time for that, Jock, get on with you!" slapping the mountainous rear gently with a flat rein, and the buns appeared behind the wagon under us in perfect single-file pattern like a queue of smooth-headed children, steaming slightly as they sank out of sight in the gumbo. The chinook blustered violently through trees and over a roof and suddenly Mr. Ireland roared with it as we passed the Japanese Buddhist church that was swallowing a snake of small brown children,

"Oh, he shot her through the window,
And the bullet's in her yet!"

and the dray sighed silently across Main Street at 101 Avenue on its fat balloon tires salvaged from World War II fighter planes. A huge black truck with its grain box standing tight full of Hutterites, beards and polka-dotted kerchiefs facing into the wind, rolled past and squitched all of a grey pothole at us, but missed.

"Do men have yets too?" I asked Anni.

"Yets?"

"He sang, 'The bullet's in her yet."

Anni laughed. "No," she spluttered, "only women. And you have to shoot them through their windows to hit their yets!"

But then, still laughing, she knocked one of our pails off and we had to jump anyways because we were passing the high front of the largest grocery and hardware store, Doerksen Bros. Props., and

Rudy Wiebe: Collected Stories, 1955–2010

that's where Mrs. Orleski had her Christmas trees leaning against
the wall. Mrs. Orleski usually sold *Lethbridge Herald*s at the corner
for a nickel, perhaps two or three a day since Hermie Kudreck had
the town sewed up with home delivery—Hermie owned a ccm three-
speed by the time he was ten, a Harley Davidson at fifteen, and an
Olds convertible at nineteen, all starting from *Herald* saturation of
our town—but when Doerksen Brothers started playing Christmas
carols on the gramophone at the back of their store, she shifted to
their vacant lot: one day it was white, bare, the next heavy green,
thick with needled aroma like the mountains where Mrs. Orleski said
her son worked deep in the Crowsnest mines. I could not imagine
that then, crows' nests were bundles of sticks notched high in poplars
and a coal mine was....When her son came home for one day at
Christmas you could see the coal engrained in his skin like topsoil in
the drifts of a three-day prairie blizzard. His shoulders had a hockey
player's powerful slope and were only a little narrower than Onkel
Willm's and he liked to show his favourite muscle, a bulge when he
bent his elbow that heaved up and clenched itself rock-hard and not
even Whipper Billy Watson the heavyweight wrestling champion of
the world could muster that; he knew, for he had once challenged
Watson and that dead-white mound of muscle from Toronto had
backed off. Nothing but the usual stuff in his arm.

"Jolly old St. Nicholas, lean your ear this way...." murmured the
wall of the store. If Doerksen Brothers, Anni said, leaned any farther,
they would fall over.

"You kits still lookin'?" Mrs. Orleski pulled her hands from
between her three summer coats and whatever else she wore underneath, sweaters and skirts and every kind of unmentionable. "Sell,
lotsa sell this year, see," and she gestured around with her arms wide,
a little stump of a fireplug turning as if about to break into dance.
There were only three trees left, three scrunchy trees in a trampled scatter of spruce-tips and sodden snow; abruptly she wheeled
and her nostrils flared into the chinook, opening hugely like gills in
fast water, "Here, here! They leave it, the leetle branch, they leave it
lotsa...." and she was stooping, gathering with the swift inevitable
hands of workers, "Sometimes stump, have it too much branch...."
and she thrust them at me, offering in the wimpling eddy of the

sun-and-wind-warmed wall a stinging memory of motionless feath-
ered muskeg, our black dog plunging head and tail through the
crystalline velvet sinking of it, the indented spoors of rabbits and a
slither of weasels: Mrs. Orleski's two stubby arms filled with spruce
boughs like a proffered squirrel nest stuffed fat and full and warm for
the winter, "You take it, is good, hang it some places, Mama happy
so...." Offering the wistful windy madness of a gift.

"I'm sorry," Anni said, and I stared at her in horror. "We still have
no money."

"Wha? I no take it, your money...give for nutting, you, take!"

And I took and ran. Anni behind me argued, the very bend of her
body declaring you cannot accept a gift from someone as poor as
yourself and certainly not from anyone richer and so you refuse to
accept anything from anyone, ever. And finally thanked the old lady
almost angrily, as if forced, and followed me with her long legs scis-
soring through the last sunshine past the principal's yellow and green
house and across the schoolyard. The little Japanese houses stood
one by one along the south side of our street, their double windows
with their pale never-opened blinds dreaming even in the long winter
like unfathomable Buddhas.

"It's Christmas, and anyway it cleans up her lot."

But any word of mine just set Anni's teeth more visibly into her
bottom lip, her head lower into the branches as if she would chew
needles. Both her pails were stuck full, my basket was too small for
all my armful but I didn't drop a twig all the way home and I slid
neither flat nor flying in the mud either.

Old Emma Rajcht passed us, alone like a procession in his
smoking Buick. In the rich darkness of the car his whiskers flared
from the sides of his face like white flames reaching for the side
windows as he drove without headlights, his arms braced rigid
before him and his eyes staring ahead as if to illumine the fluid road
with their glare. The chinook seeped spruce through my head; had
I known about such things then I would have known I was at least
drunk when I heaved up my branches, waved, shouted,

"Frohe Wiehnachte!"

And his head turned round to us trudging the shoulder of the
road, heavily around like a spray of cannon wheeling and he saw me,

his eyes briefly the driven ends of spikes, and the huge polished flank
of the car lurched toward me as at a recognition before his head
trundled back and cocked forward again on his long neck over the
steering wheel and his stiff arms kept his shoulders rammed back
against the seat and his beaked nose defied that lunatic wind, dared
it to squirm him into the gumbo ditch, he would not turn that wheel,
he would not raise either his right foot from the gas or his left foot
from the clutch and so he roared away into the warm settling dusk
of Christmas Eve, finally merging far ahead of us into the misty dinosaur legs of the bare cottonwoods surrounding his immense yard:
an antediluvian monster roaring in futile and foehnish anthem the
cacophonous wonders of the Christ-child season. Gifts upon gifts,
the smell of gas and clutchplate snipped in our nostrils through the
green of spruce till we saw the rectangular windows of our house
stunned golden every one with the vanished sun reflecting from the
laden, burning bellies of the clouds, and the mud squishing under
our feet and the prick of spruce on our cold wrists and fingers. I
looked at Anni. Her hair streamed flat under wind, the cloven flames
of window and sky glistened, blazed in her eyes.

"Don't say a word," she said.

And I did that. Even when I saw our father was already home
because the dairy pickup was parked beside our door, I said nothing.
But once inside, oh, talk! Our house was packed tight with smells like
nuts in a Christmas cake and we hung our branches singing everywhere until its two rooms seemed flung all over with a green and
poignant spray. Then we stepped into the fresh darkness and the
purring, dialed cab of the truck wafted us to church, a wide building
where the men sat in two broad aisles on the right and the women
in two aisles on the left and we children crammed in front directly
under the benign (for tonight) faces of the ministers leaning over the
pulpit and the choir curved around behind them, and we sang those
Christmas songs our people had brought from half a world away, so
out of place now in the treeless, flat irrigation prairies but not at all
out of spirit:

Leise rieselt der Schnee,
Still und starr ruht der See;

Weihnachtlich glänzet der Wald,
Freue dich, Christkind kommt bald!

the high beautiful voices of the women, the deep heavy voices of the men, and the bright thread of my father's tenor between them where he sat behind me among rich farmers and storekeepers and workers and teachers and unemployed labourers. Two ministers spoke, very short and mostly stories, and there were several long prayers and the choir sang, several children's groups sang, and then we all sang again,

Nun ist sie erschienen, die himmlische Sonne...

and

O Fest aller heiligen Feste,
O Weihnacht, du lieblicher Schein...

and then young men came in with long boxes and gave every child a small brown bag which we were not allowed to open in church but we could so easily feel whether we had an orange or an apple and there was at least one chocolate bar and almost a whole handful of peanuts and either six or possibly seven candies, and then we sang,

Stille Nacht, heilige Nacht
Alles schläft, einsam wacht
Nur das traute, hochheilige Paar,
Das im Stalle zu Bethlehem war
Bei dem himmlischen Kind,
Bei dem himmlischen Kind.

And then, without talking or running around, we all went quickly and quietly home. No clouds now, the sky was brilliant, clear black with crystals of stars frozen over us, the air silent as a curtain: tomorrow would be very cold. And on our front step was a small wooden box. I bumped against it as I jumped for the door trying to get in fast to see whether I had an Oh Henry! or a Sweet Marie in my bag.

The board squeaked up—what was that? Those are oranges, my father said, Japanese oranges. They can be eaten. Roundly moist in their pale wrappers, they unzippered themselves under his fingernail symmetrically with a strange, sharp sweetness like regular little oriental shelves opening. Who could have left them for us? Such a vividly useless gift, all you could do was eat it. So we did; Anni and I each ate nine.

Then my father read, as he always did, from "And there went out a decree from Caesar Augustus..." all the way to where the shepherds returned to their flocks glorifying and praising God, and then we each said a very short prayer with the house so quiet now I could hear the coal shift as it burned in the stove and Anni and I placed our plates—like always the very biggest we could find—on the kitchen table under the spruce branches all ready for the gifts we knew we would get from the *Nätklos*—always useful gifts like toothbrushes or socks or a shirt at most—and then we climbed up the narrow stairs to our two small rooms with a final, tenth, Japanese shelving itself lingeringly into our mouths.

"Who was it?" Anni asked, breathing orange in the darkness.

I said, "Who knows?"

But I did. I knew it as certainly as child knows everything at Christmas. As certainly as the hard clear sanity of the north wind's song beginning at the window, and in my ear, our little house I believe swaying gently like a cradle, very, very gently.

THREE | PARALLEL REALITIES

The Angel of the Tar Sands

SPRING HAD MOST CERTAINLY, finally, come. The morning drive
to the plant from Fort McMurray was so dazzling with fresh green
against the heavy spruce, the air so unearthly bright that it swallowed the smoke from the candy-striped chimneys as if it did not
exist. Which is just lovely, the superintendent thought, cut out all
the visible crud, shut up the environmentalists, and he went into his
neat office (with the river view with islands) humming, "Alberta blue,
Alberta blue, the taste keeps—" but did not get his tan golfing jacket
off before he was interrupted. Not by the radio-telephone, by Tak
the day operator on Number Two Bucket in person, walking past the
secretary without stopping.

"What the hell?" the superintendent said, quickly annoyed.

"I ain't reporting this on no radio," Tak's imperturbable Japanese-
Canadian face was tense, "if them reporters hear about this one
they're gonna—"

"You scrape out *another* buffalo skeleton, for god's sake?"

"No, it's maybe a dinosaur this time, one of them real old—"

But the superintendent, swearing, was already out the door yelling
for Bertha who was always on stand-by now with her spade. If one of
the three nine-storey-high bucket-wheels stopped turning for an hour
the plant dropped capacity, but another archaeological leak could
stop every bit of production for a month while bifocalled professors

stuck their noses...the jeep leaped along the track beside the conveyor belt running a third empty already and in three minutes he had Bertha with her long-handled spade busy on the face of the fifty-foot cliff that Number Two had been gnawing out. A shape emerged, quickly.

"What the..." staring, the superintendent could not find his ritual words, "...is that?"

"When the bucket hit the corner of it," Tak said, "I figured hey, that's the bones of a—"

"That's not just bone, it's...skin and...." The superintendent could not say the word.

"Wings," Bertha said it for him, digging her spade in with steady care. "That's wings, like you'd expect on a angel."

For that's what it was, plain as the day now, tucked tight into the oozing black cliff, an angel. Tak had seen only a corner of bones sheared clean, but now that Bertha had it more uncovered they saw the manlike head through one folded-over pair of wings and the manlike legs, feet through another pair, very gaunt, the film of feathers and perhaps skin so thin and engrained with tarry sand that at first it was impossible to notice anything except the white bones inside them. The third pair of wings was pressed flat by the sand at a very awkward—it must have been a most painful—

"The middle two," Bertha said, trying to brush the sticky sand aside with her hand, carefully, "is what it flies with."

"Wouldn't it...he...fly with all six...six...." The superintendent stopped, overwhelmed by the unscientific shape uncovered there so blatantly.

"You can look it up," Bertha said with a sideways glance at his ignorance, "Isaiah, chapter six."

But then she gagged too for the angel had moved. Not one of them was touching it, that was certain, but it had moved irrefutably. As they watched, stunned, the wings unfolded bottom and top, a head emerged, turned, and they saw the fierce hoary lineaments of an ancient man. His mouth all encrusted with tar pulled open and out came a sound. A long, throat-clearing streak of sound. They staggered back, fell; the superintendent found himself on his knees, staring up at the shape which wasn't really very tall, it just seemed immensely broad and overwhelming, the three sets of wings now sweeping back and forth as if loosening up in some seraphic 5BX plan. The voice rumbled like thunder, steadily on.

"Well," muttered Tak, "whatever it's talking, it sure ain't Japanese."

The superintendent suddenly saw himself as an altar boy, the angel suspended above him there and bits of words rose to his lips: "*Pax vobis...cem...cum,*" he ventured, but the connections were lost in the years. "*Magnifi...cat...ave Mar....*"

The obsidian eyes of the angel glared directly at him and it roared something, dreadfully. Bertha laughed aloud.

"Forget the popish stuff," she said. "It's talking Hutterite, Hutterite German."

"Wha...." The superintendent had lost all words; he was down to syllables only.

"I left the colony, years ago I...." But then she was too busy listening. The angel kept on speaking, non-stop as if words had been plugged up inside it for eons, and its hands (it had only two of them, in the usual place at the ends of two arms) brushed double over its bucket-damaged shoulder and immediately that appeared restored, whole just like the other, while it brushed the soil and tarry sand from its wings, flexing the middle ones again and again because they obviously had suffered much from their position.

"Ber...Ber.." the superintendent said. Finally he looked at Tak, pleading for a voice.

"What's it saying," Tak asked her, "Bertha, please? Bertha?"

She was listening with overwhelming intensity; there was nothing in this world but to hear. Tak touched her shoulder, shook her, but she did not notice. Suddenly the angel stopped speaking; it was studying her.

"I...I can't...." Bertha confessed to it at last, "I can understand every word you...every word, but I can't say, I've forgotten...."

In its silence the angel looked at her; slowly its expression changed. It might have been showing pity, though of course that is really difficult to tell with angels. Then it folded its lower wings over its feet, its upper wings over its face, and with an ineffable movement of its giant middle wings it rose, straight upward into the blue sky. They bent back staring after it, and in a moment it had vanished in light.

"Oh, dear God," Bertha murmured after a time. "Our Elder always said they spoke Hutterite in heaven."

They three contemplated each other and they saw in each other's eyes the dread, the abrupt tearing sensation of doubt. Had they seen...and as one they looked at the sand cliff still oozing tar, the spade leaning against it. Beside the hole where Bertha had dug: the shape of the angel, indelible. Bertha was the first to get up.

"I quit," she said. "This job. Right now."

"Of course, I understand." The superintendent was on his feet. "Tak, run your bucket through there, get it going quick."

"Okay," Tak said heavily. "You're the boss."

"It doesn't matter how fast you do it," Bertha said to the superintendent but she was watching Tak trudge into the shadow of the giant machine. "It was there, we saw it."

And at her words the superintendent had a vision. He saw like an opened book the immense curves of the Athabasca River swinging through wilderness down from the glacial pinnacles of the Rocky Mountains and across Alberta and joined by the Berland and the McLeod and the Pembina and the Pelican and the Christina and the Clearwater and the Firebag rivers, and all the surface of the earth was gone, the Tertiary and the Lower Cretaceous layers of strata had been ripped away and the thousands of square miles of black bituminous sand were exposed, laid open, slanting down into the molten centre of the earth, *O miserere, miserere*, the words sang in his head and he felt their meaning though he could not have explained them, much less remembered Psalm 51, and after a time he could open his eyes and lift his head. The huge tar sands plant, he knew every bolt and pipe, still sprawled between him and the river; the brilliant air still swallowed the smoke from all the red-striped chimneys as if it did not exist, and he knew that through a thousand secret openings the oil ran there, gurgling in each precisely numbered pipe and jointure, sweet and clear like golden brown honey.

Tak was beside the steel ladder, about to start the long climb into the machine. Bertha touched his shoulder and they both looked up.

"Next time you'll recognize it," she said happily. "And then it'll talk Japanese."

Seeing is Believing

[1982–1983/1984]

a. "Why don't you just do it," he said, "and be done with it. Beginning, middle, end—the way stories have always been made. Go ahead, write."

"It's so boring," she muttered.

"It certainly isn't as boring as writing about writing."

"I never said I wanted to write about writing."

"Look," he said, trying to be helpful, "it's the way people live, in sequence, they meet and something doesn't happen and then they look at each other again or meet again and something does happen— somewhere in time, though maybe not connected, and that's a beginning and out of that happens a middle and maybe even an—"

"Dear god," she groaned, "it's so dull!"

"Damn it, why write at all then?"

"What is there to do that's better?" she said.

b. Once upon a time in a land not too far away there lived a young maiden. She was intelligent and beautiful as maidens invariably are, and of course she was very unhappy. You see, her father who adored her had died while she was but a child and her stunningly beautiful though not particularly bright mother, unable to cope with the large estate her husband left her, quickly remarried. Her new husband, so considerate and courteous in courtship, turned out to be a clever brute on the make who blatantly favoured his twin sons from a previous marriage. Very soon the mother, worn out by cares in the usual patient suffering fashion, and with only slightly worse timing than intelligence, died.

It seems hardly necessary to elaborate on the fate of our heroine. Her twin stepbrothers noticed her only to tease her and, as they grew older, to chase screaming around the great house. Her stepfather was too preoccupied enlarging his enormous estate to notice anything; he simply kicked her aside when she got in his way. By the time she turned ten she was strong enough to be useful, and so she was sent to work in the barns. She carried hay and oats and water all day long to the one hundred horses stabled there, and after feeding she had to clean the aisles and gutters because of course the more those strong, beautiful animals ate, the more manure there was to shovel. Often she was so exhausted that she fell asleep on the straw in an empty stall, and one day her stepfather noticed this and said she might as well live there; it would save her time and probably be better for the horses. So she took her blanket and the picture of her father, which was all she owned, and cleared a small space for herself in the loft behind the hay bales. Soon she smelled so much like the stables that her stepbrothers called her Barney.

As she grew older, Barney learned how to groom the horses as well, but of course she was never allowed to ride one. That was reserved for her stepfather and stepbrothers only. Every day at ten fifteen the brothers would walk into the stables in their beautiful riding costumes, smelling like Brut or Igor or something, and parade down the aisle poor Barney had laboured to clean, deciding which horses they would ride. Every day.

Until one spring morning. As Barney led out their mounts, the soft sunlight flickered a particular aura about her there between the shining horses against the dark opening of the barn. The twins broke off their usual banter; they stared. Silently Barney held out the reins to them, but they did not move. It seemed that both were seeing her for the very first time.

c. "De-constructionists are not smart-ass, you ninny," she said. "They are parodic, they are trying to break down our conventional under-standing of language and rebuil—"

"All language is convention, what the hell else can it be? Look, it's the one, the greatest co-operative venture known to humanity, without it—"

"Aren't there a few other 'co-operative ventures'?"

"Silly, I mean on such a massive scale, see, we both agree this thing is called 'bed,' everybody who speaks English, maybe a billion people or so all agree, this is 'bed,' otherwise—"

"They won't ever call it 'bad,' not 'bed' but 'bad'?"

"Oh, some of them will have a poor accent, sure, a handicap but we all know what they really mean, they're just not quite able to—"

"What if I know better, I can hear exactly what I'm saying and I say it that way because I mean it, this is not 'bed,' it's 'bad.'"

"Yeah, that's de-constructionist all right," he said, after a moment's thought "it probably started because they're all foreigners and can't talk properly anyway and that gave them the idea, probably Frenchmen or Marxists."

d. In the high glass and concrete departure area of an airport echoing with arrivals and leavings, with persons repeatedly paged but apparently never appearing to lift receivers and to be heard by an ear waiting for a voice, somewhere, there was a small circle of people. If they had faced outward they would have resembled muskoxen of the Canadian Arctic islands backed around young to confront enemies, but these faced in upon themselves: they were bending gradually closer and closer together, intent only upon the slowly tightening sphere they made. It could have been a family, a mother, a son, several daughters, a father. Between the slabs of echoing glass a film of quiet gathered about them, it might have been that the father or a daughter was leaving. Certainly none of them had the worn, devastated skin of someone recently hurled for hours near the edges of space. Perhaps the son was leaving, or a daughter and they were vainly trying one last time to look into each others eyes, to see as they never had all of themselves at the same instant while their hands and arms groped around and beyond the person pressed

against them for the next, trying to feel every bone in every individual body they suddenly knew they loved with an overwhelming
conviction into the very cell circle and absolute affirmation of their
own fingers meeting to clutch themselves. It seemed they should
really be hollow globes, inside and outside every one of each other, to
be touching completely every surface in the desperate singing of all
the pullulating nerves they had discovered within themselves, everywhere. Perhaps the mother was leaving.

e. "Will you write me a letter every day?"

"Then I'd have time for nothing but to write you letters."

"Really?"

"A good letter, yes."

"That would be lovely. You're a superb writer, but you've never
written me an all-day letter."

"I will write you. An all-day letter, the most perfect letter possible;
immediately, I will send it to you special delivery, Express as they say,
and every day you'll read it all day and it will tell you everything you
want to know of me and of you and of us, it will be a letter you can
read forever and never grow tired of, absolutely satisfying whenever
you so much as glance at it, you could wear out the paper reading it
so you better put it under glass and never touch it again until your
looking wears it out, wears the letters right off the paper through
glass, I will type it perfectly on an electric typewriter on hard, white
paper and you can read it forever and it will—"

"What will it say, tell me, this perfect letter?"

"Have you put it under glass?"

"Yes, of course, my eyes are wearing it out. What?"

"It will say, a b c d f g h i j k l m n o p q r s t u v w x y z. And I'll
sign it, perfectly."

"Every day I should read that?"

"Yes, perfectly complete, just arrange it, it will say whatever you
want it to say."

"I guess that's all carpenters do too, arrange lumber, or potters
mud...."

"Every day I want to say exactly what you want me to say—isn't
that good? The perfect letter."

"I couldn't even make the word 'love' in your letter."

"Why couldn't you?"

"You left out the letter 'e.'"

"What?"

"You didn't say 'e.'"

She hesitated, then said quickly, "You noticed that?"

"Yes."

"Actually," she said, "I did say it, I was talking fast and I said 'a b c dee f,' I just ran it together a little, that's all, but I rea—"

"There isn't much of a letter you can make out of the lumber of the English alphabet if you don't have an 'e.'"

"You're not listening to me."

"I am, and you didn't say it. If you had written it out you'd have no argument. No 'please,' no 'remember,' or 'beauty,' 'sweetheart'...'we'...'love'...."

"There's a lot of useable four letter words," she said, "without 'e's."

"There is only one four letter word."

"Yes," she said, "'mama.'"

"No. There is only one four letter word and I've never liked the smell of it. It stinks."

"'Gold'?" she asked.

He would not answer. After a moment she spoke again, "Could you write me a love letter without an 'e'?"

He spoke then, very carefully, "I-would-not-want-to-try."

f.   It was so dark they could not see each others' faces when the hunters finally heard the beaver coming. The sound of the creek running over stones played back to them from the cliffs in an endless lullaby and they stood still as trees against the willows, their shapes gone now from dark into darkness. They had been waiting so long for that quiet splash, that imperceptible breaking of surface in the pond before them that at first they could not recognize the sound for anything it might be: it seemed merely...noise...coming over the narrow water before them from the sand bar overgrown with willows, a small racket as if something was being dragged through willows and alder brush, an ever louder bumping between bushes. And nattering, like old workers trudging to the job and already anticipating a

weekend. And then there fell into the indecipherable black sheet
of water before them such a clumsy...plop!...one seeming bellyflop
and then another, that the hunters nudged each other in astonishment, the very turns of their heads in the darkness betraying their
utter incomprehension: were these the secret beaver they had never
seen, whose dams measured and tiered the creek in steps between
every bend and rapid where each fall weekend revealed more poplars
devastated like wheatstraw, mown down and hurled against those
still, temporarily, standing? The hunters strained to see, still touching
each other for fear one or the other would make a sound; they tilted
forward into the darkness, and then they saw upon the invisible,
suddenly silent water a string of starlight slowly being drawn.

"Okay, there," one of them breathed.

A click, the black-green water surfaced in one spot of brilliant
light. A beaver head there, a small blotch quickly turning and gone,
the larger hump of back and tail flipping, Smack!, into a roil of water
and gone, the hunters cursing each other almost aloud but unable
to finish an oath before the head again surfaced, the light centred
on it, and there was a tremendous CRASH. The cliffs hammered it
back against their heads like clubs and the water exploded, seemed
to smash in pieces out of the yellow light. And then again, an instant
too late, another CRASH smashing the pieces further into pieces.

"Shit!"

"Did you get the bugger?"

"Sure as hell you didn't!"

"Well I—"

"Sh-h-h..." the boy with the light hissed.

A head again; nose circling high out of the broken water. Was it
the other one stupidly searching in the relentless light to smell its
way into discovery, breathe invisibility there?

The tremendous crashes this time were simultaneous and so overwhelming that only a clanging hammered in the hunters' heads, on
and on, while the light wavered, searching over the pond. Gradually
the sound of the rapids returned through iron to its gentle insistence. But there was nothing on the surface of the water. Only a dark
green glister, and then white bits moving, it could have been autumn
leaves; or bone.

g. "What were you doing the day I turned sixteen?"

"I wasn't born yet."

"So what were you doing, November sixteen?"

"I was with my mother. Looking at a van Gogh exhibition."

"In Canada? Where—Montreal?"

"No, Esterhazy, Saskatchewan—or maybe it was Cereal, Alberta."

"A van Gogh exhibition in Esterhazy or Cereal?"

"Why not? They'd never had one there before."

"I suppose not."

"It was the first and only van Gogh exhibition to ever travel to North America and the paintings were hung at three-foot intervals all around the school gym, just at eye level, all those superb blazing golden Arles vineyards and bridges and canals and purple wheeling nights and thick corn fields, they made the gymnasium stinking of basketball and wrestling mats burn with rainbows, I was swimming in rainbow fire, turning somersaults like a porpoise in the Gulf Stream."

"Your mother really liked it."

"Not really. It just gave her a huge belly ache."

h. Barney, still holding the horses' bridles, looked from one brother to the other in similar amazement. Slowly she understood that, in their own peculiar way, the twins were as beautiful as any horses she had ever seen. Their very twinishness was like a mirror, doubling the seeing of them with tiny, charmingly distinctive particularities.

"Hey," one of them laughed at last, it was Astor who had a small dusting of beard, "why don't you...come ride with us?"

"Yes," Charles laughed also, "please do."

"I've never ridden," Barney said, even more amazed. "I wouldn't know how."

"We'll teach you," the twins said together, but they really did not have to. The bodies of horses were so familiar to Barney that when she at last mounted one, she felt with her legs what she had already always known with the rest of her body. So they rode all day, and if the estate had not been so enormous they certainly would have discovered every corner of it. They rode about in silent happiness: only occasionally would their glances meet and one or the other would suddenly laugh and break into a gallop or jump across a creek or a fence, and the other two would instantly follow. The sun was almost down before they noticed that their horses were exhausted and that they themselves were hungry.

"Come to the house for tea," Charles said.

"Yes," Astor laughed, "please, please do."

So after they had rubbed down the horses together, they went up into the house. In the rose arbour opening off the library, they were served tea. Through the glass doors Barney could see the room she remembered better than any other of the house she had once lived in: the foldy leather chairs, the globes and maps, books scattered and stacked, the dark bookshelves to the ceiling; it was almost as if she could smell her father's pipe, the faint sweetness of it. Then she realized that the twins had bent towards her; that each was holding one of her hands!

"Let's get married," they both exclaimed together, laughing.

Barney was puzzled. "Which one?"

"It doesn't matter," Astor said, and Charles finished his thought, "Not even father can tell us apart—one day Astor has the beard and the next day I do."

"We're both exactly the same," Astor said, "you want to see?"

And indeed, Charles and Astor were as alike as two roses. Then they all three put their arms around each other in the rose arbour and laughed and laughed.

"It would be perfect," Charles said.

"Come, marry us," Astor echoed.

i. "Would you love me even if we weren't married?"

"You believe I love you now?"

"You just said so."

"That was at least fifteen minutes ago."

"But your actions haven't changed in fifteen minutes, they—"

"Actions are reflex, habitual, one's body is too lazy to discover new ones."

"I believe you love me."

"Good."

"Would you love me still even if—"

"I don't know."

"I know."

"What do you know?"

"That I want to love you, married or not."

"Good. I want to too."

"So show me you love me. I want to see it, right now."

"We've done everything seeable, a thousand times over, on three continents, or four."

"Come on, lover, you're the one with the famous imagination, now come on!"

"How about...this?"

"Very nice...but no good, you did that on June 23rd, 1981."

"I did? This too?"

"Hmm...I don't think so...no, that was on October 2nd, 1976."

"You're sure, never since then?"

"Never."

"Aw, sweetheart, there is nothing on earth so reassuring as loving a computer."

j. Under the quick knife, the body of the beaver slowly revealed itself. It was a knife-point unzippering, the gradual removal of a fur coat to expose a yellowish fat nakedness.

"You ever see a seal lying on a rock?" the skinner asked. "Maybe in a zoo somewhere?"

The woman was looking at his knife with a certain abhorrent intensity; she said nothing, and since the man did not look up, he did not see the slight shake of her head, which might in any case have been no more than a suppressed shudder.

"They're a lot longer, but they have the same kind of bloated, boneless body," the skinner continued. "Maybe all water animals do, probably whales too, though I've never seen one. Skinned. Their skeletons are so deep inside layers of meat and fat, they don't seem to have any bones at all to look at. Look here, two inches of fat, turning my big trees into fat, the bugger."

The woman said nothing. His left hand was clenched in the roll of greasy fur and was trying to tear it back under the quick, short slashes of the knife; both his hands were thick with fat and blood, she could not imagine them touching her, anywhere.

"You cut a hole in it," she said, pointing, "there."

"Shit!" his hands stopped and he looked up at her, grinning. "You're watching me too close."

"Don't you like me watching you?"

"You're the one doesn't like it," and he bent to his work again. "That's just a tiny cut, not like the bullet holes. I'll stretch it out carefully and you can sew it shut with two stitches. When it's cured, no one will ever notice."

"What makes you think I'd touch that?"

"That's the woman's work, sewing...and when it's stretched and dry you have to chew it soft too, carefully day after day just chew it, till it's cured all soft and we can wrap it around our feet, keep warm at night."

"All my six years of braces to chew a dry beaverskin?"

He laughed, "What are beautiful teeth good for?" and did not look up to see her baring them at him. "You'll make this softer than layered silk, you'll see, the inner fur so soft you'll...have you ever made love on beaver fur?"

She bent her slender legs up against her breast, wrapped her arms around them. Her chin found its notch between her knees.

"I don't know," she said slowly, "if I could make love to a beaver."

"That's not what I meant," he said. "That is not what I meant, at all."

What was left of the beaver lay on its back. When she looked at it with half-shut eyes it appeared to be a pale, bloated torpedo tipped with two enormous yellow teeth and black gaps of nostrils. Its tiny front legs with their webbed claws seemed folded in some prayerful petition. But when she opened her eyes wide, it looked like nothing more than a plastic bag of bruised fat.

k. "No language is translatable," she said.

"You're exactly wrong, the genius of language is that it is eminently translatable."

"No, it isn't. Every language has its own systems of meaning, of reflecting what you see. If you have no past tense in a language, you cannot think about pasts."

"That's exactly where de-constructionists so-called become so ridiculous. They take words with fine, perfectly ordinary meanings and break them up so you can't recognize the most usual—'desiring' becomes 'de-siring,' a beautiful word like 'ineffable' becomes a contorted obscenity like 'Effing the Ineffable.' It's dreadful."

"That has nothing to do with what I was saying; and aren't your examples rather tendentious?"

"So what's tendentious? These so-called writers use the accidents of phonemology to get their tendentious meanings, usually obscene, into—"

"All words are play."

"Don't jack around too. I'm talking about phonemes, sounds, not phenomes, facts."

"I know," she said. "All words are play and you just did it."

"You're being ridiculous! Words are the way human beings handle reality. You can make a game out of eating, but if you don't eat at all, you're dead."

"I agree. Words are the deadliest game of all."

"See, you're at it again, jacking around with words, once you start there's no stopping. It's like when you start to look for risque shapes, soon everything longer than it is wide is phallic, everything rounded is a breast—"

"Everything with a round opening, vaginal."

"Exactly, so take it one step further, to translation."

"I thought we agreed, languages are not translatable."

"We didn't agree! If that thing can be 'the slipper,' it can certainly be 'die Pantoffel' as well."

"It's 'der Pantoffel.'"

"Okay okay, German expert, now, you're taking a boat cruise down the Rhine and you buy a card showing the Lorelei cliffs and you write me in Canada, 'Hey Lover, here I am sailing down the River Clean and we've just passed Lorel's Egg'...isn't that ridiculous?"

"Hey, that's pretty good."

"It's a joke, a silly meaningless joke based on mixed-up German/English phoneme accidents!"

"Actually, I find it ironically meaningful, really, the River Clean, I'll never—"

"Oh, for Pete's sake!"

"I'll never see that miserably dirty, abused river the same way again, my sweet, and who is Pete, eh?"

"The old Pete, I'm sure, black with a glowing red pitchfork."

"Oh...I thought you had a pete—r."

"Probably, and you no doubt have a hairy!"

"Isn't she nice?"

"Oh, for—"

n. At first they could not believe it, but the fact was that the streets of the town were so narrow between overwhelming walls of white-washed stone that they could not walk two abreast. Then they simply laughed; if anyone met them they would have to turn past each other sideways.

But fortunately they met no one. The cobblestones, rough as if just gathered from a field, led them downwards toward the centre in the gradual evening and they were so excited by this ancientness, this definite Before Christ antiquity still being lived in in a clustered town they had glimpsed like a white-tiled splotch against a cove of the blue Mediterranean; so ecstatic at their own nerve of turning away from their planned route and leaving their car locked in the shadow of a wall and just walking (they had seen immediately there was no question of driving down what was obviously little more than a topless tunnel), leaving the technological safety of their car and just walking with nothing but their handbags ("never leave your travellers' checks or passport anywhere") firmly tucked under their arms; neither was even wearing stockings, just a loose cotton dress for the heat, and sandals.

They met no one. Perhaps it was the time for evening meal; they could hear voices and kettles, pots through open windows too high to look into but letting in, at last, the evening coolness though they were still perspiring from the tremendous sun all day, their skin still glowing, and then turning a corner they saw what must be people passing far below them where it seemed another street perhaps as narrow as their own crossed; but when they got there, laughing to themselves a little in anticipation, they were still alone.

"Make your photos?"

It was a moment before either realized they had been spoken to;
in English. In any case, the intersection would have forced them
to decide in which of five directions to face here where the cobblestones emerged out of their straight narrowness and circled about
themselves. Even the untrained soles of their feet could feel that; if
they had been blind, if the whole town were blind, the circled stones
would tell them exactly where they were; and then the tops of their
feet felt suddenly cold as if along one of the streets a breath had
come up from the sea. A man was standing in the fold of one wall.
And then they realized that it was he who had spoken to them. A
square camera, was it actually of wood?, stared at them, its black
cloth draped over his arm.

"Oh!" the shorter woman said, frightened. "Oh...I...."

"It's much too dark," the other woman said with certain technological assurance.

"No," the man said without moving and without inflection. And
indeed the lens at the centre of the wooden face seemed to flicker,
it clicked precisely even as they stood turned slightly away from
it, their lower bodies poised as it seemed for flight but their faces
caught exposed; perhaps quite unguarded and open. His left hand
moved, presenting a piece of paper.

"Oh, no you don't," the other woman said. "We're driving on immediately, we're not staying anywhere to pick up a picture tomorrow,
we're not going to be pressured by some unscrupulous—"

But the paper already in her hand was the picture. She recognized
herself in bright sunlight: her back, she was getting out of a taxi in
front of her own suburban house and there where her three tall children running, it seemed they were running down the curved walk to
greet her! She could not believe what she saw in her hand, her three
children, their faces....

"Where's mine?" the shorter woman demanded beside her.

The man had glanced once at the picture he had taken and now he
quickly shook his head. "No," he said, crouching back as if he would
have been happy to disappear into the wall, "it is not good, no."

"Where's John?" the other woman said, still staring at the picture.

Rudy Wiebe: Collected Stories, 1955–2010

"You're a fake!" the shorter woman spit out. "You're all alike, fakes trying to get money out of us, well, what do I look like in front of my house, eh? Show me, come on!"

But the picture she received did not show her. There was no person on it at all. Only the straight concrete walk between the two birches leading to the front door of her house. There was no one there at all.

"There's just the three kids," the other woman said, still staring.

"I did not want to take it," the man said to the shorter woman, his face hunched painfully together; his voice so deeply gentle, almost as if he were praying the Miserere.

"Where's my John!" the other woman screamed.

They stood side by side feeling the stones under their unwilling feet. They had not even planned to visit this town, their car was waiting for them, with one slight twist of a key it would carry them instantly, permanently away. But here they felt the circled stones, revelations laid before their defenseless eyes.

o. "Please, don't do that."

"Sweetheart, I want to talk to you about it."

"Why?"

"Because I like it, I want to experience more of—"

"Then why not just read it again?"

"I will, I will."

"Readers nowadays are such meaning hounds, sniffing, sniffing after nothing but meaning, yes, I get a whiff here, there's a spoor of meaning, sniff, sniff...if that was all there was to meaning a writer could just make one big stink and be done with it: the husband is a son of a bitch! Period!"

"It means a lot more than—okay, I'm not looking for meanings, it just is, okay? But...why did you arrange the parts in the order you did?"

"I don't know."

"Look, I don't believe that, when you write you're so careful you—"

"That's why they're labelled 'a,' 'b,' 'c,' etc.—you can read them in any order you please."

"But 'b' comes after 'a,' and 'h' always before 'j,' so—"

"Not when you write words they don't."

"What? Are you trying to make a word out of—"

"Try making your name, for all I care."

"My...."

"Read them in any order you please, only please!"

"A story has to have a pattern!"

"Not necessarily. It could be—a necklace, with various beads in a relationship to each other, that's all."

"Then...I don't see the string."

"Why do you have to see it? You sense perhaps it's there, some-where at the centre of things, but in good necklaces you never see the string, only individual beads juxtaposed. Don't be so damned logical!"

"Okay, the true beauty of a necklace is brought out when it's hung around a neck, right? So whe—"

"Right! You're the neck."

"Me?"

"Yes you. You've read my story, you're wearing the necklace."

"Oh. Has it..." he hesitated, then plunged on, "has it made me beautiful?"

"You always are," she said, suddenly moved by a profound love. "I don't really know, about the necklace. Maybe you don't need it."

"But I want it."

"I know. But maybe the story isn't really a necklace. Maybe it's just a...a random scatter of beads, as spilled on a bed."

"Not a 'bad'?"

"No, bed, b-e-d, bed."

"Of course," he laughed. "If you want to, right away."

Millstone for the Sun's Day

MOST OF THE PEOPLE seemed to be already on the docks when the
boy and his parents arrived, but the press parted swiftly for them.
Without hesitation the boy passed down the long dock, the ladies
smiling and the men reaching to pat his head, to where the boats
lifted easily in the quick morning sunlight. Turning on the last quay,
he saw the Yacht. Its white with imperial black piping burned under
the solstice sun and, not quite able to believe it, he turned with a
laugh to his mother just behind him.

"Mom, can I really ride on it?"

And his father's hand came down on his shoulder with his deep
voice, the people all about them quiet and looking, "Joey, just go
ahead—over there. We can't be late."

But the boy was looking at his mother still. Usually when he asked
her a question his father did not answer. When the boy had come
into the kitchen that morning to find the porridge steaming in his
bowl but with the unexpected delight of brown sugar beside it, his
father had been saying,

"Mary, it's better now than maybe later. You've never said anything
against it until—"

But his mother, usually so gentle and quiet, her back stiffly turned
and her hands slicing bananas—brown sugar and bananas both

on porridge in one day, hey, this was really a holiday—interrupting fiercely, "We don't *have* to let them!"

His father stood rigid as at a blasphemy. "What—Mary—what in all the almighty world—not *have* to?" his voice hanging on incredible pitch, the sunlight in the big-windowed kitchen gleaming on the hair of his half-lifted, abruptly paralyzed arm. Then he saw the boy in the doorway. "Joey! We didn't even hear you. And dressed already! Ready to go."

"Uh-huh—we better hurry, huh, for the ride?"

His father was smiling, bending to him, swinging him aloft so his head almost touched the ceiling, his father was so tall. The boy cried with delight as he swung up and over, and then he was plopped down facing the steaming porridge. He turned to his mother, laughing. "Mom, we can all ride the Yacht 'cause it was me drew the Lottery. At the meeting-house, eh Mom?"

But his mother did not turn or speak. When she moved at last, placing the tiny bowl of sliced bananas beside his porridge, she sat down beside him, her features tight and stiff, as now on the dock, but her eyes, now bunched against the direct sun, distorting even more her lovely face. The boy did not like her frown. She was always too happy for frowning; rather, singing in the kitchen, shaping towers and boats with his building blocks, walking in the Windy Woods and naming the birds flicking high on the tips of the ferns. Now, suddenly, the boy twisted from under his father's hand and tugged at her dress. "Mom, don't you *want* to ride in the Capitular's Yacht?"

She bent swiftly, her summer skirt flaring out like a dark blot and she was hugging him tight against her breast, silently. Over her shoulder he saw the dark lanes of the people up the lift of the dock, their pale faces turned stiff in their smiles against the dead-blue sky. His mother shivered, and he pushed back.

"Mom, shouldn't I of pulled the Lottery yesterday?"

It was incomprehensible. He could remember the disappointment of his friend, Eric, behind him in the line and all the people in the meeting-house waving and clapping for him, the Capitular's hand holding his high to show the mark, the clapping hands flickering everywhere so that he could not see his parents though he knew exactly where they were from watching them as he inched forward in

the long line. For an instant only he saw his father's black onyx ring
flash in the sunlight from the great arched window in the rhythmic
clapping at his winning draw. He was looking at his mother's face
now, but her eyes avoided him. And then, between the people beyond
the sheen of her hair, he caught a flash of white and he looked up.
A slim white figure came down the dock, floating without sound
or seeming motion, the gold-and-crimson ribbon across its breast
merging with the crimson of the cantors he knew following.

"Mom!" the boy jogged her shoulder, "Look—look! It looks—just
about, all dressed up, like—" he stopped, his recognition shimmering
away, then, "isn't it—like Miss Grierson? Look!"

His father's hand fell on his shoulder. "Joey, stand over here,
where we belong," and he was hustled to the very edge of the quay
where the Yacht waited, motionless as a castle in the water. Past
his father's black trouser-leg the boy saw the long bent line of red
figures and hats ebbing down between the people and heard the
gentle sound that wavered, rising and falling, in the still air, a sound
as he had never heard from them before though he had gone to the
meeting-house since before he could remember, as everyone once a
week, and heard them chant in the rood-loft.

"Dad," the boy tugged at the trouser. "What're they singing?"

His father's hand slid over his mouth, the wide ring clicking
against his teeth, and he could only look as the flaring baldachin
of the Capitular emerged at the head of the dock, flashing red-gold,
and the procession stopped and parted, and at long last, in the rising
sound, the Capitular at the head of the Lesser Capitulars moved
down through the dividing ranks of the cantors to stand beside Miss
Grierson in the middle of the dock before the boy and his parents.

The Capitular's benign smile broadened. "Joey." His voice was so
deep in the motionless air. "Come forward please." The boy had no
time to look to his mother. His father's hand was at his back and he
was under the Capitular's raised palm. "Joey. You won the Lottery last
evening. Therefore you are our special guest today. We will ride in
the Yacht together to Sun Rock, and then perhaps around the island.
Will you like that?"

Directly facing the Capitular, the question of what every child on
the island dreamed of doing stirred a vague apprehension in the boy,

for there was something—and then he forgot not only the correct words but also the bow for suddenly he knew and he spoke without thinking, "Sir, your Highest—but—but there aren't my friends here."

From the low gasp of the people he knew his breach of whatever was correct and shrank back even as the laugh rumbled above him.

"Of course. But all your little friends *know* you are going with us. On the Yacht. They have all gone to the picnic at the Garden in the Valley, like you did on this day last year. But you are the special one, the only child," the hand was on his head now, the great form bending over him, "that can come on the Yacht. Because you drew the Lottery. Now, don't you like that?"

This time he remembered, and bowed. "Yes. Your Highest."

The hand lifted from his head and the sound of the cantors belled. The boy stood motionless, as they all, eyes on the gold slashing of the Capitular's robe, hearing,

> The shepherd heard the sheep always
> High hummocked humitry
> The day of wrath to scath shall pass
> High seared in scarify

The diagonal gold and crimson on white of the other figure before him drew the boy's eye. So very close now, he could recognize Miss Grierson even less than from far away. Her face was immobile, as if caked in something not her own skin, and her eyes, which had laughed only days before with him and Eric building sandcastles in the schoolyard now stared away as through all the people and over the water and through the very sun itself. He stared at her in turn, the Capitular's long intoning above his head not moving him from his amazement. Then abruptly he was wheeled about and, as he twisted for one more look, his father's voice said, "Joey," and he had to turn.

Wonder of wonders to the boy, he walked up the short gangplank first, followed by his parents. And at the head of the gangplank, beard almost brushed into order, stood the old man who sunned himself day after day in the park across the street from the school. No child knew his name, or ever talked about him; no child had ever seen him do anything, but his standing there at rigid attention was merely a minor amazement as the boy and his parents, followed by the Capitular under his baldachin, stepped aboard the Yacht. In a moment the deck was filled, the motors vibrated, and they were out on the water, smoothly, as if unmoving in their dignity.

No one said a word; motionless their faces sat upon their bodies like blocks. The boy squirmed, trying to look between, around them—

"Joey." The Capitular's voice stung him to stiffness. "You wish to explore the Yacht?" He had not and could not say it but the Capitular, seated in the circle of the Lesser Capitulars and the cantors, seemed to pluck out his thought. The gentle voice continued, "Yes. They always do. You are our guest—go."

The boy's mother, the only other person seated, was holding the boy's hand tightly. But when he looked at her, she nodded hastily. "Yes. I—I'll stay here—now."

For an instant he was disappointed. But how often had he dreamed of exploring the largest, the most beautiful vessel on the island! He was gone, slipping between the people. The tall masts where the flags curled and stiffened in the breeze of their motion; the black-bronze railing; the polished wall of the wheelhouse where high above through the window glinted the skipper's glasses; the coiled ropes like barrels; the boy saw it all, and all was wonder. Finally he shouldered back, through the cluster of cantors and for a moment a press of skirts stopped him. And voices.

"—but I'm askin' yuh, why her? You'd think, of all the—" said a young feminine voice, but another interrupted.

"Look kiddo, don't bother. It never makes no difference. None. Just do what you're told."

"Well, it's a shame. And don't it make yuh think, huh?" the other insisted.

"I don't think. It never—" but the boy was pushing between them and the voice shifted, "Oh—it's Joey."

As the boy moved to avoid them the first girl stepped suddenly into his path. "Say, you're seeing the big Yacht. That's nice. Look at the view, over here," and her long bare arm was pulling him and he reluctantly ducked his head below the railing to look as she bent to him. "See the town. Looks nice, don't it, with all the nice tall buildings. And look, over there there's the boat factory." She was pointing in what he vaguely sensed was a kind of flurry, keeping his eyes away from the Yacht. "And doesn't your father work—ain't he a director at the factory—see, over there—"

He had not followed her finger for the flotilla of small boats following had held him. All the boats of the island seemed spread behind the Yacht, bumped full of tiny people, cutting through the water in their wake, but he looked then at the tall chimneys of the factory. "Uh-huh," he said. "Sometimes he takes me along to his office or we look at the motors—" his voice trailed away. "Where's the smoke?"

"There's never no smoke today. See, everybody's here, coming with us." She was erect, gesturing vaguely, pushing him ahead between several girls, and then he was behind an air-funnel, momentarily alone. From deep within the ship rose a muffled throb and he could imagine the great motors running easily, motionless as rocks in their unseeable spinning. With a twist he pried himself between the people again.

And then he saw Miss Grierson. She was sitting, clustered about by girls all dressed, as he suddenly understood the girl talking to him had been, in white but without the band of gold and crimson over their breasts. He wanted to step forward, to tell her—but he saw that she looked even more strange and rigid, sitting so motionless. His mother, now Miss Grierson. A pennant snapped high on the mast above him; he wished suddenly, overwhelmingly, that Eric was there.

He did not want to explore any more. But pushing to find his way back he came upon the old bearded man in a little gap away from everyone leaning over a great block of iron by the railing. The boy looked at it, for it seemed very familiar, but he could not quite decide what it was while the old man muttered to one of the Lesser Capitulars who was hunched down trying to work a rope through one of the innumerable holes in the iron.

"—ain't nothin' what it useta be. Naw sur. In the old days. Useta climb up there, before the sun come up, spend all night climbing, up the trail, through the dark with damn few torches. Just climb. And gettin' them up there was a job. Ha! But everything's gone soft, new stuff, and floating along in boats! Not like we useta climb, *before* sunrise."

The younger man looked up, face flushed. "Is this well enough tied, sir? This new rope..."

"It's gotta be new rope!" The old man bent over, not touching the knot. "Yeah," he said grudgingly. "I guess. And you take this platform contraption—" he struck the boards under the iron lightly with his scuffed boot. "One more o' the Cap's new ideas—" he snorted and the boy jumped a little. "Useta be tough, man. None o' this soft psychology stuff. Carried it up right, right up there. We done it right then, but now—" the old man glared with a fierce brilliance at the other, his chin bristling over the mass of iron as the crest of Sun Rock emerged out of the mass of the island beyond the wide water. The boy turned frantically, slid between the stiff pillars of people, not stopping until he felt his mother's arm about his shoulder.

He stood, panting a little. He said nothing and she did not ask. The peak of Sun Rock grew above the people's heads and the boy understood that they were approaching much closer to the highest point of the island than they ever did in their family boat-picnics. He looked to his father, but his head was high, eyes distant as if he saw nothing. The Capitular's voice was saying, "We hope you had a nice exploration tour, Joey. We were just beginning to wonder where you might be." His Highest was not looking at him as he spoke, but rather at what seemed to the boy was a watch one of the Lesser Capitulars was holding before him. Everyone stood silent, grim as if they had never smiled. The Capitular's face was the only friendly one, and suddenly the boy stepped forward.

"Sir, Your Highest, I saw Miss Grierson. But she didn't—look at me. At school we always played in the sand, Eric and me, and she—is something—" The Capitular, still smiling, threw a swift glance at the sky and stood up. The cantors began, their sound lifting unintelligibly into the warm morning, united, plaintive, strangely harrowing. The boy turned sharply for his mother but the Capitular's soft hand was on his shoulder, his voice in his ear.

"Come, my boy. I want you to do one thing, something just for me. For this you were chosen yesterday, when you drew the Lottery."

The boy gazed wide-eyed at him. The Lottery was for the ride. He twisted, one glance finding his mother now standing. Her eyes were dilated and her face pulled out of shape, but she was nodding soundlessly to him. He could not but obey and he walked forward, the heavy hand now very tight on his shoulder, through the lane opening between the people, hearing the chant merge to words as the motors throbbed and died under his feet. And then over the cantors, the high voice of the Capitular lifting and they were standing before the roped, riddled bulk of iron on its little platform, the people all about and sounding now also, the morning sun just visible over the high thrust of the Rock.

"—the-evergoodness-of-the undying-and-golden—"

But the boy did not hear, his eyes shifting from the water where there was now no bronze railing to interrupt his view of the wedge of boats sitting like gulls along the edge of the Rock's shadow on the blue-black water. In the hesitance of silence the Capitular bent to the boy, voice now almost sorrowful.

"Joey, do exactly as I say. This is the handle." The thick fingers pointed to a lever on a raised panel. "When I nod my head at you, pull it back. Just one little pull. It is very easy. But don't," the fingers closed on the boy's hand lifting, "don't touch it till I nod. Exactly then. That's my fine boy. Now, watch me. Exactly. When I nod."

The mesmerizing smile on the broad face, so close, held the boy watching the great arms lift as they did each week in the ambo, the sound of the cantors rising, rising to the top of comprehension and the world flaming with their incredible sound as the boy had never heard it from the rood-loft. He stood erect, swaying slightly to the sway of the people. Then the Capitular bowed to him, his hand found the handle and, standing all alone, facing the water now and the sun flush in his eyes over the peak of the Rock, he pulled.

The sound of the cantors was now the sound of all the people, swaying beyond the water's lift of the Yacht. The boy was the only one who saw the little platform stir and tilt at his feet and the iron slide from the deck like a living thing. Amazed, he stepped to the edge. The splattered circles of its falling fled away from the very apex of Sun Rock's shadow on the water and he saw the mass of it waver down into blackness and the white rope snake along the waterline, his eyes following, and seeing suddenly, beyond the people tight to the rail, the rope ending in a white form falling from the Yacht in one smooth motion. The form hesitated, flat, spread-eagled on the water like a great headed т crossed with a gold-and-crimson slash, before it smudged, then vanished in the black water. The boy stood, staring, remembering only the gaping hole in the mask-like face.

Under the sound of the people floating over the water, the old man was leaning over the railing, cursing softly. "—goddamn motor block, so goddamn many holes, gurgling to hear it above the chant! In the old days we used millstones. Clean, sure. Damn newfangled stuff!"

The boy's fingers dug through his mother's thin black dress as she crouched down, clutching him to her.

"Mommie—Mommie—"

"Hush," said his mother. She shuddered in the sunlight. "Hush. Just hush."

Did Jesus Ever Laugh?

[1969/1970]

AROUND THIS APARTMENT at least they haven't stuck in trees for birds to sit on and try to sing. Just bushes to keep you off the patch of grass too small for a gopher and then up blank like a north-end coulee in fall, twenty stories cement straight up and down, maybe seventeen apartments on each, say around twelve or thirteen hundred in all; you know, a grey slab box with metal windows. In twelve or thirteen hundred, a place like this, there should be one. One at least.

You'd think so, wouldn't you, but you can't count on it; I've tried a few. Football and hockey games aren't worth the snot you blow waiting and the late movie's absolutely blank. Nothing. There's too much of this people coming out now trying to jack themselves down after some man's north end been flipping through the sheets. It's just nothing like it was.

You'd think a place the size of Edmonton (over seven hundred thousand friendly people says the sign on the Calgary Trail), it's amazing with that number of people and all that preaching flushing through their heads how few there really are in the whole city. At least the few I've seen, and I spend my time looking. I'm never not looking and I know; there are but few. Bars and nightclubs have always been like you know, hopeless. The biggest encouragement I ever had about Edmonton was I found two within four feet of each other at the Willingman Brothers Evangelistic Revival Incorporated last year when they come out at the Gardens. In broad daylight! By the time I could move they had both disappeared and I nearly lost them, both. They say Billy Graham could be coming next fall, but that's probably too much to pray for.

So that's why I was on apartment blocks now, in broad daylight. Waiting actually isn't too bad there sometimes, with the clouds down and November wind prying in where the liner's torn away on the old Lincoln's doors. It's a beautiful car yet, better every year. I can see it black, from here. I work it over with hard wax at least once a week, you know really sweat it with elbow grease like I always did. All the soft parts in it are about gone and I've got these nice hard boards shoved under the seat covers where I sit. On days like that I can sit, watching and waiting, wherever I've parked and I'll get numb slowly till there's no feeling in me at all and I'm just sunk down, eyes along the bright black edge of the hood, watching. Not feeling a thing, just eyes, waiting.

But this fall's been bad; the summer was cold and rainy but now in October the sun shines as if it's gone mad and Edmonton was prairie. The leaves come gliding off the trees and it's warm and people walking around without coats. It gets so you—I—can't sit at all; all of a sudden I have to get out even when I have a good parking space and the meter doesn't have to get fed. I just have to get out, walk around in the sunshine if you can imagine that, I have to rub behind my knees where the edge of the board cuts. It's terrible; I stand there feeling my blood move. The warm air washing over my face. It's so bad then I even forget the words.

But today, no sunshine. I could sit in the car easy just off the corner where this poured slab was sticking up, holding the concrete clouds. A few dozen had gone by, in and out, but they were no good. One glance will always tell me, I never need more. You're watching and waiting; it seems like all my life now I've spent like this, watching and waiting and there always being so few, so few, for weeks it's hanging in your mind there aren't any left anywhere in the world and then it happens like it always has who knows how it's almost past before you suddenly know and you wonder how many you maybe missed just like that because you were hopeless even while you're sitting up, slowly, careful, feeling it, letting it soak into you again as you're looking and moving, always like the first time at that circus and dead-white up high against the canvas the white leg starts out, feeling slowly along something you can't see but it must be there while the drum rolls and you tighten, slowly, and then so sudden you haven't seen the move she's standing complete, alone, white arms crossed out wide, standing up there above everything on nothing. Though you know there has to be a wire. I was on the sidewalk, standing, and walking then. Not fast, just enough to stay behind, feeling the tightness work me like a beautiful dull ache towards the grey block, under the grey porch, and the tune was there, the words and tune too right there as if I was soaked with it,

> Leave the dance with me sweet Sally,
> Come with me just

walking just fast enough to stay behind because a woman with a heavy bag of groceries will not, of course, walk very fast.

With only one bag the outer door was no trouble; she swung that easily and I was slowing down so I wouldn't come up and show I had no key by not offering to open the inner one (wear a tie and always move calm, that's all) but it was all fine, of course, just fine as it always is if you've been able to wait long enough: a man all in black pushed out that very minute and held the door, she didn't have to bother with a key. I went in fast and caught the inner door as it started to shut after her. I nodded but the man was past and didn't even grunt; he went past without a look at his best deed for the day. When I see him again, I'll thank him.

Two steps up to three closed elevator doors; there was a rubber rug on the floor, and the little lobby off the front door had three bile-green couches and a coffee table with a comic book ripped like some kids had been tearing their hair out there. A blown-up kodachrome saved wallpaper on one wall. Mountain lakes! I can't stand them. Where we waited for the elevator was a trough of dark broad plants with flowers stuck in sandpails. The flowers were big as my fist and cold, just beautiful.

The middle elevator thumped and five people came out, one a woman with a wiener-dog on a string and two girls. Their stockings were mottled white so their legs looked like dead birch sticking in a puddle, but the rest of them—ugh—they were ugly, so smooth and round-faced with long straight hair the way you see them now wherever you look in the world. And tight skirts so short when they sit they'd show to the crotch, their boobs sticking out, it was obscene,

O look it's grey out.

I said bring your coat.

This lipstick doesn't match it.

O look it's so grey.

I said bring your coat.

But my ear-rings....

their stick legs tapping along the rubber rug, twitching each bandage of a skirt.

She had pushed her floor and I leaned over the panel to push the same one, just in case she was looking. But she wasn't, of course. Why should anybody look at me? They never do, especially in elevators where there are more than two people; even when there are only two. People in cities don't look at each other; their glances slide over, like the man standing beside me with a face as if he'd slept maybe two minutes in some can last night and nicotine all over his cigarette fingers, letting the smoke curl at me. That's just the way it is, always, somebody's cancer poking at your face, you can count on it like the sun rising

...with me just once more.
Follow me tonight, we'll take the boat from shore.
I will keep you warm, sweet Sally,
In your dan

the door was open and she going, I almost hummed it away. But of course I was moving (even if I'd lost my arm in the door), following like a gentleman, and turned left as she turned right, the hall carpet under my feet and one glance at a door number as she walked down the lighted hall—1808—and wheeling around after her, only three strides behind when she stopped by a door, fumbling in her shoulder purse, and just beside her as the top of the grocery bag split from her tilt and movement, split so I can stick out my hand for the box of Tide sliding out, grab the whole grocery bag, like a gentleman, just perfect, it is absolutely just perfect.

"Oh—" then softer, "oh—thanks, that—yes, thank you," reaching.

I might as well hold it now, you open up.

"Oh, yes, of course," the key is out as she hesitates, "I usually," and in the lock, "I should have put it down," turning, "but usually I manage," the door clicks and she looks up from its little movement, her hands coming up to take the bag and she'd have touched my hands doing it if I hadn't jerked away, my shoulder swinging the door in—don't for God's sake don't not yet—so I can hardly get my mouth open,

I—I m-might as well—as well c-carry it in....

Her glance flickers up at me in the dim hall light and I step in fast—don't give her a chance not a chance—1815—and in the little hall with the usual white plaster walls and the kitchen straight ahead my heart slows, settling back even as I hesitate with my back to her still somewhere in the doorway, or maybe the hall,

Where would you like it, please?

like any gentleman delivery boy. The hesitation is all I need, just a little pause you see, little things always will happen but you cut through them with calm direct action and they're no problem. Then just take a deep breath and on you go.

"Anywhere I—on the kitchen counter—my mother-in-law, you needn't—"

No trouble at all, I might as well, and among the dirty dishes I thrust the bag, I might as well, careful with two egg-marked plates, turning to her in perfect calm and look. Now. The big move left. It's starting to roll and a man in black goes past in the hall behind her but doesn't so much as glance, it's starting as I start to the door. Her face loosens like she pulled a cord. She shifts sort of sideways, smile and words start slow, then burst as she opens just a little in relief, "That was—oh, very kind, of you, I was downstairs washing and the detergent ran out so I hopped down to the grocery while my mother-in-law was..."—ooo lady you've got a long way to go—I'm hearing her,

I guess, where she stands aside against the coat closet in the grey apartment hall, talking, shifting as I move so there's thirty inches between us, steady, as I reach for the door and she is back between the kitchen's dutch doors, separating them, the light (a momentary break of sunshine outside?) from the window like bullets spraying from her black solid lovely shape as I turn from closing the door and slipping up the door chain without so much as a small rattle, can lean back then against that closed door; and look. The song really rolling now

...Sally
In your dancing gown,
Warm as the tropic sea
Far from the lights of t

rolling so I have to wrench myself erect or right then and there I'll be already into the chorus!

She is making a sound. I don't hear quite and her face is in shadow as the light fades again, but her hands go slowly up to her throat, first one and then the other. I'm standing solid now, weight even on my two feet and everything back under control. I always have to watch that, when the first stage ends. Once after too long I got rolling so strong I—well, spilt milk.

Excuse me, I move to see the lashes on her eye. You talking to me? She's now against the kitchen counter and her hands drop. Just my right height for a woman, five foot six. Her voice, well, there've been better, but not bad. With other things, the voice is fringe benefit.

"...the—no idea who you are. I thanked you for your," her arms lift a little; she has nice motion that way; "and now, go."

Of course not.

She hasn't a touch of make-up and her eyes dead grey, as they have to be. Not a speck of colour in her eyes. Her face going like stone, she turns, very nice, and walks past the table off the kitchen and around the partition into the living room and while she is still far enough away not to get hurt by something flying I put a bullet through the telephone. The silencer cost me but it's the best you can get; the shot is no louder than a kid falling on its head out of a high chair; the noise is the telephone flying apart on the bookshelf, what's left of it crashing to the hardwood. The bell clangs as it hits, something sizzles

We are all alone, sweet

but I can cut that one easy. Her move rushed me a little and I'm already in the second verse. That's not so good.

You shouldn't of made me do that. Take this out so quick. I put it away. Rushing don't help a thing.

Her back is like you pulled a lever and turned her to rock, half-tilted against the bookshelf. After a while her little finger starts to jerk back and forth a little on the spine of a book lying there; it looks like a Bible, lying with bits of black telephone on its black cover.

Where's Mother-in-law?

Her finger stops; after a while she whispers, not turning.

"Mother-in-law?"

Yeah. When we come in. Where's she?

"She—she lives in Vauxhall, three hundred miles—"

That's okay, I was born in Alberta, I know enough about Vauxhall. All right. Would you kindly show me around, you know.

"Show you...."

Just take it easy, around the apartment I mean, that's all.

She wheels so fast I think she's ready for something and look up from her tight ankles quick, but she's just on the edge of crying. That's no good at all; is she the wrong—

"Please, oh please, for the love of—"

Don't do that! and she stops very fast. You know how I can't hold my hand with a voice like that and I have to talk fast. Just don't do that, talk like that. Just business, like you wanted to sell something, okay, and I was buying? Now show me the apartment.

She's looking at me and her face hardens again—I knew it, she's the cream the real solid kind who pick it up fast—slowly hardens out of her other expression. She walks ahead of me, voice stripped like she's selling the place.

"You—saw the kitchen, dining area, living room. This is the hall closet."

That's handy, right by the door. I'm standing back a bit, looking forward mostly to be polite; hall closets don't do much for me.

"Each apartment has them there"—atta girl edge in your voice edge—"and this is the storage area, small but conven..." she's got the door open and with a twist before I start to see it she's half inside and I've got to grab her, get both my hands out and actually grab her! Yank her before she's inside and the door slammed behind her and who knows what they've got in

> *all alone, sweet Sally,*
> *Far from the dance on shore,*
> *Where your lovers wait to*

that far into the second verse and not ten minutes with her. She's rushing me, that's all I can say, she's a good one, the best maybe but she's rushing me and I can't say anything at all when I break myself out of it and get my face and hands more or less calmed down again (sometimes I've never had to use my hands at all, you know that) and she's staring at me from where she's spread against the dim wall in the hallway, staring up till I can finally get my face quiet and my hands down. My jaw unlocked.

It's that door, that one. Don't you make one move.

It was her fault, that TV trick with the storage room, and she knows it. I have the one closed bedroom door open without taking my eyes off her, bent back, hands still spread where she caught herself, back against the wall. The shades are drawn, it's even nicer dark in there, but I've got to see sharp right now so I reach in with my left hand and flick on the light. An instant is enough; a grey bun of hair on the bed facing the other way and a quilt over the shoulders. The quilt helps. There's hardly a twitch and it's done in a flick, no different from putting two into the dummy out on the range so fast and tight the sergeant can't yell a thing because if he's got two bits to his name he can cover both holes. The song and tune holding it right on

> *lovers wait to hold you close once more.*
> *But you'll dance again sweet Sally,*

As you glide on down,

Down, down in the sea far

though I'm still a little mad she pushed me so fast. It's not really right and when I think about it later it'll be such a waste, so fast now. You really should have time to think about it all, step by step. Appreciate. Well—I've put it away, and my hands are free again. The door's shut.

Into the living room, you can sit on a chair, okay?

I knew she was right. She gets herself straightened up, it takes time but she does and she walks quite steadily into the living room and makes it fine to the armchair beside the bookshelf. The couch across the room from me. Just fine. Beautiful in fact.

You understand of course it's never happened this fast before, so much and so fast. I would never have dreamed to find anyone who could handle it the way she does, that would have been out of the question to imagine seeing I had such terrible waits even finding anyone. Oh, the waiting I've done, sitting, my body going dead sitting, or sometimes walking a little, waiting outside all those buildings in a place the size of Edmonton, seven hundred thousand friendly souls and how can it be I couldn't, didn't find anyone, no one after you, and you—ah-h-h—just sitting here across from her with her slim legs decently together and skirt over her knees even when everything has exploded as it were in her usual life, to sit there and face me again with a dark solid face like rock and I don't have to begin anything. She will keep facing me I know without a word and her face set until I'm good and ready to start. When I'm ready.

There is, of course, no reason in the world why a human being should laugh.

I stop there like usual; I'm so sure now I don't have to bother at all timing it, that she'll butt in. She sits, her arms down along her thighs but she is not slumped. She does not blink and I am sitting right where her eyes seem to meet, although they don't seem quite to see me. She's alive and perfectly inert the way one can only dream and even then knowing you'll wake up before you can taste it all but there's no waking here, not now

Down, down in the sea
Far from the lights of town, Michael row

but that's trouble, the last verse starts like the chorus and if I don't
watch that—you remember don't you—I'll be on in the chorus at last
before the last verse because the first words are the same, and then
it's all been wasted. All! But now I sense it of course right away, the
second word in the last verse is "weep" and I pull up. With someone
like this I can probably keep this going—well I can try again can't I—
the complete song, every verse, she looking like she is, so I can cut
the song and continue. At my leisure.

The problem with laughing is it makes you forget. You relax, and
the bad you've done you begin to forget it. Right away. That's wrong,
you see. Don't you. You shouldn't just be able to forget about what
you've done wrong. You should have it right there in front of your
thinking all the time, know every wrinkle of it. Not wash it away with
a laugh or a grin or a big-laugh and slap on the back. You gotta keep
it in front of you all the time and that's the biggest thing that's wrong
with laughing because it washes it out, you relax and it's gone, right
out of sight and out of mind and that shouldn't happen like that
outa sight and outa mind which is where laughing gets you because
people should just hafta see and keep on seeing and staring right in
the face every bit of everything and they've done ever done....

Her expression has changed, and it's just as well because it breaks
up my talk. Maybe she said something? I know, I was stumbling
already, repeating myself. That's another thing that usually happens
when it's so long. I repeat and then I'm going in circles. I know that,
you don't have to—it's hard to stop, like some other things, unless
you get help and here again she's got it. Just the look is enough and I
can get stopped. No problem; start again.

You know these men nowadays call themselves theologians and
call others to a new morality and call God dead? No doubt you've
heard all about that, you can't get away from it hardly unless you
plug yourself up, eyes, ears, nose, everything—well, God is dead
for them, sure, because they've laughed him to death. There's just

nothing left sacred and serious but somebody cuts it up laughing. Can you think of anything they don't laugh at now? I could give you ten minutes and you couldn't think of nothing, bright as I know you are. The Devil in the Snake got Eve to eat the apple by cracking a joke about God and the Devil's been laughing ever since. You laugh and you don't keep the proper things down no more—you get rid of them, right. The stuff's got to be kept down, down where it belongs and not laugh it away, and whatever you do you've got to be able to face it, square face to face and face it right out, and not once do you laugh it away easy. You do every bit you do dead sober, you live a godly, righteous and sober life like the Bible says, right. A righteous and sober life, facing everything you do without....

She may have been saying something again. I can't be sure of course, because I was explaining something to her, but she may have been saying something because I see now that her mouth is moving and it may have been moving and it may have been probably moving for some time. Her hand has definitely moved; she has the Bible in her hand now and is brushing the bits of black telephone off, holding it clutched in front of her with her eyes closed like sleep, but her lips move.

Right like the Bible says. I know you're a Bible reader, and I believe what the Bible says too. I don't always do right, I know that, and I've been punished, don't think I haven't, but I'm never getting punished because I don't know and didn't care I was doing wrong. I'll know it before anybody else. The trouble with the world that walks past every day is they don't know they're doing wrong and they don't care if they did because they're so busy laughing it all away. Everything's laughed at. People are always looking around, hoping to see something they shouldn't see, something to laugh at. Women wear clothes—not you but there's plenty right in this building with you, you've seen them, showing things God never meant to be shown and people look and look and laugh to cover up the evil grinding in their heads when they look. Smiling everywhere, just notice it sometime. It isn't right and I've got the proof for it. You know the final proof?

I wait, like I always can afford to wait and I know from this one I'll get response. But I'm so relaxed, and the verse comes

Michael weep for dear sweet Sally
Down in the deep blue sea,
Hang your head and cry down by the gallows tr

thanks heavenly God she's been saying something again, though I haven't heard it, and her staring mouth moving helps me cut across to her and hear her saying, aloud,

"...ever done, what have I ever done to anybody that you—"

Hey hey now, I've got to jump in here fast. I can't have overestimated her, but dear God! Now that is no question for us sitting here like this. Don't do that, don't do that at all.

And she stopped, of course. She sits there motionless again, holding the Bible, her fingers dead white along the edges. The darkness has come in more from outside and someone I know is walking down the hall. You can hear him even with the thin rug there. This place was really built on the cheap, and maybe I should have figured that more before. I guess I did but I didn't think of all the possible implications of that, though by now you'd think I'd know better. Mistakes; I keep doing wrong and one of these—cut that!

You've got the proof right there, in your hand. The Bible. The Book of Jesus. You ever read in there that Jesus laughed?

She doesn't say a word that I can hear. Her eyes are wide, looking, her face rigid and her lips moving but I can't hear a word so I carry right on or I'll be through all that last verse and then there's nothing left but the chorus.

No. You never. You'll never read that we know right now, both of us, Jesus never done it. He healed the blind and wiped off the sores of lepers and threw out devils and whipped moneychangers and told Pharisees they were just so many sonsabitches and he gave the hungry food sometimes. But when did he ever laugh? Eh? You ever catch Jesus laughing? Nosir.

"...talking about Jesus after the unspeakable things you've..." she goes on talking, her face still rigid like it's been cast forever but her hand gesturing down the apartment hall.

The old woman now, right, and she went in sleep. She never knew a thing of it. We should all pray for that. She could have lived to ninety-five, here and in Vaux—the—the medicine, they have, now, and her teeth falling out and not able to control herself and you always wiping up her mess. Oh, I know, Jesus raised some from the dead, about three the Bible says, and some relatives thanked him for it but you never read nothing from the ones that was raised, do you? Not a thank you, not from one of them. He never done it for the dead ones, let me tell you, it was the living, just some of them, nagging him. Anyway, if he did it for the dead, why didn't he do it more? Tell me that. There must have been plenty dead with Jesus walking the country, and he just raised three. Nosir, There's nothing to worry about the dead. They never laugh. Not even when they come back.

I must have been talking a long time. My mouth feels dry and she has pulled herself back in her chair, as if she were trying to push back as far as she could. Has she been saying something? Perhaps. Maybe that's why for a minute the sun coming in through the slatted window, the big one in the living room where we sit, my body coming back now a bit and relaxing on what once was a good foam-rubber couch but now worn thin and threadbare, though it's really clean, I seem to have lost where I was. Even the—no—

Down in the deep—
Hang your—head and—cry down by the gall

No, that's there okay. But it's so far gone. I must have been wasting it somewhere, and she's talking too; I can hear her, so I have to talk more.

I've heard it all before, yeah, he raised three and loved them all. So in all them hundreds of years since, how many you think he killed?

That's everybody's mistake about Jesus. He had a lot more things in his mouth than love. That's the forgotten Jesus. Like hanging stones around your neck and into the sea with you, down down, or calling a woman that isn't a Jew like him a dog, just like a lot of other Jews do now, just walk down the pawn street and you'll hear. Or that about the sheep and the goats. Everybody lined up, all the nations, great and small it says right here in your Bible, Matthew, chapter 25, and the big finger coming out and the voice, "You sheep right," and "You goat left." That's judgement, and sheep and goats sliding right and left without so much as a snicker anywhere. Dead sober, dead, and the goats knowing dead sure why they're going. They know why. Because compared to a sheep a goat's a LAUGHER

Sheep   the range flat grey powdered rock dusted in hollows to grey chewed root   sheep-like clouds, white on grey-green, white in the streaky blue   the horizon so far and straight the hills turning on a shimmer of griddle heat   sheep like clouds, sheep whitish pancakes fuzzing grey in the heat, frying flat, speckled under the specks of hawks stuck on the blue for gophers   above hawks and sheep and flat grey to the horizon end in sky hang vultures, flat, sailing like dead ashes hooked on the heat over the impossible level of sage and stubble gnawed grey by sheep and gophers and the unending sun   soft at the flat edge of it, almost gentle but slowly hoisting itself higher and higher to burn over the gaunt woolly sheep panting against each other, sides thumping in the heat till their backs merge in the shimmer of flat earth sweating greyness and light under the ash of vultures endlessly turning turning   sheep. The goat standing in the one patch of shade   beside the sleeping-wagon   alone in a herd of sheep   no female to chase in a small surge through the flat backs and a momentary lunging elevation   a female of his kind   always erect already in whatever shade, on whatever elevation, a sweat-spot beside the wagon or any stone large enough for two hooves   head erect, horns curled back chewing standing and chewing endless under the ash   chewing with a twist to his mouth, head turning from the panting sheep smeared flat over the land facing ahead, a twist in his mouth   the flat blazing earth flimmering   in heat

...where's the girl?

She stops what she has been saying to me; whatever it all was. Her mouth just stops and she is looking.

"Excuse me?" she says finally. "Please!"

Your girl? She at school now I guess? She just stares. Over there, the picture. I see everything. How old is she?

"It was, just last, fall, before she started school, just last, we got that picture...." She's staring at me now and the expression on her face is changing again. She is looking at her wristwatch and her expression is changing as I watch, her fingers slowly kneading the smooth leather of the Bible.

In the dark northern lights come and go   washing out the stars
in colour with their slow twitch   alone in a world bending flat
backwards   the goat's white tail flickers   you can step off into
stars   his black head nodding. He coughs.

"...finally dressed, it was such a hurry. And like I said when we
finally got there, after all the fuss of the accident right in the underpass, it wouldn't have really caused any trouble if it hadn't happened
right in the underpass, we almost cancelled everything, but Jake said
it couldn't be helped, it wasn't his fault and Mama had come from
Vauxhall to see her start school so why go through it all again but we
were all so upset it came out stiff upset by the accident she's usually
such a happy little girl the photographer tried everything and even
got out his jack-in-the-box but she didn't want to laugh. He tried
everything and Jake almost choked but she just couldn't seem...."

down by the gallows

her mouth stops. And her face breaks. Breaks like when a hammer
hits a dried-out clod of southern Alberta gumbo

tree
Michael weep for

She is screaming. Sitting perfectly motionless holding the Bible in
front of her, staring at her wristwatch, screaming.

"God my god my god, that horrible song, stop it! STOP IT!"

I told you she was the right one. The song is in my head of course,
I've of course never sung it out loud again and I wouldn't, you know
that, even with her, but she knows. She's that kind

dear sweet

she's on her feet, screaming, moving *her dancing* coming towards me,
her hands set like claws *drifting in the tide* too fast! It's too fast, she's
coming too fast, reaching *the lights of town Michael row the* but it's
too fast! I can't finish! I just can't jam it all in so FA-A-A-A

The blanket from the shelf in the hall closet covers her easily. Even the Bible lying there, splattered out. I shouldn't have counted on her that much. Depended so much. Sitting so still, talking so long and perfectly normal—weren't you talking about your life, all those growing up things, don't you remember?—I should have expected she'd break and got it finished. But it was so comfortable, at last. That was my mistake, I know, but we have to have time or it doesn't do any good. You taught me that too. And this almost worked, you can't really say it didn't till you had to spoil it but it worked—well, it's a minute to four—all afternoon? She was better than anyone, since. In a place the size of Edmonton, to find so few! But there's still the little girl. Is there?

I'm sitting erect on the windowsill eighteen floors up. There's no balcony, this place is too cheap, and there's not even a screen but my head is very steady on heights so it is not dangerous at all. Though it has never been this high before. The black bridge, beautiful with black heavy steel, reaches over the valley, low water glinting here and there under the sodden clouds. Apartment blocks stick up all over but the black level line is the best thing about the best thing about the valley, a line straight across the green hollow, though now in late fall when the leaves are finally gone there is mostly grey left. They are gone. The valley, the river, the road and the spidered trees, the side-walk and the parking lot approach below. All variations on grey.

Four o'clock so it must be very close to time. The sun pretty well gone. A black spot of someone comes out from under the porch and cuts across the grey, passing behind my black Lincoln. I sit. She'll be coming soon. Has there been pounding on the door? I listen but then, how can you tell? The song hanging there, waiting, still waiting to be finished finally. Flat Vauxhall. Is someone pounding? Is there?

Or is it a knock? Ah-h-h-h-h-h

Believing is Not Seeing

"Because you have seen me, you have believed."
—JESUS (as quoted by John)

ONE

"Have you ever," she says, "seen a row of dead people?"

"A row of...what?"

"People laid out in a row, one beside the other, full length on the ground, say a few hundred—dead ones."

"No, no, where would..." he mutters, and stops. "Yes of course I have."

"When? Where?"

"On television, billions of people see that kind of thing on television, practically every day."

"No, television doesn't count."

"What do you mean, doesn't count? It's where we see everything."

"I know, I know, everything from any massacre anywhere in the world—but that's no more human than the 'voices' you're always complaining about on the machines that answer all the phones now, televison's just a machine image, no no, I meant literal bodies, you could bend over and touch them, one after the other, your hands

292

would actually come to a stop like this," her fingertips rest on his skin, "against dead human flesh?"

"You mean, like, seen with a touch?"

"Yes."

He has not a word to answer.

"And smelled them," she says.

"What?"

"Unless it's a very cold climate, like polar regions say, human bodies swell up fast, all those gases in the stomach, there's a extremely strong stench, very quickly."

"And flies and maggots..." he stops, and starts again. "A Dene man at Fort Good Hope once told me a body even in cold water like the Mackenzie River will come to the surface, you might not be able to recognize the face after the fish go at...no. I haven't."

"In Canada," she says, "we never see rows of bodies, really, except once in a while in disasters like mine explosions. The biggest we ever had was the Hillcrest Mine in the Crowsnest in 1914, one hundred and eighty-nine men dead. When they brought them out of the mountain they laid the body parts out in the mine wash house and tried to re-assemble them, arms, legs, heads, so relatives could identify—"

"Why," he interrupts, "are you talking about this?"

"You can go to Hillcrest, Alberta, it's practically a ghost town, and see where they're all buried," she says. "A double row of graves, several hundred yards long with a low white fence around them, hardly any tombstones or names, just the long bumpy grass and the Crowsnest River valley and mountains. A beautiful graveyard, truly beautiful."

He puts his hand on her bare shoulder. "Why are you asking me this? You know I've only seen a few bodies, one at a time, in coffins."

"Which is more than most people have," she concedes, "your father, right and—"

"And my mother, yes," he says. "And I have never seen the body of my daughter because she has never been found. Why?"

"I know, my love," she says, touching him back. "I was asking about many bodies, laid out. Strangers."

The Development Appeal Board of Leduc County is sitting to hear an appeal concerning a proposed expansion of a hog operation. L.H. Rollnick Farms Ltd. already have a huge hog complex on one farm, and the company has purchased another quarter section of land a mile away and proposes to build a further, much larger, barn there which would expand its operations by an additional six hundred brood sows, all animals to be raised in those barns from farrow to finish.

Harry and Anne Szekorick, whose home farm is halfway between the two Rollnick properties, have appealed against such a development.

There are sixteen letters supporting the Szekorick's appeal against the development, and the Board secretary is reading every word of every one of them aloud. Adam sits in the mix of presenters and spectators; as he listens he doodles numbers: six hundred sows, okay, plus how many boars? ten? twenty?, no, boars didn't matter, they wouldn't amount up to much, but each sow's litter averages, say for simple arithmetic, ten piglets—though not all would litter at the same time so you couldn't really say six thousand more—but then all would be fed to finish them off for market, which averages nine-ten months, and every sow litters at least once a year, maybe every nine months— so really, once it got into full swing, that barn would have to hold at one time an average of at least eight thousand pigs. On one quarter section of land, pigs gestating and feeding and growing and above all producing manure: eight thousand pigs minimum. Tons and tons of daily manure that would need fifty to sixty-five thousand litres (as Rollnick said in his application) of water every day to flush it away as liquid waste. Absolute stinking lakes of it.

"Have any of you ever lived near a lagoon that stores liquid pig shit?"

Harry Szekorick is asking the Appeal Board around the U-shaped council table, though from his wide gestures he might, Adam thinks, more likely be questioning the cosmos. "A lagoon where it all gets pumped into and stays open to the air for months? I have, half a mile from the one he has right now, for twenty years ago when he first built it."

Adam is seated badly, there was only one chair left in the back row of the crowd when he arrived; he can see his grey-headed childhood school acquaintance well enough, and some of the Board, but no more than the back of Leonard Rollnick's bald head and heavy shoulders. The hog breeder is not looking at Harry, who is certainly staring straight at him.

"I must ask you," says the chairman of the Board quietly, "please speak to the development. Not personally."

"Personally?" Harry says. "Orest, you know me, I'm no big company. It's just me and the wife. Every day I thank God I've woke up another day and I'm alive. And then I go out the door, I was born there, half a section of good enough land for a living, we raised five kids right there where my folks homesteaded 1907 on the bench above the Strawberry Creek—I'm on the porch and then that stink, from his open lagoon with the black, shining scum on it, it's coming down the creek again, and I smell it again, and I leave my breakfast right there. Off the edge of the porch. That's what it's like—Anne can't open a window, I can't go out my door without losing my breakfast. That's it."

An immense brush-cut man, skin burned almost black by every kind of Alberta weather. Adam suddenly feels tears start behind his eyes at Harry's magnificent gesture in standing up suddenly, arms flung wide. We always kidded him, Adam thinks, he was so kiddable, even in grade six Harry Szekorick was "Short and wide as a two-holer shit house, yeh, yeh Big Harry!" and then we'd scatter, run like hell as he came roaring after us.

"I never complained to the law before," Harry has left the presenter chair and is walking back to his seat in the audience, but he continues to speak. "I talked a lot to *him* about it but never to you guys. Farming's farming, okay, my few cattle's feedlot don't smell so sweet either sometimes, but now he'll build another barn on the other side of me, and I'm surrounded. I tried to buy that land when Joe Blinak got too old, I offered Joe sixty five, and right away Len offered him seventy, so I say seventy-five and Len goes eighty. The land ain't worth it, not for usual farming, and I can't find that kind of money. But he can find it, all the money he needs. So now there's gonna be stinking open lagoons on both banks of the Strawberry, and I'm surrounded. No matter how the wind blows, I get it?"

Harry stands there and lifts both his arms again, staring his question over the heads of the crowd and around the board table; at the chairman who is the county councillor and a farmer also.

"Is there anyone else who wishes to speak against the proposed development?"

THREE

"A mine disaster isn't like a massacre in Rwanda," he says. "When a mine explodes there's working civil order in place, with officials and rescue parties—"

"It's not like ethnic cleansing," she concedes, "of course not, but—"

"—and everyone's trying to help, police, firemen, doctors, whoever, the grieving wives and kids, the relatives are all there, the only ones dead are the miners who went into the mine, deliberately, knowing that maybe they—"

"Knowing it doesn't make them any less dead."

"Okay, but dead for them is a possible job hazard, it's dangerous digging coal inside a mountain."

"Dangerous, like being a citizen of Iraq? They're just living too, and working at their usual work and all of a sudden the world explodes and they're laying bodies out in rows, trying to assemble human parts into recognizable people, only now they're women and children and old people too, not just working soldiers."

"That's different, that's war."

"Like the mine in Nova Scotia, Westray, everybody knows it's deadly, just a question of when it will kill you so—"

"Stop playing changes on me," he says, almost angry. "Stick to one subject!"

"I am," she says quietly. "It has to do with danger, with death, with men walking a dangerous line and knowing people will get killed and still they do it. The men who control businesses where people have to work, the men who control countries where people have to live."

"Oh, men," he says. Discouraged already.

"Yes. Men organize and run the businesses, they organize and fight the wars."

"Yeah, and they're the ones who know best how horrible wars are."

"Oh, they're horrible all right."

"All those men in all the wars, even good ones like they call the Second World War, fighting fascists, they'll tell you. And you've heard them too, they were in it and they hated it and they won't say another word about it."

"Oh, they hate it," she says, "of course they do, and they'll tell you about a buddy that was killed. It's truly horrible. But maybe...maybe they won't talk about it because...they loved it too."

"What?"

"It was fun too. It was the most excitement they ever had, and they're quiet now because they can't dare tell anyone about that."

"How can you say that? You know Tom's dad, how he was, how—"

"Yes, I'm thinking of Tom's dad, exactly. He would never say anything, just went to every Remembrance Day parade with all the other vets and cried and drank a little with his old buddies—he was flying Mustangs against Germany when he was eighteen, you think he ever had that much *living intensity* again? Selling furniture in Eaton's for forty years? You think he could ever explain to anyone who wasn't there what flying a plane like that meant to a prairie boy, roaring over the huge cities of Europe, and life and death dogfights in the sky, and watching the brilliant streaks of bullets, his bullets, and seeing those Nazis, those absolute, horrible enemies, falling, trailing smoke and exploding into flames when they smashed into the ground, those monsters that herded people into ovens?"

"He didn't know anything about ovens when he was flying."

"Don't quibble, he knew it later, and it just made him feel more right, the intensity better, yes."

"No, no, you're distorting it. I agree with you, war is a male thing but—"

"Sweetheart," she says, "you know it, women don't fight like that. Rarely among themselves physically and never, in any military sense, do they fight men. War is a completely masculine business."

"Okay, just you're pushing it too far. Fun! Tom's dad was a father, he loved his kids, he loved life, he couldn't—"

"Yes, yes! And a man never wants his son in a war, I know that, and yet...in a way I think he does. To know that life-and-death intensity, every bit of you on the line, living through the most paralyzing fear and knowing you found the courage somewhere to do it. And the incredible comradeship, a little group of you, a platoon of soldiers on patrol with machine guns poised, a cluster of pilots trained to perfection in those slick, beautiful machines fighting a malignant enemy together, life and death—look at it! How can a six and a half percent mortgage, shopping till you drop at the mall compare, eh? Playing golf...for god's sake!"

"Oh, sweetheart," he can only groan, "sweetheart." Because she has boxed him in on his own unutterable, inchoate and well past middle age apprehensions. He has never lived at such intensity; he knows he never will.

"Listen," she says against his ear. "Robert Graves wrote that his main inheritance from World War I was 'a difficulty in telling the truth.' Tom's father wouldn't lie, he just didn't tell us anything. No stories. He hinted at a story once, remember, about when he was escorting a bomber squadron and his best buddy from Claresholme was the tail gunner in one of the Lancasters? He got back okay and then his buddy's Lancaster came back all shot up and crash landed with only the pilot alive, and then he died too before he could tell what happened. That's the classic male war story, it tells you nothing, it's told to keep you, who weren't there, in the dark, you are left ignorant and so he can say, 'That's the way war *is*, it *means* nothing,' and therefore it can mean everything."

"So..." he mutters at last. "What's the classic female story then? That means nothing, and so it means everything?"

"What do you think?"

"Childbirth?" he says.

"You really think so?"

"Yeah. Maybe. I think so."

"You and your 'maybe.'"

"Well, it's sure exclusive. Okay, for women it's childbirth."

"That's an old one," she says.

"Yeah," he says. "As old as they come."

On the back of his Notice of Appeal, Adam has been jotting down names and reasons from the letters that support Harry and Anne Szekorick against building the enormous breeding and feeding barn. No one argues against the hog business itself: they say fine, let Rollnick build the eighty by two hundred metre barn—it will cost three million dollars, but money is no problem, apparently—but his company owns land at various places in the district, why build it exactly there to hem in the Szekoricks? And, even more particularly, why on the high banks of Strawberry Creek where the valley acts as a funnel to bring the stench down on them and everyone else downwind? One Szekorick daughter's statement is particularly moving: their families can no longer come to the home where they grew up and visit Grandma and Grandpa outdoors, no more barbecues because of the continuous stench; and beyond the unbearable smell itself, her youngest boy has asthma, the odour gives him dangerous attacks.

The Szekorick daughters and sons are in the room, but none of the neighbouring farmers have come to speak in person; perhaps they don't want to confront Rollnick's glowering face. But two of them several miles downwind from the present barns write letters that testify to the putrid odour. Apparently the Alberta Environmental Board holds that air pollution alone cannot be a deterrent to development—Alberta may have the worst pollution legislation in Canada, Adam thinks: most fitting then that the present premier, whose only political principles seem to be i) Stay in power, ii) Hold a draconian "bottom line" on the budget, most fitting that he was the environment minister when the act was passed—the letters say that bad air definitely does ruin their "enjoyment of life." Isn't part of the attraction of the country life supposed to be the freshness of what you breathe?

The farmer letters raise a further ominous matter: for years Rollnick has dumped and sprayed liquid waste on his land beside them and, as far as they can see, he is ruining the land for grain. So much soil saturation with such powerful manure has killed a large stand of poplars and spruce, and an entire quarter section now will grow nothing but hay. Where's he going to put all that waste from thousands of more pigs?

299

And finally: the site is barely two hundred yards from Strawberry
Creek; which flows directly into the North Saskatchewan River;
which supplies the water for Edmonton.

Around the Council table the Board members shift in their
suits and tight ties. They are all male and, except for one lawyer,
all farmers. They seem to be listening, but not one asks a question. Surely they understand something about air and soil and water
pollution. Adam cannot tell from their set faces, and wonders if there
is any point to this effort: money and politics far away from this table
will probably decide it anyway.

The chair declares that the statements of those opposing the hog
operation are concluded, and the developer may now speak.

Rollnick is a large man, he can begin softly. Adam thinks his
accent gives him an appealing Canadian sound: his is the classic
story of the immigrant who in this land of opportunity and endless
individual initiative gets the chance to achieve his most unlikely
dream—own large chunks of farmland and become so rich he can
vacation in homeland Éurope for six weeks every year. And so now,
of course, he declares he wants nothing more than to benefit his
community with jobs.

The magic word; the very prime minister utters it a hundred
times in every speech he makes. Leduc County people need jobs, and
Rollnick declares he'll provide them.

Smart man, Adam thinks, very smart; he implies he'll bring more
money into the district in a few months than labouring, unimagi-
native Harry has in a lifetime of personally shovelling manure for a
hundred head of cattle where his father shovelled for thirty.

Rollnick continues: he is an agri-business company, he has built
a car wash in town because his hog-trucks must always be clean,
he has bought the town's bankrupt lumberyard because he's always
building something, he needs concrete and carpenters and tonnes of
feed-grain and labourers and electricians and truck-loads of bedding
straw, he will provide endless hogs to keep the packing plant ship-
ping more and more dressed pork to Asia. Alberta young people need
work, there is a world market demand for Alberta farm products, and
Leduc County farmers can compete in it!

Watching Rollnick speak, Adam thinks: he can do all that because he has German money connections, he can talk tight Canadian bankers into lending him more and more money until he hangs himself on the interest—but he probably won't, not this guy. He negotiates tricky farm English idiom flawlessly with his unstoppable German drive: no, he's much too smart and—obsessed—to go broke and get foreclosed on interest.

And concerning waste disposal? Rollnick declares that, yes, that's the biggest problem of hog raising, and his farms—he does not say he himself did it—his farms were the first to devise a unique waste sprinkler system now used across Canada: every few months an engine pumps the waste stored in the lagoon out through a six-inch pipe and hose to a nozzle set on wheels. This nozzle moves forward while spraying the waste over the field in an immense, circular jet; in a few days the lagoon is empty and the liquid fertilizer is where it will do the most good: helping the next crop grow. He has calculated he will need an acre per sow to dispose of the waste properly, and since he has only a half section of land at the new site, he has reached a cordial agreement with the neighbouring Warspite Hutterite Brethren Colony: he will spread his waste on their land.

The business manager of the Warspite Colony states tersely that they own eleven sections of land adjacent to the proposed site, over seven thousand acres, and yes, they will accept all the waste Rollnick Farms Ltd. will produce. They will rotate the spreading in the most productive way.

Adam studies the county property map again: the Colony certainly owns that much land; it also adjoins the Szekorick land on the one side Rollnick Farms does not. No wonder Harry is appealing the project: if it goes ahead, his home place will be completely surrounded by flying manure. And finally Adam also understands why the cluster of black-suited Colony men is in the room; the business manager is heavily middle-aged, so who then is the stout, white-bearded man beside him? Has the Colony Elder, their minister, come to this business appeal? Why?

What does it matter on what land they spray? Everyone knows the ground in that area is grey wooded bush soil, a thin layer of it no more than three to five inches thick above forty feet of solid clay. Every bit of natural run-off, rain or snow or manure spray, must drain into Strawberry Creek. The rich, vivid plants, the innumerable animals and birds living all along the beautiful green water of that small, meandering creek will—

But the white-bearded man is getting up: ancient, dignified, his face set and his very movements measuring out the veneration it is his absolute right to receive. It seems he will say what he does because he has divine authority to do so.

"My name is Elder Joseph," he says, and Adam thinks perhaps the ministry fell to him because he has such a deep, imposing voice. "I am the spiritual leader of the Warspite Hutterite Brethren Colony, and it hurts me really deep when there is conflict between neighbours. Our Good Book teaches, 'If it be possible, as much as lieth in you, live peaceably with all men.' That is what we have done throughout our history, and that is what we want to do here, now, yes, we do."

Adam is abruptly convinced; this old man is about to begin a prayer meeting on how to make piles of money out of spraying pigshit.

FIVE

"So," she says, "there we are then. Our unique experiences, women and men. In birthing women give life to children, in war men kill them. Neat, eh?"

"That is brutally unfair."

"Oh? Why?"

"Because men are involved in birth too, life can't begin without them, and most men never, not even soldiers, ever kill anyone."

"That's true, but the Idi Amins or the Joseph Stalins organize things so well, or the Napoleons, they kill quite a few more than your average quota, that's true so—"

"You don't have to get sarcastic."

"Why not? Otherwise I'd only cry. You saw that spot in Belgium, the one they always point out at Waterloo where five thousand men were killed. Five thousand men slaughtered by cannon and sword on two city blocks—well, try Bosnia now, or Rwanda, Burundi...."

After a while he says, "Some women kill in wars too."

"Yes, a few, sometimes, do. When they get themselves trained by men they of course behave like them."

"Maybe..." he is thinking hard, "pre-historic, when the hunter went out to face the wild animal and the women stayed behind to care for the children—maybe when women have to live life on the edge of death too—I mean, live their life beyond the life/death of their child being born, when they have to face it that their necessary acts can mean they either live or die—then maybe they behave like men do too: they fight to the death too. I think that's just human nature, survival takes over and they're juiced just as high as men. It's not male, it's *human* intensity, eh?"

And oddly, she laughs at him. "No more sending the men off to war, eh, with tears and hugs and staying home and feeding the kids and wiping their little asses and waiting, waiting with such deep longing for the brave boys to come back, no! just get in there, girls, trench warfare and machine guns and tail gunners and see what happens to your gentle, tender mothering instincts!"

"Yeah! Push women like you push men, all-or-nothing. See what happens."

"Everyone admits," she says, "the adrenaline of war heightens all the appetites, and who knows, it's imaginable that that might happen to women too. In fact it never has happened to women in massive armies like men but...say, if I believed I was facing certain death and you, now, were the last man I'd ever make love to, what an incredible rush that would be—eh?"

"You're changing the subject."

"We'll get back to the other one...that would be something, eh? Last woman, last man, last time."

"I hardly need that, with you I can't imagine how much—"

"I didn't say if you could *imagine*, I said if you could *believe*: this is the last time. It would be...well...and you can't?"

"No, I can't imagine believing that."

She laughs. "Oh, you are tricky, you 'can't imagine believing,' well, okay leave sex out of it and—"

"Why leave sex out?"

"For the moment! Try a different heightened appetite, say, an awareness of beauty, any beauty. The amazing design, for example, of deadly weapons. A trimmed down, slick and graspable Kalashnikov rrrrrrrr! spraying out bullets like a steel spider drrrrr! or a CF-5 Freedom Fighter as they call it, a fusion of aerodynamic grace and purpose moulded into stunning power and available to you, at the fingertip control of you alone—wouldn't any man alive want to fly

304

that if he could, and be gone over the curve of the earth before the sound you were coming arrived? Or that newest B-2 Stealth, whew, such an ominous, thin black wedge that even radar can't detect, there's only twenty of them in the world and 2.3 billion dollars each, imagine the body surge, you're in command, you can fly it, the deadliest, most complex machine man has ever concocted, compared to this the invention of the stone hammer for smashing skulls is like spitting to stop the ocean—you control it all! How can a man possibly resist? An incomprehensibly powerful machine of incomparably beautiful design. No matter what its purpose."

There are no words in his head, but something leaps inside him, his entire body springs together.

"I've seen it, I don't have to believe it."

"Seen what?"

"The Stealth."

"But you haven't flown it! Can you see yourself doing that?"

He clamps his arms around her and holds on.

"Oh-h-h," she breathes out; he can feel laughter bubbling beneath her ribs. "You're brainwashed, my dearest."

"We're at war," he whispers into her hair. "You talk and my appetite is uncontrollably heightened."

He is holding her so tightly she cannot laugh, nor gasp.

SIX

Adam cannot believe his ears. He is frantically writing down the words the minister of the Warspite Hutterite Brethren Colony is speaking aloud in the crowded board room of the Leduc County offices, but even then he cannot believe what he sees scrawled in blue across his notepad. His difficulty is not the three simultaneous acts of seeing what he has heard, the momentary delay of his memory of hearing it, and the ongoing fact of continuing to hear more and more even as he writes and sees and remembers: no, that he can handle; his difficulty is in what Elder Joseph is, quite literally, saying.

He is not leading in prayer; he is preaching a sermon on the supreme blessedness of breeding and feeding and slaughtering pigs. Because if you do that right, on a large enough scale, you will achieve the eternal salvation of unending money.

"...and all this talk against our grey wooded soil, it's too thin, it's not as good as some other places where it's two feet deep—okay, but we know how to farm it. We Colony people have shown it's as good as any soil in the world for farming, all the barley and oats and other feed grains for animals it grows. So there's a problem, animals on farms smell, well sure they do, we know that, so why don't you stay in the city if you don't want to smell it? We smell our barns and feed-lots all the time, our houses are closer to our barns than any one's and we don't complain, it's like Mr. Rollnick says, that is the smell of money. Big money, and that keeps all of us busy, working hard, who's got time for little picnics? And I've said to Harry Szekorick, you don't like the smell, we'll buy you out, you don't have to live here, we'll buy your land and you go live in the pretty mountains, you can't smell nothing there, just plain air.

"Leonard Rollnick told you all the businesses in Warspite he keeps going, from the packing plant to the car wash and the bankrupt lumber yard he took on. My Colony supports him, we work with him, we give him business and we rent all his land to crop and then we sell him our grain. But the people in Warspite, the small farmers that complain, run to the County, to Edmonton, even Ottawa and complain—I don't know. Maybe I shouldn't say this but we have to keep some businesses going here and the people of the town don't do much, they don't know what they believe or where they come from, they haven't got any ideas of how to expand and make money. Without the Rollnick businesses and us Colony, the people of Warspite are nowhere. They're nothing."

Adam considers this aged man in his seventeenth-century beard and clothing. He wrote his words down: the humble, peace-loving (as they insist they are) Brethren, who are so selfless as to not even

305

own personal property, for them all is communal, and their spiritual leader has just stated publicly that he thinks his neighbours should just leave their homes and family's life's work and go live in the mountains. Because they are nothing. Dearest god.

The Board secretary takes an occasional note but no tape record is being kept of these presentations. Memory only, except for Adam. He looks around the table. Impassive faces—as if the Board members themselves weren't the third and fourth generation descendents of the homesteaders who first cleared this land and have just now been called "nothing." They are all so uniformly expressionless that Adam suddenly feels they may be more shrewd than he suspects: their official appearance will never betray anything. That may be why they're on this Appeal Board.

But as long as he has known Harry Szekorick—which is all his life—Adam knows Harry has never known how to hide his thinking, and he won't now. When the hearing is concluded and the Board decision declared as coming within two weeks, the audience empties out into the bright sunlight of noon. And sure enough, the big farmer ignores Rollnick as he strides by heading for his vehicle; Anne Szekorick is at her husband's elbow, trying to pull him away but he is talking furiously at the Colony business manager.

Everybody knows, he declares, the Colony has crawled into bed with Rollnick on this development. And of course they have, how much property, how much land does one man need anyway, and him over sixty? The Rollnick girl works in the city, she can't come home except sometimes in winter because she's so allergic to the stink, and the son could never manage that much of—everybody knows the Brethren are letting Rollnick set it all up and then they'll buy him out, it's just a way for them to get bigger, some of the Colony men have been bragging already!

The Colony manager just stands there in the parking lot surrounded by his black-suited fellows; he shakes his square-cut head.

"No, no," he says very quietly. "Nothing like that."

Adam walks directly towards Elder Joseph, already standing beside his van and waiting for his driver; four women in polka-dot kerchiefs sit in the back seats, they must have been there throughout the three-hour hearing. Not bothering with a greeting, Adam says in German, "I was very interested in your sermon on money, I was so enlightened by your commitment and faith in pigs, how they will help this whole county prosper. I'm sure you know the story, in your Good Book, about Jesus and the pigs?"

Adam stops; behind him Harry isn't arguing any more; the only sound is the drone of traffic on the nearby highway and the roar of a jet taking off from Edmonton International Airport.

"You speak echt Dietsch," the old man says mildly, acknowledging nothing.

"Jesus found that poor madman in the hills," Adam continues in German, "it wasn't much with him either, poor guy, not even wearing clothes, certainly not making any money like the Gadarene farmers with their big herd of pigs. You know that story."

Elder Joseph's hand lifts to stroke his white beard, attentive but politely silent. Adam begins to feels a bit foolish, so he can only continue: "Jesus seems more concerned with that poor man than he..." Adam stops; he detests sermonizing, especially when he hears himself doing it—but there's nothing else to be done with this mono-lithic face confronting him. "Jesus kicks a legion of devils out of him by sending them into the pigs, and the pigs charge down a cliff into the lake and they all drown. That's how Jesus deals with pigs."

The Colony minister remains expressionless.

"You understand?" Adam insists. "Jesus prefers people to pigs?"

The pale eyes staring into his do not so much as blink. Adam is suddenly, furiously, angry: this arrogant, self-righteous old ass.

"Do you think," Adam is shouting in English, "Jesus was crucified just so you can ruin your neighbours and make mountains of money from *pigshit*?"

Finally the bearded mouth opens, a deep, rumbling voice: "The Good Book says, 'Believest thou that there is one God? Thou doest well: the devils also believe, and tremble.'"

SEVEN

She is half-chanting, half-singing something; he is too drowsy to open his eyes.

"'Oh, I have slipped the surly bonds of earth

And danced the skies on laughter-silvered wings....'"

"'Surly,'" he mutters, "what's that?"

"From 'sir-ly,' the way a Sir would act, a lord—arrogant, nose in the air, sir-ly."

"Oh, sort of 'overweening pride'?"

"Yes," she says. "The most deadly of the seven deadly sins."

"So—'*surly* bonds of earth'?"

"It's a derived meaning, sweetheart, meaning 'rough and gloomy.'"

"Oh, contrast to 'dancing the skies.'—what is that?"

"A poem, *High Flight*, an American soldier wrote it while flying for the RCAF."

"Is it all full of that nice romantic stuff?"

"Yep, every bit of it, he's an American fighter pilot volunteer in the Canadian Air Force, he's flying the Battle of Britain, 1941, and it's nothing but 'tumbling mirth' and 'soaring' and 'wind-swept heights' and 'easy grace'...."

"Wow. No shooting anyone, nobody shooting back?"

"Nope. Just 'chasing the shouting wind,' just 'sunlit silence.'"

"Never a Nazi anywhere, never a hand on the gun triggers?"

"Oh, he uses his hands. What he does is, while treading 'the high untrespassed sanctity of space,' in the last line he puts out his hand and...'touches the face of God.'"

"Whewww. Worse than *In Flanders Fields*."

She chants again,

"'In Flanders fields the poppies blow

Between the crosses, row on row,

That mark our place an....'"

She breaks off. "That's actually very good," she says. "McCrae was a doctor, I think it's pretty hard for a doctor operating on men blown apart in trenches to rhapsodize about them."

"'And in the sky,'" he recites sarcastically, "'the larks, still bravely singing, fly'—eh?"

"Finish it," she says. "'Scarce heard amid the guns below.'"

"You're right, yes, as always, sweetheart. Good. So, what happened to this romantic American? Big hero? Lots of fun shooting lots of Herman Goering's boys?"

"I don't know. He was killed December 11, 1941, flying his beautiful fighter-plane."

"Oh."

"Maybe that's what he meant," she says, "in the last line. He obviously worships his plane, so when his hand touches his guns, he does touch the face of—his—God."

"What?"

"It's the power, leave this surly earth...power. Touch God."

He can utter nothing but a groan.

"Here we lie," she says, "side by side in bed. Alive, and safe, and filled with love and lovely philosophic thoughts. I keep thinking of bodies laid out, row on row."

"For me, one particular body'd be enough. But then, as long as I don't see it, I can still believe...."

He stops. She touches him; he knows she is there.

"Have you ever," she asks him, "seen a row of dead people? Children and women, and men, wailing over them?"

He says, "I have never seen that."

Life Story

[1998/2010]

IT BEGAN when John was born, when his mother was almost fifty. His father, sixty-seven, said it was an accident, that for years now he had thought his thing was set on play only. John did not speak English or French until he began school, where he learned to sing a song, two lines of which he could never forget:

But it stopped, short, never to go again
When the old man died.

He understood after reading a Bible-story book that Jesus had never laughed nor made love, though he had wept out loud and beaten several salespeople and money changers, nor had he ever touched a woman—except perhaps his mother—unless she first touched him. In high school John played hockey, and once almost scored a goal in an important game. He did not, knowingly, ejaculate while awake until he tried to kiss the woman he was convinced he could marry. She was not convinced, and that was that. After seven years he stopped trying to teach school when he noticed a girl staring at him in horror just as he was prepared to murder, at last, by manual strangulation, one of his utterly unteachable students. For two years he collected and arranged stamps. A choral society

310

he attended sang a song, several lines of which continued to pass
through his mind:

Nothing is here for tears, nothing to wail,
Nothing but well and fair.
And what may quiet us....

He could not recall the ending of the third line, nor did he ever try
to discover it. He began to sell real estate, there were vacant houses
and shopping malls everywhere, it became obvious the world was
designed to be sold. He touched a woman's anus once, and circled it
softly with his fingertip. "Please," she said in her Canadian way, and
that was that. There were times when John suspected he might be
happy, though he could not discover any reason why. He suffered a
heart attack while speaking on his cellphone; fortunately his car was
halted at a four-way stop, in neutral, and no one was hurt. His will
consisted of a single sentence stating that his remains, such as they
were, were to be cremated. Despite his enormous gifts to foundations
for afflicted and famine-ravaged children, his estate was so large
that his nine older siblings and their spouses, their children, grandchildren and great-grandchildren, seventy-one persons in all, were
momentarily at a loss as to what to do with it. Momentarily.

All final arrangements were handled by the Hurlburt and Zoom
Funeral Home. The crematorium was outside the city, hidden behind
poplars so that no passing motorist on the nearby highway was likely
to notice the dense, oily smoke billow from the silver chimney, churn,
and fray into elements that vanished in the sheer, sunlit air. Or, if
anyone did notice, they would not recognize it for what it might be.

Crash

DAVID BOUGHT THE MAP at the Santiago tourist booth for its
title, "Travel Vision Map, Rutero Chileno": a thin booklet for a long,
extremely thin country. As he paid, the fingertips of a woman also
standing in the staggering sunlight of the Paseo Ahumada touched
his arm; her hand offered him a paper. "My dearest Josepha": the
single English sentence explained that "All my Love! John" would not
return from the United States. David glanced at the woman's face, so
anxious, so beautiful. "Verzeihung," he said, and handed the paper
back. "Ich spreche nur Deutsch."

Under shelters along the middle of Ahumada's noise, painters
smeared canvases with snow-lined peaks, shimmering water-
falls. Over the heads jostling him he could recognize the classically
Spanish Plaza de Armes: circling the fountain, Santa Clauses sat in
sleighs attached to wooden reindeer, sweating children laughing in
their laps. But the single star of Chile's flag drooped below the dome
of the Catedral; its door opened into a high, amazing silence.

Only an infant laughing; delicate, like a continuing scatter of
beads in darkness. Near the transept in the left aisle Mary's virgin
china face was crowned with a golden cross, Jesus on her arm her
tiny mirror image, exact to crown, eye shadow, pertly bowed lips,
curly hair and brocade dress. "Maria, Hija Predilecto Del Padre Dios,

312

Ruega Por Nostros." Yes, plead—please plead, you and your baby daughter Jesus, her tiny forefinger pointing up.

Coloured lights outlined a creche beyond the burning gold of the altar; blinking like a Canadian house memory, but here the snow was cotton, the manger empty. Tonight at mass the necessary doll would be laid there.

Suddenly loudspeaker crackle drifted down, muttered into organ. "Jesu, Joy of Man's Desiring." Man's desire indeed. Indelible Bach drove David past altars and stations of the cross, past an exposed "Martyris" reliquia with its half-naked torso contorted as if hanged, past an altar to "Santa Teresa de Los Andes, 1900–1920," her thin image blessed—so declared the letter screwed onto the wall—by Pope John Paul on 24 March 1993, the unrelenting tinny sounds declaring in Johann Sebastian undulations forever and forever that the bleeding wounds of Jesu Christi had set him free forever.

He was at Santiago Airport where he arrived that morning. He pointed to his opened map. "Iquique, si," the woman sang, not asking for his passport. The plane lifted him into a red Pacific sunset. The woman who had left him, or he her—perhaps it was mutual, how could either bear it being their action alone?—to fall from the sky here, smash into cinders, merge indistinguishably with this unending volcanic sand. If he were so lucky.

The plane landed safely at Antofagasta. In the shadow of the airport building he turned left into darkness. Finally the plane roared away towards Iquique, and he could search for stars. The night sky was unrecognizable; it seemed as if he had never before looked up. Perhaps he was lucky.

Urn Burial

[1999/2001]

THE BUS CRAWLED EAST up the two-hundred-kilometre incline
of the Atacama Desert from Antofagasta, past the adobe warrens
of nitrate towns left roofless to sun and wind, to Calama where
a four-hundred-year drought ended in 1971, only to begin again
immediately. David crossed the blazing street to huddled jeeps. In
Chuquicamata, he was told, they would never show him the copper
mine, the largest hole on earth ever made, but a jeep could take him
high into any mountains, he could see anything. Dollars, good, but
rental required a driver's license. "No, gracias," he said.

The perfect desert, Atacama: not one sprig of plant, but slight
rain was possible every forty years. Dew. In Oasis San Pedro the bus
stopped behind the museum, where bodies doubled into clay urns
hugged their leather knees against their leather chests. The plaza's
giant peppertrees separated Pedro de Valdivia's house (1540) from the
whitewashed church, its algarroba rafters overlaid with cactus logs. As
the afternoon cooled people strolled arm-in-arm, dogs smelled each
other intimately, bars blared rock; David joined a tour to the Salar.
The impossible stick-legs of the flamingoes walked in the water as if
on skin, their luminous, doubled bodies meeting themselves at their
black beaks while they fed. When he knelt in the salt baked jagged as
coral, it gleamed smashingly white, whiter than snow...wash me and I
will be whiter...he fled to the safe technology of the bus.

Walking, walking, David found himself high in the pukara where the Atacamas had made their last stand against Valdivia. Below him, beyond the roofs traced among trees, the desert vanished upward to an endless, undulating skyline anchored by volcanoes. Perfect cones in the moonlight, like altars. No, he thought...like blue prayers. If only.

What is to be done? He felt his mind open as softly as a book.

And remembered Lourdes: "The light of this candle is the image of my prayer."

Morning brightened behind the volcanoes; he walked again. Sheep surged out of spear grass to drink from the stream, and he turned to cliffs lightening above the valley, to the Inca fortress whose repression here was as ruthless as Spain's. He clambered up a narrowing barranca, its jagged, volcanic walls flashing minerals, and a gash opened beside him. Deep inside, where the rock layers pinched together, gleamed bits of white.

He inserted himself along the gash and wriggled in. He felt his shirt rip, bottom, then top as he squirmed closer. He touched...ribs certainly, and heavy bones with ends knotted, legs perhaps, they were held immovably in a runnel of sand washed solid as concrete. He pulled in his breath, twisted his head flat and shoved towards a light beam. Rock tore his left ear, and against his right eye bone curved up, its surface impressed like the filigree of a leaf. Then, where the rock tightened into absolute darkness, his fingers felt an edge. Rounded clay: the lip of an urn.

It seemed the earth had shrugged. David was pinioned, without breath. Held firmly at last...or perhaps long enough.

A History of the New World [1978–1979/1979]

Box 3,
Indiana, Alta. TOA 1Z0
July 30

Dear Professor.
You asked to write down my Opinion, to write makes Things clearer,
so I will tell you I have read Thousands of Books of all sorts. Some of
them Were just Picking up Here and there, what we may call collage,
to me that is ZERO. Books like you talk about for me, a free thinker,
have no purpose or goal toward light and truth. Religion believers
have lost the original goal of Civilization

= the Conquest of Man by itself with no God, no master
= doing the Right Thing because it is Right
= with no fear of God or the Devil as a way to attain Beatitude.

You look at the pictures on my wall and my book piles and ask if I am
a Socialist. I am a lot worse than that, and in Alberta that Something.
Religions (3000 in the World) have given the Ignoramus a way of life.
He can avoid developing his Human potential. If you have Religion
given to you, by Baptism or other Hoodoo Worship, it makes no

difference, the development of the grey matter cease at 27 years old when the bones of the Cranium solidify. Finish: no more growing.

If, for instance, a person has had the misfortune to be Baptize in Religion, the bones of the FONTANEL are solidly welded together, then if in some way his Brain Waken in a splurge of Energy, *he die instantly*. And that no b.s. It happen every day and they call that a stroke.

I am one of the fortunate individuals that was blessed with· a Human being for a father. A man at 8 years who was on the barricade in 1871 Commune in Paris, who worked at that age = 14 hours a day for 20 cents with his two Brothers in a Brickplant. My father at 27 was the bodyguard of old Clemenceau, the Tiger of France, and also secretary of the Radical Socialist Movement. But being primordially HONEST, He did not climb the ladder of Politic. At 6 years old He used to take me to political meetings with the Idea that to be a Citizen you start Early.

When I was 14 years old I wrote a Book in a week, 500 pages. "The History of the new World." That was so far advanced in Thoughts that friends of my father told me to destroy it as nobody would believe that a kid 14 could write it. I could do that because Thinking is Electric phenomenon with waves like Radio that never stop through the universe ad Infinitum. The thinker open himself to the Telepathic message: we think when we are open to thoughts and lost in the Dim past we have quadrillions of ancestors, making a liar of any man proclaiming himself "Self Made Man."

Sincerely yours for the Golden Rule—the only law for Real Peace

JEAN LABARGE
A 88 year old Philosopher graduate in
the University of Hard Knocks

University of Calbridge, Alberta

October 11

Dear Mr. Labarge:

I'm sorry to be so long answering your letter, but my summer was
full of travel and...well, your letters are made to ponder. I have a
wonderful memory of you standing in your magnificent garden, so
far north and the July corn already up to your shoulder and even the
horse radish knee-high, growing on the soil you made yourself from
lake sand and your wood-fire ashes (Did you buy that pike the little
boy offered, and ran? I'm surprised you don't fish yourself, the lake
lapping your land, though if those terrified little boys will sell them
for fifty cents I suppose it's not worth the bother): I can only think of
you as a French gourmet who grows all the ingredients for his vegetarian feasts himself.

But you are also a free-thinker, and if so you must be open to any
experience that will enlighten you and your comprehension of the
world. Now we all believe something; even you, who believe in the
Golden Rule. It strikes me that Jesus told stories about that Rule
and lived it as well as anyone in history ever has, so your argument
against Christian believers (since you mention baptism) cannot be
about *him*: it must be with the way his teachings have been abused,
right? So why do you throw him out with all "Hoodoo worshippers"?
That's not free-thinking. That's like throwing out Mao because some
of his followers are ignorant killers.

Also, I cannot follow you on "the goal of civilization." Our Western
"civilization" is one of many developments in history. What common
goal could the disparate (a pun if you like) millions of the world have
unless it were one given to them by the creator who started the whole
matter of universe in the first place? You may call that "creator"
anything you please (and don't throw any "six-day-creation" dust at
me either) but surely a free-thinker would be the first to recognize
that the primordial slime out of which our ancestors, presumably,
crawled, the primordial thought which somehow (as you have it)
has us all thinking, they must have originated somewhere. In other
words, something was; *before* we began. It could not have been
Nothing.

318

Rudy Wiebe: Collected Stories, 1955–2010

I can never pretend I am "free" in any absolute sense of that word: I am tied to a body, to gravity, to psychic and mental demands and limits—demands and limits both hereditary and environmental and volitional. I often have no comprehension where these limits come from, and even when I know I can do little to resolve them. Oh, I am free to think what I please, certainly, but actually I am hemmed in even there by a limited (conditioned, uninformed?) imagination. In what sense is anyone, ever, a *free* thinker? It seemed to me you were, for example, hemmed in by your hatred of Calgary Power, a hatred perhaps justified since their engineers dug up the street and then filled it so badly that contaminated water seeped through and soured your root cellar and so destroyed all your carrots; hemmed in by your fear that the town boys would tear up your garden (if you curse them every time they walk by, what can you expect?); even hemmed in by your long-set refusal to consider religious options which millions of people have, over the centuries, sometimes found gave them peace and a certain uneasy happiness. I have given up pretending I can ever be free; my freedom I believe must consist in what I commit myself to and that....

Indiana, Alta.
Oct. 14

Dear profess.
A free man live with his Brain and Exist with his Stomach. I did not read the end of your letter because I know it Already.

I came to Canada in 1910 because the Canada Immigration covered France with paper that anybody could make $10,000 in five years, just work hard to make a farm. So I come to Edmonton, $400 and I could have bought a Whole block of Jasper Avenue but those papers say Farm and I bought three oxen with $400 and started walking North on the Grouard Trail. There was land by the Section there they said, and lots of French. And lots of Priests too, they didn't say. Started June 6, 1910, and got to Grouard on Lesser Slave Lake Sept. 13, 1910, walk every Step and one Ox sank in a swamp trying to get away from Mosquitoes, the second ran home—only time he ever move that fast, I have to walk to Edmonton three years later to get him, all summer Trip, and the only one Ox left so thin he was not even edible. I farm at Grouard, McLennan, High Prairie, Girouxville, all over 45 years, and then I got Smashed in a car accident and sold the farm: $6000 and the lawyer take $2000 for fee. That's the Canada Immigration Farm Dream. How rich would I be with two blocks on Jasper Avenue beside the Hudsons Bay, eh? Goddam capitalist, and

that's no b.s. Thank god and Jesus and the virgin, if you want, I live from Ground I Made myself, I got so little I can shoot anybody wants to grab it, and I give you peas again if you come stand in my gate and talk. They're still growing, but I have to cover them every night.

You sent me a Good picture. Your nice wife knows More about gardens than you, but you know it Already.

Altogether during 1000 years of the Dark Age over 50 millions of European peoples were murdered in the name of the Cross and Jesus Christ. In 1979 years now the Atomic and Hydrogen and Neutron Bomb, Bio warfare, etc. All done with the rejoicing of all religions: a very Christian future of Peace on Earth.

Total writing time = 13 minutes.
It is crazy to worry
fifty below rain or shine
Silly enough to be Happy
to Enjoy life is no Crime

NOTE = the grey matter of Brains has enough power to push
out the bones of the Cranium ad Infinitum
To the Seeker for Know How, there is no limit. Try it.

J.L.

[1969/1971]   # Bluecoats on the Sacred Hill
of the Wild Peas*

"HEY, LOOK, up ahead, the white on that hill there, that's it!"

"What?" Only his small son responded; not even this green Montana valley could nudge them from the stupor of an all-day line of Wyoming plains.

"That's crosses, of the battlefield I think. That must be where the soldiers are buried, yeah."

His wife shifted the baby once more on her tanned legs. "They just better have a campground there, is all I say, with their thousands of graves. Sheridan was plenty far, but not for you, oh no."

"Yeah," he was saying again, more slowly, "thousands—looks like a awful lot." The hillside half a mile to his right came up quickly while he kept car and camper on the road by instinct, his sixty-two m.p.h. standard on limited access highway. "Too many. There were either 265 or 266 killed, but that's way too many, for sure."

"There's more on the hill behind," the little girl pointed across the jumble of blankets around her.

in further observance of the occasion, Robert Little Beaver of Oglala Sioux improvised a moon dance.

"Stay on the road!" his wife shouted.

"Oh—yeah, that's it, that's the hill, the higher one where they made the last stand. This in front—hey, that was the Little Bighorn, eh?"

The tires had sung loud over a bridge. His wife said, "Slow down and you'll maybe see something else."

"That in front, there, is probably a national cemetery, or something. Like the one in the Black Hills we saw."

And so it proved when they wheeled right at the sign "Custer Battlefield National Monument 1 m" and in a moment turned right sharply again up the hill to the parking lot sweating tar faintly into the evening's heat. The two oldest children converged on the running water fountain but there was no shade; and no campground.

"The museum closes in half an hour," he said, "but there's a kind of area for camping in Crow Agency up the road just two miles, so maybe tomorrow—"

"It's four nights, and today you have to make five hundred miles. I've got to bath this baby. I'm not staying anywhere where there's no hot water." The baby was beginning to laugh in the beautiful way he had which meant that in 2.7 minutes he would be screaming, whether held or not.

*after man had been on the moon at least thirty minutes,
the television sets were turned off and the coronation began*

"Yeah yeah," he said, getting in slowly. "That means Hardin. So fifteen minutes. Hey, kids. Com'mon!"

The car pulled the little camper slowly up the steep incline. The tapered squarish monument on the highest point of the ridge stood, they discovered, on a massed grave of the 225 men of George Armstrong Custer's personal command that had been killed with him. A black iron fence surrounded the white stones marking the spots on Custer Hill where forty-two bodies had been found. The level western sun washed like a green mist of sagebrush down into the valley flat with wheatfields and twists of the Little Bighorn outlined in cottonwoods.

*as Armstrong descended from the lunar landing vehicle, the
four hundred persons in the big ballroom fell silent when he
stepped from the last step of the ladder to the lunar surface,
they let out a whoop*

"There's the valley we came up," he explained. "The Indians were
camped all the way back from there where the Little Bighorn—
the Indians called it the Greasy Grass—turns right angles across
the valley. The northern Cheyenne camped first, about there by the
bridge, because they always led, the fiercest plains fighters but they
weren't as many as the Sioux so they joined together with them
against the whites, then the Oglalo Sioux whose war chief was Crazy
Horse, greatest of the plains Indian generals—we saw the Oglala
reserve now across the Badlands in South Dakota, by Wounded
Knee—and then there were some circles of other Sioux tribes like
Brulés and Minneconjous. Right in the centre there was the huge
sundance lodge. Remember I told you at Bear Butte that they usually
held their sundances there but the settlers coming into the Black
Hills, with the Army, chased them away west

*three television sets were placed around the ballroom at the
Little America, and the sight of a man stepping onto the moon
held the crowd's attention*

so they held their sundance here in 1876. That's why there were
so many Indians in one place, way more than G.A. Custer or his
commanding general, Terry, or anyone ever thought there could be.
Maybe eight or nine thousand. And right way over there, coupla
miles up the valley, their camp was so big, were the Uncpapa Sioux
with their warchief Gall and the chief-medicine man Sitting Bull, the
greatest of the Sioux leaders, who in the sundance had had a vision
of white men on horses falling into the Indian camp. That gave all
the Indians courage to fight when old G.A. showed up, because they
knew their medicine was good. Maybe four thousand warriors, at
least two."

"It's beautiful," his wife was dandling the baby between her hip
and the iron fence.

"What!"

"Everything. The hills and the sage brush—that colour—the valley and the mountains back there."

"Maybe it was like this here June 25, 1876. When Cheyenne chiefs rode into battle they often sang, 'This is a good day to die.' This was a good place, maybe."

Their little boy suddenly raced down the hill. In a minute he was back, having circled the grating with its dead-white stones, panting.

"Is that all the cowboys?" he asked, collapsing on the edge of the mass grave.

Miss Nimmo is the daughter of Mr. and Mrs. Bruce Nimmo, and Miss Powers' parents are Mr. and Mrs. Tom Powers

"There weren't any cowboys. It was the army, the US Army 7th Cavalry, fighting on these hills all over, see the stones, where cavalry—soldiers that ride horses—is stupid to try and fight. It should have been down there, on the flat, where it can manoeuvre."

"That's the colour I want for the living room. I've been thinking about it all day and that's what I want."

He stared at his wife.

"Sagebrush, the green. Sagebrush."

"It's terrible," the little girl said. She had been motionless, looking through the bars at the stones and across down into the valley. "It's not nice to kill people or Indians. Why did they want to kill them?"

"They did manoeuvre," he said to her. "Over there, at the Uncpapa end of the valley Custer sent Major Reno with three companies, about 150 men—"

"Like in Nevada?" his wife asked. "Reno, Nevada?"

"Wh—oh—I don't know. No, that was earlier—what the—"

"You seem to know everything else, that's all." His wife hoisted the baby, laughing again ominously, and went up around the monument.

"No, I don't think it was named after him," he followed her. "He never made himself famous with that charge, down the valley. They hauled him into court later because he and most of his men survived. They thought he stopped too soon. He attacked, stopped when lots of Indians charged him, retreated back to the bluffs and that left all the Indians more or less free to attack Custer and his five companies at this end. At least so some think—nobody knows for sure. How can they, the only living thing to survive of the 7th was a horse."

"I remember that," the girl said. "Comanche!"

"Right!" he grinned at her. "You can see it from here, how it happened. The whole 7th Cavalry, twelve companies, came in way down the valley from the south and east over there. Reno was ordered to attack the village—in the dust and smoke they didn't have much idea how big it was but Custer would probably have attacked anyway, he thought Indians just had to see him to run, and Custer with his five companies rides along behind these hills to attack the other end of the village—city really, it's so big—down a creek valley there to cross the river. When Reno gets chased back across the river to the bluffs—the Indians fight so hard because they have good medicine and they're protecting their women and children,

Miss Powers will be next year's queen both girls are students
at the University of Wyoming in Laramie Miss Nimmo will be
a senior next year, working toward a degree in agricultural
economics, and Miss Powers will be a sophomore

the Indians can throw everything against Custer. Gall, leading the Uncpapas, counter-attacks Custer's charge down Medicine Tail Creek toward the ford, cuts him off from getting any more messages for help to the supply train or Reno or even Captain Benteen, who's waiting with four companies back there in reserve. Custer is forced backwards up this slope, fighting all the way, men falling where the stones are, see, Indians racing back and forth around him, hanging low on one side and firing over or under their horses' necks. In the meantime, Crazy Horse and his Oglalas, the fiercest of the Sioux, have come up behind this hill from the north, see, there, and attack Custer from behind over the crest right here. That's why they're all scattered down there, just below the top. In probably half an hour it's all finished."

The little boy was goggle-eyed. "Is somebody dead?"

"They're *all* dead. Companies c, e, f, i and l of the US 7th Cavalry—old George Armstrong too, right there by the stone with the iron flag he was lying, and the Indians whooping it up. Get in, we'll go see where Reno and Benteen got besieged."

Bottle-warmer plugged into the cigarette lighter, they drove very slowly along the ridge, its west slope washed in the green mist of the falling sun, its east dark with small white clusters of stone where three companies had fallen. Over a cattle guard in the road, and down between grazing cows toward the river and Medicine Tail Creek running high after a month of rain.

"Why are so many bodies on the east slope, if Custer went down to this ford and got beaten up the west hill, like you say?"

"I didn't know, were you listening," he said. "That's a good question. Actually, nobody knows what happened because Indians at that time mostly told whites what they wanted to hear and so their reports later—when they were convinced they wouldn't get hung for even admitting they were in the fight—were pretty much contradictory. Some believe Custer never even got near the river, he just stayed back of this ridge all along, but then that doesn't explain E Company all the way down that ravine or—hey, look! They've cut the road right *through* Weir Point!"

the week-long festivities began when Miss Frontier, Marie Nimmo of Cheyenne, accepted a bouquet of roses from Milburn Stone, who plays Doc in the Gunsmoke *television series Miss Nimmo's lady-in-waiting, Carol Powers, was greeted by Ken Curtis, who is Stone's television sidekick, Festus*

So they had. He stopped by the marker explaining that in the late afternoon of June 25, 1876, Captain Weir of Reno's command had fought his way forward to this spot trying to find what had happened to Custer.

"Fifty feet in the air now above this spot," he said and drove through to the siege-works. They read the plaque and looked across the little hollow where the surviving doctor had set up hospital, the concrete paths outlining defensive lines.

"Reno retreated from his attack on the village across the river below there and up this ravine. Lost lots of men at that ford. This was the best position they could reach, but even so that point is higher and Indian sharpshooters were potting them from there."

It seemed that under the setting sun there was no one alive except they on the hill. On the grey line of concrete down the valley not a car moved. The baby suddenly, irrevocably, began his roar.

"I'll just run around the entrenchment trail, just a minute. Can't you plug him up?"

"It's still heating in the car, dear," his wife said. "Isn't it like the Cheyenne warcry of Triple Moons, or something?"

the first official event of Frontier Days, the coronation of Miss Frontier, was delayed about half an hour so the four hundred Western-clad celebrants at Cheyenne's Little America motor hotel could watch the historic event on television

"No," he said. "The name was Two Moon."

He went alone and looked down the ravine to the ford. It looked like it: the bank far below must be one of the steepest cavalry ever tried. When he turned, his boy was beside him, and they ran together along the line where M Company had lain, down and up to the point held by H Company. There were weathered trenches, and ravines folded down to the river.

"What's the little sticks?" the boy asked.

"That's where the soldiers shot from. See, that side, is where they fought their way down to the river for water—they were up here two nights and a day—and over there in the east—see the hills and the trees—that's where they came from in the morning of the 25th, when Custer was trying to find the Indians and attack." They were returning down the hollow, trotting past A Company barricade.

"They shoulda had cowboys," the boy panted. "They'da fixed em."

"It was before there were any cows around here, long before. The Army men rode horses too."

In the car the baby was snorting as he devoured his milk. They drove slowly back, past the point where Custer was last seen alive, through Weir Point. Where the asphalt bent over a little hill before dropping to Medicine Tail Creek he stopped.

"George A. and his two hundred probably charged down this hill that Sunday. When the buffalo berries bloomed on this hill the young men came here to wait for their puberty dreams."

"That enormous camp, thousands of mothers and babies?" His wife was staring across to the river flats.

"That was the way to handle Indians. Custer had cut up a Cheyenne village at Washita in '69 and instantly that made him the most famous general in the US."

"My god."

"Some say that's why he hurried so much to find the Sioux, before anybody else would. He pushed his troopers, they say they'd been marching twenty-four hours without sleep when they got here. Maybe he wanted to send back a telegram that he'd cleaned up the Indians for good and all and stampede the Democratic Convention in St. Louis that was meeting then into naming him their candidate for president. He did promise his Arikara scout, Bloody Knife, all kinds of things when he became the 'Great White Father,' Bloody Knife said later, and he could have made it if he'd got the message out by June 28. The Bozeman telegraph line was only a hard twenty-four-hour ride."

*the pull of the moon was heavy even in the Old West atmosphere
of Cheyenne Frontier Days as the seventy-three-year-old celebration got under way about the time Neil Armstrong stepped onto
the lunar surface Sunday night*

"Would he have got it?"

He released the brake and the car began to roll. "1876 was the 100th birthday of the Republic. They'd just solved the Negro problem forever with the Civil War, you think anybody would have voted against a general who cleaned up the Indian problem forever?"

"This was that important?"

"Maybe. If the Indians had just lain down and died. He was a hero when heroes still had jobs. And for fifty years Anheuser-Busch made sure pictures of 'Custer's Last Fight' were in every beer parlour in the US."

The stubby obelisk stood black against the evening sky as they wound along the ridge; the museum was locked. Even the water fountain was turned off. There was nothing left but the road to Hardin. As they passed Crow Agency the girl suddenly said,

"See, the moon."

A curved sickle riding beyond some cloud. "The man in the moon was made in USA," he said. The baby, oddly, was sleeping.

"What a time for a ten-day trip like this," his wife said. "When the rest of the earth is watching history happen on TV."

Frontier Days Moon Walk Delays Queen Crowning
Cheyenne Wyo

"Myth. We'll watch them walk onto Mars," he said. "They'll have that in colour."

"Living red," his wife said. She was sniffing a tiny branch of sagebrush.

"Are they going to Mars?" the girl asked.

"I like cowboys anyways," the boy said.

"Sure they're going. If they push it they should get there in time for the 200th anniversary."

"We are not," his wife said, "camping anywhere where there's no hot water. This child is absolutely filthy."

"Sure," he said. "If we have to drive all the way home to Alberta."

* *With a certain acknowledgement to* The Denver Post, *"The Voice of the Rocky Mountain Empire; Denver, Colorado, the Climate Capital of the World," Empire Edition, July 22, 1969, p. 17.*

In the Ear of the Beholder [1993/1995]

ON TV a woman and a very stout man were explaining why John F.
Kennedy, the first president of the United States born in the twentieth century, could not have been murdered in the way the Warren
Commission reported he had been. Adam was, as usual, clicking
through the channels to avoid boredom and himself and sometimes ads when this sudden show—so amateurish, so miserably
home video with its camera fixed on two motionless people behind
a table scruffed with papers, talking—stopped him in mid-click. He
was already two channels past when those two plain faces twitched
him back, a memory of a word, their—what was it?—their completely
TV-unnatural normality?

He fumbled buttons a moment before he understood a diagram
now filled the screen on that channel: a side view, a line of dots
marking the necessary flight of "Magic Bullet." That was its name
now, the man's voice-over explained, "Magic Bullet": the first bullet—
not the real killer bullet—from Lee Harvey Oswald's rifle which must
have gone in six different directions, first through Kennedy and then
through Texas Governor Connelly to end up as it apparently did
in Connelly's left thigh. The dotted line showed it caroming about
billiard-like, thud thud thud—off what?—political flesh so hardened
by high office? And then an overhead view of the necessary trajectory:
the bullet passing with inerrant destiny from president to governor

330

and ignoring completely the proximity of presidential lady must also have shifted itself sideways at least 1.7 feet to orchestrate those wounds—seven in all, entrance and exit—bursting from the two men.

Then the screen cut to "Magic Bullet" itself. Close-up, and never shown in the Warren Commission Report. After smashing through Kennedy's neck and into Connelly—chest, ribs, arm, and finally wrist, the bullet had come to rest at last (uneasily it seemed) in the flesh of Connelly's thigh. Job done. Perhaps because of its miraculous changes in direction, it also revealed itself quite unmarked when it was found—the doctors dug nothing out of Connelly—on the Dallas Hospital floor an hour later; perhaps discovered by being stepped on, fallen from no one knew which, if any, stretcher.

Quite unmarked, oh, marvellous Magic Bullet! Described in the Report signed by the Chief Justice of the Supreme Court of the United States of America Earl Warren himself, and six others: a bullet. The most adored of all American death dealers, always the infallible, instantaneous cure for every problem; especially on TV, drama or news.

Lovingly as it seemed the male voice lingered over the supposed image of the bit of lead, a faint gleam along its right side—such blunt photographic silence—longly bald on blank paper; framed. The voice grew so deep, so profoundly large including as it did the entire century nearly completed and every trace of humanity anywhere on the globe: the greatest, the most (greater even than the World Series and the Superbowl combined?), this unfathomable mystery of a Made-in-USA mail-order bullet. And suddenly washed over by a long skiff of laughter.

As if he had laughed himself. Adam had dropped the book he was holding, though the TV control seemed still to be in his right hand. He could feel it.

The slender woman talked now. Sitting with calm, number confidence beside the man who had explained the bullet, and listing names, ages, home addresses of witnesses and ever more volunteer witnesses. The absolute TV evidence of numbers running in such heavy lists like accumulating weather: scrolling too fast to read but clearly and most irrefutably there. Five hundred and fifty-two in all, yes...the numbers vanishing for Adam as he heard them explained: so many hundred and something (how many?) witnesses who had been around that corner of Houston and Elm where the motorcade turned in Dallas on November 22, 1963, and who had declared to someone or other that they wanted to testify to the Warren Commission, only (how many?) had actually been interviewed, most superficially and without recording or notes being taken, and of those a large percentage (how many?) were in 1991 already dead. More than (how many?) percent of these dead had died of non-medical causes: single-car accidents, suicides, fires, lightning or tornados, plane crashes, cave-ins, dropped out (of life?) and vanished untraceably and unknown even to their nearest families. It seemed that Lloyds of London had calculated the odds of such vanishment happening in that time to that number of persons gathered fortuitously in one particular place as being in the range of 17 trillion to one, Yes! that was it! 17 trillion—statistical certainty.

Who laughed? Had he, laughed? A TV audience, deliberately unrevealed by any camera?

On the hotel bed, staring along his legs stretched towards the set in its high shelf, Adam thinks: a two-inch shift of camera away from those two ordinary people talking might very well destroy the illusion of what I believe I am at this instant seeing. A shift to me sitting here, my possible cock a possible stick in my hand? As easily as the shift of his mind to the exact moment, the exact place where he had first heard of that shot.

Or those three shots as the Commission claimed. Or more than four as various people, never officially believed, insisted. He was talking to a colleague in his basement office of the Illinois college where he then, briefly, taught; the colleague wanted to stage John Gay's *The Beggars' Opera* with his English students and felt that the criminals in the play, highwaymen, thieves and murderers, would not raise an eyebrow with the College Board of Governors but that the whores and particularly the hilarious concluding bigamy in it would create certain problems: what did he think?—when the freckled student thrust her red head in at the door and gasped, "They have shot my President!"—just like that, "*They* have shot *my* President"— and fled, sobbing.

He must have smiled then, he still thought. Perhaps, stunned and
puzzling stupidly whether this might be a new student joke, he may
even have laughed. He could never forget his first clear thought: God,
you Americans! You'll try to make an Abraham Lincoln out of a TV
president even if you have to murder him! His American colleague
had been staring at him; perhaps he had laughed—or worse, said
that aloud. He must at some time have left; quickly. He knew he had
stood with several hundreds in the Students' Association Lounge
watching small-screen history being fumbled about, summary and
detail upon inadequate, inconsequential, time-filling detail in inconsequential repetition and the grey voice of Walter Cronkite, whom to
see remove his heavy glasses and hear, glancing up at a studio clock
off screen, say "...thirty-eight minutes ago," was to believe. No flight
possible for doubt.

And the murderer, with picture and full US Marine biography,
announced there too within three hours. Not to miss the evening
news from New York? And formally charged at 1:30 in the morning,
November 23.

The book lying beside him on the bed now, unnoticed where it
fell from his left hand, is *A Gun For Sale*. Adam sees it; he can pick
it up again, it has remained at his fingertips. It first appeared in a
box of books he pulled out from under a rummage sale table in the
Bloor Street United Church Hall, still spine-coded G 311 but stamped
all over in capitals DISCARDED from The George Brown College of
Applied Arts and Technology Library, Casa Loma Campus, Toronto,
last Date Due Apr 1 1986. A dog-eared Penguin whose first words
emerge out of forgotten distance like an intimate, ghostly voice:

*Murder didn't mean much to Raven. It was just a new job. You
had to be careful. You had to use your brains. It was not a question of hatred. He had only seen the Minister once, an old rather
grubby man without friends, who was said to love humanity.*

A voice created by Graham Greene. Speaking to him through a
re-ordered alphabet? Adam has never personally met Greene who
is now very aged and may be, just recently, dead. A voice out of a

past he recognizes he remembers, thirty years at least, speaking with a delicate enchantment only language can create out of fear and botched murder and luck, hare-lips and gasmasks, of a chorus line dancer tied, gagged, and thrust up to die grotesquely in a fireplace chimney but she doesn't—a novelist foreseeing the Second World War in 1936!—the dancer apparently not traumatized by hours rammed up into sooty claustrophobia; an accumulating double hunt into the black hole of criminal and business and military and individual amorality. More than thirty years actually—fifty-five were possible if he could have heard English in 1936.

The little man behind the church hall table wears a name-tag on his vest: "Hello, my name is Arnold." Too close to mine for comfort, Adam thinks, and it comes to him like words in his ear: there will be other books for me, here. And discovers his right hand already fondling one: *The Death of Adolf Hitler / Unknown Documents from Soviet Archives*, by Lev Bezymenski. In perfect hard-cover condition, including dust jacket, unmarked and undiscarded and available for one Canadian dollar. Between his fingers it falls open like a trap on two pictures: "Helga Goebbels after autopsy in Berlin-Buch," black rubber apron and gloves lifting a small head, and on the opposite page, "Burned corpses of Goebbels, his wife, and two of their children." This captioned upside down, so that the charred remains of the adults are at the bottom, the smudged but uncharred children laid out in white nightclothes at the top.

Over his skin then he feels the hubbub of stragglers and book-lovers digging for rummage discoveries in the church hall shift imperceptibly into silence. Everyone in the room is standing with him, motionless, an exploded book in each hand which has, the instant before, blown the faintest sound with itself into unexistence. And silence breathing, an animal run to ground.

"That's quite a book, eh, for Monday?"

"Wha—?"

From his open mouth it would seem Hello-my-name-is-Arnold has spoken, in a voice as small as any expectable Canadian apology. But precise too, in the texture of his lumpy sweater—without hearing him, Adam would have understood him even if there had been another sound in the grubby hall with its grey, dappled windows

grinning. The small voice clamours at him along the dusty book
spines crammed in boxes, in jumbled heaps on the folding tables
more accustomed to serving coffee and unsold doughnuts to people
hunching in from sleep somewhere under Toronto cardboard: Adam
is standing on a book. He feels its edge slip, crunch aside under his
feet, oh oh, he kicks it hopefully away. Anywhere.

"Remembrance Day I mean, next Monday, that beast," gesturing at
his book.

"Oh him, yes, that...shouldn't insult the beasts of the field!" and
he feels fine about his smart literary rejoinder but oddly ashamed
as well, closing the book softly on the gruesome pictures as if they
might squash while nevertheless unable to put the book aside. The
little men of rummage sales should shut up and shuffle books and
leave you alone, who wants to confess their ashes of words into
pictures here? It was enough to walk down the north side of Bloor
with November sunlight almost warm off the brick and concrete
walls with the careful, heaped trash of transients buried in the
corners of cemented parks and not be required to make a sound
louder than breathing in a charity hall or pretend there was purpose,
pattern in what you were doing in this enormous city when you were
avoiding everything by doing nothing at all—where did this mouse
Hello-Arnold get the gall to utter a word? He must have made the
mistake of catching his eye. Not consciously, hell—and why should
eye be connected to mouth, and voice, and being forced to listen?
Could you catch someone's ear? By the mere pass of hearing?

He is at the left corner of the cashier's table—a card table—with
his two books in hand, or three, and he lays them down, fumbles as if
he were looking for—and discovers himself inside romances. Tender
pastel chapters always ending when Eric's or whoever hard but
gentle hand just brushes Isabelle or whoever at some sensitive place
oh so gently. He cannot pretend long—shit who here would bother
to watch him?—and he turns to see the belted man who may at some
point have been standing beside him hand the Bezymenski Hitler
to the cashier. Are there two? He has been spared?—his own is no
longer on his small pile sweet jesus gone surely he can resist going
back to see if another one—yes! His heart leaps quick as if he had
bolted oxygen, there is cosmic design, *all has been taken from me,*

and in his hand he finds one more air-brushed woman, one Regan O'Farrell to be exact, being undressed by Ashley Darlington Rockford III in *Wildfire Dreams* by one Megan Flanders:

Last night, with one shattering kiss, with one endless moment of hard hands against soft skin, she had discovered that, like all steely things, she could be as weak as rubber when raised to the right temperature.

Already, on page 15? How will you ever "she knew he must set the pace" reach page 187 "like the stab of a white-hot poker" unpenetrated? "First, tell me. Is it safe for you?"

Romance # 1,267. There is no one at the table before the oddly young cashier. And her slim hand is pushing *The Death of Adolf Hitler* aside. The belted man is gone, did not buy it. Perhaps he accidentally picked it up together with his own worn selection and, seeing it when he paid, said, "I don't want *that*." The cashier girl—she is very young, so young as to be untemptable?—has pushed it behind various plastic containers of paper money rolled on edge, a huge map of coins spread at her fingertips. That's the way to treat money, he thinks with enormous weariness: stand it indistinguishably on edge in recyclable plastic, dump it in a heap in front of you, all this careful ordering, this dedicated veneration of numbers, this penny-counting of taxes on every goddamn copper—throw it on a pile, pluck out whatever you need whenever, and then scrape it all, paper, coins, plastic, dirt off the table-top from too many dirty books into a sack when finally you're done with it—he puts his few books down, reaches, places Hitler on top.

"This one too."

"Great!" exclaims the girl, so inviolably cheerful. She is no Hello; unlabelled her hands fly. "One dollar for the hardback one for two paperbacks two dollars in total thank you have a nice day!"

And no tax. Trying suddenly to focus her he bobs his head, but his bifocals fuzz in both areas: to see her exactly he would have to lift his glasses and bend to within eighteen inches of her good, round face, perhaps even take her by the shoulders and lift her firmly into place so his eyes—you cannot touch a woman in public, not any more, it will always, and rightly be misunderstood, into a scream perhaps. She is not even looking at him but for one instant, it may have been at the cut between distance and close-up, it seems her focused mouth actually means what he heard. A good day: have it. Good god. He sees the third paperback he has bought, there in his left hand with an indelible clarity: big, folio size, a dark, glowering bald face, by Roderick Stewart *The Mind of NORMAN BETHUNE.*

Sitting on the hotel bed with his legs spread and glasses beside him, beside Greene, the afternoon light in blotches careening about the room and the steady TV drone of the stout man continuing until he finds the right spot at his fingertips and the sound fuzzes away too, Adam is amazed. At his thoughtless, probably stupid innocence of walking west along the north side of Bloor in Saturday November sunlight. Approaching the venerable brick assemblage of Bloor Street United Church, a good church presumably, a church with the goodness to overflow in a memorial service for Margaret Laurence. Goodness. Why doesn't goodness lurk in dark corners, under dust, behind old brick and cracked concrete, in urine-soaked corners and around peeling trees grown lopsided with the desperation of survival, why not that waiting patiently through a January funeral to waylay you and knuckle you, overwhelm you into purity and care and enduring tenderness and compassion which all humanity prayed for before you were aware of it and can set yourself against its willful seduction? Ugh, always a coward, always such a fucked-up weakling, goodness. Hiding, if anywhere at all, among the venerable dead.

And he has already gulped Hitler to page 51, the indigestible brutality of DOCUMENT NO. 12:

Concerning the forensic examination of a male corpse.... Splinters of glass in the oral cavity, yellowish glass splinters.... The remains disfigured by fire were delivered in a wooden box.... A smell of bitter almonds developed upon dissection.... Height 165 cm. (5 ft. 4.35 in.).... The corpse is severely charred.... Part of the cranium is missing.... Berlin-Buch, 8. V., 1945.... In the upper jaw there are nine teeth connected by a bridge of yellow metal (gold).... The heart muscle is tough and looks like boiled meat.... The lower jaw consists of fifteen teeth, ten of

*which are artificial.... In the scrotum, which is singed but
preserved, only the right testicle is found. The left testicle could
not be found in the inguinal canal.... Crushed glass ampule.... A
smell of bitter almonds.... The left foot is missing....*

A male so far right as to have no left foot or testicle? No left cranium
as well? That actually made sense.

There is a knocking at the door. And again, like a memory. His
door? No one knows him, or that he is here—and the rattle of keys
with another, gentle knock makes it obvious, and he calls,

"Yes? Come in?"

Adam hears the door open, steps, the hotel maid. The skin of her
bare arms and her face is not quite so black as the stockings on her
slender legs; her hair, if possible, blacker.

"Oh, excuse me, sir. I'm here to turn down your bed."

She may have said something, who knows. He is looking at her
and after a moment she comes towards him, between the two beds
very close since the room is not that large, and places what he knows
are two rectangles of silver-wrapped chocolate beside the telephone
on the table nearest his elbow. Then she turns her back to him, lifts
counterpane and blanket from the bed on which he is not sitting,
folds it back with one smooth motion to the white sheet, the white
pillow; her fingers slender and powerful, their inner skin so pale
sharpen that edge straight at herself quick as a gesture.

She is bent forward to her business. Such textures of slender
blacks; such tightness. There is a seam of uniform tucked at her waist
and he speaks to that,

"Would you care to make some extra money?"

Her back straightens into an instant of hesitation, then she
turns—the beds are so close he could touch her—her right thumb
and elegant finger offer between them at the exact point of his short-
sighted focus a plastic package. A condom. Safety available in any
public washroom.

"You will have to include the 7 percent Good Service Tax."

She could not have said that. No one would. He swings his legs
off the edge of the bed and she is standing between his knees, so
close his nose brushes that tuck of her uniform below her waist. The

uniform, a button, it is buttoned grey up between her breast to the dark vee at her neck, down to the middle between her long thighs, one straight line which he does not need to move his neck to know is there, five buttons for easy egress, ingress, aggress under her fingers they are opening, top to bottom, he does not need to move his head, he can hear it, and she wears nothing underneath, he can hear that too, only the stockings—pantyhose, black textures changing in the light tighter than glistening skin; her body absolutely there. As it of course always has been, somewhere.

> *We carry within us the wonders we seek without us: there is all Africa and her prodigies in us.*

The goodness of Sir Thomas theological Browne, given to silent powerless words. Adam gestures and she shifts slightly, aside, and with long fingers (the plastic still gripped between the thumb and finger of the right) widens the stockings out at her hips, slides them down over her hips, down her long legs, together with the shoes off her feet, first left then right.

"Is there anything else?"

Her endless skin laid it seems against his very eyes. But he tries to tilt back, to see her face and she is towering so valley and mountain over him that he cannot discern what he knows, what she must be— nor does it matter since she is already doing what he would certainly imagine were he still capable of it: an ineffable movement of her arms lifts both her hands to her breasts, pushes them up so that the nipples beak forward, out between her spread fingers, and it is obvious her breasts are so full and her neck so long that if she bowed her head over him she could curl her tongue around either nipple, whichever she chose, left, right, it is as if she spoke these possibilities into his very eyes, numbered them in his ears.

"Everything else? Too?"

"Slow...slow..."

His senses stagger, perhaps he is tilting, but her hands continue to push at her breasts, up, and they are completely distorted now, they are being lifted up from her ribs smoothly grotesque, she is hoisting them up past her face, over her head and she drops them both somewhere behind her without a sound, her hands quick as water everywhere flowing down her torso and stripping off her hips and buttocks, the hollowed lines and folds of her thighs, the full backs of her legs (that obscene little plastic square safely flickering) and her hands rise to her round belly, her groin, the black centre of her curly mons which ever since she turned to him has always been right there and so he delayed looking because it was most certainly there a tongue-length from his face, and it is gone. She is become, suddenly, the thing itself. And once her dreadful hands reach the stunned beauty of her face, who could admit she is there at all. This poor, bare, forked, stick.

"Is there anything else I can do for you, sir?"

She stands at the door. It may be Adam shakes his head. When the door closes he recognizes she has left her breasts behind, the long, curved sheen of her legs.

On the TV the woman and the man sit motionless, still talking. Inside the electrical box with them swirl particulations: backs, faces, breasts, hands, bunched buttocks, nipples, knees, hair, thighs—all possible human parts available except cunts and cocks—presumably the TV expects the viewer to contribute what s/he can, a handful of whatever—bodies in whole or in part pumping and gasping and moaning away with relentless endurance hour after hour, the buttons and sticks for search and uncovery under the fingertips. Coloured mist for the seeing eye, moving; not at all like these patterns of ink dots, these shades and density that shape Blondi's German shepherd corpse, the dog that belonged to the German shepherd—or leader, guide, chief, commander—god perhaps. Beside the six delicate Goebbels children: Hilde, Helmut, Holde, Hedda, Heide, Helga, all "H"s in honor of the one inexpressible "H" himself and no doubt falling into their last slender sleep with a Third Reich murmur of prayer,

"Händchen fallten,	"Fold your little hands,
Köpfchen senken,	Bow your little heads,
Und an Adolf Hitler denken."	And think of Adolf Hilter."

No rhyme nor rhythm (nor reason) in English. All the parts of the children when so carefully dissected: brain, tongue, lungs, kidneys, heart, offering up the smell of bitter almonds. Glass splinters in every mouth.

Bitter almonds. A few solitary corpses, so few among those European mountains of them. These few now seemingly as harmless as slender children. And proving nothing except what everyone already knows: that a human body will burn only roughly and in part, not at all properly unless placed, or stacked if necessary, inside a scientifically designed and fuelled oven. Looking is impossibly silent: what is needed to declare this is primordial scream, a vomiting OUT that would rip OUT every feeling gut. Adam's stomach heaves, a pathetic exorcism of bile and revulsion. He is looking at the other bed, folded down to its white sheets. There is no body part there. For the moment. Though he has no hope they will not be again, and that quite soon. He will make his contribution.

Pick up, clutch the glowering, almost devilish book-face of Norman Bethune: a GOOD man, it was said. Though continually and throughout his life an egotistical bastard—well, not according to Mao, but then he only met him once and never answered a single letter after. Good at least the closer he came to death, apparently better and better as his blood diligently circulated rot away from the gangrene having entered at the tip of his finger. Finger, the official record had it, though it could as easily have been the tip of his cock. If a man were in pain and dying at his farthest extremities long enough, slowly enough, did gathering goodness become a possibility? Mould you eventually into a wholeness? Not a Hitler; he came apart.

Adam cannot remember ever having a possible death pain: he laughs at the very pretentiousness of the thought sitting legs spread on a bed in the enervating comfort of a Toronto hotel where a beautiful tall woman has just turned down his bedding and left him two exquisite chocolates: he feels sick, and alone, but—unfortunately— neither is a pain unto death. Nothing possible at his fingertips in this cliché of a room will make itself or anything anywhere better.

But Bethune was a doctor involved in both the great oh *great* world killings of his final decade. On opposite turns of the globe he tried to cure wounded soldiers of whose languages he spoke not a word—so they would be healthy enough to kill again? From the Wu T'ai Mountains in China, August 21, 1938, he can write at last:

I don't think I have been so happy in a long time. I am content.
Here I have found those comrades whom one recognizes as
belonging to the hierarchy of Communism—the Bolshevists.
Quiet, steady, wise, patient; with an unshakeable optimism;
gentle and cruel; sweet and bitter; unselfish, determined;
implacable in their hate; world-embracing in their love.

Slow, slow, Bethune. You are writing about trained killers; whose
hatred and love, gentleness and cruelty conceived dreams to rule the
world and all the people in it. Mao at their head. And yet, suddenly
for Adam the deftness of Bethune's scalpel is so temporary, his disor-
dering of the alphabet too masterfully enduring:

How beautiful the body is; how perfect its parts; with what
precision it moves, how obedient; proud; and strong. How
terrible when torn. [Burned?] *The little flame of life goes out like*
a candle goes out. Quietly and gently. It makes its protest and
extinction, then submits. Four Japanese prisoners. Bring them
in. In this community of pain there are no enemies. Cut away
that blood-stained uniform. Lay them beside the others. Why,
they're as alike as brothers!

What is the cause of this cruelty, this stupidity? A million
workmen come from Japan to kill or mutilate a million Chinese
workmen. Will the Japanese worker benefit by the death of the
Chinese? No, how can he gain? Then, in God's name, who will
gain? Who will profit? How is it possible to persuade the
Japanese workman to attack his brother in poverty; his
companion in misery?

The names of God and gain and profit. Even Bethune dying cannot
avoid those enduring excuses. As if he already anticipated the coming
horrors of Mao in control of the Chinese, his behaviour thirty years
later indistinguishable from anything the Japanese ever did to them.
Well, distinguishable perhaps because it would be worse, since no
stranger, no matter how sadistic, can ever hurt a family—or a race—
as deeply as one of its own members.

This is not my country, this is not my land, this is not my race—
but of course in spirit we are all brothers, so I can come here and
be good enough to die, I can come here and be good enough to
watch: what is happening here is not happening to me though of
course I understand and sympathize so deeply—Adam sees himself
suddenly in Illinois that convulsive autumn 1963 and knows in a
flick of sarcasm he is rethinking himself—but from here I am always
writing somewhere else, writing home, even though when I am home
I cannot endure half the silly bastards who imagine they are my
friends simply because they knew me once but cannot imagine who
I really am, now. If I am any more than bits and pieces, at any given
time, now.

Like these two silent analysts on TV, mouths moving without any
visible emotion, still making sounds, still presumably explaining and
explaining why a weak-minded man like Lee Harvey Oswald, who in
a short life had been used by everyone he ever met—and by so many
organizations, both illegal and offical, both in the United States and
in the Soviet Union and perhaps even in Cuba and Mexico—how such
a feeble man could not possibly have conceived and carried out a
complex assassination with such brilliant and untraceable success.
The place where he happened to work on the sixth floor of the Texas
Book Depository as unlikely as being able to fire, with such unbelievable accuracy at a target moving away from him, three shots from a
bolt-action rifle in less than six seconds, the last shot blowing John
Kennedy's head apart so that Jacqueline Kennedy's first instinc-
tive reaction, her mouth wrenched in unutterable scream, was to
scramble onto the trunk of the Cadillac to try and collect the bloody
pieces. As if they could be, somehow, smeared back on the exploded
cranium and all will still be well and all will still be very well in
waning Camelot. The practical question was: why would those pieces
be on the trunk if the killer bullet came from *behind* the car?

The man and the woman are saying this. In ten thousand different
ways. Adam does not need to hear them, their motionless bodies
behind the desk a cipher of invisible words. The room he inhabits is
as still as a 1990 room in the centre of an enormous city can ever be:
a faint utterance of traffic, of plumbing, of heating: the omniscient

noise of twentieth-century indolence. Nothing is here for tears, nothing to wail; nothing but a tremor of sad wisdom.

There is never an end to TV; there is an end to a book. A singular discreteness. A book can be held, in your hand beginning, middle, end. Adam holds them, thus.

THE DEATH OF ADOLF HITLER: *"The corpse is that of a girl appearing to be about 13 years old, well nourished, dressed in a light-blue nightgown trimmed with lace. Height: 1 m. 58 cm. (5 ft., 1.6 in.) Chest measurement on the nipple line: 65 cm. (25.4 in.). No signs of violence on the body surface. In the mouth glass splinters."*

THE MIND OF NORMAN BETHUNE: *"Comrade Bethune's spirit, his utter devotion to others without any thought of self, was shown in his great sense of responsibility in his work and his great warm-heartedness towards all comrades and the people. I am deeply grieved over his death. Now we are all commemorating him, which shows how profoundly his spirit inspires everyone. We must all learn the spirit of absolute selflessness from him. —Mao Tse-tung. Yenan, December 21, 1939."*

A GUN FOR SALE: *"'Oh, I'm sorry,' Anne said. 'I've said it before, haven't I? What else can I...I'd say it if I'd spilt your coffee, and I've got to say it after all these people are killed. All the same,' she said, as Raven covered her with his sack; dead Raven touched her with his icy hand: 'I failed.' She began to cry without tears; it was as if those ducts were frozen.*

"'Failed?' Mather said. 'You've been the biggest success,' and it seemed to Anne for a few moments that this sense of failure would never die from her brain, that it would cloud a little every happiness; it was something she could never explain: her policeman lover would never understand it. Already as his face lost its gloom, she was failing again."

Adam drops the third book, gets himself stiffly up from the rumpled bed at last and walks past the silent TV with all its trapped pictures hammering for attention. Nevertheless, in it you can still occasionally discover individuals who believe in planning their lives; who believe in responsible actions; who actually believe there are people in control of the world who know what they are doing. Who can somehow believe with their feeble Greek minds in a vaguely Hebrew god.

He is at the inevitable window. All around him the stacked city burns in a kind of, as it seems, unending light.

He thinks, this is safe. Like Anne he thinks, Oh, I'm home. Twenty-seven stories below him a shadow moves along the base of the building. It seems to Adam he can hear footsteps; there may be a knocking at the door. He stands at the window, waiting to hear the next shadow.

And prays: If only it might be possible to love others so as not hate one's self. And touches the window with the surfaces of his ear. It is there; it is cool.

The Blindman River Contradictions

[1983/1984]

an interview with Rudy Wiebe

INTERVIEWER: *Maybe you could begin by telling me where you were born and where you grew up.*

WIEBE: There's a story around that I was born in Saskatchewan to a Mennonite refugee family but that's not true. I was really born in Alberta quite near Edmonton, a tiny hamlet which has now disappeared. My father was the son of the inspector general of the British army and he came here to homestead when my grandfather got tired of him sitting around home: he was nineteen years old and still had no idea what he wanted to do, so grandfather said, "Go out to the colonies and see if you can make something of yourself." My father ended up in Nova Scotia while his father was going to Bermuda to inspect the British military installation there. From Nova Scotia he gradually worked his way west, like everyone else.

How did a Mennonite family end up in the military?

There was no Mennonite. I'm not a Mennonite.

You aren't?

No, I'm British, I'm English. I never had anything to do with the
Mennonites; that's a fiction I made up because of course in western
Canada there's much more point to being somehow ethnic than to
being English. Actually, a Canadian writer has an enormous disad-
vantage in being English, as you perfectly well know, rather than
Ukrainian or Greek or Icelandic, or Mennonite. I had the races of
the world to choose from and I made a really bad choice; I should
have chosen Jewish, which would have given me tremendous literary
contacts in ways I can never have as a Mennonite (Mennonites generally don't read and never buy books—at best they borrow them)
but really, I'm English, and I was telling you about my father who
detested militarism but his father was the inspector general of the
British army, a professional soldier who kicked him off the family
estate in England and so he ended up on a homestead near Falconer,
Alberta. Of course, Falconer didn't exist at that time but he rode up
the Blindman River trail from Lacombe to Buck Lake I guess, and he
found a homestead easily enough.

Really? What was Falconer like as a place to grow up?

Well you see, my father and his cousin created that hamlet because
they were such terrible farmers. They were archetypal Englishmen,
they chose homesteads for the scenery they wanted on their estates
and the Blindman River valley is really beautiful, but the place they
chose had the worst soil in the entire district. If they had gone just
a bit west of Lacombe where the black soil is two or three feet deep,
they could have done very well, but they had to have a rippling
stream, scenery an Englishman could appreciate, wooded river-
banks, hills, ravines, and they didn't bother to find out that three
inches of soil is all that covers the clay. So they couldn't make a living
as farmers, especially gentlemen farmers; they had to do something
else. They were perfectly literate, they could keep accounts well, so
they ended up building a general store on the banks of the Blindman
River. There were several families living nearby already so they
named the place Falconer after one of the families.

Your name wasn't Falconer?

No.

What was it?

Are you the police?

Of course not.

Exactly.

Am I to assume you went to a one-room schoolhouse?

Of course I did, but the reason I became a writer was because I sat on the knee of the Governor General of Canada. You see my grandfather, this general above all British generals, finally got perturbed about what his son was doing in the wild Canadian West and after thirty years he decided to visit him. I was born in the middle thirties, that is a fact, and was still too young to know what was really going on, but when my aged grandfather visited us he brought the Governor General along—it was John Buchan, Lord Tweedsmuir. By that time Buchan had written several novels, *The Thirty-nine Steps*, *Greenmantle*, which I read a few years later—I was reading by the time I was three or four though I wasn't old enough to do that at the time he showed up—but I knew he was a very famous man and he came to have tea in Falconer one afternoon when my grandfather finally visited my father, the one and only time either came to Alberta. Lady Tweedsmuir came along with a huge vice-regal party and Lord Tweedsmuir picked me up, I remember this with absolute clarity, he put me on his vice-regal knee and patted my head and said, "You know, there's certainly good stuff in this boy; just keep him growing," and then he drove back to Edmonton because tea was over. History was made in Falconer that day. The house still stands where it happened, you know. It was very exciting; everyone had such English accents.

Was it a house filled with books?

No. My father rebelled against all things English. He detested the English military tradition of the nineteenth century and basically he hated English books because they propagated that militarism. I did go to a one-room school, that's a fact, but my father became secretary-treasurer of the school and he went through the library and took out all the books like *Tom Brown's School Days* and *Great Expectations* and *Rob Roy*, all those classic books that describe English life—*Winnie the Pooh* and *Wind in the Willows*—and I wasn't to read one of them so of course I read them clandestinely. I almost burned the house down once because I was using a match to read, if you can believe this, a match to read *Tom Brown's School Days* under the blankets! He punished me for it of course, but beating simply made me a more compulsive reader than ever.

Did you have any favourites that you especially enjoyed reading?

I really liked reading the nineteenth-century English novel where everybody knows exactly what they're doing. You have an ordered sense of the world in the great novels of the nineteenth century: you must get married, and get married well. You start with Jane Austen—I also read Scott but he's too romantic, so far away in chivalry and honour and impractical principles like that—the thing I loved about the English novel was its simplicity: money and marriage. Of course George Eliot messes it up by having Miss Brooke marry well and then the problems start, but basically Dickens, Thackeray, Trollope create a world that makes total sense: once you have married rich you're set, the story is finished. I liked that.

Were you a prose reader all along or did you read some poetry too?

I liked poetry a lot, famous poems like "The Highwayman" and "Sheep" and "Dover Beach," that enormous English melancholy of tides rolling endlessly up and down the naked shingle of the world. I loved that perhaps because I never saw an ocean; my father wouldn't take me anywhere near one. He himself returned to England to fight in various wars that England always has and Canadians feel obligated to help them with but he would never take us there, me or my sister. He always said, "See an ocean and before you know it you'll be standing at attention, saluting something," and he didn't want us to be corrupted by the English genteel world either so we didn't eat with napkins on the table. Now I know that English people really do eat with napkins on the table, and fine bone china, they always have that and any amount of silver cutlery. It made me angry because the one time I met my grandfather and his friend the Governor General I experienced this clear sense of class, of *correctness*. You know? The contradictions of my father were very strange; he hated the army but he served in two world wars, he wasn't any good at farming and he wasn't any good at business either.

But my father did know how to write speeches and he ended up being a member of the Alberta legislature here in Edmonton. The thing that got him elected was building the railroad between Lacombe and Breton; he worked on that for twenty years, around wars, and the MLA salary certainly helped keep the store going and then when he got the railroad built he lost his seat. Typical of Canadian politics of course, but it enraged my father even further. He got kicked in the teeth again and again for the kind of person he was; he sort of lived his life seething.

On the other hand I really did like the liberal melancholy I found in Tennyson and Arnold. Tennyson's great question standing in Westminster Abbey, that magnificent structure built to faith and the state church, "But God, what if it is not true? What if there is nothing up there?" Is Darwin really right, or the Bible? That kind of liberal melancholy—focusing the human need for doubt—it's heady stuff.

Your father was a politician and a great speaker, he must have been a pretty good storyteller too.

Well, he controlled himself when he was at home. My mother often said to him, "Don't bother, so much control!" but you know my mother was Ukrainian and he did this again in defiance of all things English. I mean what Englishman would marry a Ukrainian peasant girl, eh? And that she certainly was. My mother was the warmest, most loving person who had a far better knowledge of everything human than did my father, and her blood was the rawest, bare-footest, most up-to-your-ankles-in-the-cowshit kind of peasant that could be. This ancestry really gave me my dichotomy; I mean I go in two different directions: I don't mind calves and chickens wandering around the room and at the same time I long profoundly for white linen on the table. I can't imagine a better start for a novelist. But I felt I had to disguise this basically unbelievable dichotomy when I began writing so I invented this Mennonite persona that I'm known by, now.

Did your mother sing Ukrainian peasant songs, and tell you anecdotes, proverbs, enrich you from the treasury of Ukrainian folk culture?

She certainly did. But she had to do it clandestinely or my father would swear at her. Every time she started singing one of these beautiful lyric songs, getting all weepy the way Ukrainian people do when they get into the old songs, he would come in swearing and cursing, and if he hadn't truly been an Englishman, he would have hit her. Of course he didn't; as an Englishman he could just yell at her or slice her fine with cold sarcasm, but he never touched her in anger in his life. I would sometimes hear them through the bedroom walls, "You know, Charles, if you would hit me sometimes, you might get over it." I understand this now. I didn't then, that if couples really love each other, sometimes if they can fight physically they can settle some things. My father could never do that; an Englishman's sense of fair play will not allow him to beat women or children. It's impossible, so they lived this kind of profound, almost terrifying contradiction unresolved.

Did you have any teachers that made a lasting impression on you, that helped you develop the promise the Governor General saw so intuitively?

What can I say? I was the archetypal Canadian prairie kid who always has to walk three miles to a one-room school; always through deep snow at forty below, always poor and during the Depression. Well, we *were* poor. My father and his cousin owned a store but it was a terrible business. People think that storekeepers have lots to eat, but they don't unless they eat their own wares and then they're just making themselves poorer. And the multiracial "ethnic" Canadians all around us never believe you can possibly be poor if you spoke English like my father. You should have heard his accent when he was mad.

When did you get bitten by the writing bug?

I had a good childhood to be a writer because I had all these contradictions at home and I longed for a world out there that I believed must be really attractive. It was, and so I read more and more. Reading is a way of ordering the world better than the world that surrounds you. If you can say that a critic is a reader of a text, that a critic takes a text apart and orders it more clearly, then the writer takes the world apart in effect and orders it according to his thinking. And that was always appealing to me. The world I lived in was such a miserable world; why not make a better one? You couldn't make it any worse.

So you picked up the pen to do social work?

No, no writer is a social worker but one of the effects of writing, of thinking and putting stories on paper is that you do create a particular worldview, if people are patient enough to read it all, carefully. Most of them aren't of course. Many readers just want a diverting story but if you write serious fiction, as I hope I do, then eventually you do create a particular worldview; it is there in your work, hidden, and reading uncovers it. A good reader has to be willing to follow wherever the writer leads. Many people aren't; if the trail is too tough, they'll just go off and ride easy on some railroad track laid to somewhere else. But if they have to walk and cut their way...you know, following a good writer is like following a good scout through Alberta bush. Maybe the trail is half disguised and you even have a hard time finding it. Most people would rather sit in airplanes and circle around the world that way, looking down serenely on everything from ten thousand metres and actually feeling nothing much at all except comfortable.

Were you a child prodigy in the literary world of Falconer?

No.

Do you remember some of your earlier stories? Were you shoved up in front of the class to read, or be the star performer at the Christmas concerts?

No, no, I had a lot of miscellaneous ability...I was fairly well co-ordinated so I could play sports quite well and I could sing pretty well, I could tell stories pretty well. It would have been much more convenient if I had one particular ability, you know some people really have a voice and that's good because then all your choices are limited: either you sing or you're dead. Some people have good logical minds and they know they're going to be lawyers or doctors and of course every immigrant offspring wants to be that because they make money. But if you have a miscellaneous mind that goes in all kinds of directions, you've got no help. I could have done about fifteen different things and been sort of average at any one of them. I had problems.

When did you decide you were going to be a writer?

I am still not sure if I am one. Every book you write, you're still trying to find out if you can write it or not. I've been involved with publishing fifteen or twenty books, but that still doesn't mean they're very good or that I'll be able to write another one. You're always trying to find out, well, can you or can't you? And every time I start again I—I mean I don't even think in some ways that I *write* a story; it seems to me rather that I'm finding it. I don't know if I'll ever find another one. How can you tell?

When did you write your first story? How old were you?

Oh, probably about the time my sister died. That was right at the end of the war. It wasn't a story, actually it was a poem. Or a song. I made it up riding to school. Falconer was so small the school was in the country and I...this...thing had nothing to do with my sister who was lying in a coffin in our storeroom because there weren't any undertakers around to take away the body of a person you loved and bring it back packaged like they do now. My father was in England of course, training soldiers, but it was spring luckily so the body stiffened up nicely and didn't smell too much among the leather harness and barbed wire. I made it up...it was a kind of a song I guess, I was riding my horse to school. I was about eight years old, and crying.

How about your first publication? Was it in the Falconer Gazette *or where did you publish first?*

Well you could hardly call it publication, a local newspaper article. The write-up of a school party which I disliked so much...I didn't like parties even then so I was the perfect reporter. I stood there and watched kids my age, fourteen or fifteen, going through the charade of a party and it gave me the perfect kind of writer's stance. I was standing back and watching everyone, including a goofy, long-boned kid like me ladling out the punch, watching the older boys trying to pick up girls and the girls simpering and giggling and some of the sensible ones I admired not knowing what to do because being silly is really the only expected behaviour there. That experience gave me a sense of distance, of being an observer at the same time as a sort of participant...this sense is a necessity to any writer. In one way you are totally involved and in another you are quite apart, watching. That's a fine thing about being a writer. You're split. It helps if you're a Gemini.

Are you a Gemini?

No. I wish I was.

From what you're saying, it must have been quite traumatic for you to go from Falconer into the big city. Was it a difficult transition to make, have you ever really left Falconer?

I don't know. I'm a Libra and I balance two things at least, all the time. All my life I'm holding two things or more in my hands. Now the fact is I've never literally lived on a farm; on the other hand Canadian newspapers have sometimes had agricultural journalists review my novels. All my adult life I've lived in cities, yet I like the land, I like farms. But I can't stand the thought of myself being a farmer. It's ridiculous.

Do you enjoy going back home?

Where's home?

Falconer.

No, I never go there. It doesn't exist. I know this is a cliché but really, you can't go home again.

What else would you still like to do? Do you have any second careers in mind outside of writing?

No. Writing is one of the great arts and anybody can spend a lifetime at it and still not be satisfied with what he's done. I suppose it's that way in making the other arts too, say music, painting, but those arts aren't quite so close to daily life. Nobody naturally uses musical sounds all the time, nor makes pictures or designs, but everybody uses language. Language, both poetry and fiction—it's so close to the way we conduct our lives in one sense and in another so far away that there seems to be no connection at all with what a marvellous writer like James Joyce or William Faulkner does with language and what we do, writing letters or talking, and yet in a mysterious way there is a connection. Far more so than what Picasso does with images, or Stravinsky with sound, story is always a living closeness; there's an endless fascination in making them. Anyway I don't even think I write stories; I find them. I'm more archaeologist than inventor. You never know when, or where, but you're always looking and suddenly you unearth a marvellous archaeological site and then, if you're smart, you dig very carefully indeed.

Do you think your awareness of language or your appreciation of it is heightened by the fact that you grew up in a community with so many central European kids, people talking so many languages?

Oh, that is certainly true. I can't imagine myself being a writer without my mother who spoke to me only in Ukrainian or to her mother in German. My father had been sent to one of the best schools in England, not exactly Eton but close, because his father had military plans for him. But the polyglot world of languages in which I grew up gave me a magnificent start and my mother always said that the first word I uttered was "Baba," it wasn't anything else; it was

Ukrainian.

Then why have the Mennonites laid claim to you? What's in it for them?

Oh well, heck, they're just glad to grab any publicity they can get. I mean, they have so little artistic reputation, until my generation they've never had a writer writing in English in this country worth reading twice.

Then how did they end up with you? Couldn't they have chosen someone else?

They've certainly thought so many times since, I assure you, but after my first book came out the die was cast. They couldn't do anything about it and they just have to put up with it, now. As Osip Mandelstam says, no more than you choose your own parents, do a people choose their own poets.

Thank you very much.

FOUR | NOW AND WHEREVER

Shadow of a Rock

FOR PURPOSES OF THIS STORY you have no wife, no daughter or son, no in-laws nor siblings nor grandchildren; certainly not a small granddaughter three thousand kilometres away who mails you tiny papers of splashed yellow and vivid blue abstracts labelled "for grampa," four tiny papers or five, and once a thin black stone round as a phase of the moon. Nor did you have parents whose labours ended long ago, the bodies they knew for over eighty years disintegrating into their base elements without seeming regard for any unshakable belief that they would, in time, certainly rise again.

These comforts are not here. You are simply a human being, alone. Thinking.

❀ Of high places. Millennia before the pyramids of Egypt, before the Great Wall was draped over hundreds of mountain peaks in China, before the stories of Hebrew exodus and long before the biblical Samuel—named "a man of God" who would anoint the first king of Israel—before Samuel walked up the high hill at Ramah, in what is now once again Israel, to "bless the sacrifice"—whatever it was—in order that his people could eat; long before Jesus left his disciples to their boats on the Sea of Galilee and walked alone into the hills to pray: thousands of years before such events, on hills in what is today Alberta, Canada, high places were equally venerated. People knew

that from them you could see the long sky stretched over land formed
into endless undulations by the advance and retreat of ice oceans;
could see the moon and the sun setting and rising again unendingly; see cloud streaks tower up and boil into black thunderstorms
whose lightning slashed fangs over you until you were overrun by
stampeding sky and recognized at last that you were inside the very
flames and wind and water of the universe itself, and always had
been, though you had not known it.

And sometimes, on these prairie high places, people found
erratics, great wandering rocks carried and left by the wayward ice.
To locate the roving animals they needed to eat and live, aboriginal
people often waited in the shadow of these rocks, waited for days and
nights, waited for weeks, felt the grainy, massive boulders against
their sinking bodies as air and land and stone slowly, steadily, materialized them into their prayer. And eventually, always, the animals
came. A gift to be thankfully, skillfully taken.

On one such high place in Alberta the great rocks still remain
in their aboriginal place. Oddly remain, despite dynamite and bull-
dozers and efficient farmers who believe in stones only if they are
shoved into random heaps around which their relentless machines
can best, most mono-culturally, manipulate the soil into their concept
of profit. Even more oddly, this particular high place is easily found;
in fact, anyone can drive to it on an all-weather road, there is actually no need to touch the earth until you open your car door in the
parking lot on the very top of the hill.

But first, take off your shoes.

◉ Somewhere in your childhood you discovered that the English
words "I" and "myself" and "me" meant the same thing: you could
hold conversations with your selves. In German there were actually four such words, "ich" and "selbst" and "mir" and "mich," but
an English trialogue could be complex enough, and certainly much
better than the formidable, often immoveable Mennonite binary you
knew yourself (through no choice of your own) to be living in: "It's
either *right* or *wrong*—what else can it be? If you're not sure whether
your pants are clean or dirty, they're dirty."

Now however, if *I* said, "Do it," and *me* said, "Oh no, don't!" there was still always *myself* available for debate: "Maybe do just a little, but then stop, and if it's really wrong you can always say, 'I didn't know, I'm so sorry!' And even, if necessary, pray to be forgiven. But at least you've tried it, and who knows, it may actually...."

In your trialogue with yourself you eventually recognize that the German four-part "I" is possibly even better than the English three-part. German retains a particular I-word for the dative case, a grammatical form of indirection English has sluffed off, and when you use that word, "mir," you have the added argument of evading responsibility for an act by saying it was something done to *me, I* couldn't help what happened and therefore *I am not at fault.*

But be careful: this can easily lead so far as to imply, "The devil made me do it." Then you're right back in implacable Mennonite binary of *dirty.*

But in any case, you can pray for forgiveness? Hope?

❋ On their high place, the pre-historic Ribstones on their hill near the town of Viking, Alberta, seem small in a tufted landscape of treed farmyards which vanishes everywhere in every turning distance of fields. From your car door the two largest stones are visible against the skyline. The very largest could well be a pale albino buffalo bull lying low in the grass, the other just beyond it a slightly darker cow or grown yearling. The ground seems to shift under your moving feet as the approaching stones become even more profoundly animal. A huge backbone is incised the length of the longest, from which a ribcage of parallel ribs curves down both sides, disappearing into the grassy ground. Tiny round cupules are carved in patterns into the smaller stone, like wet curls matting a living animal fur. It is said that when these curls are drummed while singing, the grass whisper of buffalo hooves approach.

Your hands know no rhythm of drum, you have no songs fit for this place, you feel suddenly that your melodious Mennonite "Heimatlieder" (*hymns of home*, a play on 'home' and 'heavenly home') will vanish on this hilltop like a grain of sand in the Pacific Ocean. And yet...and yet...sand grains do exist in every sea, like our spot of Earth does exist in a universe whose limits no one can map,

much less fathom, and you know that even as you came walking
barefoot over this stony ground your body was humming,

> *Keiner wird zuschanden*
> *Welcher Gottes harrt....*
> [No one will be destroyed / whoever waits upon God....]

and the song continues singing, cell by growing cell you already
sang it in your mother's womb, the German words rhyming themselves through their verses as you contemplate the smaller, scattered,
stones resting in the grass, the tobacco and cigarettes and sweet-
grass offerings, the coloured clothes placed where the prairie wind
can move but not remove them. People working with stone tools on
these quartzite boulders year after year as they waited, generation
following generation, human tears and hands that grain by grain
shaped these stone prayers to Old Man Buffalo.

And white farmers have not destroyed them. Of all the numberless high places bulldozed and thrown away without memory in vast
Alberta, these solitary stones remain on the high place where the
glaciers moved them. A crest of prairie aspen partially surrounds
them; the thin trees are gnarled, broken, dead, but nevertheless they
continue to sprout from roots out of the ground and grow again and
again, relentlessly. Colour prayer-flags are tied to their stems and
branches, offerings hung, weathering into the elements of bright,
windy air.

◉ The North Saskatchewan River is running extremely low. Barely
a hundred millimetres of snow and rain have fallen from January
to the day in July when you walk along a ridge of muddy gravel
curving away from the willows at what was, after 1829, the Fort Pitt
landing. You have come to this place for forty years, and have never
before been able to walk out into the bed of the river. Only the wide,
shallow sweep of water and the long eastern valley hills of grass
and dark folds of saskatoon and aspen remain of what Plains Cree
Chief Mistahi-maskwa—Big Bear—once saw here, beyond Governor
Alexander Morris offering him a feather to touch in eternal surrender
to Treaty Number Six. The treaty spoke an unreadable language

which, though absolutely White, Mistahi-maskwa understood only too well; he would touch nothing.

You take each step carefully on the slipping stones, and beside your shoe you see the muddy shape of what may be a gnawed beaver stick. But touch tells you what you could not have dared imagine, and the river water confirms it. A buffalo horn: the mud washes away to the grey, grainy surface, pours out of the hollow shaft into which you can push two fingers. It is a curved cone the exact length of your hand: the right horn of a plains buffalo cow or yearling, with the broken spikes of its thick skull still attached.

You crouch down on the stones in the river. The river whispers something incomprehensible to the luminous grey horn in your hand. This place. No wild buffalo is known to have been on the North Saskatchewan since the Plains Cree people followed the last animals south into Montana in 1878. A hundred and thirty years. Listen.

A yell bounces over the water, "...good! Great! Now come back, but walk closer to the bank!"

An order: straighten up, turn and face the movie camera tracking you.

You must walk back, along the riverbed under the looming sand banks of green willow. But you will not raise your eyes from the river stones, you walk towards the spot where wooden York boats from Edmonton and from Hudson Bay once landed with their furs and freight and singing, cursing voyageurs, their exhausted trackers. High on your left a fringe of poplars tower along the edge of the valley plain where the palisade and worn log buildings of Fort Pitt once stood; where once their smoking ruins sank into the muck of April snow; where you first saw nothing but a ripening barley field planted by the Hutterite Colony that, the Canadian government declares, now *owns* this land. But walking that first time in their plow cut along the poplars, you found a bright shard of Blue Willow China plate. Now, watching your feet, you remember the white Hutterite buildings, how they are visible in that fold of valley hills where Wandering Spirit and his warriors appeared in April 1885. And at that instant you glimpse another muddy shape half-hidden in the gravel bar.

Truly a beaver stick, also as long as your hand. No gentle curve lengthening to a blunt point: this is the diving shape of a dolphin head abruptly gnawed off at the shoulders, complete with long bill and a black spot for its bulging eye. The dry feather weight of grey wood.

You shout at the camera: "What do you want, buffalo or beaver?"

"Both!" Like any Canadian.

❁ From Ribstone Hill, the high hill beside Iron Creek is a tiny bump on the southeastern horizon; smoke on one hill would be clearly visible from the other. But as so often happens on the prairie, you do not comprehend what you are seeing. Iron Creek itself is traced on every Alberta map, but you discover its name and its high hill in a letter written in 1869 by the Methodist missionary George McDougall:

> *August 23rd, Iron Creek. —This beautiful stream derives its name from a strange formation, said to be pure iron. The piece weighs 300 lbs. It is so soft you can cut it with a knife. It rings like steel when struck with a piece of iron. Tradition says that it has lain out on the hill ever since the place was first visited by Na-ne-boo-sho after the flood had retired. For ages the tribes of Blackfeet and Crees have gathered their clans to pay homage to this wonderful manito. Three years ago one of our people put the idol in his cart and brought it to Victoria [a settlement the McDougalls built on the North Saskatchewan River]. This roused the ire of the conjurors. They declared that sickness, war, and decrease of the buffalo would follow.*

It is said that it was young David McDougall who obeyed his reverend father's orders and dragged the black "idol" off the hill for display in their Methodist churchyard one hundred and fifty miles away. And the native Elders were only too correct in their prophecies of coming disasters, though they never assaulted or killed any Christian, nor stole anything in order to return their sacred stone to its high hill. Truly exemplary heathen (Christian?) behaviour.

As the sad years of prophecies fulfilled themselves among starving prairie peoples—during the smallpox epidemic of 1869–70 some three thousand people died, including three of George McDougall's

daughters—the black stone was dragged even farther away: over
two thousand miles by cart and river boat and wagon and train to
Victoria College in Ontario. There the thin, roughly conical stone
was "scientifically" examined and declared to be a meteorite twice as
large as the Holy Black Stone of Kaaba in Mecca. Finally, after over
a century in eastern Canada, it was "repatriated," back west; to a
corner of the Royal Alberta Museum in Edmonton where only proc-
essed air and certainly no sunlight will ever touch it.

This gleaming black, pitted iron that once blazed to Earth from
outer space, now variously called "Iron Creek Meteorite," "Iron
Stone," "Iron Creek Manitou Stone"—why did George McDougall,
having seen this "wonderful manito" high upon its magnificent landscape, explicitly connect it to the Hebrew story of Noah's flood and
the eastern Saulteaux tradition of Nanabush, the creator of Earth
and animals? Why did he not recognize its Blackfoot and Plains Cree
name: *Old Man Buffalo*? Because to this day, even under the low
roof of a mechanically controlled museum, as you contemplate the
dazzling, shifting surfaces of the stone, it is possible, sometimes, to
see Old Man Buffalo's awesome face.

❈ You and your friend stand side by side in the stark museum light.
He asks: Can you see him?
And you ask: Where?

❈ The questions lengthen into the landscape: from what high hill
of veneration was Old Man Buffalo stolen one hundred and forty-
three years ago? Without your friend you might never have known.
Together you travel parkland prairie grid-roads, looking. A kind
woman in the Sedgewick District Archives offers several copies of
papers and you angle towards Iron Creek where it loops south to the
Battle River. Gradually you both begin to comprehend that, rising out
of the northeastern horizon, is the cone of a solitary, spectacular, hill.

"Straw Mountain" is its official *Alberta Gazette 1995* name. The
closer you come, the more it grows into your childhood homestead
memory: the golden straw blowing from the threshing machine
shapes itself continuously, higher and higher, into a mountain of
straw before your wondering eyes. Here the road allowance cuts

straight through the mountain's base, leaving a gravel scar where your car can stop along a barbed-wire fence. Your friend says: You climb at your speed, I'll climb at mine.

No matched slabs of steps to guide you up towards a pillared temple. Only the steep earth, growing with brush and wild grasses.

You look and look. Your friend is beside you, looking. Slowly you turn until you return to what you first saw: Iron Creek twisting south within the bends and escarpments of its valley, the wind washing like water over squared miles of grain to surround the bare massif of the Wolf Ear Hills. A pickup truck crawls up the road between the ears in a banner of dust. Here Old Man Buffalo rested; for uncounted millennia; guardian of the great animals that grazed around him in their millions. And when he was dragged away, within a decade those animals were completely and forever gone.

Your friend murmurs: Here, I think, even I could have a vision.

※ This high place. Straight roads, square farmyards hidden in trees, machines, rectangles of grain; enormous oil tanks gleam on the southern horizon—not one animal, anywhere.

You sense the air as motionless, but the bright clouds above you move in two directions, they pass over and under each other both east and west. Beneath your feet the hilltop is flat, almost hollowed out as if scooped away by shovels, and you remember some papers said that local farmers had dug gravel from the hill until they blundered into a human skeleton. Homesteaders first settled Iron Creek valley in 1906, but there was no written record of anyone buried here, so the county council declared the hill "protected as part of the prehistory of our country."

The tintinnabulation of silence. Your friend stands with you... but...more are needed, a gathering, one that would together completely circle this mutilated hill with human beings. A smell: saskatoon berries ripening, and a strangeness wraps itself around you...you cannot quite feel what it could be. As if, seeing this land, you must forget yourself and move through an immense curtain into another space that would look exactly the same, yet is different. Into a comprehension of *beyond*. You need patience, to wait together, wait. Until you all are given raven eyes to see in every direction simultaneously, until the entire circle of the earth inhabits your bodies. And Old Man Buffalo is here. His gnarled and pitted face, like Mistahi-maskwa's after his spirit wiped aside death by smallpox. Old Man Buffalo's black face shimmering in the unbearable light of the sun, his long bent nose, his great mouth open, will you listen! Don't you know "listen" is simply an anagrammatic flexation of "silence"— *si...lenss, liss...sen.*

If you can see in silence, you can also hear. Listen. Look. Feel this enduring stony earth, under your knees.

The Shells of the Ocean

1. ALL LIFE COMES FROM THE SEA. It would seem reasonable then
that all life must return to it. Reasonable. He sits under the palm
trees, or sometimes under one of the tiny frond-thatched roofs served
by the solicitous waiter; watching the sea; listening. Sometimes he
contemplates the two volcanoes floating so high above the bay; or the
sound of bare feet in sand. On the curve of reef paralleling the shore
the swells break, smash down like a continuous and interrupted
rhythm of wall toppling from left to right, climb up and smash down,
again, and again, both their beginnings and ends lost beyond edges
that he cannot see. Only the shadows of one or the other volcano
occasionally in the clouds insist on land somewhere; certain and
reasonable there, beyond or above the water.

2. All seas everywhere are the same sea, and so he has come to this
one where they never were together. The creatures in and on them
were always the same. Again and again the porpoises crossed the
wake of their ferry between Honshu and Hokkaido; she of course saw
them first, playing as it seemed, beside the ship, and together they
watched those dark shapes torpedo into the ship's wake, back and
forth, whiter bellies arching...why was the word for that "wake"? The
killer whales off Galiano Island revealed their enormous black backs
once and then the sea swallowed them, but the porpoises of Japan

followed as far as he could see despite the ship's turbulence—perhaps because of it?—until it left them behind while the several hundred Japanese high-school students aboard in their navy and white, almost military, uniforms came to crowd around her testing their rudimentary English, "what your name?", "what age you?", "where you live?" until her blondness swam above their gleaming black heads. She was a celebrity signing books, bits of paper, diaries, and he was in an eddy beside her with his greying beard, and they were begging her to accept the tiny carved key charms, the bells, the chains they were supposed to be taking back to their parents from their school outing, and soon the delicate girls reached for her with fingertips like leaves, her unbelievable pale skin and golden hair, the grey porpoises riding unnoticed far away in their wake. Was the sea also asleep? Did ships, like intruding bodies, wake it? Sweetest heaven, what a lifetime he had been asleep! Death itself could not at first jolt him out of that; but now he was most certainly awake. Had he slept a minute since... would he ever?

Only last summer they had travelled the arched coast of Wales. Among the massive ruins of Edward I's enslavement of the Welsh in the thirteenth century she had seemed no more preoccupied and sad than he: their mutual melancholy a closer companionship than they had been certain of before in their lifetime together. He thought then her occasional singing under her breath made her sound almost happy again, and he certainly could have done with a little happiness; again. "Oh, it's just a folk ballad, it's turning circles in my head, you know, just the tune." But she knew words, at least one verse, and her sudden silence when the three students like medieval musicians laid their instrument cases open in the inner ward of what was left of Aberystwyth Castle and piped the melody she had been humming, and the lean girl haltered in a peasant dress sang with aching sweetness,

"There is a deep valley—"

"Hey!" he had exclaimed, "that's your...now you'll hear the words."
But her face was wiped blank. Stiff, broken like the wall against which they were leaning, blown apart by Cromwell's self-righteous

English cannon destroying the Welsh for the last time. The falling sunlight glanced up off the sea there, lit the tiny particularities of her face he had studied, cared for, adored since he held her in his arms within hours of her birth, oh God, God.

3. Wherever he may be looking makes no difference. There is nothing to see but the inside of arid eyelids. The endless roar of the reef has hardened into moments of crash as the tide falls steadily higher and higher up the beach.

"Another drink, sir?" a soft voice in his ear.

"A mixed juice," not opening his eyes.

If he began with alcohol there would be no stopping. The waiter is gone without a sound, dark feet no doubt bleached in the livid sand. Without opening his eyes he knows her song is floating in his head like the volcanoes, now this one, now that one, dreaming on their bed of cloud. He should ask the waiter: which way do you prefer that it come? From the solid flanks of the mountain you know are always there inside that mist, or from the sea which you can never not hear? From the flanks of mountains that sometimes adjust themselves, shrug once or twice every generation and run fire and molten rock over you? Or from frightful shapes coming through the white wash of the sea about which you never had any warning either: a thousand years ago the Hindus from India, then the Chinese, then the Arabs, each bringing in turn slaughter and new overlords and religions, and then the ultimate invasions of unstoppable Christians: the Portuguese and Roman Catholicism, the Dutch and Calvinism, the English and Capitalism, until finally the Japanese turn the deadly circle back to Asia again with no government or religion or ideological reason for killing except power. Each in turn destroying and building, destroying and building in a millenium of invasion from the sea with knives and spears and arrows and cannon and machine guns and grenades and diving planes until now the ultimate incomprehensible bomb hangs over them with all the rest of the world, and he sits here day after day remembering one single life, fingers through that thread by thread. How can you comprehend centuries and millions when one day, one life overwhelms you?

There are so many ways to be destroyed: sliced, skewered, smashed, shot, blown to bits, incinerated, overrun by flowing, molten rock. Or by the single irrefutable needle of longing.

4. There is only the sound of her voice and the words she never sang:

I never will marry,
Nor be no man's wife.
I expect to live single
All the days of my....

Never sang word for word; never that he heard. All she murmured once, it was on the northwest tower of Harlech Castle, where seven centuries of sand dunes now separated its massive inner wall and cliff from the white line of the sea and they were staring in a kind of mutual resignation across the miniature railway and the golf course and the campground and the trailer park parked tight window to wall with holiday tenants, on the tower wall she murmured something about the Carter Family. Later, much later that emerged like flotsam in his memory: the Carter Family was his sad mother humming in the log house in Alberta, those peculiar Carter guitars laying a clanging riff on the static of battery radio, turning and turning in melancholy, rhythmic whine until Maybelle alone or Sara alone or together or both joined by A.P. droned their flat voices into ineffable tragedy as if the gentle knives of misery were sliding flat through your gut and you would never really know where all the pain was originating, would discover tomorrow you had been disembowelled and filleted yesterday, were already eviscerated, dead, though still so sadly walking about the day after yesterday.

5. There are beautiful palm trees here, yes, but where can you pray, since the molten mountain or the sea are certain to bring some new and previously unimaginable horror? Rice fields now rest like stamps brushed onto the mountain, the endless fish in the sea...but there is never any warning and you never want to believe it anyway and always hope, hope, hope, hope until factuality crushes you and to what then, when you are crushed, can you pray? Both oh both, oh

bring back, bring back o...mountain or sea oh *fish of the sea come
listen to me for my daughter my life the joy of my*...there is no rhyme,
only rhythm to this run of words behind his eyelids, he is an old dog
circling in the endless curl of his unnamable, unfindable place and
there is no circle into forgetting, into painlessness. She has forever
drawn her life like a chisel along every trace of feeling and he is
hacked down to a skeleton by her disappearance, not even skeletal
bone, no, no, down to nerves only; primordial ganglia.

There are no gulls here over the windy sea; there are none
anywhere, he has noticed with amazement, there is nothing thrown
out to gobble up, there is no garbage. Their wheeling he has known
as a life-long ritual, their voracious appetites like the hunger and
thirst for righteousness he has only in despair. Above his father's
plow folding back the grey-wooded soil of their homestead, the gulls
circled in thousands for an occasional offering of worms, that gentle
bush piety becoming for him such a certain quicksand that it must
be escaped, fled. And having fled he discovered he could offer her
only folktales, paintings, classical music, ballet, her small sleeping
body in his arms swaying to Brahms and, at best, deep, inarticulate
(to him) Russian harmony. The Cossacks singing a discovery so deep
he broke the record. But her baby face, her perfect tiny fingers curled
against it are caught in a newer detail: the buttons down her blouse
as they walk through wind in Wales. They do not open, the blouse
would have to be pulled over her head. "*I expect to stay...all the days
of my*...." Maybelle Carter sang in her voice like a taut string and his
clear mind is avoiding the rest of the song branded onto the clarity
of sky like the blue volcanoes, now this one, now the other, in their
remorseless bed of cloud.

He found the record under the Coca Cola sign at Piccadilly Circus,
the song she hummed before Aberystwyth but never after. There
is always somewhere to find what you are really looking for if it is
something as simple as a man-made thing.

6. And he has looked, he would certainly always look now into every
crowd: so many people, especially in cities, thousands, millions.
If he stood at Yonge and Bloor or the overpass on Waseda-dori at
the Iidabashi Subway Station or sat at a restaurant window above

Leicester Square long enough it must be inevitable that eventually he would see her, again. There were so many people it was utterly impossible to be so indelibly different that somewhere on earth you could never be found again—sometimes he did see her, even among the black heads of Jakarta and Singapore, the incredible complexions of Lima, Kuala Lumpur, Sao Paulo: bits of her, a profile, a momentary back, a jacket fold or flip of hair and shoulder shift, and his heart would lurch for he already knew he must certainly be disappointed; and he was. Nevertheless, the first betraying detail always crushed him—the walk wasn't quite right, or the length of leg, or nose. The hands too large. Millions had been born on her day, her minute, her second no doubt and he would have found every one in every country on earth if one were only she. He had since then never actually seen anyone, he realized at some point, except those who in some detail suggested her because the very day after he had been somehow walking in or through a park where young women were suddenly playing something, field hockey perhaps, running and he had to crouch behind a tree holding his ears shut, unable to stand erect leave alone walk past their bodies—why were they all there, running, quick, laughing, he would not have missed or groaned for a single one of them if they had not been there, and yet they were all—and one of them had come and touched him with that terrifying girlish tenderness he knew and he could barely shake his head; trying to cover his eyes then also.

But he had found the words, all of them. The earphones clamped to his head in the store above Piccadilly Circus. They had chiselled themselves into the acoustic tile of his mind, connecting the numberless holes like runnels; he heard them, mouthed them, hummed them. There was really nothing so referential needed, not really, but they were hammered onto the sky wherever he happened to be:

The fish in deep water
Swim over my head.

7. So he has come again to the sea. A part of the great sea he has never seen before, where they had never been together. Not Peru and the ocean breaking like mountains after a run across the entire

Pacific to slice up the beach faster than her child's or his adult legs could run; not the hissing warmth of undertow at Copacobana hedged in by extravagant cliffs of buildings; not their flight through the middle of one night and in San Juan she curled into the bed, "I want to sleep, Daddy, sleep," when he threw open the curtains of their hotel window to the night surf crashing just below: not any of those beautiful seas he now remembers with despair.

The shells of the ocean
Shall be my deathbed;
The fish in deep water
Swim over my head.

The musicians at Aberstwyth began, "*There is a deep valley...*" What were the rest of their words? Were there any? Had he dreamt them? The prairie where he was born, she too, was always being compared to the sea. Praise be, the first time he had seen the ocean was from a ship after a long summer day moving majestic as a mansion through Quebec down the long throat of the St. Lawrence when ships still carried passengers and there was a boat train waiting in Liverpool, the grey heaving Atlantic still so imprinted on the cochlea of his mind that the green English fields and hedges lifted under him like the breathing sea itself. Somewhere the sea held her.

Milton once wrote: "I cannot praise a fugitive or cloistered virtue, unexercised and unbreathed." Good for him: was the greatest virtue, love, fugitive and cloistered also if unexercised and unbreathed, untested by opposite and contrary? So what is most contrary to being? Nothing. Exercise nothing, Mr. Poet Milton: great love is greatest when it is gone...yes...breathe that if you philosophically please. Sit on a tropical beach, paradise by any northern definition, and discover your thoughts are the same as if you were stretched on your standard bed at home hearing the furnace groan and noticing the ceiling turn slowly; sometimes. What a waste, yes waste...where is she? Surely I have been exercised and breathed enough, I changed her diapers streaked with baby shit and cradled her around the room against my chest to Handel and Vivaldi and Cree drumming and Vivaldi and last summer she led me through every clean and

stinking hall and cranny in Harlech and Carnarvon and Beaumaris
and Conwy and Rhuddlan and Flint and Beaumaris again because it
was so symmetrical, so perfectly preserved and historically useless,
and ruined Aberystwyth also; as if by necessity, returning to it again
in daylight after we walked there in night rain and we would never
have heard the musicians except for that three centuries of grass, the
sudden sunlight on the exploded stones. Already then she must have
been wearing her necessity everywhere we went, where were my eyes,
my goddamn eyes? Didn't at least my gut insist? But she was brilliant and quick and laughing, dearest sweet Jesus how I had longed
for that again, even the faintest trace of it and there it was at last.
Apparently, certain.

8. Only last summer on the Friesian coast—how often his thoughts
are triggered by "only"..."just"..."if only"..."if"...and his mother's
unassailable Low German peasant wisdom, as proper on her gentle
tongue as profane on his own: "If 'if' wasn't if, sheep's shit would be
grapes"—only last summer in Schleswig-Holstein they had seen the
sea slowly making land.

"The winter storms are so good, they bring ground," the young
man guiding them said carefully, "the heavy wind piles up the muddy
water against the coast and—"

"The wind does what?" she interrupted.

"The steady winter wind of course, day after day, blowing," the
guide said into it, his accented words almost lost with all their hair
streaming across their eyes, "it is the friction of the wind on the
water, friction piles up the water against the dikes and slopes of the
watte, here, we call the whole area outside the dike 'watte,' and as
the wind dies the water has to run back of course and that is why
we build these low rows of twisted willows, reeds, across the watte
because when it runs back the mud in the water sinks down of
course, settles against the rows and builds up, you see, grain by grain
here, land."

Like snowdrifts caught on prairie fencing, he thought then, but
low, slimy soil drifts creating eventually ridge and ditch growing
imperceptibly out of the frothing sea that played over them.

"So, after some twenties or thirties of years of course the rotting willows are covered over like over there and then there is land, enough for sea grass and the grass catches mud out of the high tides and the storm flooding even better and then soon the sheep, you see over there, graze in summer and only the high winter storms, very high, come up here and you see it keeps building. Fresh land then of course, not salt."

She was squinting past the young man's pale hair into the sea light. "The rows are all so...straight," she said. "Right angles."

"It's easiest to make, straight."

The sea light was relentless, like her voice. "But if the sea is muddy here, it must be tearing down the land somewhere else."

"Well of course, the sea is always tearing down and—"

"And since there is more sea than land, eventually there will be nothing but sea everywhere and..."

"Well," he laughed, "there are such very big land, and mountains."

"...the mountains will be levelled, the Himalayas into the Sanda and Philippine Trench and the Andes into the Chile Trench and the whole earth will..."

He and the pale young man were staring at her; it was the hard wind finding water in his eyes.

She said, "When the sea has levelled all the land in the world, the entire globe will be two hundred feet under water."

The young man said very gently, "But it will take a very long time. And here," he was bending down and he might have been taking her arm if she had been the kind of woman a man could easily touch, "...of course here the land mostly comes up from the sea bottom, you see."

His fingers dug in the muddy silt. They were standing on the buried line of woven willows, the grey slime stretching flatly ridged away to the indistinguishable edge of the grey sea.

"Many shells, bones" he said, spreading the mud across his hand. "Ground to pieces."

9. It couldn't have been the marrying, no not that. How many times was she asked, asked herself and then said no, better think a bit more about it. Marrying itself wasn't all there was in anyone's life,

especially a woman's now, she said and she would peer at one of them, her profile like her mother's had been so direct, a Dutch beauty that cut her personal image into any man's core. What was it? Just...never?

"*Hello, Central, give me he-aven,*" she sang that Carter twang in Wales,

> "*For I know my mother's there;*
> *With the angels there a-waiting,*
> *Waiting on the golden stair.*"

"Please," he said. "I can't stand that."

A kind of gradual, inevitably accumulating never-ness that became its own personality, its own certain aloneness even when they were together.

Across a crowded concert lobby he had seen the back of a friend whose wife he knew was dying of cancer. He had known for months but had avoided him, unable to endure even the thought of the words they would have to try to say, his own inevitable evisceration, again, but suddenly he was beside him, touching him and his friend turned instantly and they embraced so hard, so quickly between clusters of concert chatter. "I've been thinking about you," he murmured against his ear, and his friend murmured back, "I know, I know." They could hear violins tuning in the auditorium, some elementary Mozart delicacy—neither of them would have dared a Mendelsohn or full-organ Bach—and his friend was describing something, a sigmoidiscope or something like an eye at the end of a hose with which doctors had seen the enormous cancer, and drew a map with his finger on his own shirt-covered abdomen, tucked right in there and they had cut that all out, every bit of that. But the liver was beyond any scalpel. And they stood together almost easily, they found they could speak this factuality easier than a hockey score and it was only later that he remembered he had kissed his friend beside his ear, that they had held each other's hand while they were talking those facts only, things themselves; that mirrored nothing, presumably, if they talked fast, said words fast enough. But at some point they had both said, "Miracle." Almost together, as he later thought about it. For an instant both of them blurting out such an aberrant, echoing word—

as if it had been lurking there all along under their useless facts. Stupid. Stupid.

10. He is standing on the reef. Unbelievable, marvellous coral ebullitions hump up out of it, reflect a surface in shimmers around his ankles. What may be his own thonged feet ripple there, and a purple starfish inert as stone. His toe approaches it, nudges close, suddenly flips it over. A skiff of drifting sand, it is certainly upside down now but still motionless: long before this dreadful sudden inversion it must have already been protecting its central mouth like that with itself; probably had done so forever in enduring, hopeless anticipation of this one possible act, flipped by a merciless Canadian. It will not move. He stares level over the vacant sea, avoids every faint variety of shore or wave and concentrates on what seems to be the empty line of water and sky. Count slowly. After the third quick glance down he recognizes that the top left arm is beginning to curl; under; at the tenth glance he sees a tiny ripple of water help bend the second arm. In eleven minutes the starfish has almost folded three arms under, and then a sea surge opens it upright, over, flat. But once is not enough. His toe moves again.

11. He lay on a hotel bed in Husum, the Schleswig-Holstein town where Theodor Storm wrote *Der Schimmelreiter*, and he was reading the novel in the new edition which included pictures of the latest movie. When she came through the connecting door and sat on his bed, she barely nodded at the stupendous grey horse he offered her rearing above a dike ripping through in vicious rain.

"You know I don't like horses," she said; she had not yet cut her hair short for travel.

But his mind was lost in Storm's sonorous language and the great farmsteads on their diked islands they had seen rising like ships from the midst of the sea. And the implacable North Sea wind still roared in his ears so it was some time before he comprehended that they were talking about something quite different from their words.

"What?" he said, suddenly apprehensive.

"We shouldn't have come here, now" she was repeating herself, directly. "We should have gone north first, to Denmark, Esberg, and then all the way down the coast through here right to the Ijssel Meer. We should have seen it all. If only the sea can make land then we should see it all, start in the north and drive along every dike and watte and polder right to where our ancestors started."

"We'll get to Harlingen," he said quickly. "I promise."

"I'm sorry," she said then.

"For what?"

And that too was like so many questions he had asked her: never answered. If he found that pale young man again on the watte, they would be hunched there together, her fingers accepting the smear of mud he offered, they might have been holding hands. "Within a century," he would be saying, "we'll grow wheat here where there was only the sea. This land will be unbelievably fertile."

And it seems she is holding some specks of mollusks or perhaps bone in her hand, is rolling white specks ground roundly into powder between her slim fingers, the wind whipping her hair, long again, across her face.

"That's the easiest to do," he says, "to try to build it straight. But the sea is always bending, everything of course."

And she is laughing with him.

12. He is standing on the reef in the sea. When he bends his head the tip of his chin, his nose are touched by it; the columns of his body, legs, feet are there as precise as cut crystal bent among coral, gesturing fronds, creatures perhaps moving though seeming to lie still as sand, a multiplicity of world so brilliant he cannot recognize any of it though his eyes are open. The great sea will reveal everything, of course. He simply must know at what moment to look into it.

An Indication of Burning

I

BUT HERE THE SPRING was so subtly, so aggressively lovely, the sky drifting blue as a salt block licked hollow in a pasture and clouds barely blocking the sun with their stunning whiteness and the wintered creek slopes occasionally brushed purple—Jon pulled his car over and trudged up between staring cattle. The ground slipped uneasily; it was still frozen two inches below the surface, and the purple was tall spirals of dead weeds, not short crocuses as he had hoped. He snapped one off, it disintegrated in his hand like ash.

The cows, so enormous now that he was close to them, did not move aside, though their calves sprang away between them as if on coiled steel. If there is a principle of lesbianism, cows must embody it—who wrote something like that? Al Purdy? The cows' bulging eyes followed him striding past the greenish curve of water and the black sprouts of willows where the pasture had been burned for spring, and abruptly he felt ecstatic, muscular and living and breathing immensely, the lithe silence of the hillside leeching both the winter-sanded city and rutted muddy farm town where he was to read that night out of him like one long sigh. Macho Purdy.

So then he drove round a bluff of poplars, and between pickups strung along both sides of the gravel road like a long ditch of gaudy metal bending down through a valley he saw a farmyard. On the ridge ahead, thick with machinery and the multi-coloured density of people. At his open window he heard the auctioneer's chant snoring like some variable public address chainsaw into the blue air and his heart jumped with quick anticipation. Three minutes later he had high bid on a dented stack of eight-gallon milk cans. Twelve dollars. He couldn't believe it. Twelve—

"You want 'em all?"

"Huh?"

"You bid on one can," without the p.a. the auctioneer had a normal country voice under his brown Stetson. "You got your pick, there's eleven there, how many, you want 'em all?"

Jon had thought he was buying them all. Amazed at the thick ring of reddish farmer faces surrounding the flatbed where the long auctioneer's helpers busily stacked cans about his embroidered boots: they were bidding so low Jon would have gladly paid twenty-five for them all and piled his car full and dispensed them to his friends, "Genuine Canadian milk cans, a steel taste of the vanishing West, used only by genuine Canadian scrub cows—" twelve times eleven, dear god as much as the Canada Council reading fee—how had he been such a blithering idiot—the auctioneer's sharp face peered at him. He was wasting time, money.

"Uhh...one...."

"One?"

"No...two, that's really all...."

"Two it is," the auctioneer straightened up easily. "Just give your name to the accountant here and take your pick."

"Rasporich," he blurted out, "Jon Rasporich."

But nothing registered on the handsome face; or anywhere around the ring of farmers. A monolithic blankness at his long hair and beard but not a twitch of—as he had fully expected, how could it, they wouldn't recognize Irving Layton if he gave them a thick finger in the street, but mention the star in *Hee-Haw* or—

"R-a-s-p-o-r-i-c-h," he spelled to the woman with the pen and long paper, "J-o—"

"That's okay," she waved him off with a smile, writing. "Nobody else here has your name."

"Where do I...pay?"

"The office trailer, there, but first pick your cans."

He grabbed the nearest two off the flatbed while above him the auctioneer snored the other nine away—they were stuck already at five-fifty, he could have gotten four for the price he'd paid.

"You gotta look in 'em," a voice said beside him. "Rust."

But he could get neither lid off. He heaved mightily, embarrassed beyond ignorance now, maybe they were rusted tight but he had taken these...he looked into an elderly face under an orange SURGE peak of cap.

"Burns 'em right through. You work on the rim." The man bent his broad back, hands thick as paws, levering the lid about in a circle bit by bit until it clanged off. "Not bad," he straightened, "but you gotta really watch that rust. Last summer I drunk water once outa a rusty can, last summer and I was finished like I was slugged in the gut, one dipperful and I couldn't hardly taste nothing but I was damn near totalled."

When the talking face turned to him Jon saw it was scarred; a lopsided crescent bunching the whole face left, a kind of horseshoe welt through the lips and circling up the cheek as if the farmer had once been kicked, viciously, his bottom teeth caved inwards...his occlusion must be impossible, he could live with such a face only by forcing fluids—

"I won't use them for water," Jon interrupted his thoughts quickly. "I think I'll...you know, just...."

The farmer was smiling immensely, his broad face glistening with good-natured sweat. When he closed his mouth the scar almost disappeared, faint only as a shadow; but perhaps it was the awesome contrast that made him appear so ordinary then with his mouth shut, normal.

"This can ain't bad, I ain't saying it is," the farmer said, his food-lined teeth and pale broken gums again incredible. "Just tell your wife to take some of that brass stuff she uses for pots and she can rub it right out, those spots ain't burned through yet, some of it's just dripped down from the lid there, rain maybe getting in," and he thrust his quilted arm in deep, brought out a rust smudge on his blunt finger, smiling open-mouthed. "It comes right off, see, and lotsa soap and water and elbow grease it'll come right off."

"Sure…sure, thanks," Jon clanged the lid down, crookedly only half in, "thanks a lot."

He was furious with himself, his seemingly double revulsion compounded by the man's easy friendliness…."He's tough, just sew him up, together what the hell he'll live" and every smile showing now what he had eaten in the last three days—sausage and lots of eggs with ketchup for sure this morning—Jon wheeled away, disgusted with having to force himself again and again out of his initial reactions. Then he deliberately pulled erect and faced the man; smiled at him. The farmer was broadly solid, clothes smooth from work and wearing but clean, very cle—why did cleanliness for god's sake make him feel better towards this scarred, relaxed—and the layers of clothes visible at his thick neck, clean and white, mended neatly with delicate off-colour stitches. His dreadful face smiling open-mouthed as calmly as an icon.

"Just don't drink no rusty water."

"I won't," Jon said, "promise."

And immediately after, under the northwest poplar spreading itself bare over the grey patch of spring lawn covered with furniture for auction, he again saw the woman he had seen as he drove into town. A boy leaned in the first low crotch of the tree, eyes intent over the crowd as if floating on the variable song of the auctioneer, but the woman sat motionless on a couch among the cigarette-marked chrome chairs and plastic-topped tables and veneer dressers and double-bunked mattresses and stools and cracked hassocks and clichéd photographs of mountains and impossible waves of impossible oceans enlarged to perhaps look like paintings, all so grey and somehow slicked over as if walked upon too often by impersonal flies; her chubby baby was now slumped over in the walker, asleep. Her little girl stared at him around a green hide-a-bed, her thumb in her mouth. Long blondish hair, in ringlets…what an endless labour that must be, regiment that gossamer so deliberately to endure in this spring wind, a child's head without background as if cut out of a catalogue but for the thumb and the tiny running nose…there was such a clutter of everything, people and impressions and feelings and all this dreadful cigarette-stubbed and lived-in veneer of modern existence on such a day in rural quietness—ha—rural quietness as

he had thought it would be when he drove out of the dusty city that
morning, why in god's name did he get up so early to arrive in this
money-braying sunshine? So much stuff of all sorts he could not keep
it aloft, even in his head, like seventeen balls at least in the air and
he feeling himself no better than a one-armed juggler in what he
had supposed would be quiet rural Alberta, close to the warm land,
spring....

The woman, she seemed so young as to be barely a girl. But even
in his thoughts he refused to allow himself that sexism. The woman
now no more agreed to notice him staring at her from among the
furniture than she had in town. He had driven off the smooth
highway onto the ridged spring ruts of what was Main Street, past
the closed railroad depot and the elevator, discouraged already and
looking for the amateur sign that would identify the town library
where he was to give a reading that night; there were concrete sidewalks past the Co-op store at least and the post office, but chunked
with mud by people scraping their boots clean. His car shifted sideways under him on the small incline and he turned across into a side
street and knew immediately that the gravel there was unmarked
because no one had dared drive there all spring. The front of the car
nudged into soft gravel and he stopped, gently as if easing against
butter. He swore, winding down the window to crane at his wheels,
the front submerged in mud and sinking, and he twisted his neck
towards the back, but he did not see that: he saw instead a woman
coming down the mud-clotted sidewalk.

She pushed a walker loaded with a baby framed by Co-op grocery
bags, a little girl in golden ringlets and tiny red-rubber boots
trudging beside her, reaching up for her hand. A woman—no more
than twenty, really—coming towards him with her face like a quiet
dream rising out of a long sleep. He was parked directly in her path,
she moved with a grace that gave away her long thighs as certainly as
if she had been wearing nothing—dressed up to shop in this town?—
and he could not so much as press his foot down on the gas and try
to move, waited for her to bump into him like some gawking teenager with acne and mouth open. But at the corner twelve feet away
she wheeled aside from concrete onto planks, her glance slipping by
him and dodging away—she had jerked momentarily he was certain,

her eyes had widened slightly he knew—her glance on his car and the mud of the street and she was walking steadily away in the direction he would have needed an arctic crawler designed for sloughs and tundra to follow, a slim blue-coated figure clustered about by her beautiful children who cared nothing that they saw her day and night, so erect, her calves above her black boots...there wasn't any mud on them...carrying her away like the half-circle of a vision into noon light. He felt as if a hot sliver of glass had slit sideways below his chest, a ritual disembowelling. He ducked his head, unable to watch at what miserable little shack she would deliberately enter.

"Lots of people," he said to her now. He stepped closer to the hide-a-bed between them, "They all come out, to an auction..." for a moment he could not go on. Her head had shifted at his words but she did not look at him. "Even boys in trees," he gestured up, fighting the abrupt space in his gut and chuckling. But she would not move, "Sitting up...there...."

Instead, she laughed. An oddly deep sound while bending to tuck in a corner of the baby's blanket, needlessly. Her laughter flipping him over, he might have been standing on his head.

"We celebrate," and her voice was stranger, deeper than her laugh. "Somebody else is getting out of here."

"Are there...do, many 'get out'?"

"If they have the nerve," she said. Her voice seemed completely inappropriate to a woman so delicately lovely, though she was obviously strong, very strong with fine turns of muscles across her shoulders and around her arms, he could see that very well, so close to her now that the little girl shrank against her thigh; not ducking her head, but staring at him with enormous brown eyes. What colour were her eyes?

"Nerve?"

His shoulder ached and he realized suddenly he was standing there a large lumpish bumpkin with the two rust-burned milk cans dangling from his hands. He dropped them with a clang, and the woman looked up direct as steel into his eyes. Hers were so brown they were almost black.

"It's easy to stay," she said. "You just do nothing."

"You want to leave?"

She held him steadily in her brown look. "I recognized you in town, sliding in the mud." She said, "I want to be a poet. A real one."

II

Jon read that evening to twenty-seven people, three of them men and one a boy. He read his usual small city/farming town program of lightly humorous lyrics first, then a few full page "story" poems like "The Triple-headed Snake" and "The Moose Calf," and then a few longer, contemplative poems as seemed appropriate, and a few of his translations from the German. But as usual the people were too serious about the supposedly weighty event of his presence to smile easily, even at the beginning when he tried to warm them up with off-the-cuff chatter about spring. At the first hint of a rhythm they were instantly fixed in the necessary solemnity of poetry; they could not laugh, even silently and since he never wrote poems which used the four-letter words of sex or religion or excretion he could not offer even the dullest of them the most obvious convenience of slightly shocked, mindless laughter. "I have never written poems about God or shit," was one of his set answers to questions. "I have never felt I could quite get down to the one or up to the other, take your pick," but this evening no one offered him a chance to use the line, even obliquely; there were no questions whatever when the applause stuttered out. A faintly vegetative silence, that was all.

The old man who was both librarian and caretaker had gotten up early to plug in the coffee urn; he had not returned to his seat, which was just as well because they were stacking chairs, and noisy. But the clash of chairs now released the bubbliness in several older, severely coiffed ladies. They even had questions, which they were far too shy, they laughed loudly, to ask in public, but clearly they had every intention of asking them now that everyone was clustered about him with white Styrofoam cups at their teeth. Culture large and by the beard.

"Mr. Rasporich, why do you write?"

And he could bite off Flannery O'Connor's ineffable words, "Because I'm good at it." And got the usual brightly giggling, slightly conspiratorial—Oh, he is *so* egotistical!—sideways glances at each other in return. To say that here was asking for it, have mercy upon us.

"I've been trying to write poetry for...well, years, Mr. Rasporich, working and working at it and no one...how do you write poetry, really? How do you begin?"

Such a gentle maiden no doubt, fifty-one at least with a lace-doily voice and he quickly quoted Stephen Leacock on humour as benignly as his face hunched in its permanent after-reading smile allowed him—but for the Can Cow and its $150 plus expenses who would ever endure this with burned...how can you burn coffee? They had—"Writing [poems] is no trouble: you just jot them down as they occur to you. The jotting is simplicity itself—it's the occurring that's difficult."

They all laughed then. Finally. All except the woman looking at him between heads, her large brown eyes even more intense now and seeming to widen slightly. She sat motionless, scarcely even breathing throughout the reading; he had wanted to stir her somehow, jolt her physically out of that self-contained and at the same time draining inwardness that the very set of her bones asserted, but only this smarty line moved her. Apparently. He said quickly to her through all the faceless heads bobbing with laughter,

"And that's silly, of course, as you know and everybody knows who's ever written, or tried to. But it's true too. A poetic insight, image, it's a gift. Like Bach said, 'Every tune is a gift from God.' So one is thankful...at least."

The maiden was bending towards him unblinking. "Do you ever write poems about God?"

"No!" and he laughed aloud, ready to continue but immediately felt himself skewered on that distant brown glance. "I have never written poems about God or...no," he said, very quietly.

And then her rich voice suddenly reached him: "The Rilke poem you read, 'The leaves are falling, falling from so far....'"

He smiled genuinely at her; longing like a sudden gasp that they might be alone somewhere talking. But all he could think to do with that horde of heads and bodies between them was quote the last two lines again, lines he so loved in German and was almost happy with in his own English,

"But yet there's One who holds this endless falling
Endlessly soft within His hollowed hand."

She nodded.

"It's not my poem," he said. "It's just my pale translation."

"And you cannot really translate Rilke," he said a little later standing very close and directly in front of her, "without dealing with...he's awash with God. All over the place."

"Then why translate him?"

"He's just the greatest poet of this century and who ever said I didn't *want* to write about...hey," he had manoeuvred his long arms akimbo, almost bracketing her out of the crowd, "do you live far from here? I have to go back to the city; could I give you a lift...home I mean?"

"We just live around the corner."

"On a small street," he tilted towards her, "of bottomless mud."

He noticed then the silence of people very close and listening all around them; not even the passing delicacy of a coffee sip to veil his talking to the one beautiful young woman there. Probably in town. But her dark glance passing over his face was open now, raw as a wound and he turned to his elderly host quickly as she walked towards the door. When he finally got free and was unlocking his car to the distant country singing of frogs, there was her figure still on the otherwise empty sidewalk. Moving imperceptibly through the last streetlight, a figure that in its soft spring jacket seemed slightly thickened at the waist he thought as he came alongside her; almost as if she were pregnant.

III

This warmth spreading between my legs
(where you kiss sometimes, groaning)
freezes me
the uncontrollable monthly brute
clawing inside me for a hold
to root
to grow

And it throbs on from its burning source
(where you knock sometimes, groaning)
till the inevitable red tears through
my ice, narrow branches of gore
searing me longing not
to live or
let live

"I know you hate women that write 'out of their viscera,'" she said. "You know?"

"I hear you all the time on the CBC, I've read everything you've ever written," she said, "yes."

He shifted her papers slightly. "So?" he said at last.

"For me, what is there? There's Orlando coming home every night, dusty and swearing and his kidneys rattled loose by his grader. You think there's a *subject* we have to talk about?"

He held them in his hand after the first swift glance, staring through his college office window at the distant huddle of white stone and concrete downtown. "Orlando, Orlando..." the whiff of arcane memory rising in his head and he always followed that, especially when he was at a loss, "Italian for Roland, it means 'glorious land'...'land and glory'...."

"Glory?" Her laugh, he had never heard it before, was like a jack-hammer starting. "Oh shit, glory!"

He laughed, no happier than she, his mind twisting for something: maybe she'd be able to write if somebody, something kicked her long enough, if she could laugh a little looser than that at that, but he didn't want to blast her, she was too...keep your eye on the words you fool, he thought, you fool.

"I can't care," he said aloud, "who you are or where your words or images come from or what your experience is or what your hu—talking about writing is not a sensitivity session."

"It matters to me."

"What?"

"Where my words and images come from."

"Okay, you, but why should I care?" he yelled suddenly. "Huh? Why?"

She stared at him, his abrupt noise setting her upright and rigid, her eyes so widely dark they opened beyond the depths of her small head; but with a single flick of her head she thrust him past his role, great bushy father of all.

"How?" she said.

"Not by staring at me with your beautiful face. That has nothing to do with poetry."

"No more than my forty-six-foot house trailer, my two and two-third kids."

"Or your grader-operator husband. A poem is a pot, a made thing small and precise and complete, but made with words. Just show me your pot."

For an instant they were entangled completely in each other's eyes, and then they burst into laughter, together caught in one wave of tremendous release. As if they had discovered "I can hardly believe it, you too?" He leaned back and patted his carefully regimented gut—just so far and no farther, Brother Ass—and she understood instantly and laughed with him; incredibly musical this time.

"It's a useful earthy image," he managed finally. "I like earthy images."

"How come you're so—" after a hesitation she continued past the gap, "on radio and TV you sound completely high and mighty."

"I can't be very human to a microphone."

"Well, I thought...."

The reading; he knew it with a jolt, that was what she was thinking about, and the supposed "chatting over coffee" later where he had been no more human than if a lens had been study- ing his every hair and wrinkle demanding wit and profundity and comprehensibleness all wrapped in kind of beaver-toothed Johnny Carson slick—but different too, because wisdom was expected—no, demanded—and also just plain folksiness all in one camelish beast because of course any elitism was anathema, impossible for God himself in a world where every swine swilling beer was as okay as Plato on the trivializing screen, the medium designed for quiz games and weather maps, and when he read in a town facing over-dressed women and three old men and one boy he thought of them, he had to face it he did, as that indistinguishable mass of 3.73 million who

watched *Hockey Night in*—brighten up, the 300 thousand out of
25 million watching the CBC at any given primetime hour, and at
that still a hundred times more audience than had ever bought a
single one of your books, you can't sneeze at—how did he know her
thoughts like that? She had sat opposite him now for twenty minutes,
in the city for a visit to her obstetrician—it was almost an hour but
it seemed no time at all; none at all. Not so strangely, he knew from
the way his head and body sang. Wonder of wonders, her intuition
was a greater wonder than her face, good as that was—good? No, it
was more than good—she felt every thought inside his head, he was
convinced suddenly with a jolt of true home-seeking terror. As he did
hers.

Rudy Wiebe: Collected Stories, 1955–2010

"I got them to invite you," she said. "They didn't know what a
poetry reading was, as you noticed. What one would do there."

"Is that why some were so dressed up?" Her own black dress like
the belted drapery on a Praxiteles marble.

"What can you get dressed up for? The curling bonspiel banquet,
an evening of beer at the hotel?"

"It's not so far to here, how about a monthly trip to the theatre, or
opera?"

"Orlando likes beer, TV football, and sex."

"In that order?" he said without expression.

"It's not so funny," she refused to smile now, "when you live it."

"Okay, okay," he threw his hands up in mock despair to try and
get out of it, swiveling away from her face, her body, "you're a classic
case, classic."

"And they come, and sit in this chair, every day," she drawled,
ironic too.

"Not as classic as you...seem to be, living, every day..." he petered
out, lame.

"I don't care how or what way I'm classic," she said suddenly,
fierce. "And you can damn well forget about my 'classic' face and
figure, men have always stared at me like that and all it got me was
fucking propositions and a husband too quick. I want you to tell me
if—"

"Do I stare at you 'like that'?" He was studying the black dot
caught between the double panes of his all-wall window. If you

concentrated on it hard enough, at certain moments you would swear it had moved.

The silence stretched but he refused to move his head. Let her stew, who would have imagined her so nervy?

"Yes," she said, but very quietly. "You'll have to excuse me, I've been in this body twenty years, and men...I guess I look for it, now."

"And you always get it," again without expression.

But he had to look at her then, because he knew she was nodding with her head down, the straight white part in her brown hair and her nod shifting it like a thick curtain on either side of her hidden face. He leaned back, contemplating the ceiling.

"Being formidably ill-proportioned myself," he said with comradely philosophy, "I have always considered the problems of great beauty to be greatly exaggerated, a special of comforting 'sour grapes' perpetrated by the excessively plain and the preternaturally jealous."

"Since thirteen I've been our town's favourite four-wheel-drive pickup."

He looked at her; blanked.

"You know, 'Hey Hank, think you can get into *that* for a good ride?'"

All your conscious adult life. Ugh.

"Mr. Rasporich, all I want is that you tell me, can I or can't I be a poet?"

Oh to be God. Oh to be God and create out of nothing. Oh to be God and reconstitute seething oblivion.

"I was trying to write poetry before you were born," he said at last. "Sometimes I write it, far more often I don't. I try to translate from the great poets, I try to teach the skills of writing in this college, I talk with you for some minutes and read one sheet of what you've written and...."

He gestured, staring at her. But her brown eyes burned into him remorselessly.

"If you've been doing one thing for over twenty years," she said, "you should be some good at it."

"Yes!" he exploded. "Yes! But one page of...I have to read everything you've written, and no matter what you're writing now, for you to improve will take years, and it has to be work and work, endless work. How do I know you've got the iron guts to stay with that? A bit of talent—I see hundreds of people with a bit of talent for writing, that's common enough."

"Try me."

"You've got how many more appointments with your doctor?"

"Three. But I could develop complications."

"How often?"

"Every...two weeks?"

"Sometimes every week?"

"I...I don't think so. He'd get worried and come along."

"What about his...gradering?"

"Oh, he'd just take time off. He's very committed to me as a mother."

Jon drew his hand over his face, riffling through the sheets with the other. All untitled...

On that day when mountains began to come...
A gentle hour touches me like silver...
There is a rider riding in black/steel...

she's so lovely and strong, at this rate he can get at least seventeen or eighteen out of her before her insides burn out, all his handsome little boys gradering the roads of Rosebud County flat and all his lovely little girls one by one dropping their regular litters...such a swell of hatred for a man he had never seen was stupid, stupid, there were images here that hooked...perhaps, perhaps—

"Can we...talk a little," she said, "now, about those?"

He remembered then to look at his watch again. "In ten minutes I have to see a student..." her face changed and he felt a surge of he did not want to analyse what, "but I could leave a note on the door—Unavoidable Call, Had to Leave—we'd have to get out of here right now though."

"But this person is coming—"

"I see him every day, he's," he gestured "forget it," on his feet and scribbling the note. "Let's get out of here, fast."

She was standing already: as tall as he, her unbelted summer coat veiling her slender and elegant.

"Do you want to come to my place?"

Rudy Wiebe: Collected Stories, 1955–2010

"Yes," she said, "yes."

Her tone was so open and gentle and warm he suddenly did not want to resist her face, her eyes, and he could only twist his tone into banter, light sarcasm to keep his balance.

"I warn you, it's the lair of a middle-aged bachelor."

"You said it yourself, talking about poetry is no sensitivity session."

He jerked open his door and stabbed the note onto the board there, laughing uproariously.

IV

"They just took off," the farmer grinned through his food-glazed teeth. "Somewhere three-four weeks ago."

The street was bone dry now, and the space where the house trailer had obviously stood was empty except for the power pole and the stumpy plumbing pipes in the grey rectangle. Uncut grass to the sprawling caraganas. She had looked at these branches and dusty leaves, again and again.

"He had that four-wheel-drive Ford, he didn't even have to hire nobody. They're laughing over at the hotel," the farmer leaned confidentially out of his truck window, thick blotchy arms on the glaring metal, "Orlando just come out one morning, hoisted her up and put the wheels under and dragged her off, whole kit and kiboodle like he just dreamt it up that night."

"Where's this...Wandering River, you said?" Jon asked into the noon heat. In the cab beyond the heavy shoulders a boy sat, without motion or face like a shadow.

"Nah, *Meander* River, it's damn near the Northwest Territories, you know where they plugged up that big oil fire."

A thousand kilometres northwest of Edmonton, on the gravel ridges and stubby muskeg spruce where Orlando gets seventeen bucks an hour and thirty-five overtime ripping his kidneys loose on a cat and you can wait for your time in the High Level Hospital while the blackflies crawl, gnaw at your brown eyes all summer. Oh my darling, my darling of the words and the terrible, terrible longing... Rilke was right, as always

Whoever now cries anywhere in the world
without reason ["cause" really, the word meant both] *cries*
   in the world,
   cries over me. Thee.

But there was both reason and cause here, more than enough of
both. Meander River on the Mackenzie Highway. Gravel strip to the
inhuman north.

"Never said nothing, to nobody. Always was a loner, that Orlando."

You have to go with the big, quiet kind because at least they have
never molested you and you can always imagine there's really something going on under all the silence. Pray there is. He could see her
sitting on his couch, careless of where her dress fell open and talking
through a poem—she did write poems, yes and she would write more,
she was unstoppable—with the quiet inevitability of a glacier moving
in on him; grinding him so small he had to re-make himself out of
detritus when she left. Try.

"Aren't you that writer," the farmer said slowly, "the one that read
outa his poems here a while back?"

"Yes."

Whoever now laughs anywhere in the night,
Without reason [cause] *laughs in the night,*
   laughs at me.

"I also bought those two rusty cans," he added.

"I knew that right aways," the man smiled immensely, the horseshoe crescent of his scar a torch lighting up his pleased face. "My boy
here heard you."

The faceless shadow did not move.

"We ain't never had any writers around here, not even to visit."

"Have you heard of Robert Kroetsch? He was born near here, at
Heisler."

"Kroetsch...Kroet...oh, you mean Kretch—yeah, when I was a kid a
Kretch come around to build the barn, but he was a carpenter."

"Bob's father. He built barns all over, you've got a Kroetsch barn?"

"Sure. Standing over fifty years, not a lean or crack in it. Oh yeah," the gnarled face moulded itself in thought, normality. "He had five daughters and then a son. The son went bad on him."

"That son 'went as good' as anybody I've ever known," Jon said fiercely. "You ever read one of his books?"

From the truck's hot darkness the boy's voice suddenly spoke precise as a perfect bell ringing. "They took all his books out of the library."

"Why?" Jon burned his hand leaning forward and trying to see inside.

The boy's voice said again,

"The librarian read one of them."

"What?" Jon peered, but the farmer's broad face would not move aside.

"We don't need to read any of that shitty stuff around here," he said steadily. "If we want it, we can think it up and do it ourselves."

"Robert Kroetsch doesn't write any—" Jon exploded, but stopped.

"That Orlando," laughter sprayed through the split mouth, "never says a word, just all of a sudden do it. Like marry the prettiest girl we ever had around here and leave all them loud-mouth cocky bastards standing around with their pants stiff...heh!...and here he just up and pulls out!" laughing aloud now, clearly he had played a tremendous joke on the town, the district, the whole world presumably, that Orlando.

The farmer abruptly peered at Jon. It seemed his washed-out eyes had seen everything there was in the world for eyes to see. "You looking for her?" he said slowly.

It would have been better, much better if he could see the boy's face. What had the boy said about that evening? Well...he would have said nothing, he would have needed to say nothing because rumour never depended on the evidence of discerning children; the old women would have been enough. But Jon wished he could remember the boy's face: had looked at it with the intention of remembering, as he must if he was to take with him one exact human detail. There had been more here that night than he had recognized. Or imagined. As there almost never was.

"I am writing a series of poems about small prairie towns," he said. Not lying this time either.

"There's something here to write about?"

"Oh?" Jon shrugged. "There, that's an interesting image...picture right there, the old house basement filled in, and the rectangle of dead grass left by the trailer on top of it. There's layers of a past, here already, what will there be in the future?"

"Nothing."

Jon looked up as the farmer laughed, and he realized suddenly that his uncontrollable antipathy toward this man had nothing to do with revulsion at his scar; in fact, if there had been no scar he knew now he would have understood his feeling earlier: there was a kind of malign, almost satanic glee in that knobby reddish face. Like the Bashkir in the Tolstoi land story, fat, chuckling, looking for the seam of failure, the soft rust spot for his blunt finger....

"I've got every empty house and lot in this town," the farmer said.

"What?"

"Every year I buy three, eight, every one that comes empty. I never rent 'em, or build nothing on 'em either."

"And when you own the whole town," Jon slowly thought through the tone, the expression, "you'll level it all, raze—"

"Right!" the farmer roared with delight. "Clear it like my granddad cleared the useless bush off our homestead! But I'll do it with a bull-dozer, smash all this crap trees and houses and roads into windrows and burn the whole kit and kiboodle, and then sow it to wheat. One nice big open field of wheat."

"A real Doc Murdoch," the boy said calmly.

The farmer did not turn his face from Jon, but he said in the sour tone he obviously always used on his son, "There's no docs left around here and you know it." He added after a moment, smiling again, "Not that I couldn't figger circles around them if there was."

But Jon was inwardly laughing. Who could ever tell where miracle lurked, biding its time? He felt like chanting a hymn to Bob Kroetsch for aiding and abetting this invidious young treason.

"And all the people that live here?" he asked.

"They can just pack off to any one of them dirty oil towns, like Orlando—he's smart, goes before he gets pushed. Say, you ain't so slow yourself," the farmer chuckled appreciatively. "I was wondering there a bit, when you bought them rusty cans."

"Hazard LePage," Jon said past the scar to the immovable shadow in the truck, "looked for twenty-four years till he found what he wanted. It had been in his own yard all along."

He heard the farmer's hiss breathing behind him to keep him there, but he ignored it and walked through the gap in the caragana then. Where she had walked often as if caged, the grass thick, the edge of the old foundation crumbling; rotten with alkali. He had been translating Rilke's "Einsamkeit" and she had heard the English resonance of the poem without knowing a word of German: as if she too had walked through Paris all one rainy night and felt that...felt it before she was born, the black glisten of stone streets on September 21, 1902:

> *Loneliness is like a rain.*
> *It climbs up from the sea to meet the evening,*
> *It climbs up from the world's far distant prairie*
> *Toward heaven, which has it forever.*
> *And only then, from heaven, does it fall upon the city.*
>
> *Rains o so gently in those barren hours*
> *When all streets bend themselves to search for dawn;*
> *And when those bodies, which have still found nothing,*
> *Bereft and disappointed, let each other go;*
> *And when these people who can only hate each other,*
> *Must sleep together in one common bed:*
>
> *then loneliness moves onwards with the rivers....*

He was looking in the grass for something, a plastic toy, a broken dish, something, anything discarded. But there was not so much as a trace of the walker's wheels in the impersonal earth; every single touch gone in oblivion. Meander River.

The truck at the caragana gap whined into life, bounced heavily away.

"'Scar,'" he was reading a dictionary page in his head, "'a variant of "eschar"...a hard crust or scab as from a burn...Greek *eschara*, brazier, coals; an indication of burning.'"

The Good Maker

IN THE SUBURB of a large Canadian city there once lived a man and
his wife and their two sons. The two-car garage attached to their
bungalow contained an older Canadian station wagon, which could
pull their trailer or carry all of them and their skis depending on the
season, and a smaller Japanese car; also a lawn mower and thirteen
cases of empty pop bottles and thirty-seven stacked bags of old newspapers which the man had not yet given to the little league hockey
team or the girls marching band because on Saturday morning he
was never up when these groups came around to collect. Besides
the four people, the bungalow contained all the standard middle-
class furniture and kitchen appliances, a large stereo, an imitation
old-fashioned jukebox and one and a half TV sets: their aged black-
and-white set only worked on the odd-numbered days of the month.

It was on one of the even-numbered days, when his wife was in
the basement throwing the usual clothes into the washer and his
younger son was at hockey practice and his older son in the family
room had turned up the stereo to a level where, if such sound had
attacked anyone in industry, the unions would have classified the job
as hazardous to health, it was on such an ordinary winter evening,
just after supper, that the man began to think about God.

After a moment the man was startled with himself. Usually
he thought about God a little on Sunday, whatever few thoughts

398

the pastor of his church managed to persuade him into, but these thoughts had come to him on his own. In the middle of the week. He sat at the kitchen table, the Bible open to its first page. The words seemed to be pricks of light, coming in small clusters, from a distance, and growing so huge they exploded in his head like rockets fired at him in a movie, "God made...God said...and God said..." the chair he sat in, the table, the whole house was vibrating with the mindless chords thundering from the stereo but the small words drove on, "God said...and God..." He saw his wife come up from the basement and shrug something to him with that twist of her shoulder he had loved the first time he saw it; he got up and went to the doorway of the family room.

After a moment his older son saw his hand signals and with a grimace distorting his handsome face reached for the earphones, jammed them on and flicked the switch. The sudden overwhelming silence did not alarm the man, as it usually did, about all that hammering now in the narrow confines of his son's head.

"The dryer is on the fritz again," his wife said. "We never should have bought all our appliances at once. When we bought the house, that was silly, all at once."

"Oh," the man came back to the kitchen table.

His wife shut the dishwasher and threw the switch; nothing happened. She kicked the washer in a particular spot and it groaned immediately and began to function. "See," she said. "You buy them all at once, they break down all at once. It'll cost a fortune."

"You know what it says here?" the man pointed to the book. "It says, 'So God created man in his own image.'"

His wife looked at him expressionlessly and he went on, "I was just wondering what that was, 'image,' what...." His wife's puzzled expression made him stop.

"'So'?" she asked.

"What?"

"You read, '*So* God created man,' so the 'so' must mean something happened before so that *then* God decided to make man, after something else happened."

"Oh," he said in relief. "Well, sure, lots had happened. He had created more or less everything else already, light and the waters and all living creatures according to their kind, and 'He saw that it was good' (the man was reading by now) and then God said, 'Let us make man in our own image and likeness to rule the fish in the sea, the birds of heaven, the cattle, all wild animals on earth and all reptiles that crawl upon the earth. So God created man in his own image, male and female he created them.'"

"Oh," his wife said. "Then who's the 'us'? 'Let *us* make man.'"

"I don't know," the man said slowly. Then he had a latent Sunday morning revelation. "Hey, maybe it's the Trinity, you know, the three of them?"

"The Father, Son and Holy Spirit," his wife said.

"Sure," the man said. "I bet that's what it is, who it was." He was very happy suddenly; he had made a connection with something he hadn't known he knew and he had answered his wife at the same time. That was wonderful.

"So man is made in God's image," his wife said. And he could tell by her tone that he had not answered her at all; as a matter of fact he was immediately convinced that she had just been setting him up. "So we've got created human beings now, and we should be able to see something about God from human beings, right?"

"I guess so," he said, already feeling hopeless.

"Okay, there is God the father," pointing at him, "and there is God the son," pointing towards the family room, "so who," the woman said, "in this analogy who would be God the Holy Spirit?"

He met her clear bright eyes for a moment. "I don't think it is what you're thinking," he said at last.

"Why not?" she said, but her tone was no longer aggressive; as if she herself was apprehensive to say it. "In the human image we have father, son...mother. Why can't the third person of the Trinity be called God the...."

They looked at each other for a moment in a kind of consternation. Why not indeed?

And suddenly he burst into laughter. "There was a young woman walking down the mall yesterday noon, wearing this t-shirt with big yellow letters on it, 'Trust God, She Will Provide.'"

They both laughed so that the kitchen rang. Finally his wife said, "And she wasn't wearing a bra either, was she."

"I don't know," he said.

"If you were reading all that on her chest, you know."

"I guess I do," he said. "She wasn't. But look here, God had already established the male-female principle with the animals, before man, so he makes man male and female too, but human beings alone are said to have the image of God. Then the image cannot have anything to do with sexuality, which animals have too."

"Okay, I guess so," his wife said. "But the image surely can't mean man's shape," and the man laughed again.

"Yeah, I wouldn't want God to be in my shape."

"Nor me," she laughed with him. "I should lose ten pounds."

"Ahh, your ten pounds." He dismissed her usual longing with a flip of his hand, "But if you think about it, man sure does have an odd shape."

"Odd?"

"Yeah, you know, we're used to peoples' shapes, but if you'd never seen a human it'd look pretty funny, long gangly appendages sticking out at all the corners, arms, legs, head, from a sort of bulgy little trunk in the middle."

"No funnier," his wife said, "than an elephant with its nose long enough to scratch its rear, or a giraffe's tiny head sticking up at the end of that long—"

They were both laughing again.

"God must have had a lot of fun," he said finally, "thinking up all those crazy shapes. I mean, even in one species like dogs you can get a hundred different variations."

"That's mostly man messing around with breeding," his wife said. "But it's handy having all these crazy things sticking out of my 'bulgy little trunk.' I can pick things up, step over them."

"If God had a shape," the man said, "it would be a perfect shape. What would it be?"

"Sure not an old man with flowing beard sitting on a cloudbank, that's for sure."

"Yeah. We see too many Michelangelo paintings, old God with his long arm stretched out and Adam happening at the end of his fingers."

"There's only one perfect shape," his wife said.

"What?"

"A sphere."

"Round like a ball," the man said slowly, and his hands formed themselves into that as he looked at them. "Perfect, everything complete, perfect."

"Maybe before the fall Adam and Eve were round like globes," his wife said. "Wouldn't that be beautiful, all of us perfect balls rolling around."

"Smooth and perfect like roller bearings," he said, "no edges to bump into anything, anybody."

"No hands to grab anything, no legs to kick," she added. "And you'd never have to lose weight, everybody'd just be a little bigger or smaller ball, that's all."

"No," the man said, "that wouldn't be so interesting. No faces, no oddities, you know, noses, or one leg shorter than the other, and anyway it'd be no fun, having no arms to put around each other."

She grinned at him. "That's a Greek story anyways. Plato says man was once round like a ball, complete in himself, but Zeus didn't like that so he split him in half, right down the middle, and that's why everybody goes around now looking for their better half."

After they stopped laughing he insisted, "In some way, like it says here, humans are like God. What way?"

"What has it said about God up to that point?"

"Nothing much, just that he made things."

"How?"

"He just said things, and they were there."

"Just like that, out of nothing?"

"I guess so. It just says. 'And God said, Let there be light, and there was light.'"

"Maybe," his wife said thoughtfully, "maybe that's the image...I mean, man can't make things out of nothing, just by saying so, but man *is* a maker. He can certainly *make* things."

"What has man made?" he said after a moment.

"Generally," she said, "a mess."

They both pondered that, staring at each other in the abstracted way of two people who have together suddenly understood something which is a revelation to them both and after a moment

Rudy Wiebe: Collected Stories, 1955–2010

comprehend that the revelation has opened them to an even larger mystery. The man was thinking of rockets and computers and robots and television and...he saw like a picture the city he lived in, humming like an incredible organism with all the wonders man had made, and yet every day city people were more and more worried about the quality of life they had to live, worried about their families, worried about crime, about lies in high public places, about hunger and accidents and suicides and the poor. When he flicked on a switch in his office, light brilliant as sunshine sprang up, yet on winter days the power plant covered the city with a grey, filthy shroud of smoke.

"What have you messed up now, Dad?"

The man and his wife looked up. Their older son stood in the doorway, looking curiously at them bent over the Bible on the kitchen table.

"We're...just talking..." the man felt a little self-conscious suddenly, but his mind was so fixed in a certain direction he couldn't think his way into an evasion, "talking about God."

"God made a mess outa you?"

His son was peering at him with a sudden frank interest, but his wife immediately cut in,

"No, it's humans make the mess, we're talking about God, the good maker."

"Boy, a mess," their son said. "Our teacher told us today if the world's population keeps on growing like it is now till the year two thousand one hundred, the whole surface of the earth will be covered with one solid building seven stories high and on the top level they'll have all the usable soil that's left and the people who grow the food up there will be the only ones that ever see the sun. Boy."

The man looked from his son to his wife. Bad as history was, somehow the future could always sound even more horrible.

"I hope," he said, "God will make something better than that."

"Sure, he'll make something good," his son said heading for his bedroom. "He'll make us dead before it happens, that's good."

Which was what the man himself hadn't wanted to say. But it was "image" and "making" that he was still thinking about when he got on the bus to go to work next morning (his station wagon was getting a valve grind), and suddenly he looked at the people crowded above him in the aisle, really looked. Like always in a Canadian winter, the people were so wrapped in parkas and down-filleds and sheepskins that he could see nothing but the centres of their faces, but that focused attention like a telescope...what an awesome variety of mouth, nose, hair in colour and texture, skin, eyebrows. After a moment he realized that the perfect face above him was not a young man's but a girl's; he knew that immediately from the way her body moved in the crowd's surge towards the door. What inimitable grace, so absolutely particular and distinctive, no matter how her body was covered. He felt his own body to the very tips of his limbs, powerfully, as he walked down the crunching street, the hard air sharp, brilliant with cold in his nose and lungs; he seemed to see everything as if it were drawn new in crystal clear ice. And when he went up for coffee, the woman who had staffed the office cafeteria...she must have served him for five years and he had never really seen her. She was slicing tomatoes into the small salads she always prepared for lunch and seeing her water-swollen, expert hands, that crisp food, he said suddenly before he thought,

"Maria, you make beautiful salads."

Her face lifted and for a moment they looked at each other openly, in amazement.

"What a...lovely thing to say. Thank you."

And her face ducked away again, shy, almost embarrassed; as he was. But he could not forget how he had seemed to see through to the inside of her head, her flush of happiness...had he revealed all that to her too? Because he had said a few, almost banal, words? Words. "What a lovely thing to *say*." God said, and it was. A word. The Word became flesh. There was something somewhere in the Bible about the Word and Jesus Christ, and all things being created by the Word. In John, he would have to look that up when he got home. And find out where human language began in Genesis, that was it, when did man first say a word? He puzzled about that all day, even when he picked up the station wagon and began jerking his way home through the usual clotted traffic. Where was the power in "word," why did the Bible—it said somewhere else, funny how all this about "word" kept coming back to him, things he had long ago forgotten he knew, "By faith we know that the world was made by the *word* of God..." and just as he had decided again to find out about man's first word, a traffic light turned red and the cars in front of him stopped but on the icy road he did not until he smashed into the car ahead of him.

"Oh God," the man said, "oh God."

There had been a chain reaction through four cars. The driver of the car ahead was out on the road, swearing clouds into the air. "What the blazing zeros are you thinking of!"

"I'm sorry," the man said. "It's all my fault, I was thinking about God."

The driver, who was dressed in the cool beard and leather of a cool intellectual, stumbled out of his curses; to stare.

"It's really my fault," the man said again. "Will you forgive me?"

The driver looked at the smashed rear of his Citroën. It had collapsible bumpers but of course they did not match heights with the Canadian car and therefore had not come into play until they met the man's lights, fenders and radiator. So the two men stepped out of the steam rising from the antifreeze on the icy street and then the other furious drivers from the cars ahead joined them and after a time they began the familiar ritual of exchanging numbers.

The man told his wife later, hanging up the phone, "Thinking about God will cost me $247 more in insurance next year."

"Maybe the church will give you a receipt for it," his wife said, and he laughed with her. She was alternately tossing a green salad and stirring something on the stove that looked vile but gave off a delicious aroma.

"Joker," the man took a swipe at her left ear with his lips. "Now listen, the key to God's making is his word, right, God said and it was so. And Jesus, 'The Word' as John calls him, 'was with God at the beginning and through him all things were created.'"

His wife stopped stirring the pot. "What are you getting at?"

"Just look here," he said pointing to the second chapter of Genesis. "It tells about the origin of language, man's first *word*. 'Then the Lord God said, It is not good that man should be alone; I will make him a helper fit for him. So out of the ground the Lord God formed every beast of the field and every bird of the air and brought them to the man to see what he would call them; and whatever the man called every living creature, that was its name. The man gave names to all the cattle, and to the birds of the air, and to every beast of the field; but for the man there was not found a helper fit for him. So the Lord God caused a deep sleep to fall upon the man, and while he slept took one of his ribs and closed up its place with flesh; and the rib which the Lord God had taken from the man he made into a woman."

"That's a beautiful story," his wife said. "But what are you getting at about 'word'?"

"Man names things. It's his first act as a maker, he makes names for everything around him and while he is doing so he discovers, he understands something profound about himself and his world: there is no partner fit for him. Words are man's creative acts, with them he gains knowledge and understanding. Words, language, that's how man makes things. With a good word we make the best thing we can make, and with a bad word we destroy the best thing."

His wife looked at him in wonder. "'And if you confess with your mouth that Jesus Christ is Lord..'" she murmured.

"Make that word," the man said. "Yes, yes!"

"Hey you guys!" Their youngest son stood in the kitchen doorway. "What's that awful stink?"

With a gasp his wife wheeled to the stove. The boiling pot now smelled a great deal worse than it looked. After a supper of tossed salad and toasted-cheese sandwiches, the man took his young son to play hockey.

It seemed to him he had never seen boys skate before. On the treachery of ice his small son wheeled, twisted, raced, glided, stopped dead with swift, unconscious grace; even when he fell, he let his body slide without concern and was up again on the narrow steel of the skates as the culminating movement of his fall. They lost the game and, back home again, after tinkering with the dishwasher a little the man helped his older son organize his school history essay on the topic of the greatness of Napoleon. They had been arguing about it for a week: the man insisted Napoleon was the exact oppo-site of great because he had slaughtered hundreds of thousands of people and with his massive armies really destroyed the manhood of France. His son however argued Napoleon was great because he had conquered most of the world and forever affected the course of world history. What could be greater than that? "Well, it's your essay," the man agreed finally, and while his son recopied the essay, he paged through texts. Suddenly his glance fell upon a few words spoken by the French historian de Tocqueville in 1842:

"Napoleon was as great as a man can be without virtue."

His son's eyes brightened as he read that. "Hey, that's the perfect ending to my essay. Great!"

"You see," the man said later to his wife in their bedroom, "the right word, and you understand."

His wife was propped up in bed and, though it was the odd-numbered day of the month, she was not watching the old TV. She was reading in a thick book.

"It says here" she said, "that we can only talk about God by analogy. If we can't say, 'God is like this...or like that...' then all we can say is 'God is who he is.'"

"Which doesn't explain much," the man was getting into his pajamas.

"Explains nothing," his wife said. "But listen here. 'In the being of God there are not three individuals but we must speak of three personal self-distinctions within one divine essence. God expressed his thought in a Word; the word of God is the creative power, as the spirit of God is the bringer of life and order.'"

"Okay," the man said getting into bed. "It's as if I would try to write a poem. There is myself, there is the idea I am having, and there is the word I am writing. Three parts of the same thing, me. The word written down is simply the manifest part of *my* thought."

They studied each other a moment in the bedroom light. Shapes so familiar, so loved.

He said, "This will do with a bit more thought."

She smiled. "I think so. I'd like to make something good other than words."

"Yes," the man said. "That's another whole aspect of God we haven't talked about yet."

And he leaned over her, and switched off the light.

There's a Muddy Road

"WHY DON'T YOU TAKE YOUR SHIRT OFF TOO," Mary said, and laughed. That nervous little spasm of a laugh again. "I've never seen a naked man who didn't have a beard."

"I bet."

But she ignored his tone. "That wasn't so bad, now was it," she said. Her slender hand seemed to be curling around, among the red hair of his thigh. If he hadn't been staring at it, sitting knees up and forehead against his propped-up fists—Rodin's thinker no less, no, wrong position—he wouldn't have known she was touching him. Compulsive talker.

"No."

She laughed far too loudly for the empty room. Her tent dress— that she hadn't taken off and he didn't want her to take off now—loose around her. He was feeling absolutely nothing at all. He found he could even look at her, down directly into her brown eyes in her unrecognizable upside-down face and not even blink. "It takes time, we've both been married too long," she said.

A child called outside again.

"And besides, you always want something more, of course."

"More!" his snort exploded in his nose.

"I'd say this was barely a start," she said, laughing. That husband of hers she no longer loved flapping around playing word games, straggle-haired in blue jeans at the university, over thirty and on an eternal scholarship or assistantship or whatever it was the government kept forking over in tax money so he wouldn't have to finish his degree and get to work if he could find any, fuddling around with words, his care-for-nothing-but-love attitude was carved into her every laugh and sentence. He was even called "Harry."

"How'd you dare get married?" he had asked her once. "With names like you've got."

"They sang a song at the wedding, 'Mary and Harry will reach Tipperary.' The names were real fun, maybe that's why I married him when I was looking for a husband."

"Huh."

"My daddy said I was on my own, he wouldn't send me to school and the easiest way seemed to get married. I was a child then. He loves me too, and he's always been good to me."

"In his own way of course."

"Better than you in yours."

"Who started this?"

He realized he had said perhaps that last aloud. Perhaps all of it had been out loud, and he didn't care about that either because they'd been round and round with themselves on that so many times; it was all they ever had to do together with her twenty-minute coffees or hour lunches, talk, though sometimes it was really laughing fun and the days and sometimes weeks when he knew there wasn't a chance he would see her, talking was the last thing he thought of doing with her. Sometimes there grew these great stupid plans of some night together in some luxury hotel in some city where no one knew him and not one other soul in the whole world would ever know about it to be bothered, simply one complete thoughtless perfect night, one "*Wow, outa sight!*" as his daughter would say, and that was it, exactly, that would wipe out the whole mess once and for all clean so he and she too would forget what she kept insisting she felt for him: love.

"It might have been okay, eventually," he had said. "We could have been friends and had our good laughs at lunch and maybe you could have got me to where I'd been willing to have as they say 'an affair' with you. When you first showed up I even thought about that. Any man always thinks that about any new girl that looks like something walking past and he sees her, nothing much personal about it, and he thinks the girl's young and has any number of chances and won't do it anyways so what the heck it's something to fiddle around with when houses aren't moving. You hear the guys."

"And that's what you thought of me."

"A passing thought, they go by all the time."

"Like your salesmen?"

"Look, I don't kiss women, or just accidentally rub past them. I don't have 'affairs.' This whole *now* thing, it's nothing new anyway, makes me sick because there's never anything to it but mess and more mess. Believe me, I've seen enough. I don't believe in living like that. I'm honest, I believe a man should love his wife for life and live with her and with his children. He's got to provide for them, why do you think I'm still in business? If it wasn't for them you think I wouldn't have cashed it all in long ago and done what I've always wanted? I could have too, if I just said like your lovely Daddy, 'It's your life, you're on your own.' I'd be a doctor right now, don't you worry."

"You can't love me, and Alice and your children too?"

Mary was still lying stretched out beside him. Her very short unbelted dress as if flung on the gold rug, her right leg bent so that foot touched her ankle. Her legs were the best part of her, he had seen that the first time she walked in before he looked up and saw he knew her face. He remembered legs better than faces. The fast, lopsided grins of men whose glance brushed past his, knowing, down to skirt lengths shamed him, but he was always looking there anyway before he became aware and deliberately looked away. She lay with her face upside-down to him and steadily looking up out of her dark eyes, which were the other good part of her, with her hair once you thought of it. Her body was too thin, her nose a bad turn and her complexion erratic. For the men an affair meant somebody stacked, some liberated thing on pills that didn't give a damn tomorrow. No part-time office help with a seven-year-old daughter and a bad teenage marriage, no matter what the legs.

He couldn't remember, had they said a word since he took off his shirt? He had taken it off. He was trying to think of something but he somehow felt nothing at all inside him; nothing, just an empty sack all over which could feel the coolness of the vacant house. Beyond the curtains behind him the sun would be baking the pavement. Several children called there.

"I don't like to leave the scene of a defeat," she said.

She reached up and tried to pull him down but her very words, straight out of her stupid Freud bible or Reich or whatever she was always reading—if they weren't from there they sure sounded like it— stung him and he pulled away. He put his hand against her shoulder, stood up and reached for his clothes crumpled against the drapes.

"This house is on multiple listing," he said out loud. It was only three seventeen; he couldn't believe so little time had passed and he had told Mrs. Rostok he was on a call the rest of the afternoon. Yeah.

"What happened if some salesman walked in?"

"I'd forgotten to unlatch the door, I was in the basement with my customer, you, and didn't hear the bell for a while. So."

"I like being your customer."

"You're not."

"Even just in case, and you had it all figured out?"

"Yeah."

"At last, a plan."

"Yeah." He was buttoning his shirt but he did not feel noncha- lant. Had he ever? Maybe that was a lot of what had been wrong. He had felt just nothing, almost as if he had decided deliberately, a plan today, yes, and then the kids shouting beyond the drapes, rattling their wagons over the pavement of the bay and once earlier when he looked out the kitchen window a teenager who should have a job for the summer was leaning on the fence across the alley, studying his gleaming Buick. He should have parked in front, what salesman took a customer in from the alley? What had he been thinking of?

"Where's the bathroom?" She was up, already walking towards the hall.

"Straight ahead. There's one off the master bedroom too."

He observed himself in the bat-winged mirror; adjusting his tie. Exactly like in the narrow one at home, not a wrinkle, not a mark. Absolutely nothing. He settled his coat straight as he heard the water pipes singing. She had left the bathroom door open so he had seen the bend of her knees, and he stayed in the bedroom a moment. Its window also faced the alley, the kid wasn't leaning there now. All high-back fences around the alley curve like pens at the stockyard. Her shadow shifted across a corner of the hall, and he went.

"I wouldn't buy this house, it's kitschy suburbia."

"You couldn't afford it, nobody can, they want far too much and think leaving the drapes will fool a stupid buyer."

"How convenient." She was standing at the steps of the back entrance, looking across dining and living room to the drapes. "They're gaudy."

He was putting on his shoes he had left at the door. "They want thirty-seven five."

She laughed. "It'd be better in a tent."

Her laugh was no happy sound and because their best times had always been exactly such triggering back and forth and hounding down of double entendres, the last thing he wanted was to pick that up. And it was only three seventeen. Twenty-three now.

In the Buick she said, "Would you drive round the front?"

"Huh?"

"I'd like to see it from the front."

"I can give you the address too but the pho—"

"No, I don't want..." she interrupted and stopped as quickly. For an instant he almost felt pity. "Just see it."

He shrugged, backed all the way out to the street, then forward around and slightly into the bay and stopped. The children, three girls and a spindly boy, stared at them, ready to scatter from hopscotch. "The mauve front with the empty planter and yellow-brick fireplace. That means it's four years old and next year it'd have to be new 'old brick' which style has already reached BC from California."

She said nothing and so he backed up and drove down the street. Through one grey-roofed Edmonton suburb and then another, his mind registering out of the corner of his eye the price of any house by size and exterior, out to the arterial street. The house market wasn't this year what it had been last, though still good; he should have cashed out three years ago. Every year helped, and made it a little harder too. The radio was murmuring; he turned into a service station he had never used before on the highway now and bought four dollars worth of gas and three bottles of Pepsi because he saw the machine and felt suddenly thirsty. He got the attendant to clean the windshield again, properly, and then they were on the Calgary Trail. He kept just two miles under the speed limit, pushing down immediately when the signs were readable. From the radio came the echoed picking of electric guitars, that was, yes, The Sounds of—"*Hello darkness my old....*" He turned it up.

He had first heard that the Friday evening he had promised to take Alice to see *The Graduate*: "It tells you everything about today's generation," which wasn't why the office was talking about it. That same afternoon Mary had come in with her last sheaf of letters because Mrs. Rostok was over having her baby and would be back Monday, and he watched her body move and her legs disappear thinking nonchalantly as he had more than a few times in those three weeks, "It would be nice having you here all the time, every way girlie," and then suddenly she was standing there again and he looked up to her face and saw she was crying. He had sense enough to get up and close the door.

"Sit down," he said. "What's wrong?"

He hated having women cry. That was one thing Mrs. Rostok never did, among others, like getting whistles just walking through the office. Mary's shoulder bag had slipped and when she was seated she reached for it. He thought she was getting something to blow her nose, but she unearthed her pocketbook and from the inner compartment behind some bills took a small blue paper. Despite her continued crying her slim hands moved efficiently as they always did. She held the paper to him without looking up. It was just a scrawled note he had placed with the first letters she had done for him: "You're one girl from Office Overload that can type *and* spell. I *like* that." He looked down at the white part of her hair. Her pocketbook?

The radio sounds were humming, echoing on and he managed another long swallow of Pepsi as he drove carefully. Once he heard a certain song repeated when he was in a certain mood, he could not hear the song again without the same feeling rising to him. He had first become aware of this strange retention of sound and feeling the summer he finished high school and finally got a job pouring concrete that might make him enough to get to university. The crew was completely refugee, no one except the foreman could speak a word of English to him and all week he shovelled gravel for sidewalks into that scrapping mixer to the unintelligible shouting of those men in a small town out on the burning prairie and they slept in tents behind the town workshop where a generator thumped until no more electricity was needed and when it cut out in the middle of the night he always woke startled into the silence and with the snores of the muttering men he felt the terrible loneliness of that song drive into him, a song he heard every day sitting with them at the counter in the town's one Chinese café and the radio blaring, always this one song. The tune wasn't actually that sad: it was hearing it there, again and again, as if the one station that could be reached had only one record.

The guitars clanged out on "...silence..." and he cut it off just before the announcer screeched. He knew suddenly he could not remember that other song. Twenty-four years. That was impossible, it had been sung by Elton Britt. Elton Britt singing...he couldn't remember. There was only this haunting sadness he had first heard that night during that almost unbearable movie. Poor Elton driven under, wiped away.

He slowed, turned right towards the river. The road was gravel, potted with water. He slowed even more; he was just getting mud on his car. Mary was talking. He became aware of that as he looped his empty bottle over the car into the opposite ditch. He'd heard it before, there was probably nothing she had to say he hadn't heard before.

"...and we'd moved there just that spring when you came home from graduating from Alberta and their star basketball player too and the principal had you talk to the whole school assembly. He was so proud, smiling, and I was ten then in grade four, without a single friend. Daddy had moved us there practically the end of the year. You talked up there so tall and confident and that's when I started to love you."

He had admitted to her once, when she really pushed him, that he liked to remember her saying that. "Okay, I'll be honest with you. Knowing you've said that gives me confidence. It helps me when I feel in a corner." But he could not understand it: he could not believe a woman could have *loved* him all those years, to the very summer twenty, and he not know a single thing of it, hardly even have heard her name for eighteen. Glimpses he'd never known about when he visited his parents, far away, down streets. How could that be love? If only one person knew about it and never so much as made a plan to say a word until a pure job accident pushed in? Eighteen years, with jobs and marriages and kids all thrown into the mixer by both of them and all of a sudden she pulls out this stupid little note and cries for love. It sure shafted friendship. Or anything.

"I can't think of what baloney I said there."

"It wasn't so bad. You were going to work awhile and go back to school, just the usual thing about working and doing your best."

"So why in the world?"

"You need a reason?"

"Oh sure," and that was believable about her, her frankness, but he couldn't believe what she told him. "I can't stand this mad running around. It's never anything but a mess, a hopeless mess believe me and I've never done it, not that I didn't have the chances."

"I know that."

"Okay, and when I first saw you I thought, 'Well, like usual the one with the best—figure is married, but I think something like that of any girl, I can't be a saint and when I found out who you were I remembered you from back home, of course, and I thought we could be friends and was going to invite you over or something with Harry—"

"And I spoiled it?"

"Yeah."

"Then why didn't you leave me alone? After that? I said my bit and you didn't believe me. I'd been holding that so many years and when I worked for you it was—I knew for certain why I had wanted to love you and did and do, more than ever—why do you keep calling up and we have lunch and coffee together and getting me to talk? Why don't you leave me alone?"

"I like to hear you talk. I like being friendly. You're from my home town and I like you."

She was staring at him; he could see that as he looked ahead and avoided a puddle; took the car over a rise and slowly down into the valley. It wasn't the river yet, just a creek crossed by a narrow bridge; a track led into the summer-green poplars beyond it on the left.

"Okay," he said, "that's not all. I've said it before, you give me confidence. And," he hesitated, then said fast, "when you're not around I think of all kinds of things we could do together, some place alone but when we're together I don't want to. You just don't do anything like that to me, as you know now, not even..." he was far enough into some lie, he didn't know exactly which and it certainly wasn't all lie either, so he could stop. He turned the car down into the crooked track. It was even muddier than the gravel, the car bounced violently and then he stopped. Out of sight from the road anyway, under the trees.

"You don't know anything about love."

"Have it your way. Like always." He got out, carefully onto the grass, into the cool air that smelled of rain still. What sky he could see was absolutely blue; not a puff of cloud.

She was walking away on the muddy trail toward the sound of the creek. He followed on the grass, watching the bare brown feet lift, sink gently into the black mud. Her ankles seemed a little thicker than he remembered them but her tanned legs without stockings or heels were fantastic.

"You think it's some fantastic club that will clout you, knock you silly and forget everything, jab you in the groin. That's all. Have you ever loved anyone, have you ever loved Alice, have you?"

"I love Alice."

"I know she's very beautiful, much more attractive than I but she's not happy and you aren't. I'd never said a word to you if I hadn't felt you were desperately unhappy. Why do you think I said nothing for so long? You were getting all those calls from her, and the children too, then, and I could hear you holding down your anger and frustration and you were so cruel to them, and that isn't like you. I couldn't stand it. You were so terrible on the phone, you couldn't love her. You never talk as if you do."

"You can tell that, just like that."

"Yes."

"You should talk."

"I don't love Harry any more and I've told him. He knows, and he still loves me and has made me very happy at times, but we're frank with each other. We talk through what is and what isn't. What do you and Alice tell each other? How much is in the bank? You sound as if you've never talked to her."

"Sure, you can tell that too."

"That's the trouble, I can. You never deny what I say and—"   .

"Some things between man and wife you don't talk about to anybody."

"—and you keep on with your boy's dream of being a man of great knowledge and healing some day when you do perfectly good things like selling houses, honestly, and people need salesmen who sell houses honestly as much as they need doctors. And that's something that's good about you too," she added sadly, sitting down without a glance. "You keep thinking you want to do it."

They were at the creek, she sitting sideways a little above the mud of its bank. The water was swollen a glossy brown with rain and whorled in the sun turning past them, out from under willows against the high clay it had sheered off at their right, held straight for fifty yards and then bent sharp out of sight to the left. The willows just below them were almost completely submerged. As she said nothing he saw three boys appear out of the bushes on the left and run down the incline to the creek.

One had a knapsack, another an air rifle; they seemed the age of his oldest son. They did not look up; laughing and pushing they walked right into the water spinning from its turn as if it wasn't there, as if they had already taken off their shoes and clothes. The now generation all right, his daughter walking into the lake with jeans on just like that, ducking around and screeching with her friends "Wow—Wild!", water running off them and sticking their tee shirts to their bra-less chests it was obscene and answering nothing to his yell but "Oh shut dad!" But the current here made these boys aware, staggering them nearly to their waists while they laughed, still grabbing each other and pushing until suddenly the kid without the knapsack or rifle slipped, vanished into a blaze of light off the brown water, and in an instant his head resurfaced against the bank, sputtering. His two friends seemed to go berserk with laughter, staggering about in delirious imitation, then they were all three drag-ging themselves up the slimy groove in the opposite bank, laughing, leaping to watch the water squitch out of their shoes, slipping down the groove again to the edge of the creek and grabbing legs and roots and willows to clamber up somehow. Finally they were all up on the level and shrieking they ran off, directly through the puddles on the path, scattering them like spray as they disappeared.

"That kid really soaked his gaunchees," he said. "That would have been something, if he'd disappeared and I'd had to help fish him out."

She should have caught up something smart, like how would he have explained his muddy pants to Alice, but she was staring up the trail where they had gone.

"I've had enough," she said, "you and your absolutely spotless Buick."

"You've only had one ride in it."

"That's enough. There are other men. I'm going to make myself beautiful."

"How'll you do that?" But she refused even that tinge of nastiness. "You've said that a few times before too."

"It's really enough now. You'll never make up your mind, you just want everything, and neat and clean too. I've loved you very much and you won't do anything about it. You think it would be nothing but a mess if we were together and that I couldn't make you happier than Alice. I know I could and she'd be happier too, but you won't believe me. I've made Harry happy and I don't love him, the only thing that makes him unhappy now is you. Knowing I'm always thinking about you and you such a dog."

"Dog?"

"It's his word for your kind."

"I'm a 'kind'?"

"To him yes, not to me. And you haven't even told Alice I exist."

"She knows you took over when Mrs...." it was too inane and he stopped.

"Two years." She was tossing tiny stones into the spinning creek, one by one. "I know that if we could sleep beside each other, peacefully and happily, it would be very beautiful. Even when I was a girl I always thought there had to be a God for how else could I explain love and the strange pull of it in such strange places in my body?"

"That's just sex."

"Love has everything to do with your body. And with everything else too."

"Mary," he said suddenly, "I always thought that the most beautiful, the most divine thing was that somewhere among all the world's billions of people there was one woman, and one only, who was my true love. I believe that."

She said nothing. Her long fingers kept on finding stones beside her bare, muddy feet.

"I'm going to leave him," she said. "I don't know when, maybe soon. He's a lovely father, he'll take better care of Ruthie than I, and we've been really happy together. The happier a man and a woman have been the sooner they separate once the happiness is gone."

"You're just saying that. They'd work at it all the harder."

"They know too well what's missing, and they can't take it."

"That's too easy," he said. "I don't believe it. No. I can't."

Sleeping (Uneasily) with Franz Kafka [1992/1993]

CLOISTER

The memory of mirror. Nothing of its size or shape or what must
have been its inevitable baroque trim, merely the angle in it of that
enormous room and window before him, following him in through
the tall door. Was it that echoing space which first lured them into
never closing a bathroom door? The morning light there slanted
up, as it appeared, into long vanishing emptiness. When Adam still
thought that Kafka was something else Karan could eventually be
persuaded into forgetting.

"Would it help," he called, trying to recall the deep-set eyes, the
long, bumpy nose, and doing so only too well: in generalities the face
might have been tilting forward on his own naked shoulders, "say, if
I parted my hair in the middle? Trimmed it up sort of high, sort of
furrish, like a cap?"

Out of sight, she was laughing about the vegetarian fuss in the
restaurant the night before. Her voice echoing: "Such people play
around with their health as if it were a sickness."

"You're quoting again," he said, very nearly bitter.

Perhaps she hadn't heard him; she was still laughing.

"How about I prop my ears out," he called, "like sort of big scoops...."

"Oh shut up and get back here."

420

She was there, her body then still waiting like a tender child's. The ancient, noisy bed too tiny in the room under ceilings that vanished upwards, somewhere in air; a body seemingly as forgotten there as all other possible nunnery purposes that empty building once had. Only hidden under the close warm tent of sheets, and skin along skin, could they see each other and escape its cavernous echo.

"Why do you always want me?"

"An unfortunate state of mind. For me."

"Don't you mean 'state of body'?"

"Not at all."

"The body is a state of mind?"

"Abso-loo-loo-lutely."

"'The applicant,'" Adam quoted in German between her breasts, "'is fluent in the German and Bohemian languages, in speech and writing, and further he commands the French, partly the English—'"

She tugged fiercely at him, "Stop it! It's hopeless. You never had a huge ambitious Freudian father to finally hate."

"''It's a unique apparatus,' said the officer to the research traveller and considered, with a certain look of wondering admiration, the to him very familiar'"—ugh! that hurt—or should one translate 'Apparat' as 'machi—'"

Karan was astride him, his arms pinioned back, flat. "I'll kick you out," she pronounced through her perfect teeth.

"Okay—but please, please not—not in!" He was trying to laugh at his feeble pun, her tense knee thrust now between his legs and threatening to jerk.

STREET

A microscopic image of his face shone in her black eyes. Was he that small to her, always so tiny? Tiny as the archaic keyhole they in turn peered through in some unreadable Josefstadt street of Prague, a keyhole she had found too—she was a superb research traveller. As she had quickly found the air-blackened bust with its unreadable Czech on the corner of what had once been, she told him, Karpfen and Engegasse, everything of the building torn down and rebuilt except the original entrance and even that obscured by scaffolding so ancient it might have been clamped together there since 1883, bleeding such rust and obviously no workman near it for decades.

No Intourist official in Wencelas Square who could speak either English or German or French would admit knowing the least thing about a Kafka bust or corner, the site of that building now built over and into the baroque profusion of the St. Niklaskirche behind blue hording, the nine-spired towers of the Tienkirche shrouded in iron in a tight angle of roofs beyond. Nevertheless, the youngest female guide did acknowledge *sotto voce* as they all bent together around the mapped bend of the Moldau River pulling the city together that oh yes, Franz Kafka of course was born and lived his life in Prague, but everything in the old centre had to be repaired and rebuilt after the war. The Peoples' memorial to the horrible Nazi elimination of all Jews once living in Prague, one person safely dead in 1924 could be no more important than any other in a rabid, genocidal destruction of an entire race, though Prague itself had not been bombed by the Allies like all those other defenseless European cities and of course the Grand Soviet Army had not fired one single shot more than absolutely necessary to wrest it from the last Nazi Gauleiter, shooting him down in the street, she thought—what were they really looking for, exactly?

Karan said nothing as Adam bent to the keyhole, expecting inside the bolted planks of the door an insect's legs to be wavering in the unresisting air. Oddly, the cemetery door was at street level, though the long brick wall stretched away a metre above his head, and grave-stones stuck out over it to the far walls of buildings, stones shaded in brilliant sunlight by the moving branches of trees. With stones so high—could a city be sinking even as it was torn away, levelled and rebuilt?—the remains of the dead must be buried at eye-level, an elevated cemetery in an ancient city quarter dug out of slums and bordellos? Was the patient earth dragged away to eliminate the sweat of poverty and lust soaked into it? Where could you bury that? But inside those ancient planks—they couldn't have been that old then, the wood should be more rotten—the graveyard apparently dropped to the level of the cobbled street, and an insect remaining would have been too much to expect from relentless National Committee cleaners. Gravestones only, thick as files in a cabinet. But unrif-flable; unreadable. Each stone thin as a graven hand reaching up and carved edgewise, blundered with moss through what might be Hebrew, or German, or conceivably even Bohemian notations that continued their centuries of settling over the bodies layered in this long-suffering earth, every tiered body pulling its slab down at its own sagging angle into rot and falling slowly, surrendering nothing of its irradicable stone. Peered at through this crack in the door, and ignoring the drone of the city, the tall sunlight made it appear a gentle, mossy garden of crusted knives.

Or had he actually been looking *below* the cemetery protruding *above* the brick wall? Had Karan somehow found and shown him the real graves hidden below a tourist surface, the true, green bottom-lessness of burial?

"He isn't buried there, not there," a voice says behind them. Gravelly as small water in a streambed long dry. Like her dessicated face.

"Whom do you mean?" Karan asks.

"They'll charge you five korunas to go in and look. But you won't find him."

"Whom do you mean?" Karan asks again in her delicate German.

"In the graveyard in Prague-Straschnitz, there's his stone." A dark round mound of a woman, her crushed face held together snugly by a cowl. "Though who knows if he has a body."

"We're interested in Franz Kafka, where he—"

"Who else?" her mouth gums words. "On this street." Laughter ripples, a small wind shivering over her. "But I wouldn't make the effort to look. If he still has a body, it's been dug up seventy times over."

Karan steps close to her. "Dug up? They dug him up? When?"

Adam understood every word, but could not fathom them together. A sunlit summer street in a huge city roaring with markets and voices and cars, its historic centre designated heritage and so saved from the grotesque castings of 1980s subway tunnels. Nevertheless this apparition in siblesque charcoal transfixing his beautiful friend between baroque building, cobbled street and an iron-studded door in a contradictory brick wall with uttered apho-risms. Like a pretentious movie—except they were together standing in it. Listening, more than a little frightened.

"Heh heh, oh they were such organized hunters, where was there earth enough to hide Jewish bodies, dead or not?"

"When?" Karan repeats. Her hand has lifted, she may be about to tug the next, true word out of this featureless human hiding.

"If he was ever there, and his parents lying right there too."

Karan's face slowly freezes, mouth slightly open to the icy tips of her teeth. The sunlight is so brilliant he understands why Hermann Kafka once lived here in a house called "To the Golden Face."

"Where? Where do they lie?"

"Go to Straschnitz. There you'll see what they had to do when they died, the few Jews that ever got rich in Prague."

"We have, it's just...an ordinary...graveyard...."

The crumpled face actually crumples further, into what must be accepted as laughter. To all appearances sympathetic; or ghoulish.

"That poor Franz! Only for seven years sheltered in the earth, alone—ach and then his heavy Papa lies down on him again."

Mama too. That's what the stone said: "Dr Franz"...."Hermann". "Julie".... Franz, not Frantisek, as the river for him was "Moldau," not "Vltava"—but their quest seems so ridiculous to Adam, suddenly: to know *all* the facts about someone you'd have to literally relive their entire life, stupidities and all, thank god this one lasted only forty-one years and not like Goethe eighty-three. What the hell anyway did it matter where Kafka lived, or if his body was still rotting some-where? They hadn't wiped out his stories and novels, even though his literary executor Max Brod published the bulk of them after death in direct contradiction to the requirement in Kafka's will that they be, without exception, burned. Max Brod. What kind of a shit friend, or executor, was he, huh?

"You're the shit. You never listen," Karan told him, striding back. "You see and hear what suits your prejudiced preconceptions. And remember even less."

He should have looked through the keyhole once more. Or let her walk away, wherever, left her and gone past the brown and the yellow Skoda to the cut-stone building at the corner and paid the five korunas and gone in past the inevitable girl asleep at the entrance, her hand waiting for a ticket. Perhaps if his misconceived ignorance had searched among the broken stones under the trees he could have found something he could not now misconstrue, or forget.

An entrance opening down. A helpless beetle on its back. A printer ripping back and forth, buzzing out a bloody text between its fixed margins on folded automatic-feed skin not yet, quite, turned into parchment or paper. As she once said, with Kafka who repeated and anticipated everything about humanity like certain writers in the Old Testament, with Kafka any horror is possible.

CLOISTER

"I told you. He lived his life in Josefburg, an entire life within two hundred metres of where he was born. Grew up, was sent to a Hapsburg dying Empire German school, to Charles University, graduated a doctor of laws, went into work recommended by his business uncles but didn't stay—his father moved the family incessantly from one Jewish Quarter house to the next and when he was twenty-five not a single building in which he had lived remained, anywhere—not one. Can you retain that one simple fact?"

"Aren't you distorting? If all the buildings were gone—"

"Can you understand anything? I'm talking *vanishment*?"

"My parents homesteaded in Saskatchewan, I can't even find the cellar depressions."

"God, you are a self-important bastard."

"You're talking about vanish—"

"You travel the world and talk nothing but yourself!"

"And you're a bitch, with keyhole vision! Franz bleeding Kafka, middle-class, educated, super-achiever Jewish suffering, oh such endless suffering on a permanent disability pension from the Workman's Compensation Insurance Comp—"

"You're being an ass—"

"Who the hell hasn't suffered? See anybody, ask them, they'll yell it in your ear—who?"

Very quietly: "I'm talking about the writer of *The Metamorphosis*."

"And suffered without full pension, without beautiful women in every spa and hotel in every great city of Europe more than willing to sweetly lick the goddamn sweat off your goddamn suffering brow!"

"Did you hear me?"

"Every opera heroine dies of tuberculosis, lungs gloriously unclogged, singing full tilt!"

"Did you?"

"Yes. And also 'The Great Wall of China' and *The Castle* and *Amerika* and *In the Penal Colony* and whatever else he scribbled and scribbled, hundreds of pages. Most of which he wanted burned."

"What do you know what Kafka wanted?"

"He wrote it, so why shouldn't he ash it?"

"Who told you?"

"His will! But Max Brod and his dear Momma decided it was worth too much—"

"You think anything he ever wrote was that simple, even his will?"

"Maybe he didn't write it—he just signed it."

"Well...?"

"Well what?"

"Do you know? Did he write his own will, word for word? What it said?"

"Karan, he had a PH.D. in law, his will—"

"And if he wrote this very personal document, his will, he meant it to be taken literally, word for dictionary word?"

"Arrrggggh," he groaned, "you of course always know—everything! Your endless overload of ironic facticity. I'll tell you what I know Kafka wrote, because he published it while he was still alive! He didn't burn it—*A Country Doctor*, Munich and Leipzig, Kurt Wolff Verlag, 1919. And in it a postage stamp story—as translated by Willa and Edwin Muir in 1933, or a little later:

THE NEXT VILLAGE

My grandfather used to say: "Life is astoundingly short. To me, looking back over it, life seems so foreshortened that I scarcely understand, for instance, how a young man can decide to ride over to the next village without being afraid that—not to mention accidents—even the span of a normal happy life may fall far short of the time needed for such a journey."

"There," he said. "Fact enough?"

"What happened to your favourite, in the first book he ever—"

"Answer my question, please."

"Oh yes, fact, to the very comma...to his first collection, *Betrachtung, Achtzehn kurze Prosastücke*, dedicated to Max Brod, Leipzig, Rowolt Verlag, 1913. I refer to the one-sentence story, 'The Wish to be a Red Indian'?"

"I have, as you know, vowed never again to mention that one, to you abhorrent, *word* in your presence," he said reaching for her shoulder, which for a moment wasn't there, but came.

"You have an outstanding selective memory."

"Never to mention it, in any form, either as 'native' or 'aboriginal' or 'Amerindian' or 'first nation' or 'indigene' or—"

"Ree-ally—'indigene'?"

"Yes, nor even to quote it from the writer whom you have now so conceived of in your mind as to worship. I will no longer express any wish, ever, in your presence, aloud, to gallop spurless, reinless, over the smooth prairie (which is never actually smooth but then your idol, never having seen any, wouldn't know that and perhaps didn't care to try and imagine it—even the ambiguous greatness of Kafka eventually finds that some writing 'types' are necessary) when one's 'horse's neck and head would be already gone.'"

"Facts, dead on," her kiss nuzzled tongue and lips in his ear. "Correct to the very semi-colon, my lovely camera-eyed lover."

And she was running ahead of him. Along the wall of that devastated nunnery, past the locked and boarded chapel doors singing,

"Come run in the woods...come run in the woods...come in the woods...come come."

CLOISTER TOWER

But, very oddly, the double tower doors open when he hesitates following her, and tries them. A small, square space scattered with straw, mouse and rat leavings, with bird shit. It must be the pigeons, when he looks up he sees a beak protruding here and there at him where the black cross braces angle into corners. Bobbing out, and back again, single eyes, perhaps they are brooding there in the lengthening summer. A fine tight space with beams to pattern the long emptiness up and up, upward openness for an only son who at thirty-one (be accurate, from 1883 to 1915) has not yet left the clutching itinerant house of his parents. High beyond the fluttering pound and landing of pigeons, there, where inside the dome the light dusts long beams into existence.

He can rest, and lean his hands on that light as if it were oak. The sustainable iridescence of air. Far below him her beautiful face—that is memory of memory only, he was certainly too high to see—rests on the tiny roundness of her bared shoulders. Her body dropped away, gone, and as unrecognizable as his own face upside-down.

"Come down."

Her voice climbs the off-set sections of ladders upward so cautiously, so thinly; when it reaches him she is stretched into a single word,

"...sweetheart...."

And then he desires suddenly, overwhelmingly, to climb higher than possible, higher, so he will see only the backs of the pigeons as they open and lift their dappled wings wide to escape, even momentarily. She will have to be terrified; with him.

Up is always the easiest. In the empty cupola he has to jump a little to clasp the empty bell-beam, and then he swings out. But he can't get his feet to lift high enough over his head to catch himself up and hook them, they seem too distant at the end of his sudden body. Hand-width by width, the squared beam cutting his wrists, he manoeuvres himself nearer the arch of the wall, then walks his feet up until he hangs at right angles and parallel to the long column of space below. But his body will not pull over, onto the hewn beam. Not like he once lifted himself and walked the two-by-four rafters of houses in southern Alberta wind, or swung over scaffolding onto the slender parallel facts of strapping—the beam is straight between his straight arms, he does not look down, he will listen only to the beat of birds below him, the blotches of medieval stucco fallen away, the air now straight as a bed of needles beneath him which he lies on like solid silence, his clenched stomach and crossed ankles and hands may hold something somewhere and feel nothing. Nothing. Like resting in a brief moment of freefall. Or possible prayer.

He finally caught up with her where the beech branches reached into space. The forested ravine sheered level below them by the evening sunlight, and he was gasping.

"'And there in the wood,'" she sang, "'a piggywig stood with a ring at the end of her nose, her nose, with a ring at the end of her—'"

"Toes, her toes, come toes or come nose, we will come to blows."

"You blow or I blow?"

"We'll blow together...."

"And come together...."

"Can't—it won't rhyme."

"Piffle," she swirled that away with one naked arm flung out over the ravine of the world, "flow together, grow together, stagger to and fro together...."

The branches and their perfect leaves moved beyond her black hair against the sky, bits of light opening in his eyes like the slow elliptical movements of all-night stars. There was a jagged branch under him, he was aware of it with a quick stab of pain and he thought, I'll carry a scar on my ass for life. But he forgot about that then; completely at her movement.

CLOISTER

It was only visible in a mirror, bent over and backed up looking between his legs; and only for a few months. That wasn't where he carried a scar.

"Always looking for new angles on yourself?" she asked. He said nothing. "The pucker of your piles?"

"I don't have any."

"I know that perfectly well, my love. I've kissed your every pain away."

"Not every pain."

"Oh you poor darling," she nuzzled his head into her opening lap. "I'm not as good at it as Momma was, am I, only your poor big bruised and aching body, your tender little ass?"

"Kissing is supposed to make you feel *all* better."

And she turned the tables on him, again. She said,

"Our kissing doesn't, does it."

Perhaps they were seated on the bed in that cavernous room. Or he was kneeling against her knees after she had folded herself into the stuffed chair—was there a stuffed chair?—when she said that. Actually, it must have been much later, if there was no visible scar. At the time she thought they might have to find a doctor, the skin was really broken and who knew what infection lay scattered in a German forest, she was always more concerned with his bodily ailments than he. Perhaps because he had so few. If he could only be sick sometimes, he thought then, or have some small, trivial but very visible wound on his body—even a barked knuckle would have helped—then for a short time at least they might not have forced each other to find such furies.

STREET

"And his three younger sisters," the old sibyl laughed, "they were all very close, the four children, Elli who travelled with him to Hungary and at last to Müritz on the Baltic, and good little Valli, and Ottla the youngest, she gave him his last summer cottage when he almost couldn't eat anymore. Ottla he loved best, but he died in the arms of Dora Dymant."

"So...where are the three sisters buried?" he asked, so stupidly. Karan turned, stared at him.

"Look in the air," the old woman croaked. "Buried in the air, like garbage!"

"The official word was 'Assanierung,'" Karan told him. "You knew, why did you ask?"

"I did, but..." he can never explain how he could have, even momentarily, forgotten the long list of women whom Kafka loved, as much or as little as he could, who within twenty years were murdered one way or another so grotesquely. "Only Felice Bauer, whom he refused to marry, every five years, and...."

"Only refused twice."

"All the fives he had time for."

"And Dora Dymant. London, 1952. The human 'Assanierung' of Prague."

"I...what does that mean?"

"The word they used—clearance, architectural cleansing—tear down every house in Josefburg, after 1893, and build this imitation Vienna. Kafka said, 'Our heart still doesn't know anything about this completed "Assanation." The sickly old Jewish town is much more real to us than this hygenic new city around us.'"

"God, you've memorized every word, even his letters."

"At least I don't pretend they're the Eternal Word of God."

"Hell no," fury exploded in him, "you never pretend, you know! Everything!"

The jumble of Friday market in the Great Ring he was striding through was so much like the mess of his feelings that he could have smashed, thrown, crashed over—it didn't matter, do something physical, violent, break something absolutely and forever irreversibly—DO!—when she sliced him, her brilliant, perfect angling of the slipping knife, his mind just—disappeared. He had nothing but legs with feet to kick something into disintegration, long cramped arms and empty hands clamping onto something, heave it up, smash it—a heap of cobblestones rammed against his toes, the mason looking up at him calmly from his padded knees. His hammer poised for another tap on the last stone he had placed in its necessary angle of concentric curves; speaking to him some words in Czech. Could it be "comrade"? Wearing a bruised grey leather apron. Adam discovered his arm was raised, a stone there high in his hand.

He was looking at the great clock in the City Hall tower above him. Low as it was, he doubted he could throw the cobblestone that high. Such an incredible clock of interlaced faces, built when you couldn't buy Japanese time at any stall in the market and carry it away, Emperor Franz—Franz indeed!—Josef should be riding by with his white beard and inbred Hapsburg mustache, in medals and fourteenth-century uniform on a perfect black horse.

Karan lifted the stone from his hand, so he let his hand drop. She handed it to the mason, who placed it in the sand at his knee and chose another black one. He was talking to her, Czech perhaps or some dialect of it, and she nodded, answered in perfect accent with the few words Adam knew she knew—"Yes," "Why?" "Thank you."

As if she understood every word the man was at length explaining. "Goodbye."

"This," she said in his ear, "is the Clock of the Apostles—all except Judas. And that," her warm arm turned him slightly, pointing across the stones circling themselves one by one for those thick hands, "that is the Kafka house 'Minuta.' You ran right to it."

How often he has dreamed since that he looked at her then; could remember the exact openness of her obsidian eyes. *You ran right to it.*

"His three sisters were born in that very house, the family lived here seven years. They moved to Zeltnergasse just before his bar-mitzvah in the Zigeuner Synagogue."

"'Gypsy,' oh gypsy," he muttered. "When?"

"June 13, 1896. 10:30 in the morning."

Saturday no doubt, and Leap Year. But he didn't look at her watching him, still knows exactly why he wanted to say nothing. Lived there to age thirteen, when everything new and unknown in a life has already happened; when it is all over but the variations of ruthless repetition. The building stood there, attached to all the others, three stories above arches and below a steep tile roof. Blank as a cobblestone. The attempt to assemble a life out of the minutiae of accidentally preserved grocery lists or laundry overwhelmed him with futility. Especially creative genius.

"Come," she said. Kissing him with her particular softness among the rushing comrades of the Great Ring. "We'll go to Ottla's rented house in the Street of the Alchemists. It's across the river."

Where in the last years of The Great War, as they thought it then, he wrote most of the "little narratives" published in *A Country Doctor*. Little perhaps to suit his daily routine in the little black house. Two odd windows, a chimney, a door below the immense gothicly castellated cathedral on the hill where the kings and queens of Bohemia were crowned, when they still had bodies to bury.

CLOISTER TOWER

The arches where bells should be are older than baroque or gothic. He hangs beamed like a bell bat above the forest and the never distant clearings of German fields, bent roads, villages, the perpetual whine of Autobahn somewhere like its national drone, but he is resting calmly in a great silence. He knows he cannot jump back to the beam on which he stood, it's impossible, and he thinks, suddenly, that he would like to hear the cantor at a bar mitzvah sing the dark, strong songs of sorrow and dedication, of lament thick as an unaging human secret. For all their endless, imaginative articulation, the words between Karan and himself, not even the very simple ones like "go!" or "come," ever quite found them home. Never completely. Never as they desired of them, search as relentlessly as they might. It seems he knew even then that words would never be enough, so why did they groan themselves into each other's bodies as they did, searching and momentarily on the brink but never quite finding what even they could not express to the other they sought?

And if they couldn't express it to each other, who could there be to say it to? Would there ever be? Why must it be said? What was it? Who?

The sound of the nuns comes to him on irridescent air. The tower does not open from the nave, nor out of the choir, it opens up to end with itself. But nevertheless their ancient song has been waiting for him to climb to, to sway into, has been held here for him throughout the centuries of air they have already been forgotten, high and weightless into his hanging, free from every sorrow and transparent as ice, voices of women obsessive in adoration stretching so high, free, slender as silk, the spin of spiders floating without end beyond the tips of the tallest trees into sacrifice, their white wimples wrapping their throats so tight and opening their faces like bells up into the light, voices faceless, soaring together indistinguishable and pure. Song without body, there cannot be any such thing as body, its very memory forgotten, only a yearning upwards together and solitary as the point of candle flame.

"'History is a needle, for putting you to sleep....'"

She is there very nearly beside him, reaching, reaching for him. She can barely touch him but does. When his feet let go the maw of space swings up from under him and his heart lurches wauggh! his hands open. But she pulls him across air and in to her strong as steel.

"You ass," she breathes in his ear. "You goddamn ass."

The beam is exactly wide enough for their interspaced feet. The air, swaying, wraps them around each other, brief summer clothes, skin, bones, hair.

"'Annointed with the poison,'" he whispers over her bare shoulder into that medieval void. "'Of all you want to keep.'"

"You misquoted."

"So did you, I used your word."

"Nor is Montreal Cohen Kafka."

"You started it."

Up is always so easy. He climbed up and then she climbed up. Or did she climb and he climbed after? They are held by nothing but air on a beam perhaps rotten, they enfold each other into each other's terror. But their hands, their implacable bodies find the relentless movements of love, imperceptibly she opens her thighs, imperceptibly he pulls her harder against him. Here. Their bodies intensify, this shell of air is all that needs to hold them, is the sheet enclosing them under unseeable ceilings or stone floors, is always their own small sufficient place in the unrelenting voyeuristic multiplicities of the world.

"Will you come when we fall?"

"Always."

"Why Kafka, why not Rilke?"

"Too much Catholic guilt."

"At least Catholics have the Virgin, better than Moses."

"Not Moses, I love the virgin Susannah."

"She was no virgin, Kafka never wrote a word about her."

"He didn't have to, she destroyed those Elders herself."

They sway gently as one, the clapper of a bell a memory too light to strike sound; hang on falling off the lip of terror into ecstasy. Endless at last.

"We could search for Rilke," Karan breathes in Adam's ear. "Their lives overlapped, they lived in Prague, they never met."

"But Rilke...wasn't a Jew."

"He didn't have to be. Like you."

Swaying him so gently.

WHEN HE CAME FORWARD, quickly, the stewardess was alone in
first class, contemplating the flawless face reflected in her nightcase
mirror. He cut into the right seats. Already the plane had edged up to
the river, lying north and south here but in the distance bending in a
long curve back, east, and farther ahead there was the tiny blackish
spiderwork of trees arranged by loops upon river loops into a wider
valley—that had to be the Red Deer—it was all so fast, too fast.

He slid across to the left seats—that deep cut angling southwest
must be the South Saskatchewan. He pressed his forehead against
the window; six miles below, between white prairie and white river,
the brownish fringes of cliffs crumpled back up ravines until the
river gradually straightened as if drawn into the far blue mist of land
barely yellow and grey in the white. He pushed, harder, but directly
below the incredible raw valley was steadily drawing away behind
them—that stupid pilot was flying dead-centre over the confluence,
he would need a bomb-bay to see exactly where the two rivers joined
their ice...had needed, it was already inevitably past, and he had not
even a memory to—

"It looks so cold down there, doesn't it!" The perfect face of the
stewardess tilted on the seatback, smiling her perfectly trained excla-
mation. He stared at her.

"The Oldman River is always..." she began after a moment, and stopped.

"Then what's the river below now," he said. "The Waterton?"

He was past her legs, unflawed nylon marble; back in his own seat. Strong plastic trayback, strong plastic window. The Red Deer River looped back and forth across its shallow drift, again and again swinging almost back to touch itself in shadows carved by the winter sun. The window hardened his face with cold, gradually hardened, straightened the river out of curls into curves, then simply bent lines among the grey-white mushrooms and striated egg-cups of badlands. Soon that too had vanished in a long valley northwest, but he had a memory to lay on the white ordered land outlined by faint webs of fences, by squares and oblongs of texture. The memory of a little man, on a summer day, white sleeves looped by gold links, a hand passing over his face like a kiss and suddenly holding...holding an unbelievable curve of teeth, teeth which have just emerged out of the man's head.

He must have seen that standing, he remembered now, carefully, in front of the cabin where he was born, on the spot where his mother stood once when a greyish picture was taken, she small in an apron like a white yoke against the greys of mudded logs, the even smaller figures of his two sisters already whitely aproned on her right, and himself a tiny greyish bump smudged against her other side. In front of the door, the screen door where in summer he had often stood fearfully, waiting to hear the cowbells return from the free-range stretching forever west of their homestead, knowing his mother would surely bring the cows if she could find them in the mosquito-whining bush, knowing if she went too far she would have to find them to guide her back home, the smudge-smoke waiting too, a blue flat cloud caught above the corral in a motionless net of poplars. He had stared, rigid, at the teeth cut with such inhuman precision out of, what he had thought till then, a living face. The man's blurred voice asked him if he could take his out too, and he could not so much as shake his head when he had never thought it possible to try. And his mother leaning beyond the sheen of screen door, not laughing like the grey man when with a sudden jolt of terror he clawed inside his own mouth, tearing at his tiny, oh blessed be Lord Jesus, immovable teeth.

"That's not for us, Bengelchi," she said reaching out, nubbling his head. "We're not that advanced yet."

But she was soon advanced enough, the first in the family, after she wrenched her left arm out of its socket falling between the split poles of the hayrack and after two years of sporadic paralysis finally getting to a doctor who told her she should have been sewn together immediately when it happened, that she would never heal properly now, and that her teeth were broken pipes draining poison into her body. Her teeth then no more than grey or black stumps, destroyed systematically by chewing salt whenever their unending pain became more unbearable than the sharper, but briefer, agony of killing them.

His tongue slid around his own teeth, capped, filled, so solid and strong the dentists always said, all those turnips and boiled cabbage grown in Alberta bush that had destroyed his mother's...she was younger then than he was now. His body shuddered in the foam seat; he tried to somehow comprehend that. She had always seemed so... ancient...was that the word? Bits of pictures, touches, words would be falling on him like rain as long as he lived, and how would he ever recapture her, the feeling he understood when her eyes were still level with his and she would say a word to him, her hand now soft as weathered cloth then firm, unshaky in his own.

"Die letzte Nacht im Eltern Haus."

In English that sounded merely silly, perhaps it was her rhythm of saying "Eltern" that made the equivalent "parents" so bony: words she first said when he first left and almost every time he returned, even for a day, even the short day he brought his wife through the door, married in a ceremony across an ocean and for which she could do no more than airmail a poem he never knew where she found. The poem was doddery, stale to him snoring lyric Rilke daily under his breath, though the feelings were right, for her. He could hear her voice sounding the words as her hand slowly moved them across the page, perhaps out of her head: "Wohl dir, du hast es gut...."

The Calgary airport was khaki metal walls and fans blowing through heaters hung from exposed pipes; after an L10-11, the next plane barely a basket. He folded himself in with some others, it quivered like a Model A, though the airvents and window were plastic. And the white mountains, the Bow and Oldman rivers sifted him out of his jet-lag, out of the staggering weariness of walking momentarily on cement. Among the trees of these valleys—the plane seemed in rather than over them—buffalo had wintered with the Blackfoot, bedded in those folds. The voice of the long-distance operator trying to hammer him awake, to make him understand. How had they found him at that Montreal hotel?

It had to be wrong, they would never have carried the tub up those pole stairs, leave alone the hot kettle, yet he always remembered her bending across the tub in the angle of the rafters under which he slept at night curled into wool on a straw sack, the house logs cracking fearfully in the cold when he rammed himself out of a bad dream, the stovepipe standing straight up into darkness at the edge of his bed. In that memory she leaned forever at the angle of the rafters, clawing at the kettle from which his older sister poured boiling water into the tin tub and thoughtlessly onto his younger sister—her thigh—squatting to bathe in the tepid water he had just left: that scream must have echoed in the kitchen below, and his mother's too, the kettle now in her hand with his older sister suddenly rigid in the soft steam of her pouring, her mouth fallen open and her hands still up, crooked as if still holding the blackened kettle. That might not have happened in winter, any more than it happened in the sleeping loft; it might have been the summer when the gigantic bull stalked out of free-range, roared about the yard all afternoon so that none of them dared open the door, not even his mother, and he prayed if only his father would appear, oh help him to come, now from wherever he is, somewhere, help him to come home early for Sunday, help, and then there he was, coming steadily down the wagon tracks with a green stick in his hand and going to the bull pawing dust over himself, head down and roaring, and had hammered him across the nose and jammed the stick into the bull's ring and led him west out of the yard; had broken the poplar on the bull's silently retreating rump.

He could not have been thinking in English then—how could he have thought? In the *Low German* she still spoke to him, that he screamed into the telephone to make her understand, *Joh, Joh!* he would come! Her removable teeth perfect and even as though carved from marble filling her mouth, moving her jaw down out of the folds of face to shape her strong chin again, the uneasy evenness of her sudden smile which no longer depended only on her eyes, her cheekfolds.

There was no language necessary, only pictures. She stood with her left arm crooked against the belly of a shaved, decapitated pig hung from a beam between two poplars in snow, the long knife in her hand ready to slice down that belly and spill the guts into the waiting kettle; guts she would pull inside-out and clean and stuff with ground meat and boil in the bubbling fat cauldron that winter evening; where he would stand stirring with a long pole, waiting not for the sausage but for the short chopped ribs to be crisp, stuffing split wood under to keep the fire leaping. She herded chicks across the grass mat of farmyard to their log shelter, away from the night coyotes. She tramped manure into the clay mud of a shallow pit and smeared that between and over the crooked poplar logs of the house. And once, when their dog Carlo had torn the neighbour's dog apart and she had had to accept all that neighbour's obscenities because his father was not there—he was never there, always away from home, somewhere, working like an animal for someone who would give him orders to work like a beast—Carlo lying complacent, his red tongue lolling—why can't you ever be home like other husbands, work here like you work for others? And his father stood so easily, his arms hung motionless at his sides, the sobs of a wife far easier to manage than that a neighbour think him less of a fine fellow. With Carlo panting in the corner shade of logs, the beautiful fur still perfect at his throat for almost one more year.

World War II hangars and brown sheds intact at Lethbridge Airport, shingled together now into one U-Drive office available with two cars. White mountains and, as always, wind. Almost too much to climb home against at right angles on a bicycle, singing in the nostrils with slivers of a February spring. The town elevators still stood, grew larger, centred in the highway.

She lay sleeping. Her face held between her hands, mouth bunched like delicate, weathered rags. Despite his all-day coming he had to lean against the curtained doorway; she was still here, suddenly, as if half his lifetime had never been so much as a sound swallowed in an empty room. The sound of her songs, sad as he

439

Home for Night

always thought them then, offering a faith used as it seemed for nothing but to long for "the Home over There," though there were always edges of happiness in her voice as she cooked berries for winter, sweat running down her unwrinkled cheeks, her left arm bent against her side while the other moved swiftly for both, her high clear voice rising like a cobweb into the summer heat gathering black with thunder over the spruce. His stare must wake her; if she lay like this when he pounded on the door, shouted her name in the kitchen as he came around into the living room, what could not walk into the house when she slept? Alone, like this, just the tiny shape half curled towards him; barely breathing. He turned quickly, past the empty bed in the corner of the living room, out again. Backed the car away.

"He was so old, he really wanted to go," his sister said. "And such a look, of peace, just all of a sudden." She faced him, her legs folded sideways, crossed at the ankles. "Always even when he was sleeping with the pills, you know he breathed so loud, like gasping, his face all—but there was this look, as if something just beautiful...as if he saw it all, all of a sudden, really beautifu...."

For the first and only time he felt tears prickle along his nose and behind his eyes. His sister leaning forward on the chrome table, her warm voice talking and tears sliding on her cheeks she did not shift her hands to wipe away. It was not there again, not even when he came through the door and his mother was tight against him, when after a moment he let her go so he could bend down and kiss her, he did not feel that. Past her cheek he saw her grey hair pulled into the same bun she made when she combed it out and he knew that either visitors were coming or they were going somewhere, other-wise she would never have time for combing. He was bent forward so awkwardly, his back kinked by the plane anyway, as if trying to kiss a child without either lifting it in his arms or hunkering down—he could not do that to bring his face level with his mother's—but she pulled back and his hands caught on her two shoulders, her bones there fragile as willows.

"For a whole year he lay there, in that bed, in the corner," she said. "And I took care of him."

She was looking up into his eyes. Her teeth clacked and he wanted to pull her close, against himself; out of sight and sound.

"I haven't cried for three years, the Heavenly Father has taken my tears away. Even now. I cried too much then, you know, yes?"

He pulled her to him, floundering for the murmurs of under-standing, the indiscriminate sounds of whatever language to get past her wavering right arm.

"Mom...Mama...I wanted to...I really...."

"Don't," she said, thin and dry against his chest. "Don't lie. Not today."

Except God, Who Already Knows [1989/1990]

Turning to the open sea
she speaks in low German.
No one can hear us now she says....
—SARAH KLASSEN, *Journey to Yalta*

THE ERRATICS *wait along the skyline of eskers like im-memorial stones—a land not to be believed or uttered,* Adam is writing in his journal. *Sometimes there is sky under them. They sit balanced on three or four small stones like a massive table waiting to be set, or an altar. Now when I look up, through the tent's mosquito mesh I see only white water. To the endless, stony grumble of this unnamed river north of the Arctic Circle (where else in the world would you find one?—Siberia?)—we will sleep well tonight.*

And they do. But suddenly Adam jerks erect—"gronk!"—that's Eric's bear-horn not working again at the instant it must if it is to protect them, he is staring through the mesh in the tent door away from the river—the danger will come there, not from the water—everything shimmering through the screen and blurred naked without his glasses, he is groping for their protection in this strange night brightness and something tiny, brown, flits by, running low like some swift flow disappearing between the scattered rocks—"gronk!"—

certainly not the bear-horn, certainly animal—very loud and dignified as if it were a statement of processional entrance but so close too, on the very ground outside the tent, that he shudders, violently, despite the soft warmth of his sleeping bag hooked about his shoulders; stares at the nylon just beyond Joel's sleeping body. Claws will slash through, there, the low, snaking head and he cannot move, fear opening wider inside him, his breath—

A magnificient ptarmigan struts slowly past. The bird's tiny head cocked brown, its lower body and legs mottled white, it seems to float on the misty lichen, on the light darkening between rocks, moving toward the boulders heaved up by permafrost where their packs lie, and on against the edge of the northern sun lining the horizon as it has all night: a small, fat bird with the pomposity of total unawareness walking its habitual path—the faint trail they all puzzled over leading to the water, of course, that was ptarmigan, birds so dull the Dene say they snare them like bush rabbits. The endless tundra to scatter over and they insist on one trail, even run along it if you chase them and the two hollows in the river's sandy pebbles must be where they bathe. They're as stupid as barnyard chickens and almost as large, they—"gronk!"—it declares from beyond the boulders, and Eric's bear-like shape materializes where the other tent stands out of sight beside the white river: the ptarmigan's regal walk lies between them. It is gone. The July polar night glows lemon yellow where light touches earth, the sky flushed blue upward to a brilliance of indigo through green mesh; Adam feels his body shrink around himself.

He is being removed, distanced into somewhere beyond time. As if he were smothering under ice, the deep voice of the river and the light already here all those millennia since the slow melting of the continental glaciers spread out the body of the global sea.

He can feel his hand touch himself. He is here, yes, he is. Outside Eric turns to his tent; both his hands scratching innumerable mosquito bites.

Adam sinks back, lengthens out again inside his sleeping bag. Between stones too deep to clear away for their tent floor he can feel the pressure from his body softening the permafrost; when he and Joel fold up the tent they will see their shapes there side by side, momentary body prints of moisture rising from the tundra. Beside

a nameless river somewhere between lakes labelled on survey maps
Winter and Starvation. Who knows what the Dene call them. The
bag is too tight for his shoulders, though that makes it warmer. Too
narrow, almost a zipped body bag though he has never seen one,
much less been in one. Actually, they aren't north of the Arctic Circle
either. Through the sphere of his mind's eye the globe slowly turns
its enormous Arctic face and he follows those straight male lines that

try to organize and control (on paper they appear to organize and
control) the incomprehensible space of ocean and land and flowing
ice; follows until he recognizes that he is lying precisely on the
parallel of the Magadan Gulag. There, beyond the Kolyma Mountain
Ranges, somewhere in that immeasurable desolation between the
Yukagir Plateau and the swamps and rocks of the Omolon and
Kolyma rivers, his father's brothers were destroyed digging out gold
for Stalin. And his mother's brother on Sakhalin Island—but that
is not north, no, the longest part of it stretches south even beyond
Regina or Vancouver. Why does he always think of Sakhalin as north?
Exile. For him like any Canadian, exile is up the map.

"You're paddling all over this tundra," Joel says to him, "and you
still just think about your lost uncles."

"Not just," Adam says.

They are paddling across a placid, nameless lake. That morning
they negotiated a series of runnable rapids, then a long rock garden
where wading with the canoes was just barely possible, and finally a
steep boulder-trap of a shallow fall in the middle of which Eric stood,
immoveable as any erratic, handing the loaded canoes through while
the rest of them scrambled over shore rocks trying to control the
painters, the water smashing up into spray against him and the boulders and the wild, leaping canoes all at once.

"This land makes you think," Adam laughs. "What are you
thinking about?"

"Mosquitoes. Look at the buggers," Joel lifts his dripping paddle
and smacks the roped packs in front of him, "they ride along out into
the lake, then come drill you, even out here."

"Keep your head-net down, your paddle in the lake, I'm doing all
the work!"

"You're just muscle up there, I'm keeping us straight."

"You still have to think to J stroke?"

"Ha!" Joel laughs his abrupt, explosive laugh. "Just don't stop pulling when you think Siberia. I see it every time."

The lake is sheet steel. Ahead of them Eric and Christina's canoe slides though the long ramp of an exact, inverted esker. No sky or water, a double of horizontals forged by relentless ice.

Joel says, "What did Oncle Jahonn say, about your uncles in Siberia? How come he knows, more in Paraguay than you in Canada?"

"They tell stories better, not so busy making money."

"Stories?"

The old man and his circle of eight sons sat under the para-todo tree passing the matte cup back and forth between them. The Paraguayan night, cooling slightly so that Adam's evaporating sweat became a gentle comfort, sang with insects and frogs as one by one the men were satisfied drinking around and drifted away. Joel had no language, neither High German nor Low, to speak with any of them, but one laughing grandson, both handicapped and mute who happily offered an eloquence of gesture which made some facts as compre-hensible as the most delicate language, beckoned Joel out past the darkness into the moonlit fields to look at the Southern Cross.

"It wasn't Oncle Jahonn who said it," Adam says over his shoulder between the rhythm and grunt of paddling. "It was Taunte Aunna."

"Hadn't she gone in the house."

"No no, she was there. The women don't drink matte, but she was there under the tree, saying nothing."

"She's the nicest little mama," Joel's chuckle is like the sound of the lake against the gliding canoe.

"She said it, Oncle Jahonn never would have."

"What?"

"Fifty-eight years in Paraguay, and still their Russian Mennonite villages, are so real to them. And all the relatives, what's happened to every one of the relatives."

Joel says suddenly, "Maybe she thinks about it more."

"What, thinks? Old Jahonn's the one who knows everything, talks and talks all the time. You saw him, he never stopped, as long as we were there."

"I just mean, I couldn't understand them but she always does the same things, clean up, cook, and he's always running around. Maybe she dares to think."

Adam stops paddling and glances back at his lanky son. The lake opens without edges; his head is down, his paddle driving through the water with a relentless rhythm that surges the canoe straight ahead with a tight, curved stroke. Before he had seen Joel heave up and invert the canoe on his shoulders and begin that first carry across the tundra, Adam had not yet imagined him so aggressively strong.

"Dare?"

"It's hard to think sometimes," Joel says, "some things. What'd she say?"

Not a story to be told over a shoulder in quick phrases between breaths, kneeling in a shifty canoe where his knees again already alternate between groan and scream. But not easier either, he finds, to utter flat on his back in their domed tent, his words bunched into the angles of taut nylon hammered so loud by the summer Arctic wind. Suddenly he can barely speak, or even breathe, the flow of his possible words spinning that ancestral past tighter and tighter until it threatens to become a winding sheet for him and his son stretched out beside him; lay them out wrapped and still under the ceaseless wind of the tundra. Perhaps words spoken to the open, quiet sky, the lake...where on earth could you ever say this?

"Exile...well, exile...they were always being forced into exile, the Loewens leaving Antwerp in 1590...even Adam Wiebe when he maybe gets lured from Holland, his travel from Harlingen to Danzig in 1616 is really exile. He drains the Vistula River swamps, sure, and when he invents the cable car to build the walls of Danzig to protect the city from Gustavus Adolphus and the Thirty Year's War, all that ground he brings in buckets on an endless cable over the swamps from the Bishop's Hill...actually, it's like he's making land, the way his people had been making land from the sea in Holland for centuries. He probably would have taken it out of the sea the way they did and at the same time deepened the harbour of Danzig if there had been time, but the Swedish army was already sailing across...."

Joel says flatly, "Dad. A military bastion is not a wheat field."

Rudy Wiebe: Collected Stories, 1955–2010

This is easier, this usual repartee, these mostly genial disagree-
ments. Adam concedes, "Sure. But...you can graze sheep on bastion
walls if they're made of earth. You saw all those sheep on the dikes in
Holland. The new land made by the sea, the watte, isn't just a field.
At a certain point, when the watte's built up high enough they have
to make dikes anyway to protect it from the sea, and that's all a city
wall is, a protection. In Danzig Adam Wiebe builds a dike not to hold
back the violent sea but to hold off the brutal people coming over
it. You see, he's still doing exactly what he did in his homeland, he
is simply trying in exile to make again...if he doesn't make this dike
of city walls even his place of exile will be destroyed, and what new
exile will he have to find then? If he survives at all."

"Dad!" Joel shouts above the tremendous wind that is pounding
the tent like a spastic drummer, "Taunte Aunna was *not* talking about
Adam Wiebe and his cable car."

"Our family's had all kinds of exiles," Adam avoids him.
"Hundreds, and sometimes the Mennonites themselves did it to each
other. Did I tell you about our relative on the Loewen side who was
a portrait painter, and he got exiled for painting? The Mennonite
Church did that."

"A Loewen was a painter?"

"The seventeenth century was full of great Flemish painters,
this one's name was Seeman, Enoch Seeman the Elder (there was a
Younger too), the Seemans were one branch of the Antwerp/Danzig
Loewens and Enoch the Elder was appointed the official artist of
Danzig and painted all the portraits of the councilmen to hang in
the City Hall. But the powerful Mennonite Bishop George Hansen
decided he believed painting portraits was wrong, after all there is
the second commandment, and so he ex-communicated him. Seeman
fought the Bishop, maybe even in court, and lost, so he left Danzig,
but not before he wrote a little book, anonymously of course, called:
*Revelation and Sentence of George Hansen's Folly Brought to Light
for Everyone's Brotherly Admonition and Faithful Warning by a
Lover of The Truth*, 1697. Enoch the Elder found a kind of royal exile
in Dresden with Elector Augustus II of Saxony and at the time King
of Poland, and finally permanent refuge in London, England, where
his son Enoch Seeman the Younger painted the official full-figure

portrait of King George II and Queen Caroline which can be seen to
this day in the National Portrait Gallery just across Trafalgar Square
from Canada House, and also the Duchess of Buckingham with her
son Edmund and an oval bust of Queen Caroline (again) in the Royal
Gallery at Hampton Court and his self-portrait was hung in the
magnificient Zwinger in Dresden just before—"

"Dad!"

And Adam concludes gently in a sudden quiet of exasperation and
the wind catching its breath over the tent, an uneasy quiet which at
last, like open water, makes certain words possible "…the Zwinger
in Dresden before the firebombing, February 13, 1945. Yes, Joel, yes,
Taunte Aunna in Paraguay knows nothing about Adam Wiebe, or
Antwerp, or dikes and sheep on land made by the sea…and certainly
nothing about Enoch Seeman, Elder or Younger. Yes yes."

So lying side by side in a shuddering tent on the rocky permafrost of an island barely fifty strides long in Little Martin Lake in the
Mackenzie District, the Northwest Territories of Canada, what can
Adam Wiebe tell his son Joel of Taunte Aunna's story of Sakhalin
Island? Taunte Aunna knows nothing about Sakhalin Island, not even
the double-dagger map shape of it as if roughly chipped from stone
(does it point south or north?) in the Sea of Okhotsk because she has
no atlas, in fifty-seven years will not have seen one except in Spanish,
which she cannot read. Besides, Sakhalin Island is not Taunte
Aunna's story, what there is of it. She is a Wiebe, Oncle Jahonn is the
Loewen and it was he who brought the story (though he cannot tell it
to Adam) of the Loewen brothers from Canada to Paraguay because
Adam's mother told it to him when he visited her in Alberta, Adam's
mother who for sixty-five years was Mrs. Heinrich Jakob Wiebe,
born Elizabeth Loewen, Jahonn's cousin. But it is Taunte Aunna
who must tell it to Adam that Paraguayan night under the dazzling
yellow flowers of the paratodo tree, tell it quick and flat as she tells
everything, as if she were explaining a receipe for buns or borscht
or verenike, something every Mennonite in the world must already
know except someone born into the stupefying wealth and privilege
of Canada. She says:

"Your mother said they sent her brother Benjamin Loewen
into exile on Sakhalin Island and then her half-brother (If he ever

translates this for Joel would he have to say "*their* half-brother"? In Low German the definite article for the feminine singular possessive is the same as the plural possessive and it is true that Elizabeth and Benjamin were full siblings? Isn't it? Which did Taunte Aunna mean, "her" or "their"? Both?) half-brother Isaak Loewen, the Communist, he travelled there to that place and murdered him."

Her flat, quick Low German, the tropical night so black that Adam cannot see the bright flowers above her, or her worn face, barely her pale cotton dress in the light reflected from the kitchen where daughters are clattering dishes, their husbands peering over their shoulders.

She has used words much quieter than English "murder." Four little ordinary words twisted together in an untranslatable, horrifying, idiom: *Hee brucht ahm omm.* Literally: "He brought him around."

Over Oncle Jahonn's head clutched between his massive hands, she adds abruptly, "They say he just brought a knife. And stabbed his brother."

Speckje: poked. Like a needle wandering through cloth.

Isaak Loewen the Communist. His photograph is in the album Adam's mother left; head and shoulders, a morose, handsome young man with a shadow of mustache wearing a flapped woollen cap rising to a peak in the centre of his head, fronted with a star. An unreadable number bar on his erect collar. Was that the uniform of Trotsky's Red Army? Or the later one of Stalin's? The cardboard picture is pasted onto the black pages of the album with flour; when he finally gets it separated from the album, between blotches he discovers a message angled across the top left corner in a beautiful German gothic script which he slowly puzzles into comprehension: "With artelistic greetings from your brother, brother-in-law and uncle, Nove...." the date and place ("....ovka.") torn out forever by paste and black paper. That Isaak who never married, except perhaps the Communist Party, rubbing it in with a Party word they must have instantly hated without ever quite understanding.

Uncle Benjamin is nowhere in the album, but Grandfather Loewen is, stern and bald, white goatee, his thick legs sheathed in gleaming knee boots stretched out black before him and his last wife (no older than Elizabeth, whose best friend she was before she, to Elizabeth's horror, married him) standing slightly tilted and unsmiling behind him. Nothing is written on the back.

Poked...they say...half-brother...the Communist. Nothing on paper; just a few dreadful words uttered at last into the unwitting air. Lives wrung out, dripped long ago into an oblivion.

If Adam's father had been alive when his mother told Oncle Jahonn that, his father would have murmured, "Isaak...Benjamin... those aren't the names."

And his mother would have answered, "They're close enough," and all three of them would have been weeping. Who could say how long. Their minds unable to imagine a Sakhalin, but knowing enough horror for it to suffice; their old bodies dragged around the world and destroyed by work and poor food and ultimately by cancer, hunched together in a prayer for mercy, mercy at last, Oh please, mercy. The Alberta sunlight caressing them with gentle, bitter mockery.

"Listen," Adam can say in a sudden quiet of wind catching its breath over the tent; say to Joel who has not moved for perhaps hours, who may be sleeping or dead, "listen. Your Ooma never said one word to me about this, not even when we were looking through the albums in the hospital and she talked and talked, you remember she said everything so easily then, but no, not a word. After Grandpa died she hardly spoke, when we'd drive somewhere in the car you remember she just sang a little, flat, off key because she was so deaf, or recited lines from the Psalms—'the cattle on a thousand hills are mine' driving into the foothills in summer, 'the heavens declare the glory' but she would never finish that sentence, it drove me crazy, 'be still and know that I am'—she never even cried again and she said almost nothing until the last visit in the hospital, as if she knew it was the last, and then she spoke without stopping but she never said a word about this, not one word."

After a time Joel stirs, sits up. "Where'd you put the blue bottle?" he asks so quietly Adam can barely understand.

"Right there," he gestures between them. "Somewhere, you piled your clothes on it."

He lies staring at the tent roof; he does not want to see what-ever may be on his son's face. They laughed uproariously, a bit embarrassed when Eric first offered the bottle to them, but they discovered that no matter how instantly one drew the tent zipper closed around the other's body, they could not go out and re-enter without dozens of mosquitoes somehow whining in with them, a new horde that had to be squashed against the splotchy mesh before they could expect to sleep.

"Shit!" Joel mutters.

"Spill?"

"A bit, yeah...how do you...?"

"It's better not lying down, on your knees maybe, keep it completely upright," Adam shifts his position noisily. "Hey, leave some space for me before morning."

Joel snorts through his nose. "Good luck!"

"You filled the whole thing?"

"It's just a litre."

They are both laughing then. Adam settles himself elaborately; Joel reaches to the screen at his feet and then stretches back. It is almost two a.m. Adam has written nothing in his journal today; there is a warm trace of urine, a whiff of body intimacy in the cool, bright air of the tent. He cannot remember when the wind stopped abusing the tent, but if it stays quiet he knows Eric will be up at three-thirty and they will paddling Little Marten Lake before six to skirt its length, headland to headland, in all possible calm. If the whitecaps stop running, crashing on the rocks below.

Joel says, "Maybe your uncle the Communist wanted to end his brother's suffering."

"Yeah. But how would he know where he was? And he would have had to get past the guards into that camp—very dangerous."

"Well...maybe he had to, Stalin's orders."

"That's possible, sure, but why? Stalin was using Benjamin, killing with work. Why bother?"

"Hell, I don't know," Joel is suddenly loud, "I'm just a middle-class kid from the suburbs who's been driven to school and music lessons all his mixed-up life. All you ever do with your relatives all over the world is talk about suffering and what the hell would I know about that, suffering huh!"

Adam skates over that with a quick joke, "You aren't suffering a little, mile-long portages on the tundra?"

"Oh yeah, and you pay thousands so I will. Scheduled, three weeks of summer suffering complete with freeze-dried food. Mostly I think your relatives who got away from the Soviets to Germany don't even like *not* being forced to suffer, they can be so nice and sad now with their nice West German pensions for the rest of their lives."

But Adam avoids him, with mildness. "If Cousin Peter there were alive, he'd know that story."

"Did his wife?"

Gentle, crippled Helen sluffing about their small Gladbach apartment, her black kerchief covering the tight bun of her hair. In the kitchen, Peter's chair stood exactly where he had always sat, watching her prepare meals. She says, "He was happy to sit a lot, here we always had as much food as we wanted. And then he died so quick, almost before I noticed it."

"No," Adam says aloud up into the tent which seems to be shuddering again under wind. "She never heard the Sakhalin story. Or she said she hadn't. But she said she remembered Benjamin Loewen, his kids were about her age and he was her village teacher until the war, and then he disappeared. Arrested. And that's really strange—Benjamin a teacher—my mother never mentioned that either. Maybe he was a Communist too."

"What," Joel says, startled.

"To be a Soviet teacher you'd probably have to be a member of the Party...at least a sworn atheist."

"Would they arrest a Party member?"

"Oh, the purge was very popular, with Stalin...ha!...but how would they ever accept a Mennonite as a member by the thirties? All those relatives and family history, the separated villages, German—to prove himself reliable he'd have to do so much horrible dirty work for the Party—I can't see how Benjamin would ever convince them."

Joel says slowly, as if thinking aloud, "Maybe that's why your uncle the Communist had to travel to Sakhalin Island. To prove himself."

Strangely, Adam has not thought of that. "Sure," he says. "Prove himself. Over and over."

On that double-pointed stone dagger of an island barely separated from the Soviet coast by the rising of the glacial sea; which end was the haft? Certainly during the Second World War Japan held the south—so the north must be the blade, a Soviet fist was always closed on some blade aimed at heart or throat. As perhaps Benjamin's fist closed on the blade also, momentarily, when he understood the purpose for which Isaak had come holding it. In the bow of the canoe Adam digs his paddle relentlessly into the midnight bronze of Little Marten Lake. His banned uncles would have found such unrequired labour inexplicable, such travel forced by weather alone insane; however, that their own work and travel were decided by the infinitely blacker, public madness of a dictator (or perhaps they recognized him simply as worldly wise, brilliant like the Ghengis Khan in the labyrinthine, quintessential cruelties of absolute power) would certainly not have escaped either the Wiebe brothers somewhere in Kolyma nor the Loewens on Sakhalin. But gold, coal, timber, asbestos—whatever technicality killed them, it did so with the massive impersonality of cosmic law; even Isaak Loewen travelling for weeks with a knife intended solely for the brother who perhaps pretended to be a Communist to stay alive and keep his job to feed his family, whose bed he had shared throughout his childhood, even Isaak became merely inevitable. After fifteen years of Stalin and then facing Hitler, there was no "I will do this," no "I will not do that"; no more than if, once you had begun to fall from a bridge, you could at some point personally decide to stop falling.

Thunder rumbles over the lake and Adam's body continues to bow in the implacable rhythm of the canoe, but his mind staggers. The endless, universal interweavings of evil, Oh, the horror, horror.

South in front of him, over the bronze water, Dogrib Rock humps up like a granite loaf between the angles of two eskers spaced by distance. All day they lay in the lee of the tiny island, hammered by the wind that bent and finally split their tent poles before they realized they would have to take the tents down to save them. But evening brings a sudden quiet, an eery calm to the breakers as if a hand has been laid over them, and they paddle south quickly on the waveless lake, the long, unbreaking swells that gleam like oil under the level sun directly behind them. The lake narrows between rocks, darkens imperceptibly into the base of high western cliffs; suddenly, as if framed, Adam recognizes a picture. Here young Robert Hood of the His Majesty's Royal Navy, with John Franklin on his first disastrous expedition to the Polar Sea, sketched *An Evening View of Marten Lake 29–30 August 1820.* That strange jumble of rocks on the right like an immense temple toppled over by antediluvian giants against a pyramid: he painted exactly that—at midnight also, night and storm soaking up from below?—the cliffs for him crowned everywhere by erratics and inquisitive, artistically spaced caribou with antlers like lyred fronds contemplating the great voyageur canoe that effortlessly sailed Englishmen in picturesque beaver top hats aiming rifles over the romantic water and a flight of snow geese rising left like arrows up a beam of light heavenward. And Hood, poor fool, dead a year later, shot within a glance of here just before he could die peacefully of overwork and starvation. A voyageur's bullet, a brother's knife: how was nineteenth-century exploration in the Canadian Arctic different from twentieth-century exile in Stalin's Siberia? Personal choice? How much of that did the naval ensign or the village teacher have? The starving Mohawk who shot Hood, or the terrorized Party Mennonite? Adam feels the canoe surge under his aching knees, driven by his son's powerful stroke. It had to be. Everything was personal, it had to be.

Including travel and travail—really the same words: a journey; a laborious torment, suffering or painful effort. On his knees in the narrow canoe Adam knows that this Arctic journey he and his son have chosen for their time together is both. So why did they choose it? Because someone had, because someone had not, travelled it before them? The landscape here recorded time like an unwinding scroll. Their journey lies over one of the large scattered remnants of prehistoric, glacial Lake McConnell, formed from the melting of the Wisconsin Laurentide ice sheet which for millennia covered the eastern half of North America; the eskers they pass mark the leavings of its sub-glacial rivers. Sometime, somewhere to the north and west when ice lay here kilometres thick, Asiatic peoples traversed Beringia and travelled south along the narrow corridor of glacial drift between the eastern and western continental ice sheets—what

Moses with what rod parted those frozen waters for them, piled
them up in mountainous oceans of ice on either hand so that they
could walk safely through that sea on dry ground? God again, always
Yahweh, the God of Wandering and the Journey, of Unending Travel/
Travail. His temple and habitation a movable tent, his altar a rock
in the barren valley—not on the heights, that was for other gods
fixed and motionless—promising always meat, water, and yet leading
always deeper into some holy desert. This land is a desert now, an
arctic desert with less rainfall than the Sinai, water preserved in
its folds only by the dreadful blessing of cold. But always travel,
journey, always the laborious suffering of travail. Even when a stone
temple was finally permitted them on a mountain, its Holy of Holies
remained hidden behind the veil of a tent. Here, when the glaciers
turned to water and melted back into the oceans, the Plano Indians
seven thousand years ago conceived canoes and travelled the streams
and lakes of that melting north again. And always hunger; always
fear. Always the restless, inexplicable, wandering back to where you
have been, or have not.

Thunder. Thunderbird speaking out of darkness surrounding
Dogrib Rock. With an apprehension like sudden fear Adam
recognizes that the open water before him leads straight to that overwhelming monolith.

He rests his paddle across the bow. Thunder again, echoing itself.
Did Thunderbird speak to the Plano Indian Dene? Who can know now.
He balances forward and looks back. Joel raises his wind-darkened
face, grins. Behind them Christina and Eric come on in that silent,
timeless motion of human beings together in the small moving
community of a canoe. For once there are no mosquitoes.

Carefully Joel lifts himself from kneeling, onto the thwart to ease
his legs a moment. "Over there," he points with his dripping paddle,
"left of the rapid, maybe a good campsite."

Adam bends to the aerial picture under plastic in front of him.
The rapid's deep roar wavers in the midnight air; he feels warmth,
then cold move over his face, his aching body.

"Maybe it's steep, too rocky," he says. "Maybe we can't run it."

"How long a portage?"

"About two, three hundred metres."

Joel laughs, dismissing that. "Just find us a flat place to park that goddamn tent," he says, settling down again, digging in.

Tiny trees bristle here and there—spruce, willow, a shimmer of perhaps birch—at the knotting of lake and river. Adam thinks: we have almost reached the treeline. And when this particular journey is over he will be amazed at his own stupidity, at how oblivious he was in anticipating certain dangers of this summer journey. As if rocks and rapids and tundra and running waves and animals were all one need prepare for; as if words spoken into the wash of thunder, rain and falls might not eventually work the more lasting devastation. All those days together and stupidly he will anticipate nothing when Joel asks, well past the middle of that night when they have together cleared their flat site and are stretched out inside their snug tent again, asks with such beginning innocence,

"How many wives did your grandfather have?"

And he answers so easily, "Which one?" Serenely content with his understanding of family history.

"Grandma's father, all those half-brothers and half-sisters in Russia."

"Women died a lot in childbirth then. Four, I think. Each one younger than the last, Mom's mom was the first, the oldest."

"Too bad more of the babies didn't die," Joel says so flatly Adam cannot for a moment trust his ears. "Saved them a murder or two."

For a moment he can say nothing, and suddenly Joel continues,

"'A woman when she is in travail hath sorrow because her hour is come.'"

"What?" Adam manages finally.

"I read that in a book—Jesus says it somewhere. Sorrow probably because of what's been done to her and all the mess this kid for sure is bringing with it, all this travail and sorrow."

Travel/travail Adam tries to remind himself; but his mind seems to have stopped. And then Joel rises toward him, on his elbow in the strangely chiselled Arctic light that etches faces into skulls and his words drive in with a final twist.

"So where's Trish, my gorgeous full-sister Trish who I never see or hear from since our little family bust up without any help from the Communists. Where is she, huh?"

The icy spray from a standing wave in the turmoil of rapids is nothing compared to this sudden cold in the comfort of his sleeping bag.

"She's...travelling. You know that."

"Exile?" Joel asks. Adam does not try to answer. "Like a woman taken in travail?"

"She's not pregnant," Adam says stupidly.

"I know that, but that's not all she's not."

"She's in Greece. I told you she called me just before I came, I told you she said she's fine, she's with friends in Greece."

Under the slight, scudding rain now and the wavering roar of the rapids, Joel sinks back and says something which Adam knows he must hear; he cannot control the sudden insistence that overwhelms him.

"What...what did you say, Joel? What, what?"

And after a moment his son repeats, "The father," his voice as thin as if speaking through clenched teeth, "the father is always a motherfucker."

"Why...why say it that, way it...."

"I read that too," his son tells him. "In a book called *The Dead Father.*"

Bowman in their battered canoe on Little Marten Lake, Adam has not the slightest premonition that, when the storm arrives, he and his son will have said things to each other from which neither will ever be able to retreat. For this moment, paddling with all the strength he has in his hard body, he can still contemplate with warm, genial happiness their travel across the tundra which has now brought them almost to the treeline. In front of him, beyond a mist of rapids the southern darkness of storm blackens around Dogrib Rock, but he is certain that behind him, north, behind Joel whose J stroke holds them on course, the midnight light is steadily broadening over the horizonless Barren Lands. For a few more moments at least he can still think that today the sun will not set. And believe it too.

Bears, All the Time Bears [1978–1979/1979]

WHY IS IT, all summer all you hear in Alberta mountain parks is bear
stories? I mean "stories" as in "jokes," so-called. Like the old klunker a
otherwise pretty guide told us on the Maligne Lake boat cruise in
Jasper: How do you stop a bear from charging? Answer: Take away
his credit card. And she expected us to laugh. Some idiots did.

You see more deer than bear in parks, but nobody tells stories that
are supposed to be funny about them. Nor mountain sheep. They're
pathetic, mooching along the highways all summer and nibbling junk
from some kid's hand while mama shrieks, "Be careful—Oh—they're
so cute!" and papa squeezes off another fifty feet of 8 mm. and then
in fall with their digestion wrecked and the tourists gone, either
the long-distance truckers wheeling through smash them or they go
belly-up because there's no barbecued potato chips growing in the
grass. I mean, I take pictures too, sure, but any junk food I buy my
kids eat; their stomachs can take it.

My son—I only have one, also four girls, all older—my son Havre
and I took that Athabasca River Raft Ride and there we heard the
silliest bear story of all. You'd figure that for a two-hour ride at $12.75
per adult and $6.50 under twelve—since when is a thirteen-year-old
adult?—they'd have quality stories when there's nothing but the usual
scenery sliding past, which is most of the time with Edith Cavell
sharp and frozen enough but looking more or less always the same in

the background. Our raftsman with muscles like Pete Rose handles the raft's big sweep easy as a toothpick through rapids and you figure in the calm he'll come up with a man's story, but he pulls one out about a guide, four nuns, and a grizzly!

They meet this big grizzly on a mountain path and the guide tells the nuns just keep calm and take one step back. They do, and the grizzly takes one step forward. The guide tells them just keep calm and take two steps back. They do, and the grizzly takes two steps forward. By then the nuns don't think too much of their guide's advice so they try their own technique: they kneel down and start to pray. And sure enough, the grizzly kneels down and folds his paws just like he's praying too and the nuns get real happy, see, he's religious, he won't bother us. "Nah," the guide says all grey and shaking, "he's the worst kind. He's saying grace."

Some clods practically fall in the river laughing at that one. I had to give little Havre a bat, he was laughing too. We ran through the long rapids then just opposite Belchers Cabins and for a while that kept me busy hanging on with Havre yelling like a Red Indian and all the women aboard—I had sent my wife and the girls to take some good pictures of flowers—shrieking, grabbing their men like they wanted to throttle them right there in their own life jackets, but then I got to thinking: would that story have such a kick had it been a bull moose? No. And just tourists, not nuns? No again. The joke is in the danger: like this raft ride, you want to be scared but you want to know for sure it isn't really deadly—they tell you three times when you buy the raft ticket they've never lost a passenger yet, not even bust a neck—just the *feeling* of danger maybe. That's it, that *and* the religion: danger and making fun of religion, there you've got the biggest laugh multipliers of all. Kneel down to pray and nowadays somebody will kill himself laughing.

The wife says there are worse ways of going. That night a bear—no grizzly, just ordinary black but big enough that's for sure—a bear comes out of the bush by our campsite. I like to get close to nature and they give us a site—they've got over seven hundred of them, all full all summer—on the outer edge, right up against Whistler Mountain. So of course where does this bear come first?

Rudy Wiebe: Collected Stories, 1955–2010

One of my girls screams and two others drop their wieners into the fire and my wife says, "Into the truck, quick!" and shoos all five kids in the back there where we all sleep, but the bear doesn't come to us: he goes next door, number 29-A, where they've got a nice blue tent beside a table piled up with utensils and they've gone to see the nature film at the amphitheatre. That's the modern way, nature happens on screens. Anyway, it's 10:45 and this bear starts a rumble on that table and campers come running, gawking, and some idiot is taking flash pictures at sixty feet and I'm yelling at this bear to stop busting good equipment, waving my yellow plastic waterpail but he doesn't even bother to give me a side-glance until he's knocked everything over and it's clear there's nothing to eat there and without looking up he comes toward us, number 29-B, in that slope-shouldered easy sideways four-wheel-drive motion they have, ha! The wife and I are around the corner of the truck and the campers are screaming at their kids to get back and I peek around the corner and Holy Maloney there sits our silver food cooler!

On the table, stuffed full of our breakfast. This flashes through my head and the bear is still coming—the campsites really are nicely spaced—and all of a sudden there's Havre out of the truck heading for the cooler too! Thank god the bear beats him to it. Havre's yelling and waving his arms like he was shooing a chicken and I've got him by the seat of the pants and throw him behind me and the wife catches him before his head bounces off the truck bumper and then that bear looks me in the eye: his two front paws are up on the cooler but it's good stuff, it doesn't open or bend and when I throw the water from my pail at him his head swings up and he looks at me and I know he'll charge, never mind the credit cards, and I try to scramble back, scrunch, and of course I fall flat on my can.

You know that old one about your whole life flashing by before your eyes? Forget it. When you look into the little close-together eyes of a black bear swinging his head around mad, your ticker stops dead and there's nothing but simple flush-everything-out-in-one-whoosh terror. I'm on my back, my wife is grabbing for my arm and screaming, Havre is grabbing and screaming, the girls are all screaming in different keys and I'm trying to move and I don't know if I'm still alive and I *am* still alive because that bear has not charged!

The screams don't matter to him. He has knocked that cooler off the table and is rolling it backward under the trees, end over end, and walking backward like a circus dog doing tricks and finally the lid pops off and he stops, fifty feet away, to have a look. Four pounds of hamburger, two of bacon, a dozen eggs, two loaves of bread, butter, four quarts of milk, mayonnaise: could be worse. He settles down right there and has a picnic. Half an hour; nobody, but nobody bothers him.

Eleven-fifteen. Out on the prairie it would still be light but against the mountain we can barely see him, nothing but a dark blotch when he pushes the cooler away, stands up and swings his head around, then continues on to 29-C, 29-D, perfectly alphabetical. But everybody's stowed everything in their vehicles and he's sniffing around 29-M when the ranger finally gets there and throws a firecracker at him that explodes like a cannon and he, without any rush but like that was some sort of signal, lopes off sideways into the dark. He'll be back now, the ranger says looking at me sour as pickles, tomorrow for sure and they'll have to try and shoot him with a tranquillizer and haul him away, way back into the mountains.

So I got dirty looks besides all the embarrassment. When our neighbours got back from their nice nature film about twenty people told them why their equipment was so messed up and then they all looked at me trying to bend my cooler straight—all that was left in it was the jar of mayonnaise, open but uneaten—and sort of chuckled. We pulled out for the Columbia Icefields real early next morning. And I'll tell you one thing. If I ever hear some guide tell a story about some hell-fire preacher in a big Winnebago trying to shoo away a bear rattling empty cans at his neighbours while he's got a full hamper of food standing right beside him, I won't be held responsible for what happens.

Someday Soon, Before Tomorrow [1963/1974]

IT WAS THE FIRST DAY OF MAY. The spring sunlight lit the patchwork flatness of Manitoba countryside, the straight roads and the twisting rivers, the pinpoint farmyards and the clustered towns, the bare lines of the shelterbelts and the sprouting whiteness of willows along the creek-beds. It spread like beneficence over the winter-wan land, but it also revealed four men grouped on a municipal road who were talking almost fiercely, their arms swinging out at a wide expanse about them that should have lain black and heavy with expectation. But there was only the level gleam of water.

A small truck halted behind the column of vehicles strung on the road's shoulder and a heavy-set man stepped down. The other men silenced and, one by one, turned toward him. A tall lean man said, "Morning, I G."

"Morning Walter, morning men," the newcomer's glance slid over the weather-hardened faces nodding in greeting. "I couldn't just drive past friends. You're gathering early."

A man in bibbed overalls snapped, "You've as little to joke about now as most of us will in a couple hours. You expect the water to rise this fast?"

I G drawled, "Can't say I'd have done much if I had, Harry."

Walter Kostiuk turned impatiently. "We're not laughing, I G. See that?" His bony finger jabbed at the two eddies in the water below them in the ditch. "Them two two-foot culverts have been over their tops since last night. It'll keep on backing up on your and my land now, and the same thing's already started on Harry's on the next road. And it'll keep on like that for another mile before it gets to the Granmere ditch. Everyone of them damn culverts is too small. Before the marsh is drained we'll all of us be three-quarters under water!"

Eyes intent on his own fencepost that poked a foot of its length and one of its three wires above the water, I G said, "I didn't vote for Royer. And I didn't get on the list for haying rights on the marsh."

An uncomfortable shuffle stirred the farmers. It was true enough they had eagerly followed Jake Royer when he ran for reeve on an "Improve our Municipality" platform.

"Huh! Royer!" snorted another, and spat. "He's watched too much TV. Even with lotsa spring water we used to have only little puddles along the creek and the marsh could just stay where it was—"

"Ah shut up, Jim," growled someone.

"Yah," Walter said. "We know now, all of us. What are we gonna do now?"

They stood, hard bodies bent, eyes brooding on the silt-scummed water that chuckled as it whirled into the narrow crib of the culverts and sprang away at its release, easing down the imperceptible fall of the land until a mile farther south another pair of culverts too tight for its girth would spread it relentlessly over the crumbly soil, building up pressure to squeeze it faster and faster through the steel strictures until they too were buried and the water would gurgle into another eddy and ram its way through to glide sedately on. And after another such delay of some hours or days or perhaps weeks it would ease itself into the huge Granmere Drain to be led, without discomfort, to where the Red River squirmed across the plain and through the city and around oak and poplar bends to the immensity of Lake Winnipeg. Eventually some stray stubble now rimming the curve of the eddies before them would reach the lake, but the men had no thought for that. What they needed to know was, hedged by the physical circumstances before them and the legal ones all realized were there but which few of them could have pinpointed, leave alone countered, how they could drain and dry their land fast enough so they could do what farmers are meant to do: seed a spring crop. And they looked not to Walter Kostiuk, who could and would speak for them when the time came, but to I G Loring, under whose careless surface, somewhere, lay the agility of thought and comprehension which, could they but prod it, might puncture the dam of their dilemma. And, oddly enough, they all knew that his being in that dilemma deeper than any of them at the moment was not the factor which would stir him.

Rudy Wiebe: Collected Stories, 1955–2010

I G said, "Did you call Royer?"

"Yah," Walter replied. "The council's meeting this afternoon, but he doesn't think they can do much. They've no money—the big road contract was signed last week."

"Sure," I G laughed and his voice rose to mimic level. "'I tell you, farmers of La Crosse, our municipality could and *will* be the finest and most progressive municipality in Manitoba. We'll make people sit up and take notice. We have the farmers; we have the land and,'" he made a grand gesture, "'—now we have the water!'"

No one guffawed. Jim said harshly, "Damn it, I G, will you quit horsin—" he stopped for a black car with a white door had sighed to a halt beside them. The officer in it looked up at them but did not get out.

"Good day, men." All nodded in greeting. "Anything wrong?"

They did not move; no one said anything. The policeman looked right and studied the water pouring from the culvert into the watercourse that led south across the land, the creek marked here and there by half-submerged willows. He turned to the farmers, but they had not moved so he backed his car slightly to see the water sprawling over the fields to the north. With a jerk he pulled even with the glowering men. "Culverts can't take it, eh? Does this happen every year?"

Walter said, gesturing, "No. Just since that so-called drain was dug last summer."

"I see." The policeman was obviously trying to be understanding but the belted elegance of his voice did not help him. "Why didn't they put in bigger pipes?"

Walter flicked his cigarette over the car hood into the ditch as I G drawled, "Farmers hardly tell engineers from Winnipeg what to do."

The policeman looked up sharply at I G's bland, direct glance, then at the others who stood, sullen, eyes on their boots or far over the fields. "You're being put in a bad way, all right," he said. His radio sputtered and he listened for a moment, then flicked it off, "But I wouldn't get any quick notions about pulling up a few culverts to stop the back-up. Destroying municipal property is a criminal offence." His glance locked with I G's, who smiled abruptly.

"Wel-l-l now. When you drove up, sir, we were in a slight quandary as to what could be done. But if, without even leaving your car, you could help us solve our problems—"

Flicked to the raw, the officer interrupted, "What's your name?"

"I G Loring."

"Where do you live?"

"Sure—" after a slight pause, "right over there, beyond the big puddle in the house among the trees."

"It was to you I was talking then. Don't get any foolish ideas on how to—"

"Hold on one damn minute," Walter Kostiuk was beside the car in two strides. "You're new here, but just what kind of a stupid accusation is—"

I G's big hand was on his shoulder. "Walter, don't be rough on our friend. He is doing his duty. I'd be kinda peeved too if every workin' day of my life I hadta say things to people they didn't like, all the time wearin' puckered britches with a yellow stripe down my leg."

The tension split with a roar from four muscular throats. The officer, his face black with anger, said rigidly. "The Mounted Police brought law to the West in 1874 and—"

"Sure," I G said, "and my grandfather broke this half section with a walking plow in 1888. History doesn't need a uniform." The big farmer smiled again, and now his smile was broad, warm. "I'm sorry if I had to bother you—ah—Constable Ribbing, isn't it? We're under a bit of pressure right now."

"All right," Ribbing ducked his head a moment, then put the car in gear. "I can see it's rough. Just remember what I said."

When the black car had vanished in the dust of the road the farmers crowded around I G, voices urgent. "Listen," I G battered them down, "it won't work. People'd come driving along and get wrecked—hurt—"

"We could put up road blocks at the sections," Jim interrupted.

"Coupla days open running and the whole mess woulda moved into Granmere," rumbled another.

"You heard him—it's illegal! Wait till the council meeting this afternoon."

Walter spoke at last, bitterly. "They won't do nothing. We know you don't care much for farming—probably laugh if you couldn't get on the land for a year—but we've got to work together; every hour a few more acres of my land is under, and Harry's is starting, and soon—"

"You want to try pull this thing up with your bare hands?" I G turned away. "At least give Royer a chance. One day won't make that much difference." He walked back to his truck, but the others only stared after him. As he idled by them I G leaned from the cab and said softly, "You want some inside dope? With that new road cut-off, its only forty miles to Winnipeg. We could open a resort. Complete with mucky-loam beaches!"

But there was no grudging smile even on I G's face late that afternoon when he hung up the phone and went out again. The municipal council was over its head in commitments; it could only try for a court action against the engineers which, Walter had assured him grimly, Rick Wenman the lawyer had said could take months, perhaps years, to prove because the drain followed a natural watercourse. I G studied the dike he had spent the afternoon building around the barn, then looked at the water creeping but inevitably advancing up the pasture. He had not thought it could come so high. The cows were huddled in one trampled corner.

He had driven them into the higher loafing yard and was closing the gate when Georgie came running up the lane from the road.

"Hi!" I G shouted.

The boy dropped his lunch-kit on the house-path and ran up to the barn. "Daddy, will we get flooded?"

I G smiled down into his anxious face. "It's started, but it won't rise much higher. It'd run over the south road first."

"But what about the land?"

"It won't reach the house, and the barn's okay with that dike, see. The water won't get at us."

"But the land," Georgie insisted, "it's almost all under water. All the kids in the bus yelled when they saw it. Ours and Mr. Kostiuk's land!"

I G said quietly, "Maybe we won't have any crop this year. You better feed your rabbits. I put them up in the loft, out of the way."

Georgie was studying him, small face pinched in concentration. "Aren't you going to do *something*?" he asked.

"There's too much water for the culverts, that's all." I G gestured. They were in the barn now, and abruptly the boy turned and began climbing up the ladder to the loft. But his look seemed to hang there in the familiar gloom of the barn and I G sensed himself forced back, with a sudden clarity, upon himself. There had been a time when he really wanted to do something. He had a vision for a great new breed of wheat and it had been barely begun when, within days of each other, the news came of his brother's fall at Dieppe and his father's death, and grandfather Loring had come to the university, sharp eyes glittering under his bristle of white hair, "Isaac, you have to take over the farm." So he had come back to the farm, to the land his grandfather had won from wilderness, to the huge stone house his grandfather had built and at which he was now staring through the barn door. He had done all the many things that had to be done, year after year, and in the busy, easy circle of the years he kept on; he did not particularly like farming, but neither did he particularly dislike it either. If the crop was poor one year, it would probably be better the next; the work was easy; one could avoid strain. And now, in the eyes of his son he had begun to comprehend that year by year the belief which every human must embody if he is to see himself as more than a trace of ink on income-tax records had shrunk in him until, even now when he was finally, abruptly, forced to face the thought head-on, momentarily it seemed less than an inanity; a spasm of electrons flitting amok over his neural connections.

As in a trance he walked out and stared past the corner of the house, across the water that lay master over the land. An unwonted, gut-clutching oath welled as if it would burst in him. God knew he had never wanted the farm! George was to have it! He could now easily rationalize why he had come when he did not want to, under the numbness of the deaths, under the will of his grandfather, and

467

why through the years it became inevitable to simply stay, to work hard physically, and flap a few more self-concocted jokes. And now the water had cornered him.

A hand touched him, and he looked down, at his son smiling wanly. In the very line of the jaw he could see his grandfather. As they stood, motionless a moment, I G could hear as if it were a physical voice: "That forty down by the creek's good land. A bit low, but full of silt. I saw that soon as I got here in '88. First year—first breakin'. I walked that plow through the buffalo chips and your grandma drove the oxen. Land never touched by iron since God made her. She was a good woman...." The story's warm cadences spoke themselves in his mind, complete to the strange land-woman intertwine the old man always wandered into, the patriarch who he knew bestrode his life like a colossus to nail him to this particular bit of earth, now inundated, helpless.

His son's face had disintegrated in his comprehension, but he could feel the boy's shoulder under his hand. I G shook his head, several times. "Com'mon," he said, and they went together into the massive house. Elaine, his wife, looked up from the kitchen stove as she heard him speak quietly into the telephone: "Walter? Yeah. Yeah. I'll be over in fifteen minutes."

It was almost midnight before they were ready to try. An overcast hid the night sky and the water lapped high on the road shoulder, unheard now over the idling tractors. The road surface was broken wide along the line of the two culverts and I G, dressed again, his head wrapped in a heavy towel, waggled his torch at Walter, then aimed it down at the exit ends. One tractor revved, the cables tightened with groaning hoist. I G tensed forward, but nothing moved. He signalled faster; the tractor's roar deepened; he dropped his light, seized a pick and sprang into the rip above the near culvert. In a frenzy he struck again and again along the ribbed curve of the steel, trying to jar it loose, his huge arms driving the pick down unerringly in the murky light. The towel-end slid over his face and he knocked it from his head. The tractor was grinding down, stalling nearly, when the thing stirred under his feet. He backed a step and struck again with all his strength. A suck smacked on the night; I G staggered, then leaped aside as one and then the other culvert scraped and heaved up like gigantic murky worms spouting into the darkness.

"Georgie!" I G bellowed above the noise, grabbing his light and waving. The other tractor laboured, but the road's hold was broken and with a whoosh! the still submerged intakes of the culverts broke its surface. The tractors backed slowly, and the two thirty-foot pipes lay on the road, bridging the gaps. For a moment the wall of earth between their former beds held against the flood, then piece by piece it collapsed, vanished, and a ten-foot crest of unleashed water charged through.

The tractors ceased and the scrape of cables being unslung could be heard in the calm above the singing water. Walter Kostiuk emerged on the far side. "Your idea worked good! First heave."

"It was close for a bit," I G's hand fell to his son's shoulder. "Nice work."

Walter said into the quietness, "Handled that tractor like a veteran. Make a good farmer some day."

"He is one already," I G returned, even as they heard the putter of a motorcycle behind them. In a moment, Jim Magyar drew up.

"Hey, you got her up okay, eh?"

"Sure. How about you?"

"Slick as a whistle! She's open straight to Granmere. And every crossin's blocked."

"Good," I G said. "Then we'll just sit here and let it run." At his feet the gap was almost brimming with black, slightly undulating water. "Get me that other towel from the cab, Georgie. The one I had is heading for the lake."

The sun was well up when they heard the first car approach. I G roused in the back of his pickup, got out, and joined Walter leaning against its fender. The second fence wire was visible now, draped with soggy stubble gleaming in the level sunlight. Walter slowly rolled a cigarette.

Ribbing was out of his car and around the tractor before the dust settled. Tall in shiny knee-boots, he studied them across the running water. "So you wouldn't listen. Was that your one-way I had to scrape around at the intersection, Kostiuk?"

The big rumpled farmers returned his look without expression. Walter finally said, "We've got nothing to say to you."

Ribbing's face stiffened. "All right. That's the way it will be." He pulled out a notebook and went around the tractor, striding off distances, sketching, making notes. He crossed on the culverts; his tone as he worked was almost conversational. "I've been on the radio to headquarters. The attorney general will lay what charges he sees fit against you and your friends south of here. I'm impounding every vehicle obstructing public roads, and Reeve Royer is already getting a crew to make these roads passable again. You want to say anything, now?"

Suddenly, into their silence, Georgie's head appeared at the truck window. His eyes drooped, sleep-heavy.

"Hello!" Ribbing said, astonished. "What's your name?"

The boy looked quickly at I G, then away across the water.

The officer's voice was tight. "All right," he said. He clambered back to his car and began speaking rapidly into the radio.

Reeve Royer arrived some time after a crew of men with trucks and a caterpillar tractor had pulled up. The foreman did not look at the two farmers across the gap leaning against the pickup, but set his men to work pulling Walter's tractor down the road. The reeve, however, balanced his precarious way over the culverts, his face suffused.

"Boys, boys, what have you done! Roads torn up for three miles! All this expense! The west farmers have to haul their eggs and milk to town. How—"

Walter spat. "Stow it, Jake."

"But boys, you can't rip—"

"We just did."

As Royer stood, gesturing wordlessly, the roar of the caterpillar burbled down. Someone yelled,

"Hey! Get that kid off there!"

All turned, and stared. The crew had hitched to the culverts to lift them from their straddle and down into the road again. Only as they stepped back and the cat was about to hoist did they see Georgie. He sat astride one culvert. If it moved, he would slip into the racing water.

Ribbing pushed between the workmen. "All right, all right. Get him off there!"

I G peered at his small son, bent and clutching. He said nothing.

The policeman strode to the edge of the rip. "Loring! What's the matter with you! Get him off!"

Even Walter looked at I G then, puzzled. I G had come forward a little, but an odd smile shaped his lips as he looked over his son at the officer. The water ran, silent, impenetrable, under the boy's feet.

"I G," Royer squeaked.

"What the goddamn hell!" Ribbing's control broke and he stepped onto the culvert. But before he could advance more than one unsteady step I G was on the other end and in the instant they confronted each other, teetering, balancing on the mucky roundness, glaring. The cat, its cable taut, chortled almost humanly. Then I G touched the boy's shoulder.

"Com'mon son," he said.

Someone charged through the workmen, gasping, waving a press camera. "Officer! officer! just a sec—would you—"

Ribbing was off the culvert on the instant. "No! Get the hell outa here, you!"

Across the tear I G and Walter looked at each other, then at the cursing reporter. "The man wants a story," I G gestured. "We'll see you, Walter. We're going home."

He and Georgie walked up the road together, past the truck and tractor which, though already impounded, could not actually be possessed until the road was closed, and when they turned from the road and started across the field for the house among the trees they heard the culverts splash behind them. They trudged over the plowed land, their feet sinking in its soft, warm blackness. Their eyes found the wide line of the water's retreat and the land, opening itself completely to the sun. And they were laughing, together.

The Funny Money of 1980

I NEVER WANTED TO BE A POLITICIAN, least of all premier of the province of Alberta. I refused to accept a nomination in the election of 1935, but when the Social Credit League swept fifty-six of sixty-three seats (there were entire polls where not a single vote was cast for United Farmer or Liberal or Conservative candidates), every one of our elected members offered to resign if I would accept the leadership. I always considered that election to be my call from God through the voice of the people and was premier until my death, almost eight years later. May 23, 1943. And now most Albertans know little more about me than some faint whiff of "fire and brimstone" preaching, of "funny money," of....

There is no need to defend my record. If my leadership of this province during its greatest crisis is seen as a deviation, a disorder of standard politics, then I say "Hallelujah!" Standard politics had almost destroyed us by 1935, and there is a real danger in the 1980s that they will do so again. Listen, listen to me and—in my day I never had to tell people twice to listen. I stood six foot two, weighed an eighth of a ton, and on the windiest Alberta day I never needed a microphone to get the biggest crowd's attention.

"Mr. Aberhart," all those frank, weathered faces begged me, "tell us the truth."

And I did.

Albertans in 1980 are like a man making a journey into a strange country. Towards the end of a beautiful day—the finest he has any memory of—he comes to a crossing where five roads meet. He is aware suddenly of the sun sinking, that the hills into which the roads disappear are covered with heavy night clouds, but ahh, there is a guidepost—fallen to the ground! Five directions, how will he ever find his destination? After pondering for a time, he asks himself, "What do I know that will guide me? I know which road I came by, and where I came from." And with that he picks up the guidepost, turns it until the correct marker points in the direction from which he came, and immediately he knows the destination of the four other roads.

In case you weren't here, or have forgotten, let me tell you where Alberta came from. In 1930 it was the most desperately poor province in all of Canada because it had been settled last, very quickly, and the people who flooded in had borrowed enormous sums against the land in order to buy machinery to work it. When Depression wheat dropped to twenty cents a bushel, hogs to two cents a pound, it was impossible to pay ten percent mortgages; life became a war and Albertans lost everything. Do you know how many of our young men were rejected for the army in 1939 because they had rickets from malnutrition? I know, and that's only the men; no one bothered to count the women and children.

There was real starvation in Alberta in the 1930s not because the land would not produce. The coal was always in the ground, the wheat always grew to an extent (there was never total drought in all areas), but the mine owners allowed only enough coal production to keep prices up; mortgage companies had taken the land and the machinery away from farmers, so how could they farm? People starved while wheat rotted in storage, was dumped into the sea to keep consumer prices high. Because Big Money always protects its investment.

You think many rich people became paupers after the crash of '29? Let me tell you, they were paper millionaires to begin with, their supposed wealth based on the speculation numbers of a speculative stock market. Those who actually owned property, land and resources, the Rockefellers, the Masseys, the J. Paul Gettys, became richer than ever during the Depression, and distillers like

the Bronfmans who prey on human beings in misery joined them
in a luxury unknown to the wealthiest kings of antiquity. Have you
heard of a single Canadian bank, a single brewery that went broke in
the thirties? You could look forever. Their money power controlled
our country, and it was stronger than the elected power of the
people because the traditional political parties were under the Big
Money thumbs too. Private enterprise had been allowed to expand
far beyond the public good, and that is wrong, wrong! So, when our
Social Credit government passed revolutionary legislation that would
have put rightful power back in the hands of the people, the Supreme
Court of Canada, never once speaking to the issues we tackled,
simply ruled our legislation *ultra vires*, "beyond provincial compe-
tence" because those federal judges were of course Big Money people
too. We starved until Hitler attacked Poland, and then just like that!
at the first shot of a gun, we were wealthy enough to fight the most
expensive war in history—why? Because Big Money knows that the
biggest profits of all are made by blowing people up! So they let us
produce again, as we could have all along.

Ohhh, when I think of it I am so enraged I could pray for the
wrath of God to flame down from heaven and—but I wanted to set up
the guidepost for my beloved province in 1980, the seventy-fifth anniversary of our beautiful province.

I want to ask you one question: Is it possible that Alberta, with
the exploitation of its marvellous natural resources—especially the oil
sands—is becoming like one of the propertied rich of the Depression?
It allows Middle East potentates and American monopoly oil companies to set unbelievably high oil prices and then says to its fellow
Canadian consumers, "Well, you'll have to pay because that's the
world price, now isn't it. Sorry." Windfall profits, profits that for
the most part have little or nothing to do with legitimate earnings:
profits at the expense, the exploitation of the general public.

Well, does Alberta at least use these enormous profits to help
people? For example, encourage research in new methods of conser-
vation, to experiment with more efficient production and distribution
of food to the world's starving, to say nothing of aiding refugees in
their flight from oppression and misery? Have you heard anything
about that? No. Instead, taxation on the big foreign oil companies

is eased so that they can increase their gigantic profits even more quickly—after all, that promotes investment! At the same time, school and hospital budgets are cut by inflation and the poor and unemployed people increase all over the province. Alberta has the highest divorce *and* suicide rate in Canada, why? Because wherever the rich and fortunate cluster, there also the social contrast is greatest and the unsuccessful are driven to the greatest despair.

What do Albertans really want with their enormous wealth? The temporary—resource wealth is *always* temporary, and fluctuating, it's always Boom or Bust—the temporary satisfaction of standing at the top of the sandpile and thumbing their noses at the rest of Canada and chanting, "Haha on you, we're on top! We've got the money, now we'll call the politics! Go on, eastern Bastards, freeze in the dark!"? I cannot believe we are so childish.

If our memory of the Depression is any kind of guide at all, it should teach us that the people of Alberta *deserve* their present wealth no more than the people of Alberta *deserved* their Depression poverty. We have had some good resource management in the past, but resource wealth is a gift oh so easily squandered; it is the business of a democratic people to elect those to leadership who will use and build on those gifts wisely: for the wider human good. If they do not, they will soon suffer for it, together with their short-sighted politicians.

And if this sounds a lot like a sermon, don't be surprised. I was a preacher a lot longer than I was a politician; or have been dead. Do not be deceived by fleeting resource prosperity. Let me assure you, there is a larger and ultimate justice that rules the world, both the living and the so-called dead.

The Oil Capitals of Canada [1978/1979]

THE OIL CAPITALS OF CANADA are of course in Alberta, and they
both tell you what they are on nice large billboards, it doesn't matter
from what direction you drive in. The signs are lit up bright at night
and that's really important around December when there are only
seven or eight hours between sunrise and sunset anyway. Of course
that's balanced by the more or less round-the-clock-twice daylight of
June, but when you drive a car and the snow has been slashing out
of the darkness at you for hours, it makes you feel nice and warm
just to see those signs, "Welcome to Calgary, Oil Capital of Canada!"...
"Welcome to Edmonton, Oil Capital of Canada!" And since they're
297 kilometres apart, you're not likely to see them at the same time
and wonder.

I almost never fly, but I know the roads of Alberta better than the
If you fly in, Calgary wins hands down. As the plane taxis to an
airport that's so modern it's out of date already, you suddenly see
three oil donkeys, close together, pumping relentlessly. No sign,
no word, just those pumps so close to the ramp that a 747 has to
time it just right or its wing-tip might get heavily nudged. Neither
Edmonton Industrial nor International has anything so ominously
stunning.

I almost never fly, but I know the roads of Alberta better than the
stubble I scrape off my face every other morning. Since the fifties the
roads here are probably the best in Canada and the gas is cheaper,

by twenty cents, than anywhere else so I'm like the average Albertan in that way, around on wheels most of the time and most likely in a pickup at that. I was born and have lived here all my life—away just long enough in 1943–45 to learn that the mud of Holland was something I never wanted to slog through again, especially while getting shot at—but don't ask me to explain Calgary and Edmonton. A lot of people living in them now moved in from far away, but still the largest number are like me: born on Alberta farms or in small towns and come to live in them for the jobs, the money, the good living. That one prairie province should have two such big places, so much alike and so different, is kind of amazing.

Edmonton got going first, 1790s, because the Hudson's Bay Company wanted to trade with the Indians but was too scared of the Blackfoot (there was a good reason: four different posts got burned down) so they stayed north among the friendly Cree on the North Saskatchewan. Calgary started in 1875 when the North West Mounted Police built a little fort where the Elbow River runs into the Bow so that they could chase out the American traders who were killing the same Blackfoot with disease and rotgut whisky. Then in 1883 Calgary got the CPR transcontinental. Edmonton had to wait till 1891 to get the railroad—from Calgary!—but Edmonton got the government in 1905 and, by Premier Rutherford's sharp trick, the university two years later. Calgary always had the prairie and the foothills and then eastern money and ranching; Edmonton always had the deep black soil of the parkland and then the Ukrainians and mixed farming, but the big action, so Calgarians say, started southwest of Calgary in 1914 when the Dingman Well opened up the Turner Valley oil field. Edmontonians will tell you it started southwest of Edmonton in 1947 when Discovery No. 1 blew in the Leduc oil field. So now the two cities anchor either end of the four/six-lane highway that's the north/south stem of the province (or you can fly between them in thirty-five minutes either direction, every hour) and Calgary will tell you it's got all the oil company headquarters and Edmonton that it's got all the refineries. They're both right, of course; even.

My grandfather Blake came west after the Riel so-called Rebellion got everybody in Ontario excited about the North-West Territories and he was lucky: he met Dan Riley (later senator) who gave him a

job wintering cattle up the Highwood River and then my grandma
saved him from the lonely and dissolute life of a cowpuncher. At least
that's my grandma's version, and she outlived him by twenty-seven
years so it mostly holds in the family. She was the fourth English
governess the Cochrane Ranch brought into the country (the first
three got married away too) but my grandfather always said she
wrestled him down to a homestead and look at what happened: such
a big spread on Mosquito Creek, the home place and the township of
lease land running with chunky English Herefords and the log house
they built so full of English books that he never had time, one year
to the next, even to ride into Nanton for a drink. Nothing but work,
work, and raise four sons to try and keep ahead of more work. I was
William son of William, second son of second son, and after Holland
I tried working on that family ranch. The Stoney Indians call the
foothill country west of Nanton and High River "Paradise." They say
there the Great Spirit made all the women and put them into one
big ravine and then he made all the men and put them in another
one and they lived like that, apart, until one day a woman met a man
hunting. They told each other how lonely their camps were, and that
night all the men moved to the women's ravine. I don't know why
they didn't move the other way around but that, as the Stoneys tell it,
was The Beginning of Things.

I can believe it. I've never seen anything like standing on one of
those hills, the white mountains shining behind you and the long
green foothills levelling out with creeks and rivers to the prairie
as far away as you can see, the horizon misting away until it slips
into sky, and the cattle all over the round hills grazing. I remember
one fall roundup, when we trailed our herds down from the mountains the sun was rising, the scarlet edge of it just a paper cut on the
golden horizon and the light spraying up like glory; it made you feel
like doing what the Indians sometimes did: lie down on a high rock
and die. But I couldn't work there; the place was too small for all the
grandchildren and half my lungs and most of one leg was gone from
the war. I had to try something in the city.

Calgary then was clumped down in the Bow/Elbow valleys, a
few clusters of big houses on Mount Royal and all the little places
no farther west than the Louise Bridge with the CPR Palliser Hotel

478

Rudy Wiebe: Collected Stories, 1955–2010

the tallest building downtown, like it had been for forty years, and
the Grain Exchange kitty-corner from it second. "Sandstone City"
they called it before World War I, and the best business fronts along
8th and 9th Avenue were still that; nothing much had happened
since the fast cheap building boom of the twenties, and Leduc with
all the new eastern and American money hadn't started to move
much yet. There were lots of ads in the *Herald* and the *Albertan* for
"seismic crews," and I had no idea what that meant but went around
anyway and they took one look at my leg and said sorry. A couple of
the exploration men, veterans too, tried to give me desk jobs and I
finally took one, a kind of woman's job (I thought then) talking on
the radio-telephone and trying to keep track of where everything and
everybody was with all the new expensive equipment, but after a few
months I couldn't take it. Everything was running crazy, everything
should have been done an hour ago if not yesterday, there was paper
falling off my table and piling up in the corners of the closet where
I couldn't move my chair, just swivel around in and out, and they
were always making new strikes that made anything they'd found till
then look like peanuts—as if the whole earth under Alberta was one
hellish fire and if they only poked a pipe down deep enough it would
explode out, flaming gas and oil on everybody. After a while when the
telephone rang such a strange grimace would come over my boss's
face that finally I realized what it was: greed.

There's a world in every city, rich Alberta too, that fits in/around/
between the obvious one of everyday business, of the ordinary people
who make up the solid core of any working world and pay their taxes
and have some civic pride and make sure the buildings are warm
and maintained. It's a world these ordinary people—you—walk past/
through a dozen times a day and you never notice it because maybe
you don't want to and anyway it tries, with all the skill it has left, to
fit between the spaces your world leaves so it won't get noticed. But
it's there all the time downtown, and sometimes in the evening and
at night when it really comes out you can't help seeing it. It's the
world of the derelict, the "bum" as most people call it but that name
doesn't mean as much as the other, a world mostly of men because
women usually don't let themselves go in that way and if they do they
do what they have to in small closed rooms they pay for by the hour

so you hardly see them unless you go looking for them. The world of scavenging, of rescue missions, of rubbing alcohol and dying.

I had a bit of veteran's pension, like many of the men I met—you sometimes have a partner for a while in that world but you never live with anyone—but toward the end of the month I'd be stealing after-shave lotion from the night drugstores and sometimes in winter I got thirty warm days in the Crowbar Hotel out of that, but terrible days too because then you're forced cold turkey dry. After a while the taller buildings of Calgary's boom that's still going on started to pile up, all around us, between the abandoned businesses and houses where we lived in the summers to save the two bits a Salvation Army bed would cost, but the only difference to us was that the construction workers sometimes gave us a dime. They're usually easier to touch than the up-and-running businessmen because they usually walk down the street in bunches, bragging to each other and they won't look at you to admit you're there, but if you ever get one of them alone you—

Two weeks ago I was in Edmonton at the new, dazzling Chateau Lacombe and after breakfast, before the next conference session I was there for, all of a sudden I got this fierce longing to walk along the top of the riverbank again, the places I can never forget anyway. It's all changed now of course. Where the old public library and the Edmonton Club once stood is the AGT tower, thirty-seven stories up, but the brush below the Macdonald Hotel was still there, bare brown with autumn but still thick enough to hide you and sure enough the path was still worn and I came around the cement corner of the air vent below the Mac—and there is a man, I knew it, squatting against the grating like we used to, and not too badly dressed because these heavy nylon parkas now wear well and keep their colour even when they're slick with dirt. He is gnawing a small bone carefully, chicken I think, a tall can of hairspray on the ground beside him. Nine-thirty in the morning, the cloudless autumn sun hitting him straight on warm and the blast of air from the vent so moist and hot my glasses fog, again and again. At least I think it's from the air. He glances up and his eyes change, as I know mine always did when I saw a comfortable Canadian man facing me alone, but he has a nice little routine. He drops the bone between his boots and digs in his parka pocket, studies the three coins he finds there, then looks up smiling

Rudy Wiebe: Collected Stories, 1955–2010

pathetically. Under the bulgy parka, inside his big solid skull he looks terribly sick.

"I got twenty-seven cents for starters," he says. "If I had two bits more...."

I have to say something; I can only gesture at the hairspray.

"Why'd you...get that?"

"Last night. I don't feel so good now," he says. "I kinda lost my head there, last night."

"You've got to eat food, solid food," I say and he sees the five-dollar bill in my hand. His tone changes:

"My god man, I'll pray for you every day, I'll get some real good food, I know just the place that'll—"

"Don't promise!" I'm yelling at him now. I have to get out of here. "Just get some food!"

It was stupid of me to walk along here, what got hold of me? I get up the path and onto Jasper Avenue screaming traffic and across it by a dug-out space where they're putting together the steel crane to build a skyscraper and past that there's the new Citadel Theatre, all square glass and open for everyone in the world to see how beautiful everything here is. I get behind some hoarding so I can cry in peace.

Well, I never said I was an Alberta he-man with gravel and concrete in my jaw. Or head. Actually, most people you'll meet out here aren't either. I grew up in the foothills, parents, uncles, aunts, cousins, family all around and not one of the so-called Big Four ranchers in the bunch. I never knew what hunger was, or want, and my grandma telling me stories about cowboys and dukes and Indians and a Prince of Wales and storekeepers like they had always belonged together, just naturally. But I lost myself; something went wrong in the world I saw growing around me and I lost myself, I didn't really understand how or care maybe till very early one morning, autumn like this, when I noticed a bent old man leaning over one of those garbage cans they bolt onto lampposts, digging down carefully and I looked and looked and all of a sudden I knew I was looking through plate glass at myself. I saw *my self*, if you get what I mean. When I got myself back home then my mother couldn't say anything, just "Billy... Billy..." and my father came into the room and looked at me in the bed and after a while he said, "We all thought years ago you were dead."

In my grandma's library that winter I discovered my namesake:
William Blake, the English poet.

> *Does the Eagle know what is in the pit?*
> *Or wilt thou go ask the Mole?*
> *Can Wisdom be put in a silver rod?*
> *Or Love in a golden bowl?*

and

> *He who binds to himself a joy*
> *Does the winged life destroy;*
> *But he who kisses the joy as it flies*
> *Lives in eternity's sun rise.*

and my favourite, I think:

> *I laid me down upon a bank*
> *Where love lay sleeping.*
> *I heard among the rushes dank*
> *Weeping, Weeping.*

> *Then I went to the heath and the wild,*
> *To the thistles and thorns of the waste*
> *And they told me how they were beguil'd,*
> *Driven out, and compel'd to be chaste.*

So the fall after that I was at the University of Alberta, a bit long
in the tooth but not too much out of the veteran line. Some English
architect, I believe, was once hired to plan a kind of imitation Oxford
Colonial on the south bank of the North Saskatchewan and they actually built a few buildings at opposite sides of a possible quadrangle
before the poplars and the river valley got too much for them and
they scattered buildings around odd clearings. When I got there it
was mostly quonset huts between the distant brick, but there were
good songs in Mixed Chorus for the bass voice I found I had and
several professors knew Blake enough not to ruin him. I became a

teacher, high school by mistake for two years and then grade five ever after. Twenty years, watching the city sprout up higher than the Legislative Building out of the oil-soaked ground in glass and concrete all along "the beautiful river valley that makes Edmonton," as Bob Kroetsch writes so carefully, "one of the three most beautiful cities in Canada. It is a valley that on a January morning might shelter ten thousand buffalo. Edmonton with its high towers illumined at six o'clock on a winter's night is a blue-green vision of a city, hung from the stars above a black chasm." I couldn't say it any better so I won't try. Twenty years, and then I said to my wife, "Let's take a year off."

"What?" she said, quite loud for her.

"Wouldn't it be nice, a year in Calgary?"

"Well...." She was born in Edmonton.

We rented out the bungalow we had bought long ago for twice the old mortgage payments (rent in Edmonton is unbelievable now) and for the extra we leased a very small house under the Bow valley bluffs, Sunnyside, across the river from downtown. I sold our truck camper for $4,800 and that means we've got $400 a month to live on, plus about $50 extra from savings. I hope the Ford doesn't break down, we need it to visit all the cousins in Nanton (they always say, "Go ahead, fill up at the yard tank," and I do, I gladly accept gifts) and to take young Bill to hockey practices and games. His coach doesn't wear a white Stetson, at least not behind the players' bench, but he's a genuine Calgarian of a certain kind.

"That kid of yours, he's so terrific, big, strong, if he'd just push himself a little he'd be the second coming of Bobby—"

"He doesn't want to be terrific," I try to comfort him.

"Did you see that shift, did you see, he shifted that winger right out of his jockstrap, did you...."

Thank god young Bill has more sense. If he really put his back into playing, somebody would show up with half a million dollars and wreck him for good.

Out of our living-room window through the trees on Prince's Island we can see all the squarish skyscrapers. Some smart alec in a big eastern paper (not the silly one that tried to count all the bathroom taps made of gold that were sold here), this guy wrote that Calgary would be a city all right as soon as they got around to uncrating it, but if you walk north up Nose Hill you get the right view of things. Don't drive; walk through the prairie grass in autumn or in the first light snow of November and feel your muscles work inside your jeans against the cold so you've got hard proof you're alive. Up there you'll see that even if another seventy office skyscrapers get knocked up, as they say they will, even if one of them is half again as high as the Calgary Tower and there's a million people spread out of the valley and onto the flats, most of them at least will stop trying to crawl to work in single cars all at the same time: they're planning Light Rail Transit now just like Edmonton already is building, and no matter what happens the hills can't be destroyed, nor the hundred miles of mountains you can see stretched down the west and totally unbothered by people. No world is really changed by money and skyscrapers: not if you don't want it to be.

The oil capitals of Canada. I have to laugh. They're right, of course, both of them, and soon they'll be grown up enough to know they don't have to mention it. I used to get so mad at people knocking Alberta, and a few years ago when the Ford was new I drove one of those bigwig speakers we always get to our teachers' conventions back to his hotel in Edmonton. It was February, a nice solid cold front well settled in and he'd been in Calgary the day before offering freely (for a big fee) of all his wisdom there. The sky was blazing blue sunlight, the wind coming straight as a knife down the valley from the Arctic and the tires groaned and bumped on the High Level Bridge like they do in a windchill of about seventy below. He just hunched up, curled inside his coat in the warm car. Finally he delivered himself:

"Why the hell'd anybody ever try to build cities up here?"

I just had to laugh in his face. It isn't polite but I figured somebody owed him that, it might as well be me who paid.

"You'll never know," I told him. "Not if you don't have the guts to live here."

Finally, the Frozen Ocean*

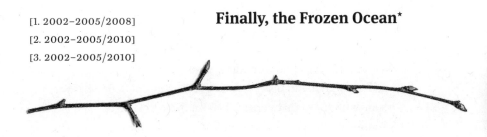

1. YALTA

"And in this room, at that desk," the guide declares in his mellifluous English, "Anton Chekhov in January to October he wrote *The Cherry Orchard*, 1903. Writing slowly, for him slowly, he was only forty-three here but by thirty years he had written over five hundred stories, novellas, and three tremendous plays, and already a doctor too, before thirty, but at this desk, *The Cherry Orchard*, his masterpiece, he was spitting blood and could not go to Moscow for rehearsal. His masterpiece, he died with TB on July 2, 1904."

Not here in the white Dacha, Liesel thinks, he died in Badenweiler, Germany. She watches the guide's elegant hand gesture over the table and its untouchable inkbottles, like the profound Orthodox blessing of an eight-part chorale sounding through a cathedral, and she is certain he will not mention that fact as her mind slips aside to her own small triangle of Germany a lifetime ago: *Universität* Tübingen on the green Neckar for study and Baden Baden for Dostoevsky pilgrimage and Badenweiler for Chekhov, sulphur vapours prickling in your nostrils like feeble ghosts sifting up from the pools, and castle crags on immense, forested cliffs—she always imagined Chekhov's Yalta studio must face the sun and the open sea, but now that she

485

is in it at last she finds only a rectangle of sky and low vine terraces
covering hills.

Du gehst, dass du kommst.
Du schläfst, dass du erwachst.
Du—

What was the third line? A natural triad,

You go, that you may come,
You sleep, that you may awaken,
You....

that could have been written by Chekhov but wasn't, it is an Egyptian
sarcophagus text from 2000 BC, there in the museum that occu-
pies Tübingen Castle now, not when she was a student half a century
ago; then the Castle was headquarters for the French Army soldiers
who stared at you over sub-machine guns when you arrived at
the train station, now gnomic translations between emptied stone
sarcophagi—the third line

Du atst, daut du—waut?—schitst?
You eat, that you may—

Ever a dirty old Lowgerman woman. She is alone, back in the
other room with the piano where the young man said Feodor
Chaliapin once sang "Boris Godunov." Was he accompanied by
Rachmaninov, who escaped the Bolsheviks in 1918 and died exiled
forever in the desert of California? The young man had not said who
played, though Liesel thinks she knows, oh, if she could only have
heard that voice, alive, singing words believed so utterly as only a
Russian basso can.

1938. She was eighteen, come to Buenos Aires the year Chaliapin
died, it was possible he could have given a concert—in South
America, the year he died?—oh sure, and she an empty Mennonite
girl but too book-smart for the miserable Paraguayan Chaco would
have had the money to buy a ticket, the brains to do it—she'd have

done it if he'd sung Mephistophiles! Russian and that word alone would have lured her.

She is laughing at herself; her ridiculous, invented memories of a childhood, as if she wasn't crammed full of enough actual ones. Schluffing about in this empty room, looking at the felt *Schlorre* they made you wear over your shoes to save the floor. She feels her body trying to register details the way she always does on tours, automatic life-long research, a learned paper can sound so evocative if you have an exact image—"Anton Chekhov's Yalta Studio: The Crack in the Floor," where is there a crack?

From the other room: "...Chekhov wanted his actress wife to act Charlotta Ivanovna, the German governess, she comes on in the first scene leading a small dog and goes off again in the end leading it back...."

And suddenly Liesel feels herself overwhelmed with a feeling of... hollow...as if in this high, empty room a cave were opening into the belly of her life, a hollow of longing at all her years so often and forever with nothing—face it!—no one to fill her with anything but relentless working texts and facts and minutiae of endless ridiculous—dear god five quick years of Jose Cereno when she was a child—listen, here, in this empty room packed with voices and music and laughing and Anton Chekhov talking with Olga who certainly loved him, Maxim Gorki bringing *The Lower Depths* and Stanislavski who would play *The Cherry Orchard* lead at the Moscow Art Theatre with his vivid hands, Chekhov trying simply to breathe, gagging, spitting out his genius—and Liesel feels the eight decades of her single life stuffed with relentless gathering like some peasant woman hording every kernal of corn against a famine that will never come, a banquet no one will ever eat: what are you doing here? Hollow old woman. Go home to your Calgary penthouse and shut down. Die.

That was the sarcophagus triad line:

Du stirbst, dass du lebst.
You die, that you may live.

Tell me, oh Tübingen Egyptian: how?

◉ Liesel is walking along the Yalta promenade towards the sun half gone behind the western headland of the Black Sea. She walks the edge bordering the stones and black water, her deaf right side can easily ignore the noisy restaurants, the bars, in her long life she has eaten and drunk enough, she need never bother with that again; though she might, tomorrow, if the young guide appeared for breakfast and she could speak properly to him, watch his long jaw shift into his own language. The reddish-blond hair he was always sweeping back with his quick hand would hide the side of his face as he dipped down to his coffee cup.

Rudy Wiebe: Collected Stories, 1955–2010

But he won't be there. He's a day guide and gone now to wherever he lives, some tiny cubicle in one of the enormous concrete apartment slabs built by Khrushchev forty-five years ago and crumbling everywhere you look, he will sleep on a lumpy couch in the kitchen-eating-living space of his grandmother's flat—who will be ten years younger than Liesel and certainly have no natural teeth.

The endless racket of bars, the swish of cars passing above her on the promenade. Liesel concentrates on her steady footfall along the quay, the white lappings of the sea she watches at the edge of the stony beach. His voice in the other room: "She comes on the first scene leading a small dog and goes off again in the end leading it...."

The play—the superb short story. She stops, facing the darkening sea. She, Elizabeth Driediger Cereno at eighty years of age is walking on the promenade at the Black Sea resort of all the czars and the Communist comrades that destroyed them, walking alone, but unlike Chekhov's heroine Anna Sergeyevna she is neither young nor blond nor beautiful nor wearing a hat and she is certainly unaccompanied by any dog—endless translators played around with that little dog, trying to be distinctive: "The Lady with the Toy Dog," "The Lady with the Dog," "The Lady with the Pet Dog," "The Lady with the Lapdog"—perhaps Chekhov met his lovely wife here, on this quay with a white Pomeranian trundling at her heel, that was why he wanted her to play the small, vivid role of governess in *The Cherry Orchard*. See her enter and cross the stage with the tiny dog, which would not again be seen until the very end when she would lead it across in the opposite direction and leave the sister and brother to weep quietly in each

others' arms, and then the stage would be empty. Silent, except for
the sounds of axes chopping at the beautiful trees in the orchard.

And their ancient servant Feers coming on, alone in the deserted
house:

They've gone. They've forgotten me.

An old man. After the elegant lady and her dog are gone, the sister
and brother weeping, an old, old man dares to say to himself:

Your life's slipped past...you haven't got any strength left,
nothing's left, nothing...Oh you...you old *nyedotyopa*.

Liesel thinks, I should lie down here, turn the noise of the quay
into a distant knocking, lie down as if this promenade were a lumpy
couch left behind. A superb word, *nyedotyopa*, a word Chekhov
invented because there wasn't one good enough in all Russian for
what he needed. You old *good-for-nothing dim-wit*, you Lowgerman
Schlosäwendoot, literally "beat seven dead," where did that—

"Madame Cereno," a voice behind her. "Good evening."

She knew him; after a moment she turned slowly and quoted in
Russian:

"'A new person, it was said, had appeared on the promenade:
a lady with a pet dog.'"

His long jaw sagged in astonishment, but he responded without
hesitation, "'Gurov thought, if she is here alone without her husband
or a friend, it wouldn't be a bad idea to make her acquaintance.'"

They laughed together. Liesel said, "One of the greatest stories
ever written."

He bowed to her; they walked. She could feel him shorten his
stride to fit hers. She thought, there truly is that strange light coming
over the sea, and beside her he said Chekhov's next words aloud:

"'The water is warm, deepening lilac, and soon the moonlight
will lie on it like a golden path.'"

"This promenade was certainly quieter, then."

"There were crowds when the steamer arrived. They took a carriage to Oreander."

Liesel said, in her most cynical tone, "Do you also remember, the lace on her lingerie reminded Gurov of fish scales?"

But he continued, unrufflable, "Oreander is there still, even the church building, high above the sea."

"And also the bench where they sat?"

"No," the young man said. "Long ago the wood was used for firewood. You speak Russian so perfectly."

"Perfected at my father's knee, in Paraguay."

"Paraguay!" Surprise: an emotion at last.

"I went to school three years in Russia, I was born north of here in a village on the Molotchnaya River." She hesitated; he was too polite to look at her but she could feel his tension now, so she added, "I was born in 1920."

"Ahhhh," he said softly. "Your family fled the Revolution."

"No, fled Stalin, almost too late, in 1929. But Canada would not accept us, so we landed in Paraguay."

"Canada." After a moment he said, "My grandfather was born in 1930 and he says that they never…" he stopped, as if the growing eagerness of his voice betrayed him. He continued in his usual tone, "My grandfather never saw his father, and his mother died very young, she was a worker on a collective farm. So…how many languages did your father teach you, so perfectly?"

"Russian, High German, Lowgerman, the others I learned on my own."

"What is that, 'Lowgerman'?"

"The Mennonites spoke that, here in Russia. A good home-speaking language."

"Mennonites?" he said, turning the word on his tongue. "My grandfather says there were Mennonites near where he was born."

"Yes, many of them lived in Ukraine, before they fled," Liesel said. "Did he say any names?"

"He once said his mother worked for Mennonites, a little while… before The Big Change."

"The Five Year Plan in 1928? When Stalin collectivized the land?"

"Perhaps..." he said apologetically. "I'm too young, we learn very little in school now of Soviets, nothing at all about Stalin."

"I have often thought," Liesel said, "all history teaching should be stopped, completely, for good. Oppression, war, horror—all history teaches children is whom to hate, how to hunger for revenge."

"Or...perhaps...how to hate revenge?"

"You are very clever," Liesel stopped and looked at him until he turned his head to face her. The last light from the sun glancing up from the obsidian sea lit his long face framed by red-gold hair. "You are excellent with languages. Why do you stay here, spend your good talk on passing tourists?"

"My grandfather lives up there," he gestured to the lights on the darkening hills of the city.

"In America, if they saw your face and beautiful hair, they'd straighten your teeth perfectly and a hundred cameras would be in your face, you'd be an instant model, a star to be stared at by thin girls in advertisements, or draped on their arms, you'd make thousands of dollars a...."

She stopped herself. Eighty years old and still like this...yet there was something so strangely *true* in the beauty of his face, and his voice—she could not understand her own silliness, true...true?

"I live with my grandfather," he said, as if he had not heard her.

"He is very fortunate."

Slowly they began to walk again. Soon the promenade lights would come on, but for the moment they were moving into the comfort of darkness.

"Where did you learn your English?"

"A technical school, in Trewoj Rog. Not a very good school, but two years we had a Canadian volunteer, she taught us."

"Trewoj Rog?"

"A city four hundred kilometres north from here. But my grandfather was here, alone..."

She felt him glance at her quickly, but it was too dark to read his expression. "You are probably wondering," he said, "how my grandfather could possibly get a pension apartment in beautiful Yalta. What he did for the Party."

"I wasn't really thinking that, no."

He insisted, "Of course he was a member of the Party, all his life, and he always worked for it, but he has never told me what, not exactly what he...."

Liesel said gently, "I was thinking that once, before the 1920s there was a Mennonite colony near Trewoj Rog, with many villages, it was called Karatov."

"Yes, yes, that's a name my grandfather said. He was born there."

"Born in Karatov!"

"Maybe not born," he was apologetic again. "But that's a name he says. Would you like to meet him?"

"Could I?"

"We're walking in the right direction—but the street is very steep."

"Perhaps we could hire a carriage?"

He glanced at her, and then they both laughed, thinking of the Chekhov story over a century ago and the car drivers that now swarmed everywhere in Yalta, offering ancient Volgas, offering Mercedes.

She said, "We could find a taxi. But it is very late."

"My grandfather is blind and cannot walk, but he hears everything. I don't know if he ever sleeps. He is always awake when I am—to hear you speak would make him very happy."

"Perhaps, he knows Lowgerman?"

"He...he has never said a word to me."

Liesel was trying to imagine herself blind, unable to move, always awake. And with a grandson with such a voice to bring the world into the tiny space of a Soviet apartment. Sitting or lying forever, awake with memories.

And she remembered Gurov, his thought when he left his small daughter at school and walked on to his rendezvous with Anna Sergeyena:

the only interesting life of every individual goes on as under the cover of night, secretly. Every individual existence revolves around a mystery.

The cover of night. A mystery.

The sun was gone now, and there was as yet no moon over the black sheen of the water, the dense cliff of headland rising out of it.

The young man beside her asked in English, "Should I find a taxi?"

"Yes," she said. "Tell me, what is your name?"

2. BERLIN

Thin streamers of blue Berlin sky shone through the enormous glass and cable dome hung over them, a spiderweb of angled wedges suspended from ribs fanning together into the circles of a steel pin pointing straight down at them.

David exclaimed, "It's like the Eiffel Tower!"

"What?" John asked, distracted.

"Upside down, an umbrella handle holding up the centre, see, it sprays out like an upside-down Eiffel Tower—it's crazy! How can they make it all hang like that?"

David was gesturing, his hands up and drawing a circle as if amazed at himself because he could hold the newly created world of Potsdamer Platz high over his broad shoulders. Irene laughed at him; she was turning too, the immense glass and brick geometry of the Daimler-Benz and Sony buildings that surrounded them flickering through the dome in shadows over her face.

"They build things so people can live in space," she said, staring up, "for years...but this is really crazy. Why on God's earth...if a really big wind got under it, it would tear away!"

"That glass," David pointed to the transparent building wedged over them like a spear into the sky, "it'd split the force, and they don't get winds like—

John muttered, "I think in *Wings of Desire*, where the two angels stand in the open space, it's all weedy and the wrecked couch in the grass, I think that spot was probably right here—the seventies, just the Wall and bare dirt and junk...."

"That scene was here?"

"The Wall was over there, the old Platz was bombed to rubble anyway, they had this dead space in old Berlin Centre facing the Wall."

"And a hundred billion D-marks later..." Irene murmured.

"A field of weeds," David said in wonder, staring around at the cliffs of buildings that enclosed them. "Remember when that angel sits on the golden wings of the Victory Column? You can see right across to here, and nothing, just stubby trees, grey grass—"

"He's sitting on the wings of Die Goldene Else."

"Else? Who's Else?"

"Com'mon," said Irene, turning, "I've had enough of money and impossible architecture, I need coffee."

John took her arm. "I think I need a bit more Rembrandt," he said. "I'd like to go back to the Art Gallery."

"Ahh Dad!" David followed them towards the street through the business crowds flooding in every direction. "We were gonna go to the Brandenburg Gate, past Hitler's bunker, that stuff."

"There's nothing there," John said. "An empty hole in the ground."

"So what? It was there! Just because you've seen everything already doesn't mean—"

"Com'mon, Davie," Irene reached for her son, and he gave her his hand, always that loving gesture, "just let him," Irene was smiling, John did not have to look to know, "run back to the seventeenth century, we'll go see an *über-historisches* hole in the ground, right now."

"Are you okay?" David was looking at John. "This is supposed to be your holiday too."

"More Rembrandt is my holiday. But I want a coffee too. First."

David laughed, "Good. I like your credit card."

They all laughed; Irene pointed at the café sign across the roaring street. The sidewalk was crowded with people talking in languages impossible to recognize. At the corner where they waited to cross, a huge board covered in plastic displayed THE BERLIN WALL in cards, books, drawings, to swarms of people pointing, buying, trying to recognize something; across the streams of traffic, among the endless construction barriers, fences, concrete accretions where the Wall had disappeared, the remains of a watchtower stuck up. Its slanted roof looked like the erections they had seen in German fields meant to drive birds away.

"Crazy, eh?" David said. "All it needs is a farmer with his shotgun."

Rudy Wiebe: Collected Stories, 1955–2010

"More likely a border guard ghost," Irene said, suddenly grim. "With a real Kalashnikov."

❉ But John did not again see the enormous Rembrandt painting that simmered in his head: *The Mennonite preacher Cornelius Claesz. Anslo and his wife Aeltje Gerritsdr. Schouten, 1641*. Walking the curved sidewalk alone from Potzdamer Platz to the Kulturforum, he found himself deflected back into the Museum of Applied Art; trudging up the wide steps he gradually comprehended that he wanted to buy another ticket beside the thick catalogues and enter again the dazzling circle images Sandro Botticelli drew of Dante's *The Divine Comedy*. An unconscious impulse and desire and he did it, following a whiff of longing unnecessary to explain to anyone; if he was on retreat, spiralling back five and seven centuries was even better than trying to find three.

He strode through hell and heaven, between the curves of intense viewers bunched before every Canto in Inferno and in Paradise, between people hunching into the light concentrated on each wall image like a radiant heavenly body, walked round and round directly to Purgatorio, Canto xviii, and stopped.

All last night Rembrandt's magnificent painting of Anslo and his wife Aeltje flickered in his memory: the brilliant faces, the hands, the thick pages of bibles flared under the burning candle—but this image was engraved into his sleeplessness. As if Botticelli's ink were molten in his brain beyond any possibility of vision or dream.

There were fewer people in the Purgatory curves: only two before this strange revealing. The label read like a mathematical number poem:

Purgatorio Eighteen:
The Chamber of Love,
Stage Two: *Defective Love*;
Ring 4: "Virgil explicates for Dante the Principle
of Love and the Role of Free
Will: Repentance
of the Slothful.

Dante's Mountain of Purgatory had three stages of misguided human love. The first stage was *Perverse Love*, lived out in Pride, in Envy, or in Anger, while the third stage was *Excessive Love*, expressed by Avarice, by Gluttony, or worst of all, by Carnality. Love was everywhere and in everything a human being did, but it could be Perverse: that is, it could express itself excessively in those things that by right ought to grieve us; or it could grow into Excess, as in our longing for those things which ought to be of secondary importance to us but became primary. First and third categories with three heavy but forgivable sins each, and only the second, the middle stage, Defective Love, had a single misguided expression of a deadly sin to balance those massive threes: the pivotal transgression between Perverse Love and Excessive Love was Defective Love embodied as *Sloth*.

There it was: that five-hundred-year drawing of seven-hundred-year words. Why were these naked sinners, condemned to the sloth level of purgatory, running so dreadfully? And as they ran, bunched, tipped forward, why were so many biting their hands? Gnawing themselves?

"'*Busse der Trägen*,'" he read again the translation of whatever Dante's Italian said. And suddenly German tasted bitterly foreign, he had to feel English sounding in his head: "Repentance...Contrition of the Lazy," speaking half-aloud to himself, "Remorse of the Slothful—" and the end of the word flipped further forward in his mouth; *fuul*. In Lowgerman that word would be the full Mennonite judgement on the faintest whiff of *lazy*.

He said it out loud: "*Fuul*."

Yes, abominably lazy. But that same word also said "rot." In Lowgerman if you were called LAZY you became an echo of ROTTING. Verb and adverb: to rot, or be rotten—even a noun: a man could be a *Fuula*, a woman a *Fuule*.

He stared at the naked figures bunched on the wall: in his oral home-language Dante's central repentance for the seven deadly sins was poised on the pivot of escaping self-rot. For a Mennonite to be lazy meant not only that you were doing nothing, were completely useless, but also that you were decaying bit by bit into filth, vaporizing into stink.

No wonder they ran to escape the purgatory of Sloth. Call this image *The Rue of the Rotting.*

And before their crowded flight Virgil and Dante stood robed in the drawing as calmly as imperturbable saints: all medieval intellect and purity. Virgil's right hand lifted in lecture, Dante with head bowed and hands folded low, forever seeking correct instruction. The animal sound of "sloth" grew in John's head beyond all his stuttering languages of omission and distintegration and commission into a shaggy cluster of apparent leaves hung from a jungle branch, the sweating arm of the Amazon hunter pointing his black spear until John finally saw it, motionless, ruminating, asleep, alive—who could tell unless you actually touched it? Intellectual, spiritual sloth, too lazy to contemplate the goodness of the Creator, completely satisfied with your coming golf and pension comfort, just grab around for whatever branch your world offers your sharp claws, for you there is always endless abundance even if you are comatose, perhaps already hanging there dead, if someone touched you, you would fall to the ground and instantly begin disappearing into the pincers of insects, the nuzzling lips of slugs. Disintegrate. Bit by bit rot.

"With rue my heart is laden"...but not for "golden" friends; for things undone, things begun and left undone, for things unrecognized in a Canadian life no matter how consciously he tried to live, things he had not imagined needed doing until it was too late to do them. And those who imagined they knew him thought he had done so much: at the Good Service Dinner, the ultimate that worldwide Inter-Mennonite Service could allow itself in celebrating anyone, they had listed his years in IMS, beginning in Algeria and then Paraguay when he was too twentyishly idealistic to know what he was actually doing, and then descending deeper with East Pakistan and Benin and Thailand and Sierra Leon and East Pakistan again while it became Bangladesh and now Africa, again, unfathomable Afr—and of course those honorifics avoided the centennial gap of 1967, the crack inexplicable to even the most empathetic IMSers, fit only to be omitted, when he wandered western Canada dragging the heavy wood, he knew it now, of his brother Samuel and did not know what to do with it except walk and walk and talk with whoever would walk beside

him; in the hopeless hope that he might eventually, finally, understand what it was he was doing; or should be. Walking all that love,
what other word could you find for it? Worship? Something he felt
then was possibly very good, yes, but now also somehow *defective*,
profoundly unrecognizable, deeply sluggish; he was gaunt as a tree
from relentless walking and yet filled with the sloth of a spiritually
lazy, inadequate recognition of what he truly might have been. Been
doing? Be.

That crevasse ran through his life for a decade. Until one evening
in Vancouver, when he had given an IMS report, told stories
mostly, about how people tried to hold their lives together on the
Brahmaputra River, at the reception a thin woman came up to him
while he was stirring his coffee; stirring slowly to blink his eyes clear
so no one would see him crying. The legs of the woman stood there
until he looked up. A small boy and smaller girl were holding her
hands, and she said without warning:

"My father once offered you a ride, in his car."

Her reddish-blond hair; though the children's hair was pitch
black: he knew her.

"A Cadillac," he said. "Maroon leather seats."

"He died in that car."

"I know. The road people near Edmonton told me."

"You could have come," Irene said.

Now before Botticelli's Purgatorio XVIII a black-haired woman
stood beside him. Pale blue along the edge of his left eye, studying
the deranged rush of the slothful, she had been there motionless for
as long as he. At them biting their hands, their wrists forced criss-
cross into their contorted mouths, those ahead with scarred and
bitten hands reaching forward even more desperately, a naked man
was stumbling, falling, he would smash his face, they were almost
all naked men with perhaps three or four women half-hidden among
them but biting too, one straining forward had thrown her curly
head back and three left fingers splayed wide before her nose, she
had thrust her thumb and forefinger back deep between her clamped
teeth. All naked and in agony.

A long sigh beside him, like a whisper; truly a German *seufzen*,
such an eloquent word for that release of breathing, especially from a

woman, she too was filled with loving, longing desire, such misguided love—and at that instant John's body hit him. Without warning, bile exploded in his gut, surged, it rammed up into his throat, his mouth surged full, his cheeks bulged, he could only clamp his hands over his mouth and plunge past blue and between people startled into abrupt curses, he would never find a washroom in time, his stomach heaved, again, he saw the large potted fern where the wall turned an angle, there, and his stomach roiled in fire and he was running with his head thrust forward and he dropped his hands to split the stems apart as his mouth burst open. His bile poured out.

A desert, a jungle, a mud village street: his necessity would be perfectly understood there, been smiled at with compassion. But at an exhibition of priceless art in the new creation of Berlin?

The fern fronds fondled his face; that felt so gentle. And the stench was dreadful, the taste, he had to lift his head out of them. He fumbled for a tissue in his pocket, wiped his lips, jabbed into his mouth and swallowed the vile taste of himself with his eyes shut, he was too ashamed, too sour and stinking to open them.

When he did, finally, he was facing the lightness of the distant angled lobby across the gleaming floor, the shaped glass streaming with the light of fathomless air: oh to be somewhere far away in air, alone.

The people who stared at him from the Purgatorio Hall were turning away; he had humiliated them, startled them into rage for having to witness something so ugly, so body and brutishly human. Only a uniformed attendant remained to face him, glowering. In this polished palace of perfect art and cleanliness, John's body had ungorged itself into an immaculate tropical plant. He looked at the plant: it appeared perfectly unperturbed, it's delicate fronds hiding every bit and spittle he had retched onto its roots—he could have laughed at the guard, at the abhorrence he read on that perfectly shaven face, and it came to him that the guard must be told in impeccable German,

"I and you, also, we both carry this stench and sour burden within us, every moment of our lives, there are matters more vile and deep than this within us, and when our body understands it must purge itself of some of that burden, it will not be stopped. It will spew it out. You also know this, of course. So why glare at me?"

499

Finally, the Frozen Ocean*Finally, the Frozen Ocean*

But he said nothing aloud. He wiped his hands on another tissue and took out his pocket book; two fifty-mark bills. He offered them to the guard.

"This is most regretful to me," he said. The convoluted impersonality of formal German: "An impossibility of prevention."

The guard spoke abruptly. "Use the goddamn floor," he growled. His accent was so thick he could be a Brecht caricature. "Anywhere, easier to clean. Why murder a plant?"

"It's not poison," John said, "the plant won't...here, I'm extremely regretful, for your trouble. And the smell...."

The man scorned to move a muscle; John bowed deeply, laid the bright bills side by side at the toes of the polished boots reflected in the gleaming floor.

"Don't worry," as he unbent his hand brushed the fern, "it's not poison, the plant—" and the gentle touch wiped away his language, leaving only a blink of biblical King James to mock him. "The plant will..." he heard himself say, but he saw the enormous mango tree spreading itself wide beside the clay and grass village, the gaunt African children gathering around him in its magnificent shade and each holding a tiny twig, ready to write the first letters of their names in the sand.

"It will flourish," John declared in English, "flourish like a tree planted by the rivers of water."

And he fled towards the glass light.

❋ "If we bought one good coffee-table book," Irene said, "we'd have good, clear pictures of everything we've seen, and more."

David was stretched out on his sofa bed beside their queen-size, reading, holding a small guidebook in both his hands above his head. "No," he said, "I like these area ones better—you can't carry those monsters around, or read them in bed."

"Ruining your eyes."

"Dad's done it all his life."

John wasn't reading. He lay on his back, left arm over his eyes, trying to think nothing; and he was almost there, wife and son voices making everything feel like *Tüss*, as his mother said every day when he came from school, *So, nü best du wada Tüss*, so, now you are home again, it was profoundly comforting not to be alone in a hotel room as it seemed to him he had been, most of his life—to feel the voices he heard bounced from satellites far more often than breathing the air with him—

"Dad!" David exclaimed. "That Reichstag, that's one fantastic building! Baroque and postmodern."

"Never been inside," John murmured, but wide awake now.

"The dome especially, it opens high over the seats in the parliament, there's this layered stack of mirrors in the centre that holds up the dome, it's shaped sorta like the shaved meat on a donair stack, you know, the meat sliced off from top to bottom on a rotating skewer, only this one's all inlaid rectangle mirrors and you walk around and around it inside the glass dome.."

"On a spiral ramp," Irene said, stretching out beside John. "It really is incredible, you see everything walking in a circle, higher and higher, it's like Berlin is sinking around you, you see more and more of it until you're above it, all."

"Glass and mirrors," John said. "You know that story by Borges, what he says about glass and mirrors."

Irene nudged him, "Not glass, silly, it was mirrors and copulation."

"What are you talking about?" David asked.

"Borges wrote, 'Mirrors and copulation are abominable because they increase the number of men.'"

"Or," said Irene, "as the case may now be, women."

"You guys!" David laughed. "This sofa bed wasn't my idea, I said I'd take a separate room."

John teased him, "And architecture reminds you of food, so why don't you go downstairs and have a long, slow meal alone."

"John," Irene's fingers were on his stomach. "Be decent."

They were all laughing. "At your age," David said, still studying the booklet at arms-length over him. "The Brandenburg Gate reminds you of nothing, it's completely covered with scaffolds and plastic, not a crack to see."

"What about Hitler's Chancellery?"

"Huh, nothing at all. Fenced off, it's like it's on this map, lots of buildings around it but, on the spot, blank. Where you can see through hording there's a few scattered bricks, grass sprouts, a billboard that says something about maybe a museum but it's been rained on for years. Just a big hole."

"The old and Hitler's new Chancellery were there," John said slowly; he had once walked along Wilhelmstrasse in East Berlin, and after the Wall collapsed along the three steets around the place. "That's where he and his ss planned everything. And the beautiful Chancellery Garden, the last four months he was in a bunker fifty feet under that garden, while his marble Chancellery was bombed to rubble."

"Yeah, right there, surrounded by those old government buildings all fixed up—why don't they do something with it?"

David's words sat there in the air, in the empty space of a room in the living, roaring city of "the new" Berlin.

"It's too infected," Irene said. "The very place."

They could hear the traffic on the Kurfürstendamm moving unendingly to and from the Kaiser Wilhelm Memorial Church, the re-enforced ruins of the tower and the octagon Hall of Worship with its amazing walls of square, blue light. And in a wall niche on the right the tiny charcoal Madonna of the siege of Stalingrad curled around her baby: *1942 Weihnachten im Kessel*: Christmas in the "kettle," where nearly half a million German and even more Russian soldiers had already been, and would be, boiled.

"I was thinking," Irene was saying, "why don't they dig it out, say a hundred metres out below the bunker, the whole area where the Chancellery stood and the garden—dig it out straight down from the edge of the street and haul it away, barge the dirt down the Spree to the Elbe and the North Sea, dump it far out in the ocean. Every speck of it."

John said, "The place remains. It's there."

"Leave just...space?" David pondered. And after a moment, "Yeah. Put a glass wall all around it, build bleachers so people could go sit, think about everything that happened. Around an empty hole."

"Fill it with thinking?"

And in the darkness behind his covered eyelids John saw the brown clay walls of the devastated church in Rwanda, the black opening through which the United Nations officer was pointing while holding his handkerchief over his nose and mouth, perhaps over his eyes as well:

You must be the witness. You are here, you must go in, you must count the bodies of the slaughtered. You must bear witness.

It does not matter what he will breathe or see as long as he lives: now he must look. Not for the sake of "justice," for there can be no solitary, identifiable murderers here, because this is no death dealt by organized killers doing their daily work in some hidden location for a Hitler or a Stalin or a Mao or Amin, oh no, here every citizen in the nation left alive may well have physically beaten or shot or chopped at least one person to death so that no one can ever be, as they say, "brought to justice" because there is no one left to "sit in judgement" on anyone.

Nevertheless, witness must be borne.

"It wouldn't be enough," Irene said heavily. "A hole. People can't think about 'nothing,' not our TV age. Maybe they should fill the space with rock, rock from inside the Alps that's never been seen or touched by humans, ever, just steel machines dig it out, haul it, dump it. Fill it level."

David said, "But the place would still be there." After a moment he asked, "What have they done with Berchtesgaden?"

John had been there once, before Irene with little Simon and Christine met him, years before he imagined having a son to talk with. He said, "Now, I don't know."

David dropped the guidebook to the coffee table as he swung his feet down and sat up.

"Time for some good jazz," he said. "In the bar."

Irene sat up. "Good idea." She looked at John; both his arms now laid over his face. She touched his shoulder.

"You come too," she said as the door closed.

"Didn't you want to call Vancouver?"

"Christine's already at work."

"Taunte Marie will be waiting too."

"Taunte Marie is ninety, she's always waiting. Come."

John lowered his arms. The red-blond Friesen he had first glimpsed while he was sitting in the highway ditch between Calgary and Edmonton. Such a slim girl then, quick and lovely and playful, and he dragging the wooden cross he had made of two-by-sixes from the pig barn his gentle brother Sam had never finished. He had selected that wood so carefully; no knots. Take whatever you want, Sam's wife Emily said, weeping. Go and proclaim peace in Vietnam.

"Come," Irene leaned down and kissed him, her nose feathering his. "I'll call her tomorrow."

He thought: thirty-three years. Half a lifetime, thirty-three years.

Rudy Wiebe: Collected Stories, 1955–2010

◉ The clock on the bedside table clicked to 3:37 as he looked. John dropped his head back to the pillow. Irene moved in his arms, sleeping deeply, and suddenly she moaned, her usual night sound trailing up into a whimper of fright, but then she was quiet again and he used her motion to slide his right arm from under her. When he slipped his legs and then body out of the bed, she remained asleep under the blankets as if still curled into him. Oh, my lovely love.

The room felt cool, right for standing in pajamas. He walked around the bed, looking at Irene, but over her the darkness was not filtered by enough light to see her face change continually as she slept; there was only her marvellous hair flared into the blankets bunched against her. His hand instinctively reached to touch it, to play it together as they always did fumbling laughter and kisses.

There was a sound...a faint hissing. As if this German hotel at night were lying in wait for a coming intruder. A moan, a sound, any sound starts from nothing and ends in nothing, but while you hear it there is only one possibility: it is there, Sam, Sam...Sam always said go to sleep, there's nothing, but there was, but it's gone now, yeah? but there was...and Sam always told him in the daylight there was never anything, when you wake up in the morning there'll be nothing there and he'd hunch up under the thick blanket, closer into the warmth of Sam's hard back and sure enough in the morning there it was...nothing.

John straightened into the silence of the room. An aging, sleepless man trying once more to watch his young wife's sleeping face change. Or his son's. A lighter shade through the curtained window crossed David's narrow face: it rested forward on the edge of the wide couch. When John hunkered down on his heels the way Africans could sit for hours, his son's face was as brilliant as a black and white photograph.

That moved. David's face moved as he slept, his jaw, lips, cheeks, his eyelids…as if a hand were shifting slowly under his skin, reaching, rearranging a shape already always there, but hidden. My only son, eighteen years old, is a shapeshifter; in the world where he lives in sleep he's making power, though he does not seem to know it when he is awake. Not yet.

John bent closer; a frown was now twisting David's smooth face, the lips suddenly stretching into a grimace of such abrupt fury that John twitched, frightened. But as quickly as the expression came it vanished, David's jaw dropped open in a small snore and his whole body under the coverlet turned with a massive roll, his face blank as it vanished over, into the pillow. Just a long young man sleeping.

When he was a baby David slept through the night, eight to eight, not a move or expression, how often he had watched him and not a squirm: put him down and he slept. He never awakened himself screaming, they always had him in the most distant bedroom so Simon wouldn't wake him, thirteen then, or less often Christine, eleven, Irene would crawl into bed with either of them and try to cuddle them out of their uncontrollable terror, or, as it went on and on and she was crying too, John would carry Simon's hunched, sometimes violent body around the dark room in his arms, "Lightly, lightly!" Irene would whisper, "so he knows he's warm, not held *hard*," and sometimes she would be screaming as loudly as her distraught children, "That! That!—" there was no curse obscene enough to name their father, "if only he wasn't dead, I could murder him!"

And Irene would be cursing herself, her unbelievable stupidity, her father gone and destroying the last years of her sorrowing mother, so worldly helpless until Taunte Marie in Vancouver had found her and hauled her and her babies out of that stinking basement, Taunte Marie who had always had such a strong head that as soon as she had a husband whom she could tell what they were going to do, in 1934 they left Paraguay to return to Canada, if the rest of her family wanted to go on cat-scratching themselves among those bugs and sand, *na*, let them.

John straightened up, his knees creaking. Sixty-one, Sam would be seventy-five. In the shadows of the pillow he could see the darker shape of David's rumpled head. Vomiting was like a sound, like a moan or small snore in a hotel room, like ecstatic Beethoven performed in a magnificent concert hall dazzling with chandeliers: it started from nothing, it was, and then it stopped and that was the end of it.

Like any life, come, there, gone.

He could not believe that. Not nothing. Never.

The telephone rang. Like a siren blast, and he grabbed it up in its second ring even as Irene stirred, jolted upright.

"What in God's name!"

"I'm extremely sorry, sir, a call from Canada, an emergency, they say an—"

"From Vancouver?"

"I—I'm not sure, sir, but Canada, an old lady she says it's—"

"Yes, yes, put her on!"

Irene's arms were around him tight, her face cuddling his and the telephone.

"*Jahonn?*"

"*Joh, joh, Taunte Marie,*" he said in Lowgerman. "We're all good here, is something wrong? What is it?"

3. ELLESMERE ISLAND

This arctic valley with its grey river of braided floodplain opens east, wide and flat between the white-creviced slopes of mountains into the Nares Strait. Below me, the black beach is rimmed with crusted ice, but in the strait icebergs and pan ice float free. I look, and look, but the world is too immense for my eye to rest anywhere: as if, an instant before I looked, I and the whole of Ellesmere Island had risen, shedding water and ice, out of the frozen sea.

you always go away forever mom and ever why can't I come I'm
hardly bigger than your suitcase mom

Over the strait the sunlight sprays through high banks of cloud; if I
were light I could step across on those pans, glint over smaller icebergs
onto that one with a high hook, lean back and rest as easily as I do
on the shoulder of this nameless mountain; and continue walking
to Greenland, there it is past the small hump of Hans Island, layered
white and brown and flat as a cake disappearing into all horizons. Only
forty kilometres away, a bird could in minutes; or a polar bear.

From the cliff below me a snow bunting leaps straight into the air,
sings its tiny rapturous song over me and drops straight down again,
disappears into silence. A dazzling surprise in this arctic desert: a
sprig of flight and music, of happiness.

*it's like legs shining down through the clouds look they're
walking along the sky*

I have to move, concentrate on angling down the mountain
towards the beach, look for a nest in the stony clay cliffs. A massive
conglomerate perhaps worthy of geological analysis, The Chief
should look at it. But no buntings; the male would sing his song leap
within earshot of his nesting mate but not give her location away.

The white tents of the Geological Survey of Canada, Ellesmere
Island Case 9, 2000 are behind me, a small dust up the valley four
kilometres away. I can still see the white spot, set apart, inside which
I sleep: its exact GPS co-ordinates North 81 degrees, 15.939 minutes,
West 66 degrees, 15.489 minutes, give or take a metre. This summer
twelve people are living here briefly, shadowed by the bare peaks
of nunataks thrust through a glacier spread along the east coast
of Ellesmere as far as a helicopter eye can fathom, or a Twin Otter.
Places never, ever, walked by a human being, seen perhaps by a few
small birds or a muskox. I've found saxifrage bunched over muskox
droppings on slopes eight hundred metres above rivers, but when
they have climbed that far, snuffling between rocks and scree after
whatever is edible, do they suddenly see those immense valleys below
them, recognize shining in the vees between peaks the vast icedome
of Greenland?

Here, all I can fathom, is. Uncomplicated. Unbreathed. Twenty-
four-hour sunlight and I am alone. Here the mountain goes down

under the bay, a snow bunting fleets by, a scatter of muskox spots
search above me on the slopes, the perfect purple bells of saxifrage—
a duck bursts away at my feet, an eider, I almost stepped on her
crouched flat in her nest. A compact of charcoal down in a dry water-
rip of stones, five elongated eggs the buff of the leather on my gloves
tinged green. Warm down contains the eggs like a shimmering mist;
the duck circles me, her wings whistling.

I'll call every evening sweetheart on the radio phone just two
weeks of school with aunt Angie and a week of art camp and
three weeks holidays like usual with your dad and you'll ride
every day and ten days in the mountains and before you know
it August 13 I'll be home and you and I'll be together, we'll walk
B-J every day and swim and sweetheart sweetheart

At my very feet. In the supposedly barren Arctic there is still
far more than I notice. Good for you, Uncle John said, now you're
an historian thinking in thousands of years. I told him if I were a
geologist it would be billions, but he said that surely an archaeologist was more human, the rock folds of mountains like the picture I
showed him over our camp last summer were, he thought, like cells
gathering together in the womb, observable perhaps but somehow
unimaginable, too profoundly *beyond* any fathomable human experience, still. Whatever he meant, talking and smiling a little and
staring at the ceiling as if it might be the universe about to split open
and reveal a creator bellowing, "TO BE! TO BE!" Which, according
to him, was the name God gives him/her self in the Old Testament,
it's always been so badly translated, no noun, just the bare, most
elemental verb. What else could that name be?

My feet have brought me above the beach. On black gravel
between me and the shelved and broken, slightly wavering ice in the
bay are the meagre remains of human beings. Rings of stone to weigh
down their shelters against wind off the sea. The Independence Fjord
people, as they are called after the Greenland place where their traces
were first found, searching these shores four thousand years ago.
Jane, Jane, sweet Uncle John will say when I tell him, you have done
Canadian archaeology marvellously proud: a good Reimer Mennonite

finding a new human site eighty-one degrees north, on the rim of the abysmal plains of the Arctic Ocean!

Not quite the rim. I walk down the shifty ridges shoved up by the sea until my feet are beside the largest stones. They are well above the rotting ice stranded on the black gravel. I step over, into the centre. This is not proper scientific technique, altering a site with my feet, my weight, but I suddenly need to stand inside these small, disturbed lines, if I wanted to lie down between them I would have to hunch up, if there was someone with me even an eight-year-old daughter we would be bundled together, tight. There are several straggles of stones opening or closing into one another, chunky rocks just the size to lift and carry against your belly, even smaller ones fit for a child and green splotches of moss, every tendril a relentless search for a speck of nourishment. Live, grow.

mom o it was so horrible B-J jerked the leash away and I was calling her so loud and she ran away from the street no dad said I was big now I should she ran across the tracks and I saw her between the wheels and the engine stopped I was screaming and she came to me under the train she was so scared mom mom dad said

I will touch nothing but I have to sit down. As gently as possible, legs folded. I concentrate on the jumbled sequence of stones curving towards the strait: I see a three-stone hearth opens there, an intimate place for a tiny fire—of what twigs?...whale blubber?—to cook food, to bend close and warm your face when ice breathes off the sea. To huddle around, the solid feel of one another's arms, shoulders; eating together.

A family once lived here. However briefly, perhaps five or six people, when I come next year with a crew we may discover more bits about them. The hearth is a large tan stone on the left, a slightly smaller grey on the right, and a low granite straight as if split by fire between them. It is hardly possible that a bone shred will remain from muskox or whale or seal, an eider barbule; more possible a sliver of microblade, if we're very lucky a burin for cutting bone. A kilometre along the bent beach is another site, more heaved than

this by the sea; I must list as many sites as possible for fuller investigation next year. It seems these people did not build their shelters
within sight of one another, nor did they live long at any one place.
Perhaps, beyond the necessities of their continual, and meagre, hunt,
the ghosts of their ancestors followed them like the relentless wind to
every new hearth—and who can know what a ghost may do.

Perhaps, if I sat long enough between these stones on the Nares
Strait lifting with ice, the unending July light would reveal how well
I am attended, watched over by ghosts. Far beyond any familiar I
already know, from four millenia ago they could come, so few and
strung along the edge of Ellesmere and Greenland between the ice
and the mountain, still searching for—what? Eternal rest? Speech?

If only Homo sapiens had developed ghost technology, beyond our
irrefutable apprehensions. Endless regrets.

I contemplate the white haze over Greenland, the blue slivers of
sea in the vast plain of icebergs and gnarled pans. The delta of the
river and the tilt of grey and reddish mountains reach beyond the
sprinkle of our camp to the flat blaze of glaciers far along the western
sky. The exact, unmoving, seemingly unchangeable world we flew
into, Twin Otter roaring. When the engines stopped, not a sound. Go
and proclaim peace in Vietnam. One night, in a Manitoba Mennonite
village, my father Sam Reimer heard those words. He wrote them
down on a grocery list.

From the inner pocket of my Gore-tex I pull my Uncle John's
airmail envelope, the postcard inside. 1641 Rembrandt in the
Prussian Art Collection, Berlin: three enormous, golden books
stacked on a damask table, one tilted open and the man's hand
gesturing towards it, his bearded mouth talking below his immense
beaver-felt hat, the delicate face of the woman listening with her
hands dropped in her brocade lap. Draped fur and superb lace ruff:
the nurtured merchant wealth of unimaginable profits from the
Thirty Years' War—a war of religion and politics.

The back is black with words, tiny as though inscribed by an
obsidian stylus:

Berlin June 21, dearest Janie: I greet you on the last land on
earth with this magnificent painting so large [5 feet x 6] it has

a wall to itself, of the Dutch Mennonite minister Cornelius
Anslo and his wife Altje [though there is evidence she may be a
rich widow come for instruction]. North is in his name: "Anslo,"
an ancient form of "Oslo" where his father was born, 1555, a
merchant moved to Amsterdam 1580. Preacher Anslo gestures
to the open Book, speaking, and I beg you in the highest Arctic,
listen. You remember our discussion [I do not use your word,
argument], the Socinians with whom he debated insisted
Jesus was not divine and scrapped the Trinity, but their core
teaching was the intellectual free will of man [excuse me!] and
man's [sic] natural knowledge of God *through observation and
God-given reason*. When Rembrandt painted this portrait the
poet van den Vondel advised him: "Paint Cornelius's voice; he
who would see Anslo must hear him." You know the image in
Genesis is that God SPOKE the universe into existence, and
behold, it was VERY GOOD. I pray you this blessing: in the
silent Arctic: may you hear the Creator wherever you look.
Love, John.

Talking man, listening woman, Uncle John never utters that name
when we talk and talk face to face, but when he writes—cards from
wherever in the world he may be—there's my father's name for me:
Janie. I didn't even know I'd had it until he told me, my sweet, stupid
mother thought she could wipe Samuel U. Reimer out of her children's memories by selling everything, moving over the mountains to
Vancouver, marrying an accountant and telling us our "wonderful"
father had "passed away due to a congenital heart ailment." "Due
to"—like a mislaid letter at a post office. But her campaign somehow
succeeded, perfectly. I have no visual memory of my father, none,
except the one air-brushed on their wedding portrait; I have no
child Manitoba image at all except a dark circle of machinery: I am
six years old, I am sitting in what I now know is the aisle of our old
attached barn in what was once Gartental—there's nothing left of it,
the street is a prairie road allowance between sunflower fields—and
I sit surrounded by the separated parts of a tractor. I only met Uncle
John at his marriage to Irene Williams; he told me the words my
father knew he heard, though neither Uncle John nor I ever heard

that infamous tape or saw the words scribbled over the grocery list. How is it possible a whole childhood can be blank?

As my father wrote Uncle John in Paraguay, his one and only letter I have seen: a man shot point-blank doesn't need to see the bullet to know his wound.

I long to lie down, to do my weeping hidden in the folds of my arms. Next summer I can have my team excavate other stone circles, not this one. Except around the hearth.

The sun shines high above the mountain behind me, the relentless midnight sun that is already day by day inevitably sinking towards the long darkness of winter. Uncle John walking his cross never found this north. When I first told him I was coming here he "confessed" with his lopsided grin that, even in "pre-historic 1967," to reach such north he would have needed technology more developed than an ancient execution symbol of two two-by-sixes hammered together.

next year sweetheart just wait you'll be big enough you can come next year oh sweetheart just wait

I am lying curled, my knees drawn tight against my breast. I was the youngest, it may be my mother has had a good life since I left; cards every New Year need to explain nothing. At the edge of my eyes the dark frame of land remains fixed, but the seascape is changed.

Changing continuously: with an infinite slowness it is in steady motion, perceptible because the hooked iceberg far out in the strait seems to be grounded and, lying down, looking out between the circle of hearthstones, I gradually comprehend that the entire strait is moving past that hook; moving south. Here it begins, and ends: the everlasting sea ice seeking its dissolution in this sound, this motion. Whoever once lay here inside a muskox-hide shelter looking across this hearth and blackstone beach, lay here together, must have felt beauty, must have heard happiness.

A possible chapter 14 for The Blue Mountains of China, *1970.*

APPENDIX

THIS SMALL STORY was written when I was eighteen; it won the
fiction writing prize in the church high school I attended at Coaldale,
Alberta. I find little to say about it now, except that it is completely
imitative. Almost every fiction element in it: time, place, character,
action, I had never come close to experiencing. I had seen gloomy
churchyards, though certainly without oaks, and there was a federal
prison outside nearby Lethbridge, but I knew no guard who worked
there, nor ever saw an inmate, least of all a multiple murderer. Too
much shallow teenage gothic, I suppose, and the weakest of Hugo,
Scott, Zane Grey; the O. Henry twist ending. This is the original text.

Predestined

IT WAS A CHILL NOVEMBER WIND that filtered through the stark, towering oaks. The moon rode pitchedly above the racing clouds, casting her rays upon a panorama of utter desolation—the ragged little copse of trees, with the bodies of their former children a crunching layer beneath them, the withered brown line of the fence, the earth, bare in places, dark and decaying. The ancient crumbling outline of the cathedral deepened the gloom which enshrouded the weathered pillars and low mounds of those who had once been, but rested now forever.

A narrow unfrequented footpath led past this spot, while an even narrower part of it gained entrance at the creaky gate in the enclosure. Only an occasional hardy traveller hurried by this dreary place, and not without several timorous glances cast over shoulders hunched against the thin night wind. The forelorness of the scene was enough to affect the most callow, even without the weather-beaten signboard attached above the gateposts. "Pauper Cemetary."

On this unfriendly autumn evening, someone mounted the steep path who did not hurry past. He pushed at the gate, which swung groaningly open, and with a pick and shovel upon his broad back stepped boldly into the shadow of the ruinous old kirk. As if to bolster his spirit among these depressing surroundings, he commenced to whistle. The thin high crescendo rebounded eerily among the rafters and he stopped as suddenly as he had begun. The immediate dead silence was broken by a groan from the oaks as a squall of wind brushed his face. He stepped back sharply, bumping against the fence, the sound and touch causing an unpleasant sensation to quiver down his back and his heart to thump quite audibly.

"My goodness," he muttered, angered with himself, "you'd think it was the first time I'd come here on a dark night. What am I, a superstitious fool?" and the self-imposed tongue-lashing augmenting his courage, he resolutely grasped his implements and strode to the farthest corner of the churchyard under the bare sidery branches of a tremendous oak. Setting to with a will, he began to break the silence with heavy blows of the pick upon the frozen ground.

After half an hour's arm-tiring work, he paused to wipe his brow and muse a bit. Certainly would come in handy, the $2 he'd recieve for this job. Being guard at the prison was steady work, but the pay wasn't very much. Still, on the other hand, it was more than most people got (if they had a job) in these hard times. He was probably lucky he could work steadily, leave alone wanting more pay. If they only had a few more executions, he—, but that wasn't a very nice thought. Certainly Jenny wouldn't approve of it. Sure was a bad one, him they were going to illiminate tomorrow at midnight. Assault and murder of three respectable citizens. No pardon for him. Only plea his council had set up was temporary insanity, and even that wasn't enough to get him life imprisonment, although he probably was quite mad (at least everyone at the jail thought he was). Well, he'd be dead and buried by 12:45 AM tomorrow (they didn't like to slow up things like that in these hard times. Made a good impression—swift justice—on the poor starving population), and he'd have the $2 extra to give Jenny. Might even be able to get her that badly needed dress. Ho-hum, better get back to work.

By eleven thirty he was down one half of the required eight feet. He didn't know why the "bad-uns" had to be 2 feet deeper than the usual six, but they paid more and he wasn't afraid of work. He'd call it off for tonight, and finish it tomorrow evening. He should have it finished easily by midnight.

He left his tools under the big tree and walked rapidly to the shabby tenement he called home. A church clock farther in the town struck twelve as he was about to enter. "Twenty-four more hours, Mr. Slayer, and you will never again commit a crime." With these thoughts, he entered quietly to lie down and sleep the sleep of the serene.

When he arrived at the prison next morning at 7, the place buzzed with the escape. It was whispered about that the officials had not taken the proper precautions in guarding so dangerous a criminal, and being very understaffed, the prison had proved vulnerable to the crafty mind. He had added another death to his list of crimes, while yet another guard was severly wounded by a knife the prisoner had recieved no one knew how.

But his crimson liberty was to be short lived. It was observed by the remaining guards that he ran into the little wood southwest of the old pauper cemetary on the hill when the alarm had sounded. The small grove was immediately surrounded by men readily hired for any avocation. No one, however, seemed anxious to enter and capture him, so it was decided to wait until he made an attempt to escape and then to shoot him down. Without food or water it wouldn't take very long and it was much safer this way. It was no use endangering more lives. The man was desperate, but they as good as had him.

The day for the prison guard passed with its usual routine. The watchers around the copse chatted with alert eyes open to any disturbance. Nothing happened, but the general opinion was that he would make a break for it after dark. The cloudy overcast weather favoured the outlaw and the watch was strengthened as dusk approached.

After twelve or thirteen hours at the prison and a frugal supper, the same man appeared at the church gate, but this time he had company there. Under the very oak where he had been digging, sat a watchman with a long musket over his knees. After a quiet greeting, the digger lowered a short ladder, scrambled down and began to work. They'd have the man soon, two days at the very most, so he might as well finish now as after. Better to get these long working days over as quickly as possible.

Time passed. It was very late and all was silent save for the muffled scrape of pick on stone and then the dull thud as another shovelful of earth was thrown out. The watchers were silent, wary for the least sound. None came. The moon at last disappeared behind an overhanging, ominously black thunderhead and only the faint lantern glow of the digger, a hazy flickering light coming from the very earth, so it seemed, was visible to the alert sentries.

It was done. He extinguished the lantern and slowly climbed the ladder, carrying his tools. He put them down softly, leaned down and pulled up the ladder. He was about to take his silent departure when a suppressed "Hist" from the watchman arrested him. He slipped to the wood-ward side of the huge tree and knelt beside the other man, striving to pierce the opaque blackness of the leafless grove.

There it was again. A faint snap as though caused by a foot being carefully pressed down to avoid noise, and unexpectedly encountering a dry twig. Nothing more could be heard by the straining ears but the watchman, trying to muffle it in his mackinaw, cocked his musket. The faint but clear click quivered in the expectant air and suddenly resorting to speed, the criminal broke from the trees, running swiftly but silently towards the old church, evidently to escape towards the north, away from the town and the pursuit. Before the long barrel could be raised, the huge tree was between it and its quarry. Then there was a stumble, a short bitten curse, a dumb thud—and silence.

The two men needed no light, but as they scrambled over the mound and looked down, the moon shot a spidery ray into the pit—upon the still twitching face and the twisted broken neck. The grave had received its rightful occupant.

The clock down in the village struck twelve.

[March, 1953, Alberta Mennonite High School]

SELECTED BIBLIOGRAPHY

❋ SHORT STORIES

Page numbers in square brackets indicate where the story can be found in this volume.

"A History of the New World." *Alberta, A Celebration.* Edited by Tom Radford. Edmonton: Hurtig, 1979. [p. 316]

"A Night in Fort Pitt, or (if you prefer) The Only Perfect Communists in the World." Commissioned and read at Sir Walter Scott Conference, University of Alberta, Edmonton, August 1987; published in Scott Conference Proceedings, 1988. Also in *Saturday Night,* Toronto, v. 104, no. 8 (August 1989): 42–47. Various reprints. [p. 94]

"After Thirty Years of Marriage." *Canadian Forum,* Toronto, v. 58: 685 (November 1978): 36–40. Also in *Alberta, A Celebration.* Edited by Tom Radford. Edmonton: Hurtig, 1979. Various reprints, including Norwegian translation, 1985. [p. 156]

"All On Their Knees." *The Mennonite,* Newton, KS, v. 83, no. 46 (December 17, 1968): 778–83. Also in *Where is the Voice Coming From?* Toronto: McClelland & Stewart, 1974. pp. 73–85. Various reprints, including Hungarian translation, 1985. [p. 178]

"Along the Red Deer and the South Saskatchewan." *Prism (International),* Vancouver, v. 12, no. 3 (Spring 1973): 47–56. Also in *Where is the Voice Coming From?* Toronto: McClelland & Stewart, 1974. pp. 113–23. Frequently reprinted; also in Spanish translation, 1989. [p. 52]

"An Indication of Burning." *Canadian Fiction Magazine*, Kingston (Summer
1980): 150–64. Also in *The Angel of the Tar Sands*. Toronto: McClelland &
Stewart, 1982. pp. 123–40. [p. 379]

"Bears, All the Time Bears." *Alberta, A Celebration*. Edited by Tom Radford.
Edmonton: Hurtig, 1979. [p. 458]

"Believing is Not Seeing." *Alberta Views*, Calgary, v. 1, no. 1 (January 1998):
46–53. Several scenes in chapter 7, *Sweeter Than All the World*. Toronto:
Knopf Canada, 2001. [p. 292]

"Bluecoats on the Sacred Hill of the Wild Peas." *The Star-Spangled Beaver*.
Edited by John H. Redekop. Toronto: Peter Martin Associates, 1971. pp.
46–54. Also in *Where is the Voice Coming From?* Toronto: McClelland &
Stewart, 1974. pp. 103–11. [p. 321]

"Broken Arm." Part 1: "In the Beaver Hills." *Aurora: New Canadian Writing
1978*. Edited by Morris Wolfe. Toronto: Doubleday Canada, 1978.
Complete two-part story, "The Broken Arm," *Canadian Forum*, Toronto,
March 1982: 24–29. Various reprints. Complete story adapted in May,
Two and May, Four of *My Lovely Enemy*. Toronto: McClelland & Stewart,
1983. [p. 3]

"Chinook Christmas." *NeWest Review*, Edmonton, v. 4, no. 4 (December
1978): 8–9, 12. Also in *Alberta, A Celebration*. Edited by Tom Radford.
Edmonton: Hurtig, 1979. Various reprints. Adapted version published as
children's book: *Chinook Christmas*, with paintings by David More. Red
Deer, AB: Red Deer College Press, 1992. [p. 235]

"Crash." Traces in chapter 21, *Sweeter Than All the World*. Toronto: Knopf
Canada, 2001. [p. 312]

"Dialogue at an Exhibition." First read as "Conversation in a Gallery" on CBC
State of the Arts (April 1988). Published as "Dialogue..." in *Prairie Fire*,
Winnipeg, v. 11, no. 2 (Summer 1990): 88–95. [p. 133]

"Did Jesus Ever Laugh?" *The Fiddlehead*, Fredericton, no. 84 (March–April
1970): 40–52. Also in *Where is the Voice Coming From?* Toronto:
McClelland & Stewart, 1974. pp. 57–71. Various reprints. [p. 276]

"Except God, Who Already Knows." *The New Quarterly*, Waterloo, v. 10, no.
1&2 (1990): 224–38. An altered version: chapter 13, *Sweeter Than All the
World*. Toronto: Knopf Canada, 2001. [p. 442]

"Finally, the Frozen Ocean." Original title "The Unknown." Possible chapter 14
for the 1970 novel *The Blue Mountains of China*. Part 1: "Yalta." *Rhubarb*,
Winnipeg, no. 20 (Winter 2008): 15–19 [p. 485]; Part 2: "Berlin."
Previously unpublished [p. 493]; Part 3: "Ellesmere Island." Previously
unpublished [p. 506].

"From Montreal, 1848." *Alberta, A Celebration.* Edited by Tom Radford. Edmonton: Hurtig, 1979. [p. 72]

"Games for Queen Victoria." *Saturday Night,* Toronto, v. 91, no. 3 (March 1976): 61–67. Also in *The Angel of the Tar Sands.* Toronto: McClelland & Stewart, 1982. pp. 42–60. [p. 75]

"Growing Up in Rosebud." *Alberta, A Celebration.* Edited by Tom Radford. Edmonton: Hurtig, 1979. [p. 221]

"Home for Night." *NeWest Review,* Edmonton, v. 1, no. 9 (April 1976): 6–7, 9. An altered version in: May, One of *My Lovely Enemy.* Toronto: McClelland & Stewart, 1983. [p. 435]

"In the Ear of the Beholder." *Stag Line.* Edited by Bonnie Burnard. Regina: Coteau Books, 1995. pp. 132–46. An altered version: chapter 17, *Sweeter Than All the World.* Toronto: Knopf Canada, 2001. [p. 330]

"Lake Isle of Innisfree." *Alberta, A Celebration.* Edited by Tom Radford. Edmonton: Hurtig, 1979. [p. 213]

"Life Story." Previously unpublished. [p. 310]

"Millstone for the Sun's Day." *Tamarack Review,* Toronto, no. 44 (Summer 1967): 56–64. Also in *Where is the Voice Coming From?* Toronto: McClelland & Stewart, 1974. pp. 37–44. Various reprints. [p. 267]

"Oolulik." Originally chapter 4 in *First and Vital Candle.* Toronto: McClelland & Stewart; Grand Rapids, MI: Eerdmans, 1966. Also in *Where is the Voice Coming From?* Toronto: McClelland & Stewart, 1974. pp. 87–102. Various reprints. [p. 116]

"Sailing to Danzig." Broadcast as radio drama on CBC *Arts National,* July 20, 1986. Published as story in *Malahat Review,* Victoria, no. 76 (September 1986): 64–73. Also in *River of Stone: Fictions and Memories.* Toronto: Vintage, 1995. Frequently reprinted. An altered version: chapter 2, *Sweeter Than All the World.* Toronto: Knopf Canada, 2001. [p. 167]

"Scrapbook." Original title: "Eight and the Present." First published as "The Midnight Ride of an Alberta Boy." *Liberty,* Toronto, v. 33, no. 7 (September 1956): 22, 64, 66. Revised as "Scrapbook" in *Where is the Voice Coming From?* Toronto: McClelland & Stewart, 1974. Various reprints. [p. 204]

"Seeing is Believing." *Kunapipi.* Aarhus, Denmark, v. 6, no. 2 (1984): 1–14. Several scenes in chapters 7 and 15, *Sweeter Than All The World.* Toronto: Knopf Canada, 2001. Various reprints. [p. 252]

"Shadow of a Rock." Previously unpublished. [p. 358]

"Sleeping (Uneasily) With Franz Kafka." *Malahat Review,* Victoria, no. 103 (June 1993): 28–40. Definitive story version in *Boundless Alberta.* Edited by Aritha van Herk. Edmonton: NeWest Press, 1993. pp. 509–29. An altered version: chapter 11, *Sweeter Than All the World*. Toronto: Knopf Canada, 2001. [p. 420]

"Someday Soon, Before Tomorrow." *Where is the Voice Coming From?* Toronto: McClelland & Stewart, 1974. pp. 27–36. One-hour cbc tv adaptation by Rudy Wiebe and Barry Pearson, 1975 ff; produced by Ralph Thomas and broadcast in numerous countries and various translations. [p. 462]

"Speaking Saskatchewan." *More Than Words Can Say*. Toronto: McClelland & Stewart, 1990. pp. 144–49. Frequently reprinted. An altered version: chapter 1, *Sweeter Than All the World*. Toronto: Knopf Canada, 2001. [p. 231]

"The Angel of the Tar Sands." *Alberta, A Celebration*. Edited by Tom Radford. Edmonton: Hurtig, 1979. Also in *The Angel of the Tar Sands*. Toronto: McClelland & Stewart, 1982. pp. 188–91. Frequently reprinted, including Spanish translation, 1989. [p. 248]

"The Blindman River Contradictions." *Camrose Review*, Camrose, AB, no. 5 (1984): 40–44. Also in *River of Stone: Fictions and Memories*. Toronto: Vintage, 1995. Various reprints. [p. 346]

"The Darkness Inside the Mountain." *Alberta, A Celebration*. Edited by Tom Radford. Edmonton: Hurtig, 1979. Various reprints, including Spanish translation, 1986. [p. 224]

"The Fish Caught in the Battle River." *White Pelican*, Edmonton, v. 1, no. 4 (Fall 1971): 33–37. Also in *Where is the Voice Coming From?* Toronto: McClelland & Stewart, 1974. pp. 125–33. Various reprints. [p. 107]

"The Funny Money of 1980." *Alberta, A Celebration*. Edited by Tom Radford. Edmonton: Hurtig, 1979. [p. 472]

"The Good Maker." *Mennonite Brethren Herald*, Winnipeg, v. 18 (February 16, 1979): 7–10. Also in *The Angel of the Tar Sands*. Toronto: McClelland & Stewart, 1982. pp. 178–87. [p. 398]

"The House Smashers." *Alberta, A Celebration*. Edited by Tom Radford. Edmonton: Hurtig, 1979. [p. 210]

"The Naming of Albert Johnson." *Queen's Quarterly*, Kingston, v. 80, no. 3 (Autumn 1973): 370–78. Also in *Where is the Voice Coming From?* Toronto: McClelland & Stewart, 1974. pp. 145–55. Very frequently reprinted. [p. 142]

"The Oil Capitals of Canada." In *Alberta, A Celebration*. Edited by Tom Radford. Edmonton: Hurtig, 1979. [p. 476]

"The Power." *New Voices: Canadian University Writing of 1956*. Edited by Earle Birney, et. al. Toronto/Vancouver: J.M. Dent and Sons, 1956. pp. 128–33. [p. 191]

"The Shells of the Ocean." *Malahat Review*, Victoria, no. 86 (March 1989): 112–23. An altered version: chapter 15, *Sweeter Than All the World*. Toronto: Knopf Canada, 2001. [p. 367]

"The Year We Gave Away the Land." *Week-End Magazine* (*Toronto Globe and Mail*), July 9, 1977: 14. Also in *Alberta, A Celebration*. Edited by Tom Radford. Edmonton: Hurtig, 1979. Various reprints. [p. 63]

"There's a Muddy Road." *Where is the Voice Coming From?* Toronto: McClelland & Stewart, 1974. pp. 45–55. [p. 408]

"They Just Won't Believe." *Alberta, A Celebration*. Edited by Tom Radford. Edmonton: Hurtig, 1979. [p. 216]

"Tudor King." Original title: "For His Friend." *Christian Living*, Scottdale, PA, v. 11, no. 12 (December 1964): 10–11, 31–32. Various reprints, including German translation. NFB film adapted, directed by Allan Kroeker, Winnipeg, 1977. [p. 197]

"Urn Burial." Traces in chapter 21, *Sweeter Than All the World*. Toronto: Knopf Canada, 2001. [p. 314]

"Watch for Two Coyotes, Crossing." *Saturday Night*, Toronto, v. 113, no. 3 (April 1998): 50–62. Various reprints. [p. 32]

"Where is the Voice Coming From?" *Fourteen Stories High*. Edited by David Helwig and Tom Marshall. Toronto: Oberon Press, 1971. pp. 112–21. Also in *Where is the Voice Coming From?* Toronto: McClelland & Stewart, 1974. pp. 135–42. Very frequently reprinted; also in German (1976), Spanish (1997), Serbian (1999), and Montenegrin translation (2009). [p. 22]

⬤ CHRONOLOGY

Short Stories

Dates indicate when each short story was written. Original titles appear in square brackets.

1955	"Tudor King" ["For His Friend"]
	"The Power"
1956	"Scrapbook" ["Eight and the Present"]
1963	"Someday Soon, Before Tomorrow"
1964	"All On Their Knees"
	"Oolulik"
1965	"Millstone for the Sun's Day"

1969	"Did Jesus Ever Laugh?"
	"Bluecoats on the Sacred Hill of the Wild Peas"
1970	"Where is the Voice Coming From?"
1971	"There's a Muddy Road"
	"The Fish Caught in the Battle River"
1972	"Along the Red Deer and the South Saskatchewan"
1973	"The Naming of Albert Johnson"
1975	"Games for Queen Victoria"
	"Home for Night"
1977	"The Year We Gave Away the Land"
	"The Good Maker"
1977–1982	"[The] Broken Arm"
1978	"After Thirty Years of Marriage"
	"Chinook Christmas"
	"The Darkness Inside the Mountain"
	"The Oil Capitals of Canada"
1978–1979	"Lake Isle of Innisfree"
	"They Just Won't Believe"
	"The Angel of the Tar Sands"
	"The House Smashers"
	"A History of the New World"
	"Growing Up in Rosebud"
	"The Funny Money of 1980"
	"Bears, All the Time Bears"
	"From Montreal, 1848"
1979	"An Indication of Burning"
1982–1983	"Seeing Is Believing"
1983	"The Blindman River Contradictions"
1986	"Sailing to Danzig"
1987	"A Night in Fort Pitt, or (if you prefer) The Only Perfect Communists in the World"
1988	"Dialogue at an Exhibition" ["Conversation in a Gallery"]
	"The Shells of the Ocean"
1989	"Except God, Who Already Knows"
	"Speaking Saskatchewan"
1992	"Sleeping (Uneasily) with Franz Kafka"
1993	"In the Ear of the Beholder"
1996–1997	"Watch for Two Coyotes, Crossing"
1997	"Believing is Not Seeing"
1998	"Life Story"

1999	"Crash"
	"Urn Burial"
2002–2005	"Finally, the Frozen Ocean" ["The Unknown"]
2009–2010	"Shadow of a Rock"

Other Works

Dates indicate year of publication.

1962	*Peace Shall Destroy Many* [novel]
1966	*First and Vital Candle* [novel]
1970	*The Blue Mountains of China* [novel]
	The Story-Makers [ed.; anthology of world stories]
1972	*Stories From Western Canada* [ed.; anthology]
1973	*The Temptations of Big Bear* [novel]
1974	*Where is the Voice Coming From?* [short story collection]
1974	*Double Vision: An Anthology of 20th Century Stories in English* [ed.]
	Stories from Pacific and Arctic Canada [ed., with Andreas Schroeder; anthology]
1977	*Getting Here: Seven Women, Seven Stories* [ed.]
	The Scorched-Wood People [novel]
	Far As the Eye Can See [with Theatre Passe Muraille; drama]
1979	*Alberta, A Celebration* [ed.: Tom Radford; stories: Rudy Wiebe; photographs: Harry Savage]
1980	*The Mad Trapper* [novel]
	More Stories from Western Canada [ed., with Aritha van Herk; anthology]
1981	*A Voice in the Land: Essays by and about Rudy Wiebe* [ed. W.J. Keith]
1982	*The Angel of the Tar Sands: Selected Stories by Rudy Wiebe* [short story collection]
	West of Fiction [ed., with Aritha van Herk and Leah Flater; anthology]
1983	*My Lovely Enemy* [novel]
1985	*War in the West: Voices of the 1885 Rebellion* [ed., with Bob Beal; illustrated history]
1989	*Playing Dead: A Contemplation Concerning the Arctic* [essays]
1992	*Chinook Christmas* [illustrated by David More; children's fiction]
1994	*A Discovery of Strangers* [novel]

1995	*River of Stone: Fictions and Memories* [short story collection]
1998	*Stolen Life: The Journey of a Cree Woman* [with Yvonne Johnson, biography]
2001	*Sweeter Than All the World* [novel]
2002	*Place: Lethbridge, a City on the Prairie* [essays: Rudy Wiebe; photographs: Geoffrey James]
2003	*Hidden Buffalo* [illustrated by Michael Lonechild; children's fiction]
2006	*Of This Earth: A Mennonite Boyhood in the Boreal Forest* [autobiography]
2008	*Big Bear* [biography]
2010	*Rudy Wiebe: Collected Stories, 1955–2010* [short story collection]

ABOUT THE AUTHOR

RUDY WIEBE was born on October 4, 1934, near Fairholme, Saskatchewan, where his parents were carving out a bush homestead after their escape from Soviet Russia in 1930. The family moved again in 1947, to Coaldale in southern Alberta. Growing up, Wiebe read omnivourously, from the Eaton's Catalogue and the Bible to *Pickwick Papers* and *Les Misérables*. He completed his BA in English Literature at the University of Alberta in 1956, where he began writing stories, plays, and poetry, and won a national prize for fiction. He continued his education in literature and theology as a Rotary International Fellow from 1957 to 1958 at the University of Tübingen in Germany. Here Tena Isaak of British Columbia joined him, and they were married. Together they returned to Edmonton, where Wiebe began his MA in creative writing.

Between 1960 and 1966 Wiebe was a federal foreign service officer, a high-school English teacher, the founding editor of *Mennonite Brethren Herald*, and a college English professor. In 1962 he published his first novel, *Peace Shall Destroy Many* (McClelland & Stewart). During this period he also completed his MA (University of Alberta, 1960), a Bachelor of Theology (Mennonite Brethren Bible College, Winnipeg, 1961), and a program in creative writing at the University of Iowa. From 1967 until 1992 Wiebe taught as Professor of English/Creative Writing at the University of Alberta. During his career there he supervised fifteen creative and academic theses, and mentored a wide variety of writers including Lorna Crozier, Caterina Edwards, Minister Faust, Katherine Govier, Frances Itani, Myrna Kostash,

Suzette Mayr, Thomas Trofimuk, Thomas Wharton, and Aritha van Herk. He was visiting professor at various universities, including Concordia, Montreal (1973), Calgary (Writer in Residence, 1978–1979), Kiel (1984), Copenhagen (1990), Marburg (1995, 1996), Ningbo, China (2005), and Canadian Mennonite University, Winnipeg (2007, 2008).

During this time Wiebe also wrote essays, movie scripts, novels, plays, and stories, and he edited and co-edited seven short-story anthologies. In addition to *Peace Shall Destroy Many*, Wiebe's novels are *First and Vital Candle* (1966), *The Blue Mountains of China* (1970), the Governor General's Award–winning *The Temptations of Big Bear* (1973), *The Scorched-Wood People* (1977), *The Mad Trapper* (1980), *My Lovely Enemy* (1983), the Governor General's Award–winning *A Discovery of Strangers* (1994), and *Sweeter than all the World* (2001). He has also published collections of short stories, including *Where is the Voice Coming From?* (1974), *Alberta, A Celebration* (1979), and *The Angel of the Tar Sands* (1982); an Alberta Book Award–winning children's book, *Hidden Buffalo* (2003); collections of fiction and essays, such as *River of Stone* (1995) and *Playing Dead: A Contemplation Concerning the Arctic* (1989); and biography and autobiography, the multi-award-winning *Stolen Life: The Journey of a Cree Woman* (with Yvonne Johnson, 1998), *Big Bear* (*Extraordinary Canadians* series, 2008), and *Of This Earth: A Mennonite Boyhood in the Boreal Forest* (2006). Wiebe is also known for his television scripts, which include the four-hour CBC miniseries *Big Bear* (1998); it won the best script award at the American Indian Film Festival in San Francisco in 1998.

Wiebe has given hundreds of readings and lectures on four continents, from Igloolik and Singapore to Adelaide, Stockholm, and Dnepropetrovsk. He has received many forms of recognition; in addition to winning the Governor General's Award for Fiction twice, Wiebe has received awards from the Alberta and Saskatchewan Book Awards, the Writers' Trust of Canada Non-Fiction Prize (1998), the Writers Guild of Alberta Golden Pen Award (2007), the Charles Taylor Prize for Literary Non-Fiction (2007), and the Grant MacEwan Author's Award (2007). He has been awarded honorary degrees from the University of Winnipeg, Wilfrid Laurier University, University of Brock, University of Waterloo, and the University of Alberta. In addition, Wiebe holds the Lieutenant Governor of Alberta Distinguished Artist Award (2009), the Lorne Pierce Gold Medal from the Royal Society of Canada (1987), was inducted into the City of Edmonton Arts and Culture Hall of Fame (1995), and was named an Officer of The Order of Canada in 2000.

In turn, Wiebe has been a juror for numerous Governor General's, Writers' Trust, Giller, and provincial book awards. He was founding vice-chair of The

Writers' Union of Canada (1973–1974, chair 1986–1987) and founding chair of the Writers Guild of Alberta (1980). Wiebe was also a founding member of NeWest Press in Edmonton (1977) and president of that press in 1983, 1989–1993. He edited the first book NeWest published as well as more than twenty others. The time he has volunteered to further literary culture in Canada has been gratefully accepted by agencies such as the Canada Council for the Arts, the Government of Canada, the Alberta Foundation for the Arts, and the Edmonton Arts Council.

Rudy Wiebe's contribution to Canadian literature and culture is vast and varied; his represents a rare and wonderful talent that combines teaching, writing, mentoring, and community service, all of which have been true gifts to his readers and students.